WESTERLING

PRINCE OF WESSEX

The sequel to

LINDISFARNE: *Fury of the Northmen*

WESTERLING

—❧—

PRINCE OF WESSEX

Feran Chronicles: Book 2

OWEN TREVOR SMITH

Swa cwæð eardstapa

Old English: 'So spoke the wanderer' (lit. earthstepper)

First published in New Zealand by
WordsmithNZ 2023

ISBNs:
978-0-473-66904-1 (paperback)
978-0-473-66905-8 (hardback)
978-0-473-66906-5 (epub)
978-0-473-66907-2 (Kindle)
978-0-473-66908-9 (Apple Books)

While some of the events and characters are based on
historical incidents and figures,
this novel is entirely a work of fiction

Cover Image: Steven Novak
Novakillustration.com

FOR TINA

<u>The Seven Kingdoms (Heptarchy) of Anglo-Saxon England</u>

Northumbria, Mercia, East Anglia, Essex, Kent, Sussex, Wessex

WESSEX AND CORNWALL (South-West England)

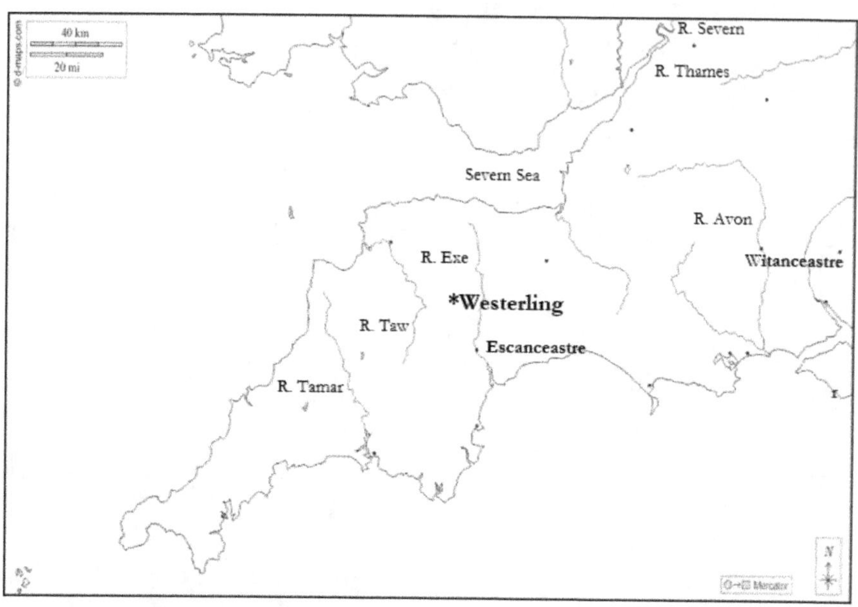

Witanceastre (Winchester)

Court of King Beorhtric and Queen Eadburg of Wessex.

Escanceastre (Exeter)

Market town on the River Exe. Closest large town to Westerling.

River Tamar

Formed the border between the Kingdom of Wessex and the Kingdom of Cornwall.

River Thames

Formed the border between the Kingdom of Wessex and the Kingdom of Mercia, and also between Wessex and the sub-kingdom of Hwicce.

Severn Sea

Early name for the Bristol Channel.

HISTORICAL CHARACTERS

Although this novel is entirely a work of fiction, some characters are based on historical figures. The following historical persons appear or are referenced in the novel.

Eadburg	Queen of Wessex (789-802), wife of King Beorhtric, King Offa's daughter.
Beorhtric	King of Wessex (786-802), Kaela's father (*in novel only*).
Worr	Ealdorman at King Beorhtric's court, Witanceastre (Winchester).
Beauduheard	King Beorhtric's Reeve (deceased).
Cynewulf	King of Wessex (757-786) (murdered), succeeded by Beorhtric.
Offa	King of Mercia (757-796), father of Eadburg and Egfrith.
Egfrith	Offa's son, King of Mercia (796).
Ine	King of Wessex (688-726) (deceased).
Ingeld	Ealdorman of Hwicce (deceased).
Ethelmund	Ingeld's son, Ealdorman of Hwicce (796-802).
Oswallt	King of Cornwall (775-780) (deceased).
Hernam	King of Cornwall (780-810), Oswallt's son.

Hopkin   Hernam's son, King of Cornwall (810-830).

Eahlmund   King of Kent (784), (deceased), father of
                        Egbert and Alburga.

Egbert   King of Wessex (802-839).

                        Son of Eahlmund, half-brother of Alburga.

Wulfstan   Ealdorman of Wiltonshire (Wiltshire) (?-802).

Alburga   Wulfstan's wife, daughter of Eahlmund,
                        Egbert's half-sister.

Alfarin   Jarl of Alfheim (region in Sweden) (79?-804).

Widukind   Duke of Saxony during the Saxon wars (772-
                        804) against the Frankish King Charlemagne
                        (Charles the Great).

Charles the Great   King of the Franks (768-814). Appointed Holy
                        Roman Emperor in 800 by Pope Leo III. In
                        Latin he was known as *Carolus Magnus* and later
                        as Charlemagne.

The sequel to

LINDISFARNE: Fury of the Northmen

The story so far...

On the 8th of June, 793CE, Fenn is a young apprentice scribe at St. Cuthbert's Monastery on the Holy Island of Lindisfarne in Northumbria. He is just beginning a promising relationship with Yseld, a milkmaid. His close friend Olgood serves the monastery community as blacksmith and carpenter.

Their world is shattered on that summer's day when two strange ships thrust their towering dragon-headed bows onto the beach. Viking raiders swarm ashore, led by two huge men — brothers Ragnall and Olaf, intent on plundering the monastery for its riches and ruthlessly slaughtering all who get in their way.

Fenn tries to save the Lindisfarne Book of Gospels, a priceless manuscript, but the fine leather cover, inlaid with gold and silver and encrusted with precious jewels, is contemptuously torn from the Book and seized as Viking plunder. With twenty others, Fenn and Olgood are dragged to the Viking longships, leaving behind the bodies of monks and friends sprawled in the dust — the monastery in flames — the fate of Yseld unknown.

The ships carry the captives across the wild North Sea to Ragnall's home village of Lognavik in mountainous southwestern Norway, to be sold or serve as thralls (slaves). Another thrall, Hakon, speaks Fenn's language and acts as an interpreter. They meet two more house thralls — an attractive young woman, Gisele, who works in the kitchen, and a youth, Kael — dirty, surly, and uncommunicative. Kael is a thrall belonging to Askari, mother of Ragnall and Olaf, a 'medicine woman' who lives in the hills but is in Lognavik for her sons' homecoming.

As summer turns to winter, life as a Viking thrall in Lognavik is harsh and brutal.

In spring, Fenn is taken on a hunt for a bear and demonstrates his skill with a sling by driving off the bear when it threatens a deaf child. At Askari's hut he meets Kael again. In a startling secret admission, Kael reveals himself to be Kaela, female, who was mistaken for a male when captured four years ago on a Wessex beach and, knowing life as a thrall could be much worse for a woman, has continued the deception. She has learned the language of the Northmen and knows the mountains.

Fenn's hope for freedom and his interest in Kaela are both kindled.

An inter-village conflict escalates and Lognavik is attacked. In the chaos, Fenn seizes the opportunity to escape. He retrieves the stolen jewelled cover of the Book of Gospels and vows to return it to Lindisfarne. Fleeing into the mountains with Olgood, Hakon, and Gisele, he picks up Kaela and the group attempts to cross a high mountain pass but they are woefully unprepared for the harsh conditions and suffer almost disastrous consequences.

Their hopes are dashed when they are out-thought by Ragnall, recaptured, and imprisoned in an apple cellar, to be returned to Lognavik and face their fate. Viking law dictates that the only penalty for thralls who attempt escape is death.

When Ragnall and his men celebrate too heartily with cider, the prisoners are freed by an ally, and the five fugitives steal a boat and set sail for the land of the Danes, relentlessly pursued every step of the way by the brothers Ragnall and Olaf.

As they journey south through current-day Denmark and Germany, relationships develop within the band, fuelled by their shared struggle,

They make a further deadly enemy of the leader of an outlaw band, Lothar the Hun, when his brother is killed by Kaela who, revealing one of many hidden talents, displays extraordinary skill with a sword.

After a life-threatening incident, Fenn regains consciousness to find himself abandoned, confused, and injured. A clue left by Kaela eventually leads to Lothar's camp deep in Skyrvid forest where Hakon is imprisoned and Kaela is destined to die a horrible death. A vengeful Lothar has tied her to a stake inside an enclosure with starving dogs. Fenn discovers that Olgood and Gisele have also been captured and are being brought to Lothar's camp.

Fenn executes a daring rescue of Kaela and Hakon from under the nose of Lothar, and the three set out to ambush the cart transporting Olgood and Gisele to the camp. At a crucial point in the resulting skirmish, Fenn is aided by Gunther, an unwilling member of Lothar's outlaw band, and the five companions become six.

Fleeing from Ragnall, Olaf, and now Lothar, heading ever southward, the fugitives find themselves entangled in a desperate war between Franks and Saxons. They help a woman, Mathilde, and her children by escorting them to Hammaburg (Hamburg) Castle. Mathilde knows Widukind, the Duke of Saxony, who asks Fenn and his companions to help defend the castle against an imminent attack by the Franks.

The Franks besiege the castle and a brutal battle rages. Fenn's prowess with the sling and his leadership earn him respect but the castle walls are eventually breached by the Franks' superior numbers. During the hand-to-hand fighting in the courtyard, the strength of Olgood and the skill of Kaela stand out.

In a bold counterattack, the fortunes of war are reversed and the Franks are defeated — at least for now. A grateful Duke offers to secure passage for the fugitives on a trading ship bound for Northumbria.

Kaela reveals the secret she has been concealing to protect her father — she is the daughter of Beorhtric, King of Wessex. The news initially causes Fenn to despair, thinking himself unworthy, but with further revelations, that feeling is reversed.

Finally, Fenn stands before the gates of St. Cuthbert's monastery on the island of Lindisfarne and remembers the fateful day more than a year ago when he was bound and dragged over this very ground to be taken across the sea to a foreign land.

He has returned the stolen cover of the Book of Gospels as he had vowed and fulfilled his promise to lead his companions back to Lindisfarne. The rebuilt monastery community warmly celebrates the return of their lost son.

The circle is complete, but a new journey beckons. Fenn's eyes turn south, to the home of the woman standing beside him — Kaela, Princess of Wessex.

It is an end and it is a beginning....

PROLOGUE

Kaela knew the Queen had murdered Lord Orvyn the moment she learned how he had died.

A man who complains of stabbing pains in his stomach and a band of iron around his chest moments after drinking from his wine cup; who falls from his chair, face beaded with sweat and struggling to draw his next breath – the screams of a kitchen girl filling everyone's ears, and the wooden plate she had been about to place on the table splitting in two on the stone floor beside her Lord, peppering his contorted body with onions and peas – such a man has been poisoned.

And poison showed the Queen's hand as surely as if she had used it to thrust a knife into his heart.

By the time anyone had knelt beside him to give what aid they could, Lord Orvyn was dead.

Orvyn was a wastrel, a glutton, a drunkard, and a fool who spent his days in aimless indolence, neglecting his estate. His neglect stemmed from disinterest, as Orvyn much preferred the excitement and intrigue of the court of his childhood friend, King Beorhtric of Wessex, to the lonely concerns of his newly-acquired estate, Westerling, inherited six months ago from an uncle he barely knew. It was no secret that he considered his ancestral holdings, while vast, to be far too remote, being a week's ride to the west of Witanceastre, close to where the Kingdom of Wessex bordered the lands of the Dumnonian Cornish.

To spend time that far away from court was equivalent to exile.

For all his faults, Kaela had liked Lord Orvyn. He was a fool but a kindly fool. When Kaela had been younger, Orvyn had often allowed her to hide in his rooms to escape the wrath of Queen Eadburg, the new wife of her father, King Beorhtric.

Kaela had not known her birth mother, Aedra of Mannin – she had died giving Kaela life. From Prudy, the kitchen servant who became Kaela's substitute mother, she learned that Aedra was famed for her beauty and skill as a dancer. Prudy said Aedra had gifted Kaela her eyes, her high cheeks, her flame-red hair, and – Prudy would wave her hand vaguely in the air – 'her natural *grace*'.

Prudy revealed a tale of true romance, eagerly enacted by two players in love who had eyes only for each other; a story which would undoubtedly have continued with the King making Aedra, had she lived, his Queen.

When Beorhtric married Eadburg, the daughter of King Offa of Mercia, to seal an alliance between Wessex and Mercia, the new Queen's contempt for the King's bastard daughter intensified as the years slipped by and Eadburg failed to produce a legitimate heir to the throne of Wessex. Kaela's very existence was a threat to Eadburg's influence with the King, and constantly reminded the Queen *she* was the outsider in the family and a second choice. She did everything in her power to make Kaela's life a misery. She had successfully urged that Beorhtric 'advance' Kaela's education by sending her to the court of King Charles in Francia, but the assignment had only lasted a few all-too-short years. If Eadburg could have arranged for the girl to be sent even further away, she would have, but on that matter the King was adamant. He wanted Kaela at court.

Then, five years ago, the Queen's fervent desire was realised when Kaela's curiosity led her to be on a Wessex beach at the wrong time. During a skirmish with Northmen who had landed on the beach to steal sheep, she was abducted and taken across the sea to serve as a thrall. The years as a captive were harsh and brutal, but she had eventually escaped and, together with several companions, including Fenn, Olgood, and Gisele, endured a long and dangerous journey back to Wessex.

The Queen did not bother to conceal her intense displeasure at Kaela's reappearance.

Kaela was not the only one to suffer from Eadburg's jealous rages. The Queen could not abide competition of any kind, especially regarding the King's attention and affection.

Finally, her blind unreasoning hatred towards anyone King Beorhtric favoured had resulted in murder.

CHAPTER ONE

Court of King Beorhtric, Witanceastre (Winchester), Wessex, 795 CE

'**H**ow *dare* you enter this room with a weapon!' hissed the Queen.

'Your guards must know who I am,' Kaela replied calmly. 'They didn't ask for my sword.' She deliberately let her hand rest on the hilt of the sword and smiled. 'But you needn't worry; you're quite safe….' She left the impudent '*for now*' implied but unsaid.

Queen Eadburg conveyed her disapproval with a stony stare.

Kaela looked away, letting her eyes roam the room. 'Why did you summon me?'

'I'm sure you're aware the King has left for Tamworth to visit my father, King Offa of Mercia.'

'I am. I watched them leave.'

The Queen's head jerked up. 'Them?'

'The King and Ealdorman Worr.'

'So, he took that slimy weasel Worr with him, did he?' the Queen said to herself but not quietly enough. Her face clouded. 'Damn him. That man has too much of Beorhtric's ear.' She had to take a moment to control her anger.

'But that's of no matter for now,' she said, her voice deliberately calm. Her lips creased into a semblance of a smile, and she clasped her hands together, dramatically taking in a breath and letting it out slowly.

'I wish to present you with a very generous gift,' she said, attempting to sound sweet and genuine.

Kaela grunted in amusement. 'A gift for me? I'm shocked.'

The Queen's eyes narrowed at the remark. 'I'm sure, nonetheless,' she stated curtly, 'that even you will find *this* gift substantial.'

She strolled to the centre of the room with a swirl of clothing and selected a necklace from the array of jewellery pieces arranged on a tiered table, holding the large centre stone up for examination.

Kaela sighed. Eadburg's prominent display of her extensive collection of jewellery was a demonstration of wealth and power that Kaela found unnecessary and vulgar. Did the Queen intend to present her with a necklace? Why?

The Queen replaced the necklace with exaggerated gentleness, turned, and extended her hand toward Kaela.

'I am bequeathing to you the Westerling estate of Lord Orvyn,' she said, '…which, as he is without an heir, was recently forfeited to the King.'

Kaela's eyes widened at the audacity. Although she was certain the Queen had killed Orvyn, she could not prove it.

'The lands are extensive,' Eadburg continued, 'encompassing several villages, I'm told. So you will appreciate my generosity.'

She gave a slight bow of self-congratulation and waited for Kaela's reaction.

When Kaela said nothing, Eadburg's voice became solemn.

'Unfortunately, it has been reported to me that there are urgent problems on the estate, and my *proposal…*' her emphasis indicated this was more than a request, '…is that you attend to these problems.' She paused, then said with finality: '*Immediately.*'

As an afterthought, she added: 'And you will take your new friends with you.'

Despite her desire to show no reaction to Eadburg's words, Kaela could not suppress her astonishment. With her father away from court, she had expected to be sent on some meaningless task so the Queen could be rid of her for a few days. This bald-faced attempt to banish her to a far reach of the realm, especially being presented as a gift, was unexpected – even from Eadburg.

'You can't *do* that,' Kaela protested.

'Oh, but I *can*.' Eadburg beamed a wicked smile. 'With the King away, *I* rule Wessex. The decision, in the circumstances, is rightfully mine.' The smile disappeared. 'However…' she lifted her chin, '…I had considered that you may not wish to accept my gift, so I've arranged an alternative option….' She allowed a few dramatic moments to pass, then called loudly: '*Guards!*

The door was flung open and two men appeared, drawing swords as they entered, their eyes searching the room for a threat.

Eadburg pointed an imperious finger at Kaela.

'*She* has dared to enter this room armed with a sword and has threatened me.' Eadburg's eyes were piercing. 'A serious offence which merits serious punishment. Seize her!'

Their faces hardened and the two men advanced.

Kaela gave a resigned groan. Eadburg had left her no time for negotiation and she would never provide the Queen the satisfaction of a meek surrender. Her hand gripped the hilt of her sword, easing the weapon from its scabbard. It escaped with a sighing sound.

'And *now* she has drawn a weapon *unbidden* in the presence of the Queen of Wessex,' Eadburg intoned, widening her eyes theatrically and shaking her head in disbelief.

She whispered so only Kaela could hear. '*This could mean death.*'

The guards approached confidently. The girl held a sword but she was only a girl. The men split, circling in opposite directions, assuming flanking positions.

Kaela waited until they were well apart before she moved.

She took three long steps toward one of the guards, isolating him. With perfect timing, her sword swept aside his laboured attempt to lunge at her. Maintaining contact with his blade, she drove his sword arm across his body, upsetting his balance. He took an unsteady step back, expecting her to do the same to regroup. Instead she moved with him, as if in a dance, closing the gap, and before he could recover she reversed her sword and struck him solidly on the temple with the blunt pommel. The man crumpled to the floor.

The other guard stopped moving, frowning and uncertain. His companion's rapid and unorthodox removal was not an expected outcome. He looked to the Queen for guidance – did she want him to continue? That look was his undoing.

Kaela crossed the floor at a run. Hearing the movement, the man's eyes snapped back and his sword came up – but too late. With a flick of her wrist, Kaela's blade struck his from above. Her speed and leverage combined to force the guard's arm down but before full advantage had been taken, she abruptly lifted her sword and slapped the flat edge sharply onto the man's exposed knuckles. He yelped in pain and the weapon fell from his loosened grip, clattering noisily onto the wooden floor – accompanied by a shriek of alarm from Eadburg.

The man's second mistake was to drop his eyes to check the damage to his hand. Kaela dealt him the same swift blow to his head and he, too, fell senseless.

She turned to face the Queen.

The choice Eadburg offered was clear. Withdraw to a faraway estate or face the false but serious charge of threatening the Queen.

The two were alone. All the injustices Eadburg had dealt to her in the past flooded Kaela's mind. Until this moment, the charge of threatening the Queen was fabricated – but a unique opportunity presented itself. Impetuously, Kaela extended her arm until the tip of her sword hovered a few inches from Eadburg's neck and was pleased with the result. Eadburg gave a quick intake of breath and her eyes widened with fear.

'Are you m-mad?' she stammered, her voice quivering. 'What are you doing? You can't kill *me*.' She took a step back but the sword followed. It was rock steady.

Kaela's eyes narrowed. She slowed her breathing, contemplating her next action. An involuntary whimper escaped from the Queen's throat.

'*Please*… Kaela….' she begged, her horrified eyes fixed on the blade.

Kaela smiled. The pleading words caressed her ears like a beautiful musical refrain. She was tempted to close her eyes and relive their memory, but she contented herself with inhaling a sweet breath of deep satisfaction.

'Lower your sword, Kaela.' The male voice came from the door.

Eadburg's eyes flicked away from the threatening blade. 'Sergio! Thank God!' She sobbed with relief. 'You see what she's done. She has a sword at my throat! A hanging offence.' She finished with a guttural choke. Kaela's sword had not moved.

Sergio stepped into the room. A small man, tight dark hair and a trimmed beard, fancily dressed in a jacket edged with white lace, he moved with a confident and natural grace that, for some reason they could not explain, made people wary around him.

'Put down your sword.' Sergio repeated his request. His hand rested on his own weapon, as yet undrawn. 'This play is over.'

Kaela groaned inwardly. She relaxed her wrist and let her sword fall from Eadburg's neck. She turned to face him, automatically adjusting her stance.

Sergio nodded slowly.

'Yes…' he acknowledged, '…you are the one person in the kingdom who could best me, especially with that blade.' He tilted his head back and regarded her gravely. 'But that would not help the situation, would it?'

Kaela let out a breath of exasperation. Of all the people who might pass by the Queen's chambers at this moment, it had to be Sergio, the Lombardy sword master retained by her father. The very man who had trained her mercilessly in her youth, drilling her for endless hours every day for years – until the skill of the pupil had exceeded that of the tutor.

She twisted her hand and slid her sword into the scabbard on her belt – the weapon returning to its home with the same sighing sound.

Sergio nodded and glanced at the two bodies sprawled on the floor. 'These pitiful fools had no idea they were up against a master trained by *Sergio*,' he said. 'But at least they're still breathing. It could be worse.'

'*Not much worse*,' the Queen whispered behind Kaela. '*This can only end badly for you.*' She paused, then added meaningfully: '*Unless….*'

She was once again in control.

Kaela regretted her rash action, but the opportunity to invoke real fear in the Queen's eyes had been too inviting to ignore. Unfortunately, there was no escaping the facts – she *had* threatened the Queen with a sword, and Sergio had witnessed her action. Even her father may not be able to protect her from the consequences.

'I'm sorry about these two,' she said conversationally, gesturing at the men lying on the floor. She was facing Sergio but speaking loud enough so the Queen behind her could hear. 'I hope they recover quickly. I don't know them. Are they new?' She waved a hand in the air. 'You're right, Sergio; they were slow and clumsy – a poor choice for royal house-guards. Neither did *you* know, it seems, Eadburg, that Sergio had trained me – but that's not surprising since you took no interest in anything I did.'

Eadburg gave a grunt of dismissal – the matter was of no consequence.

Kaela turned abruptly and the Queen gave a frightened gasp, reflexively raising her hands in front of her face.

Kaela leaned in. '*I know of your part in Orvyn's death,*' she breathed in the Queen's ear. '*And you'll pay for that.*'

'*Was that another threat?*' Eadburg's return whisper was snarled through thin lips. Kaela noted she didn't deny the accusation.

'Not at all,' Kaela said, leaning back, 'merely a hope.'

Louder, so Sergio could hear, she said to the Queen: 'I accept your proposal.'

CHAPTER TWO

An encounter in the market

The thief was small, probably a child.

Fenn watched an arm sneak out from beneath a dark hooded cloak, watched fingers curl around a shiny red apple that was enfolded inside the black clothing in the blink of an eye. If that were all that happened, Fenn would have thought no more about it. The boy was probably hungry – it had been a bad year – and nobody would miss one apple.

The small figure moved away from the market barrow, skirting around the puddles, heading in the same direction as Fenn, not hurrying, blending with the crowd. Fenn's stride was longer and he gradually closed on the thief. It would be interesting to see whether he was a boy as Fenn suspected or a small man. When he passed by, he would try to get a look at the fellow's face.

His intentions were altered a few moments later.

The same hand that had deftly snatched the apple emerged again from the cloak, but this time the thief's attention was not set on fruit.

A stout man, wearing clothing that immediately marked him as wealthy and important, his fine tunic elaborately embroidered and fur-trimmed, had stepped down from a wagon and was reaching up to help an equally stout and well-dressed lady descend. This action opened his tunic and, without looking in the man's direction, the thief's bony fingers slipped beneath the man's arm, appearing less than a heartbeat later in possession of a fat purse – a bounty so large that the small fist struggled to hold it. Fenn blinked in astonishment. Even as he recognised the gravity of the offence, he also admired the thief's speed and the skill involved. The victim was entirely unaware he'd been robbed.

The thief quickened his pace, wanting to be away before the theft was discovered, but he was too late. Before he'd taken two steps, Fenn's arm reached out and grasped the small figure firmly by the shoulder.

An apple was one thing, but a man's purse was another.

The thief was quick, as one would expect. His entire body instantly became a ball of frantic movement. He let himself fall to the ground, twisting in several directions, scrawny fingers clawing at Fenn's hand, shoulders wriggling in an attempt to shuck off the cloak. A foot kicked blindly backward, looking for a shin. Fenn had hold of a squirming, writhing, wild animal. Those nearby drew back, leaving a clear space around the struggling pair. On another occasion, had the grip been less secure, the thief would have slipped free and disappeared into the crowd, leaving his captor standing bewildered in the street holding nothing but a small cloak to show for the experience. Even so, it was becoming difficult to restrain the squirming bundle with one hand alone.

Fenn took a step closer, his other arm encircling the small writhing body, pinning the flailing arms and stifling the wild thrashing. In the final violent struggle, the hood of the loosened cloak fell from his captive's head.

The long hair that broke free was as black as midnight, and, as it fell aside, the features thereby revealed proved the thief to be neither boy nor small man.

THE STOUT MAN HAD recoiled back against the wagon when the flurry of action broke out beside him, but he quickly surmised what had occurred, patting the side of his tunic for confirmation that his purse was missing. Seeing the thief was pinned securely, the man grunted with satisfaction and reached into the wagon, retrieving a coiled leather bullwhip.

He squared his shoulders and puffed out his ample chest. 'You dirty thieving whelp,' he growled. 'I'll teach you a lesson you'll never forget! Nobody steals from *me*!'

He shook the whip loose and drew it back, raising himself slightly onto his toes. Fenn held the thief close and the man tried to peer around him to see who had taken his purse.

'Stand aside,' he said to Fenn. 'He's mine! I'll curl my Jenny around that worthless hide before he even thinks of taking a step. I'll strip the skin from his bones.'

'Hold, sir! It's a girl, and a young one at that,' said Fenn.

Still holding the girl, who had twisted her head to stare wide-eyed at the whip, Fenn turned his body to shield her from the man. To the thief he said quietly: 'Give him back his purse.'

The girl shook her head. Fenn frowned down at her. 'Do it quickly and he may let the matter go.'

The girl shook her head again. 'Never!' she hissed. 'The purse is *mine*. Fairly won.'

Her voice was surprisingly deep with a husky tone. Was she older than she looked? Despite her brave words, he could feel her body trembling – she was clearly terrified of the whip.

'What are you two whispering about?' the man growled, his suspicion and anger growing. 'Are you in this together? Stand aside, I say, or I'll turn the lash on you both. It matters naught to me that she's a wench.'

The man snapped his wrist and the heavy twisted leather whip snaked out, the knotted triple-flailed tip flicking to within a hand's breadth of Fenn's head. A vicious *crack* sounded close to his ear. The long whip was handled with well-practised ease and the gleam in the man's eye reflected the pleasure he gained from his skill and maybe from the fear the whip produced.

'I'm suggesting she give you back your purse,' said Fenn, keeping his voice calm, 'and perhaps we can all go on our way.'

'I'll pry my purse from her limp fingers when she's senseless in the mud,' snarled the man. He widened his stance. 'For the last time – stand aside!'

Fenn gave the man a quick appraisal. He had a rotund shape, but his bulk was more the result of physical work rather than gluttony, despite the image his clothing presented. His arms were thick and his shoulders broad. For all their finery, however, his clothes had been poorly tailored and did not fit well.

Fenn was tall and the man was half a head shorter but he outweighed Fenn by a considerable margin. His stance was firm and well-balanced. Even with his ill-fitting attire, he looked capable of carrying out his threat.

Fenn spared a glance at the woman on the wagon. She had paused in the act of stepping down. At the moment Fenn's eyes caught her, the corners of her mouth crinkled into a small smile of satisfaction. She seemed to be anticipating the upcoming action as potentially enjoyable entertainment, as if she had experienced similar scenes before.

The girl was breathing in quick frightened gasps and her body tensed. He adjusted the grip of his encircling arm in case she was preparing another escape attempt and his fingers touched a hard object under her armpit – the stolen leather pouch, full of coin. He twisted the girl around, reached beneath the cloak, and found a pocket sewn into the side of the fabric. In one swift movement, he freed the leather pouch from its hiding place – the removal also dislodging the red apple from the pocket. The shiny fruit appeared to leap from beneath the cloak, falling into a puddle at the girl's feet with a splash.

All eyes followed the apple. Fenn saw the whip lower as the man leaned forward and dropped his gaze to see if it was his purse that had fallen. He seized the moment and released the thief, pushing her away from him.

'Run,' he said urgently, 'and don't come back here.'

He expected her to leap for the safety of the crowd. Instead, she took a moment to reach down and smoothly scoop the apple from the puddle. Then, before the stout man could react, three quick steps took her to the edge of the crowd, where she stopped. One more step and she'd be gone. She sensed she was safe – too close to other people now for the man to use his whip. She turned to look back at Fenn, her black hair falling aside to reveal a pretty face. She was young, about ten or twelve. Her long eyelashes framed large dark brown eyes, but her skin was pure pearl.

She mouthed the words 'Thank you, sir' and took the time to flash a genuine smile that brightened her face and brought a sparkle to her eyes.

In the next heartbeat, she was swallowed by the crowd.

FENN TURNED TO THE man, holding out the purse.

'Your purse returned, sir, and I bid you a good day.'

The man made no move to take the purse. He raised the whip again, ready to strike. Fenn stepped up to the wagon and balanced the purse on the wagon wheel.

'One moment there, youngster,' the man said slowly, his voice gaining a sharp edge. He shook his whip hand, the menace clear. 'Seems to me you were in league with that thief. I'd wager if my trusty Jenny hadn't been to hand, you'd both have been away and sharing the proceeds by now.'

There were murmurs from the crowd which the man took as support for his words. He gave a grunt of satisfaction and glanced around, nodding his head.

Fenn had been raised in St. Cuthbert's monastery on the Holy Island of Lindisfarne in Northumbria. He was an orphan, left at the monastery gates as a baby and taken in by Lenglan, the stonemason, and his wife, Aerlene. He had never known any other parents. However, his wavy black hair and tan complexion, which darkened readily with exposure to the sun, hinted at an ancestry that may have had its origins in lands well to the south. This appearance, combined with his piercing blue eyes, marked him, in the view of many, as a foreigner. In the northern monastery where he had spent his childhood, he'd been accepted and no one commented that he looked different from the paler skin more common to the people around him. In contrast, during the short time he'd been in Wessex, he'd noticed that walking in any public place drew frequent stares. He saw those same suspicious stares in the faces around him now.

'Turn out your pockets,' the man growled, 'and no doubt we'll discover whatever else you've stolen today.'

If the man expected meek compliance, he was quickly disappointed. Fenn moved up to him, standing close enough to nullify the threat of the whip. This close, their height difference was accentuated. Fenn looked down on the man.

'Be careful who you accuse, sir, and with what. I have returned your purse to you and if I had not been handy, both purse and contents would be long gone. I've done you a favour today, and your gratitude would be a better response than your misguided accusations.'

'Why, you snivelling young pup…' the man blustered.

He took a step back to give himself room but this brought him up against the side of the wagon. Fenn moved with him, crowding him. The man pressed himself against the wagon, surprised. He sensed that if he moved to the side, Fenn would just move with him, making him look foolish.

Fenn bent his head to speak so only the man could hear him.

'We can leave this here,' he said, 'with nobody hurt and nobody out of pocket, or we can continue along a path with an unknown destination. It's up to you.'

The man was clearly unused to his authority being questioned. His anger flared but at the same time his brow furrowed with uncertainty and his eyes flicked again to the crowd. If there had been support before, it was faltering. A row of eyes stared back in silent but eager anticipation of the next move. The show may not yet be over.

'Do you know who I am?' the man said as forcefully as he could, trying to assert his authority.

The boy in front of him was young, but he was tall and broad-shouldered. The man was confident in his strength. In his position, it had been a long time since anyone had challenged him physically, but that lack of challenge made him unused to confrontation and unsure of the outcome on this occasion. The boy looked capable. He was showing no fear and he was certainly not backing down.

'I see a man visiting the market – just like me,' said Fenn.

The man hesitated, breathing deeply, weighing his options. The boy had annoyed him but hadn't physically assaulted him or threatened him. There were too many witnesses to create any other story.

With a grunt of dismissal, he snatched his purse from the wheel.

'You're not worth my time or trouble,' he growled.

He turned so that his shoulder deliberately made contact with Fenn's chest but Fenn had anticipated the move and it was the man who unexpectedly recoiled from the exchange. He staggered, his back striking the side of the wagon, forcing him to use the hand holding the whip to steady himself. Disbelief showed on his face but it was quickly replaced by annoyance. He brushed dismissively at the sleeve of his tunic.

'Don't cross my path again,' he said gruffly to cover his awkward stumble. Twisting the whip into a coil, he shook it in Fenn's face. '…or I'll make certain you feel the bite of my Jenny.'

His lips curled into a scowl and he drew his head back to spit in Fenn's direction but at the last moment he thought better of it and swallowed instead.

'We'll visit the market another time, my dear,' he said to the woman, 'when there are fewer unsavoury characters about.'

From the final looks that both of them gave Fenn, he was left in no doubt of the strength of their ill feeling. Many faces in the crowd expressed the same resentment. *He* was the stranger. He didn't belong.

Did he belong? It was a question he'd asked himself several times since his recent arrival in Witanceastre.

'ALL I DID WAS ensure he got his purse back,' complained Fenn, raising his voice above the hum of the alehouse. 'I did nothing to antagonise the man, but I'm sure if we ever meet again, he'll not look upon me kindly.'

He shook his head and leaned forward, circling his hands around the mug on the table before him.

'Trouble follows you like an obedient dog,' observed Olgood. 'We leave you alone for a few moments and you spend the time upsetting the locals and aiding thieves. And…' he added, '…I see you've returned from the market empty-handed. If I'm not mistaken, you went to buy apples.'

At Fenn's apologetic shrug, he smiled and raised his mug of ale to his lips but caught a meaningful look from Gisele.

'Oh…' he said, lowering his hand, '…I almost forgot. Well, no, I didn't forget… it's just that….' He gave up trying to explain. 'While you were disturbing the atmosphere of the market, Gisele told me some news.'

He paused with a strange look on his face. Fenn stared at him, but if he was supposed to deduce the news from the expression Olgood now wore, he failed.

'What news?' he asked. 'Is it bad, or…' He glanced at Gisele. Her expression was less enigmatic. 'Ahh… *good* news.'

'Yes. *Good* news!' repeated Olgood enthusiastically. He banged his fist on the table and stood up, smiling broadly at her impatient frown telling him to get on with it. He raised his mug in the air.

'Gisele is with child,' he said.

Fenn jumped to his feet, upsetting his chair which toppled back, colliding with another chair. The noise turned heads, but interest quickly waned as soon as it was determined it was not the beginning of a brawl. Placing a hand on the table, Fenn nimbly leapt over it and enveloped the startled Gisele in a hug.

'That's not good news; that's *great* news,' he said, his voice muffled by her hair. He squeezed again gently and stood back, hands resting on her shoulders. He looked at Olgood.

'You should have told me this straight away, you big lump, instead of letting me rattle on about my adventures in the market.'

Gisele gave a grunt of agreement, but she reached up and squeezed Fenn's hands, beaming her wonderful smile up at him. In her unusual accent, she said: 'Thank you, Fenn.'

He reached out a hand to Olgood who grasped it. 'The best news I've heard in a long while,' said Fenn. 'I congratulate you both.'

Olgood nodded, beaming.

'We must celebrate,' Fenn said, his voice rising again. He reached across the table for his mug. 'I drink to….' He hesitated. 'Have you chosen names?'

'A name?' Olgood snorted. 'I only learned a few moments ago that I'm to be a father. Our discussion has yet to reach the matter of names.'

Fenn laughed. He raised his mug. 'To a very fortunate child.'

He waved at Olgood to follow his example and enthusiastically drained the mug's contents. There was more ale than he expected and a proportion escaped from the sides of his mouth onto his chest.

'Another!' he shouted, undaunted by his damp tunic.

'No more!' Kaela's sharp voice came from behind Fenn. 'We need to leave.'

Fenn twisted around to face her with a wide smile. 'Have you heard Gisele's news?'

'I have some news for *you*,' said Kaela, her tone serious.

She opened her mouth to speak but stopped, looking at Gisele, her eyes widening. 'Oh…' her voice softened, '…but first, Gisele, you must tell me *your* news.'

Fenn shook his head – in resignation but also admiration. She *knew*. How could she know already?

When Olgood repeated his proud announcement, Kaela clapped him heartily on the shoulder then stood on her toes and pulled him down so she could kiss him on the cheek.

She turned to Gisele and gently took her hands.

'Oh, Gisele, that's *wonderful*,' she said, bending to kiss her, then holding her in a long embrace. She stepped back, dabbing at her wet eyes with a finger.

'We've just started the celebration, so we can't possibly leave yet,' said Fenn. 'You've arrived at just the right time. I'll get a mug for you and more ale.'

He took a step but Kaela stopped him with a hand on his arm.

'No,' she said. 'The celebration must wait, unfortunately. When I said we must leave, I didn't mean leave the alehouse. We need to leave Witanceastre *now*, and men are waiting outside to make sure we do.'

To the questions mirrored on their faces, she said: 'It's complicated. I already have our belongings on a cart. I'll explain on the road.'

CHAPTER THREE

The journey west

'Was the Lombard Sergio's arrival a coincidence, or had the Queen asked him to come to her rooms a short while after you?' Fenn asked. 'Do you know?'

Kaela looked at him across the fire. 'No, I *don't* know – I didn't ask him. You think it was part of a plan?'

Fenn spread his hands.

She considered the question. 'Coincidence or not…' she said ruefully, '…if I hadn't drawn my sword, we probably wouldn't be here. The charge of threatening the Queen would have rested on her word only. She may not have been able to carry it through.'

'That's the point,' said Olgood. 'She needed to weight the scales in her favour to ensure she got what she wanted. I agree with Fenn – the affair sounds staged. With each action, she made her desired outcome more likely.'

'But she was angry that I entered her rooms carrying a sword. If that was an act… it was a good one.'

Olgood leaned forward, raising a finger. 'That's the first part of her strategy. The guards should have demanded your sword. She must have instructed them *not* to. Entering her rooms with a weapon was your first offence – a minor one.'

He raised a second finger. 'She then gambled you *would* defend yourself when she called for the guards and thereby draw your sword in her presence – and there we have a second, more serious, offence. *But…*' he lowered his fingers and smiled, '…she didn't know how skilled you are and expected you to be easily subdued.'

He paused then said: 'Even if you somehow prevailed… with two of the Queen's guards down by *your* hand – that would be the third and most serious offence. You'd be completely at her mercy.'

He waited for her acknowledgement. 'In any case,' he continued, 'a witness would seal the matter and it's too much of a coincidence for the Lombard to appear at the perfect time.'

Kaela sighed, nodding again. 'It's possible,' she conceded.

After a moment, Fenn said: 'Of course, her cause was helped immensely when you turned a false threat into a real one by putting your sword to her throat.'

'Ah,' said Olgood with a wry grin. 'The final escalation. I'm sure *that* wasn't in the Queen's plans.'

Kaela looked up at Fenn, surprised at the criticism, but the smile on his face told her the words were teasing. He reached out to touch her arm.

'I'd bet a hundred of Offa's silver pennies it was worth it.'

'Oh, it *was*,' she said, returning his smile. 'It most certainly was.'

Her eyes narrowed. She reflected for a moment.

'My thoughts hadn't gone beyond conceding that Eadburg had achieved her long-held desire to divorce me from my father's court – an action that is *semi*-legitimate but only if you discount her murder of Lord Orvyn. But I wonder…. did Eadburg conceive a broader plan to remove *both* Orvyn *and* me from court in one stroke? She's undoubtedly devious, but is she *that* clever?'

Nobody offered an answer to either question.

KAELA TOOK STOCK OF her three companions.

Despite the forced and hurried departure, they were relaxed and looked content. Together, not so long ago, they had endured many days and nights on the road when escaping from the Northmen, days that mixed despair and danger with equal portions of beauty and happiness. Like her, she suspected, a part of each of them missed the life on the road – missed the camaraderie that facing danger and experiencing good times together brings. It was good to be back around a fire.

The heat of the day had eased into a warm night. The leaves above their heads rustled in response to a welcome night breeze that was pleasantly cool on the skin. Kaela took a deep breath and released it slowly, savouring the night air. Even in the circumstances, it was a pleasant evening.

'Whatever fate brought us to this point, here we are,' she said. 'With Nyle and his men supposedly along to see that we reach our destination but less for our protection and more to ensure we obey the Queen's… *request.*'

She turned her gaze toward the second fire, where six men sat or lay in various poses. As if on cue, a raucous laugh rang from that direction.

Fenn followed her eyes. Five of the six were young. Kaela said they were farm boys, recently recruited to the royal house-guard and still inexperienced, still more at home behind a plough than behind a sword. He hadn't spoken more than a few words to any of them.

He automatically assessed the boys. They could perhaps prove useful in a fight because they possessed youth and strength but, with their skill untested outside the training ground, Fenn knew it would all depend on their will to fight. Would they stand and fight when they needed to stand and fight? Or would their courage desert them at the first sight of an armed foe? He smiled to himself. He had little right to judge them – he was no older than the farm boys in age, but he at least had recent experience of battle.

The sixth man was different.

The young boys had been sent because Eadburg didn't want to waste good men on this task, but even she recognised that raw recruits needed a competent leader. He picked out Nyle, tall and wide-shouldered, lounging on the far side of the fire – older than the others but only by a few years, casually resting on one elbow with a leg drawn up. He looked relaxed, but Fenn doubted if he ever really relaxed. When introduced to Nyle outside the Prancing Pony alehouse in Witanceastre, Fenn was struck by the fierce glint in the man's narrow eyes. Those eyes were never still, never resting on any one thing for more than a few moments. Fenn was reminded of a caged animal, continually expecting an attack from any quarter.

He searched for and located Nyle's bow, set against a tree trunk within easy reach. Even in the short time he had been acquainted with the man, the care that Nyle lavished on his bow and especially on the bowstring which he kept close to his skin so it would always be warm and dry, told Fenn that he was probably a very capable bowman.

'I presume Nyle knows the way to our destination – Westerling?' asked Fenn.

'He knows the place. He said he fought against the Cornish nearby, a year or so ago.'

Nyle must have said something. One of the boys looked at him and then stood up, buckling on his sword. Nyle pointed towards the west and the boy walked off in that direction.

Nyle wants a night guard, thought Fenn. *A sensible precaution.*

'We could overpower them, of course….' Kaela said, '…with surprise and a little luck.' Turning her eyes to Gisele, she added: 'They wouldn't suspect the lion we have in our midst.'

Olgood grunted with amusement. 'I'm sure they're unaware of the capabilities of either of our lionesses,' he said.

Kaela smiled, then her face became serious. 'But that would be contrary to the Queen's orders and would only make us fugitives.'

She picked two pieces of wood from a pile and added them to the fire.

'We'll play the game for now. We've four or five nights travel ahead of us. Let's see what my father's reaction is when he learns of our situation.' She smiled grimly. 'I've sent him a message.'

THEY WERE A DAY from Witanceastre and travelling through a vast open forest. The trees were well-spaced and enough sunlight penetrated the leafy branches to promote the growth of lush green grasses and small bushes. The road they followed was well-defined and a few small groups had been met travelling in the opposite direction; families searching for a better place to live, tradespeople looking for work, farmers taking produce to a distant market.

Nyle and two of his men led a horse pulling a two-wheeled cart carrying their meagre belongings, extra clothing, supplies, and tools. Fenn, Kaela, Olgood, and Gisele followed the cart and the three remaining boys walked at a short distance in the rear.

Nyle carried his bow secured to his back by a leather strap, with a quiver of arrows slung over his shoulder. Each of his men wore a sword and held a round shield of wood and stretched leather, painted blue, with a spear in the other hand. In the centre of each shield was a strange winged dragon, the colour of gold, showing only two legs and a large twisted pointed tail. When Kaela saw Fenn's interest, she told him the creature was not a dragon but a *wyvern*. It was a symbol of Wessex.

Fenn and his companions were also armed.

Kaela's sword was the most notable. It was a specially crafted weapon made from the finest of materials that she had taken from Alfarin, Jarl of Alfheim, during her escape from the land of the Northmen. Housed in an elaborately decorated scabbard, it was a beautifully constructed, perfectly balanced weapon with a blade of legendary Damascus steel, renowned for its exceptional strength and flexibility and its ability to keep a razor-sharp edge. Several runes were inscribed across the handguard, bestowing the sword its name: 'Lord of the Battle'. It was unusual for a woman to carry a sword, especially *such* a sword, and this fact, combined with her shining red hair that she now wore free and long, elicited both admiring and wary glances from passers-by.

Olgood carried a Northman's axe with a wide curving blade at the end of a long handle stained the red colour of blood. The axe had once been one of a pair belonging to Ragnall, the leader of the Northmen who had captured Fenn and Olgood from Lindisfarne. Olgood had taken the axe during the escape from Ragnall's village, Lognavik. He preferred the axe to a sword, saying that the weight and shape of the deadly weapon suited him perfectly.

Olgood was a striking figure, even without the axe in his hand. A full head taller than most, with sun-bleached blond hair falling onto broad shoulders, Olgood had developed a thick and heavily muscled body bestowed by nature and from years of strenuous physical work as both blacksmith and carpenter at St. Cuthbert's Monastery in Northumbria where he and Fenn had been raised. His strength was prodigious, matching his height and impressive physique. Such physical attributes could have made him intimidating were it not for his genial nature and relaxed attitude – never seeking trouble but ready and willing to deal with whatever came his way.

Fenn also had an axe slung in his belt. Like Olgood's, this weapon had also belonged to a Northman, but, in contrast, Fenn's was a gift from Thorvald after Fenn saved his deaf daughter, Agatha, from a bear. The weapon had been created by a master craftsman who added an unusual feature – a thin flat strip of iron wound around the handle, enhancing its strength and enabling it to parry a blow from a sword.

As remarkable as the axe was, Fenn did not consider it to be his primary weapon. Tucked into his belt, out of sight, he also carried a sling – a length of braided cord with a loop at one end, a knot at the other, and an oval-shaped webbed leather pouch in the middle. On his belt, alongside the sling and tucked inside his tunic, hung a small bag of smooth hand-picked stones.

Gisele's belt held only a long curved knife, used primarily to prepare food. If appearances alone were considered, Gisele looked to be a fair-haired defenceless waif who would cower from the slightest confrontation. In fact, she had proved herself to be quite the opposite. Kaela's reference to her as a lion stemmed from several incidents in which Gisele had been highly resourceful and surprisingly capable when danger threatened. Until a few months ago, her life as a thrall had consisted of relentless hard work with cruelty and suffering as daily companions. Rather than being crushed under the weight of circumstances, she refused to be bowed, instead taking what lessons she could from those harsh experiences. Her knowledge of the forest and its treasures was vast, and she was without equal as a skilled hunter and forager. As for her cooking talents, none of the group doubted her ability to create magic from nothing. Despite the trials dealt to her in the past, her attitude toward life was reflected in her cheerful and optimistic disposition, which matched Olgood's perfectly.

THE NIGHT CAMP WAS set up beside a river Kaela said was called the Avon. Wide and slow-flowing, it provided both a welcome source of fresh cool water and plentiful fish for the evening meal.

As soon as the road met the river, in the late afternoon, and turned to travel along the wooded riverbank, Gisele had diverted several times to pick what looked like young grass shoots, which she accumulated in a pouch. When preparing the fish she and Olgood had caught, Gisele inserted the grass shoots into pockets sliced into the flesh.

The aromas released by the fresh fish cooking wafted from the fire and filled the air. When added to the sound of sizzling juices, it became difficult to think of anything other than the imminent meal. Judging from the frequent glances thrown their way by Nyle's men from the second fire, the same tantalising sounds and aromas easily crossed the distance between them. Gisele had promised there would be enough for everyone. She had also collected a bunch of wild onions from somewhere, which she added to the embers, retrieving them just as the outer skins burned off.

When she declared the fish ready, Gisele carefully placed three onto a wooden board and scattered onions over the fish. She rose to take the meal to Nyle and his men, but Olgood stood too and insisted on carrying the board. She gave a roll of her eyes but smiled and handed it to him. Fenn and Kaela shared a look. The thought of Olgood as a father would take some getting used to.

The men eagerly accepted the gift; Nyle stood back suspiciously at first but readily tried some when it was offered. Gisele's fish melted in the mouth and had a pleasant tart and tangy taste that reminded Fenn of lemons, wonderfully augmented by the sour onions.

Fenn was halfway through his meal, enjoying each mouthful, taking his time, when there was a commotion at the other fire. After loud urging from his companions, one of the farm boys rose from his position and approached. He stood in front of Gisele, wringing his hands nervously.

'Miss…' he said to Gisele. 'Excuse me, but we would all like to thank you for the fish. It was unbelievably delicious. I've had many a meal of trout but I've never eaten anything like… *nothing* like that at all.…' He stopped, embarrassed, and bowed. 'Anyway… we would like to thank you Miss. I think you're quite the best cook I've ever known… a wizard.…' The boy coughed, then quickly turned and hurried back to his fire.

Fenn smiled to himself. He remembered the times in the past when Gisele had produced memorable meals using seasonings and herbs he had never tasted before. She surprised him with every meal.

He finished his portion, wiped his hands then stood and crossed to Gisele, kneeling before her and hugging her shoulders.

'You've lost none of your magic, Gisele,' he said. 'As the boy said, that was indeed delicious.'

Gisele smiled her thanks and that simple action reminded Fenn how much his life had changed over the past two years. Gisele's beautiful smile was so much like that of Yseld, a milkmaid at St. Cuthbert's monastery – a young girl with whom, not so long ago, Fenn had hoped to spend the rest of his life. Time and circumstance had combined to change everything.

He glanced around the fire. Through the trees, the light was dimming but there was still some time before it would fade into twilight.

He stood up, reaching beneath his tunic for his bag.

'I think I'll use the last of the daylight to search for some river stones.'

Kaela reached up and laid a hand on his arm.

'It may be best if Nyle and his men don't know about your sling,' she said.

Fenn frowned, but he nodded. He had learned to trust Kaela's instinct. Maybe she still thought there may be a confrontation with Nyle and his boys.

'Very well,' he said, 'I'll be careful. But if you want to be cautious, shouldn't you cover your hair? I saw the way people looked at you today.'

Kaela's hand reached up to touch her flame-red hair. She bent her head and for a while she didn't speak. When she did, her voice was soft and thoughtful.

'Nyle also suggested I cover my hair. But…' she turned her head to include Olgood and Gisele before looking into his eyes, '…I've spent a long time keeping secrets and pretending to be someone I'm not. I don't want to hide anymore. I *won't*. I'd rather be myself and accept the consequences. Does that make sense?'

He bent and cupped her cheek in his hand.

'Perfectly,' he said.

Olgood nodded and he and Gisele shared a glance.

HE BENT TO PICK up a stone but it was too spherical and was discarded, tossed in a high arc into the river. Several others were initially promising but they were also dropped or thrown away. His bag of stones wasn't full but if he was to add any, he wanted only the best. Stones smoothed and rounded by river waters were good candidates for his sling and he searched for a particular shape. Experience had taught that when his sling released a spinning stone in the form of a slightly flattened bird's egg, that stone flew true.

He turned his head, methodically searching the riverbank, his eyes adjusting to the gradually fading sunlight. His roving eye was arrested by an unusual sight – a mound of small stones surrounded by a group of large river boulders. He walked closer and examined the ring. There seemed to be an order to the scene. Had the boulders been deliberately placed to form a protective circle?

He was reminded of the ancient standing stone circles he'd seen in Northumbria and also in Wessex. According to the locals, such places contained a mysterious energy. Could this miniature ring also enclose secret forces?

Fenn reached out to rest his hand on one of the taller stones and felt a tingling in his fingertips. He withdrew his hand immediately and the tingling stopped. Slowly extending his hand again, he lightly rested his fingers on the stone. This time he felt nothing unusual as if he'd been tested and accepted. He placed his other hand on the neighbouring boulder and when he felt only hard cold stone, he stepped between the two.

It may have been his imagination, but inside the circle the air was unusually fresh. It had the sweet new smell that air takes following a shower of rain. He knelt and selected a handful of stones from the centre pile. In contrast to those he had previously checked on the riverbank, he could see that many were close to the shape he sought. He sorted through them and quickly selected five that looked perfect.

He picked up another handful.

CHAPTER FOUR

The ash tree challenge

Olgood pulled himself out from under the cart and stood up.

'The wheel isn't running true because the axle's cracked and needs replacing. It'll break within the next mile if we continue.'

Like the men, the cart Eadburg had provided was barely fit for purpose, but for the opposite reason – it was old, many years past its prime.

Nyle bent under the cart to examine the axle. He ran his hand along the wood, then straightened with a grunt. Although he nodded, he seemed annoyed that he had to agree with Olgood.

The axle was not the only part of the cart in danger of not lasting the journey. Many of the wheel spokes were so bleached and thinned with time they could snap at any moment. Olgood saw where he was looking and nodded, shrugging his shoulders.

'I can't rebuild the whole cart while we're on the road,' he said, 'but I can do enough to keep it going a few more days.'

'Are you sure you can make another axle?' Nyle asked.

'Of course.'

Nyle did not seem convinced.

Olgood ignored him. He placed his hands on his hips. 'First things first. Unload the cart, and then the wheels need to come off so the axle can be removed. I'll put the cart onto its side so you can remove the old axle while I go into the forest and find a new one.'

Fenn smiled. Where working with wood was involved, he accepted that Olgood would take charge.

Nyle thought for a moment then waved to his boys who lowered their spears and shields onto the ground and set to the unloading, helped by Fenn, Olgood, and Nyle. Kaela and Gisele unhitched the horse.

Nyle placed the last sack on the pile and released a heavy sigh, stepping back and stretching his back with his hands on his hips. He called to three men standing close by: 'Don't wander away. Help Olgood put the cart on its side.'

Olgood gave a snort. 'No help needed. I said I'd do it. It's only a small cart.'

Nyle stared at him. He shook his head. 'One man can't….'

Olgood frowned and Nyle stopped, narrowing his eyes. Then, dipping his head in mock acceptance, he spread his arms wide and stepped back, giving Olgood room.

'If you insist…' he said, 'I'd like to see you try. But if the cart is damaged….'

Nyle left the warning unfinished. He folded his arms as Olgood stepped forward.

Nyle's boys moved closer to watch. Gisele wore an anxious look. She glanced at Fenn and he smiled back, trying to reassure her. She returned the smile weakly, but her eyes were still worried. Fenn knew Olgood's strength. He didn't doubt Olgood could lift the weight, but it may be awkward to lower the old cart safely onto its side.

Kaela led the horse a short distance away and turned to observe. Fenn moved to a position where he could quickly assist Olgood to lower the cart if necessary.

Olgood steadied himself. He took a hold on the underside of the cart with one hand, slipping it between the spokes of the wheel. With his other hand, he gripped the front corner. He bent his knees. The huge muscles of his arms and back tightened and the wheel rose from the ground.

For a moment, the weight of the cart was supported by the other wheel and one of the harness poles. Olgood straightened his arms and the cart rose higher. At the point of equilibrium, he shifted his grip to the top of the cart and stepped around the front and over the harness pole to get enough leverage to ease the cart down.

The cart descended as smoothly as it had risen and gently came to rest.

Nyle's disbelief was evident on his face. Exclamations of admiration and congratulations from the boys were stifled when Nyle glanced in their direction.

Olgood regarded Nyle steadily and used his forearm to pretend to wipe sweat from his brow. Nyle stared back at him. He gave a slow nod.

'*Now* I could use a little help…' Olgood said pointedly, '…to fell a suitable branch and cut it to shape. With your permission, I'll take two of the lads and find a good oak.' He waited for Nyle's answer.

Nyle's suspicion showed in his eyes and a slight lift of his chin. Fenn sighed – the man was suspicious of everything.

'You two go,' Nyle said, pointing at Fenn and Olgood, as much to disagree with Olgood, Fenn thought, as for any other reason. 'My men will guard the cart.'

'Guard the cart?' said Olgood incredulously. 'With the wheels off, it's unusable. Guard it against what?'

He made a show of looking around, checking both sides of the road. It would be a poor choice of location to stage an ambush. The surrounding area was flat and the forest floor was carpeted by grass and moss-covered boulders. The nearby trees were well-spaced, providing excellent visibility in all directions.

Nyle didn't reply. Fenn thought he would arrogantly ignore Olgood, but after a moment, he grunted and said: 'Cedric the Bald has been active in this area. He's been known to confront travellers and take their possessions, however meagre.'

Fenn had heard of Cedric the Bald – talk of the outlaw was commonplace in the streets and alehouses of Witanceastre. Many travellers arrived through the West Gate with a tale to tell of Cedric the Bald. Usually, Cedric or some of his followers had been seen some distance away, on the horizon, or on the other side of a river, but even so, the travellers had only just escaped with their lives.

Olgood laughed. 'Cedric the Bald…' he said derisively. 'I've heard he's an old man, hiding away in the woods.'

'Cedric may be many things but he's certainly *not* old, and he doesn't hide.'

Nyle's words were said matter-of-factly and had a ring of truth. He wasn't trying to argue, just making a point. Had Nyle seen the outlaw, or maybe even had an encounter with Cedric the Bald?

Olgood was about to protest further but Fenn laid a hand on his shoulder.

'Come along, Olgood, let's find you a mighty oak.'

Olgood looked at him. Softly, so only Fenn could hear, he said: *'Three men would be better, then two could hold the branch steady while….'*

Fenn held up his hand and mouthed the words: *'I know. We'll manage.'*

Olgood shrugged. He drew his axe from his belt and checked the edge. Fenn grunted with amusement. He knew Olgood always kept the blade in perfect condition. Olgood turned toward the trees, laying the axe across his shoulder.

'Don't you think you should measure the axle first?' asked Nyle, his tone suggesting Olgood had forgotten an obvious point.

Olgood didn't turn around. 'No,' he replied, tapping his head. 'I have all I need here.'

Fenn found satisfaction in the fact that Nyle could not disguise his surprise.

OAKS WERE PLENTIFUL IN the forest and several had long straight branches of sufficient thickness but one after another, these were rejected by Olgood because smaller branches sprouted along their length.

'If I cut off the small branches,' he explained, 'the part left inside the wood would show as a dark spot, and the axle would be weak there. We don't want any weakness.'

They walked a mile and a half before Olgood found what he sought.

The huge oak stood proudly dominating the centre of a clearing thickly carpeted with leaves of all shades of brown shed from its massive spread of branches – a monarch of the forest. Olgood circled the enormous tree and grunted his approval. He pointed to a thick branch twenty feet above the ground sprouting horizontally from the trunk.

'Help me up,' he said.

Fenn bent in front of the trunk and Olgood used his back to reach the first massive branch. He climbed quickly, moving smoothly upwards, surprisingly agile for a big man.

When Olgood was just below the branch he'd chosen, he shuffled along its length, carefully examining every part. It was twice as thick as Fenn's eye judged it needed to be, but when he mentioned that, Olgood assured him: 'The axle we want is waiting inside this branch.'

From his lofty height, Olgood scanned the ground, checking where and how it would fall. Satisfied, he steadied his footing on two lower branches and leaned back to give himself room to swing his axe. It took a series of heavy blows from the sharp blade delivered at a precise point to sever the branch – the final blow delivered with extra force to make a clean cut.

The limb fell, landing with a crash that shook the ground, sending a flurry of leaves swirling into the air. The noise was followed by an eerie stillness as the forest held its breath, startled into silence by the assault.

Olgood scrambled down from the oak. Fenn held the fallen oak limb steady while further blows cut it to a rough length.

Olgood stood up and wiped the sticky wood shavings from his hands and sleeves. Leaning his back against the trunk of the mighty oak, he scanned the clearing, pointing to a group of stones protruding from the leafy carpet.

'If we wedge our branch between those stones, it'll be held off the ground. I can turn it and form the axle there,' he said.

The same blade that had just brutally separated the branch from the tree was now used to delicately trim the outer bark.

When only a length of pale bare wood remained, Olgood sat back and regarded it. He rotated the naked branch several times, running his hand along the now smooth wood, communicating with the oak by his touch and previewing the upcoming process in his mind. After some time, he patted the branch and took a deep breath. He was ready. He tested the edge of the axe with his thumb, laid the axe against the wood and sliced a long strip from the branch. He continued, precisely shaving the wood, turning it every few moments to ensure the slicing was applied evenly.

Fenn sat on his haunches and watched him work. Olgood treated the wood with gentleness and reverence. He showed no hesitation, each movement deftly and surely releasing the axle that Olgood saw buried within the branch; the axe in his hands equally obedient when taking broad slices or tiny chips.

After a while, Fenn tired of watching the repetitive strokes and turned his gaze to the study of his surroundings. A group of birds had followed the men in the latter part of their walk through the forest, probably interested in whatever insect delicacies their passage disturbed. They were birds he hadn't seen in Northumbria – their long tails gave them incredible manoeuvrability in the air. While idly watching the birds and marvelling at their skill, his eye was drawn to the movement of a bush that swayed momentarily in opposition to the wind.

He slowly rose from his crouch.

'Maybe there's hare or quail about,' he said quietly. He drew his sling from his belt and shook it loose. 'How long will you be?'

'As long as it takes,' replied Olgood without pausing or looking up.

Fenn smiled. He drew a stone from his bag and fitted it into the pouch of the sling. Cupping the pouch in his hand, he slowly walked towards the bush where he had seen movement, placing his feet carefully on the leaf-covered forest floor to minimise the sound of his footfall.

At the edge of the clearing, he stopped. If the movement he saw had been made by a small animal, he should have heard rustling or seen some activity in the foliage as the animal moved away, but both the bush and the surrounding undergrowth had remained still and quiet. Had the movement been caused by something other than an animal? He transferred his sling to his left hand and drew the axe from his belt with his right.

He took a quick step to the side to see behind the bush.

Nyle casually stood up.

Fenn shook his head, more irritated than surprised; his suspicion confirmed.

'So, Olgood – it seems we are being spied upon,' he said, fitting the axe to the loop on his belt.

Olgood looked up, saw who it was, and returned to his task without a word.

'I thought you were ensuring Cedric the Bald didn't steal our broken cart,' said Fenn.

It was Nyle's method of approach that annoyed him. The man had come to check on them, but he could easily have approached openly to enquire about progress. It matched Nyle's nature to be sly and furtive.

Nyle ignored Fenn's words. He took some time to study Olgood's methodical trimming of the oak branch, then, still watching Olgood, he said: 'As Olgood said, it's an unlikely place for an attack. My men have their instructions. The cart and the goods are safe.'

He finished his inspection and casually turned his attention to Fenn.

'What have you there?' he demanded, indicating the sling Fenn held wrapped in his palm. 'A toy to hunt squirrels?'

Fenn dropped the stone-filled pouch from his hand, holding the cord, and let the pouch swing at his side. He checked Nyle's bow, held against his back by a leather strap, and noted that the quiver was full.

'No, ' he said stiffly, 'it's *not* a toy. This sling is a weapon, and I'll wager it's better than your bow at any distance you care to choose.'

Nyle's eyes widened and he laughed in astonishment. It was the first time Fenn had seen the man remotely happy. With a smile on his face he looked a different person.

'Better than my bow?' he laughed again, this time derisively. He leaned back, appraising Fenn. 'And what would you have to wager?'

'A mug of ale when we reach our destination.'

Nyle's eyes became a little wider. 'Ale?' he said incredulously. He obviously expected a more substantial bet.

The wager amount hardly made the exercise attractive but the opportunity to impress his authority with marksmanship could make the contest worthwhile. He looked down at the sling. He saw a length of braided cord with one end formed into a loop and the other knotted. In the middle was a leather pouch housing a small stone.

He nodded and grunted an acceptance.

'I accept the challenge,' he said.

Nyle placed his hands on his hips and arched his back, then brought his elbows forward, stretching the long muscles of his back. Reaching over his shoulder, he withdrew the long bow from its leather strap and, with his other hand, felt inside his tunic for the string. He took some time to examine the bowstring, then bringing it up to his nose, he smelt it.

Fenn watched him. Was he checking the string was dry?

This was the closest Fenn had been to Nyle's bow. Immediately he noticed it was taller and thicker than most, as tall as Nyle himself. Even so, in its unstrung state, it was no more than a slender strip of wood. Only when the bowstring was slipped over the end and the bow bent and strung did the wooden pole become an instantly recognisable weapon.

Nyle drew on the bowstring to test its tension. Satisfied, he turned to look in the direction Fenn was facing.

'What's the target?'

Fenn searched the forest for a moment, then grunted with satisfaction. He pointed.

'That young ash,' he said.

There was a natural corridor through a row of trees to a pale ash standing sixty paces away. Its tall straight smooth-barked trunk was thin enough to be encircled by a man's hands and light enough to show the mark of a stone or arrow.

Nyle raised his eyebrows. 'Will your little stone reach that far?'

Fenn pretended to consider the question. 'I think so,' he said thoughtfully. 'We'll see, won't we.'

He bent and picked up a fallen branch, snapped off some twigs and dropped it in front of his feet.

'We'll shoot from here.'

Behind him, the sound of the axe chipping at the oak branch stopped and Fenn heard Olgood approaching.

'A contest, eh?' said Olgood at Fenn's shoulder. 'What's the wager?'

Fenn told him and Olgood laughed. He regarded Nyle with a broad smile. 'Can you afford that?'

Nyle mumbled something dismissively, then said: 'Who first?'

Olgood's voice took a formal tone: 'Traditionally, the one who was challenged shoots first.'

Fenn stepped back. Nyle took his place and twisted his feet to find firm footing.

'One shot or best of three?'

'Best of three,' said Fenn.

Fenn was confident of his ability with the sling. His father Lenglan had presented him with a sling when he had been a small child and he had taken to it immediately with an affinity that seemed inborn. As he grew, the spare time necessary for practice became a precious commodity that was difficult to extract from his days in the monastery. In his early years, the day was spent at school and later, as an apprentice scribe, in the scriptorium. At most other times he was expected to be engaged in one of the many chores that monastery life demanded – harvesting, feeding animals, tending gardens.

But Fenn persisted. Whenever and however he found the time, he would sling stone after stone at increasingly smaller and more distant targets, often until the gathering darkness made it impossible to see.

In the beginning Lenglan had tried to teach Fenn to swing the sling vertically – 'Like the slingers in the Frankish army' – in both directions, so the stone could be released either at the top or bottom of the circle. But Fenn had found a nearly horizontal swing above and behind his head more to his liking, and soon Lenglan could not argue with his results. The pupil improved rapidly and the teacher became unnecessary as Fenn learned to adjust for wind, distance, and, if necessary, the movement of the target. The cord and pouch became an extension of his body and eventually his arm could place a stone wherever his eye directed it.

But constant practice was essential, and lately Fenn had had little. A thriving, bustling town like Witanceastre offered neither space nor opportunity for such activity. He was grateful for the few throws he had been able to take on the riverbank the previous evening.

NYLE STOOD SIDE-ON TO his target.

He flexed his shoulders and looked at the treetops, checking the wind. His eyes dropped to the forest, moving left then right and finally resting on the distant ash tree. He stared silently at the target for a long moment.

Nyle took a deep breath, released it slowly, extended the arm holding the bow, and curled two fingers around the bowstring, locking the arrow between them. He raised his arm so the shaft pointed high on the target tree. Fenn watched him smoothly draw back on the bowstring. For this bow, with its extra height and thickness, Fenn knew that simple action would require considerable strength.

With the bow at full stretch and the hand holding the notched arrow tucked hard against his cheek, Nyle lowered his arm in a slow easy arc and released his shaft while the bow was still moving. The soft twang of the bowstring resonated in the forest as the arrow silently sped down the corridor of trees. It struck the trunk of the young ash on the right-hand edge. There was an explosion of splinters, and the arrow gouged a furrow in the wood before flying beyond the tree and deep into the forest.

There was a grunt of surprise from Olgood, and Fenn nodded his approval.

'Good – *very* good,' he said. To hit the slender tree at this distance was something Fenn was sure not many of the King's archers could achieve, and certainly not consistently. In battle, archers usually depended on volume – putting as many arrows into the air as possible – rather than accuracy. With that one shot, Nyle had proved himself to be the marksman Fenn had expected.

Nyle seemed surprised that the compliment was genuine. He lowered the bow and stepped to the side. Fenn took his place.

He examined the stone he had drawn from his bag then closed his hand and held it tightly in his palm. He checked the direction and strength of the wind in the trees. It was blustery, but there was more movement in the treetops than on the forest floor – he would need to compensate for that, just as Nyle had. He placed the stone into the centre of the pouch. He slowed his breathing. Like Nyle, he stood with his left leg forward as he started the sling whirling over his head.

Four times the sling spun in its tight circle; on the fifth spin – when the balance was right – he brought his hand forward and, with a flick of his wrist, released the knotted end of the cord, freeing the stone. There was a small whistle as the stone left the pouch, after which, like the arrow, the missile flew in silence. Fenn held his breath as he followed the flight. Where this first stone hit would tell him if other corrections were needed.

The stone struck the tree below where Nyle's arrow had hit, also on the side of the thin trunk. It bounced away from the ash and hit a neighbouring tree with enough force for the second strike to be audible. The damage to the ash was less than that caused by the arrow, but it was still noticeable.

The mark of Fenn's stone was closer to the centre of the trunk by the width of a finger.

Olgood gave a grunt of satisfaction.

Nyle regarded the ash. He released an audible breath but said nothing. Fenn knew what he was thinking – it would be the *second* shot that showed whether the first had been lucky or not.

'The wind is a little stronger than I thought,' Fenn said. 'It seems to have affected the stone less than the arrow. What do you think?' As he spoke, he took another stone from his bag and held it tightly in the palm of his hand.

Nyle stared at him.

After a moment he said: 'We shall see.'

He examined the arrows in his quiver and selected a second arrow. He stepped up to the mark.

Again the bow was raised with the arrow pointing to the sky and slowly lowered. Again the arrow sped through the trees and struck the ash with a force that shook the tree. This time the shaft remained fixed in the ash, toward the right edge but higher and closer to the centre – closer than the mark of Fenn's first stone. Fenn had to acknowledge it was impressive marksmanship.

Nyle nodded his approval and stepped aside. His look did not need words: '*See if you can do better than that.*'

Fenn opened his hand and examined the stone he had chosen. It was rounded and flattened, just as he liked. This stone, like the first, was one of the set he had found on the riverbank last evening. It had been held in his hand long enough to be warmed. He wasn't sure whether the temperature of the stone affected its flight, but he liked the idea that he should gift the stone the warmth of his body. It gave them an affinity.

He placed his foot behind the branch, steadied his stance, and set the sling moving.

One, two, three, four times, again, it whirled – its speed increasing with every turn. His eye, his arm, and his fingers compensated for the first stone's strike by moving his focus a fraction to the left. The stone gave that same unusual whistle as it left the pouch and then flew for a few heartbeats in silence as it sped towards the distant ash. It struck the tree trunk in the centre, and that fact ensured the stone did not bounce to left or right but stayed where it had hit, embedded in the tree.

Nyle stood for some time silently regarding the young ash. His eyes dropped to the sling held between Fenn's fingers, assessing again the weapon he was competing against. He released his breath slowly between his lips and nodded.

'Interesting…' he said. 'A perfect shot. Your stones fly as fast as an arrow and hit with more force than I expected.' He held Fenn's eye before returning his gaze to the tree.

'But I have one more arrow.'

He stepped up to the branch and stood there calmly, his bow held at rest by his side. His eyes flicked once more to the treetops and he wet his lips. He took a third arrow from his quiver, examining the shaft, the feathers, and finally the tip. Satisfied, he notched it to the bowstring. Slowly, he drew back on the string until the tips of his fingers nudged into his cheek, and the bow started its steady descent in an arc to the target. He stopped breathing a moment before his fingers released the string.

The arrow struck the ash in the centre of the trunk, an inch above Fenn's embedded stone.

Olgood gave a small cry of astonishment and approval.

'Also a hit in the centre,' said Fenn. 'Truly an excellent shot.'

It was not his habit to dwell on the importance or otherwise of a task. If it needed to be done, he simply did it to the best of his ability. So he wasted no time thinking that his next shot needed to be perfect to win the contest. He needed to place his third stone into an area the size of the tips of three fingers on a target sixty paces away. Many factors were in play, only some under his control. A gust of wind at the wrong time. An unsteadiness of foot on the rough ground or a slip of sweaty fingers. A tiny miscalculation of angle. An imperfection in the stone. Any of these could affect the outcome by a small margin. And a small margin would be enough.

He checked the stone he held in his hand. It was another of the stones from the mysterious circle on the riverbank; it looked to be a perfect shape. It already felt warm as if it was radiating its own heat.

He placed the stone in the middle of the pouch and started the sling whirling above his head. He felt his body tune to the sling, to the movement; felt the combination of hand, arm, and eye come together, become *one*. He was the cord, he was the pouch, he was the stone – and the stone was part of him.

On the fifth revolution, he gave an extra flick of his fingers at the precise moment, the moment that felt *right*, and the stone flew free.

There was the same unusual whistle on release. A moment later, all three heard the stone hit. To Fenn's ear, the sound had a strange sharpness.

For a long moment, there was silence as three pairs of eyes studied the distant ash.

'Where did that stone strike?' asked Nyle. It was a genuine question; his voice held no sarcasm. 'I don't see its mark, but I heard it hit.'

The ash was unchanged. It showed no evidence of Fenn's last stone. The trees surrounding the ash had darker and thicker bark than the solitary ash so if it had hit a different tree, the mark of the stone may not be evident at this distance.

The throw had felt good with nothing out of balance. Fenn had followed the stone's flight toward the tree. It looked to be on target. He could think of no reason why the stone should not have hit the ash. But the evidence was unmistakable – whatever the cause, his last attempt *had* failed to find its target.

He shrugged. 'I owe you an ale when we reach Westerling,' he said to Nyle, 'but I offer you my congratulations now. That was impressive marksmanship.' He held out his hand to Nyle. 'You, sir, are a true master of the bow.'

Olgood shook his head in disbelief. 'Fenn's stones always go where he wants them to go,' he said.

Nyle accepted Fenn's handshake with a firm grasp. 'I'd call it an even contest,' he said. 'You've taught me a valuable lesson today. I wouldn't have believed a sling could be so effective if I hadn't seen it for myself. Even at this distance, your stones hit with a force that would disable or even kill a man.'

Fenn nodded. 'But a wager is a wager, and an ale is an ale.'

Nyle smiled. Again Fenn was struck by the difference Nyle's smile made to his usually dour face.

Nyle bent the bow to unstring it. The oiled wood glistened in the sunlight.

'Your bow…' said Olgood, '…what wood is that? It looks to be yew but I see you've banded different woods together.'

Nyle eased the string over the end of the bow and looked up at Olgood. For a moment his eyes narrowed, suspicious of the question. Then he grunted.

'Yes, it's yew,' he said, 'I made it myself. Heartwood *and* sapwood. Combined, they're stronger and more flexible than either alone.' He paused but then held out the bow for Olgood to inspect.

Olgood took the bow, examining the wood from tip to tip. 'And the shine?'

'Oil and wax. To keep the wood supple and dry. I also use a mixture on my string for the same reason.' He held the string up to his nose again.

Olgood nodded in appreciation. 'It's a masterpiece. I've never seen a bow like this one.'

'There's not another like it in the land.'

Olgood handed back the bow. Nyle took it then regarded the tree where his two arrows sprouted like budding branches.

'I'll retrieve my arrows,' he said. 'And I'd like to find the shaft that flew further into the forest. Unlike your stones, each arrow takes time and effort to create.'

And a good stone takes time and effort to find, Fenn thought. He remembered the unusual whistling sound his stones had made as they left the sling. He'd like to examine the one still in the tree for damage and find where his third stone had hit.

'I'll help you look,' he said.

'Good hunting,' said Olgood. 'I have an axle that still needs shaping.'

Fenn followed Nyle down the corridor of trees toward the ash.

He lagged behind Nyle, in no hurry. He knew Nyle would need time to remove his arrows. A breeze touched his face, then it was gone. Had a sudden puff like that affected his last stone? It would need to be much stronger than that gentle waft, but it was possible. Thinking of the third stone drew his thoughts to the stone circle on the riverbank.

He had felt a difference in atmosphere when he'd stood inside the ring of boulders, but it was nothing he had words to describe, and he had to admit it was probably imagined. Nonetheless, the stones he'd used today flew as true as any he'd ever thrown. *Except for the third,* he had to remind himself. Perhaps that one was flawed, twisted in some way that had caused its path to curve out of line. He thought again about the short whistle each stone had made leaving the pouch. It was strange that all three should make the same sound. They seemed to be announcing that they were different from other stones. Maybe these stones *did* have a mysterious quality.

At the ash, Nyle reached up to grasp the closest arrow. It had penetrated the trunk with force, and he took his time to carefully ease it out of the wood without overly bending the shaft. When it was free, Nyle thoroughly inspected the metal tip for damage, turning it over several times. He then examined the feathers at the other end of the shaft. Even while giving the arrow such close attention, Nyle remained alert, his eyes regularly pausing in his examination to search the surrounding forest, even twisting to look back down the tree corridor. Fenn also turned his head, sweeping the forest with his gaze. Nothing seemed out of place.

He sighed. He was catching Nyle's habit. He pulled his axe from his belt – he'd need to use the point of the blade to pry out his stone. He relaxed and waited for Nyle to complete his retrieval.

When the second arrow had been removed, Fenn expected Nyle to step aside to allow him access to his stone. Instead, Nyle used the point of an arrow to extract Fenn's stone from the trunk.

Fenn smiled, pleasantly surprised that Nyle would do that without being asked. He replaced his axe.

Nyle suddenly jerked back from the tree and became still, his whole body motionless as if a poisonous adder had appeared – a hand's width from his face. Nyle was as tall as Fenn. Fenn could not see past him.

'What's the matter…?' he asked, his concern growing. He stepped to the side to get a view around the tree but couldn't see any danger.

'*That's not possible,*' said Nyle, his voice no more than a whisper.

'What…? Nyle, what is it?'

Nyle turned to Fenn, an expression of disbelief on his face. He extended a closed fist and slowly opened his fingers.

In his upturned hand lay two identical riverbank stones.

'The third stone followed the *exact* path of the second,' said Nyle. 'How could that be?'

Fenn stared at the stones, a smile spreading over his face. He remembered the sharpness of the sound as the last stone hit.

He accepted the stones from Nyle and examined them. Both were undamaged, showing no sign of their encounter with the tree or with each other. He closed his hand, cradling the stones.

'I would have *sworn* it flew true,' he said.

Nyle shook his head and blew out a breath.

'Nobody will believe me.'

CHAPTER FIVE

A nocturnal abduction

They halted early to set up camp. The sky was clouding over and darkening in the northwest, threatening rain. When a thick grove in the forest promised good shelter, Nyle decided to stop for the night.

Olgood and Nyle were under the cart, examining how the new axle had travelled. Gisele searched the forest for herbs with one of Nyle's boys as a guard. The others were building their fire a short distance away.

Fenn brought an armful of dry branches to the tree where Kaela had a fire already showing good flame. He added his wood to the pile and sat down beside her.

'That should be enough.' He wiped his hands on his knees.

She leaned against him and kissed him.

He held her and they rested together for a while, comfortable with their silence, surveying the surrounding woodland. The breeze had turned to the west and was trialling its strength with forceful gusts tugging at their hair – another harbinger of the storm.

'What do you know about Nyle?' Fenn asked.

'Nyle? Why?'

'He came to meet us in the forest when Olgood cut a new axle this morning. At first I thought the man was overly nervous and suspicious, but now….'

When he didn't continue, Kaela prompted: 'But now – what…?'

'I may have been wrong. Maybe he's just a good leader who takes his charge seriously.'

Kaela leaned back and regarded him. 'Hmm…' she mused. '*That's* an interesting observation. So you think he may be a good leader of men….' She stopped, teasing him with a half-smile on her lips.

Fenn smiled. He wagged his finger at her. 'Don't play with me. Do you know anything about him or not?'

'Well, he *is* an interesting man, or, at least – I've heard interesting stories about him. You could say he's almost infamous, in fact, according to some in my father's household.'

'What do they say?'

Kaela added some larger branches to the fire to build the flame.

'I can only tell you what I've heard,' she said. 'It may or may not be true.'

She folded her arms over her knees.

'A few years ago, Nyle was a *proven man*, a status he'd earned by performing some noteworthy action in a conflict against Hernam, King of the Dumnonian Cornish. Beorhtric rewarded him and his family, his father and brother, with a small parcel of land in Hwicce, a province between Wessex and Mercia. When Hernam again raided across the border, Beorhtric called on his Ealdormen in the north and west to raise their fyrds. He remembered Nyle and ordered that he be made a leader in the fyrd of his shire Lord – Ealdorman Ingeld of Hwicce.'

'A fyrd? I don't know that word. What's a fyrd?'

'Ah, I forgot about your sheltered monastic upbringing,' she smiled. 'In these parts, a *fyrd* is the force of men a shire Lord gathers to fight either for the shire or for the King.'

'What if a man doesn't want to fight, or if the harvest is due?'

Kaela widened her eyes, acknowledging his question.

'That depends on the circumstances. If the shire is attacked, everyone fights. But if the King asks the shire lord to provide a fyrd for a more distant conflict, the Lord decides who stays for the harvest and who fights. Most will fight willingly because defeat could mean death or capture as a thrall.' She shrugged. 'But all men are bound to serve their Lord. If they refuse when called, they'll be fined or punished under Ine's Laws. King Ine realised both the harvest and the defence of the shire were important – putting all your efforts into one and ignoring the other will equally result in disaster. From that came the idea of the fyrd taking both into account.' At Fenn's puzzled look, she added: 'Ine was King of Wessex seventy or eighty years ago. He issued a written code of laws. Beorhtric has retained most of his laws.'

'I see,' Fenn nodded. 'So, Nyle became a leader in Ingeld's fyrd.'

'Yes, but he was appointed by request of the King, not by Ealdorman Ingeld.'

'Is that important?'

'I don't know the detail, but there was bad blood between Nyle's family and the Ealdorman. Nyle's father had accused Ingeld of plotting against Wessex and being a spy for Mercia. Ingeld would *not* have made Nyle a leader.'

'But Mercia and Wessex are allies, aren't they?'

'Beorhtric treats Hwicce as part of Wessex, but it's traditionally been a sub-kingdom of Mercia. It was probably part of the marriage agreement when Beohrtric married Eadburg. At the moment, this bizarre arrangement allows Beorhtric to collect taxes in Hwicce and require the fealty of the Ealdorman.'

'How do you know all this?'

'I had good tutors, and I find the relationships interesting.'

Fenn reminded himself that Kaela was raised a princess of Wessex, taught by leading scholars, had been sent to the court of King Charles in Francia to further her education, and spoke several languages.

'Of course.' Fenn smiled at her. 'So, the fyrd was formed by Ingeld….' He waved for her to continue.

Kaela leaned forward. 'The fyrd was formed with Nyle as a leader, and marched to the River Taw in the west to join fyrds from the western shires.' She looked up at him. 'Our destination, Westerling, lies close to the Taw – between the river Exe and the Taw.'

He raised his eyebrows but said nothing.

She continued: 'At the river, they met Hernam. Under somewhat mysterious circumstances, Ealdorman Ingeld was killed at the start of the battle, or maybe just *before* the start. Now… this is the interesting part. Prudy told me there was a rumour that Nyle had killed him. The story said that although Beorhtric had positioned his fyrds for a dawn attack, Ingeld ordered Nyle to cross the river with a small force during the night. Nyle refused. The next morning the Ealdorman was dead. Nobody seems able to say whether the killing was an accident or deliberate, but the word from others who served in the Ealdorman's fyrd was that the man was an idiot and a brute and deserved his death. No one admitted seeing the act, and no one would talk against Nyle. But even so, only his past service, the lack of willing witnesses, and the mercy of my father saved him from the death demanded by many of the Ealdormen of Wessex. As it was, Beorhtric took away his land and he now serves the Queen, as you see, in her house-guards, trusted only with minor duties…' she waved her hand to encompass their small gathering, '…such as this.'

'I see. And the battle…? What was the outcome?'

'Hernam was outnumbered and got the worst of the skirmish. He agreed to retreat to the River Tamar and recognise that river as the border between Cornwall and Wessex. Everyone went home.'

When Fenn was silent, she gave him a questioning look.

'So Nyle will be returning to the scene of his alleged crime,' he mused. He paused for a while in thought.

'There may be more to Nyle than meets the eye,' he said. 'He certainly is a master bowman. I've only seen one other as good – do you remember Manfredi at Hammaburg?'

'Of course.' A frown creased her brow. 'You said you met with Nyle in the forest. What did you mean? Did you see him use his bow?'

Fenn had been looking for an appropriate time to tell Kaela about the contest. He had so far held back for two reasons – firstly, he didn't like to boast and secondly, she had thought it best to keep his sling secret. But now he had no choice.

'He came to check how Olgood was faring with the axle. He saw my sling and called it a toy.' Fenn shrugged. 'I challenged him, sling against bow.'

'What was the wager?' Kaela asked warily.

'A mug of ale.'

She laughed. 'I see.'

'Yes. At sixty paces, Nyle hit an ash tree about this size….' Fenn formed a circle joining the fingers of both hands, '…with all three arrows.'

Kaela raised her eyebrows. 'Sixty paces. Impressive.'

'Yes…' Fenn nodded. 'Yes it was.'

When Kaela was silent, Fenn stood up and stretched. He looked to the west where the setting sun was being swallowed by dark stormclouds approaching from the northwest.

'There'll be rain tonight,' he said. He glanced towards the road. 'I'll see if they've found any problems with the axle.'

Kaela held up a finger. 'One moment please, sir,' she said in a sing-song voice.

Fenn sighed.

'Who won the challenge?'

Fenn was glad she hadn't asked who'd won the *wager*. It could be difficult to explain that although his sling had won the challenge, he'd conceded the wager before the ash had been examined.

'I did, but only with a fortunate shot of my last stone.'

'Ha!' Kaela exclaimed. '*He* hit the tree with all three arrows but *you* won the contest. I've said it before – that sling of yours seems to produce a large number of fortunate shots.'

She patted the ground beside her. 'Tell me the details.'

FENN ADJUSTED HIS BEDDING and placed the folded cloak he used as a pillow so it rested at a comfortable angle against a tree root. He took his axe and set it on the ground beside the blanket, then removed the bag of stones from his belt and placed that by the pillow. He pulled Kaela's blanket closer so that it touched his. Standing, Fenn threw his arms out and backwards until his shoulders creaked, then clasped his hands above his head, stretching the muscles of his back.

Kaela had left to check the horse and he'd just heard its whinny of greeting. He sat on the blanket and then reclined, letting his head fall onto the cloak. Absentmindedly, his fingers felt for the handle of his axe, checking it was where it was supposed to be. He reached up and touched the bag of stones with his other hand. Satisfied, he covered his eyes with the crook of his elbow and waited for Kaela's return.

A short while later, she folded herself against him and the touch of her lips brushed against his.

'I've missed you,' he whispered, returning her kiss. 'You were a long time. Where have you been?'

'You know where I've been.'

She started to pull away but he stopped her with his hand on the back of her head. 'And where do you think you're going now?'

His reward was a deep chuckle.

As if in harmony, a soft roll of thunder sounded far away.

FENN OPENED HIS EYES.

It was dark.

The thick foliage and clouds combined to shade any light from the moon and stars. The fire had been reduced to embers and the glow they projected barely extended beyond the perimeter ring of stones. He was thankful it hadn't yet started to rain.

He wondered what had woken him. Some sound, he supposed, but he couldn't recall it. He automatically reached out to check his axe but froze with his hand in mid-movement.

A foot had stepped into the feeble light cast by the fire. It was encased in a sandal. Nobody in the group wore sandals.

He allowed his hand to resume its slow creep toward the axe. His fingers touched earth and he spread them wide, searching for the weapon. It was gone. He started to rise but something hard – the tip of a sword – pressed against his chest. Somebody threw a handful of leaves and sticks on the fire and, when it flared, followed with an armful of branches.

The sudden blaze of light revealed a dozen men standing by the fire.

A man with a drawn sword stood at Fenn's feet. He was big-chested with solid legs. He wore a vest of chain mail, and the firelight glinted on a metal helmet. He extended his sword so that it again rested against Fenn's chest. Another man's sword threatened Kaela. On the other side of Kaela, a third man was tying Olgood's hands together behind his back. Olgood was allowing this to happen because the sword of a fourth hovered above Gisele's throat.

Fenn's eyes were drawn to an unexpected sight among the men revealed by the firelight – two young barefoot boys aged about seven or eight.

A deep voice said: 'Bring the other men to this fire.'

There was the sound of annoyed grunts and curses as Nyle and his men were coaxed away from the dull coals of their fire and directed to the one beside Fenn that was now burning fiercely.

When he saw that Gisele had a sword to her throat, one of Nyle's boys started toward her with an exclamation of alarm but the protest on his lips died when he was struck solidly on the head and roughly bundled back into line.

Nyle strode into the firelight.

'What has happened to my sentry, Cedric?' Nyle demanded. His tone was surprisingly belligerent.

There was a slight pause before the man he'd addressed answered.

'He lives.'

The two men stared at each other. Fenn moved his head for a better view of the man Nyle had called 'Cedric'. Was this Cedric the Bald? The man looked bald but only because his hair was cut very short.

'Well, Brother,' said Cedric. 'It's been a while. How have you fared?'

Fenn saw the resemblance immediately; high forehead, thin face, hooked nose. Cedric looked to be the elder. Fenn took a measure of the man, his eyes roaming from head to foot. With a start of recognition, he saw that Cedric held Fenn's axe in one hand and Kaela's sword and scabbard in the other.

Nyle didn't answer the question. 'Is my man hurt?'

'He'll wake in a while.'

Nyle gave an annoyed grunt in his throat. 'Why have you come here? What do you want from us? We don't have much.'

'I wanted to see *you*,' Cedric said in a mocking voice. 'You haven't ventured west for some time.'

'You know what I think about how you choose to live,' said Nyle.

Cedric was suddenly angry. 'When that bastard Ingeld had our father killed, I didn't *have* a choice.'

He calmed his temper with an effort. 'Anyway, when I was informed you were travelling this road, it was an opportunity to belatedly thank you for the Ealdorman's death.'

Nyle neither admitted nor denied his hand in that matter. 'Yes,' he said simply. 'He's dead.'

'This land is much the better without him. What of his son, Ethelmund?'

'He's never done us serious harm.'

'Not directly, perhaps. But to others, certainly. You know he's as bad as the father. Now that he's Ealdorman of Hwicce, who knows....'

If he expected Nyle to comment, Nyle didn't oblige.

Cedric stared at his brother for a moment, then shrugged.

'Ah well, time enough for that to unfold. I'm keeping my eye on Hwicce.'

He turned in a half-circle, his arm extended, introducing the forest.

'I've made my life in the forest and I have a *good* life here, one I've been undertaking for so long now that I couldn't change if I wanted to.' He paused and added forcefully: 'Which I *don't*.'

When Nyle still didn't speak, Cedric motioned for the men holding Fenn and Kaela to allow them to stand. Fenn's hand covered his bag of stones and in the act of adjusting his clothing, he tucked the bag safely under his tunic. He checked that his sling was where he expected it to be.

When he straightened, Fenn saw two men hitching the horse to the cart.

'The King will hear of this,' said Kaela.

Cedric shook his head. 'Unfortunately, not soon enough. The King is with Offa in Tamworth.'

'He *was*. He'll be returning with all haste to Witanceastre as we speak.'

'No,' Cedric said firmly, shaking his head, 'I'm afraid he won't. The messenger you sent to your father was stopped by the Queen.'

At her intake of breath, he said: 'There's very little happens around here that I don't know about, and, yes, I do know you are Beorhtric's daughter, Princess Kaela.' He smiled, waving a hand toward Nyle. 'Firstly, you're travelling with my brother, a member of the Queen's house-guards, and then there's the matter of your hair, which, even in the firelight, is hard to ignore.'

Kaela shared a pained look with Fenn, but he shook his head. It didn't matter.

Fenn knew Queen Eadburg forbade that Kaela be referred to as a princess, so Cedric's use of the title indicated he was no friend of the Queen.

Addressing Nyle, Cedric said: 'We will, of course, take your horse and cart and your weapons. I'll take the Princess and *you*...' he indicated Fenn '...you seem to be a pair... as hostages. I'm sure I'll be able to ransom you for a penny or two.'

He waved for the men to separate Fenn and Kaela from Olgood and Gisele.

The outlaw gave a rueful smile. 'I'd like nothing more than for the King to hurry home. Indeed, I'll be praying for his quick return. If what I've heard is true, the Mercian bitch he married wouldn't part with a bent penny for his daughter's safe release, so the sooner the King is in Witanceastre and can pay me, the less I'll need to feed you.'

'He may decide to pay you in your own blood rather than coin,' Kaela said.

'Let him try. He has to find me first.'

He glared at Kaela, daring her to reply. She regarded him silently.

Cedric placed his hands on his hips and stretched his back. Fenn was reminded that Nyle had performed the same hands-on-hips stretch before shooting his first arrow in the forest.

'You'll come along too, Nyle,' Cedric continued. 'When I've been paid, the three of you will be freed.'

'Cedric, is this necessary? Why not just let us go on our way?'

Cedric's eyes narrowed. 'As you remarked yourself, Nyle, this is what I do. It's how I'm forced to make my living.'

Nyle sighed. 'Then why take me?' he asked. 'I'm not worth anything.'

Cedric gave a wry smile.

'It may occur to you to try to retrieve these two *before* I get paid. I know you, Nyle, and I don't want you and your bow free to try.' He held up a finger. 'And I wouldn't want you hurt in any foolish attempt.'

Nyle stared at his brother. He took a deep breath and let it out. 'Make sure my bow is not damaged.'

'I'm aware of what that bow means to you,' said Cedric. 'We'll take good care of it and you'll get it back.'

He turned his gaze to Olgood and Gisele and then Nyle's men.

'I've no need of the rest of you – unless you'd like to join me. You can shrug off whatever chains are binding you and live as free men in the forest.' He paused, waiting for a response. When there was none, he smiled again. 'Ah, well. An opportunity missed.'

He waved a hand at Olgood. 'That big one looked like he wanted to break me in half and I think he could have done it. He can be untied after we've gone and in the morning you can all go on your way.' He spread his hands, offering an apology. 'Unfortunately, you'll be without your weapons.'

Cedric lifted the axe and sword he held. His gaze flicked to Fenn, then back to Kaela.

'You were both carrying unusual weapons. The axe is interesting, but I have no use for it, and you'll get that back. But the sword….' He dropped his eyes to Kaela's sword, the flickering firelight reflecting on the fine metalwork of the hilt and scabbard. 'This is a real beauty and an unexpected bonus. A particularly fine weapon. I'll keep it as part of your ransom.'

Fenn's glance caught the narrowing of Kaela's eyes.

One of the children came up to Cedric and tugged at his cloak. Cedric bent down and the boy whispered in his ear.

'Of course you can,' Cedric said, ruffling the boy's hair. 'Both of you.' The boy collected his mate and they ran towards the horse.

Cedric noticed Fenn watching the boys run off.

'Our little rats scampered silently over the ground and lifted your weapons without a single clink to disturb the night,' he said. 'I gave my word they could ride on the horse if they did well, and I stand by my word.'

The light from the fire had dimmed - the armful of wood it had been fed was all but consumed. A brief flash of lightning penetrated the tree cover and another roll of thunder sounded, closer than before. Cedric took in a breath and glanced upwards. His genial mood turned serious.

'We need to hurry.' He circled a hand over his head. 'Back to the camp,' he ordered. 'You all know what to do.'

There was instant movement as his men took to their tasks. They were disciplined and well-organised. Cedric detailed four men to take care of Fenn, Kaela, and Nyle. One motioned them to move with his sword. Fenn reached out to invite Kaela to go ahead.

'No touching and no talking!' Cedric said sharply – then, to his men: 'Keep them well apart.' He came up to Fenn. 'I'm not going to tie you,' he said. 'You may think it a simple thing to escape in the darkness, but if one tries, the other will suffer for it – even if that person is a princess.'

Cedric turned away and walked to where Olgood, Gisele, and Nyle's men were still seated. Looking over his shoulder and pointing towards the east, Cedric's voice carried on the night air.

'Your companion is seated against a tree in this direction at two hundred paces. He's tied and gagged but unless he's fallen on his face, he should be comfortable.'

The fire was quickly dying, and once again the only light in the clearing came from glowing embers. The cart was already out of sight and Cedric and the men beside him were visible only as dark silhouettes.

A hand pushed at Fenn's shoulder, wanting him to turn and walk into the forest. Fenn tried to catch Olgood's eye but the light was too dim. He took a few steps backwards, trying to keep Cedric in sight and hear what he was saying.

Cedric addressed Olgood's group: 'Some of my men will stay with you until we've had time to get some distance from here.' He pointed at Olgood. 'The big ox stays tied until they leave.'

A sword prodded Fenn painfully in the chest – a more insistent request to move. He looked at the man behind the sword. It was the same man who had woken him, wearing the chain mail and helmet. He was standing close, so close that Fenn could smell the stench of his breath. The man placed his sword alongside Fenn's cheek.

'Will it take blood to get you to move?' he snarled.

He had an accent similar to Gisele's. His comment was overheard by a second man who diverted his path towards them in case the big man needed assistance.

Fenn turned. At first, looking away from the fire, he could only make out the vague forms of trees. He took a few careful steps in the direction indicated by the sword. With his eyes adjusting quickly to the gloom two figures could be distinguished, Nyle and Kaela, waiting ahead between a pair of tall tree trunks. He took another step, feeling rough tree roots underfoot.

The wind was strengthening as the storm closed in, gusting and moaning with growing force. The rain would not be far behind – Fenn could smell it.

Cedric raised his voice so those who remained could hear. Fenn heard his last words clearly over the wind rushing through the trees, the rustling of leaves and branches, and the shuffling of feet on the forest floor.

'We are well practised at this,' Cedric said. 'There won't be any tracks for you to follow, even from the horse and cart.'

His voice hardened. 'I'm warning you not to try. I'll be checking our trail. I'm willing to spare you now, but I will *not* be as lenient if you try to follow where you're not wanted....'

'You will pay with your lives.'

CHAPTER SIX

A river barrier and an outlaw camp

Cedric the Bald stared at the dark rushing water and cursed.

'It's too high,' said Nyle, standing beside his brother. 'You won't get the cart across here.'

'*Almost* too high,' Cedric corrected. 'There's no other place for a horse and cart to cross for miles.' He turned his gaze upriver. 'It's risen fast. The rainfall must have been heavy in the hills.'

The downpour started soon after they left the campsite. The rain streaked their faces, soaking their hair and clothing, but the centre of the storm passed some distance to the north. Luckily, as the night wore on, the wind also decreased, reducing the chill of damp clothes clinging to their skin.

With the storm's passage, the clouds parted, allowing the pale light of a full moon to filter through the trees, providing faint visibility of their surroundings. However, the storm's legacy was still ominously present in the churning waters blocking their path.

'Abandon the cart,' suggested Nyle. 'Maybe we can carry some of the goods across.'

'What we'll do is waste no more time,' Cedric said. Beckoning to a group of men close to the cart, he called: 'You four hold the cart. Push it forward and keep it steady.'

He waved to the man holding the horse. 'Lead the animal in.'

The man looked anxiously at the swift-flowing water. He didn't move. 'I don't think the horse will....'

'Give it to me,' Cedric said sharply, snatching the rope from the man's hands. He stepped into the river, the water immediately swirling about his knees.

The horse was reluctant and moved forward nervously to the tug on its rope. Cedric turned and shuffled backwards, feeling with his feet, twisting his head, trying to keep an eye on the horse and the river.

Fenn searched for Kaela and saw she was close by. Their eyes met and she nodded, telling him she was well. During the night, he'd been kept apart from Kaela and Nyle so they couldn't speak, but the stoppage on the riverbank had concentrated the band.

He glanced at the men beside him at the water's edge. All were watching the scene with apprehensive expressions. Fenn agreed with their assessment; it was risky to attempt to cross with the river in this state.

He had another worry.

Cedric used several manoeuvres to confuse anyone attempting to follow. Fenn would have thought the storm alone, while it raged, made pursuit impossible. Whenever he raised his eyes to see where they were headed, the wind and driving rain forced him to focus instead on the ground in front of his feet. Even in the worst of the weather, they still walked across hard rocky ground and crossed and re-crossed streams, and they had also waded through a broader expanse of water that may have been a shallow lake or a swamp.

Nonetheless, he was sure that Olgood and Gisele *would* follow Cedric's band, just as he would if the situation had been reversed. His worry concerned the ten men Cedric had sent to check their back trail, four of whom were archers. Olgood, he knew, would be careful. Cedric had warned the path would be watched, but would Olgood expect *ten* men? Fenn wasn't sure about Nyle's boys – assuming they were accompanying Olgood. They were inexperienced, but maybe, being country-raised, they would know a little about tracking game. His brow wrinkled. Could Olgood keep them under control?

Too many questions without answers.

The four who'd been detailed to steady the cart took up positions with two on each side. They searched each other's eyes for encouragement then added their weight to the cart. The horse gave a high whinny as it entered the water. It tried to back up, stamping and splashing its feet, its eyes wild, but Cedric's hold on the rope was firm and the cart held the horse in place.

Now that they were committed, the men on the sides of the cart added their voices, urging the horse forward. Cedric was up to his waist and having difficulty finding solid footing on the riverbed while leaning against the flow. The front wheels of the cart rolled off the bank and stuck firmly on the edge of the riverbed for a moment until, with an extra push from behind, the entire cart and its contents entered the river.

Immediately the force of the water made itself known, threatening to drive both horse and cart downstream. Only a massive effort by the men and a hearty tug on the rope by Cedric kept the cart under control.

It's going to get worse, thought Fenn. The horse had yet to enter the centre of the river and feel the full weight of the churning water. Nyle seemed to catch Fenn's thought. He spoke quietly, almost to himself: 'He'll need more men.'

Cedric was in the centre of the river, the dark rushing water swirling now about his chest. It required all of his strength to stand against the power of the river.

'Cedric, this is madness,' called Nyle over the roaring noise of the water. 'The river's too high.'

Cedric didn't answer; his total concentration was focused on the need to stay upright and move backwards.

The water lifted the cart and it slid downstream. Feeling the cart move, the horse panicked and tried to bolt for the far side, lunging forward against its harness.

Fenn and Nyle moved together, leaping into the turgid water. There were splashes behind them as other men followed, seeing the danger. Even at the edge, the strength of the flow was greater than Fenn expected, threatening to take his feet from under him. The water was icy cold, fresh from the hills – enough to cause an involuntary intake of breath. He had to use the cart to steady himself and for a moment was adding to the problem rather than helping.

As soon as he found firm footing, he pushed his way along the cart, around the men already there, all the time leaning his weight against it. He could hear Nyle following behind him. He intended to reach the horse and try to calm it, but it was soon apparent that his help was more urgently needed to simply hold the cart and prevent it from being swept away.

The forward pull from the frightened horse steadied the cart and with the addition of the extra men, the sliding was temporarily arrested, but the position was far from secure. The frame of the cart was trembling with the force of water as the river gave notice of its intention to rid itself of this unwelcome intruder.

Whenever he moved his feet, Fenn recognised the difficulty Cedric was having finding solid footing. The stones of the riverbed were uneven and greatly varying in size. The flood had scoured what may have once been a smooth ford, leaving behind a bed of rough and jagged rocks.

Fenn understood the gravity of his position. If the battle was lost and the old cart suddenly moved or broke apart, he and the men on the downstream side would be pushed under or crushed.

The rescue was hampered because some helpers were trying to straighten the cart while others attempted to push it forward. Fenn looked to Cedric to coordinate the effort, but Cedric was fully occupied keeping the horse under control.

The pressure of the water against the cart was relentless. The river seemed to suddenly sense it could win this contest, and a surge lifted the cart. It moved only a few inches, but the men on the downriver side tensed, ready to leap aside. The river seized the advantage presented by the lessened resistance and lifted the cart again – another few inches, then another.

The power of the river was irresistible – they were going to lose it.

Fenn saw the men preparing to jump out of the way, their eyes flicking left and right, but if they abandoned the fight, Fenn, and Nyle beside him, had nowhere to go.

He shouted above the noise of the river: *'Just hold it! Hold it!* Then we can all push together.'

Cedric bellowed, echoing Fenn's call: *'Hold the cart!'*

The men obeyed him, putting their shoulders against the cart and digging in their feet. The slide halted. A moment, then another, went by. The cart remained fast; its wheel, hopefully, wedged against a rock.

Fenn caught Nyle's eyes and a look of understanding passed between them. That was close – they weren't out of danger yet, but for the first time since Fenn had entered the water, the cart felt stable.

Although the sideways movement of the cart had stopped, he could still feel the unrelenting power of the surging water.

'Get ready. We'll push forward together…' shouted Fenn.

Cedric roared: *'Come on! Come on!'*

Fenn pushed his shoulder into the side of the cart, yelled *'Now!'* and heaved.

The cart moved forward.

The terrified horse twisted in its bindings, desperately trying to free itself. Unable to go ahead, it attempted to turn around, rising high on its hind legs and twisting its head back to face the way it had come. The powerful wrench of its neck tore the rope from Cedric's hands. He lunged forward to retrieve it just as the horse found it couldn't turn and instead tried again to jump towards the far bank.

Its flailing hooves came down squarely on Cedric's head, driving him under the water.

FENN DIDN'T HESITATE.

Positioned at the front of the cart, he was closest to Cedric. The instant Cedric's head disappeared, Fenn thrust himself away from the cart and dove into the turbulent muddy flow, hands outstretched. The water, frigid from its journey originating high in the ranges, chilled him to his bones. He knew he had only a slim chance of catching Cedric's body before the river swept it away. The savage blows the man had taken to the head had probably killed him, or at least knocked him senseless, but while there was a chance he still lived, Fenn had to try. The water was only chest deep but moving so swiftly that, as Fenn's head went under, the power of the river snatched at him and took him in its embrace. He could be dashed against a tree branch or a river boulder at any moment, but if that was to be his fate it was out of his control. He knew opening his eyes in the black water would be useless, so he searched blindly, frantically, with his hands. If he didn't locate Cedric immediately, he would never find him, and he'd be fighting for his own life.

His fingers brushed clothing and, reflexively, his hand clenched tight. With one hand anchored, the river tossed him, rolling him over, upside-down, pulling his limbs in different directions, every movement twisting his wrist, attempting to tear it from its attachment. He put all the power he could into maintaining his grip and swung his other hand over, feeling it break the surface of the water, searching for another hold. The current swerved and the water sped up as they were swung around a boulder or part of the riverbank. He'd been underwater only moments, but the strenuous effort was draining his energy, and his lungs demanded air.

His second hand felt a hard rough surface but there was no hold there. His body was twisted again and his free arm was driven back over his shoulder. He fought against the power of the water, straining to reach forward, realising he'd touched Cedric's head. He knew he was fast running out of time; this struggle needed to be concluded quickly. The bitter cold of the water was draining the strength from the fingers locked onto Cedric's clothing. Unless he could support that hold, it would inevitably be torn free.

He put all his effort into getting another grip on Cedric. His flailing hand met skin and slid along the smooth surface, finding no purchase, but then it touched fabric that could be the collar of a tunic. He grabbed for the cloth. His need for air became urgent, and if *he* needed air, so did Cedric.

He strained his head upwards – or the direction he thought was upwards – kicking with his legs to reach the surface. It wouldn't be wise to attempt to stand. At the speed he was moving, he could easily break an ankle or a leg.

His head broke free of the river and he gasped for breath. At the same time, he opened his eyes and saw the shadows of exposed tree roots moving above him at an incredible speed. A blow on his shoulder twisted his body and almost tore Cedric free. His head was dragged under. His mouth filled with the foul water and he had to use the breath he'd just taken to force the water out as he was spun around, tumbling, his legs rising above his head. He tucked his chin into his chest – if his head hit the riverbed boulders, he was dead. He fought to turn himself and get his legs under him, but the river reversed his move, tumbling him again. He lost sense of which way was up and which was down. Water filled his nose and he resisted the immediate urge to sneeze. Just as he accepted that he was powerless against the river, a mere plaything, his feet contacted something soft and sandy – the riverbank? The contact slowed his spinning and, all at once, the deadly urgency was gone from the water.

He was still moving and turning, but the speed had slackened. The irresistible power had gentled. He pulled Cedric's body toward him, holding it close. A side eddy, perhaps, out of the main current. He took a chance and thrust his legs out, his feet striking soft earth and stones. Pushing blindly backwards, hopefully in the direction of the bank, he finally released his first grip, folding that arm around Cedric's body, under his arms, to lift his head above the surface.

Their heads broke free of the water together, Fenn gulping, taking in both air and water. He exhaled quickly, spraying the foul mixture from his mouth and nose, clutching Cedric tight against his chest. Cedric's head flopped lifelessly. Even in the pale light, Fenn could see it was covered in blood flowing freely from gaping wounds the horse's hooves had sliced into his scalp. His eyes were closed. He looked dead.

Fenn twisted his head to look about. Much of his surroundings lay in shadow, but he could make out enough to get his bearings. His head and shoulders were thrust into the earth of the riverbank. The flooded river had eroded the bank and there was rough newly-exposed earth and scraps of vegetation beside him and hanging from the bank above his head. He fought to calm his breathing. The water in his throat caused a painful cough to accompany each breath. He spat river water from his mouth and could feel and taste a thick coating of grit on his teeth.

Water was swirling about him but its force was weak, pulling at him but not strong enough to drag him back into the centre flow. He dug his feet in, pushing against the bank to secure his position. The effort caused his arms to tighten around Cedric's body and water leaked from the man's mouth, mixing with the blood flowing down his face.

Fenn couldn't feel Cedric breathing. He squeezed the man's chest again, hard. A gurgling sounded in Cedric's throat. Fenn could feel the rhythmic beating of a heart but wasn't sure whose it was. He tightened his arms using his full strength and was rewarded with a cough. That was a good sign. Dead men don't cough.

Without any help from Fenn, Cedric coughed again, this time explosively. His body convulsed into a series of coughs – a prolonged harsh hacking sound. Water spurted from his mouth. Cedric's arms erupted from the water, reaching out; his eyes flicked open, and he gasped – a huge inward gurgling breath. He immediately tried to twist himself free from Fenn's grasp, coughing and spluttering. The struggle threatened to take them both back into the river.

'Be still!' commanded Fenn, tightening his arms. Talking was painful; his throat felt rubbed raw. 'Nasty wound on… head… but… safe.'

Cedric stopped struggling, his eyes looking up, searching for the speaker.

Fenn met his gaze. He saw confusion in Cedric's eyes, then a flicker of recognition.

'Wha' happ'n…?' Cedric's voice was slurred; Fenn barely recognised the words.

'Kicked by… horse,' Fenn said. It took an effort to speak. It hurt now to even breathe. The chill of the water surrounding him seeped back into his awareness. Exhaustion swept over him. His limbs felt suddenly unresponsive and lacking strength. He gasped involuntarily, his body desperately needing more air than it was getting.

Cedric's body went limp and became heavier, hard to hold, slipping through Fenn's hands. Had the man died? No, he could feel breathing.

He attempted to tighten his grip but couldn't find any place on the wet clothing to get a secure hold. The deadly cold from the water leached into his body, numbing him, rendering his fingers useless. Spasms of involuntary shivering shook his arms. He heard a clicking sound before realising it was his chattering teeth.

Why was he struggling so hard to keep this man alive? Cedric had abducted him and would sell him like a prize pig if he could. When the horse kicked Cedric under the water, Fenn's reaction had been instinctive. But now? The only answer he could find was another question. Now that Cedric's life was in Fenn's hands – he could hold him or let him go – were his actions sufficient that Fenn should let him die? In his mix of thoughts, he remembered the man was Nyle's brother.

In the moonlight, a movement on the opposite bank caught his attention and he watched in amazement as Kaela appeared through the foliage. She scanned the bank and located him, staring at him across the water. Cedric slipped again and Fenn's weakened arms struggled to hold him. Cedric's waist was underwater. Fenn could feel the swirling current tugging insistently at Cedric's body, dragging his legs to the side, trying to draw him back into its domain. He shifted an arm to find a new grip. Without a word, Kaela strode into the river.

'No!' Fenn shouted and winced as the word tore at his throat. He well knew Kaela's fear of deep water. This water was not only deep – beneath the wildly turbulent surface shimmering in the moonlight, ran an angry, foreboding, deadly current.

He shouted again: 'Kaela! Stop!' He swallowed, trying to ease the fire in his throat, but it only caused him to cough again. He spat out a mixture of grit and foul water. He tried to call, to tell her to go back, but couldn't get any force into the words.

She didn't hear him, or she ignored him. Fenn twisted his body in an effort to slide Cedric onto the riverbank so he could help Kaela, but it was like handling a giant greasy eel. Had she forgotten she couldn't swim? She'd be swept to certain death. Cedric's body was immovable, a dead weight. Kaela pushed her way into the dirty, writhing water until it reached her waist. Fenn strove to get a permanent grip on Cedric's clothing, but the more he tried and failed, the more Cedric's body continued its slow drift into the river. The water was now covering his chest. He was slipping away.

Fenn tore his eyes from Kaela and concentrated on finding a solid hold on Cedric. His belt. If he could reach the belt of Cedric's tunic….

He may only get one chance. He let go one hand and searched beneath the water. He touched leather but the river chose that moment to jerk Cedric to one side, sliding the belt away from Fenn's grasping clumsy fingers. The hand holding Cedric also lost its grip. Fenn struggled to secure a hold under the man's chin but his hands could find no purchase in the blood. The swirling water lapped triumphantly at Cedric's shoulders, the river claiming him piece by inevitable piece. Time had run out. Fenn couldn't hold him. The pull of the water was strengthening. In a moment the wild river would drag Cedric back finally into its keeping, and he'd be lost.

He swung his arm across Cedric's body, cupping the man's chin in his elbow in a desperate attempt to keep his mouth and nose out of the water. His elbow pressed into Cedric's throat, probably cutting off his breath. The blood from his wounds had not slowed. The river was claiming him.

Death was waiting for Cedric the Bald behind more than one door.

Fenn lunged frantically again for Cedric's belt. His fingertips touched the leather and he snatched at it, curling his almost unresponsive fingers around the strap.

He lay back panting heavily, air rasping noisily in his throat. Could he maintain his grip? Fenn couldn't answer the question because he couldn't feel his fingers. He waited. Cedric didn't move. A grunt of relief. Cedric's slide into the water had paused, but there was no way Fenn could do anything more than just hold the man, he could make no gain, and there was no way he could help Kaela without losing Cedric. He lifted his arm to ease the pressure against Cedric's throat. He couldn't tell if Cedric was breathing. His efforts may have been in vain.

Behind Kaela, three more men pushed through the foliage. Fenn squinted in the gloom. One was Nyle. Like Kaela, the men stared at Fenn and Cedric, then all three strode into the river. Fenn couldn't risk freeing a hand to point, to tell Kaela help was behind her – she didn't need to risk entering the water. In a feeble voice he managed: 'No! Kaela… *behind you*! Nyle's there…' before a spate of coughing prevented more words.

She didn't hear him and didn't hear Nyle. He shook his head violently, negatively, hoping she would notice, but she wasn't looking. Her total focus was on the river and she continued to wade forward, deliberate step by deliberate step, making sure of one foot before placing the next. Why didn't Nyle call to tell her he was there? Because Nyle didn't know she was risking her life. He didn't know of Kaela's fear and didn't know she couldn't swim.

She was chest-deep and struggling to stay upright against the river's relentless force when, to Fenn's horror, she flung herself into the churning water at the point where the current was strongest. The river seized her and hurled her downstream at an impossible speed. Fenn wanted to scream her name but the sight of her locked into the merciless grip of the river robbed the breath from his lungs and struck him dumb. In an instant she was swept twenty yards. Her arms flailed like a windmill in a strong wind, her legs thrashing at the water as if to beat it into submission.

Once Kaela had reluctantly confessed her fear of deep water, Fenn had helped her on many previous occasions when crossing rivers or in the ocean. She said she had never learned to swim, and that was evident – this was *not* swimming; she was trying to *claw* her way across the river.

Fenn strained his neck and eyes to keep her in sight. Her head was underwater; she was making no attempt to see where she was going. The river's downstream rush was relentless and unstoppable – but so were Kaela's limbs. How long could she keep up that frantic motion? Just when it seemed she could be making slight headway, he lost sight of her behind a tree that had collapsed into the river when its roots had been undermined.

As long as she stays on the surface, he thought, *she might have a chance – but if the river drags her under… if she cannot hold her breath…*

He watched Nyle point at him, then point upriver. The men turned and waded in that direction. To get to Fenn and Cedric, they'd need to enter the main flow well above him.

He closed his eyes, not interested in the progress of the other men.

He braced his back against the bank, tightening his shoulders and digging in his heels, concentrating on keeping his grip even though he couldn't feel his arms. His body shook and his teeth were beating a continuous rhythm. He strengthened his resolve, clamping down with his will, focusing on maintaining his embrace and his position. He thought he could feel Cedric's chest moving.

He *would hold* until help arrived.

What happened after that would depend on Kaela's fate.

Time became unimportant. He could feel blood beating like a drum in his temple. He waited and let time flow by at its own unchangeable rate. An eternity passed – an eternity in which the only constants were the irregular chattering of his teeth and the regular, physical, insistent, almost painful beat of his heart.

A hand touched his head, and he heard her voice.

'Are you so comfortable you want to sleep? Time to wake up, I think.'

Fenn grunted with relief. He didn't need to open his eyes.

'WHEN THE RIVER TOOK you away, we knew at least one of you was still alive,' said Kaela. 'Arms and legs kept popping out of the water – until you were swept around the bend.'

Kaela checked the blanket wrapped around Fenn, pulling it tight around his neck. She brushed some hair from his eye.

'She sprang into the forest quicker than a startled deer,' said Nyle. 'She was along the riverbank and out of sight before anyone else reacted.'

Fenn sat beside a fire, his back against a tree trunk, separated from the main camp by a small grove of silver birch. He held a large wooden mug filled with warm mead in his hands. For the first time in a long while, his strength was building rather than dissipating. The mead eased his throat, warmed his stomach, and helped restore his flagging energy.

He'd been offered food but, possibly due to the water he'd swallowed, he wasn't hungry.

Cedric was being cared for in the camp. He was alive, but Fenn had heard no more than that.

Together with the men and two boys, the horse and cart eventually safely crossed the river without further incident. Fenn was lifted onto the horse while Cedric lay in the cart. Fenn remembered someone tied a blindfold around his eyes, although he was taking only minimal note of his surroundings at the time. He'd heard Nyle protest, but another voice said: 'What you don't know, you can't tell.'

The outlaws didn't want the location of their camp known.

After a seemingly endless and uncomfortable journey through the night, the noises of people signalled their arrival at a substantial camp deep in the forest. The blindfolds were removed, and the sight that greeted Fenn's blinking eyes was dew misting above the grass in the early light of dawn – the sky streaked with orange and red. The storm clouds of the previous evening had been replaced with high wispy trails that promised a fine day.

From the number of fires already visible, the camp was more extensive than Fenn had expected, and more fires were being lit as people rose to greet the new day.

The three were alone around their fire and no longer guarded. Fenn was uncertain whether that was because they were now part of the camp and everybody was a guard or simply that his status was unclear.

He raised his head and looked at Kaela. She held up her hand. 'No need,' she said. He nodded. No need to voice his gratitude. She knew.

'So now you can swim,' he said, relieved he could speak without pain.

She laughed, and he enjoyed the sound. 'Yes, it seems so. But…' she waved her finger at him, '…only in an emergency, and I did it only because I didn't take the time to think.' She shuddered. 'The river was far more powerful than I thought. I know it almost took me. I was lucky. On another day….' She shook her head. 'I would definitely *not* like to repeat the experience.'

'Master Oswald used to say persistence and determination make their own luck,' said Fenn. 'I saw you. I wanted you to stop, not to enter the river, but I knew you wouldn't give up.' He reached out for her arm. His stomach clenched at the thought he could have lost her.

Kaela leaned forward so their heads touched. 'Never….' she said.

A noise drew them apart. A man approached through the trees, walking up to Fenn. He was a large man, heavy and broad in the shoulder but he moved with a long easy stride. There was a thick scar across his cheekbone, under his right eye. His face was hard-set and rugged and the hardness was reflected in the glint of his eye. He reminded Fenn of Gunther, a companion during their escape from the Northmen, who was liberated from an outlaw band like this one. As far as Fenn knew, Gunther was now with Hakon, another former friend, the two intent on becoming spice farmers on the southern coast.

'My name is Silward,' the man said. 'I'm the Reeve of the camp. Cedric sent me to fetch you. Can you walk?'

So this was Cedric's enforcer. Fenn took a mouthful from his cup of mead and placed it on the ground. He rose to his feet, taking the blanket from his shoulders and handing it to Kaela.

'I can walk.'

Silward gestured for Fenn to follow, leading the way through the birch grove to enter the main camp.

Despite dawn only just breaking, the camp was already busy. Fenn estimated he could see at least fifty people of all ages beginning their daily activity. An old lady mending clothing shared a fire with a younger woman nursing a baby while two children played with straw dolls alongside her. As Fenn passed, something was cooking in a pot, the fire emitting a cloud of smoke and the aroma of stewed meat. A man brought a steaming mug to the old lady who stopped her work to accept the drink and thank him. Above the hum of the camp, the man called out a name – time to come in for breakfast. Fenn watched a boy carrying bags of water stop for a rest by leaning against a tree. The boy was barefoot but looked healthy and well-fed. A peel of laughter came from two women huddled together in the doorway of a thatched hut. They clung to each other's arms sharing a story or an experience. A barrow filled with wood came into view on a forest path, a small girl keeping the high load from toppling by holding a rope that tied the bundle together while a thin white-haired man strained to keep the barrow moving. A woman hung a dripping white cloth over a rope strung between trees. An old man sharpened a knife on a stone, the rhythmic scratching sounding familiar, reminding Fenn of Olgood in his workshop at the monastery.

Four goats were penned beside a pig, and horses were visible grazing among the trees – beyond the horses, a pair of oxen in an enclosure.

It was more than a camp; it was a community.

Dogs were everywhere, roaming among the huts or lying beside the fires, and Fenn's entrance into the camp provoked a high degree of interest. Ears came up and noses swivelled in his direction – a stranger. All at once the camp dogs were on the move, heading toward him from many corners, their warning barks attracting more attention.

Silward glanced over his shoulder to check Fenn's reaction.

'Here come the dogs,' he said with an amused grin. 'You can try to kick them away but you won't escape without a nip or two.' Silward seemed disappointed when Fenn's response was only a slight raising of the eyebrows.

The first dogs arrived as Silward finished speaking. They approached barking and growling with bared teeth, but as they came close to Fenn, curiosity replaced aggression and their barking stilled. Each dog stepped up to inspect the stranger silently with nose and eyes, walking around him. Then, instead of leaving, the dogs backed away a few paces and milled about, still curious. As more arrived and repeated the inspection process, the circling pack grew larger, drawing looks of amazement from the people nearby.

Silward shook his head in disbelief, staring at the surrounding pack of dogs.

'I've never seen them react like that before.'

Fenn shrugged. 'Animals accept me,' he said.

AT A LARGE WOODEN building with a tented awning forming the entrance, Silward attempted to disperse the dogs with threats and kicks. Some wandered off, losing interest, but many only retreated a short distance and sat watching.

The two guards stood aside and Silward led Fenn through the entrance.

Inside, a bed was set on a wooden floor in the centre of a large room. A fire was burning on top of a stone platform and two women were in attendance, one stirring the contents of the deep pot set above the flames, the other tending to the fire. Beside the bed stood a long table with chairs. Men were seated around the table. It looked like a council was underway. A group of women and children sat on a rug in a corner. Cedric's family?

The talking of both groups ceased when Fenn entered.

It was dim inside the house. Coming from the bright daylight, it was difficult to make out faces, but Fenn recognised Cedric the Bald propped up in the bed with cushions behind his back and neck – even in the poor light his face looked pale. His head was bandaged with strips of linen circling his scalp and passing under his chin. Blood had seeped through the bandages on the top of his head, but the patches of red were not growing, so the bleeding had stopped.

Cedric looked up to see who had entered. He beckoned to Fenn. Silward took up a position beside the doorway.

Fenn had only taken a few steps when there was a shout from the group of women. A figure, one of the children, detached itself from the group and ran to Cedric's bed, bending to whisper in his ear. Cedric said a few words – asking a question, which resulted in more whispering.

The child had its back to Fenn and was blocking his view of Cedric, so Fenn didn't know if he should proceed. He decided to wait for the interruption to resolve.

The child straightened and turned to look at Fenn.

With a start, Fenn recognised the girl. The long black hair and striking lustre-of-pearl face were unmistakable. It was the thief from the market who'd snatched the bulging purse from the big oaf with the bullwhip. What was she doing here – three days from the Witanceastre market?

Cedric peered around the girl and beckoned Fenn again.

Fenn nodded to the girl to show he recognised her, receiving in return a bright smile that was immediately reflected in her sparkling eyes.

'It seems you have already met Rowena,' Cedric said. His voice was hoarse but it had strength. He paused, then said: 'I'm not sure whether to thank you for saving her from a whipping, or to have you beaten for preventing her from lifting that bastard Grimbold's purse. Obtaining *that* bounty would have been very satisfying indeed.'

Cedric stared at Fenn, who said nothing. The silence grew until Cedric broke it with a sigh.

'But nothing is uncertain about my debt to you in the other matter,' he said. 'I've been told what you did. I owe you my life. *That* debt I can repay in one way only, and I will strive to do that before I die.'

Cedric patted the bed beside him.

'Please, sit.'

Fenn stepped up to the bed. Rowena smiled again and greeted him by laying her hand on his arm as he sat. She sat beside him, looking up at him with large eyes.

'Can I offer you some ale?' asked Cedric.

He would have preferred more of the soothing mead, but Fenn nodded. 'Thank you.'

Cedric waved a hand. One of the women stood up and left the room.

'Have you recovered?' he asked.

'Yes. A little tired, perhaps. I didn't sleep well.'

Cedric gave a loud laugh. 'No, I should think not. Even exhausted, it's difficult to sleep on horseback when you're cold and wet.'

'I'm pleased to see you've also recovered,' said Fenn. 'I'm glad my efforts were not in vain.'

Cedric looked hard at Fenn, assessing him. 'I'm grateful for your *efforts,* as you call them,' he said solemnly. 'You were my captive. Many would understand if you did not act.' He paused, narrowing his eyes.

'If you hadn't caught me – and you were the only one who *could* – the river would have swallowed me. The horse had kicked me senseless. I was gone. Everyone who saw it was surprised you could maintain your grip in that angry water.'

'It wasn't easy,' said Fenn.

He'd always been embarrassed by praise. He was simply doing what he was able to do. In his experience, everyone who did their best deserved equal acknowledgement, even if the outcomes were different. As a youngster, he excelled in his schoolwork at the monastery and progressed quickly in the scriptorium because he enjoyed learning. The forming of letters and drawing were demanding but presented no difficulty to him. He didn't consider that made him better than many others who found the lessons hard. He respected anyone who gave an honest attempt.

Cedric laughed. He turned his head to the men at the table. *'It wasn't easy*, the man says. By God, we have a rare one here.'

He returned his gaze to Fenn and held up a finger. 'Before I forget, I'd like to return something to you.'

He stretched out his arm and reached toward the far side of the bed, suddenly stopping and shutting his eyes in pain with the movement of his head. He motioned to one of the men who bent down beside the bed and rose, holding Fenn's axe. Cedric took it from him and passed it to Fenn who took the axe in both hands.

'Thank you,' he said. 'This axe has special significance for me.'

'It's certainly unusual,' said Cedric. 'Someone put a lot of care and skill into the making, and I dare say it has a story. I'd like to hear it sometime but perhaps when my head allows me to concentrate.'

Fenn nodded, remembering the promise of Thorvald, the previous owner. Through this axe, Thorvald would always stand beside Fenn in battle. He slipped it into his belt.

'Yes, it does indeed have a story,' he acknowledged.

A woman arrived at the bedside carrying two mugs of ale. She handed one to Cedric and the other to Fenn. Cedric raised his mug in salute.

'You're free to go on your way,' he said. 'The Princess and Nyle too. It's the least I can do for the moment.' He motioned Fenn to lean closer and quietened his voice, talking only to him. 'But if there's any way I can help *you* in the future, I will. I give you my word on it – and my word, as I've already told you, I *will* honour.'

Cedric lifted his mug and drank from it, watching over the rim to see that Fenn also drank.

Giving a long sigh of satisfaction, he smacked his lips together: 'Take your cart and horse and the weapons your men were carrying. The river will be back to normal by tomorrow. Until then, you're welcome in my camp.'

Fenn waited a moment, then asked: 'Kaela's sword?'

Cedric frowned. 'Ah… that sword.' He looked away and took another swig from his mug. It was several moments before his gaze returned, his eyes not quite holding Fenn's. He'd made a decision but was uncomfortable with it. Reluctant to deny Fenn's request in the light of the offer of help he'd just made, but even more reluctant to return the sword.

'It *is* a magnificent weapon,' Cedric said. 'I've never seen its equal… I'm sorry, but….'

'Could I propose a contest?'

Cedric frowned at the interruption. After a moment, his head tilted, showing his interest.

'A contest? What kind of contest?'

'Your best swordsman against ours. First blood keeps the sword.'

'*You?*' Cedric laughed, and his laugh was echoed around the council table. 'No disrespect,' he said. 'You're tall and solid but not far past a boy, and I have men who've survived many battles and killed many times.' He pointed at the door. 'Silward is one example. I have others.'

'Pick your best,' said Fenn.

Cedric narrowed his eyes. He glanced at the table and the men seated there. Their gazes flicked among themselves and then returned to Cedric, each one giving his nod in favour of the proposal.

'It seems my men are bored,' observed Cedric, 'and in need of entertainment.' He thought for a moment. 'It could be interesting. You would abide by this contest and leave freely without the sword when you lose?'

'I give you *my* word,' Fenn said. He held out his hand so Cedric did not need to lean forward.

A slow smile spread across Cedric's face. He grasped Fenn's hand.

'And I give you mine,' he said. 'So be it.' He stared at Fenn. 'I'd take this on myself if I didn't have *this* to consider.' He pointed to his head. 'Are you sure *you're* recovered?'

'I'm fine,' said Fenn.

Cedric turned to the table: 'So, who shall it be? Silward or Galvaron?'

'Galvaron,' said one. 'He's killed the most on the field. He's our best.'

'No. Silward,' said another. 'I've watched him practise. He's more… *resourceful.*'

'Giffre?' suggested a third.

Cedric considered, nodding. 'Yes, Giffre…' He brought his hand up to his chin and rubbed along his jawbone. Then he shook his head.

'No, Silward it is. He's my Reeve, and he should be my champion.'

A low groan came from Rowena at Fenn's side. She looked pained and slowly shook her head, telling him she did not think this was a good idea.

Fenn glanced at Silward, standing by the door. He was quietly listening and did not seem concerned that he was the one being proposed to fight. He caught Fenn's glance, and his lips creased into a thin smile that did not touch his eyes.

FENN MADE HIS WAY through the camp, but he didn't walk alone. The group of dogs that had waited outside Cedric's house accompanied him, trotting silently in his wake – with one exception. A huge grey wolfhound walked in front of Fenn, his head at the height of Fenn's waist, leading the way but looking back every few steps to confirm he was heading in the intended direction. Their passage through the camp drew stares, but Fenn quickly learned that the dogs were not the only reason. News of the contest had already spread and his passing caused fingers to point and whispering to start.

As he entered the birch grove separating their fire from the camp, the pack of dogs spread out among the trees. The wolfhound stopped in front of Fenn, looked back at him and gave a low grumbling woof. Was the beast trying to tell him something? The dog spoke again, a friendly bark, his tail wagging. Maybe he was just pleased to have successfully led the way here. When the dog didn't move, Fenn stepped to the side to walk around him.

An urgent whisper came from behind, above the dogs and the rustle of the leaves.

'*Don't turn around.* Stop and talk to Balthazar.'

Fenn halted. The wolfhound remained as he was, but its gaze was directed behind Fenn. Was this Balthazar? Fenn reached out to pat the dog, and the tail swayed harder. Fenn scratched behind the dog's ears and other dogs approached seeking the same treatment. None of the dogs seemed worried about the existence of the other person in the grove. It must be someone they knew.

'I shouldn't be here,' the voice said. 'If Cedric found out he'd be angry.'

The voice was female and it was familiar. In a moment he had it.

'Rowena?' he said. 'What..?'

'*Listen to me,*' she hissed, interrupting him. 'If you're going to fight Silward, I must tell you… On the battlefield he's known to work himself into a rage – a blind rage. Even his friends keep well clear when he's like that. And…' she paused as the sound of someone calling filtered through the trees, '…this is important… he'll try to kick with his legs – it's a mark of his. *Watch his feet.*'

Just as he thought she'd finished, she added: '*Please… please be careful. He's a killer, that one.*'

Was there anything more? Fenn waited.

'Thank you,' he said, but there was no answer.

Fenn straightened and turned slowly. Apart from the dogs, the birch grove was empty.

'DID YOU TALK WITH Cedric?' asked Kaela. 'What did he say?'

'We're free to go,' replied Fenn. 'Tomorrow, when the river's lower, we can leave with the cart and our belongings.'

'Good,' Kaela and Nyle said together.

Kaela frowned, looking at the axe on Fenn's belt.

'Did he return my sword?'

'Ah…' said Fenn. 'There's a small problem with that.'

CHAPTER SEVEN

A show of swords and a new companion

Kaela stood with her arms folded on the edge of a grassy clearing surrounded by trees. Beside her, Fenn put his arm on her shoulders. At first she tensed, frowning at him; she wanted to concentrate and didn't need his comfort, but her attempt at annoyance faltered and she smiled her thanks, reaching up to take his hand in hers.

At first, she was surprised that Fenn had committed her to fight without her agreement, but once he'd explained the circumstances she agreed it was probably a better course than the only other option – attempt to steal back the weapon. If the contest was resolved at first blood, the sword would be returned at little cost.

Nyle was there also, his bow strapped to his back. The bow and a full quiver of arrows had mysteriously appeared unnoticed on the riverbank while he was washing after the midday meal – another example of the skill of Cedric's lightfooted camp children.

Nyle had expressed his concern regarding Fenn's challenge more than once. He knew of Silward, he said, and he had forcefully given his opinion that deliberately standing in an arena against such a dangerous man was foolhardy in the extreme.

'You won't be able to use that sling of yours,' he said. 'Silward by reputation is a brutal monster in battle when he gets his heat up. You'll be lucky if he doesn't – accidentally, of course – take off your head.'

Nyle didn't notice the look that passed between Fenn and Kaela. They had agreed that it may be an advantage to keep the identity of their champion secret until the last moment.

They were a half-mile from the camp and it seemed that the entire population had surrounded the clearing to observe the upcoming spectacle. Children had climbed into the trees and were scattered throughout the branches, chattering to each other, their faces eagerly anticipating the afternoon's spectacle that had given them temporary relief from their chores.

One item that worried Fenn was whether Cedric would allow Kaela to use her sword. Because it was the prize in the contest, Cedric would likely bring it with him, but that was by no means guaranteed. Fenn knew she could fight well with any sword, but the weight of a heavy battle-sword forged for a warrior the size of Silward could eventually become a problem if the fight was prolonged. The noble sword she had taken from Alfarin, King of Alfheim, was, for her, perfectly balanced and weighted. He had no doubt as to Kaela's skill, her fitness, and her strength and will. With Lord of the Battle firmly in her hand, she could fight all day.

His thoughts were interrupted by the arrival of Cedric with Silward walking beside him, followed by four of the advisors Fenn had last seen seated at the table in Cedric's house. Two other large men brought up the rear of the party. Fenn recognised the one wearing mail and helmet as the man who had been his guard. Cedric also wore a helmet made of leather that covered the bandaging on his head, but the strips of linen wound under his chin were still visible.

'The one wearing mail is Giffre,' said Nyle. 'He's a Frank and also has a well-deserved reputation. I don't know the other.'

'I suspect that's Galvaron,' said Fenn.

He noted that Silward wore sandals, unusual footwear for such a contest. He mentioned it to Nyle.

'I've heard he always fights in sandals,' said Nyle. 'He's a superstitious man. Sometime in the past he believes it's brought him good luck.'

Fenn looked at Kaela to see what she thought about Silward's footwear. She seemed unconcerned.

Fenn turned his attention to Cedric. He saw, with relief, that Cedric was carrying two swords. In one hand was a common long sword, unexceptional, worn by men up and down the land. In the other, he held the Lord of the Battle – Kaela's sword. A glance confirmed Kaela had also noticed.

Cedric stopped and gathered his group around him, conferring. Silward looked pointedly at Fenn then leaned toward Giffre and whispered something to him, nodding in Fenn's direction. They both laughed loudly, Giffre slapping Silward on the back.

The group broke up. All except Cedric and Silward continued to the far end of the clearing where seating had been arranged. Cedric walked directly to Fenn with Silward a step behind. Cedric's jaunty gait announced his mood. Apart from the bandaging, he showed no sign that he'd sustained a serious injury. The change from the pale man Fenn had met in the morning was striking.

'I trust you're ready?' Cedric asked. He smiled broadly as he gazed around the clearing taking in the assembled crowd. A few people were still scrambling to find the best remaining vantage points. 'It seems everyone else is.'

Cedric was about to hand Fenn the second sword when Fenn held out his hand.

'May I?' he said, indicating the other sword – Kaela's sword.

'You want to use *this* sword?' Cedric looked down at the sword then back at Fenn for confirmation. He hesitated – unwilling to part with the prize but also aware that choice of weapon was an accepted part of such a contest. He looked at Silward to see if he had any objection. Silward nodded his agreement without taking his eyes off Fenn.

Cedric hesitated again, frowning, then grunted.

'Very well,' he said gruffly. He held out Kaela's sword.

Fenn took it and handed it to Kaela.

Fenn found satisfaction in the expressions that crossed Cedric's face. The man's eyes flicked rapidly between Fenn and Kaela as disbelief was followed briefly by puzzlement and then annoyance – his brow furrowing as he wondered if he had somehow been tricked. The furrows deepened with Cedric's struggle to recall Fenn's exact words when the contest had been proposed. Fenn hadn't stated who would oppose Silward, but he also hadn't corrected Cedric's assumption.

Nyle's face mirrored Cedric's initial disbelief and Fenn was pleased to see that even Silward could not suppress his surprise, tearing his eyes from Fenn to stare at Kaela.

Kaela ignored their stares and took the opportunity to buckle on the sword. The sun caught on her long flame-red hair as it flowed back and forth across her shoulders with each movement of her head. She drew the sword from the scabbard and held it up to the sunlight, twisting it in her hand and inspecting both sides of the blade. Satisfied, she replaced the sword, the Damascus steel issuing a soft sigh as it slid home. She stood back on her heels and folded her arms again – relaxed and ready. At that moment she reminded Fenn of Birgitta, renowned shield-maiden of Lognavik, as he had last seen her – striding unafraid into battle with the half-light of sunrise on her golden hair. Kaela displayed the same fierce confidence and resolve. She was every inch a true shield-maiden.

'This is madness,' protested Nyle. 'She's Beorhtric's daughter! Cedric, you can't let *her*....'

Cedric held up his hand, stopping him. Satisfaction had replaced suspicion when he realised the only change was that the contest had become *more* one-sided. Instead of a tall youth who may have proven fleetingly useful with a sword, Silward would now face a girl. It was foolish not to accept an advantage if one was offered. Fenn could see his thoughts written on his face; the sword was already his, but he was disappointed that the affair would almost certainly be short-lived.

'Are you sure?' Cedric asked Fenn, to seal the terms. 'The Princess?'

When Fenn gave only a slight nod in reply, the hint of a smile formed at the corners of Cedric's lips.

He grunted and said with finality: 'So be it!'

He stepped back, raising a finger to Silward. 'First blood only,' he warned.

Silward nodded.

Cedric studied him. '*Do not* mark her face,' he said.

Silward stared back at him, his face expressionless.

Cedric matched his stare. 'Very well,' he said. His eyes flicked to the sword at Kaela's side. A fragment of annoyance remained that the prize at the centre of the contest would be used in the fight, but that couldn't be changed now. It wouldn't matter – the girl may not even get a chance to present it before a trickle of blood stopped the bout.

Cedric raised his eyes and regarded Kaela for a few moments. His stern expression softened and he smiled at her.

'Be careful with my sword,' he said. 'I would not like it to be damaged.'

SILWARD WAS QUICK, much quicker than might be expected for such a big man.

The instant the red cloth dropped from Cedric's hand, Silward leapt forward and lunged with his sword at her shoulder. Had the thrust found its target, the contest would undoubtedly have been over, but the blood shed would certainly have been more substantial than the required trickle. Silward had made his intentions clear.

Kaela leaned away from the blow and smoothly parried the sword so it passed harmlessly to the side. Instead of withdrawing, she swept the Lord of the Battle under his outstretched arm, aiming at the big man's thigh, but he was too experienced to leave himself vulnerable. The quickness of his initial lunge was matched by the speed with which he twisted his body back out of range. As fast as he was, he was only just fast enough. The tip of Kaela's sword sliced cleanly through the cloth of his leggings.

If he'd been a fraction slower or he'd leaned a fraction closer....

Each took a moment to assess the brief exchange. Fenn could see that Silward's speed had surprised Kaela, just as her lightning response and her willingness to strike at him rather than retreat had surprised Silward.

Silward glanced down at the tear in his leggings. By no more than good fortune, the skin beneath was untouched. The closeness of his escape seemed to trigger something in his eyes. They narrowed, and his face hardened and twisted into a snarl, reflecting a new resolve. If this had begun as a game, it was no longer. He realised his opponent was dangerous. The sun caught on the scar beneath his eye, further distorting his face into a fierce mask. He lowered his head – more wary but also more determined.

Kaela waited for him, the tip of the Lord of the Battle dancing a slow invitation in the air.

Rather than rush in as before, Silward stepped to his right, circling but also edging closer. He varied his speed of step, slow then quick, watching Kaela, sword raised and ready. Just outside the range where they could touch blades, he stopped and stood with feet apart. *He's tempting Kaela to make a move*, thought Fenn. Kaela waited, the two remaining motionless, presenting a momentarily frozen scene for the spectators. A hush of anticipation spread over the clearing as if each person was holding their breath.

Silward leaned to the side, appearing to continue his circling, then stepped swiftly forward, raising his sword and swinging forcefully in a downward motion at her neck. It was a blow deliberately intending to maim or kill rather than merely draw blood, as a collective gasp from the crowd recognised.

Kaela stepped back, Silward's swing passing harmlessly in front of her neck – but Silward moved with her, reversing the sword and swinging with the same force from the opposite direction, attempting to overwhelm her with speed and strength, a bear-like growl escaping from his throat with each swing. He handled the heavy sword like a feather, switching direction continuously and effortlessly to produce a deadly blur of steel.

Fenn was puzzled when Kaela continued to move back, avoiding the whirlwind of powerful strokes rather than engaging them as he knew she could. Silward was a strong man and it would take equal strength to directly oppose his massive swings, but Fenn had previously seen Kaela skillfully deflect such blows, moving them to the side then countering with her own weapon. Did Kaela realise her opponent was building himself into the battle rage Fenn had told her about – a fury that would drive him to attempt to kill her rather than merely mark her?

Fenn's hand reached inside his tunic to retrieve the sling but stopped. He should trust that she knew what she was doing.

Kaela backed towards the trees at the edge of the clearing, the spectators scrambling to move out of harm's way and allow her free passage. She moved calmly and smoothly, weaving her body, only engaging with her own blade to deftly counter Silward's sword when it came close, undaunted by the man's display of skill and strength. With each step she took away from him – each piece of ground she gave, each blow she effortlessly avoided – Silward's frustration rose, and his growls grew in volume.

As soon as Kaela entered the forest, passing between two trees, the wide swings that Silward had used in the open field were no longer possible. She was using the trees to restrict him, but her own movement was also hampered.

Silward made an immediate and dramatic change. He pivoted on one foot, using the strength of his wrist to convert the next swing into a thrust aimed directly at her head – but the lunge was a feint and was immediately followed by a powerful kick with the other foot at her stomach. He was counting on the first strike distracting her from the second, but Kaela had heeded Rowena's warning. This time she did not retreat. Instead, she ducked under his sword and presented her own blade to intercept Silward's kick, the keen edge of Damascus steel slicing cleanly through the leather of his boot and into the flesh of his shin. Kaela reacted as steel met bone and she instantly withdrew so Silward would not lose his leg. Her withdrawal, combined with the force remaining in the kick, sent her stumbling backwards. Her heel tripped on a tree root and she sprawled on her back sending a cloud of dead leaves swirling into the air.

Silward howled with pain and rage, blood from his wound already streaking his lower leg.

Technically, the contest was over, but the big man showed no sign of acknowledging that fact. His kick had intended to achieve this very outcome – his opponent was on the ground and helpless before him. She had wounded him and would pay for it.

He limped toward her, his knotted face and the animal growls issuing from his throat betraying his murderous intent. His wounded leg faltered, and he had to take an extra step to steady himself before he leaned forward and raised his sword high above his head.

Cedric called: 'Stop!' and cries of protest came from many others including Fenn as he rose to his feet and leapt forward in horror, his hand reaching for his axe. *Silward was going to kill her.* From the corner of his eye, he saw Nyle fitting the string to his bow. He hadn't noticed him retrieve his bowstring.

No matter – they would all be too late.

In the time Silward took to get his footing, Kaela twisted her body, and, in an impossible movement, she launched herself from her back and landed in a crouch on the balls of her feet. Her hand whipped upwards with the speed of a striking snake, the tip of her sword unerringly catching Silward's wrist just as his arm was motionless at the apex of the swing that would have become the fatal blow.

It was a bold and daring counterstroke, demonstrating extremes of both risk and skill.

Silward froze. His arm was fully extended and he could not withdraw it further. Any attempt to step back or move an inch could result in severe damage to his wrist. His shocked intake of breath developed into a low rumble of anger and frustration.

Kaela slowly rose from her crouch, perfectly balanced, ensuring the pressure of her sword remained constant against the underside of his wrist. A drop of bright blood formed at the tip of the sword and ran down the blade.

Silward met her eyes. They stared at each other. His lips curled, but he gave a single nod.

A SMALL GROUP GATHERED beside the cold and smokeless pile of ashes that had been the fire shared for two days by Fenn, Kaela, and Nyle. Cedric stood in front of Fenn and Kaela with Silward on one side and, on the other, Rowena and the wolfhound, Balthazar. Nyle was kneeling a few paces away, collecting his bow and quiver of arrows. A group of onlookers, including some children, watched the farewell from the trees.

Kaela was wearing her sword, which Cedric acknowledged with a nod.

Fenn tried to determine Silward's mood. Was he angry, resigned, humiliated? Silward's face, as always, was blank and unreadable. He seemed to be suffering no ill effects from his leg wound and was walking normally.

Within sight, through the trees, the horse and cart stood waiting. The cart carried its original contents plus the shields and weapons of Nyle's men and some extra goods supplied by Cedric – apples, fine wheat flour, cakes made from honey and oats, and fresh game – venison, geese, and a string of hares.

Cedric addressed Fenn. 'Our encounter has been an interesting one,' he said. 'We will meet again, of that I'm certain. Until that day, I wish you and the Princess a good journey. Nyle says your destination is Westerling – I know the place.' He held his hand out and Fenn accepted the handshake.

'I owe you my life; I'll not forget that,' said Cedric. 'Remember my offer, as I will.'

Fenn nodded.

Cedric turned to Kaela. He bowed his head and regarded her for a moment before he spoke.

'You won the sword fairly, Princess,' he said. 'I didn't think that was possible. Whether the way it ended was due to luck or unusual skill, or some mixture… it was undoubtedly memorable. It will be talked about for quite some time.'

He put his hands on his hips and stretched his back, then folded his arms.

'One thing is clear,' he observed. 'You and that sword belong together. You've reminded me that the outer appearance may not always reveal the core – the heart – beneath. I saw you as another spoiled member of the privileged nobility to be exploited for profit. I see now that, despite your youth, you're someone to be taken seriously.' He glanced back at Fenn. 'You *both* are.'

His eyes remained on Fenn. 'Nyle has spoken well of you,' he said.

Fenn glanced at Nyle. What could he have said? Had he revealed that Fenn carried a sling?

Nyle didn't meet his eye. He stood and slung his quiver over his shoulder. Cedric stepped away from Fenn and placed a hand on Nyle's shoulder.

'Farewell, Brother,' he said. 'I hope to see you again soon.'

Nyle hesitated, his eyes narrowing. Then he relaxed and reached out to clasp his brother's arm. 'Be careful, Cedric,' he said. 'You have many enemies.'

Cedric nodded. 'I'm always careful.' He matched Nyle's clasp on his arm. 'I wish you were with me… I could use a bow such as that one.' He raised his palm to forestall Nyle's protest. 'I know…' he said, '…you have other plans.'

In contrast to Silward, and despite the loss of the sword, Cedric the Bald was in a good mood. Turning back to Fenn, he pointed at Nyle. 'You may be surprised to know…' he said confidentially, '…that my little brother is a master archer, among the best in the land.'

'I *already* know that,' said Fenn firmly, his emphasis causing Nyle to turn his head and Cedric to raise his eyebrows.

Rowena ran past Cedric, Balthazar at her heels, and threw her arms around Fenn.

She hugged him for a moment and then looked up into his face.

'Thank you for saving me from that *horrible* whip in the marketplace,' she said, her voice unsteady with emotion. 'I'll also wait and hope for the day when I see you again.'

She reached up, pulled him down, and kissed his cheek. Balthazar caught her mood and raised himself on his hind legs, his massive paws hitting Fenn in the chest, knocking him backwards.

Fenn recovered his balance and laughed, putting both hands on Rowena's shoulders. 'As your father said – it's by no means sure that I helped you. If I hadn't been there, you wouldn't have been caught.'

To his surprise, she gave a hearty laugh. 'Cedric's not my father.' Her smile vanished and her face turned serious. 'And you *did* save me. You shielded me and would have taken the whipping for me. I've *never* seen anything so brave.'

Tears formed in her eyes. Abruptly, she detached herself and ran toward the camp, her hair and long skirt flying. Balthazar bounded around Fenn, excited. He stopped to watch Rowena go, ears raised, but didn't follow her. As she passed through the trees, some other children turned to run with her.

'Call your dog,' called Fenn, 'before he knocks me down.'

Rowena stopped and whirled about.

'Balthazar's not *my* dog,' she called back. 'He's his own dog and nobody else's. Maybe he's *your* dog.' She wiped her eyes, smiled, and gaily waved before running to catch the others.

Silward's eyes were on Kaela. In turn, Cedric was regarding his Reeve with raised eyebrows.

Fenn frowned. Silward had violated the rules of the contest. Was Cedric expecting him to apologise? It was too late for that. Fenn would not forget that if Kaela had not ended the fight miraculously, Silward would have killed her. In his heart, he knew there was nothing he could have done to prevent it.

Kaela held Silward's gaze. To Fenn, she said: 'You go ahead. I'd like to talk with Silward.'

Fenn hesitated. Kaela smiled at him and repeated her suggestion by inclining her head toward the cart.

Cedric brought his hands together. 'Very well,' he said. He stepped back and extended a hand in the cart's direction.

To Fenn and Nyle, he said: 'If you're ready… let's set you on your way.'

He reached inside his tunic and withdrew three strips of cloth to be used as blindfolds.

SILWARD LED THE CART through the forest for a mile – with Fenn, Kaela, and Nyle walking blindfolded – before Silward stopped and removed the cloth from their eyes. He pointed out the direction they should follow and then stepped aside and watched as they started the horse moving. He nodded to Kaela and then raised his hand to her in farewell before walking away.

Fenn shook his head. First with Gunther and now Silward, Kaela strangely elicited respect from men she defeated with the sword, where it could so easily have been resentment or even hatred. He could understand that they recognised her skill as swordsmen, but it was more than that. With Gunther, it may have been because he knew she had him at her mercy and could have killed him. Was it the same with Silward?

In Silward's case, she must know he would have killed her if he could, yet she was friendly, even respectful toward him. Fenn shook his head. He didn't understand it – but he admired her for it.

As if she could read his thoughts, Kaela surprised him by asking: 'Fenn, what do you think of Silward?'

'The man is quite simply a brute,' said Fenn.

Kaela looked at him. 'That's how he seems, but he's more complicated than that. He's a disturbed man; I could see it in his eyes. He's seen too much, fought too much, and finds it hard to hold it all together. Battles have that effect – life or death hangs in the balance. Cheat death often enough and you feel you have nothing to lose. He told me the only thing he felt he was good at was killing people. His life was empty, with no worthwhile future, nothing to hope for. The only unknown was which battle would be his last. Cedric saved him, brought him back from that edge.'

'You seem to have learned a lot in a short conversation,' said Fenn, 'But I agree he does seem devoted to Cedric.'

Cedric said this path would lead them back to the Avon but Fenn hadn't recognised any landmarks, even though the sun told him they were heading in the right direction – north and west. Two nights ago, it had been dark and he'd been cold, wet, and exhausted, but he was sure this was not the path they'd followed after crossing the swollen river. He could understand Cedric's concern. Even though they hadn't taken a direct route that night, Cedric was cautious about his camp's location. But was it just caution, or was there another reason to send them along this route? Fenn found it hard to form a judgement on the man. He was forthright and honest, at least according to his own code, but he always hid something up his sleeve.

The path was overgrown and not well-travelled, making it difficult to follow. They'd had to backtrack when the path had disappeared under a lake of new-fallen leaves. After half a mile, it became clear they were just heading deeper into the forest. Turning the cart and relocating the track had not been easy – costly in both time and effort.

Fenn walked in front, leading the horse, with Kaela alongside him. Balthazar had been ranging about, exploring the forest, but, for the moment, he was trotting at Fenn's side. Nyle walked behind the cart, ready to assist when it caught in mud or was impeded by thick bushes.

Fenn had expected Balthazar to turn back after a while, but the hound had stayed with the group and showed no indication of wanting to leave. Maybe Rowena was right; Balthazar was now his dog, although, if that was the case, *he* was the one who had been adopted, not Balthazar.

'It seems Rowena knows you,' said Kaela. 'She said you saved her from a whipping? Anything I should know about?'

Fenn looked at her, surprised. He realised she didn't know about the incident in the marketplace.

For some reason, her tone made him feel defensive.

'I'm sorry,' he said. 'I should have told you.' He felt like a boy having to report an indiscretion to his mother. 'It's easily explained.' Why did he say that? It made him sound guilty.

He gathered his wits. 'I was in the market the day we left Witanceastre,' he said. 'Rowena attempted to steal the purse of some fat oaf. I intervened, and the fool thought I was part of the robbery. He wanted to whip us both. I allowed Rowena to escape and convinced him to reconsider.'

Kaela looked at him, her eyebrows raised.

'He wanted to *whip* you? Do you know who he was?' she asked.

'Cedric knew him. He called him Grimbold, I think.'

'Of course. *Grimbold.*'

'Do you know him?'

'When Rowena mentioned you saved her from a whipping, I thought it might be him. Grimbold is my father's High Reeve. He administers the law and collects taxes and oaths of loyalty. He was appointed when Beauduheard was killed. He's Beauduheard's cousin. I'm told it was Eadburg who was behind his appointment. I think he's more *her* man than my father's.'

She put some sting into her words: *'He's an arrogant idiot!'*

The name of Beauduheard reminded Fenn of Kaela's story of her capture by the Northmen. Five years ago, she had followed the former King's Reeve, Beauduheard, out of curiosity when there was news of three strange ships landing on a nearby beach. They hadn't known the intruders were Northmen and when Beauduheard foolishly tried to collect taxes from them, thinking they were traders, they reacted violently and he and his outnumbered men were all killed. The colour of Kaela's hair had saved her from death that day – an important god of the Northmen, Thor, had red hair. Instead, she was taken captive and eventually sold to Ragnall, who gave her to his mother Askari in Lognavik where Fenn met her.

Kaela took a deep breath to calm herself. She looked up at him and smiled.

'So… you convinced Grimbold to *reconsider.* That would have been interesting to see. I imagine he wouldn't have taken that well. He does like to exercise his damned whip whenever he can.'

'We didn't part on the best of terms,' agreed Fenn.

He could only trust that now he was moving away from Witanceastre, he need have no future dealings with the King's High Reeve.

He lifted his hand to push aside a tree branch. He held it back so it wouldn't strike the horse and glanced behind to check on Nyle, receiving an 'all's well' wave motioning him forward. The horse stared wide-eyed at the branch. It moved its head to the side, gave a whinny and pricked its ears forward, staring ahead. At the same time, Balthazar gave a bark and followed it with a low growl. He turned his head to look up at Fenn.

'I think she likes you,' said Kaela.

Fenn looked down at the dog. 'Balthazar is a *he*.'

Another deep growl from Balthazar. The dog knew his name.

'I wasn't referring to the dog.'

'Then who…?' Fenn frowned. 'Do you mean Rowena? She's just a girl.'

'I think she likes you,' repeated Kaela. She hooked her arm through his elbow and looked up at him with a teasing smile.

Fenn shrugged. 'She thinks I saved her from a whipping. It's gratitude, no more.'

Balthazar tilted his head, barked twice, and growled again. Fenn looked at him. What was he trying to say? Balthazar avoided Fenn's gaze, staring ahead. Absurdly, Fenn thought the dog might be agreeing with Kaela.

Kaela's smile widened. 'I think she really *likes* you,' she insisted.

Fenn raised a finger to stop her. 'Kaela, that's….'

A bizarre figure stepped onto the path ahead – so close that Fenn and Kaela were forced to halt abruptly. Fenn felt the horse's nose push into his back before it, too, stopped. Balthazar barked loudly. It was deep-throated but more curious than aggressive.

The figure was man-shaped but covered in foliage tied to his body with strips of twisted grass.

Kaela had her sword partly out before Fenn's hand reached his axe. Both froze in mid-action.

From behind the mask of mud smeared on his face, Olgood grinned.

'Good day to you travellers,' he said.

Behind him, the bushes at the side of the path moved, and a barely-recognisable Gisele appeared. In front of Fenn's amazed eyes, one by one, five more weirdly disguised figures stepped into view.

THE SMALL STREAM TRICKLING amongst rounded boulders provided good water for the horse, and Olgood, now stripped of the leafy branches of his forest costume, suggested a stop so he and the others could remove the mud from their hands and faces.

Olgood was the first to rise from the stream, his face dripping. He shook his head, the water spraying from his hair. Nyle waited out of range until it was safe, then offered the choice of an apple or a honey oatcake from the items Cedric had provided. Olgood accepted the cake with his eyebrows raised. Nyle passed the offerings around.

'Yes,' said Nyle in reply to the looks of astonishment. 'These are a gift from the notorious and dangerous outlaw, Cedric the Bald.'

Olgood inclined his head. 'A gift, you say…. I wouldn't have expected him to give you gifts – or…' he turned to look at Fenn, '…indeed, to release you.'

Fenn nodded. They had much to tell each other.

Olgood took a bite and made a pleasantly surprised face.

Gisele was more appreciative. 'The cakes are good,' she said. 'We 'ave 'ad nothing like this to eat….'

One of Nyle's boys protested: 'That's not true. The birds you caught last night were delicious….' Gisele smiled her thanks, and the boy stopped, embarrassed.

'Do you know where Cedric's camp is from here?' Fenn asked Olgood.

Olgood nodded. 'We were close to it yesterday.' He shook his head again to dry his hair and pointed. 'On the other side of that ridge, there's another wide valley. The camp sits in the foothills on the far side – about ten miles from here if you flew as straight as a crow.'

Fenn smiled. So much for Cedric's attempt at secrecy.

He bent down and picked up a dead branch, snapping off twigs for kindling. Balthazar froze, his body tensed for action, his gaze intently focused on the stick in Fenn's hand.

Fenn shook his head. 'I was intending to use this stick for the fire, Balthazar,' he said.

'BUT BALTHAZAR DOESN'T KNOW you,' Fenn mused. 'It's a poor guard dog who doesn't warn of strangers. He certainly made his share of noise in Cedric's camp.'

A haunch of venison was roasting on a spit. The fire had been allowed to die until a bed of glowing coals surrounded a group of heated stones standing like islands in a demon sea. There was no wind and the fat dripping onto the stones added a regular sizzling to the noises of the night.

'He *did* give a warning bark, several in fact,' Olgood replied. He waved an admonishing finger at Fenn. 'But you were engrossed in conversation with Kaela and didn't notice.' He turned the spit and sat back while Gisele sprinkled salt and herbs onto the glistening meat. 'The dog barked and growled and stared directly at where we were concealed. The horse noticed us too.'

Fenn smiled and shook his head. 'I remember now. It wasn't an angry bark. He must have recognised you weren't a threat. I thought he was agreeing with Kaela.' He broadened his smile. 'Well…' he tried to explain, '…we were talking about Rowena, and Balthazar probably knows Rowena's name….'

Kaela and Gisele rolled eyes at each other and laughed, with Olgood and Nyle joining in. Fenn stopped, recognising defeat. He reached to Balthazar lying beside him and ruffled his ears.

'I'm trying to learn your language,' he said. 'I'll be more attentive in the future.'

Balthazar gave only a cursory flick of his eyes in response to Fenn's apology, unwilling to divert his attention from the leg of roasting venison revolving mere inches from his twitching nose.

Nyle had detailed two of his men as sentries, even though, as he acknowledged, they were unlikely to have trouble from Cedric the Bald. The others gathered around the single fire. Fenn noticed that Olgood and Gisele were on friendly terms with Nyle's boys; they were laughing and talking easily together. It was good to be back together again, especially with the two former groups now becoming one.

Olgood was relating the events that had occurred since they were parted.

'Not one hesitated when I asked if they were willing to follow Cedric, despite his warning,' Olgood explained, 'and each one of these men proved helpful and competent on the trail.'

His reference to the farm boys as men was not lost on Fenn.

Olgood placed his arm around Gisele. 'This lady…' he said affectionately, '…was our *fox* – she was a spirit of the forest, and, to make sure we fitted in, she dressed us in forest clothing. She knew instinctively where the hens, as we called Cedric's men, were hiding. She pointed them out and led us around them.'

While Nyle and Kaela talked about the river crossing, Cedric's camp, and the contest for Kaela's sword, Fenn leaned back contented and studied the fire. The voices blurred and his mind drifted.

When he decided to come south to Wessex with Kaela, one expectation was that his life would become more settled. Kaela's position at her father's court was complicated, but he knew she harboured no ambition to become the ruler of Wessex. She had told him with a smile that her father had educated her to rule, but he knew as well as anyone that the Ealdormen of Wessex would never allow it. They didn't resent her; she was simply not legitimate.

Thankfully denied a life at court, Fenn imagined he would eventually become a farmer or something similar, trading times that had contained excitement and adventure but also anxiety and danger for those of peace and quiet enjoyment.

So far, he had to admit, his life showed no sign of heading in that direction.

CHAPTER EIGHT

Weyhill and Westerling

The rain, when it came, was a deluge. For most of the afternoon they had watched clouds darkening to the southwest. They met fewer and fewer travellers on the road as people wisely sought shelter. The first few drops were heavier than expected – a promise of worse to come.

Nyle stood to one side to allow the cart to pass by, waiting for Fenn and Kaela to walk up to him.

'There's a village called Weyhill up ahead,' he said. 'I know it; it has the only inn for miles and sure to be full on a rainy night. The food is edible. I suggest we shelter there – this won't be a night to be spent on the open road.'

The prospect of warmth and proper shelter from the rain was attractive.

'How far to Westerling?' asked Fenn.

'A day and a half,' replied Nyle.

'We don't have much coin. Can we afford a night at an inn?'

'The Queen will pay. I'll give a note to the innkeeper. He won't like it, but he'll have to accept it.'

The rain became steadier.

'We'd better hurry,' said Kaela, just as the clouds unleashed their full force.

AS NYLE HAD FORECAST, the inn was well-populated and noisy.

Fenn found an empty table in a corner and waved to Olgood. He took some unused chairs from a neighbouring table and arranged them, then shook the water from his shoulders, wiped his face, and stamped his feet before sitting. Olgood pushed his way through the crowd with Gisele following in his wake. Those who noticed him coming moved readily aside; those he surprised took one look at the huge man with an axe swinging at his side, and any belligerence that might have been considered, evaporated. Olgood reached the table and moved a chair to allow Gisele to sit. A man made to unwittingly step into her path but Olgood changed his direction with a firm hand on his shoulder. The man turned to protest at being handled, but again, Olgood's size dissuaded him from voicing his dissent.

Nyle was out of sight, seeking a discussion with the landlord. The horse and cart had been led to the adjacent stable, with Nyle's men tasked with seeing to the cart and its contents while Kaela took the horse's care and feeding upon herself.

Gisele smiled at Olgood and sat down, tilting her head towards Fenn. 'So much noise,' she said, cupping her hands over her ears. Olgood sat beside her. He bent his head and ran his fingers through his dripping hair, trying to wring it dry.

A woman leaned across from the next table and touched Gisele on the shoulder. She pointed at Olgood, making an appreciative face.

'Here… you got a big one there, girl,' she said with a chuckle. 'Mine ain't half that size.' She reached out to grasp the head of the man beside her and pulled it into her ample bosom. 'But he also ain't half *cuddly!* Her roar of laughter echoed around the table.

Fenn and Gisele joined the laughter. Olgood sat up, puzzled at the sudden burst of amusement around him.

A buxom woman appeared, carrying four empty mugs in her hands. She leaned close to Fenn's ear. 'Ale?' she enquired. At Fenn's nod, she added: 'And food? We have hare and beef stew and bread baked today.'

'Ale and food for ten,' said Fenn. 'We have more joining us.' He was still worried about their ability to pay but trusted that Nyle would be able to make a successful arrangement.

The woman straightened and leaned back in mock alarm. 'Food and drink for *ten*, is it? Well… we'll have to see if we can handle such a mighty order.'

She gave a cackle of laughter and swayed into the crowd, holding the mugs to the front to make a passage.

Fenn leaned back in his chair and surveyed the people. By their clothing, he surmised most were farmers, and from the way they knew each other, they were local.

A group at the table in front were different. Their clothing was not farming clothing. It more closely resembled that worn at Fenn's table – travellers. These men were not locals. The six men were gathered around the table, leaning in, engaged in close and private conversation. While Fenn watched, several heads nodded at something one of them said. The man at the head of the table thumped the table with his fist and stood up. The others drew back from their huddle and followed his lead, three reaching down for packs which they shouldered as they stood. Fenn noticed the men wore swords, further proof that they were not farmers.

A lull in the hubbub of noise allowed Fenn to hear the man at the head of the table say: '…meet the day after tomorrow, he said, but that fool, Grimbold, had better be paying well, or he can kiss my…' the rest of his sentence was swallowed by another bellow of laughter from the 'cuddly' table.

'Did he say Grimbold?' Fenn asked Olgood.

'That's what I heard. Why? Do you know a man named Grimbold?'

'I do,' said Fenn. Was Grimbold recruiting men? These looked more like mercenaries than recruits.

The leader bent to drain the last of the ale from his mug, wiped his lips, and made for the door, the others trailing behind.

'Their business must be urgent to be heading out in this weather,' Olgood observed.

As if cued by his words, the door opened, bringing the clatter of the heavy rain into the inn. A giant clap of thunder exploded through the open door, stilling all conversation.

All eyes turned to the door as Kaela walked into the inn.

Two or three people had arrived since Fenn, hunched and cowed by the weather, taking a moment to shake themselves or shed clothing before looking up to greet the room – but the rain had in no measure dampened Kaela's spirit. Hair plastered to her head and water running freely from her clothing, she stood on the threshold, head high, scanning the room, ignoring the group of men who had come to a halt in front of her.

To Fenn, she had never looked more beautiful.

Kaela half-turned and pushed the door closed just as a man moved around her and reached for it. The man growled at the perceived snub and snarled at her: 'What d'ye think yer doing?'

The leader stopped him, a hand on the man's shoulder pulling him back.

'Well, well,' he said with exaggerated appreciation, taking a step to the side. 'What do we have here, lads?'

He inspected Kaela as one would a prize horse.

'A fine young filly,' he said, '…and will you look at that sword. Worth a fortune, I'm sure. Only a high-born could own a sword like that.' He looked around at the other men, eyebrows raised. 'Or… maybe it's *stolen.*'

Fenn slowly stood up.

Olgood said: 'This should be interesting.' He turned his chair so his legs were freed from the table.

Kaela noticed Fenn rising. She held up a hand to stop him.

'I'm sorry if I'm in your way,' she said, stepping to the side. The leader moved with her, blocking her path.

'You're all wet,' he said with mocking concern.

He reached out a hand to touch her hair. Kaela slapped the hand away and took a step back.

'Oh, a *feisty* little filly,' the man said, laughing. 'Just my type.'

'I have no quarrel with you unless you'd like to make one,' said Kaela. 'Let me pass.'

'Answer my question,' said the man.

'You haven't asked one,' Kaela said calmly.

The man frowned. The girl wasn't acting as he expected.

'If the sword is stolen, then it's fair game,' he said gruffly. 'So… is it stolen?'

'Yes, it is,' said Kaela.

The man stared at her, another frown creasing his heavily-scarred forehead. He'd expected a strenuous denial.

Kaela rested her hand on the sword's hilt.

The man held up a hand to warn his men. 'Ooh, is she going to show us her fancy needle? Stand back lads.'

'That's enough!' said Fenn, pushing between two men to reach the leader. He pointed to the door. 'I think you were about to leave. I suggest you do so before someone gets hurt.'

The man turned. The scars on his forehead extended down the side of his head to under his ear. He was thick-set, broad at the shoulder, with big hands.

'Ha!' he exclaimed, '…and who in the devil's name are you?'

'A friend.' Fenn pointed again to the door. 'I think you should leave now.'

'Oh, is that what you think?' the man said sarcastically, his voice rising. 'I don't give a tinker's damn what *you* think, boy, and I *don't* like interference in my affairs.'

The man drew back his arm and swung a gnarled fist at Fenn's head. The man's blow was powerful but slow. Fenn ducked, stepped to the side and punched the man hard in the stomach. The man doubled over, winded but not hurt. Fenn kicked out with his heel at the man's bent knee. The knee crumbled and the man toppled to the floor. Fenn heard the scraping of tables and chairs being moved out of the way behind him, followed by the crash of splintering wood and the scrambling of feet. The sound of a brawl broke out, but he daren't shift his attention from the man.

The man came off the floor with a roar, arms outstretched. If he got those arms around him, Fenn had no doubt the man would use his thickly scarred forehead to pound him senseless. He managed to get his own arms under the man's shoulders as he met the charge. Fenn was driven back but he twisted his body and used the man's momentum to throw him off balance. Both crashed to the floor, Fenn's head making painful contact with a table leg. Slightly dazed, he managed to get to his feet first. While the man was only half-erect, Fenn moved forward and brought his knee into his face, hearing the crunch of bone as his kneecap met the man's nose. The man reeled back with a cry of pain, blood pouring from his broken nose, his hands coming up to his face.

He looked up at Fenn, eyes blazing, one hand clawing for his sword.

'*You're a dead man!*' he screamed.

Fenn reached for his axe, but Kaela stepped between them. The Lord of the Battle whipped left and right, slicing long cuts into the man's coat.

'The next one will pierce skin,' she said. The point of her sword hovered over the man's hand, daring him to continue to draw his sword. The man stared at Kaela, stunned by her speed and accuracy.

He stumbled back a step, his balance unsteady on his injured knee, glancing over his shoulder.

Four of his men were scattered on the floor. Olgood stood in the middle. There was blood on his hands.

'You left me with five while you went off to dance with this idiot,' said Olgood, nodding at the leader. 'A tall order. Luckily, circumstances whittled them down to only three.'

Fenn looked at Gisele, standing over a man with a broken chair in her hands. The fifth man sat on a stool holding a cloth to a bleeding hand, a sword discarded on the floor in front of him – Kaela's victim, no doubt.

The leader spat blood onto the floor. He breathed heavily through his mouth, deciding his next move.

He rounded on his fallen men. 'Get up, you lot,' he snarled, his voice distorted by his twisted nose. 'Look at you – I'll be lucky to get more than a few pennies for the lot of you… *Get up!*'

He bent to grab the shoulder of a man groaning on the floor. The man staggered to his feet. The leader pushed him towards the door and limped after him. One by one, his men followed.

At the door, the leader turned, pushing the last two men past him through the entrance.

He looked down at his tattered coat. 'I'll not forget you – all of you!' he snarled, his eyes rising to glare at Kaela and Fenn and pausing to measure Olgood head to foot. The blood ran over his top lip and dripped from his chin. He spat again, ducked his head through the door, and forcefully pulled it shut behind him.

The slamming of the door was a signal. The noise of conversation resumed in full intensity, sweeping like a wave across the room, everyone with something to say, gesturing at each other and towards Fenn and Kaela.

Nyle appeared beside Fenn. 'What happened here?' he asked. 'You made quite a noise.'

'I'm not sure,' said Fenn, rubbing at a bump on the back of his head. 'A lack of respect.' He looked at Nyle. 'Do we have a place to sleep?'

'We've reluctantly been given a corner of the barn,' said Nyle. 'I suspect it's going to be crowded.' He shrugged. 'But, for now…' he waved at the woman beside him.

'Are you returning to your table, darlin'?' asked the woman, her hands filled with ales.

'Yes, we certainly are,' said Fenn, suddenly thirsty. He looked at Olgood.

'We still have a child to celebrate,' he said with a grin.

THE WIND HAD BEEN strong and blustery all morning; broken clouds scurried across the sky like flocks of seagulls. Leaves swirled in disturbed eddies of air and the trees shook and swayed noisily – producing a continuous rushing sound that made conversation difficult.

It may have been coincidence, but as soon as they crossed the river Exe and Nyle announced that Westerling was less than ten miles ahead, the wind eased, the forest became lighter and greener, and patches of wildflowers appeared more frequently. Fenn heard snatches of clear birdsong. When he paused to admire a beautiful meadow carpeted with daisies nestled among elm trees, he had the bizarre feeling they were being welcomed. He turned to share the feeling with Kaela – she looked at him, but he just smiled. She'd think him mad.

The forest thinned and abruptly ended in an area where several trees had been felled and the foliage cleared around them. The cutting had happened some time ago but, even so, the pale stumps jutting out of the ground were starkly defined in the brief flashes of sunlight that pierced the clouds.

The cluster of buildings that came into view was more substantial than Fenn expected.

A half-mile away atop a low hill stood a large hall with a cluster of adjacent buildings and livestock pens. A wide well-trodden path, bordered by stones, led from the road to an opening in a palisade of thick sharpened logs surrounding the settlement.

'Welcome to Westerling,' said Nyle.

He spread his arm in a circle.

'All that you can see in every direction and beyond for some distance is the estate of the late Lord Orvyn, including several small villages and groups of houses past the fields to the west and over the hills to the north and west.' He turned to the south. 'You can't see it from here, but there's a stone church on the other side of the hill, past the hall, by the river.'

Placing his hands on his hips, he faced the group of buildings on the hill.

'The river Yule runs by the church. A good source of fish and fresh water but too shallow for boats. The nearest large town, Escanceastre, is in that direction.' He pointed southeast.

He waved his hand in the air. 'All of this…' he bowed to Kaela, '…is now yours, my Lady.'

Nyle drew in a breath. 'When I was here last, Lord Cormwurst, Orvyn's uncle, was the Thane of Westerling. As far as I knew, he was a good and wise man. Westerling was prosperous.' His gaze scanned the area. 'It saddens me to see the poor state of the place now.'

Once freed from the forest, the line of the road was easily traced by the eye, as straight as an arrow heading west. Nyle said the road was Roman. Adjacent to the road, on the northern side, stood fields of winter wheat and barley and also large open areas left fallow. The bare fields were divided into several long strips, each separated by a line of stones. Some showed signs of previous ploughing, but most had been left untouched and were strewn with weeds and thistles. Where the land had been worked, the furrows were rough and uneven. Thick weeds were also visible among the storks of the nearest wheat field.

At the far edge of one of the strips, moving away, a solitary ploughman was labouring behind a pair of oxen. Behind him, a woman carrying two large baskets strapped to her body was spreading something, probably manure, behind the plough. The ploughman's progress was slow, each yard needing several attempts to roll the soil.

Fenn walked to the side of the road – to the edge of the strip being ploughed. He bent and took a handful of the heavy earth, mixing it in his fingers as he straightened. He brought his hands to his nose as two of Nyle's boys joined him. One also knelt to check the turned earth, and the other lowered his head to examine the soil in Fenn's hands. He reached out, raising his eyebrows with an unspoken query. When Fenn nodded, he took some dirt from Fenn's hands, pinching it between his fingers.

'This soil is too heavy for a single pair of oxen,' he said. He looked at Fenn, who nodded thoughtfully. The boy turned to watch the ploughman. 'He's making hard work for himself.'

Fenn let the earth fall from his fingers. 'And why are these two the only ones working?' he asked aloud. 'The wheat and barley are both overdue for harvest, and there's plenty of work to be done in weeding. On that high hill to the north, good grazing land, I see only two sheep. Where's the rest of the flock, and where are the cattle that should be in these lower pastures?' He turned to the cluster of buildings on the hill. 'There are oxen tethered behind the hall; why are they not being used to plough? There's something strange afoot here.'

'It was said that Orvyn neglected his estate, but I didn't think it would be this bad,' said Nyle. 'Where are all the people?'

'Eadburg said there were problems at Westerling,' said Kaela. 'Those are good questions. Perhaps these two can give us some answers.'

She placed her hand on Fenn's shoulder, inviting him to accompany her. Together they stepped off the road, Balthazar bounding ahead. The two boys standing with Fenn followed. The others looked to Nyle, but he motioned for them to remain with the cart.

Olgood called out to Fenn. 'We know nothing of farming.' He put his arm around Gisele's shoulders and pulled her close. 'Gisele and I will wait here.'

'IT WAS I WHO travelled to Witanceastre to report our problems to Lord Orvyn,' said the man.

He was a head shorter than Fenn but had the robust and sturdy look of a man tied to the land – a farmer who could labour in the fields from dawn to dusk, day after day. A man who knew his craft. Fenn had no doubt there would be a good reason why this man was attempting to plough alone and with insufficient oxen.

'But I didn't get to see him,' the man continued. 'Instead, after waiting two days, I was given an audience with the Queen.'

Fenn and Kaela shared a glance.

'The Queen listened to my plea for Lord Orvyn to come immediately to Westerling. She said she would inform our Lord of my concerns and I was dismissed,' the man said.

'When did you see the Queen?' asked Kaela.

'Three days before the ides,' said the man. 'I stayed until the ides hoping to see Lord Orvyn, but I feared the situation at Westerling could only get worse if I waited too long. I had to return. I had to trust he would come as soon as he heard of my concerns. When I saw the armed men with you, I thought our Lord had arrived....' He stopped and gave an apologetic shrug.

Kaela sighed. She moved closer to the pair. 'I'm sorry to disappoint you and be the bearer of bad news.'

The stricken expression on their faces told her bad news was the last thing they wanted.

'He's not coming, is he?' the woman said softly, despairingly.

'I have to tell you that Lord Orvyn is dead. He died while you were in Witanceastre.'

The shock for both was genuine. 'While I was *there*?' said the man incredulously. 'But... *how*? How did he die? He wasn't an old man.'

'He was murdered,' said Kaela.

'*Murdered*,' breathed the man. 'Oh, my dear Lord...' Beside him, the woman made the sign of a cross on her body.

'Yes. It happened on the ides, in fact.'

The man and woman looked at each other. 'I didn't know him well, but... to be *murdered*...' the man shook his head. 'Who would do such a thing? Why?'

'God has abandoned us,' said the woman, her voice choking. She closed her eyes. 'Lord Orvyn was our last hope. Who can help us now? We're lost... Mother of God, we're truly lost.'

Tears formed beneath her lids and slipped down her cheeks. The man put a hand on her shoulder. He clenched his other fist and looked desperately to the heavens to find salvation.

'No,' said Kaela firmly, reaching to take the woman by her arm. 'You are not at all lost because *this* is your new thane, Lord Feran of Lindisfarne, now of Westerling. A true and honest man. You can trust him. He's come to set things right.'

IT TOOK AN EFFORT for Fenn not to appear as astonished as the two people now staring at him. He resisted the urge to look at Kaela. Can she declare him to be the Thane? His mind raced.

Queen Eadburg, acting for the King, had bequeathed Westerling to Kaela. Now Kaela had announced that *he* was the thane, the Lord of Westerling. It could be a legitimate appointment, but maybe she was saying Fenn would act in her stead. He was not well versed in such procedure.

Over Kaela's shoulder, he saw Nyle react to Kaela's words with the surprise Fenn felt. Nyle also looked puzzled, and Fenn understood why. Kaela had presented him as Lord *Feran*, the name he had been christened by Master Oswald at St. Cuthbert's Monastery on the island of Lindisfarne. The name meant *wanderer* in the old language. But Fenn's baby brother Mikhael found 'Feran' hard to say – he had called him *Fenn* instead, and the new name had stuck.

He'd explain it to Nyle later.

Realising he should speak, Fenn said: 'Please… what are your names?'

He immediately questioned his choice of words. Thanes probably didn't say 'please'. It sounded like pleading. But it was also polite. Even so, perhaps something more profound would have been a better opening.

'*You* are our new thane?' asked the man. 'But you're…' he glanced from Fenn to Kaela and back. Fenn realised his youth and perhaps his foreign appearance were the probable cause of the man's confusion.

Kaela understood also. 'I am Princess Kaela, daughter of Beorhtric, King of Wessex. Lord Feran *is* your new thane,' she confirmed.

The man's expression changed to concern – in case he'd caused offence. He spoke quickly.

'My name is Edelred, my Lord, and this is my wife, Bronwyn.' While he bowed his head, his wife remained staring teary-eyed at Fenn, her arms wrapped tightly around the baskets hanging from her shoulders, seeming to gain some comfort from them.

'Is it true?' she mouthed silently.

Fenn looked at her and saw the need in her eyes. He abandoned his concerns about how a thane should act.

'I have a lot to learn, Bronwyn,' he said. *About my new position as much as about Westerling.* 'I hope you'll be able to help me.'

Bronwyn released the baskets, clasping her hands before her in a gesture of prayer, her tear-stained eyes glistening.

'Praise the Lord,' she said.

'THERE ARE OTHER OXEN behind the hall,' Fenn said. 'Why aren't you using more oxen for the ploughing.'

Edelred grimaced, raising his hands: 'I went to Witanceastre to complain to Lord Orvyn about Galastan, our new tenant-in-chief….'

'…*who shouldn't be*….' whispered Bronwyn.

Edelred frowned at her interruption. 'Yes… well… he won't release the other oxen because he says they're diseased. We think that's a… it's not….'

'It's a *lie*,' said Bronwyn firmly.

Edelred nodded. He patted one of the oxen on the rump. 'These two had been lent to Wyeford, the village over the hill…' he pointed to the northwest. '…to pull some logs. They're the only oxen in Westerling not held by Galastan. But I can't plough properly here with only two – this time of year I need a team of six.'

He raised his eyes to Fenn's, a touch of hope in his voice.

'The oxen he's holding belonged to Lord Cormwurst… no, I mean Lord Orvyn… well… now they belong to *you,* I suppose… don't they…?'

Fenn understood the question. But, even if he was the Thane of Westerling, he was no descendant of Cormwurst. Did *he* now own the oxen or not? He felt unprepared and confused, an untethered boat in an unfamiliar ocean. He stole a glance at Kaela but she stared back at him, her face expressionless. His decisions were his own.

'I'll address the problem with the oxen in due course,' Fenn said. 'But what else has happened here? Why are you working the fields alone?'

When Edelred didn't answer immediately, Nyle added: 'Where are the other people? What's stopping the people of Westerling from working together to bring in the harvest?'

Edelred looked at him. He started to speak but just shook his head. He looked back at Fenn, a mixture of hope and despair on his face. His fists clenched in determination.

'The harvest this year is poor,' he said. 'Last year also. But still Galastan has demanded we give him two-thirds. The plain truth is – if we give two-thirds of a small harvest to Galastan, we cannot survive.' His voice gained strength. 'You can see the wheat is in poor shape and should have been harvested already… The barley even worse….' He raised his hands in the air. 'We're weeks past Lammas when the first loaf baked from the new wheat should have been brought to the church. Galastan has ordered us to start the harvest, but the people are refusing to work. They won't work hard when the end is certain starvation which the weakest will not survive – at least by *not* working, they'll deny Galastan his tithe and his satisfaction. They're hoping he'll change his mind.' Edelred shook his head. 'He *won't*.'

'You don't agree with those who refuse to work…?' asked Fenn.

'I'm one voice….'

'We're two,' corrected Bronwyn.

Edelred nodded. 'We are two, but only two. Bronwyn and I don't want to give in to Galastan's demands, but we also don't want to give up – to sit and do nothing. Those tactics won't work with Galastan. I can't harvest on my own but I can try to prepare the field even though I know it's hopeless….'

Edelred's voice trailed off and he shook his head.

'We're all slowly starving *now*,' he said. 'Except Galastan, of course – he's keeping last-harvest grain in the tithe barn. *Our* stores are empty.' He looked up at Fenn. 'With no grain and not enough vegetables, we've only the livestock to eat. The sheep and cattle have already been culled to survival numbers. The pigs are gone. So are most of the chickens and the eggs. It's far too early – in the past we've only killed livestock as a last resort to survive the final weeks of winter. The forests are overhunted and bare of game, no fish in the river – the hunters are gone for days and return with only hares and pheasants, and only enough to feed a few. We haven't seen boar or deer for weeks.'

He paused, weighed down by his words, then waved a hand. 'And all the while, the wheat is wasting in the fields.' He shook his head wearily. 'Lord Cormwurst would never have let this happen.'

He looked at Bronwyn and she took up the story. 'Every morning, we pray at the church, asking God to grant us deliverance from our trial – to show us the way. We look for a sign that the sacrifice the people have chosen to make is the path he wants us to follow – but our pleas have been ignored. We've had no sign. I don't know what great wrong we've committed to deserve such terrible punishment. The folk here are *good* people. But… the morning prayer numbers become fewer each day as people give up hope and accept their fate.'

Edelred nodded. 'Some families have left Westerling in desperation,' he said. 'Anywhere must be better than here. Treddian left only two days ago with his wife and new child. They've abandoned the land they tended for years and left with nothing. It's been a hard year – they won't be welcome anywhere; they'll only be seen as extra mouths. They'll probably die in the forest.'

He looked up at Fenn. 'You've arrived just in time, Lord. Galastan has threatened to make an example if the harvest is not started tomorrow.'

Fenn frowned. 'An example? What kind of example, I wonder?'

Edelred shrugged and stared at him, then his eyes widened and he straightened.

'But, Lord, we're forgetting our manners. Please forgive me – I've been dwelling on our woes when we should be welcoming our new Thane to Westerling.'

He bent to unhitch the oxen.

NYLE'S MEN HAD CUT hazel switches to help keep the oxen moving in the right direction. The massive animals moved readily, grateful to be freed from the hard labour. Their heads, each framed by a pair of curved horns, swung rhythmically from side to side as they walked, but their wide eyes never left the huge dog that bounced happily around the group, oblivious of the scrutiny.

'How many tenants are there on the estate?' Fenn asked. 'Can't you all band together – refuse Galastan his two-thirds and take the oxen you need? How many follow him?'

'There are still about sixty of us living within the palisade,' said Edelred, 'and maybe a hundred and twenty more in the other villages. We're farmers, not fighters. Galastan doesn't need anyone else – he has the Ariochs to do his bidding. Since *they* arrived in Westerling, everyone's learned to fear them. They're big and mean-tempered… and… *different*. They're both *white* like ghosts.'

Fenn frowned. *White? What did that mean?*

Bronwyn didn't allow him time to ask. She touched her fingers to her head. 'They're simple up here…' she added, '…like children.'

Edelred nodded and continued: '…they do whatever he says… they enjoy hurting….' He grimaced, noting Fenn's frown, and spread his hands in frustration. 'I'm sorry, I'm not explaining things well.'

Fenn stopped walking. 'I don't understand,' he said. 'Who or *what* are the Ariochs?'

'The Ariochs are brothers, twin brothers,' Bronwyn explained. 'You can't tell them apart. We don't know what their mother named them – if they *had* a mother. They call each other the same name – just 'Arioch'. It probably has some meaning in their language.'

'*Their* language…?'

She looked up at him. 'They don't talk much,' she said, 'but when they do speak, they have a language of their own that no one else understands. They sound like animals.' She spread her hands, showing similar frustration to her husband. Her face twisted in anguish and her voice rose.

'*They don't feel any pain!*'

When Fenn's puzzled look deepened, she took a breath to calm herself.

'Gerwent tried to protect his daughter Erenweth and put a pitchfork into an Arioch's leg. The brute didn't seem to feel the injury. He just stared at it then pulled the fork out and struck Gerwent a vicious blow on the head with it. The poor man's senses were knocked clean out of his skull. He's still not right. He can't even feed himself properly.'

A long groan from Nyle. When Fenn turned to him, he said: 'My father suffered a heavy blow to the head like that. He was never the same. I know full well the lasting damage such an injury can cause.'

Cedric had mentioned that their father had been killed by Ingeld of the Hwicce. Fenn wondered if that head injury had something to do with the 'bad blood', as Kaela had called it, between Nyle and his shire Lord, Ealdorman Ingeld.

He brought his mind back to the present and glanced at Kaela. Her face was calm but her eyes were thoughtful. He resumed walking toward the road. Meeting Galastan and the Ariochs was going to be interesting.

He caught a whisper from Bronwyn. '*You need to tell him about the salt.*'

Edelred replied: '*No. He won't want to know....*'

Fenn smiled. 'Salt?' he asked.

Edelred winced. 'Ah… It's just that….'

Bronwyn cut in. 'Galastan refused to pay a fair price for the salt this month.' She spread her hands. 'A man comes each month from Escanceastre to sell salt. We usually trade eggs and wool and clothing, whatever we can, but we had nothing to trade. He said he would take coin and asked a fair price, but Galastan refused to pay. So now salt is scarce. When we run out, what meat we have will spoil. It's a small thing, but….'

'But it's yet another problem,' said Fenn.

'Yes, Lord,' Edelred said wearily.

'You say you're farmers, not fighters,' Fenn said. 'You may need to become both.'

Balthazar bounded up to Fenn, easily evading the lowered horn of an ox. Fenn playfully pushed him off. The dog leapt away, running in a circle, barking at the oxen.

'Save your energy, Balthazar,' Fenn said. 'We have no quarrel with these beasts.'

He turned his head to speak over his shoulder. 'Nyle…' he said, stepping from the field onto the road, stamping his feet to remove the thick soil from his shoes, '…we should arrive at Westerling with your men formed and fully armed.'

Nyle touched his forehead. 'Yes, my Lord,' he said.

Fenn's glance at him was swift enough to catch the smile that was quickly hidden.

WESTERLING HALL WAS A vast structure with walls constructed of vertical tree trunks chosen for straightness and similarity of size, topped with a high sloping thatched roof. Holes in the thatch suggested an upper storey. The solid walls were broken only by long slitted eye-holes. In Fenn's estimate, the Hall's length was at least a hundred paces. The entrance wasn't visible, so he concluded it must be at the far end.

The palisade enclosed a substantial area – a low hill with a flattened top. In the centre was an earthen yard with a stone well covered by a wooden roofed shelter from which a rope could be turned to raise and lower a bucket. Surrounding the well were various buildings and dwellings – crafting rooms, storage sheds, a large cattle barn, and several animal pens. Most of the pens were empty but one contained the oxen that Fenn had seen from the road, and two horses stood in another. Tables and chairs were visible through the doorway of a larger structure – perhaps an alehouse. The familiar open layout of a blacksmith stood next to a place Fenn took to be a butchery but only because of the single pheasant hanging outside. Some other buildings stood in a row, possibly more craft houses – tailors, coopers, and cobblers. On the southern side of the area, there were rows of huts that looked like family dwellings.

Fenn and Kaela entered through the arched palisade doors with Balthazar, keen to be at the front of the group, trotting ahead. Behind them came Nyle and his men in a line, and Olgood and Gisele leading the horse and cart. Edelred and Bronwyn followed, driving the lumbering oxen before them.

Their arrival provoked considerable interest. Many people were standing in the courtyard and outside the buildings, staring.

Edelred called a man over, handed the care of the oxen to him and caught up with Olgood, who had stopped the cart and walked back to examine the arch and doors of the palisade.

'The palisade is well built,' observed Olgood, running his hands over the underside of the arch.

Fenn ran his eyes along the wall of sharpened tree trunks. The stakes were even and solidly set. This barrier was intended to keep out more than just wild animals. A narrow step had been built halfway up the wall allowing the palisade to be defended.

'These trunks are well-chosen and fitted by a master who knew his craft,' Olgood continued. His eyes inspected the doors. 'Half-trunk hardwood, very thick… and… very heavy.' He turned his head and called to Fenn. 'Look how the doors are attached to the arch….' He tested a door moving it back and forth with one hand. '…their balance allows them to be moved easily.'

'That's Hardwain's doing,' said Edelred.

Olgood glanced up. 'Then Hardwain is the man who built the Great Hall also. I see the same excellent handiwork there.'

'He was a wizard.'

When Olgood looked at him puzzled, Edelred smiled. 'Not a true wizard, just a wizard with wood. Wait until you see *inside* the Hall. There's not another like it in Wessex.'

Olgood nodded. 'I'd like to meet him.'

'Sadly, Hardwain caught a fever and died two winters ago. We miss him.'

Olgood grimaced and groaned his disappointment.

Fenn stopped, letting Nyle and his men move past him. When nobody was close, he bent to Kaela's ear.

'Some warning would have been appreciated,' he said.

'Regarding your new position? I had no warning either. It came to me just before I said it. I thought there may be difficulties with a woman thane. It seemed a workable solution.'

'What's expected of me?'

'You're the Lord of Westerling. You're responsible for your tenants and the governing of the estate. You'll be a good thane.'

Fenn raised his eyebrows. 'That remains to be seen.'

Edelred came up to him. 'Galastan will be in the Great Hall,' he said.

'SO ORVYN IS DEAD.'

Galastan sniffed. 'A pity,' he said. 'Just when things were going well.' His voice was heavily nasal, and he had a way of speaking that made every word seem critical or sarcastic.

His lips creased into a smirk.

'You are young to be a thane, especially the Thane of Westerling, and you're not from….' Galastan paused, then he shrugged. 'But I suppose the King can appoint whoever he chooses.'

He gave a forced laugh and spread his hands, attempting to pass the comment as a joke. When nobody reacted, he sniffed again, wiping his nose with the back of a hand.

'Westerling needs order and authority like any community,' he said. 'Allowing people to do as they wish would simply result in chaos. Someone has to be in charge. It was my duty as the servant of our righteous and all-knowing God to keep the estate operating efficiently while Lord Orvyn was away.'

Galastan was a small man whose large dark eyes dominated a thin face with a jutting chin sparsely covered by the wispy threads of a meagre beard. His hair was long and slick with grease and his hands danced in front of him while he talked. He finished each sentence with the same thin and insincere smile, a habit Fenn quickly found irritating. The tenant-in-chief's voice and appearance heightened the air of insolence that he wore like a cloak.

Fenn had been surprised when entering the Great Hall to find that the entire floor was wooden. He had expected a thatched or earthen floor.

The wizard Hardwain's work. Olgood had bent immediately to examine the rough planks.

At the far end of the Hall stood an overlarge and ornate leather-covered chair raised on a platform. Stools and other chairs were scattered around the Thane's Chair. Large, rich tapestries adorned the walls. To Fenn's eye, they were the equal of those on the chapel walls of St. Cuthbert's monastery at Lindisfarne. The skill of the Westerling crafters was fully displayed.

In the centre of the floor area was a fireplace. The wooden planks ended a step from the fire on all sides and smooth flat stones filled the gap. The bed of ashes, now cold, was covered with another surprise – a construction of crossed iron bars to hold the cooking pots clear of the fire. Three iron pots of differing sizes sat on top of the rails. Stools and low tables were set around the fireplace. More wooden chairs and long tables lined one wall.

As Fenn and his companions walked the length of the Hall, three sets of eyes silently watched the newcomers approach. The first set belonged to the small man lounging in the leather chair, and the two others belonged to a pair of strange beings, one standing either side of the chair, the like of which Fenn had never before seen. These two must be the Ariochs.

'Give two-thirds of the harvest to me?' Galastan continued. He laughed as if the thought was preposterous. 'As God is my witness, that's a simple misunderstanding. A *third* to the thane is normal as rent for the use of his land, and I recommended we send another third to *market* this year. It may result in a lean year and some hardship, but it will enable us to improve things around here, buy stock, and better prepare us for the year to follow.' Galastan raised his eyes defiantly to Fenn's. 'In Lord Orvyn's absence, it rightly fell to me to make such decisions under God's watchful eye.'

As he finished speaking, Galastan leaned back in the Thane's Chair and pointedly allowed his gaze to rest on Edelred.

Edelred glared back at him and Bronwyn's shock was clearly painted on her face. Edelred's eyes flicked to Fenn and then shifted to the two men standing on either side of the chair.

These two presented a bizarre mirror image of each other.

Their heads appeared small but only because of the vast bulk of their hairless bodies, on the shoulders of which a bald head sat without the apparent support of a neck. The Arioch twins seemed as wide as they were tall, with thick arms, and legs like tree trunks – their corpulence contrasted sharply with the leanness of the other inhabitants of Westerling.

Fenn understood Edelred's reference to the Ariochs as white. Their exposed skin looked to have never seen the sun, being a deathly pale hue. They stood perfectly still, resembling a pair of carved alabaster statues.

One item of the twins' appearance stood out from their other unusual and distinctive features.

Their eyes.

In contrast to Galastan's large dark eyes, those of the Ariochs were tiny, enfolded inside pockets of skin atop prominent cheekbones. They delivered a sullen unblinking stare – and, bizarrely, from deep within their caverns, they shone *a fiery red.*

It was easy to see how these creatures could invoke such fear among the people of Westerling.

Fenn found it difficult to tear his gaze away from the twins but he returned to Galastan.

'And the oxen?' he asked.

'The oxen?' Galastan repeated, frowning as if the question made no sense. He ran his hands through his hair and wiped them on his shirt.

'Why would you not release the oxen for ploughing?'

'Ah… for a reason that would be obvious to anyone who bothered to observe the creatures…' he paused and sniffed, raising his nose into the air, waiting for Fenn to ask him to state the reason.

Fenn said nothing.

Galastan waited until the silence became awkward, then slowly drew a breath through his teeth and pronounced: 'One of the beasts has developed scaly mouth.' He glanced at Fenn. 'If you haven't heard of it, it's a serious condition that readily spreads among oxen. I'm holding all of them to see if others contract it.'

'How long has the ox had scaly mouth?'

Galastan waved a hand in the air. 'A week or ten days.'

'Did you isolate that beast?'

'That's not necessary.' Galastan chuckled, implying the idea was ridiculous. 'If others are going to get the disease, they will. Best to keep them together and get it all over with at once.'

He looked down his nose at Fenn, his lips curling into the now-familiar smirk. Fenn heard Bronwyn muttering a frustrated response to Galastan's excuse. He was about to contradict Galastan but changed his mind – he didn't want to get into an argument on the care of oxen.

Time to bring another matter to the fore.

He leaned back on his heels and folded his arms.

Galastan scowled, but Fenn could see he knew what Fenn wanted. The tenant-in-chief feigned bewilderment, then allowed realisation to theatrically creep over his face. He threw his hands dramatically in the air and thrust himself up from the chair. Sitting at Fenn's feet, Balthazar came immediately erect and issued a deep growl. Galastan visibly flinched at the movement and the menacing tone, retreating a half-step with his arms coming up awkwardly to protect his throat. When the dog made no advance, he coughed and attempted to recover his composure. He bowed low and gestured with his hand.

'Please, Lord… Lord *Feran*, is it?' He sniffed, mocking the name. 'I apologise for appearing so rude. This is rightfully the chair of the Thane of Westerling. And…' he straightened and immediately bowed again, this time exaggeratedly even lower, '…as you've explained, that is *you*.' His leer robbed his words of any sincerity. Under his breath but still intended to be audible, he muttered: '*God moves in mysterious ways.*'

He sniffed again. 'I also apologise if I have acted in any way that you think is improper. I was merely trying, as best I could, as I've *said*…' he gave a short forced cough, '…to exercise my rightful duties as tenant-in-chief while our Lord was absent.'

He flicked a hand to the Ariochs. One muttered something unintelligible and they both stepped back from the chair, causing Balthazar to switch his gaze to them and repeat his rumbling growl. They took only two steps back, a token gesture that would still position the twins uncomfortably close and behind Fenn once he sat down. Fenn heard the soft rustle of clothing as Kaela's hand moved to the hilt of her sword.

He waved for the Ariochs to move around the chair to the front. The Ariochs stared blankly at him and didn't react. In unison, they turned their heads to face Galastan. From the corner of his eye, Fenn saw the smirk on Galastan's face lengthen. Galastan caught Fenn's look and shrugged his shoulders.

'They're not my *dogs*,' he said. If the Ariochs were waiting for his word, he wasn't going to give it.

Nyle and Olgood stepped forward together, but Olgood held out his arm to stop Nyle.

'Please…' he said, '…allow me.'

'Olgood,' Nyle said pointedly, '…there are *two*.'

'I know.'

'Olgoo-od…?' Gisele said softly, elongating the name in her concern.

Olgood brushed his hand gently over her shoulder and arm. 'Don't worry,' he said. He drew his Northman's axe from his belt and handed it to her. 'Hold this for me.'

Gisele accepted the axe and appealed to Fenn with her eyes. Fenn smiled to reassure her, then turned to Olgood and nodded. He had never known Olgood to fail at anything he chose to do. If he insisted the big man accept help now, it would show a lack of faith. If Olgood said he would handle the Ariochs, Fenn would respect his decision.

He glanced at Galastan. The man was unworried, looking on with interest. He caught Fenn's glance and his smirk appeared.

Olgood stepped around the great chair, moving slowly but with purpose. The Ariochs turned to face him. Olgood inclined his head and repeated Fenn's gesture, inviting the Ariochs to move around the chair to the front. The invitation was met with motionless blank stares.

Despite Olgood's size, the confrontation was a mismatch. Together, the Ariochs outweighed him. Although Olgood was much taller and broader in the shoulder than either, Nyle's comment was valid. They were big men and *there were two.*

Appearing to read each other's mind, the twins silently took a simultaneous step to the side, separating and giving themselves room. A movement from Galastan caught Fenn's eye, but the tenant-in-chief was just folding his arms and leaning back on his heels. He issued an amused chuckle, evidently expecting to enjoy the spectacle.

Balthazar uttered a low growl, sensing the growing tension in the Hall. Fenn reached down to hold the dog.

Despite his confidence in Olgood, Fenn was worried. He knew his friend would wait for the Ariochs to make the first move and, in this case, allowing these two huge men who seemed to think and move as one that advantage could be a dangerous mistake.

For a moment the Great Hall was frozen in time. A silent stillness covered the scene as though each observer had simultaneously stopped breathing.

Fenn expected the Ariochs to try to pin Olgood with their thick arms then wrestle him to the ground where they could strike him with their hands and feet. In his limited experience from his boyhood at St. Cuthbert's, that was how most unarmed fights were concluded. Olgood had never been defeated at the monastery, but he had never faced opponents such as these.

The first movement, when it came, happened without warning. There was no adjustment of the body, no shifting of weight, no repositioning of the legs in preparation. There was also no way the form of the attack could have been anticipated.

Two massive arms flashed out, one from the Arioch on Olgood's right and one from his left. Again, through some unseen communication, the action was identically timed. Both closed-fist blows were directed at Olgood's head and, had they landed cleanly, either one would have knocked a man senseless.

Balthazar barked twice, deep and low, his muscles tensing. If Fenn hadn't held him, he would have leapt forward to join the fray.

Olgood leaned back, causing the blow from the left to pass harmlessly in front of his chin. An instant too late, he also rocked his head to the side. The fist thrown from the Arioch on Olgood's right connected with his cheek, but much of its power was dissipated by Olgood's movement. Olgood continued to bend away from the blow, flowing with it, twisting his body in the same direction, his own arm rising. Before the Arioch could withdraw, Olgood locked his fingers around the man's wrist. With a powerful wrench, he pulled downward, twisting the wrist to rotate the arm at the shoulder, dragging the Arioch off balance and forcing him to take a step forward. The Arioch tried to resist but even with his bulk he was unable to oppose Olgood's force. Olgood continued the twisting motion but changed direction to drag the arm high up behind the stumbling Arioch's back, at the same time turning him so his body created a shield between Olgood and the other twin.

Olgood's second arm curled beneath the man's chin, where his neck should be, clamping the head in a tight vice. For the first time, Fenn saw an Arioch register an emotion. With his arm wrenched behind his back, forcefully twisting his shoulder to its limit, the man's face changed from its usual implacable blank stare to a grimace of concern.

His brother uttered a squeal of rage, raised his arms with his fingers spread wide and took two thumping steps forward to attack Olgood from the side. Olgood turned to keep the Arioch he held as a barrier, dragging him to face the assault, but the man bent his legs and used his weight to slow Olgood. The second Arioch grunted in triumph and reached out, fingers grasping.

With both arms occupied, Olgood seemed defenceless.

Fenn heard the Lord of the Battle sigh as it left its scabbard and Balthazar strained forward against Fenn's grasp on his neck.

Olgood leaned back and away from the reaching hands. He flexed his shoulders, using their power to lift the feet of the sagging man in his grip clear of the floor, supporting his entire weight with the arm below his chin and, at the same time, he increased the pressure on the tortured shoulder by pulling the locked wrist even higher. The Arioch's shoulder was visibly distorted and on the point of dislocation. It was an impressive feat of strength – the Arioch weighed as much as two men. The afflicted twin's pale face flushed a deep red to match his eyes.

139

Bronwyn had said she thought the Ariochs didn't feel pain. This one at least understood what would happen if his arm was twisted any further. He screamed – a piercing squeal like a tormented pig – and the scream resolved into a word. It was the first word Fenn had heard either of the twins utter that was both intelligible and audible.

Issued from beneath the constriction of Olgood's arm circling his head and between his own clenched teeth, the desperate word was:

'*Arioch!*'

It was a command. His twin froze in mid-motion. His face remained contorted in anger, eyes blazing fire, a rumble like a growl sounding continuously in his chest, but his arms slowly relaxed and fell to his side. Then, like the thaw of a frozen river, his distorted features flowed back to their typical blank state. He stood immobile with his arms lowered, staring at his twin.

Kaela lowered her sword. When she noticed Fenn's glance, she murmured: 'The monster would not have touched Olgood.'

Galastan was watching Fenn and Kaela with narrowed eyes. The eyes dropped to take in Kaela's sword. Had he heard her comment? He screwed his face into an expression of distaste and released a breath of frustration. Or was it disappointment?

Olgood eased the pressure of his arms. With his head still immobilised, the Arioch twisted his eyes backwards as far as he could and said: 'Let me go. We move.' His unrestricted voice was high-pitched, like that of a young girl.

Olgood released him. The Arioch's feet hit the floor with a thump and he staggered to the side before regaining his balance. The man grimaced, a hand instantly moving to check his shoulder. Both twins glared at Olgood with eyes like hot coals. Although their expressions were once again unreadable, the anger and raw malintent conveyed by their eyes was not.

At some silent signal, they turned in unison and walked around the chair toward Galastan. Olgood gave a smile of satisfaction. He nodded after the Ariochs as though thanking them for their cooperation and turned to rejoin Gisele.

As one of the Ariochs passed close to Bronwyn, he used his shoulder to knock her out of his way. She only prevented herself from falling by grasping onto Edelred's arm. Olgood started forward but Fenn held up his hand. Tensions were high. He caught Bronwyn's eye and she nodded at him; she wasn't hurt. The provocation, although deliberate, was minor – any response could escalate and possibly lead to bloodshed.

'Warn your dogs, Galastan,' he said firmly. 'I want no more trouble. No more of that….' he pointed at Bronwyn.

Galastan looked at him innocently.

His attitude annoyed Fenn, but he had to try and work with the man.

'We don't want to begin our relationship with a misunderstanding or a false step, do we?' he said.

Galastan bowed instantly. 'Of course not, *Lord* Feran.'

This time there was a deliberate pause between his words and the appearance of his characteristic insincere half-smile.

FENN KEPT HIS EYES on Galastan as he eased himself into the chair, resting his hands on the leather-covered armrests. The seat was cushioned and surprisingly comfortable for a chair that was primarily a symbol of authority. He waited a moment and breathed slowly and deeply to ease his own tension.

He leaned forward. 'Edelred,' he said. 'You and Bronwyn go now and check the oxen. Isolate any with scaly mouth. The disease will normally run its course in a week, so it should have cleared by now. Tomorrow, take all the fit oxen and complete your ploughing. Whose strip is next to yours?'

'Wyllard tends the next strip.'

'At the end of the day, you'll feed and care for the oxen, then give them to Wyllard.' He circled his hand to indicate the process should continue.

Edelred could not suppress a broad smile of satisfaction. '*Thank you*, Lord Feran.' He stole a glance at Galastan who had folded his arms again, his adopted air of nonchalance betrayed by the whiteness around his compressed lips.

'Any excess grain from the tithe barn will be distributed,' Fenn continued. 'I will forgo my third this year. Tomorrow we'll also begin to salvage what we can from the harvest.'

Edelred's head was bobbing continuously. Galastan had clenched his fists and was staring at the floor. The Ariochs stood by him, faces blank, seemingly unconcerned with events.

'One more thing,' said Fenn. 'Send a man to Escanceastre to buy salt.' He glanced at Galastan whose head had risen sharply at the mention of salt. 'I presume Westerling has coin to pay?'

Galastan stared blankly. Fenn took his lack of denial as affirmation.

Fenn returned his attention to Edelred. 'I'd like an assembly in this Hall today, at sunset,' he continued, 'so I can meet with the people of Westerling. Please let the locals know.'

Edelred stopped nodding. 'Yes, Lord,' he said. His eyes searched Fenn's. Was that all? He bowed and turned to Bronwyn. She reached for his arm with both her hands, her eyes misting. Together, they walked purposefully toward the entrance, Bronwyn murmuring in his ear. She turned once to glare at the Ariochs.

'If people 'ere to meet you, we should 'ave food,' stated Gisele at Fenn's side. 'I prepare food Cedric give us.'

Olgood offered his help, but she said he should rest – she'd use the two of Nyle's men who'd been left to guard the cart and its contents. Olgood objected but was silenced by Gisele with a shake of her hand as she took her leave.

Fenn was unsure whether Kaela's smile indicated approval, amusement, or both.

'Galastan, can you take word of the assembly to the villages?'

Galastan was silent for a moment, then said: 'I'll send someone.'

'No, I'd like you to do this yourself. I saw two horses outside. Olgood will go with you so he can learn the layout of the estate.'

Galastan's large eyes got even wider. He ran his hands through his hair then waved one hand in a negative gesture.

'A tenant-in-chief,' he said, trying to put authority in his voice, 'does not carry messages.'

Fenn looked directly at him. 'I imagine no one knows Westerling as well as the tenant-in-chief,' he said, keeping his voice calm. 'Who better to show Olgood the lie of the land?'

Galastan did not reply. A strong emotion, poorly suppressed, distorted his face – anger or frustration, probably both. He held out his hands.

'Lord Feran…' he said in a condescending tone, as though advising a child, '…you *must* be tired from your journey and probably thirsty. This…' he waved his hand, '…this *misunderstanding* with the Ariochs was, as you say, an unfortunate beginning. I'll arrange a place for you all to rest and I'll send for some special Westerling ale. Why not relax for the remainder of today… gather your strength… and have your assembly tomorrow when you're refreshed?' He tilted his head to the side, his mouth creased into his habitual thin smile.

Fenn had already known the man long enough to be wary of Galastan's apparent concern for his comfort and wellbeing. He seemed to want to avoid being sent to the villages. Or did he want to delay the gathering?

'I'd like to meet the people as soon as possible,' Fenn replied. 'There's time enough today and I don't want to waste it.'

Galastan's eyes narrowed. He hesitated, considering his options, his gaze flicking to the Ariochs. Without turning his head, the eyes swivelled to check Nyle and the men standing beside him. They were only three, minus the two left at the cart, but Nyle and his men stood ready and capable. Each man carried a sword on his belt with a spear in one hand and the Wyvern shield of Wessex in the other.

The tenant-in-chief vented his annoyance with a hiss through his teeth. With deliberate disrespect, he twisted on his heel, lowered his head, and strode toward the Hall entrance. Olgood moved to block his way. Galastan thought about pushing by him but, up close, Olgood's bulk dwarfed the small man. Fenn heard a heavy-footed shuffle from the Ariochs. He resisted the urge to look at them. He knew Kaela would be watching, her sword hand ready.

He fixed his eyes on Galastan and waited until the man felt the silence and turned to look back.

'You may leave now, Galastan,' Fenn said formally. 'The Ariochs will wait here.'

His eyes met Olgood's and the big man stepped aside then turned and walked toward the entrance, looking back after a few steps to wait for Galastan.

Galastan blew a slow breath through his nostrils. His hands clenched. He glanced again toward the Ariochs, his large eyes blinking rapidly. He turned abruptly and followed Olgood, each deliberately slow and heavy footstep on the wooden floorboards proclaiming his resentment.

Fenn leaned back in the chair. Was Galastan's strange blinking another sign of his frustration or something else? A message? A command to the Ariochs? The thought drew a smile. Surely *he* was now the one being overly suspicious? He regarded the Ariochs. They turned their heads and his look was met by faces that could have been carved from stone.

White stone faces with eyes of fire.

IT WAS WELL BEFORE sunset but already a crowd of around fifty men, women, and children stood in the Hall, respectfully forming a half-circle before the great chair, the adults murmuring amongst themselves, the children taking advantage of the lack of attention to chase each other around the Hall. If Fenn had to use one word to describe the appearance of the people of Westerling gathered before him, that word would be *gaunt*. To a person, they were thin and hollow-cheeked with the harshness of recent times reflected in their dull eyes.

The children had seen better care, their eyes had sparkle and their bones showed a firmer covering of flesh, confirming to Fenn where the effort to feed the community had been directed.

The primary topic of conversation was evident from the frequent stares directed toward the Thane's chair where Fenn sat. But the eyes also took stock of the lanky form of Nyle and his men standing to one side, the flame-haired, sword-wearing Kaela on the other – and the massive shaggy hound stretched contentedly at the foot of the chair caught a fair share of the attention.

He scanned the crowd, acquainting himself with the faces of the people of Westerling. Although thin, those faces that met his eye were friendly and honest. He was reminded of the inhabitants of Lindisfarne, the Monastery where he had been raised. Simple, hard-working folk – the core of any stable and prosperous community.

A man came through the entrance. He was walking slowly with hesitant steps, supported on his unsteady legs by a young woman. People made way for the pair as she guided him to the front of the gathering. Nyle noticed their arrival and he quickly gathered a stool and took it to where the woman could seat the older man. She thanked Nyle and he remained to talk with her.

The long gown the woman wore stood out as being particularly finely made. It was pale fawn in colour and embroidered with intricate stitching. It reminded Fenn of the beautiful gowns his mother, Aerlene, produced – a skilled dressmaker and mistress of the craft room at St. Cuthbert's monastery. He thought of the last time he had seen his mother, waving tearfully to him from the monastery gates as he left with Kaela to journey south to Wessex. Sad at his leaving after having so recently returned to Lindisfarne from more than a year's absence, but happy for him also. He let his mind drift back to the monastery – to a life only removed in time by a few months and in distance by a few hundred miles, but a life to which he would never return.

Edelred came to stand beside Fenn. 'That's Gerwent and his daughter, Erenweth. To look at him now, you wouldn't know only a few months ago he was a strong man and a leader in the community – a former tenant-in-chief.'

A *former* tenant-in-chief? How did that title change hands?

Edelred had brought a youth he introduced as Wyllard, the tenant whose ploughing strip was adjacent to Edelred's. Wyllard was younger than Fenn expected for a tenant – about his own age.

Edelred also brought the news that his wife Bronwyn was helping Gisele prepare what Edelred excitedly called a 'mighty feast'.

His excitement was cut short by the approach of an elderly man whose grey beard reached almost to his waist. After a short conversation with Edelred, the man was about to turn away when Edelred stopped him.

'Lord Feran, I would like to also introduce our physician, Acwellan. His great knowledge of the healing arts serves Westerling well.'

Acwellan nodded to Fenn. 'So you are our new thane. I did hear of your arrival but I was busy.' There was a twinkle in the man's eye. Fenn felt the physician was testing him to see if he was offended by the remark.

'I'm glad to meet you, Master,' Fenn said, '…although, forgive me if I hope not to have need of your services.'

Acwellan smiled. He held up a finger. 'But everybody does, once in a while.'

'Acwellan has just told me that he thinks Gerwent's head injury will heal in time,' said Edelred. 'His control of his limbs has improved.'

Fenn glanced at the man on the stool.

'That's good news,' he said. He noticed Nyle was still speaking with Erenweth.

Acwellan nodded. 'I have much to do,' he said and turned away without waiting for an acknowledgement.

Fenn watched him go. The physician stopped beside Gerwent. He put a hand on his shoulder and bent to talk with him.

Recalling that an Arioch had caused Gerwent's condition, Fenn's eyes narrowed with the realisation that the twins were nowhere to be seen. He leaned toward Kaela.

'I don't see the Ariochs,' he said. 'I'd feel better if I knew where they were.'

Kaela looked about. 'So would I,' she said. 'I'll find them.'

'Bring them back to the Hall, where we can watch them,' said Fenn. The Ariochs could be dangerous and difficult to persuade. 'Take a couple of Nyle's men.'

'No need.'

She threaded her way through the people who parted readily before her.

Edelred said: 'I didn't notice them go either. I've been watching the people coming through the entrance – I think I would have seen them if they'd left that way.'

A hidden exit? It wasn't unknown for halls such as this to have secret passages for escape if threatened. Perhaps the idea of Galastan conveying some message to the twins with his blinking eyes was not as absurd as it had first sounded.

He dismissed the Ariochs. They were gone. How they disappeared was not important. If they were within the palisade, Kaela would find them.

'Are any of the tenants from the villages here yet?'

Edelred shook his head. 'They should be. They've had plenty of time to arrive. I've been watching for people from Wyeford...' he pointed to the northwest, '...it's the closest village, just over the hill. It would be the first place Galastan visited.'

Fenn frowned.

'When would you expect Galastan to return after visiting all the villages?'

He had no idea how long the journey he'd requested should take, but both Galastan and Edelred had accepted that the task could be accomplished before sunset.

Edelred looked worried. 'On horse, they should be back by now.'

Fenn tightened his lips. What was keeping them? Was Galastan playing some game? He hadn't wanted to go — was he deliberately staying away to make a point? He should have sent more men with Olgood. He shook his head, annoyed with himself and the situation — the big man could take care of himself, but... best to be sure.

'Can you send a man to Wyeford to see if there's a problem? Take another horse if there is one.'

'I'll go, my Lord,' offered Wyllard.

He straightened the cap he'd been holding and set it on his head, staring up at Fenn with eager eyes. At Fenn's nod, he bowed and ran for the door.

Fenn pursed his lips thoughtfully.

'Edelred... How did a man like Galastan become tenant-in-chief of Westerling? He has a poor knowledge of livestock. He's no farmer.'

Edelred sighed heavily. 'Gerwent was tenant-in-chief under Lord Cormwurst. When the Lord died, Gerwent went to Witanceastre to inform Lord Orvyn of his uncle's death. While he was away, Galastan and the Ariochs arrived at Westerling. Within days, Galastan appointed himself tenant-in-chief. The Ariochs made sure there was no opposition. On his return, Gerwent had the altercation with the Ariochs that Bronwyn told you about. Gerwent was injured and, as you see, still hasn't recovered.'

Fenn looked across the Hall at Gerwent. The man was looking at the people near him, but his gaze was vacant. Nyle and Erenweth were seated together now. Erenweth had a comforting hand laid on her father's arm but her attention was on Nyle.

'There will be changes when Galastan returns,' Fenn said.

KAELA BROUGHT NEWS that the Ariochs were not inside the palisade. Her eyes told Fenn she shared his thoughts – that was bad news. With Galastan and Olgood overdue and the Ariochs missing, an ominous feeling was settling in Fenn's stomach.

The size of the Arioch twins and their appearance made them hard to miss. Someone must have seen them leaving the Hall or leaving the palisade.

'Edelred, ask the people here if anyone has seen the Ariochs. Ask the children too.'

'Yes, my Lor….'

Balthazar interrupted his reply by leaping to his feet, uttering a bark loud enough to startle everyone nearby. His warning was followed by shouts from outside the Hall. The hum of the crowd quieted and Fenn heard the hoofbeats of a horse. Balthazar gave another series of loud barks. A moment later, Wyllard lurched through the door, supporting a man Fenn didn't know who was clearly exhausted and on the verge of collapse.

Edelred gasped and cried out: 'Treddian!'

Fenn frowned, then recalled the name. Treddian was the man Edelred said had left Westerling a few days ago with his family, desperately looking for a better life.

Edelred rushed forward to help, but several men were there before him, easing the man to the ground.

As soon as Wyllard had been relieved of his burden, he called out:

'Lord Feran! Come quickly. You need to hear what Treddian has to say. He brings a warning!'

CHAPTER NINE

A duo of dilemmas

Fenn rose and crossed the room, Kaela and Nyle on his heels. Excited by the sudden activity, Balthazar bounded instinctively toward the door, scattering folk before him, but swerved to follow Fenn when he didn't head in that direction.

Treddian recognised Edelred and strained to rise, reaching out with his hand. Only grunts issued from his mouth as he gasped for breath and struggled to talk, his face creased with effort. Edelred took his hand and, with his other arm, eased the man back to the ground. A rolled cloth was placed under his head.

'Rest a moment,' Edelred said. 'Get your breath back.' He turned. 'Please…' he called, '…some water!'

Fenn looked at Wyllard.

'I found him collapsed at the turnoff to Wyeford, Lord,' said Wyllard. 'He'd run himself to exhaustion. He couldn't talk. The only words I could understand were *'Warn Westerling'*. On the horse, he was mumbling about somebody or something headed this way.'

A woman asked: 'Myfanwy and the baby?'

Wyllard shook his head.

A cup was handed to Edelred. He lifted Treddian so he could drink. Balthazar chose that moment to push his shaggy head forward and sniff at the man on the floor. Treddian's eyes widened and he recoiled from the startling apparition thrusting itself at him.

'The dog's friendly,' said Edelred, adjusting his hold to support Treddian's head and adding under his breath: '*I think.*' Then, louder: 'Drink. It'll ease your throat.'

The man's eyes searched Edelred's to confirm the truth of his words. He threw one more nervous glance at Balthazar before he drank eagerly, coughing as the water caught in his throat. The coughing seemed to exhaust him – he groaned, his head sank onto the pillow and his eyes closed. Immediately, they sprang open again and his body jerked upwards, a hand clutching at Edelred's shoulder.

'Please…' he breathed, '…Myfanwy needs help….' His eyes swept the faces leaning toward him. 'Galastan? I should tell him….'

'Galastan's not here,' replied Edelred. 'You can speak to our new thane, Lord Feran.' He looked up at Fenn who knelt beside Edelred.

Treddian's eyes flicked between Fenn and Edelred. 'New… thane…?'

Don't worry about that,' said Edelred. 'What's happened? Where's Myfanwy and the baby?'

New strength came into Treddian's eyes.

'Armed men! Cornish!' he said with sudden energy. 'At…' he coughed, '…Magog's Ford.' He stopped, breathing heavily from the effort of speaking. His next words were forced out in gasps: 'Hid Myfanwy… in… old Roman villa… ran as fast as….' His voice died.

Fenn heard the news spread around the Hall in urgent whispers.

'How far away is this ford?' he asked.

Edelred: 'On the river Taw. Ten miles.'

Fenn turned to Treddian: 'How do you know the people you saw are Cornish?'

'The black crow… on their shields. King *Hernam*. Please…' Treddian gasped, '…Myfanwy…'

Fenn felt a hand on his shoulder. 'A word…' said Nyle's voice in his ear.

Fenn stood up and Nyle drew him aside. Kaela came to join them. Still whispering, Nyle said: 'Treddian is a name from West Wealas and so is Myfanwy. By their names, these people have some connection with the Cornish. Can we trust what he's telling us?'

Nyle had fought against the Cornish – he had a right to be suspicious. Fenn beckoned to Edelred, who eased Treddian's head onto the pillow, then rose and hurried over.

'How well do you know Treddian?' asked Fenn. 'Where do his loyalties lie? Can we trust him?'

He explained Nyle's concern.

'Treddian's *father*, Lord, was Cornish, and he was driven from his home by King Oswallt, Hernam's father, when Treddian was a young boy. Treddian's no friend of Hernam or the Cornish, and I would trust him with my life.' He spread his hands. 'He's headstrong but solid. He's near killed himself to bring us warning.'

Fenn looked at Nyle, who nodded and said: '*Hernam then.* Across the border once more.'

'Only a raid, it seems, this time.'

Nyle glanced at him sharply. 'We'd do well to treat Hernam seriously. He's a proud man.'

'Of course.' Fenn nodded his agreement and took a moment to study Nyle. How did Nyle feel about meeting the Cornish again? The bowman met his eyes calmly.

'Beorhtric needs to know,' Kaela said. 'And the ealdormen of the western shires.'

'We'll send a rider as soon as we know more,' said Fenn. He drew in a breath. 'Why would the Cornish be raiding now?'

Edelred thought for a moment. 'It's been a harsh season for us and it will have been the same for Hernam – no rain at all, then too much. This late in the season, they'll expect our harvest to be gathered and our barns to contain the winter grain. So, they'll want that grain and maybe our livestock.' He gave a wry laugh. 'In both respects, we're sure to disappoint them.'

Fenn and Kaela grunted in agreement. Nyle was silent, his face pensive.

He patted Edelred on the back. 'If it comes to it, we'll try to make them a little more than disappointed.'

Bold words with little to back them up.

HE MOVED TO AGAIN kneel by Treddian's side – Nyle, Kaela, and Edelred joining him. He waited while Treddian took another sip from the cup.

'How many men did you see?'

Treddian shrugged. His voice was stronger. 'I saw a group at the ford. Ten or twelve. There were others….'

'Did they see you?'

An insistent shake of the head. 'Didn't see us… I heard them talking… about Lord Orvyn… and Westerling… had to hide Myfanwy and the babe… so I could run….'

Fenn stood up. His eyes sought out Kaela, who said immediately: 'I'll go for the wife and baby.'

'Myfanwy first, but try to find out….'

'…how many,' finished Kaela.

Fenn smiled. 'Be careful,' he said. 'They're far enough away that I expect they'll camp for the night. It's important to confirm they *are* stopping and where they're headed.'

She nodded and turned to Wyllard. 'The Roman villa? Where is it?'

'It's hundreds of years old… just ruins now…' began Wyllard. He stopped and said: 'Better if I show you.' His eyes widened as a thought came to him. He turned to Fenn, his lips forming a strange smile.

'Galastan has a pair of mares, Lord. They're the fastest horses in the three shires.'

'Take them,' Fenn said. 'I'm sure he wouldn't mind in the circumstances.'

Wyllard ran for the door, Kaela on his heels.

Balthazar caught the excitement. He shaped to jump up, but Fenn restrained him with a hand on the dog's neck which he then converted to a rub along his muzzle.

'Easy, Balthazar. If you're looking for action, you may not have long to wait.'

Balthazar seemed to understand. A whine of anticipation came from his throat as he stepped back, his eyes searching Fenn's to see what might happen next.

Fenn bent to place a hand on Treddian's shoulder.

'Thank you,' he said. 'Your courage and efforts have given Westerling good warning.' He straightened. 'Someone is going for Myfanwy now.'

The man's face registered his relief. Air escaped from him in a long breath, then, his reserves gone, he sagged in Edelred's arms.

Fenn straightened. 'How many other horses are available?' he asked.

A man answered: 'There are two more in the stables.'

Fenn sought him out. 'We need to warn the villages. The Cornish will certainly raid them before they come here.' He pointed at the man. 'You…' his finger moved to an equally tall lad alongside him, '…and you. Take the horses. Tell the people of the villages to come inside the palisade and bring their weapons.'

If it was only a small raiding party, he may be disturbing people's lives unnecessarily, but until he knew better – his instinct was to prepare for the worst.

The surprise on the man's face changed to determination.

'Yes, Lord. What about any livestock they still have?'

'Yes. Hide what they can. Bring what can't be hidden. Oh, and….'

The man supplied the name Fenn was seeking: 'Merewyn, Lord.'

'Merewyn. Ask about Galastan. See if you can learn why he and Olgood have been delayed.'

Merewyn touched his hat and caught the boy's arm. 'Come along, Peada. Work to be done, son. We'd best be quick about it.'

Edelred called to him: 'You know the horses Galastan took?'

'We know them,' replied Merewyn.

Fenn looked at Edelred, puzzled by the question.

'You've picked a good pair there, M'Lord. Merewyn can track a fly across a hog's back, and Peada has been taught the same gift. If Galastan has been to any of the villages, Merewyn will know it without needing to ask.'

Fenn nodded. He swept his gaze around the Hall; the eyes that met his were apprehensive.

'What happened the last time the Cornish came, Edelred? Were you here?'

'They haven't come this far east for… I don't know how long… many years. A large force was turned back by Beorhtric at the river Taw a few years ago.' Fenn glanced at Nyle, who nodded, '…but it's been… let me think… at least fifteen, maybe more years since they were at Westerling. I was here. Lord Cormwurst offered them gold, I think. But they still took what they wanted.' He shrugged his shoulders. 'We started again.'

'Did they take people?'

Edelred hesitated. 'People? Do you mean as thralls? No, they took no people from Westerling, but I've heard the Cornish do hold thralls.'

His own experience had naturally coloured Fenn's thoughts on the practice. After a raid or battle, the taking of thralls was common among the Northmen, but he knew it also occurred in this land.

He had to ask the question. 'Edelred, are there any thralls in Westerling?'

'No, Lord. Lord Cormwurst was once offered thralls as payment for a debt, but he refused.'

Fenn nodded his thanks. He breathed deeply to relieve the tension that had built across his chest. His mind sought to change the subject. He inspected the gathering. Who could fight?

'Who are your hunters?' he said. 'How many have bows and can shoot?'

'Ah, well, most of the men….'

'Good. Tell anyone with a bow to report to Nyle tonight.' He glanced at Nyle and saw he didn't need to ask. Nyle would check the bows and the bowmen.

When Fenn looked back, Edelred was staring at him. 'So we are not going to let them take what they want?'

Fenn hesitated. That thought hadn't crossed his mind. He smiled. 'We are *not*.'

Edelred nodded, but his eyes were wary.

Fenn walked to the chair. The people were restless, shifting on their feet, uneasy faces echoing their concern. As he stepped onto the platform, each face turned to look at him, seeking hope, perhaps? Reassurance? Leadership?

Before he spoke, he searched the Hall for a place to keep the people who couldn't fight – the children, the old, the infirm. Fenn pointed to a door underneath the stairs that led to the upper floor.

'What's that room?' he asked Edelred.

'A storeroom. Food, pots, jars of fruit, chairs… the old Thane's chair that Hardwain replaced is in there.'

'Could the room be cleared and used as a refuge for the children and elderly?'

Edelred shook his head. 'It's too small.'

There was no other obvious place of safety in the Hall and nowhere that could be easily barricaded. He thought of the barns. Hard to defend. Would the stone church be suitable? He didn't know its situation. It may be defensible as a last resort, but it was isolated.

'Is there somewhere, perhaps in the forest, for these people to hide? The sick, too, if there are any?'

Edelred took a deep breath and exhaled, the question bringing the reality of the situation into focus. 'Perhaps…' he said. 'There's a cave….'

'Large enough and dry enough?'

Edelred scanned the room, estimating numbers. 'I think so.'

Fenn put a hand on his shoulder. 'Good. And Edelred…' Edelred looked up at him. 'Thank you,' said Fenn. Edelred's brow creased. 'For being someone I can depend on,' Fenn explained.

He looked up at the people gathered before him. They'd had time to think. Their faces were tight, their eyes showing a mixture of apprehension and fear. They saw he was ready to speak and the Hall quieted, waiting on his words.

'As you may have heard, a Cornish raiding party has been sighted.' He remembered Edelred's comment and raised his voice. 'You may be thinking you're farmers, not fighting men,' he said. 'It doesn't matter. This is *your* land and one thing you must remember is that we are strongest if we face this together. The people of Westerling probably outnumber these raiders, but…' he paused and spoke even louder, '…*we don't need to defeat them. We may not even need to fight. If we just make it hard* – too difficult for them to get what they want – they'll leave.'

There were some murmurings of agreement but most still looked unconvinced.

Fenn pointed in the direction of the palisade doors. 'Tomorrow morning, if this band of Cornish raiders see the palisade crowded with bowmen and people who *look* ready to fight – ready to defend Westerling Hall, they'll see we've not been caught by surprise.'

He let his eyes roam over the people. 'This is your land, and it's soaked with the sweat of your years of hard work,' he said. 'It's the land of your fathers and those before. This land and the produce it bears, and the life it gives to you and your children, is worth fighting for. *Your land!* Your home.'

Someone cheered, and then several more. The Hall buzzed with muted conversations.

'So…' Fenn called over the noise. 'Gather what weapons you have… swords or spears if you have them, but pitchforks, scythes, even sickles. Be ready for an alarm in the night, but if there's no alarm, everyone will meet outside the Hall at sunrise.'

He needed to talk about the children and the elderly. 'One thing more….'

A tug at his sleeve was followed by Gisele's soft voice.

'Fenn, if we are to fight, per'aps we can 'ave food in our bellies first.'

Fenn looked down at her. 'We 'ave prepared the gifts of Cedric,' she added. 'We ready to eat now. The food is 'ot. Where we set the table?'

Fenn shook his head and smiled. 'Thank you, Gisele. You're right, as usual. In the middle by the fire, I think.' He pointed.

Gisele stepped up beside him and waved toward the door. All heads turned in that direction, and there was a collective gasp as a large table was carried into the Hall laden with steaming platters of meat – venison, geese, and hares – plus bowls of vegetables, and soups. From their expressions, the people of Westerling hadn't seen this much food together in one place for some time.

'Help yourselves,' called Fenn. 'There's enough for everybody.'

He looked at Gisele. 'I hope that's true….'

She shrugged.

'I must 'elp with the food,' she said. 'But Olgood? When is 'e back?'

Fenn grimaced. 'I don't know,' he said. 'He's overdue.'

She frowned. 'Overdue?'

'I expected him back by now.' No need to mention the missing Ariochs.

The instant concern on her face was hurtful. Fenn put a hand on her arm.

'Try not to worry. Olgood can take care of himself. I've sent riders to the villages. We'll know more when they return or when people from the villages arrive.' He knew his words offered poor comfort.

Someone called out Gisele's name – Bronwyn, beckoning her to the table. Gisele gave a weak smile.

'I bring you something to eat,' she said and hurried away.

FENN LOOKED THROUGH THE Hall entrance to the yard outside. The setting sun cast an orange glow bathing the bare packed earth with an unreal light.

He suddenly wondered if there were more Cornish about. Had Galastan and Olgood met another band? Could that be the reason for their delay? He shook his head. It made no sense for Hernam to split his small force. Somewhere out there Olgood was alone. Fenn told himself there was nothing more he could do other than wait for news, but the heavy feeling in his stomach persisted.

Edelred was standing close. Fenn motioned to him.

'Can you arrange for those who cannot fight to go to the cave tonight – with food and water and bedding? Send a few men to look after them.'

'Yes, Lord.' Edelred turned and hurried over to a group of people. Fenn watched as they listened to him and nodded their heads. Edelred was proving himself a capable leader.

He walked over and looked down at Treddian, whose breathing had slowed. A lighter colour was replacing the flushed red on his cheeks. The man kneeling by Treddian looked up at Fenn's approach.

'See that he gets some food and his needs are met,' Fenn said. The man nodded.

Fenn stepped back to join Nyle. 'I haven't forgotten that there's a matter of a mug of ale that was to be settled when we reached Westerling,' he said. 'That will have to wait.' He looked Nyle in the eye. 'I have need of you and your men,' he said. 'What are your plans? How long did you intend to stay at Westerling?'

Nyle took a moment to think before he answered.

'I haven't forgotten you saved my brother's life,' he said. 'I owe you for that.' He smiled. 'Our task was to escort you here, but the Queen set no time for returning, so… I'll stay awhile.' He turned his head to where Gerwent and his daughter were sitting. 'I may have found another reason to remain at Westerling.'

'And your men?'

Nyle flicked his hand toward where his men were standing in a group talking to some Westerling tenants.

'They seem quite happy to be back among men of the land. I wouldn't be surprised if they all ask to join in the harvest – when the Cornish allow it.'

'What will Queen Eadburg have to say?'

'It will be much the same to her if I return or if I don't. I'm sure this assignment was to get me out of sight as much as anything. I doubt the

Queen will be giving us any thought at all. She wouldn't be concerned if the six of us just disappeared.'

Fenn nodded. 'Good. Now… what can you tell me about Hernam? What sort of man is he?'

While Nyle took his time to answer, Fenn returned to Gisele's concern. Olgood and Galastan were overdue, and the Ariochs were missing… he needed to find out why… but the group of Cornish raiders nearby was a more pressing problem….

One crisis at a time.

CHAPTER TEN

A confrontation and an unexpected message

Fenn stood on the narrow step of the palisade overlooking the people of Westerling gathered in the yard below. The step allowed defenders to shoot arrows or throw objects over the top of the sharpened stakes and use those same stakes as a shield.

The early rays of the sun leaked into the eastern sky, dispelling the gloom and painting the tops of the tallest forest trees yellow and gold. A stiff wind tousled his hair. The air was fresh in the pale morning, chilling his arms and face. A cold start – but the clear sky promised a hot day.

Kaela had returned by the light of the moon, carrying Myfanwy and her baby on one of Galastan's black mares. She reported there were eighty Cornish camped near Magog's Ford. She'd left Wyllard to learn where they were headed once they broke camp in the morning.

Starting at twilight the previous evening, a steady stream of people entered the palisade bringing sheep, cattle, pigs, horses, and dogs. Some arrived with hens in cages – they would be the prize layers, the remainder being left to forage free-range. One group's arrival in the night was heralded by the strident honking of a gaggle of geese kept under tight control by a master and his dog.

The first arrivals brought the news that Galastan had not been seen in the closest village, Wyeford. Merewyn and Peada returned to confirm that Galastan had not visited any of the villages of Westerling. The tenant-in-chief had simply disappeared, and the Ariochs and Olgood with him.

Fenn asked Kaela and Nyle to check the newcomers and assess them and their weapons as they arrived.

Once the flow of people had slowed to a trickle, Fenn ordered the palisade doors shut and barred, to be opened again only to allow latecomers through. His last action for the night drew on his experience at the battle of Hammaburg – he had a semi-circular barricade built facing the doors. If the doors were breached, the barricade would form a second wall. Although the doors were double-barred, they were still the weakest part of the defences. The palisade had no towers beside the entrance to allow defenders to shoot at anyone assaulting the doors.

The stream of people passing through the gate was constant through the night, but when Fenn was persuaded to retire, both the noise of intermittent arrivals and the intrusion of Balthazar who adopted a position at the foot of the bed, went unheeded. Fenn had never lain in such a bed as he was directed to in the room above the Great Hall of Westerling. He marvelled at the soft linen-covered feather-filled pillows. His tiredness infected his bones and allowed sleep to arrive without effort once the comfort of the bed surrounded him.

His last thought was a repeated attempt at reassurance – *Olgood can take care of himself.*

HE DREW IN A BREATH of crisp morning air and checked that the groups of bowmen standing at each corner of the wall and at a regular distance along the step had their attention properly focused on the surrounding countryside outside the palisade.

He'd toured the palisade at first light, observing likely areas of the forest where people could be concealed, and pointing them out to the sentries.

In each case, his information was met with an acknowledgement and a nod that said: 'Thank you, but I'm already aware of that'.

He was concerned that the forest was quite close on the side of the palisade next to the Great Hall, only a hundred or so paces from the stakes. Due to the contour of the hill upon which Westerling stood, the sharpened logs of the palisade were tallest on this side, so it was the least likely to be scaled. Nonetheless, Fenn noted that it may be worthwhile to clear the forest further back and extend the clear space between the trees and the wall – when he had time.

He waved his hand, indicating the people standing before him. 'This is Kaela and Nyle,' he said. 'Orders from them are orders from me.'

Balthazar chose that moment to issue a series of deep barks. Fenn immediately twisted his head to scan the landscape, remembering his failure to heed Balthazar's warning when Olgood had appeared on the road. The scene was clear of movement. The fields were empty, the forest quiet. When he looked down at the dog, Balthazar returned his gaze, his head tilted slightly to the side. Fenn had the absurd thought that Balthazar was piqued at being left out of the introductions.

'And this is Balthazar,' Fenn conceded, waving his hand toward the hound.

Balthazar wagged his tail on cue, drawing amused murmurs from the crowd.

'If the Cornish appear,' Fenn said, 'we'll crowd the palisade step and yell and jeer at them at the top of our voices. I want them to see and hear as many people as possible.'

Despite Edelred's assertion that the people of Westerling were farmers and not fighters, there were many swords and spears to be seen among the scythes and pitchforks. Kaela moved into the crowd, gathering the swordsmen and inspecting their weapons. Nyle sought out people carrying bows, checking the supply and quality of their arrows.

Fenn saw him stop to talk with a woman holding a bow. Nyle indicated the man standing next to the woman and she raised her voice in reply. Fenn jumped down from the step and walked over to join them.

'I will not!' the woman said. 'This was my father's bow and I can shoot an arrow better than he ever could.' She pulled a fistful of arrows from a bag attached to her waist and thrust them in front of Nyle. 'I made these arrows myself.'

'I've no quarrel with your arrows, but this will be dangerous work,' said Nyle.

'I know that!' she retorted. 'I'm prepared.'

Nyle sensed Fenn alongside him. He turned his head. 'She won't give up the bow.'

The woman glared at Fenn with determined eyes. Fenn noticed her eyes were black, like Rowena's. She was young and looked capable, but the bow had been built for a man's strength.

'Show me you can draw that bow,' said Fenn.

The woman gave a wry smile. She bent the bow and smoothly notched the string, then extended her arm and drew the bowstring back to her cheek, holding it there, staring ahead. After a few moments, the effort to keep the string in place showed on her face. Her eyes flicked defiantly to Fenn.

'Well done,' he said, motioning her to relax. 'She's proven herself to me, Nyle – how about you?' The woman released the string with a sigh.

'She can draw the bow, but….'

'Look around,' said Fenn. 'Everyone in this yard has come prepared to fight. There are women here with pitchforks. Over there beside Kaela, that woman has a sword, and she looks like she can use it. The Northmen invite women into their ranks, and I've seen them fight. These people have made their decision. If *they're* willing, I'm willing to let them fight for Westerling.'

Nyle placed his hands on his hips. 'How do you know about the Northmen?'

'It's a long story. I'll tell you when we have time.'

Nyle regarded Fenn thoughtfully.

Fenn smiled and clapped him on the shoulder. 'Put her somewhere useful. She won't take kindly to being hidden away.'

Nyle smiled. 'I agree,' he said. He turned back to the woman. 'You can keep the bow.'

The woman took Fenn by the arm. 'Thank you, Lord,' she said, dipping with a slight curtsy.

'What's your name?'

'Brianne, Lord. I won't let you down.'

Fenn covered her hand with his. 'I've no doubt of that, Brianne,' he said.

A SHORT TIME LATER, Kaela came to Fenn. She held the elbow of a young boy, drawing him along with her.

'This young lad and a group of his friends didn't go to the cave,' she said. 'They say they are very good at throwing stones and they've gathered a pile from the river. They want to stay and fight.'

Fenn looked at the boy. He saw a skinny youth standing with the insolent awkwardness of adolescence. The swathe of unkempt hair on his head made him look younger than he probably was. Rather than being overawed, the lad returned his gaze unblinkingly, his eyes fierce, his determination evident. Fenn knew the type. The only way to stop this boy from doing what he intended would be to tie him down.

'What do your parents say to this idea?'

'My mother and father are dead. My grandfather has gone to the cave.'

'This is not a game,' said Fenn.

'We *know that*,' the boy snapped. He immediately held up an apologetic hand. 'Sorry, Lord.' Before Fenn could speak, words came in a rush. 'We're all old enough, Lord, to throw stones with force. We want to fight for Westerling, and we'll give a good account of ourselves – I'll promise you that.'

Fenn regarded him thoughtfully. He found himself admiring the boy's spirit, Brianne's spirit, the spirit and the heart of the people of Westerling.

'I'm sure you will,' he said.

The boy looked up at him expectantly. 'Does that mean…?'

Fenn turned to Kaela. 'Ask Edelred to seek out the parents of the others if he can. Only those who have permission, or…' he turned back to the boy, '…those for whom permission is impossible to obtain, can fight.'

The boy's face broke into a wide smile. '*Thank* you, Lord.' His feet shuffled happily. He held out a skinny arm. 'My name is Beric, Lord.'

Fenn took the boy's hand. 'I repeat, Beric,' Fenn said sternly, 'It's *not* a game.'

The boy froze and acknowledged the rebuke with a nod, his face instantly serious.

'So… you like to throw stones….'

'We practice all the time. Once I killed a hare.'

'Come and see me when this is over,' said Fenn. 'I'll teach you how to make a sling and how to use it.'

The boy's mouth opened in astonishment. '*Yes*, Lord. *Thank you*, Lord.'

'Put them back from the doors,' Fenn said to Kaela, 'high if possible, covering the barricade.'

As the boy turned away, Fenn said: 'If the Cornish breach the barricade, you *run*.'

RESTING HIS HANDS ON a pair of thick palisade stakes, Fenn stared at a point in the forest. After a moment, he moved his eyes to examine the adjacent area. Nothing was out of place. His eyes moved on, taking the time to focus and inspect each small piece of ground. He felt blindly with one hand, checking the bag of stones hanging from his belt while his eyes continued their painstaking examination of the forest, methodically searching. Was there a man crouched behind that bush? He knew much could be missed by scanning a scene too quickly. His mind needed time to examine the detail of the image his eyes presented.

The sun was well above the forest, the glow of the sunrise replaced by a misty haze as the dew on the fields evaporated in the early heat. The air was still, allowing the mist to gather over low-lying areas in patches of grey-white, like vast floating blankets obscuring the ground beneath.

Nothing moved.

He examined the ground immediately outside the palisade. It was firm as expected, firm enough to provide a solid foundation for the palisade wall – and firm enough for ladders. Fenn remembered his only previous experience defending the parapets of Hammaburg castle. There, on the eve of an attack by the Franks, Duke Widukind had lamented that the moat was only partly dug and did not offer the barrier it should.

Ideally, Fenn would have liked to improve Westerling's defences by digging a trench in front of the palisade doors and adding a rampart to slow and concentrate attackers and make the use of ladders more difficult. Unfortunately, Westerling's walls had been designed to deter minor raids not full assaults, and there was no time for such work now.

A shout.

Fenn followed a pointing finger. A horse and rider coming fast along the Roman Road from the west. Wyllard? It was too far away for Fenn to be sure. The galloping horse brought the rider rapidly closer. After a few more strides, Fenn's question was answered by an archer standing alongside him.

'It's Wyllard on Galastan's mare,' the archer said. The news was picked up in the yard and quickly conveyed to all ears, creating a buzz of whispers.

Nyle called out. 'Don't watch the horse. Keep your eyes to the front! Open the doors.'

Three men scrambled to lift the thick beams that barred the doors. Fenn watched the horse and rider maintaining full speed on the road. Wyllard rode well and the mare was fast.

Wyllard turned the mare, leaving the road and cutting across a bare field, heading directly for the palisade doors. Fenn scanned the hilltops and the trees in the distance. Was he being pursued?

He glanced at Nyle. True to form, Nyle was looking everywhere but at the rider, his eyes flicking to different points on the horizon.

Wyllard only slowed his gallop when he reached the doors which had been opened just enough for him to pass through. Even before the horse had drawn to a halt at the barricade, Wyllard was off in a single fluid motion. Hands took the horse from him as his eyes searched the crowd, looking for Fenn. He ran to the palisade.

'The Cornish broke camp before dawn,' he said breathlessly. 'They're headed this way, coming through the forest. They won't be long.'

'How many archers?'

'Several, Lord. I counted twenty.'

'Do they have ladders?'

'None that I saw, but….'

Fenn nodded. Ladders could be quickly constructed with wood from the forest. As could a battering ram. He turned to Nyle.

'Put everyone with a bow or spear onto the palisade step. Don't throw the spears; use their length to repel anyone attempting to come over the palisade. Give the archers room to shoot and then crowd as many others on the step as you can. Let's show our strength. Remember, as soon as the Cornish are seen, everyone should yell at the top of their voices. If we *are* attacked, the extras can drop off the step and join the others at the barricade.'

Nyle nodded and motioned to a group carrying bows. He pointed to positions on the palisade.

Fenn felt again for his bag of stones. 'Kaela, take charge of the barricade. Remember Hammaburg? Form Nyle's men into a roving group who can go quickly to where the need is greatest.'

'Yes, my Lord,' said Kaela smartly. He looked at her, surprised by her use of the phrase 'my Lord', suspecting she might be making fun of him, but he saw only sincerity in her face. She smiled and drew her sword, Lord of the Battle, partway from the scabbard then let it slip back, checking the ease with which she could bring the weapon into action.

THE HEAT OF THE MORNING grew, driving away the mist and leaving a clear day. Birds and insects went about their business in the forest undisturbed by intruders. Only the wind was unchanged, its bluster keeping the trees moving and ensuring the clouds made steady progress across the sky.

Fenn caught Wyllard's eye in the yard. The youth shrugged and spread his hands, confirming he expected the Cornish would be here by now. Had they decided on a new direction or were they taking their time at the villages? Should Fenn send someone to check? He raised a hand to beckon Wyllard.

A shout from a sentry. 'A rider!'

Another horse and rider had appeared on a hill to the northwest, trotting down the hillside toward the Roman Road, heading for Westerling. He rode at a steady pace – purposeful but not urgent. Fenn stared. Was he friend or foe? Someone who hadn't heard of the Cornish threat or someone sent by the Cornish to check on the Westerling palisade? The rider was making no attempt at concealment, so the latter was unlikely. Fenn turned to the man alongside him, the archer whose keen eyes had recognised Wyllard earlier.

'Do you know this man?'

The man shaded his eyes and stared at the rider. He maintained that pose for a long moment, then dropped his hands.

'I don't recognise him, Lord. He's not a Westerling man.'

The rider continued his path down the gentle slope of the hillside. Fenn narrowed his eyes to reduce the glare of the sun. If the man kept to his current heading, he would pass close to a spur of the western forest. Fenn strained to see if there was anything stirring among those trees.

'Archers look to your front!' Nyle's shout came from directly below where Fenn stood. 'This rider may be a ruse to draw our eyes.'

Fenn didn't move his gaze in response to Nyle's call. He thought he had seen something in the trees – a movement. He used a hand to further shield his eyes from the sun.

The rider abruptly turned his head towards the trees, searching, as if he'd heard an unusual noise. Immediately, he leaned forward on his horse, spurring it down the hill. A flock of birds emerged from the trees soaring in a high arc as the horse leapt ahead, the man bending low over its neck. The birds flew directly towards the horse and its rider.

'Arrows!' shouted Fenn. 'The Cornish are here!'

Although the flight of arrows engulfed the horseman, the headlong dash was not slowed. The horse descended the hillside at a gallop, heedless of the danger of crossing the rough terrain at such speed. A half-dozen men emerged from the trees and sent more arrows after the fleeing pair but the shots were wild. Amazingly, the horse reached the foot of the hill and crossed the fallow ground beside the wheat fields without stumbling or breaking a leg. It swung along the road at the same breakneck speed, then, just as Wyllard had done, cut across the empty field, taking the most direct path.

'Oh Lord,' the archer beside Fenn gasped. 'They're hit!'

Two arrows sprouted from the horse – one in its rump and one high in its neck. The man had fared worse. There were two shafts in his right leg, above and below the knee; bad but not fatal. A third shaft protruded from his back, below the ribs.

Moments away from reaching the safety of the palisade, the horse's gait suddenly faltered and the animal lurched to a stumbling walk. A collective groan came from those watching. The horse's head lowered. It faltered to the side, then the front legs collapsed and the animal dropped to its knees, toppling onto its side, bright red blood spraying from its nostrils, staining the earth.

Now Fenn could see that behind the arrow in the man's thigh was another that had entered the side of the horse – penetrating deeply – the exposed belly was awash with blood. How the animal had managed to run as far as it did after sustaining such an injury, he could not imagine.

He looked at the archers who hadn't bothered to retreat into the trees. They waited in plain view. There was now clear movement of other men in the forest.

The man outside the palisade was feebly struggling to free himself but his uninjured leg was trapped beneath the dead horse – the two were held as securely as if they had been lashed together.

Fenn tore his eyes from the sight and searched for Kaela. She was at the barricade. She caught his gaze.

'The rider's badly injured. His horse has fallen and trapped him.' Fenn found his voice surprisingly calm. 'In the field… a hundred paces from the palisade….'

Kaela didn't wait for more. 'Open the doors,' she called.

To Nyle, Fenn said: 'Fill the step with people. Let them see and hear us.'

BY THE TIME KAELA and her helpers had detached the rider from the dead horse and carried him through the palisade doors, the archers on the hill had been joined by a large group of men.

Three men on horseback rode from the trees, one carrying a banner. One of the other two was a tall man on a light-coloured horse.

'That's Hernam,' said Nyle on the step beside Fenn. 'On the grey.'

The three horsemen conferred with the men on foot then the horses turned toward Westerling Hall, moving at an unhurried pace down the hill. A woman uttered a high-pitched scream and the cry was taken up by other voices on the palisade. The morning air rang with the noise of defiant shouting.

The mounted men did not appear worried by the cries. They reached the road and turned along it, taking the same path as the unfortunate horseman. Fenn scanned the forest. It was impossible to estimate how many more men were among the trees.

In contrast to the morning's previous arrivals, the Cornish kept to the road and only turned toward Westerling Hall when they reached the wide stone-bordered path.

They stopped just out of arrow range and waited.

'Kaela, fetch Galastan's mares. You and I will meet with these Cornish.'

Fenn jumped down from the step as Kaela called for the horses. She also called to Bronwyn who ran to her side.

'I don't expect trouble,' Fenn said to Nyle. 'They appear to be asking for a truce and want to talk, but… just in case….'

'We'll be ready,' Nyle replied. 'But there are three Cornish. Maybe I should also come to the meeting?'

'One is there just to carry the Cornish standard.'

The crowd parted as the horses were led forward. For the first time Fenn saw Galastan's mares up close. They were magnificent creatures, a matching pair, as black as midnight, beautifully muscled. They were stepping, more from suppressed energy, Fenn thought, than nervousness. He couldn't tell which one had recently been ridden by Wyllard – the mare had recovered quickly from its morning run.

Edelred steadied one of the mares while Kaela mounted. Bronwyn had quickly tied and plaited her red hair so it was pulled back from her face and hung in a tail down her back. Her cheeks and high forehead were accentuated, lending her a distinctly regal look.

When Kaela was settled, Edelred moved to the other mare, but when Fenn approached, to Edelred's surprise, the mare quieted, standing perfectly still as Fenn lifted himself into the saddle. The axe in Fenn's belt prevented him from sitting comfortably on the horse so he withdrew it and handed it down to Edelred who stared back at him, puzzled.

'Lord…?'

'Keep it for me.' Edelred nodded and stepped back.

The mares held their heads high, ears forward. They were eager to be moving, but their apprehensive eyes followed the huge dog pacing back and forth by the barricade.

'Stay here, Balthazar,' said Fenn. He wasn't surprised when his command went unheeded. 'Can you please hold him, Edelred?'

'Hold him?' echoed Edelred. He shifted Fenn's axe from hand to hand. 'I'm not sure….'

Peada, the tall lad who had ridden to warn the villages the previous evening, stepped forward and grasped Balthazar by his shaggy mane.

'I'll hold him, Lord.'

Balthazar looked up at Peada, and Fenn waited to see how the dog would react. He'd never seen Balthazar act menacingly toward anyone – with the possible exception of Galastan the previous day – but the sheer size of the dog could make controlling him a problem. Surprisingly, Balthazar sat down happily.

Fenn looked at Kaela – she was ready.

'Open the doors.'

He could feel the coiled power beneath him as the horse passed through the gap in the barricade and beneath the arch of the palisade entrance. The mare wanted to run, eager to release some energy, but Fenn kept her checked, allowing only a walk. As he passed through the doors, he turned in the saddle and waved to the people in the yard, indicating they should add their voices to those on the palisade. He raised a clenched fist of satisfaction at the resulting roar.

The doors closed behind them. Over the shouting, the voice of a man on the palisade came clearly to Fenn. 'Our Lord does not even bother to wear a sword to meet the Cornish….'

He met Kaela's eyes. 'Our Lord must be very brave…' she said softly, so only he could hear, '…or maybe he wants to make an impression… or maybe he's just forgetful….'

He should have replaced the axe with a sword; it was foolish not to wear a weapon, but he couldn't turn back now. He realised that when it came to close fighting, he had unthinkingly placed his trust in Kaela. After all, there were only *three* Cornish waiting on the path.

Fenn didn't hurry. The volume of the shouting behind him had increased once he moved away from the palisade. He smiled to himself. It sounded like there were hundreds of defenders behind the sharpened stakes.

The mares were wary of the dead horse in the field, flaring their nostrils and widening their eyes. Fenn pushed his mount on, sparing a glance at the carcass as he passed. Again, he could only admire the heart of the critically wounded animal that had steadfastly carried its rider to safety.

The shouting died as Fenn and Kaela approached the waiting horsemen. One man waited a little behind the others, the black crow banner he carried – the standard of Cornwall – shifting lazily back and forth in the stiff breeze.

The older man nodded an acknowledgement when Fenn stopped before him. He was riding the horse that was light grey, the colour of smoke.

He wore a metal helmet and a cloak of chain mail covered his chest, but beneath that was a pale tunic, the edges of which were decorated with coloured gems and beads. A brown finely-woven woollen cape was slung around his neck and covered one shoulder, fastened by a brooch that may have been gold. A belt with a similar buckle held a sword in a decorated scabbard. Fenn felt distinctly underdressed in comparison; he had given no thought to his clothing.

This was Hernam, King of the Cornish. His eyes took in the horses Fenn and Kaela rode and his appreciation was evident.

He spoke, and his words were incomprehensible.

Fenn frowned, annoyed with himself. He hadn't considered that they wouldn't be able to communicate. He should have asked if anyone spoke the Cornish language – Treddian, perhaps? Should he admit his ignorance? Should he reply in his own language?

Kaela spoke in Latin. 'We both understand *this* language, King Hernam.'

To Fenn's astonishment, Hernam smiled and nodded in agreement.

'The old language of the Romans and of the church of our Lord. Many still find it convenient in trade. So be it.'

His gaze flicked between Fenn and Kaela, a question on his brow. Who had come to meet him?

'I am Hernam,' he said. 'This is my son, Hopkin.' Hernam did not introduce the third man, the standard-bearer.

Fenn glanced at Hernam's son. He looked young, but a closer inspection showed a boy's face on a man close to middle age. Hopkin stared back at him, his lips curled in a sneer. He was clearly impatient with the diplomacy and finding it hard to sit still, his eyes darting from Fenn to the palisade.

'Am I to presume Orvyn is unavailable?' Hernam said – a hint of sarcasm in his voice.

'Lord Orvyn is dead,' said Fenn. 'I am Lord Feran, the new Thane of Westerling.'

'Dead, is he? How did he die? *Overeating?*' Hernam gave a gruff laugh.

'Father, this is pointless,' Hopkin interrupted. 'It doesn't matter who's the thane here. They won't *give* us what we want. We need to *take* it.'

'Forgive my boy,' Hernam's smile was forced, 'he's not experienced in negotiation. He rarely thinks before he speaks.'

Hopkin's eyes narrowed and his face grew sullen. He stared at the ground beside his horse.

Hernam continued as if there had been no interruption. 'And you, young lady? Who are you?'

'I'm not important,' Kaela said.

Hernam regarded her. 'So, a new thane, very young and unarmed, and an unimportant girl, also young, wearing a nobleman's sword. I find that interesting. Don't you think so, Hopkin?'

He turned to his son, but Hopkin only stared back silently. Hernam drew in a breath and gazed up at the sky. He slowly released the breath and his eyes snapped back to Fenn's.

'Hopkin's right,' he said. 'It doesn't matter.'

He straightened in his saddle, his face serious, the preamble over.

'I've come directly here,' he said. 'Orvyn's estate is the largest in the shire and you will have what I need.' He flicked a hand over his shoulder. 'I have two hundred men in the forest. We can overrun your low walls quickly – but no one wants to fight if it's not necessary. My men found no grain in the barns of your villages. You must have it all here.' He waved his hand again, this time apparently granting a concession. 'I'm a reasonable man, but we need grain. Give us half your wheat and some horses and milk cows and we won't disturb you further.'

Hernam's eyes flicked to Fenn's mare, leaving him in no doubt which horses the Cornish King had in mind.

'King Beorhtric will hear of this,' said Kaela.

Hernam frowned at her, surprised she had spoken.

'No doubt,' he said, 'but the King is not here, and we are.'

He stared at Kaela as if she puzzled him, then returned his attention to Fenn.

Fenn took a moment to study Hernam. He saw a man whose hair was greying but whose height, bearing, and breadth of shoulder still showed strength. The cape was an accessory and would be put aside when the time came, but the clothing under his armour although finely made was also practical. He was ready to fight. This was not a king who directed affairs from the rear. His eyes held the confidence of his position – he was used to getting what he wanted.

'If I were in your position,' said Fenn, 'I would overstate my numbers in the hope of a quick surrender.' He noted the tightening of Hernam's face. 'You can see that neither wheat nor barley has been harvested, so there's no grain for us to give you.' Fenn paused to allow Hernam to consider his words. Herman's face did not change.

Fenn continued: 'Should you still decide to attack, we are well prepared. The only outcome is that you'll leave many of your men dead on this ground. Men who will not be returning to their fires and families. And that is *all* you will achieve if you are foolish enough to attack Westerling with such a small force.'

From the corner of his eye, he saw Hopkin's face crease with fury.

'He mocks us!' the prince shouted, his Latin laboured. 'Let it be… *you* who is the first… ah… to die, Thane!' He reached for his sword.

In a blur of movement, Kaela's sword checked his before it had cleared the scabbard – she'd clearly anticipated his move. Hopkin's arm was awkwardly restricted, his elbow high in the air, and he fumbled to retain control of his weapon.

A bellowed 'No!' came from Hernam.

Kaela controlled her horse with her knees as the tip of the Lord of the Battle flicked up and a line of red appeared on Hopkin's cheek. The man's head jerked back. Kaela's sword descended and in a clash of steel, Hopkin's weapon was knocked from his grip, tumbling to the ground. It hit point first and stuck upright in the earth. Fenn heard the soft sigh of the Lord of the Battle returning home.

The entire action, three quick movements from Kaela, was over in the time it took to take a breath.

The third horseman had remained facing straight ahead, his hand still gripping the staff of the Cornish banner. The only thing he moved were his eyes. They darted nervously about, but the affairs of the meeting were not his concern.

Hernam's face registered astonishment, then anger. Fenn wasn't sure whether the latter was directed at Kaela or Hopkin. Hopkin's hand went to his cheek. It came away red with blood.

The skirmish reignited the shouting from the palisade. Fenn had to raise his voice above the noise.

'I've heard your request. I'll talk with my people and let you know my reply.'

An enraged cry erupted from Hopkin's throat. It was followed by a string of angry words in his language, but the meaning and intent were clear. The man had evidently taken no heed of the ease with which Kaela had marked him. He bent to pull his sword from the earth.

Fenn heard the sigh of the Lord of the Battle being readied, but before Hopkin's hand could touch the hilt of his sword, Hernam used his horse to push his son's mount aside. The Cornish King reached out to grasp Hopkin by the arm, pulling him upright in his saddle.

'Leave it!' he said sharply. 'You broke the truce once – you won't do so again. You don't deserve the sword.' He continued to push Hopkin away, forcing his horse to retreat down the path.

When he had turned Hopkin completely, Hernam twisted in his saddle.

'I'll return to this spot at midday,' he said. 'You have until then to meet my demands.'

Hopkin muttered something angrily. Hernam replied sternly then turned back to Fenn.

'I see there is wheat unharvested,' he said, 'but you will deliver half of the grain you have to me if you want to save the lives of your people. If we don't hear from you, *we'll take it all!* We'll discuss the cows and horses. Refuse, and *you* will be responsible for the consequences.'

Fenn didn't reply. He turned his horse, Kaela following.

A volley of cheers sounded from the palisade. Fenn looked up, then at Kaela, puzzled.

'They see the sword left in the ground, and the Cornish retreated before we did,' she said. 'They've taken those as signs we had the better of the meeting.'

He smiled and shrugged. 'Anything that keeps their spirits up is good.' He turned his head with a puzzled look. 'How did you know King Hernam spoke Latin?'

'I didn't. Not for sure. But I think Charles mentioned that when he traded with Hernam for clay and tin, their common language was Latin.'

'That was fortunate,' observed Fenn.

'Yes,' Kaela agreed with a smile. 'And I have a question for you.' Her smile changed to a frown. 'I expected him to order his attack when you didn't agree immediately to his terms. Why has he given us so long to decide whether to give him our grain?'

'He's had a good look at our palisade,' replied Fenn. 'I suspect he's decided he needs time to build ladders.'

He looked over his shoulder. Hopkin's abandoned sword stood starkly in the middle of the path, marking the site of the encounter. The King and his son were climbing the hill, followed at a respectful distance by the third man carrying the Cornish banner. Fenn watched as the trio joined the group standing at the edge of the forest. Together they drifted back into the trees.

'That sword could be useful,' Fenn said. She nodded.

FENN FELT A TUG on his arm. Edelred.

'The injured rider wants to talk with you urgently. The man told me he has a message you need to hear. He will only speak to you. Acwellan says Death is calling this man's name and may take him at any moment.'

Fenn checked the palisade. People were at their places.

The rider carried a message? From whom? Cedric? Eadburg? Beorhtric?

'Very well. Take me to him.'

Balthazar followed obediently behind Fenn as Edelred led him to a small hut beside the south palisade. Thankfully, the dog lay down readily when Fenn indicated he should stay outside, but it was impossible to determine whether that was because he obeyed the command or just didn't want to enter. Maybe he detected the odour of death inside the hut.

Fenn had to duck his head to enter the dim interior. Edelred followed him in but stayed by the entrance.

A man lay on a low bed. His chest was bare except for bandages wrapped tightly around his waist. The exposed skin on the man's face and chest was slick with sweat. Acwellan sat beside the bed, a cloth in his hand, wiping the man's brow. He withdrew the cloth, dipping it into a bowl of water set on a stool and wringing the water from it before resuming his brushing of the man's face.

The bandages and the bedding were heavily stained with fresh blood. The arrow had been removed from the man's back but the two others still protruded grotesquely from his leg.

Acwellan looked up and saw Fenn's eyes were on the arrows. Softly, he said: 'Removing them will only provoke more bleeding and hasten this man's meeting with his maker…' he lowered his voice further, '…which will come soon enough.' He dropped the cloth into the water bowl and moved to the side.

Fenn took his place beside the bed. At the sound of his movement, the man's eyes opened.

A whisper. 'Lord Feran?'

Fenn bent close.

'Yes,' he replied.

The voice gained strength. 'Nobody but you can hear my words.'

Fenn frowned. He didn't have time for such mystery. But if it would help the man relay his message quickly….

'Please…' he asked, '…leave me with him.'

Edelred and Acwellan exchanged glances but bent their heads and left the hut. The man's eyes watched them go.

He breathed heavily, building his strength. 'I have a message from Galastan….'

'What…? *Who?*' Had Fenn misheard?

The messenger was in pain. That was evident in the twisting of his face and the grunts forced from his throat. His breathing was noisy, a rasping in the throat that had its origins deep in his chest. He waved his hand in a 'don't interrupt' gesture.

Fenn's body had tensed at the name. He forced himself to relax.

Instead of continuing to speak, the man issued several involuntary groans and screwed his eyes shut, arching his back. He held that pose for an agonising moment until, with a prolonged release of air through a tightly-clenched mouth, his body relaxed. His eyes opened and searched the room until they found Fenn's. He strained his head upwards, fresh sweat beading his brow.

'Galastan said… you must come… to Moloch Tor… at midday on the Kalends of the Holy Month.'

The man's head fell back, unable to maintain the position. His eyes closed. Fenn could hear the man's breath still forcing a passage in his throat, so he hadn't died.

'Is that all?' he asked. His first thought was that he had no intention of doing whatever Galastan wanted.

The man reached out and took hold of Fenn's sleeve, pulling him closer with surprising strength.

'I was to return with you, just you and I… but I… won't… no one else… now you must go *alone* Lord,' the man coughed, 'he'll be watching… and you must bring with you….' He stopped.

Fenn waited. '…bring with you….' the man repeated, '…the iron box….'

Another cough splattered his chin with drops of blood. He tried to clear his throat. Words were forced through his teeth: '…bring the box… hidden… beneath the Thane's seat….'

Then a rush of words: '…if you want to see your friend Olgood… alive.'

Fenn clenched his teeth.

The man's face twisted into a grimace. His hand moved to grip Fenn's arm.

'Galastan said… the box is sealed – he will know if it's been opened.'

His body contorted as a spasm took him. His mouth opened and closed with the struggle to force more words from his throat.

'*Please…*' the man wheezed. '…I beg of you….' His voice had returned to a whisper. His eyes drooped and closed. Fenn checked the man's breathing.

The eyes suddenly snapped open, staring up at Fenn with a startling intensity. His chest bucked with the effort of drawing in the next breath, a grunt accompanying each attempt, his whole body rocking as it strove to cling to life for a few more precious heartbeats.

'Those white monsters…' he groaned. 'Those devils… took my *wife*, Kuralin, to force me….' An intense grimace of pain forced his eyes impossibly wide.

'*Please*… Lord… Lord Feran… save my Kuralin… from those…' His voice dropped to below a whisper. Fenn bent closer.

Freed from the urgency of delivering the message, the words came with more ease than he had previously managed, possibly because these were the last words he needed to utter.

'*My* life is over…' he said, '…I know that – but it would give me… comfort… to believe that Kuralin's… *isn't.*'

Fenn said: 'I swear to you I'll do everything I can.'

The eyes bored into Fenn's. Slowly but perceptibly they lost focus. Fenn watched the life behind the eyes drain away. The hand dropped from Fenn's arm and the man's head fell to the side, the tortured rasping in his chest finally silent.

Fenn stared down at him. *I don't even know your name*, he thought.

CHAPTER ELEVEN

Desperate times and desperate plans

The Kalends of the Holy Month, the day of Galastan's requested meeting, was tomorrow, and the sun was already climbing towards Hernam's midday deadline. Fenn needed to conclude his business with the Cornish *today*.

As he exited the hut, Acwellan made to re-enter. Fenn stopped him.

'He's gone. Before you attend to him, I need you for a moment as a witness.'

'A witness? For what?'

'This…' said Fenn. He turned to Edelred. 'Edelred, *you* are now tenant-in-chief of Westerling.'

He clapped the man on the shoulder and nodded to Acwellan.

'Let the people know,' he said.

Acwellan nodded. 'As you wish. But I'll finish here first.'

Fenn took Edelred with him to seek out Kaela and Nyle. He told Edelred part of Galastan's message – that Galastan had threatened Olgood's life unless Fenn went alone to Moloch Tor on the Kalends. The man's eyes widened in disbelief. He shook his head and drew a breath through his teeth.

'Galastan enjoyed the position of tenant-in-chief too much. He cared little for Westerling. Be careful with him. Don't trust him. He's capable of anything.'

Fenn grunted. 'It seems so.'

'Where is Moloch Tor?' he asked as they walked. 'How far?'

'It's on the moor, Lord, the highest peak, a half-day ride. I've seen it in the distance, but I've never been there. It's a strange, foreboding place.'

'Tell me what you know.'

Edelred sighed as he gathered his thoughts. 'Moloch Tor is a group of large rocks atop the highest peak on the moor. It was a sacred place to the Druids and the ancient ones before them. The path leading up to the Tor passes through a small but dense forest.' Edelred glanced uneasily at Fenn. 'People keep clear of that forest. It's not like any other forest. The trees are all misshapen… I don't know how to describe them…. I won't say it's bewitched, but don't stray from the path – weird things are said to happen there, even in the daytime. *Men have disappeared.*'

Fenn looked at Edelred to see if he was joking. The man was serious.

Edelred shivered. 'Apart from the forest, that Tor is surrounded by barren moor for miles. Galastan will see you coming. It's a bleak and frigid place – even at this time of year there'll be snow on the ground. If you're going to Moloch Tor, you'll need warm clothing.'

FENN DREW KAELA AND Nyle to a place where they could not be overheard. He motioned Edelred to join them.

In a few short sentences, he relayed Galastan's message again to Kaela and Nyle, this time including Galastan's demand for Fenn to bring the iron box hidden beneath the Thane's chair and the messenger's desperate plea to save his wife from the Ariochs.

'Did you know about the box?' he asked a surprised Edelred.

'No, Lord.'

'What could it contain?'

'I don't know.' Edelred thought a moment. 'For many years, there have been rumours that Lord Cormwurst had a hidden treasure, a store of gold. No matter where you travelled, once it was known you were from Westerling, you'd be sure to be questioned about it. He was known far and wide as the richest thane in Wessex, but whether that was true or not…?' He shrugged. 'He never wanted for coin. When we lost sheep to wolves, Lord Cormwurst replaced them.' He paused, frowning. 'I thought the talk was just rumour, but perhaps this box…?' Edelred looked up at Fenn. 'I don't think Lord Orvyn knew about any gold.'

'It seems Galastan did.'

A thought came to Fenn. 'Galastan's behaviour when I sent him to the villages makes more sense now,' he said. 'He tried to delay the journey a day so he could retrieve the box during the night.' He held up a finger to emphasise his words. 'From now until I leave for Moloch Tor, have someone by the chair at all times. Whether the box contains gold or not, it contains something Galastan wants – he may not be willing to place all his trust in me bringing it to him. He might also convince someone else to try to retrieve it.'

'Yes, Lord,' said Edelred.

'My men can guard the chair,' said Nyle.

'Thank you,' said Fenn, 'but I need them for another task, one that needs to be accomplished *before* I go to Moloch Tor.'

Nyle pursed his lips. His expression said: *Very well. No doubt you'll explain.*

'You need to go,' agreed Kaela, 'but you're *not* going alone.'

'I must,' said Fenn. 'From the Tor, Galastan will have a good view of the countryside in every direction. We can't surprise him.'

'You can't expect to save Olgood *and* Kuralin by yourself,' Kaela insisted. 'He almost certainly has the Ariochs with him. We could enter the forest below the Tor in darkness if we leave tonight.'

Fenn thought about it. He didn't want to risk Olgood's life, but help at hand could be vital.

'It's a good idea,' he said. 'But it will depend on whether there's cloud cover for the moon tonight.'

'If it's only Galastan and the Ariochs at the tor, I suggest we just rush them with the men we have,' said Nyle.

'I share your feeling, but that's the option most likely to be bad for Olgood and Kuralin,' replied Fenn.

Kaela opened her mouth, but Fenn held up a hand to forestall further discussion.

'We don't have time now. We can resume this discussion once we've dealt with the Cornish.'

Kaela accepted his decision with a nod. 'How do you intend to do that?' she asked.

He placed a hand on her arm. 'Firstly, Gisele should know that Galastan is holding Olgood. Can you…?' Kaela screwed up her nose, not liking the task, but said: 'Of course.'

'Next…' he said, '…it's time to send a rider to alert Beorhtric that the Cornish are in Wessex. That message will carry more weight if *you* write it.' His eyes sought Edelred. 'Who is the nearest Wessex Ealdorman?'

'Lord Herewic of Somersaeteshire, but…'

'Send a rider to Herewic first. How soon could we expect aid from him?'

'I would not expect Lord Herewic to come readily to Westerling's aid.'

Fenn stared at him. 'Why not?'

'I don't like to say it, Lord, but Lord Herewic and Lord Cormwurst had a poor relationship.' At Fenn's frown, Edelred swallowed. 'Herewic accused Lord Cormwurst of being together with his wife. Even after Cormwurst's death, his feelings are bitter and his anger remains. And…' he stopped.

'There's more?' asked Fenn, his frown deepening.

'There's more… the border between their lands is the subject of a long dispute. Herewic resents the size of the Westerling estate within his shire… and its reputed wealth.' Edelred shook his head. 'I wouldn't… he cannot be relied on to help Westerling, Lord.'

Fenn glanced at Kaela, whose pained expression said she agreed with Edelred.

'Even if Westerling – and Wessex – is attacked by the Cornish?'

Edelred didn't reply.

Fenn shook his head in amazement. 'Very well. But send a rider to Herewic anyway. It won't hurt to ask.' He released a breath of frustration. 'Wessex can never be great until such quarrels end.'

He forced himself to move on. 'The message to King Beohtric becomes even more important,' he said. 'Who would be best to carry that to Witanceastre?'

'Wyllard,' said Edelred quickly. 'He's a born horseman and resourceful. He'll get the job done.'

'Good,' said Kaela. 'I'll write to my father and send Wyllard on his way. What about the other Ealdormen of Wessex?'

Fenn grimaced. 'After hearing about Herewic, let's not divert Wyllard from getting to Beorhtric as fast as he can. Let the King decide who else to alert.'

Kaela nodded.

'Keep the mares here,' said Fenn. 'We may have need of them. Find both riders another good horse.'

'It will take days to reach Witanceastre and days for Beorhtric to alert others and to send men,' said Nyle. 'It's unlikely they'll be of any use.'

Fenn nodded his agreement. 'Nonetheless, it should be done.' He spread his hands. 'Who knows the course of today, let alone the days to follow?'

He looked around at their faces. 'Now for the Cornish. We may be on our own. I've no time for a prolonged encounter with Hernam and his people.'

'Surely that doesn't mean surrender…?' said Nyle. 'Westerling has no harvest grain to give them.'

'No. It means we must take the fight to the enemy rather than wait for their next move.' Fenn paused to allow his words to be considered.

'Nyle, gather your men. Bring their swords only. The palisade entrance may be watched. The eight of us will go over the south palisade, find the Cornish, and see what we can do – what disruption we can cause to dissuade them from attack. Edelred, you'll be in charge of the preparations here.'

Edelred looked startled. 'What can eight do against eighty?'

'We'll use surprise to advance our odds.'

Edelred looked unconvinced.

'Edelred has a point,' said Kaela. 'What *disruption* can we cause that will force the Cornish to withdraw?' Her eyes widened as a thought occurred to her. 'Unless… do you intend to capture Hernam? Or kill him?'

Fenn frowned. If anything happened to Hernam, it would likely just provoke his hot-headed son Hopkin to make some rash move. He turned the frown into a smile.

'My plan is to use whatever opportunity presents itself,' he said. 'One usually does. Any other plan we make now will certainly need to change once we find the Cornish.'

Nyle did not look convinced by a plan that didn't seem to be a plan, but when Fenn glanced at him, he had no better alternative.

Fenn checked the sky. 'We don't have much time. Nyle, if you would gather your men. Meet us by Acwellan's hut.'

Nyle ran towards the Hall. Kaela said: 'I'll talk to Gisele and write a note for my father.'

'Edelred,' said Fenn, 'can you…'

'I'll find Wyllard and a good horse,' said Edelred, '…and a man to watch the chair.'

Fenn nodded. 'Be quick.'

'What shall I tell the people?'

'Tell them we've gone to convince the Cornish not to attack Westerling.'

Edelred left, but Kaela waited. She was silent for a moment, then said: 'Gisele has proven herself useful in a skirmish.'

'I know,' said Fenn. 'It would also take her mind off Olgood. But we shouldn't *all* leave. It may seem like we're abandoning Westerling.'

THERE WAS A NOISE behind Fenn. He turned to see Nyle moving past Kaela. Nyle came up to him and whispered: 'There's someone following us. They're keeping their distance and not trying to catch up.'

Fenn breathed a sigh of frustration mixed with relief. If they weren't trying to catch up, the follower wasn't coming to tell them that the Cornish had attacked Westerling.

They had entered the forest south of the palisade and followed the Yule River around the base of a hill. A few moments ago, after crossing a tributary stream, Fenn had signalled a turn to the north to begin the search for the Cornish. The thick forest provided plenty of cover but made progress slower than he would have liked.

'Stay here with two of your men to surprise whoever's following,' said Fenn. 'They'll cross the stream where we did. We'll continue to draw them forward and wait on the other side of the hill.'

They were fast running out of time and this meant another delay. Annoying but unavoidable.

NYLE ENTERED THE CLEARING dragging Beric behind him.

'There was only this one,' he said.

Fenn stepped up to stand in front of Beric. 'I thought I'd explained this was no game,' he said curtly. 'We've precious little time, and your foolishness has delayed us further.'

Beric hung his head. 'Sorry, Lord. I know these woods and I thought I might be helpful. I wanted to be there when you met the Cornish.'

'What you've achieved is to allow us even less time to search for them.'

Beric raised his eyes. '*Search* for them? Why…? I don't understand… you're headed for Wealdemere, aren't you?'

Nyle said: 'We're wasting time. We should move on.'

An instinct told Fenn to listen to Beric. 'One moment,' he said. 'Wealdemere? What do you mean?'

'It's where the Cornish will be, for sure.'

Fenn's frustration faded.

'Explain quickly.'

Beric gulped. 'Wyllard said the Cornish were at Magog's Ford last evening. A man walking from the ford to where that poor man was hit by arrows, will pass by Wealdemere. It's a lake in the forest – it's beautiful there, a favourite place for fishing and relaxation for Lord Cormwurst. There's open ground and water with grass for horses. If I had to wait in the forest for a while, that's where I'd wait.'

Fenn sighed. He'd made another mistake by not bringing someone with local knowledge.

When he, Kaela, Olgood, and Gisele had escaped from the Northmen, Fenn had assumed leadership of the band of fugitives but he had more than once questioned his decisions. It seemed that fortune sprung as often from luck as from sound judgment. His mistakes, or what he perceived as mistakes, were frequently corrected by coincidence or chance or whatever else one may call fortuitous events outside his control. He had mused that the Northmen would explain it by saying their gods were smiling on him. While he would gladly accept every favour they chose to bestow, one thing he knew was that gods were fickle. The harvest they blessed one year would be abandoned the next.

Despite his oversight, Fenn had to accept that Beric and his information were a welcome addition. Rather than causing a delay, the boy may have saved the time it would have taken to carefully search the woods.

Fenn couldn't shake the thought that it would be foolish to expect such good luck to continue.

'Lead the way,' he said.

FENN HAD A CLEAR VIEW of the Cornish.

The first thing he noted was that Wyllard's estimate of their numbers was accurate. There were around eighty men at Wealdemere and Fenn located eighteen with bows. The lake was more extensive than Fenn expected, covering a size similar to that enclosed by Westerling's palisade. If there had been no Cornish raiders there, it would be as Beric had described – a beautiful and peaceful enclave in the forest.

The lake was bordered by a wide expanse of long grass. Reeds and moss-covered boulders were scattered at the edge of the lake, but the water sparkling in the sunshine looked clear and fresh.

Soft noises drifted to where Fenn lay on his stomach, concealed behind a tree – a low hum of voices punctuated by the occasional clink of metal. Kaela lay beside him – the others waited in a gully at the base of the ridge. He was ten paces back from the point where the vibrant green of the grass surrounding the lake met the trees of the forest.

The Cornish looked relaxed but there was an excitement in the air – an anticipation of the action to come. As he had expected, a group of men were building ladders and had stacked several in a pile. Others were checking their weapons, swords and arrows and a few spears, but most were resting, sitting or lounging on the grass.

He picked out Hernam, seated cross-legged in a circle with four others, holding council. Fenn frowned. He narrowed his eyes to sharpen his focus but Hopkin was not among them. Where was the prince? A quick scan of nearby men did not locate him.

A man approached Hernam carrying a water pitcher. At the sight of the man, Fenn's body tensed. He made to rise onto his elbows to get a better view but Kaela's hand restrained him.

'I see it,' she whispered.

Apart from the fact that he carried no weapons, the man filling Hernam's cup was unnoteworthy in every respect except one. Around his neck was a collar. From its dull glint it was a metal collar – the mark of a captive, the mark of a *thrall*.

'He looks… familiar,' said Kaela.

'Who? The thrall?'

'Yes… it's hard to tell at this distance.'

Fenn had never seen the man before, but Kaela continued to stare at him.

The thrall appeared to stumble and water splashed onto Hernam's chest. A cry of anger exploded from the King. He leapt to his feet and backhanded the man, knocking him to his knees. The man scrambled on the ground to escape Hernam who raised his fist and stepped forward to deliver a second blow. Someone from the seated circle called out and the King paused. He shook his fist at the thrall, cursed him, then dismissed him with a flick of his hand and turned back to rejoin the council. The thrall rolled onto his knees, picked up the fallen pitcher and staggered away, his hand reaching up to touch his face.

Fenn didn't realise he had risen again onto his elbows until he felt Kaela's hand on his arm.

'Whoever he is – we can do nothing for him now.'

Fenn slowly nodded. She was right. They had to concentrate on their purpose. He forced himself to relax and continued his inspection of the camp.

Closer to where he lay, twenty paces beyond the forest edge, six horses, including Hernam's grey, were tethered to a low rope that allowed them to reach the lush grass. A man, the closest Cornishman to Fenn and Kaela, was tending to the horses. He was running his hands over their legs and inspecting hooves, making sure each horse was sound and ready.

There was an intake of breath from Kaela. She touched his arm. 'Is that Hopkin?' she whispered.

'Where?'

'With the horses.'

Fenn had to wait until the man bent low under the neck of a horse to confirm it was indeed the boyish face of Hernam's son, the thin line of Kaela's cut visible on his cheek.

The plan came to him in an instant.

He looked to the treetops – the wind was coming from the right direction.

He pulled at Kaela's shoulder and withdrew from behind the tree, sliding into the gully with her following, to join Nyle.

'Hopkin is close by and isolated,' Fenn reported. 'I'm going to take him.'

He pointed to where he'd been lying. 'From the top of the ridge you can see the entire camp. You, Nyle, with Kaela and your men, will watch from there. If I'm seen or something goes wrong, you'll need to keep the Cornish busy while we escape.'

Beric stepped up, offering Fenn a large rock. 'This will put him to sleep.'

'No,' said Fenn. 'That's too risky. We can't allow him to cry out.'

'Let *me* take him,' Nyle said. 'No need to risk the Thane of Westerling.'

'No,' repeated Fenn. 'It must be me. The horses won't be alarmed if I go.' Nyle frowned and Fenn held up a hand. 'I can explain later.'

Nyle looked to Kaela who nodded. 'It's something he does,' she said.

'Beric, you stay here,' said Fenn, scrambling back up the hill.

He wet a finger with his lips and used it to confirm the direction of the wind. Hopkin was still with the horses – he was checking Hernam's grey. The thrall was nowhere to be seen but apart from his absence, the Cornish camp had not changed. Fenn heard the others settling into position beside him. He glanced along the row of heads on the ridge top to see Beric lowering himself onto his stomach. The boy was not going to be left behind. Fenn had no time to be annoyed – something about Beric reminded him of himself at that age. Eager to learn – eager for new experiences.

He crawled around the tree and scurried to the edge of the forest using the foliage as cover. Speed was essential. At any moment Hopkin could complete his inspection and leave the horses to join the rest of the Cornish camp. It was encouraging that he was checking Hernam's horse – he would probably be thorough with that one. As quickly as he moved, Fenn was also mindful of placing his hands and feet carefully, avoiding twigs or brittle leaves that could alert the horses and Hopkin of his presence before he was ready.

In violation of a fundamental rule of stalking, Fenn deliberately moved to his left so the south-westerly breeze would carry his scent to the horses.

As a small boy, he had learned that animals accepted him and knew he meant no harm. He was able to easily collect beetles, birds, and small animals such as rabbits and ferrets, which he studied and drew on scraps of parchment and then released, because they readily allowed his approach and didn't mind his gentle handling. Even larger animals like goats and cattle accepted him. The creatures always exhibited curiosity rather than fear. How animals recognised him or his intentions was a mystery, but he was grateful for the gift.

The horses' ears pricked forward and their nostrils widened as they caught his scent. As he expected, they were interested but not concerned. Fenn moved to a point where the horses shielded him from the Cornish camp and Hernam's horse was between him and Hopkin. He left the cover of the trees and walked steadily but swiftly forward. The animals kept their eyes on him but none made any noise or nervous movement. He approached the grey, the horse watching him come. When he was within arm's length, the animal took a step closer and bent its head to greet him. Hopkin felt the horse move and began to stand up.

Fenn moved.

In three steps, he rounded the grey's rump, approaching Hopkin from behind. One arm encircled his neck and the other hand clamped over his mouth. Fenn quickly stepped back, pulling Hopkin off-balance.

Before he had been captured by the Northmen, people would have considered Fenn an average youth – tall, but apart from a dark tinge to his skin, otherwise physically unremarkable. As a thrall in Ragnall's home village of Lognavik, he'd been forced to endure many months of dawn to dusk strenuous and demanding work which broadened his shoulders, deepened his chest, and built strength into his body. He fell well short of Olgood in this respect, but although he was still a youth in age, he possessed the strength of a full-grown man.

Hopkin's hands came up to pull at the arm compressing his throat. He tried to open his mouth to bite at the hand, but Fenn's elbow beneath his chin and the grip of his hand held the teeth together. Hopkin still tried to shout, but only a muffled squeak escaped between his lips. The horses were disturbed by the struggle and shifted uneasily on their feet. Fenn continued to move backwards, away from the horses but keeping them between him and the camp, heading for the edge of the forest, keeping Hopkin off-balance and not allowing him to regain his footing. He glanced over Hopkin's shoulder, between the horses. The camp seemed unaware of anything amiss, but it only needed one person to look in this direction and wonder where Hopkin had gone or why the horses were restless. Would anyone investigate?

Fenn had dragged his captive to within a few paces of the cover of the trees when Hopkin stopped trying to regain his feet and deliberately let himself fall, his body becoming a dead weight. Fenn stumbled, dropping to a knee. Encouraged, Hopkin twisted his body sharply, hoping to break one of Fenn's holds. Fenn concentrated on keeping Hopkin's mouth closed. He didn't want a shout alerting the Cornish at this stage. He tightened the arm around the neck and pulled back, compressing Hopkin's airway with the crook of his elbow. Hopkin would soon weaken if he couldn't breathe.

The same thought occurred to Hopkin. He increased his efforts to break free, twisting back and forth with all the power in his body. The intense struggle pulled Fenn from his knee and the two sprawled full-length and writhing onto the grass. Fenn tried to wrap his leg around Hopkin to restrict his movement, but Hopkin kicked vigorously. He sensed he was gaining an advantage. If he could loosen the hand covering his mouth enough, he could cry out. He arched his back, trying to drive his head into Fenn's face while kicking backwards with his heels.

Kaela laid the blade of her sword against Hopkin's nose, the tip hovering an inch from his eye. Hopkin instantly became still, staring at Kaela — to move a muscle, whether by accident or intent, was to invite blindness. That steel had cut him once; he had no wish to add to his wounds.

Fenn struggled to his feet, pulling Hopkin with him. Kaela's sword remained a finger's width from Hopkin's face. As they entered the forest, Fenn glanced again at the Cornish camp. Hernam's grey horse was watching the three people melt into the trees but the others had already bent their necks to reach the grass.

No one was looking their way.

ONE OF NYLE'S MEN pulled a lump of moss from a tree, rolled it in a ball, and pushed it into Hopkin's mouth when Fenn withdrew his hand. He then pulled his belt tight between Hopkin's teeth and around his neck to keep the moss ball in place. The struggle had opened the cut on

Hopkin's cheek and a trail of blood streaked his chin. Another man tied Hopkin's hands behind his back with a thin yellow vine. Hopkin was uncooperative, resisting wherever he could, reasoning he was not about to be killed. His eyes blazed when he was approached and he drew his head back, threatening a head-butt, but his aggression quickly cooled after his attempts to kick out resulted in a forceful retaliation.

'Lead us back to the palisade the quickest way, Beric,' said Fenn.

He cast an anxious glance at the sky through the trees.

It was almost midday.

CHAPTER TWELVE

An exchange and a freed man

'So… my son didn't wander off or head home in a sulk,' said Hernam, speaking in Latin. 'Both were possibilities – although the fact there was no missing horse argued against the latter.'

Hernam stared at Fenn. His demeanour was cool – he was angry but resigned to the situation.

'Is he hurt?' he asked curtly.

'He's not injured,' replied Fenn.

The King made a noise in his throat. 'It was Hopkin who said we should post guards but I told him it was unnecessary – the people of Westerling were just frightened farmers. It seems I was wrong.'

Fenn had been on the palisade step when Hernam, mounted on the grey, emerged from the forest. The high midday sun bore down on the scene. The King was punctual.

Other mounted men followed the King, and the rest of the Cornish, footmen and archers, drifted out from the trees behind them. Hernam's force descended the hill and crossed the fields to the road where his men remained, spread out in an uneven line while Hernam, again accompanied by his standard-bearer, rode up the path to the place where Hopkin's sword once stood. Hernam's men were restless, clearly unsure which way events were about to turn. Most had their weapons drawn and shields to the fore, facing the palisade, each prominently displaying the black crow of Cornwall.

The ladders constructed at the lake were also visible, scattered along the front rank. Hernam was prepared to fight should matters not go well.

Again, Fenn and Kaela met Hernam astride Galastan's mares, but there was one difference from the previous meeting – Fenn was no longer unarmed. He carried Hopkin's sword at his side.

It was no longer necessary to shout at the Cornish but, behind Fenn, excitement mixed with anxiety created an audible murmur of noise among the people crowding the palisade step to witness the meeting.

Fenn's confirmation that he held Hopkin as a prisoner had prompted Hernam's remarks.

HERNAM TURNED TO THE man behind him, carrying the Cornish banner, and waved him away. The man turned his horse and trotted back to the road.

When he was beyond earshot, Hernam turned back. 'Hopkin is my son,' he said, 'but for your ears only, he is not the son I would have wished for. What if I don't care for his fate and don't want him back?'

Fenn said nothing. He waited.

The King allowed the silence to draw out, then he grunted. 'Very well. What are your terms?'

Fenn silently released the breath he'd been holding.

'You will return to your land across the Tamar,' he said. 'I'll deliver Hopkin to you, alive and well, where the Roman Road crosses the River Tamar two weeks from today. You have my word.'

Fenn wanted time to deal with Galastan and for Beorhtric to send the reinforcements that could still be vital should things not proceed as planned. Would Hernam baulk at the delay?

Fenn drew Hopkin's sword from his belt.

'You may take his sword now.'

Hernam made no move to accept the sword.

'I still need grain. What's to stop me returning once I have Hopkin?'

'*Your* word,' said Fenn.

Hernam leaned back in his saddle and regarded Fenn with calculating eyes. He slowly nodded his approval. His gaze switched to Kaela, took in her sword, and swept appraisingly across the two mares before returning to Fenn. He didn't seem to be in any hurry. Behind his cool stare, the King was calmly assessing his options.

Fenn gave him the time he needed. He still held Hopkin's sword, extended hilt-first toward the King.

Hernam raised his chin.

'*One* week,' he said.

From the corner of his eye, Fenn noticed Kaela's eyes turn to him. Even if Wyllard was an exceptional horseman, one week may not be enough for him to reach Beorhtric and return with whatever relief force the King decided to send. Hernam had no leverage to bargain against his son's life, but Fenn's instinct told him it would be wise to allow the Cornish King some concession.

'Agreed,' he said. 'One week.'

Hernam maintained his stare for a long moment. Then his jaw tightened. He muttered a few unintelligible words in his language, probably cursing the turn of events or his luck.

'Very well,' he said. 'I accept the terms.' His eyes bored into Fenn's. 'You have my word.'

He reached out and took the sword.

'There's one more thing,' said Fenn. Kaela frowned – they hadn't spoken of other conditions. Hernam's eyes blazed, his lips curling, angry that Fenn wanted to extend the terms a moment after he had agreed to them.

'Your men killed a man from Wessex….'

Hernam waved a hand. 'An unfortunate misunderstanding,' he snapped. 'What do you want? *Weregild?*'

'I deem it more than a misunderstanding,' said Fenn. Hernam's lips compressed. 'However,' Fenn said quickly, 'you have a thrall with you. He served you water at the lake. I'll take him in exchange for the… misunderstanding. A life for a life.'

Hernam's astonishment overrode his anger. 'You want *that thrall?*' He stared at Fenn then threw back his head and laughed loudly – his startled horse stepped nervously to the side. Hernam pulled the horse back into place. He was still smiling.

'There may be some strange justice in this day yet.' He waved a hand dismissively. 'By the crows, *take* the fool – you'll be doing me a favour. He's more trouble than he's worth. He's useless and he's mad. I should have rid myself of that one long ago.'

Hernam laughed again, genuinely amused in spite of the circumstances.

Taking advantage of his good mood, Fenn leaned forward and asked: 'How did you come by him?'

The King frowned. Fenn thought his question might be considered inappropriate, but Hernam shrugged.

'The idiot said he was sent by King Charles from Francia to trade for tin, but there's no truth to his story. If he was a trader, why did he furtively land on a beach under the darkness of a new moon? He had coin but his boat was too small to carry ore. More likely he was a fugitive. He was arrogant and insolent, and he insulted me – so I took him as a thrall. I've had him three years and he's been a thorn every day. He cannot master even the simplest tasks. I've tried to sell him; no one wants him. I'll be glad to be rid of that one and may he plague you like he has me.'

'So he's a Frank.'

Fenn knew Kaela had spent time at the court of King Charles. She had thought the thrall was familiar. Maybe that's where she saw him.

Hernam shrugged again. 'Probably. He speaks the Frankish tongue and claimed to be a Frank at first. His story changed and now he says he's from Wessex. I don't believe a word he utters. He tells many stories.' He shook his head. 'Only the crows know why you would want *him.*'

'I have my reasons,' said Fenn.

A grunt from Kaela – reminding him to bring matters to a conclusion.

Fenn moved his horse closer and held out his hand. 'My hand on it, sire.'

Hernam looked at the hand, then up at Fenn. In his right hand he held Hopkin's sword. He raised the weapon and Fenn wondered if Hernam might strike at him with the sword. Would he try to maim Fenn and then attempt to exchange him for Hopkin? Fenn recognised his vulnerability. He was too close – his arm was outstretched. Even Kaela's speed couldn't save him if Hernam struck now.

Earlier, the Cornish King had demonstrated his vehement opposition to the use of weapons at a truce, but the stakes were higher this time. Would that change his position regarding such a violation? He'd seen Kaela's skill; he must know he wouldn't escape unharmed if he used the sword. What would he do? What would Kaela do? In the heartbeat that he had to decide, Fenn was tempted to withdraw but he kept his eyes fixed on Hernam and his arm extended.

Hernam shifted Hopkin's sword to his left hand and reached out with his right, clasping Fenn's hand.

'You act like an honourable man,' he said quietly. 'Maybe a West Saxon *does* exist who's trustworthy enough for an alliance.'

Fenn did not consider himself a Saxon, and he knew he certainly did not have the look of one. Was the King making a joke at his expense? Hernam did not look amused – he was serious and thoughtful.

'Who knows in which direction tomorrow's wind will blow?' Fenn said.

They released hands and Hernam turned his horse. He bellowed a command in his language. A man at the back of a group of footmen was pushed forward. Another man used his sword to prod the thrall towards Hernam.

All three watched the thrall's approach. The man's wrists were tied together, causing his shambling gait to be unsteady.

Hernam muttered, almost to himself: 'When the time comes that you want to rid yourself of this fool, he may be of some interest to Beorhtric.'

Kaela's eyes snapped up.

'How is that?' she asked.

Hernam snorted dismissively. 'The madman's claims know no bounds. He not only says he's *from* Wessex, he thinks he's the true *king* of Wessex.'

Kaela gasped and muttered a name under her breath.

Fenn thought she said '*Egbert*'.

AS SOON AS THE horses were through the doors, the crowd burst into cheers. Fenn waved at them to quiet, but it was only when he dismounted that the noise waned. The people quietened but did not disperse, milling about as if expecting further developments.

Kaela also dismounted. She took a long look at the thrall, now walking slowly and warily under the arch of the palisade doors, which were pushed closed behind him. She nodded as though some thought had been confirmed, then gathered the reins from Fenn's mare and led the horses away. She liked to take care of horses herself.

Fenn called to a man on the palisade step. 'Are the Cornish dispersing?'

'Yes, Lord,' the man answered. 'They're leaving.'

The thrall took a few more tentative steps. He stopped and stood uncomfortably, his eyes darting about, taking in the Great Hall, the buildings, and the noisy people crowded around him.

Fenn headed toward him but was interrupted by a disturbance in the crowd. The huge grey form of Balthazar caused several people to quickly move from his path as he crossed the yard at a run and bounded up at Fenn's chest. Fenn managed to stay on his feet and struggled to contain the dog while Balthazar worked out the enthusiasm of his greeting.

The thrall watched the action calmly, displaying no fear of the exuberant hound. Restraining Balthazar by his shaggy mane, Fenn stood before the man.

'From this moment on,' he said, 'you are no longer a thrall. You're a free man.'

The man stared at him, uncomprehending. Fenn frowned. 'Do you understand me?'

'Am I in Wessex?' the man asked.

'You are in Westerling,' affirmed Fenn, 'and Westerling is part of the kingdom of Wessex.'

'And… I haven't been sold to you? I'm a free man?'

Fenn nodded.

The man straightened his body, standing taller. His voice gained confidence.

'In that case, I thank you, Lord, for my salvation on this day. Please, may I know your name?'

The man spoke like a noble. Was it an act?

'I am Lord Feran; you can call me Fenn,' said Fenn. 'And you?'

'Call me… Edgar,' said the man.

So this man was not the 'Egbert' Kaela had thought him to be.

Edelred appeared at Fenn's side, with Bronwyn behind him. Balthazar shook his head and Fenn released him. The dog remained close, nose in the air, his interest now caught by the mixed scents of the animals in the yard.

'Did all go well, Lord?' asked Edelred. 'Did the Cornish agree to return to their lands?'

'Yes, they did. We'll return Hopkin to them at the Tamar in one week.'

A murmur spread among the people close enough to hear this news.

'One? But I thought….'

'I know, but we agreed on one.'

Edelred nodded.

'Hopkin is here?' Edgar asked, surprised. 'I heard he was missing. How did he…? Did you somehow take him from the camp by the lake?'

'We have him,' said Fenn. He held up his hand to dissuade further questions.

He pointed to the collar around Edgar's neck and spoke to Edelred. 'Please untie this man and have his collar removed.' He looked down at

Edgar's feet, then at Bronwyn. 'Maybe we can find him better clothing and something for his feet.'

'Of course,' said Bronwyn. 'Leave him with me.' She waved Edelred away. 'I'll take him to the blacksmith to remove that dreadful collar.' She reached out to Edgar. 'Come with me.'

Edgar glanced at Fenn, nodded, and followed Bronwyn's lead.

Fenn noticed the men and women still crowded in the yard were looking expectantly at him. They'd interrupted their lives to respond to his call. If he now said they could return to their homes, would they be grateful or think the whole exercise a waste of their time?

He raised his voice. 'The Cornish have agreed to return to their lands. Their threat is over for now. You may return to your homes.'

There was a moment's silence after he finished speaking.

A man called out: 'Cheers for our Lord!'

There was an eruption of cheering as if a great victory had been won. The faces, previously still and attentive, were now animated and wreathed with smiles.

The crowd started to move. A man approached and bowed before Fenn, touching his cap. 'Thank you, Lord.' Another bowed to Fenn, calling to a dog and heading for the palisade doors. A family with two small children passed by, the woman giving Fenn a slight curtsy and the man touching his head in salute.

Fenn frowned, puzzled. Beside him, Edelred said: 'They're thanking you for giving them your protection, Lord. You called them under your wing and faced the Cornish alone on their behalf.'

'Not alone. With Kaela. And it was a negotiation....'

'You two are one, so it's the same thing. You faced the Cornish, and the Cornish backed down. Your people salute you, and they're grateful. With their own eyes, they've seen that Westerling has a strong thane at last.'

More groups passed, some leading animals, some walking in pairs, each acknowledging Fenn with a smile or a nod or a touch of the head.

Fenn returned the greetings and looked at the faces. He saw men, women, and children that were part of the land – a people for whom nothing came easily, but only as a result of hard, unrelenting toil, day after day; for whom the pleasures of life were few and probably enjoyed all the more because of that. They were folk a thane could depend on, and he resolved to be as dependable for them.

Fenn waved at the barricade. 'We can take this down,' he said.

'Gladly,' said Edelred.

Fenn turned to leave. He needed to attend to the matter of an iron box hidden under a chair.

'Oh, Lord Feran…?' Edelred stopped him. 'I have more news….'

Fenn looked back.

Edelred held up a finger. 'First, the oxen are all fit. Free of scaly mouth – if they ever had it.'

Another finger joined the first.

'We have agreed to salvage what we can from the harvest – starting tomorrow.'

A third finger.

'Galastan's last-harvest grain has been distributed. The first loaves are being baked now.'

He grinned broadly. Fenn walked back and grasped him by the shoulders.

'I presume we can bring our people back from the cave?' asked Edelred.

'We can indeed. Well done. I'm pleased to hear that good news is starting to arrive.'

FENN STARED AT THE great chair. It looked immovable.

He stood before the chair with Nyle and Kaela at his side. Edelred examined the platform that raised the chair a hand's width off the floor. The chair seemed part of the platform and the platform part of the wooden floor – there looked no way the chair or the platform could be lifted or separated. Nyle suggested that a hole must have been dug in the earth under the floorboards in order to hide a box beneath the chair.

Normally, Fenn would turn to Olgood on matters concerning metal or wood. He missed his advice.

'Did Hardwain build this chair?' he asked.

'Yes,' said Edelred. 'Rather than repair Lord Cormwurst's previous chair…' he smiled, '…which was old and worn, Hardwain built this one.' He bent to examine the join between the chair and the platform. 'If there's a cavity underneath the chair, there must be some way to reach it.'

He pushed on the chair from the side, trying to topple it. Nyle stepped up to help him. The chair firmly resisted their attempt. Edelred moved to the front of the chair and tried to tip it backwards. The chair didn't move.

'Hardwain was a clever craftsman,' he said thoughtfully. 'It wouldn't surprise me if there was some trick to finding the hiding place.'

'Maybe there's an opening somewhere on the chair, with something to slide or pull,' suggested Kaela. She and Fenn circled the chair, examining the wood, probing the sides and back with their fingers. The wood was unbroken and solid, showing no cracks or seams or any signs of a covered opening.

'Galastan said the box was hidden *beneath* the Thane's chair,' said Fenn. 'There must be some way to move it aside. Surely we don't need to tear up the flooring planks.'

He motioned to the others. 'Help me try to lift it.'

All four used their combined strength in an effort to raise the chair. After a few moments, Fenn stepped back.

Hardwain's construction of the Thane's chair and its attachment to the platform was robust and solid.

'What was the message exactly,' asked Kaela. 'Perhaps there's a clue in the wording.'

Fenn looked at her, puzzled. 'The man was dying. He was trying to use as few words as possible. Anyway, I've just told you what he said….'

'What were the exact words?' she insisted.

Fenn closed his eyes to think. 'The exact words were: ...*bring the box hidden beneath the Thane's seat.*' He opened his eyes and shrugged. 'That's what I just said....'

His eyes widened.

Kaela spoke the thought that had just come to him: 'Beneath the *seat.*'

The cushion covering the seat felt like it was packed tightly with wool. Fenn methodically examined the cushion from front to back, feeling for any irregularity, a sliver of wood, a knob, or a lever. There was nothing. He ran his fingers around the front, sides, and back of the cushioned seat. Again the wood was solid with no tell-tale joins. He repeated his search, slower this time, along the front, along the left side, the right, along the back – and he felt it.

A depression in the wood, the size of his little fingernail. He would have missed it if his touch hadn't been at the right angle. It may have been an imperfection in the wood, but that was unlikely from what he'd learned about the master woodcrafter.

Fenn curled the tip of his finger into the depression. He pushed downward and, with a click, the cushioned seat of the Thane of Westerling's chair slid forward, exposing a hidden cavity beneath.

THE BOX WAS CONSTRUCTED of iron, as Galastan had described.

Whatever the contents were, the box was heavy. Using the handles at each end, Nyle and Fenn struggled in the confined space to lift the box free and place it on the floor. Fenn slid the seat back into position – it closed with a click. He squatted beside the iron box to examine it.

The metal showed no sign of weathering, which indicated that the iron was pure and Hardwain's secret compartment had kept the box dry.

The seal the messenger had mentioned was immediately noticeable. The seams of the lid were covered by a thick unbroken ribbon of wax. On both sides of the box and at each end, a symbol had been pressed into the wax – a circle enclosing the head of a bird of prey with its distinctive curved beak.

Edelred saw Fenn closely inspecting the symbol. 'The seal of Lord Cormwurst,' he said. 'An eagle's head.'

'Do you know where Lord Cormwurst kept his seal?' asked Fenn.

'It was always with him, I think. Lord Orvyn may have it… or perhaps Galastan? I can look in Galastan's room, but I don't think….'

'Please look anyway. I'd like to find the seal if possible.'

Edelred nodded.

Fenn leaned back on his heels, resting in that position for a few moments in thought, then he bent closer. He touched one of the wax seals with his finger, tracing the circle and the falcon head.

'Hmm… Edelred, do you have someone who works with wax and could re-seal the box?'

'Of course, but if I don't find Lord Cormwurst's seal, Galastan will know…?'

Kaela and Fenn exchanged glances.

Nyle said: 'What are you thinking?'

'There are many things that Galastan *doesn't* know,' said Fenn.

At St. Cuthbert's monastery on the Holy Island of Lindisfarne, Fenn had been an apprentice scribe. His exceptional talent for drawing had been recognised early and the path from school to scriptorium had been set for him by the monks. Although still an apprentice, his skill was such that his duties included working on final copies of important manuscripts and creating intricately beautiful title pages and borders using coloured inks – a process called illumination. In his spare time, that same skill allowed him to produce such detailed drawings of God's creatures, from birds to beetles, that many commented they 'looked to be alive'.

'Do you think you could carve a copy of that seal in the wax?' Kaela asked.

Fenn heard Nyle's quiet 'No….'

'Yes, it's not a complicated design.'

'*Four* copies – each exactly the same size and shape?' asked Nyle incredulously.

Fenn nodded.

'Shall I still look for the Lord's seal?' asked Edelred.

'Yes. Using the seal would still be best.'

Four pairs of eyes stared at the box.

'What if he opens the box to check the contents?' Kaela asked.

'The seal is his guarantee that the box hasn't been opened. If the box looks properly sealed, why would he destroy that seal to open the box?'

Kaela looked dubious.

'Fenn,' she said, 'I understand you don't want Galastan to profit in this matter, but you're risking lives by assuming he won't open it. Maybe it would be better to just trade whatever's in the box for Olgood.'

'You're right. I *do not* want Galastan to get what he wants. He's taken Olgood, and I'll not allow him to make any gain from that.' He let out a breath. 'He may not like me, but is he a killer? It would make no sense for him to do me, Olgood, *or Kuralin*, if she's there, serious harm.'

'Even if he finds out you tricked him? And what about the Ariochs?'

Fenn put a hand on her arm. 'They're unpredictable, but we can't control everything. As far as Galastan knows, I have no choice but to deliver the sealed box to him in return for Olgood. I don't think he'll break the seal if he has no reason to.'

He narrowed his eyes. 'Talking of Olgood… I'd like to know how they subdued him. I wouldn't have thought that was possible, even considering the Ariochs.'

Kaela snorted. 'A poor attempt to change the subject. You're making a lot of assumptions.' She looked hard at him, then she sighed and relaxed. 'But you do usually choose the right path.' She breathed deeply. 'They must have surprised Olgood – he wouldn't suspect anything.'

'Even so, he'd be a difficult man to keep down.'

She nodded her agreement.

To Edelred, Fenn said: 'Look for the seal, but I'd like to talk with the person who can reseal the box. We'll open it and see what Galastan covets so dearly.'

Edelred bowed and walked quickly toward the Hall entrance.

'I wish he wouldn't keep bowing,' said Fenn, watching Edelred leave.

Kaela punched his arm lightly. 'Let him show his respect,' she said.

'THANK YOU,' FENN SAID.

The woman laid the heavy tray on the table and bowed.

'M'Lord.'

'Who asked you to bring these to us?' asked Fenn.

'The tenant-in-chief, m'Lord.'

For a heartbeat, Fenn thought she meant Galastan but of course she was talking of Edelred. She bowed again, turned from the table and crossed the floor to speak to another woman tending the fire in the Great Hall.

When Fenn had placed a mug of ale from the tray in front of each person seated at the table, two mugs remained.

'I think we must be expecting more ah… guests,' he said.

He stood up. With his mug in his hand, he extended it toward Nyle, inviting him to touch their mugs together.

'Will this Westerling ale settle our wager?'

'Before we discuss that,' said Nyle, 'we should check the quality of the brew.'

Fenn nodded. He raised his mug and took a swallow. It was bitter as expected but there was also a spicy taste that lingered in his mouth. The next thing he noticed was that the ale was strong. Even from one swallow, he could sense a buzz in his head.

In the alehouses of Witanceastre, the ale was brewed to the local taste and with commercial interests in mind. If it were too strong, the patrons would quickly stop drinking and buy less. In the western lands it seemed there were no such considerations.

Fenn looked questioningly at Nyle.

Nyle nodded at his mug. 'A memorable brew,' he said, rubbing his lips together. 'Quite worthy of settling a wager.'

He looked up at Fenn. 'However… it is *I* who should be giving *you* the ale….'

'No,' said Fenn. 'I conceded the wager before we found the last stone.'

Nyle waved the argument away. 'I didn't accept your concession. You won fairly.' He held up his hand to forestall Fenn's reply. 'But, firstly, I've sampled this ale and, secondly, I'm not sure it's mine to give. So, no, I do not accept *this* ale can be used as settlement.'

He lowered his chin and gave Fenn a stern look, daring him to argue more.

Fenn returned the look. 'So, the wager is to be settled some other time then?'

Nyle reached out and touched their mugs together. 'Some other time.'

Footsteps sounded on the floorboards. Edelred entered the Great Hall and headed for the table with Edgar beside him. He carried a sword and scabbard in his hand. He smiled at the scene before him.

'Good, the ales have arrived.' He looked pleased. 'Westerling ale is famous for miles around, even as far away as Escanceastre. It's our own recipe, and it's twice brewed by a special guild of women – that's the only secret I'm able to reveal. We usually drink it only when all work is done for the day, but I thought it was a good time for an introduction.'

He bowed to Fenn. 'May we join you?'

Fenn smiled and waved at the two unused mugs. Edelred placed the sword on the table and sat, motioning Edgar to join him and pulling an ale across the table.

Edgar's gaze swept over the people seated at the table. His smile was forced, still unsure of his status. When his eyes came to Kaela, he frowned, his eyes widening a fraction before they moved on.

'Whose is the sword?' asked Fenn.

'I didn't find Lord Cormwurst's seal,' replied Edelred, 'but I did find *this* hidden in Galastan's room. I know this sword. It belonged to Lord Cormwurst, who always said it was the sword of King Cynewulf – he was King of Wessex before Beorhtric.' He rose and lifted the sword, presenting it to Fenn. 'Now, it should belong to the new Thane of Westerling.'

Fenn stood up to accept the sword. 'Thank you,' he said. 'But I have no need of a sword, even such a fine weapon as this. I prefer my axe. Keep it somewhere prominent, Edelred, in memory of Lord Cormwurst.'

Edelred's bowed his head. 'Of course, Lord.'

Edgar stood and reached out a hand. 'May I?' he asked.

Edelred glanced at Fenn. At Fenn's nod, he passed the sword to Edgar. Edgar withdrew the sword from its scabbard and ran his finger along the blade. He held it at arm's length, turning it in his hand, assessing its weight and balance. The man looked well used to having a sword in his hand. Edgar took a step away from the table, lifted the sword high, brought it sharply down across his body, and just as quickly reversed the swing. He gave a grunt of satisfaction.

'Perfect balance,' he said. 'A sword fit for a king indeed.' He slipped the sword back into its scabbard, passed the weapon back to Edelred and pulled his chair up to the table.

Fenn looked to Kaela for her reaction to Edgar's display, but she wasn't looking at him. Instead, she was regarding Edgar thoughtfully. He turned his attention back to Edgar.

'Welcome to Westerling Hall, Edgar,' Fenn said. He turned to the others. 'When Edgar entered our palisade, he wasn't sure he was in Wessex.'

Edgar held up his hand. 'Actually, Hernam *told* me I was in Wessex,' he said. 'To enjoy my suffering, I think – to be in Wessex but still a prisoner. I just wanted confirmation that he spoke the truth.'

Although his clothes had been changed and there were shoes on his feet, his recent transition from thrall to free man was still evident by his tousled hair and the grime that streaked his face and hands.

When no one spoke, Edgar took the opportunity to continue.

'I want to thank you for my freedom. Fate has not been kind to me these last three years. It's been a trial, but I made the most of it.'

'I'd be interested to know how you *made the most* of your years as a thrall,' inquired Nyle.

Edgar smiled grimly. 'The days were hard, I can't deny that, but I tried to gain *some* pleasure from them. That pleasure came from annoying Hernam and Hopkin. I made sure I did nothing well. The more angry they became with my mistakes, the better.'

Nyle stifled a laugh. 'A dangerous course to follow,' he said.

Fenn nodded, remembering the blow Edgar had taken from Hernam while he was watching the camp at Wealdemere. He noticed Kaela was also amused, but her smile quickly faded.

'It did cause a few knocks to come my way,' Edgar said. 'But I considered the game was worth it.' He raised his mug. 'It's been a while since I've been able to enjoy anything like this ale.' Edgar sipped the ale and gave an approving grunt. 'It'll take some time to get used to being a free man,' he said. 'I can only hope I'm able to repay you somehow.'

Kaela leaned forward.

'You can start by admitting who you are.'

Fenn looked at her. What was she suggesting?

'I saw that you recognised me when you came to the table,' Kaela continued, 'even though many years have passed since we met in Francia at the court of Charles the Great. And I recognise you, even behind the dirt and your unruly hair. Your name is not Edgar. You are Egbert, son of Ealhmund of Kent. With Offa's help and Charles' agreement, my father had you banished to Francia when you claimed the throne of Wessex.'

Edgar was silent. He closed his eyes and took in a breath. When his eyes reopened, they flicked to Kaela, then Fenn, and back to Kaela. He slowly released his breath.

'As you say…' he said, '…many years have passed. I didn't recognise you outside the palisade with your hair tied back. When I last saw you, you were little more than a girl. But now, with your hair free… it took me a moment. You're Beorhtric's…' he hesitated, then said: '…daughter.'

'Were you about to say his *bastard* daughter?' asked Kaela. There was an edge to her voice, but also a smile playing at the corner of her mouth.

'I am who you say I am – I won't hide from that….' Egbert said, evading her question, '…although I did think it wise to conceal my name in Wessex. Plainly stated, I have as much right to the throne of Wessex as Beorhtric, if not more, through a different bloodline. I'm descended from Ingild, brother of King Ine. Beorhtric, I understand, claims descent from one of Ine's sisters.'

He held out a hand to her, palm up.

'However… I accept my circumstances. Things are as they are. I hold no grievance against you, Princess Kaela, and I stand by what I said – I acknowledge my debt to you and I *will* repay you and Lord Feran in any way I can.'

Fenn noted he had not said he held no grievance against Beorhtric.

'The fact remains – my father banished you from the realm, yet here you are,' said Kaela. She turned to Fenn. 'What are we to do about that, my Lord?'

Fenn took a moment to assess Kaela's attitude. She seemed more amused than angry.

'That may be of concern to Beorhtric,' said Fenn, 'but I'll judge a man through my own eyes. For the moment we have more pressing issues, and I see no need for haste.'

He looked at her. Did she agree?

Kaela raised her mug, looked at him over the rim, and drank.

FENN STOOD AT THE palisade entrance looking out over the pastures, the wheat and barley fields and the forest to the far hills. Two grazing cows were visible – only two, but good to see after the empty countryside of yesterday. Westerling was slowly coming back to life.

'Were you surprised that the box did contain gold?' asked Kaela.

'I was surprised at the amount, and I can only wonder how Cormwurst collected such a treasure.'

'What will you do with it, now that you're a rich man.'

He looked down at her. 'The gold belongs to Westerling, and I intend to put it to good use. For now, though, we'll bury it.'

She raised her eyes to meet his without replying, a slight smile on her lips. He couldn't tell if she was still suggesting he should trade the gold for Olgood.

He leaned against the archway and curled his arm around Kaela's shoulders, pulling her head to his.

'What is it that amuses you about Egbert?' he asked.

She nestled into him. 'I'm not amused by *him* exactly, rather by his part in the extraordinary turns of fate we've seen in just a few days,' she said. 'The events that brought us to Westerling, to meet Hernam, and bring my path and Egbert's back together. Is there a reason Egbert has returned to Wessex?' She turned her head to look him in the eyes. 'Our lives seem to have gathered speed. I wonder what's next.'

'I'm surprised though at your relaxed attitude toward him. Once he'd confessed readily to his identity, rather than see him as an enemy or a threat to your father, you seem prepared to accept him.'

She raised her hand to brush his face, taking a moment to think about her reply.

'I love my father and I'll support him in any way I can, of course, but when King Cynewulf was killed, Beorhtric *took* the throne of Wessex with help from King Offa of Mercia. Offa arranged for Beorhtric to marry his daughter Eadburg so that *Offa*, through her, would then be the real power in Wessex. My father dangles at the end of Offa's strings, and *that I don't like.*'

She looked at Fenn with fierce eyes. 'Wessex will never become great until it's free from the yoke of Mercia, and that will not happen while Offa and Eadburg rule.'

It was the first time she'd expressed her thoughts about the future of Wessex. He knew she had no love for Eadburg, but he now saw her feelings were deeper than just resentment at the way she'd been treated by the Queen as a child, and swirling in that mix was the conflict she felt regarding her father.

Kaela shook her head in resignation. 'Egbert *does* have a claim to the throne of Wessex and there are many who support that claim and think he should be King. What I'm not prepared to do is hate him just because it's expected of me. I met him several times when I was at the court of King Charles. He knew who I was – the daughter of his rival – but he was always well-mannered and polite to me. I respected him for that but I was young and didn't know him well. So, I agree with you in this regard – he's *here* now and I intend to make up my own mind about him.'

Fenn was surprised by her intensity. Did she think Egbert may be the one to free Wessex from Mercia?

They stood in silence, gazing out on the estates of Westerling. Fenn felt the weight of his responsibility to this community pressing upon him. Was he taking an unnecessary risk in replacing the contents of the box to be traded for Olgood tomorrow? Would Hernam honour their agreement? How would Egbert's arrival on the scene play out? Were greater forces driving events? He drew in a deep breath of crisp Westerling air and straightened his back.

'Then we'll keep a close eye on the man who was a thrall when the sun rose and now at sunset aspires to be a king,' he said, 'and we'll take his measure by how he acts.'

When Kaela didn't reply, he scanned the horizon.

'The sky's clear. Unfortunately, it's a full moon – there'll be no cloud cover tonight.' He released her and turned her to face him. 'I'll start early in the morning and go alone to Moloch Tor.'

Kaela's eyes flicked up at the sky. After a moment, she grunted.

'The conditions may change,' she said. 'If they do, I'll be ready.'

FENN PULLED THE ROPE tight, securing the iron box onto the second horse. He turned to the horse he'd be riding and drew his axe from his belt, inserting it into a sheath Edelred had tied to the saddle.

In the dim light of early dawn he stepped back to find Kaela standing close, with Nyle beside her. Edelred was holding the horse's reins, and Fenn noticed Beric was there. The boy was interested in everything and wanted to be a part. He looked for Balthazar, but the hound was not in sight.

Nyle reached out his hand and Fenn took it. Nyle said nothing but his eyes and grip conveyed his wishes for success. He stepped back.

Fenn pulled Kaela as close as the full-length cloak Edelred had given him would allow and nestled his cheek to hers. It was surprisingly warm in the chilled morning air. He felt her lips on his skin.

'Bring Olgood back,' she whispered into his hair. 'Help Kuralin if you can. But most important…' she pressed the point of her finger into his chest, '…*you* come back to me.'

'Always,' he said.

'If you're not back by midnight tonight, I'll come and find you.'

She pulled back and kissed him on the mouth, her lips lingering, reminding him of the reason to return.

As if the mention of Olgood had summoned her, Gisele appeared beside Nyle. She was carrying a sack over her shoulder.

'I 'ave some food for our journey,' she said.

Fenn reluctantly drew back from Kaela's embrace.

'Gisele…'

'Olgood is in trouble. I can 'elp. I come with you.'

Fenn placed his hands on Gisele's shoulders.

'You would be placing Olgood in more danger. Galastan insisted I come alone.'

'Bah. Nobody see me if I not want 'im to.'

It was not an idle boast. While fleeing from the Northmen, Gisele demonstrated her ability as a huntress and her gift of moving undetected through the forest each time she successfully provided game for the fire, no matter what challenge was presented by weather or circumstances. More recently, that skill had allowed Olgood to track Cedric's band.

But it would be a different matter on a desolate moor.

'The moor is not a forest,' said Fenn. 'It's barren. No trees or bushes to hide behind.'

Gisele shrugged off Fenn's hands. She turned to Kaela and spoke to her rapidly in the Frankish language, which Kaela had learned at King Charles' court. Gisele pointed at Fenn.

'She says she cannot make you understand in your language,' Kaela said. Gisele spoke again with Kaela translating.

'Since she met you, you have eaten many hares she brought to your fire. If she can get that close to a hare or a quail, she can get close to....' Kaela stopped and asked a question. 'She wants me to say she will not be seen by the eyes of a stupid man like Galastan.'

'The best and simplest way to get Olgood back safely is to exchange this box for him,' argued Fenn. 'I don't want to worry about you out on the moor.'

Gisele's eyes flashed. Her voice rose and she stabbed her finger at Fenn.

'You don't need to worry about *her*,' translated Kaela. 'You only need to worry about yourself.'

Gisele said another sentence. When Kaela didn't immediately translate, Gisele forcefully motioned for her to do so.

'Gisele says you should not try to stop her from helping her man.'

Fenn grimaced. 'I can only *ask* you not to,' he said. 'I need to go alone, and I need to know I'm alone.' He looked to Kaela for help, but she was not going to take a side. Should he mention Gisele's pregnancy as a reason for her to stay? Instinct said no. The anguish on Gisele's face was unsettling.

'Gisele, I *will* bring him back.'

She looked at him with tight lips, her eyes moist. Slowly her taut face relaxed.

'You true friend to Olgood,' she said. 'I know this. I see you do many things. Brave things. You each would die for other one. I know all this. I know you try your best. What I *not* know is if best is enough.'

She thrust the sack of food at him and walked away.

CHAPTER THIRTEEN

A meeting on Moloch Tor

Moloch Tor rose starkly against a sky filling fast with churning clouds, driven hard before a stiff southwesterly.

Patches of blue sky allowed some sunlight to filter onto the countryside and colour the tops of the clouds white, but on their undersides they carried long dark grey streaks. If only these clouds had arrived during the night, Kaela might have been able to get into the forest unseen by watchers on the tor.

As far as the eye could see, the moor was barren and bleak, the ground studded with rocky outcrops and hillocks and the whole area covered by a short, tough, stubby mixture of grass, moss, and low bracken. The forest Edelred had mentioned sat as a thick and tangled wreath around the peak of Moloch Tor. The tor itself – several piled towers of huge granite stone slabs – emerged from the centre of the forest at the highest point for miles around like a giant fist thrust from the earth.

Anyone moving across this bare landscape would be instantly visible from the peak of Moloch Tor. Fenn had no doubt eyes were on him at this moment.

He discarded the core of the apple he'd taken from Gisele's food bag and quickly replaced his glove. As Edelred had forecast, the temperature dropped noticeably as Fenn climbed towards the tor and the ground was covered with a dusting of snow which looked to deepen closer to the forest. He was glad of the heavy fur-lined cloak Edelred had insisted he wear but he could feel the cold seeping through his woollen gloves.

A shiver crossed his shoulders. Especially on a wild, windy day such as this, he could see why Moloch Tor had gained such a foreboding reputation. The great rocks of the tor glowered menacingly down, dominating the surrounding moor. People naturally kept clear of such places.

Fenn turned in his saddle to check on the second horse, carrying the iron box. It raised its head in response to his attention, ears flicking forward, but the head quickly lowered when the animal detected nothing to sustain its interest. Fenn flexed his fingers and the toes in his boots to ward off the chill. He lifted his eyes to the forest. The path led up to the edge of the trees, but they were packed so densely that the way ahead disappeared from view at that point.

The trees of the forest were strangely shaped, their trunks twisted and branches bent at unusual angles as though some force had prevented them from growing straight and tall. Maybe the ground never warmed enough for normal growth. The twisting had merged the trees together to form a dense mass of branches and foliage.

An opening between the misshapen trees appeared at the last moment. Directing his horse into the gap, Fenn was instantly swallowed by the dark cold forest.

The dim light forced him to squint to see the way ahead. The temperature dropped even further as the sun was obscured, but at least the weird trees formed some shelter against the biting wind. The snow on the ground was thick, the horses kicking up flurries with every step. No other tracks were visible, so the snow must have been deposited recently. The thickness of the snow was puzzling. How could it have filtered in such quantity through the dense tree cover?

Fenn let the horse find its way up the narrow winding trail, steadily climbing toward the weathered stone formation of Moloch Tor. Edelred had warned him not to stray from the path, and Fenn had no problem heeding his warning. With its abnormally twisted trees and thick snow covering the ground, the weird-looking forest was hardly inviting.

He hoped the upcoming trade would be concluded swiftly so he could be back at Westerling before nightfall. The iron box, now filled with the same weight of river stones and resealed with a new wax ribbon into which Fenn had carved four copies of Lord Cormwurst's seal, would be exchanged for Olgood and hopefully also the messenger's wife Kuralin – if she was here at Moloch Tor. That was all that needed to happen. A simple trade. There was no reason for Galastan to want to prolong the matter. Fenn would insist on the exchange being simultaneous. How far he could push the demand that Kuralin be included would depend on how much Galastan wanted the iron box.

He leaned forward to check that his axe was readily available, lifting it and letting it fall back. It moved easily in its sheath.

The path changed direction so many times it seemed deliberately designed to be disorienting, but two things remained constant – with each step, the horses climbed higher, and the temperature grew colder.

The twisting and turning of the path caused the journey through the forest to take longer than expected and, without the sun to guide him, it was impossible to determine whether he would arrive at the tor at the appointed time of midday. Still, there was nothing to be gained by urging the horse to hurry; it could not reasonably move any faster along a constricted path that constantly changed direction.

The scenery was unchanging and monotonous – each turn in the trail revealed the same scene; a narrow, dark, snow-covered path bordered by densely-packed bizarrely-twisted trees.

WITH A START, Fenn realised he had been staring for some time at the horse's gently bobbing head, his mind blank. He forced himself to concentrate.

He needed to be alert. The trees ahead were thinning.

The sudden brightness when he exited the forest pained his eyes, and he held them shut to aid their adjustment. When he raised his lids the minimal amount required to see, blinking against the glare, the midday sun was clear and high in the sky, fully illuminating the spectacle of Moloch Tor.

A huge awe-inspiring structure of five great towers of stone stood before him, as though an ancient giant had piled massive granite slabs like flattened over-wide tree trunks, one atop the other, to form elongated pillars, each three or four times the height of a man. The resemblance to a mighty fist, as noted by Fenn on his first sighting of Moloch Tor from the moor, was still strong. Around the towers, the peak of Moloch Tor was flattened and packed, forming a hard clay-like surface surprisingly free of snow.

Fenn hunched his shoulders. It was intensely cold on the exposed summit. The air seemed heavy, its weight pressing down, and the wind swirled its icy breath around the tor, pulling at his hair and gnawing at his thick cloak.

The finger-like towers were angled so that sometimes they touched together, and in other places the ends were wide apart. A stone wall and roof had been built between the two formations closest to Fenn, joining the two ends and enclosing the space between them. A small square hole formed a window high on the wall.

This addition had been constructed by men rather than giants.

GALASTAN HAD HIS ARMS folded, leaning his shoulder against the wall of stone. One of the Ariochs was visible, standing in the shadow of a stone tower. Both were dressed warmly, so they had found extra clothing somewhere. There was no sign of the other Arioch or of Olgood. Four horses were tethered on the far side of the flattened peak of the tor.

When Fenn's trailing horse had completed the climb up to the towers, Galastan directed his gaze behind it to the path.

He waited a moment, then said: 'Where is the man I sent to you? He was to return with you and ensure you brought the box as I directed.'

'He's dead,' said Fenn.

Galastan widened his large eyes.

'You killed him?' He snorted. 'Why? For bringing bad news?'

'I didn't kill him. The Cornish did.'

'What Cornish?' Galastan sniffed his disdain and his thin smile appeared.

'Hernam of Cornwall came to take Westerling's grain harvest. His men intercepted your messenger and put an arrow in his back, but he reached Westerling and lived long enough to give me your message.'

Galastan looked up at him, his lip curled into a sneer. 'And then Hernam went away?'

'After a while, yes.'

Galastan stared at Fenn. 'Bah,' he snorted. 'You expect me to believe that story?'

He spat on the ground and looked back at Fenn, his eyes narrowing suspiciously. Fenn returned his stare.

After a while, Galastan shrugged, dismissing the matter.

'Ah, well. It's no longer any concern of mine. If the man's dead, what does it matter who killed him? You're here, and I see you've brought the box, so my message *did* reach you and that's all that's important.'

He pointed. 'Give the reins of that horse to the Arioch.'

Neither Galastan nor the Arioch was armed. Fenn rested a hand on his axe.

'I'll need to see Olgood and the woman first.'

'The *woman*? What woman?' Galastan raised his eyebrows in an exaggerated expression of innocence. Everything the man did seemed to be an act.

'The messenger told me the Ariochs took his wife, Kuralin, to force him to bring me your message.'

Galastan smiled his half-smile and tilted his head to the side.

'Kuralin… is that her name?'

He pushed himself away from the stone wall.

'It's a nice name. I like it.'

He walked towards Fenn, his smirk widening.

'You can dismount. The Arioch will take your horses. I'll need to inspect the box and then I'll take you to your big friend. You said you'd like to see him, *Lord* Feran.'

Fenn ignored Galastan's contempt of his title. He removed the gloves from his hands.

'Where's the other Arioch?' he asked.

'Watching my prisoner. Watching him *closely.*'

Galastan's emphasis conveyed a threat. If Fenn had not met the conditions Galastan had imposed, the 'prisoner' would come to harm. Earlier, Fenn was certain Galastan would have no reason to open the box. Suddenly he wasn't so sure.

He drew his axe from the sheath.

Galastan stopped, his hands raised in mock surrender. 'There's no need for weapons. We're unarmed. This can be a simple exchange. The box for Olkid – once we've both inspected our trade goods.'

'*Olgood,*' Fenn corrected curtly. '*And* the woman.' Fenn's hackles had risen with Galastan's reference to Olgood as *trade goods.*

Galastan gave a dismissive wave. 'The woman… *Kur-a-lin…*' the way he savoured the name was distasteful '…is not mine to give. You'll need to ask the Ariochs.'

His eyes left Fenn and pointedly searched the horses before returning. He spread his hands, a derisive gesture.

'And I see nothing extra you could *possibly* offer in exchange for *her.*'

'I'm offering the box for both,' said Fenn.

A mocking chuckle. 'As I *said,* the Ariochs…' began Galastan.

'I *heard* what you said,' interrupted Fenn, his voice crisp. 'Now *I'm* saying *this.* You can have the box, but *only* for both Olgood *and* Kuralin.'

Galastan's eyes narrowed.

'You said you wanted a quick exchange,' continued Fenn. 'Bring Olgood and Kuralin here now, and I'll give you the box. As you said yourself, it can be simply done.'

'That's not possible,' said Galastan. 'Your man is restrained.'

'Is he hurt?'

Olgood hadn't been dressed for the temperature on Moloch Tor. Fenn hoped Olgood had also been given some extra clothing.

'He's alive.'

'I asked if he was injured.'

'Nothing serious.'

'Then unrestrain him.'

'I would need to have the box before I do that. He's strong, that one. He could do some damage.'

Olgood would only do damage if he had cause. Not for the first time, Fenn wondered exactly what had passed since Galastan and Olgood had left Westerling.

'The only way this will work…' he said slowly and firmly, '…is if we make the exchange together. I'm prepared to give you the box for Olgood and Kuralin.'

Galastan didn't reply. Fenn also remained silent, letting the impasse continue.

Galastan was unable to maintain his air of nonchalance for long. His lips tightened. He grew increasingly agitated, running his hands through his hair, his eyes flicking between Fenn, the Arioch, and the box.

'Very well. I'll take you and the box to them.'

So Olgood and Kuralin *were* together.

Fenn released a silent breath of relief, then drew in another breath to calm himself. He needed to stay alert. Taking heed of the caution that Nyle continually displayed, he glanced about, also turning to look behind.

'Who else is here?'

'Nobody.'

Fenn scanned the area carefully. Despite his distrust of Galastan, he saw nothing to indicate otherwise.

Galastan turned and swept his arm, inviting Fenn to follow him.

'I happen to agree with you,' Galastan said, inclining his head, his face slipping into his weak smile. 'The sooner we conclude this matter, the sooner we can go our separate ways.'

FENN DISMOUNTED.

Holding his axe in one hand and the horse's reins in the other, he followed Galastan toward the end of the nearest tower. As he approached the slabs of stone, he stopped. The Arioch hadn't moved.

'Tell the Arioch to walk in front.'

Galastan sighed. 'You're being unnecessarily dramatic,' he scoffed. 'They don't like the sunlight. It burns them. But… if you wish….' He waved his hand. The Arioch lumbered out of the shadow, his red eyes never leaving Fenn.

Fenn expected an opening at this end of the tower would lead into the space enclosed by the roof and wall. Was Olgood imprisoned inside this crude room? As he turned the corner, he tilted his head to peer around the stone. The sun shining from directly overhead placed the interior in shadow. Inside the dim enclosure, he could see a form lying on the floor against the wall. It was not large enough to be Olgood.

Something tugged his hair from behind, pulling his head back and down. An arm circled around his neck, pressing on his throat, cutting off his air. *The missing Arioch.* The horse shied away from the struggle – twisting its head – snatching the reins from Fenn's hand. He reached up to ease the arm at his neck so he could breathe, at the same time sweeping his axe blindly behind him. His hand had difficulty grasping the thick Arioch arm. The blade clanged against stone. He brought the weapon back in a reverse swing across the front of his body. The arm around his neck continued to drag him back and down, pulling him off-balance just as he had done to Hopkin. He tried to back up. His hand found purchase on the arm around his neck. He desperately pulled on the arm but was unable to get enough leverage to lessen the grip. The axe completed its swing without striking anything.

A hand fastened onto the wrist that held the axe, and another grasped the iron handle. Fenn abandoned his attempt to free the arm around his neck and reached out blindly to support his hold on the axe, but, with a violent twist, the weapon was torn from his grasp. He heard the clang of the blade against stone again as it was discarded. He kicked out hard with one leg and had the satisfaction of feeling his foot make solid contact, producing a grunt. The second Arioch was now leaning over him. He urgently needed to breathe. A blow from above crashed against his cheek, stunning him. He kicked again, but his unstable position prevented him from putting any force into the kick. The arm of the Arioch to his front rose again. Fenn raised his arms to protect his face but the closed fist penetrated the barrier, knocking his head sharply to the side and causing a wave of dizziness. The arm around his neck abruptly loosened, and a third blow drove him to the ground, where he sprawled on his stomach, dazed and gasping. He tried to rise, but his movements were sluggish; his limbs drained of strength.

He felt an instant chill as his thick cloak was dragged from his shoulders and roughly pulled free of his arms. A knee on the side of his face and another between his shoulders pressed him against the earth while his hands were twisted behind his back and tied together. He jerked his body to the side as violently as he could – if he could just get free and to his feet, he still had a chance – but the attempt was futile. The two heavy weights pressing on his head and back were immovable. He flexed his hands while his wrists were being tied so the binding might loosen when he relaxed.

He heard an urgent shout from Galastan: '*Arioch! No!*' – just before his head was struck again and darkness enveloped him.

CHAPTER FOURTEEN

The altar of the Druids

His head ached and he was painfully cold.

He was lying on his side on the floor of the enclosure. He could feel the heat from his body bleeding into the frozen earth of Moloch Tor. His legs had been tied at the ankles and the knees. He lay still, blinking, while his eyes adjusted to the gloom. The bag of stones was digging uncomfortably into the bone of his hip – a good sign – the existence of the stones told him he hadn't been searched, and his sling was still likely to be tied to his belt. He moved his legs to ease his discomfort, and his feet brushed through the remnants of a fire – the fire that had probably provided warmth to Galastan and the Ariochs last night. There was no warmth left in the ashes now.

'Are you awake? Are you hurt?' The questions were asked by a female voice.

'Not badly,' Fenn answered, raising his head to peer in the direction of the voice. The movement caused a momentary dizziness. 'Bruised only, I think.' He flexed his jaw. It hurt, but nothing seemed broken. He tested the binding on his wrists. The ropes were tight.

The woman was lying against the wall, her body bent backward, hands tied behind her back but also lashed to her ankles so that her feet were pulled up behind her. A rope was wrapped around her arms, pinning them to her side. Her binding was excessive. She'd been trussed like an animal ready for slaughter.

She was wearing only a simple long dress with bare arms, so she'd also been stripped of any warm clothing if she had any. She must be feeling the intense cold. But, rather than being downcast, even in the dull light her eyes contained a sparkle. Her pixie-like face creased into a smile.

'Before you ask,' she said, 'yes, I *am* uncomfortable.'

Fenn couldn't help but return her smile. Her mood was heartening.

She glanced behind Fenn and her smile faded. 'But not as uncomfortable as that poor man on the rock.'

Fenn turned his head at the same time as Olgood's voice came from behind.

'We've been restrained like this b-before,' he said, his words coming unevenly, 'and that didn't e-end well.'

Fenn's smile broadened. Even in the circumstances it was good to hear his voice, though it was weak and shaking. Olgood was referring to their capture by the Northmen at St. Cuthbert's monastery. They had been tied together in the monastery courtyard before being dragged to the beach and the ships and taken across the sea to foreign lands.

Olgood was lying spread-eagled on his back on top of a stone slab with his feet and hands bound by rope to iron rings set into the sides of the slab. The large rectangular stone stood towards the back of the enclosure, under the window. The purpose of the room became clear – it was a place of worship, and the stone was an altar. But what people would choose such an uninviting place as this for worship?

Fenn's mouth tightened with sudden realisation. The position of the iron rings told him the altar was *not* intended for worship. It was intended for sacrifice. *Human* sacrifice.

His hope that Olgood had been given warm clothing evaporated. He was in the same clothes he had worn when he left Westerling. His pale, drawn features were a testament to the toll taken by extended exposure to the penetrating cold of Moloch Tor – aggravated by the bare rock and the strain of his bindings. But it was the other contributors to Olgood's suffering that caused Fenn to narrow his eyes. Olgood's face and the side of his head were streaked with dried blood. Galastan had said Olgood's injuries were 'nothing serious' – they looked serious to Fenn.

'They beat him terribly, those white monsters,' the woman confirmed his fears. 'I think they almost killed him….'

Olgood said: 'It's not as b-bad as it p-proba-bly looks.' From the evidence of his voice, Olgood was being continually shaken by violent shivering.

Fenn held back a comment about how bad it looked.

'Why have they brought *you* here?' the woman asked when Fenn made no reply to Olgood. 'Do you know why any of us are here?'

Fenn turned his head back to face her. He tested the bindings on his legs. They were firm. He'd been bound by someone who knew how to tie a knot.

'Galastan forced me to bring something to him,' he said. 'Your capture, and Olgood's, were part of that plan.'

'Galastan? Is he the small one?

'Yes.'

'So will they let us go now… if they have what they want?'

'I don't know.'

When she didn't speak again, Fenn said: 'My name is Fenn. Are you Kuralin?'

An intake of breath. 'How could you know that? Have you met my husband?'

Fenn's heart sank. There was no way to avoid what he had to tell her.

'Yes,' he said, 'I *have* met your husband. He brought me a message from Galastan.'

She was silent a moment. 'How did he…? Is that why I was taken…? Why then would they attack *you*?'

Her face was twisted with puzzlement.

'Kuralin, I'm sorry to bring you bad news. I have to tell you your husband is dead.' Her intake of breath was accompanied by a groan from Olgood. 'He died bringing me Galastan's message,' Fenn continued. 'He was a brave man. With his last words, he was thinking of you....'

'Dead? How…?'

'He was killed by Cornish raiders.'

Her shocked silence was followed by a low keening wail, then an anguished cry: 'Then I'm *alone*. What will become of me *now*?'

'Where are your family?' asked Fenn gently.

'I have no family. I have no one now. I fear this is where…' her voice broke into sobs of despair, '…it *ends* for me.'

Footsteps sounded at the entrance.

Galastan strode into the enclosure, rubbing his hands together.

'Good. You've woken.'

He gazed around, his eyes checking that all was as he expected. He carried two lengths of rope looped over his arm.

'I wanted to talk with you, *Lord Feran, Thane of Westerling*,' he said, mocking the title with his emphasis, '…and having you beaten senseless was not my plan. I stopped them as soon as I could, but… the Ariochs sometimes get excited and…' he waved his hand and left the sentence unfinished.

Galastan slowly paced across the floor, stopping at the head of the altar.

'I don't like to leave matters unfinished, so I was forced to wait for you to regain your wits.'

He nodded, satisfied with himself. 'Thanks to you and the box you bought, I have salvaged *something* worthwhile from this chain of unfortunate circumstances.' He gazed around the enclosure again. 'As God is my witness, I'll be glad to leave this forsaken hilltop behind, even though it served its purpose.'

Fenn had no wish to engage in conversation with Galastan, but he found encouragement in his words. Galastan had not remarked on the *contents* of the box – so he hadn't opened it.

Galastan leaned on the altar stone looking down at Olgood and shook his head. 'The Ariochs wanted to punish Olkood because he… he *hurt* one of them. I tried to talk them out of that as well – it makes no sense to damage the goods you intend to bargain with, does it? I was only partially successful, I fear.'

His familiar smirk crept onto his face. Galastan probably intended the expression to show concern but to Fenn it showed only arrogance.

Fenn didn't bother to correct Galastan's misuse of Olgood's name again. Galastan had given Olgood's name correctly to his messenger, so the mispronunciation was deliberate. It was impossible to tell what was truth and what was part of his act.

Galastan pointed a finger and addressed Olgood. 'They tied you here and wanted to kill you on the sacrificial altar. They liked the idea of using the altar.' Galastan waved his hand in a negative gesture. 'But, no…. that's pagan thinking. It wouldn't be right before God. I don't agree with sacrifice – with killing a restrained man….'

He paused as though he expected gratitude. When none was forthcoming, he sniffed.

'If you stopped them, and you don't agree with sacrifice, why is he still bound to the altar?' asked Fenn.

'At the time, it would not have been wise to insist on releasing him. The Ariochs wouldn't have accepted that. They only stopped when I pointed out that he'd suffer more if they didn't kill him. And now… well…' Galastan leaned forward, his smirk lengthening – he tapped his head, '…you do not release a mother bear if there's breath in its body and cubs to protect.'

While Fenn took a moment to untangle Galastan's words, Olgood spoke.

'The Ariochs are no b-better than ani-mals,' he forced out the words. 'They have animal inst-incts and always r-react with violence. Why d-do you ke-ep them?'

Galastan paused. He reluctantly returned his attention to Olgood and stared down at him, deciding whether to answer. After a moment, he shrugged and gave a soft laugh of amusement.

'They act like animals because until we met, they'd been *treated* like animals and kept in a cage like animals. God directed me to free them and take them into his care. We have an understanding. *I* find them useful, and *they* need someone to guide them. We help each other.'

He straightened and sniffed loudly, wiping his nose with his sleeve.

'But that's of no matter. I'm leaving Moloch Tor now, but I'd like to ensure you all remain here, so, to that end….'

He walked around the altar to Kuralin, bent over her and tugged on the rope tying her hands to her legs. Ignoring her groans of pain, Galastan dragged her to the altar.

'Why is she trussed like a pig?' demanded Fenn.

'Hah. She fought like a she-devil,' said Galastan. 'Even the Ariochs were reluctant to hit a woman.' He chuckled. 'They were frustrated when they found it hard to get ropes on her. It was quite amusing….'

'Why don't you l-let her go?' asked Olgood. He coughed and took a moment to regain his breath. 'You don't n-need her any… any… more, and she c-can't h-hurt you.'

Galastan snorted. 'I'm not such a fool as to send a cry for help into the countryside.'

He positioned Kuralin with her back against the altar stone and used one of the lengths of rope he carried to bind her to a ring on the altar stone.

'You'll be long g-gone be-fore she c-could reach anyone on f-foot,' Olgood persisted.

Galastan paused tying the rope. He brushed his hair out of his eyes.

'Look at you,' he sneered. 'You're half dead. You can hardly talk. Why are you making such an effort? Give up and just let what is sure to happen, happen.' He stared at Olgood, then shrugged again and shook his head. 'I don't know why I'm explaining this to *you*. It's obvious, isn't it? I'd rather no one knows you're here.'

He completed his knot and walked to Fenn.

'Turn away from me,' he commanded.

When Fenn hesitated, Galastan added: 'I can hurt her if you make this difficult….'

Fenn obeyed. Galastan knotted the other rope to the bindings on his knees and also his hands before attaching it to an iron ring. He could feel the sting of the ropes chafing his wrists and ankles.

'I wouldn't want you to try to crawl back to Westerling,' Galastan said. 'That wouldn't be good for your health.' He chuckled at his joke as he completed his knot.

'There…' he said. He squatted on his heels in front of Fenn, out of reach of his legs.

He pointed an imperious finger. 'You wouldn't understand… but, left to myself, I would have had Westerling operating tightly and efficiently after a few hard seasons. The stupid Saxon peasants somehow took up the idea to resist me, but that wouldn't have been a problem if Orvyn hadn't inconveniently died and you hadn't arrived with your damned title.'

'And *you* would have made a heavy profit at the end of each season, no doubt,' said Fenn, 'by exploiting and starving the people of Westerling.'

Galastan ignored Fenn's sarcasm. 'I don't mind admitting I would have profited as would be my due…. Wessex owes me that. However, it's of no consequence now….' He shook his head and raised his hands, acknowledging those plans had changed.

He stared hard at Fenn and let his hands slowly fall.

'I have things I want to say to you.' He nodded his head thoughtfully. 'We're alike, you and I – in one way.'

Fenn drew his head back in denial, but Galastan raised a hand.

'We're both foreigners,' he said. 'You come from parts far away I think, and me….' He sniffed and wiped his nose on his cuff. 'We won't meet again, so I can tell you what I've told no one….' He allowed his smirk to linger, enjoying the moment. 'I'm from Wealas, across the Severn Sea. They call us outsiders here. Strangers. They think of us as less than human – for generations, the filthy Saxons have taken us as thralls. Offa built a dyke across half of Wealas to keep us out.' He screwed his nose into a sneer and stabbed a finger at Fenn. 'If I'd thought about it more,

I would have taken you all back to Wealas as *my* thralls. *That* would have been fitting.'

Fenn said nothing. Galastan's heightened emotions had him breathing hard. He placed his hands on his head and sighed, calming himself.

'No, no,' he said slowly. '*This* is good. This is a good conclusion.'

He lifted his eyes and stared at Fenn. 'I regret that I didn't insist you bring my mares to me. I'll miss those beauties.'

He was silent a moment, maintaining his stare. He shrugged. 'You've taken all that from me. At least Cormwurst's gold will ensure *all* is not lost.'

His voice became jovial, revelling in his moment of glory.

'It was easy to surprise you, even armed as you were.' He gestured toward the entrance. 'There's a small alcove built into the rock there – it's called Cutthroats Gap, I believe. It's completely in shadow at midday this time of year. If you don't know it's there, you can't see it. You're not the first victim of this place to be waylaid at the Gap.'

He sniffed loudly.

'Tell me…' he said. 'Did you find the opening in the chair, or did you break the chair apart to get to the box?'

Fenn didn't reply. Galastan's thin lips widened, the first time Fenn had seen a genuine smile on his face. He immediately understood why the man never smiled. Galastan's mouth displayed blackened gums and the gaps of missing teeth, with the visible teeth discoloured and in poor health.

Galastan saw where Fenn's eyes were directed and quickly closed his mouth, turning the smile into a scowl.

'I hope you had to destroy that damned Thane's seat,' he growled. 'That would give me some satisfaction.'

Galastan rocked back on his heels, his lip curling. '*You should never have come to Westerling!*' he hissed. He remained for a moment with his face twisted into a scowl, then slowly relaxed and gave a low chuckle.

'Orvyn was easy to manipulate, the stupid fool. He couldn't have been less interested in the estate and believed everything I told him. Alas, my dear Lord Feran – if only you were more like him, you wouldn't be in this… this *desperate* situation.'

Galastan slapped himself softly on the thigh in self-congratulation. He waved his hand to encompass his three captives. 'Yes, this is perfect – this *place* is perfect – and I do enjoy it when a plan executes perfectly.'

He gestured toward Kuralin.

'I see you've told her about her husband,' he said, not bothering to lower his voice. 'It looks like her will has already departed – there's nothing left to keep out the cold. Her eyes are dead already. Her body will follow before tomorrow's dawn.' He shivered dramatically. 'I do believe it's getting colder.'

Kuralin appeared not to hear him. Previously so animated and optimistic – her eyes were now dull and vacant. She didn't seem to care what happened to her.

Galastan nodded toward Olgood and bent closer to Fenn. 'That one's strong,' he said confidentially, 'but he's been here a good while already. That altar stone is fiercely cold – as cold as a block of ice, and it's eating him – *gnawing* at him. Look at him – he's already racked with the chills. With what the Ariochs did to him – they must have cracked his skull – strong as he is, he's also unlikely to survive the night.'

Galastan stood up and took a step back, towards the entrance. 'You may live a little longer, but not much. The sky's clouding. It'll be cold tonight. *Deathly* cold. I don't believe you're dressed for it.'

He continued to back away.

'If you take my axe with you,' said Fenn, 'I'll find you and take it back.'

Galastan stopped walking.

'Hah! Will you indeed?' he sneered. 'Bold words. Such a positive attitude is admirable from someone in your position. You have some spirit. Maybe I should still take *you* as a thrall; I have a spare horse.' He pretended to think about it.

'Bah. You're not worth the trouble.' His lips creased into his usual mocking smirk. 'Unfortunately, your boldness is wasted on this occasion. Oh…' he held up a hand as if a thought had just occurred to him, '…are you thinking someone may happen by and find you?' He sniffed with disdain. 'No one comes here. The people are afraid of this place. It has a bad reputation.'

He continued to back away and spread his arms.

'When will your friends become worried, I wonder, if you don't return? Tomorrow morning? In that case, they may arrive at Moloch Tor tomorrow afternoon or evening. Too late, I fear.'

He flicked his hand dismissively.

'As for your axe – I have no need of your pagan axes. The Ariochs are my weapons.'

Galastan paused at the entrance to the enclosure and bowed theatrically.

'By your leave, M'Lord… I'm glad I waited to have this talk with you. I can say to anyone who asks that you were all alive when I last saw you. If you die after I've left – then God will have done the deed, not me. My soul need not be burdened.'

A final smirk. Galastan wiped his hands on his tunic, turned on his heel, and disappeared.

CHAPTER FIFTEEN

A disobedient follower

Fenn called: 'Kuralin…?' There was no answer.

'Kuralin…' Fenn tried again. 'What was your husband's name?'

Silence.

Fenn twisted his head. 'Olgood, how are *you*? Tell me the truth.'

After a pause, Olgood said: 'Galastan gave a f-fair descript-tion. The stone *is* deathly cold. I f-feel it seeping into me, numbing me, and I can't stop shiv-ering. It feels like my body's sh-shaking itself apart. M-my head is fog-gy. They t-tied me and gave m-me a kicking. Some b-bones in my face may be bro-ken.'

Fenn sucked in a mouthful of chilled air. Olgood desperately needed warmth – they all did.

'You s-said you were att-attacked by raiders from Corn… Cornwall?'

'Yes. We negotiated a truce. But unfortunately not before Kuralin's husband….'

A whisper from Kuralin: 'Alfric – his name was Alfric.'

'He was a brave man,' Fenn said. 'I wanted to know his name.'

She was silent. Fenn said: 'It may seem of little consolation now, but if you have nowhere else to go, you will always be welcome at Westerling.'

When she still made no reply, he added: 'Kuralin, our friends *will* come and find us. We just need to stay alive until they do. Talking will help.'

'Are they coming now…?'

'Not yet, but soon.'

'Is that someone outside?'

Fenn listened. Just as Olgood had said he was foggy, Fenn's head also felt muddled, with a constant noise, a buzzing, always present. Shaking his head to clear it caused a pounding in his temples. It felt as though his blood had thickened with the cold. He held his head still and waited but heard no other sound. Maybe the continuous noise in his ears was the wind. Was Kuralin just expressing her hopes? Or perhaps she hadn't heard him correctly.

'Not yet,' he said, 'but our friends know where….'

'Shush…' she said, urging him to be quiet.

Fenn listened. He still heard nothing.

A sound came from above – a cry from the direction of the window cut high in the stone wall. It wasn't a human sound. Could it be a crow? Some other wild animal? Fenn jerked his head back to look at the window. Through the small gap he saw only clouds. Whatever had made the sound was gone. Galastan had left only a few moments ago – it wasn't likely an animal would be prowling around Moloch Tor so soon after his departure.

A high-pitched menacing growl came from outside the enclosure. It was a noise Fenn hadn't heard before, but he could sense that the animal making it was annoyed and angry. A wolf? A wolf that also sounded like a crow? Whatever the creature was, it was circling around the stone tower toward the entrance.

He shuffled towards Kuralin as far as his rope would allow.

'Kuralin,' he whispered. 'Get as close to me as you can.'

Fenn pushed his back against the altar and bent his legs so he could kick out if the creature attacked. He heard running feet. The footsteps of something big. The beast entered the enclosure without slowing and was briefly outlined as a dark form against the light of the entranceway.

It was bigger than a wolf. It looked *human*.

He heard Olgood breathe a word. It was uttered softly, painfully, and emotionally.

'*Gisele!*'

GISELE CIRCLED THE ALTAR, her knife slicing the ropes pinning Olgood to the stone as if they were straw. She was muttering to herself continuously and angrily in her Frankish language. Her reaction to seeing her man lashed to the altar was still intense. Olgood groaned and tried to raise himself onto his elbow. The arm wouldn't hold him. He fell back onto his shoulder. She helped him roll off the rock into her arms, his weight collapsing them both to the floor. Gisele held him tightly, her head pressed to his chest, a prolonged distressed keening sounding in her throat. She lifted her head, her eyes moving over him as she eased Olgood into a sitting position, running her hand gently over his face. Her words were breathed from the depths of her soul.

'Olgood, *mon Dieu*,' she sobbed. 'What 'ave they done to you?'

She touched his hair where it was clotted with blood, lightly, worried that her touch could make the injury worse.

'Gisele…' Fenn prompted.

She turned to him with wide eyes, flicking a glance at Kuralin, remembering they were there. She moved to him, but he nodded urgently toward Kuralin.

'Her first,' he said, 'she's been nearly bent double.'

With the skill Gisele had demonstrated many times whether butchering a deer or filleting a fish, the knife moved with swift sure strokes and the ropes fell away from Kuralin. Whimpers of pain accompanied each freed limb as it unfolded. There were raw bloody rings on her ankles and wrists, evidence of her struggle against the ropes that bound her.

Fenn's bindings were removed in the same efficient fashion. He sat up, massaging his wrists.

'I *tell* you no one see me,' Gisele said, her eyes blazing at Fenn.

Olgood had fallen onto his side. She knelt by him and helped him to sit up again with his back against the altar. Her hands again softly touched the hair matted with blood. She drew a water skin from beneath her cloak, pulled the leather strap over her head and poured water on Olgood's face, wiping at the blood with her hand and sleeve, gently moving her fingers across his skin, feeling for damage. Olgood's eyes were impassive, never leaving hers.

'Did you see Galastan leave?' asked Fenn.

'Yes, I come as soon as they go.' She glanced back at him. 'And no worry – in forest I step in same places as 'orses.'

Gisele passed the water skin to Fenn. She shrugged off her cloak and eased Olgood forward, draping the garment across his shoulders. A violent shiver threatened to dislodge the cloak but Gisele held it in place and wrapped her arms around Olgood, pressing him to her, her hands rubbing his back, trying to force warmth into his body.

Fenn drank from the water skin, swirling the water around his mouth and tasting blood before swallowing. He crawled to be next to Kuralin, his limbs stiff from the cold and lack of use, and handed her the skin. She stared at it blankly, then reached out a hand, turning her tear-filled eyes to his as she drank. She coughed and a violent shiver passed through her body. Fenn gently placed his arm around her shoulders and drew her to him even though he could offer her little warmth.

He was looking for words of reassurance when Gisele spoke.

'I see Galastan throw your *manteau* in forest, Fenn,' she said, miming drawing a cloak around her shoulders. 'I know where. I see other *manteau* there… from…' she gestured towards Kuralin, '…Kuralin?'

'Yes, this is Kuralin.'

'Yes… he throw same place. Olgood axe with red 'andle also there.'

Fenn removed his arm from Kuralin and reached out, placing a hand on Gisele's arm.

'Gisele… I thank you from my heart. This is not the first time you've arrived just when and where you're needed, like a bright angel from heaven. I'm grateful you ignored me and came to Moloch Tor.' He brought his fist up and touched his chest twice, just above the heart – a salute to her – then he leaned forward and kissed her on the cheek.

She tilted her head and beamed her marvellous smile at him. Admonishing him and forgiving him at the same time.

He squeezed her arm. 'We need to fetch that clothing and get warm quickly. Can you make a fire?'

'Not here.' She waved her hand. 'No flint. Forest is wet.'

'Then we need the cloaks. Tell me where they are.'

He straightened his legs and winced with the pain of moving them.

Gisele hesitated. She took in a long breath.

'Hard for you to walk,' she said. '*I get axe and… manteaux* – cloaks. But you, please….' She looked back at Olgood.

Fenn said: 'I'll look after him.'

Kuralin sat forward. 'Let me,' she said. 'I know some healing.'

She looked up at Fenn. Some of the earlier life had returned to her eyes. Fenn nodded. Focusing on Olgood would take her mind away from her own situation.

Kuralin eased herself away from Fenn and crawled painfully towards Olgood. Gisele rose with a sympathetic murmur to help her. Kuralin looked to Olgood for his permission. He frowned at first, not knowing what she was asking, but then nodded and she knelt before him. Beginning at his ankle, she ran her hands up his leg.

'My legs are fine,' said Olgood. He was still shivering, but off the stone slab it was already less fierce.

'Shush,' Kuralin said. 'I saw them beat you. Let me check.'

She moved to the other leg. Once she had checked for broken bones, she rubbed the limb with her hands, warming the muscles.

Gisele watched her. When Kuralin moved her attention to Olgood's arms, Gisele stood up, nodded to Fenn and left the enclosure at a run.

OLGOOD'S MOVEMENTS WERE sluggish but once Fenn's heavy fur cloak had been shaken free of snow and fitted around his shoulders, replacing Gisele's smaller one, he insisted he could walk.

'I need to move to get warm,' he said, 'and I'd… like to get away from this… cursed place.'

'I left food 'idden in forest. Eating will 'elp warm us,' said Gisele. Fenn shook his head in admiration.

'Fenn…' Olgood reached out an unsteady hand. 'I didn't know the Arioch was… waiting in the Gap. I'm sorry… I couldn't warn you or help you.'

'You had your own problems,' Fenn said. 'No apology needed.'

Fenn grasped Olgood by the forearm in the custom of the Northmen and pulled the big man to his feet.

He straightened and looked Olgood in the eye. 'Not today, my friend.'

Olgood smiled. 'Not today,' he agreed.

It was an acknowledgement they had used several times during their escape from the Northmen. Death's presence had been close enough to be felt, but the Reaper had been denied and would not come calling today.

Olgood swayed and reached for the wall to steady himself. Fenn stooped to retrieve Olgood's axe and handed it to him, waiting patiently while Olgood clumsily fitted it into his belt. With the support of Gisele on one side and Fenn on the other, the big man shuffled towards the entrance. Kuralin, wearing her own cloak, followed, her stiff, jerky movements improving with each step.

At Cutthroats Gap, Fenn paused and peered into the alcove to see where the Arioch had lain in wait for him. He hoped his axe would be there – he'd heard it clang against stone when it was torn from his grasp. There was room enough for a man to be completely concealed inside the gap, but the space was empty.

In the daylight, Fenn stopped to check Olgood's wounds, but the injuries to his scalp were covered by his blond hair, which was matted black with blood. It was impossible to see how severe they were without taking the time to wash him.

Gisele was watching him. Her eyes told him not to worry; Olgood was in her care now.

Fenn turned his head to scan the edge of the forest surrounding Moloch Tor.

'Must leave now,' Gisele said. 'Long way to West'ling. We not be there before night.'

'You three go ahead,' Fenn said. 'I need to find Thorvald's axe. I can't leave it here.'

'We should stay together,' said Olgood. 'We'll help you.'

'No. Don't wait for me. Olgood, you can't move fast and you need to be moving to keep warm. You must get off this peak. Galastan may decide to check the box and return.'

'What is the box Galastan was talking about?' asked Olgood.

'He forced me to bring him a box but it doesn't contain what he thinks it does. I'll explain later. So, keep a watch for him.' Fenn motioned toward the path. 'Gisele's right. You must leave now.'

Fenn held out a hand to Kuralin. 'Will you come with us to Westerling?'

Kuralin hesitated, then nodded and moved to take Fenn's place, draping Olgood's arm across her shoulders.

Gisele frowned at Fenn. 'Too cold for you to be 'ere without… cloak,' she said.

'They won't have thrown the axe far. I'll be quick. I'll catch up with you. Please, go now.'

He took a step back.

Gisele's face creased with concern. 'Only look for *short* time, Fenn. If not find, you 'urry and catch us.'

She and Kuralin helped Olgood toward the path leading into the forest. The big man was bearing most of his weight, but his arms sagged heavily on their shoulders.

FENN QUICKLY SEARCHED among the five long stone towers of Moloch Tor. He was methodical, circling the base of each tower – but he found nothing. He saw where the horses had been tethered and hoped Galastan had spoken the truth when he said he had no need of pagan axes.

From the flattened peak, he could see over the tangled forest to the moor. The sun was low and the light would soon be fading. Time was running out. He descended to the nearest part of the forest, skirting along the edge of the trees, looking for any disturbance in the snow that might indicate where his axe had been discarded. His heart leapt when he found a place where the fresh snow had recently been trampled, but there was nothing there. It must be where the cloaks and Olgood's axe had been left and retrieved by Gisele.

He moved on, searching in the snow around the treetrunks and the tangled undergrowth of the forest, ignoring the growing lack of feeling in his feet, circling the mound of Moloch Tor.

When he returned to where the cloaks and axe had lain, he realised he'd fruitlessly covered the entire peak.

He'd taken too long. The need for care and concentration in his search had hidden the fact that, despite his movement, his body was gradually succumbing to the fierce cold. As well as his feet, his hands and lower legs were now numb, and his face was aching with exposure to the chilled air. Any reserves of energy kindled by being freed from his bonds were now exhausted and every movement was laboured.

The sun was setting. It was hopeless. He needed to give up the search and escape from the frozen peak without further delay.

Reluctantly, Fenn climbed up to the stone towers and turned in the direction of the path. He had failed Thorvald by losing his axe. He resolved to return to Moloch Tor in a day or two and resume the search. He passed by the entrance to the sacrificial altar, scanning over the tops of the trees for a view of Olgood and Gisele. They should be visible on the moor by now.

From deep in the forest, a flash of sunlight on metal caught the corner of his eye. Fenn peered in the direction, shading his eyes. At first he saw only trees – then the bright glint was repeated.

His heart leapt. It had to be the axe, high up, caught in the top branches, swaying in the bitter wind, the shiny blade briefly but sharply reflecting the rays of the setting sun. There it was again, another spark of light. Fenn took a moment to estimate the distance – it wasn't far, only fifteen or twenty paces into the forest.

He scrambled down to the treeline and pushed his way between two of the warped trunks.

Immediately the snow deepened and the ground underfoot became uneven and deformed, affected by the same malady as the trees. Fenn climbed a ridge and stumbled into a hole. It was dark under the forest canopy and forms were indistinct. He kept moving forward, counting his steps. The upheaval of the forest floor and the dense undergrowth made holding a true line to his estimated destination almost impossible. Large stones hidden by the snow twisted his ankles, forcing him to tread carefully. He fell into a snow-filled hollow thick with vines and struggled to disentangle himself and climb out. The carpet of freezing snow covered everything – an unwelcome icy ally to the already life-threatening frosty air. His staggering path confused his count and he had to concentrate on only counting the steps that headed directly toward the axe. When that count reached fifteen, he stopped and turned in a circle, looking up.

Nothing.

Through the dense foliage, there was only a faint glow left in the sky. The sun had set. He moved forward a few more steps to peer around a tree and groaned with relief.

Fenn had thought his axe would simply be discarded, thrown aside – but the strong arm of an Arioch had tossed it deep into the forest. If it had fallen through the canopy to the forest floor, Fenn would never have found it, but the wide blade had lodged in the high nest of entangled branches of a tree with a trunk bent into the shape of a swan's neck. The iron handle was just visible in the gloom, hanging vertically.

Fenn grunted in triumph and forced a path up a rise through a thicket of vines. The handle was out of reach. He felt for his sling but stopped – he needed something heavier. He plunged his hands into the snow, searching for the stones that threatened to trip his every step, ignoring the cold gnawing at his exposed fingers.

It took two accurate stones striking forcefully on the blade to dislodge the axe. The weapon tumbled noisily in a cascade of snow until its fall was arrested by another branch – but this time the handle was within reach. He took as firm a hold on the handle as his shaking hand would allow and wrenched the axe from the tree's grasp, exclaiming his triumph. He ran his fingers up the iron handle, along the blade, and, satisfied it had suffered no damage, thankfully and exultantly forced his fumbling fingers to slip Thorvold's axe into his belt.

He now had but one desire. Get away from the deadly peak of Moloch Tor, catch up with Olgood, and return to Westerling.

He was suddenly weary. He turned to retrace his steps.

The forest around him was black.

CHAPTER SIXTEEN

The secret of the forest of the Lesidhe

It should have been simple to take twenty paces back to Moloch Tor, but somewhere in the darkness he'd turned in the wrong direction. He recalled Edelred's warning about this forest. Had the forest confused and trapped him?

Edelred had said ominously: *Men have disappeared.*

He was lost.

He no longer knew which way he'd just come. Uphill should lead him back to the tor and downhill to the moor, but there were so many depressions and rises that *uphill* and *downhill* were not easy directions to follow. He'd stopped shivering – he wasn't sure if that was a good sign or bad. Maybe he was still shivering but couldn't feel it. His thoughts whirled. Perhaps staying in the forest was a *good* idea. At least among the trees he had the benefit of *some* shelter from the bitter wind. But among the trees was where the snow was deepest.

He reached out blindly to steady himself and his hand curled around the rough gnarled surface of a branch. He tried to slow his laboured breathing. With every rapid intake of air, he could feel the icy cold biting at his throat.

The chill had forced the weariness from his muscles deep into his bones. It took an effort to raise his head. The intense dark pressed on his eyes. He had to blink to make sure they were open. The emptiness remained unchanged no matter which direction he turned his head.

A heavy silence surrounded him. If the wind was still moving the treetops, it wasn't evident on the forest floor. The only sense he had to guide him was touch. He lifted his other hand and met leaves and then another branch, maybe the same one. His knees sagged with a sudden loss of strength and he hung, supported only by his hands.

'No,' a voice said. 'You will not fall here. This is *not* where it ends.'

He lifted a foot, bringing it underneath him to bear his weight.

'Now the other foot,' the voice said.

He realised the insistent voice was his own. He wasn't sure whether the words had been said aloud. He dragged his second foot to join the first, fighting the resistance of the snow.

With a concentrated effort, he straightened his legs and squared his shoulders, reasserting control over his body – and felt satisfaction in achieving this minor success – but the feeling of victory was short-lived. A surge of strength was not enough to save him. He needed substantial shelter and warmth soon or he would eventually and certainly be overwhelmed by the cold. His body was already shutting down. Where could he possibly find a haven in such a god-forsaken forest?

He could use the axe to build a crude lodge from tree branches and bushes if the rising of the moon provided light enough to see by, but without something more, without fire or at least a covering to wrap around him and trap the last of his body heat, even a shelter would not be enough.

His situation was desperate. He felt caught in a trap, and the time he needed to escape from this trap was sifting through his fingers. He stared into the blackness with a new intensity, his eyes seeking relief from the blanket of nothingness that covered him.

He knew he couldn't stay here; he *must* move. Just pick a direction and go. But which direction?

The inky black was disturbed by a flicker – like a sliver of moonlight reflecting on a falling snowflake. It was there for an instant, then it was gone.

He moved his head to the side – blackness. Then the glimmer reappeared. It was real.

Whatever that light was, it was a long way away.

But it was light. Another movement. This time unmistakable. A *fire*.

He drew the axe from his belt and leant on it to support his unsteady legs, then raised a foot and pointed it toward the light.

A brief flash of light had invited him into the forest, and now another beckoning light was drawing him deeper.

ONLY THE LURE AND promise of the fire kept him moving.

It became a beacon of hope that drove his body forward, each action automatic, step after step without thought. He tripped and tumbled to his knees several times, bruising them on the stones, each fall a drain on his meagre reserves of strength – he spent as much time rising from the snow as pushing through it. Each time he thrust his bare hands into the snow to push himself up, more heat leeched from his body.

His hands became blocks of ice, unfeeling and unable to keep a firm hold of the axe which slipped from his fingers at the slightest knock or twist, causing more precious body warmth to be lost and more precious time to be wasted as he fumbled for the weapon in the snow.

He lost the light but he stumbled on and it reappeared.

THE FIRE WAS SMALL but it burned brightly in the clearing.

He dropped his axe and collapsed against a bent tree trunk, using the remnants of feeling left in his fingers to clutch at the rough bark and hold himself upright. It took him several moments to steady his breathing and gather enough strength to speak.

He called to the fire: 'I'm alone and cold and mean you no harm. May I share your fire?'

His voice sounded weak. He hoped it would reach the man sitting in the clearing.

The man made no movement and appeared not to have heard.

Fenn rested his head against the tree trunk and gathered himself for another effort.

The man spoke first. 'I heard your approach, young man. Your spirit burns very dimly. Tell me – what colour are your eyes?'

The man spoke softly but his voice was clear in the chilled air. It carried the crackle of age. Fenn heard an accent he could not place. The old man was not from this area.

He frowned at the unexpected question. He shook his head and, in his weariness, even that action made him light-headed, forcing him to take a half-step to steady himself. He dug his fingers into the tree trunk to keep himself from falling.

'Blue,' he croaked.

'Ah yes, the blue of the deep sea. Good. Come closer, Blue-Eyes.'

Fenn pushed himself away from the tree and bent to retrieve his axe from the snow one more time, fighting to force his fingers to curl around the handle. He thought it best not to approach the man carrying a weapon, so he stood, shuffling and swaying, as he struggled to replace his axe into the loop on his belt. His hands wouldn't function properly – wouldn't obey him. At the very moment when Fenn felt he'd lost control, the handle found the leather loop and the axe slid into place. During the length of time this simple action took Fenn to accomplish, the old man waited patiently, unmoving and silent.

Hunching his shoulders and tucking his hands into his armpits to keep the last traces of heat from escaping, Fenn shuffled toward the fire, each slow and deliberate footstep a leaden, unsteady plod. Even at his approach, the old man did not look up – remaining hunched over the low flames, stoking the embers with a long stick. He wore a thick cloak that shone golden in the firelight – the hood pulled forward, covering his face.

Now that Fenn was closer, what had seemed to be a cliff face behind the seated figure resolved into a trio of standing stones, each twice the height of a man. The old man sat in the centre of the triangle formed by the enormous stones. A sanctuary.

Just as at the towers of Moloch Tor, the ground surrounding the stones was strangely free of snow.

'Stop there.'

Fenn frowned again. He was only a few steps from the warmth of the fire and salvation. A few steps from the place where his body could absorb heat rather than lose it.

He stopped.

'Kneel.'

'What…?'

'*Kneel down.*' The words were said in the same soft raspy voice, but they were a command.

If he knelt, Fenn doubted he would have the strength to rise again. He was ten paces from the fire. Its tantalising breath brushed against his face and the desire to embrace that warmth and feel its healing heat soaking into his bones was overwhelming.

What would the man do if he just walked forward and sat down?

Fenn's thoughts were muddled. The voice in his head told him it would not be polite. But desperate men, he argued, might be forgiven such a breach of manners. It was more than politeness, the voice said – it was a matter of honour. If he had the energy, he would have shaken his head to rid himself of this annoying voice. Why was he having such a conversation? The situation was simply defined; his body was dangerously cold. It needed to be warmed or he would die.

He lowered himself to a kneeling position in the snow and let his head sink to his chest.

His feet were numb. His hands were numb. He could feel physical tendrils of cold from the frozen snow creeping up from his knees and moving relentlessly along his thighs, reaching for his vitals.

The man said nothing. The wind had died. The only sound in the clearing was the crackle of the fire, punctuated once by a loud crack behind Fenn as the intense cold snapped something in the forest.

After a while, Fenn summoned his strength and raised his head. The man hadn't moved. Only his beardless chin showed beneath the hood of his cloak.

Fenn could not feel his thighs – his legs had disappeared. He cleared his throat to speak.

The man spoke first. 'Ah… do you have something to say?'

'I need the fire.'

'Wait.'

Fenn surveyed the scene through half-closed lids. As far as he could tell, the moon had not yet risen to relieve the darkness – maybe it would never show its light on this cloudy night. The black of the forest was intense among the trees to his left and right. Even aided by the firelight, his visibility extended no more than a few paces. To his front, the clearing was dominated by the glare of the fire, blinding him to whatever lay beyond.

Was the old man afraid or just cautious? Were there others nearby? It was hard to think.

Even if the man now allowed him to approach, he didn't think he'd be able to rise from his kneeling position. He'd waited too long and forfeited the ability to move his legs. His choices were being stripped from him.

If he stayed here in the snow, he would die. He was probably dying now. He felt sleepy, strangely content and at peace – even with the immediate idea of death in his head. The sounds of the fire faded and were replaced by his own hoarse breathing. He was surprised his chest was still accepting air. He could not feel its rise and fall. The sounds he took to be his own breathing were too quick and too shallow, like the panting of a dog, barely keeping him alive, but it gave him comfort to hear them. As long as those sounds persisted, he was not dead. That thought stirred a memory – another situation where the only indication of life was the noise of breathing – but it wouldn't come to mind.

The voice returned to his head, sounding faint, coming from far away. It spoke three words.

'*Move… Or… Die.*'

Fenn's body would not obey. It was no longer under his command – it had surrendered to the adversary that had threatened him from the moment he had arrived at Moloch Tor – the biting, intense, almost *unnatural* cold.

He felt the frozen fingers of death invading his soul.

Silence.

A spark refused to be extinguished. He thrust his hands once more into the snow, pushing upward.

HE WAS TIGHTLY WRAPPED in a coarse blanket, lying on his back. The fire was close, *too* close. As welcome as the heat was, waving wisps of flame were stretching out, reaching for him, attempting to sear his skin. The side of his face was burning hot. He wriggled his body to ease himself away from the intensity of the flames, his limbs responding reluctantly, every movement generating the agony of a hundred needles piercing the skin.

His axe was gone – it should have been pressing into his side. The crackle of burning wood filled his ears. There were new piles of branches beside the fire, drying. It was a larger fire now – a fire for two instead of one.

The old man must be stronger than he looked if he had dragged Fenn to the fire and wrapped him in a blanket.

'You are welcome at my fire, Blue-Eyes.'

The voice came from behind. Fenn twisted his head and the old man came into view. As before, he sat with his head lowered. He looked as though he hadn't moved from his original position. A piece of burning wood fell from the fire with a hiss. Had Fenn stayed where he was, the flames from the branch would now have been licking at his blanket. The man calmly reached around Fenn and used his stick to return the errant limb to the confines of the fire.

'Thank you,' said Fenn. His voice was a whisper. His eye caught his axe leaning against one of the standing stones alongside a long staff – a thick straight pole, probably used by the old man to help him walk.

'It's a cold night,' the old man said. He formed his words slowly but deliberately. That and his accent told Fenn this was not his native tongue.

After a moment's silence, the man said: 'You could have approached without permission. You're a strong lad – even if I objected, it's possible I couldn't have stopped you.'

Fenn drew in a breath. How did the man know he'd considered that action?

When there was no immediate reply, the man continued: 'Your clothing is not suitable for the forest, and your body was desperately cold – why not just walk to the fire and take its healing warmth? We could have made our introductions later, when you'd recovered. I would have understood that, wouldn't I? You said you meant me no harm.'

Even in the unusual circumstances, there was a hint of something more at play – more than the man's accent, or the question about Fenn's eyes, or his request to kneel in the snow. Something else was strange about this man. The scene had a mysterious and unreal quality. The three huge standing stones loomed over the man's head, creating a glow like an aura around him. Was Fenn dreaming? He shook his head. His thinking was still muddled. Questions appeared and disappeared in his mind before he could find answers. The man seemed to be testing him, playing with him. He thought for a moment about his answer.

'It was *your* fire. It would not have been….' He paused.

'Would not have been what?' the old man asked. 'Correct? Polite? Honourable? Or perhaps it would not have been the way of the forest – especially *this* forest, the forest of the *Lesidhe*?'

The man was repeating the same arguments Fenn had considered, plucking his own words from inside his head. He tried to think. He was too tired.

'Yes,' he said. 'All of those.'

The man gave a grunt, appearing to be satisfied by the answer. He raised his head, and his eyes, which were still in shadow, stared at Fenn from beneath the hood with an intensity that, although he could not see them, felt like a physical force.

A moment passed when neither moved. The eyes inside the dark hood seemed to be searching – appraising him. In that moment, a strong gust of wind whistled through the trees – an eerie high-pitched groan that rushed out from the forest, flattening the fire and swirling around the tall stones.

It was as if the forest had spoken and delivered its verdict.

The old man laid his stick on the ground. Both hands appeared from beneath the cloak and Fenn saw them clearly for the first time. The firelight drew bright vivid flashes of red and blue from two large rings on the man's fingers as he eased back the hood covering his head.

Fenn saw the face beneath the hood, and he gasped.

CHAPTER SEVENTEEN

Illusions and prophecies

When Fenn had approached the fire through the trees, the figure sitting beside it was small and hunched over – an old man with a back bent by age. When the person had spoken, the voice was low and weak and contained a rasp, the voice of an old man.

The face Fenn now saw was not that of an old man.

It was the face of a woman and, although the long straight hair framing her face and tucked under her chin was the silver colour of moonlight, she was not old.

Fenn was instantly reminded that this was not the first time in recent days that he had mistaken a woman for a man – Rowena, the young girl in the market. But there was a difference – *this* time the deception was deliberate.

Again, the woman seemed to hear his thoughts. She straightened her back.

'What do you think of my illusion?' Her voice had changed. The accent had gone. The harsh crackle had disappeared and the tone was now unmistakably feminine.

'Your *illusion*? I don't understand....'

She tilted her head to look down at him and, in the flickering firelight, her eyes sparkled with amusement. They were startlingly blue – as blue as his own, but there was a depth to them. She gave a small chuckle and smiled. Her smile was amiable and expressed satisfaction, but in the next moment there was also a weariness as though she had now tired of the game.

'My deception was effective, was it not?'

'Yes, I was deceived,' admitted Fenn. 'But why?'

He felt uncomfortably hot. He tried to wriggle further from the flames, his face creasing with the effort.

She kept her gaze steady without replying, waiting for him to be still, then she tilted her head and raised her shoulders.

'A reasonable question, Blue-Eyes,' she said. She thought a moment.

'I didn't know your intentions, but...' she shook her head sadly, '...perhaps it was just a habit... an old habit that I adopted automatically when I heard the noises you made stumbling towards my fire. Why the illusion? It would have given me all the advantage I needed – had I needed an advantage.'

Her answer raised more questions.

'If I had rushed in, what would have happened?'

'That cannot be known. I cannot speak for the Earth Mother, but my companion and I would have found it unacceptable.' As she spoke, she reached out and ran a hand along the staff resting against the tall stone beside Fenn's axe.

The Earth Mother? Was she saying the forest was involved? Her reference to her staff as her companion suggested it was more than a walking aid.

She stood up. 'I think you are heated enough on one side, Blue-Eyes, don't you? We'll let the fire attend to your other side.'

Her words were uncomfortably similar to those used when discussing the roasting of meat.

Both hands emerged from the cloak again, and Fenn clearly saw the two distinctive rings, one on each hand. On the middle finger of her right hand, a thick band of gold was topped with a large blue stone. On the left hand, a similar-sized red stone flickered in the firelight. There was a design etched into the stones but Fenn couldn't catch the detail.

She lifted his wrapped feet and walked him in a half-circle. His head swung close to the fire but at just the right time, a rush of wind pushed the flames away from him – or maybe the wind was caused by his own movement.

When she sat again, Fenn was facing her. The move had tightened the blanket around him. He shrugged his shoulders to relieve the stiffness that had crept into his neck and shifted his arms to ease his confinement but was unable to loosen the blanket. He was as contained as a caterpillar inside a cocoon. Had she deliberately restricted his movement? She appeared not to notice his writhing.

Fenn relaxed. The blanket and the fire *were* warming him, and the tight wrapping ensured it was a slow warming. He knew the pain and damage a too-fast warming of a cold body can cause.

'So…' he said when he had achieved a measure of comfort, '…did I pass your test?'

She leaned forward, her eyes enveloping him. 'I wasn't testing you, Blue-Eyes; I was *judging* you.'

'Judging me? How?'

'Every action you took, the actions you did not take, every word you spoke and the way it was spoken, told me about *you* – told me your story. I presented you with decisions to make and placed some obstacles in your path, but they were only partly physical. Mostly you battled against yourself. There was no correct reaction – there was only *your* reaction.'

'But… why? Why judge me? Why not simply let me share your fire?'

'People do not enter this forest willingly, yet our paths crossed here. It was important to learn the fibre of the man the Earth Mother had sent me.'

'Who are you?' The question was out before he thought about it.

Her eyes narrowed.

'If you're asking for my name, which name would you like?' she demanded. 'The name my mother gave me? Or the name my brute of a father spat at me? The name I'm called by the common folk? Or do you want to know one of the names I've earned?'

Fenn hesitated, surprised by the intensity of her answer.

'The name you think I should know you by.'

Her face softened and the corners of her mouth creased.

'A good answer, Blue-Eyes.' She waved an apologetic hand in the air. 'As you see, the twists of my life's journey have tended me to be overly defensive at times.' She leaned back. 'You are different, Blue-Eyes. A fresh cool breeze in the heat of summer.'

She stared at him, her intense eyes seeming to lay his soul bare.

Her next words, when they came, were slow and deliberate.

'You would not break your code of honour,' she said, 'even with Death's fetid breath shrouding your face, its bony rotten fingers reaching for your soul. Even so… you overcame the selfish pleading of the flesh to lay down and surrender. You have an inner strength, a core more solid and uncorrupted than I've met in… a very long while. And… I think you already know this – I sense in you a harmony of spirit that can be felt by those attuned to it. That's a gift from the Earth Mother. You must have learned this from her creatures.'

Was she speaking of his way with animals? He put the thought aside. Her talk of many names intrigued him. He would like to know them all, but for now, the one she wanted him to use would do.

'I have only one name,' he said, 'and that is Fenn.' Immediately he realised that wasn't true.

'Mmm? Are you sure? Maybe you're unaware of your other names.'

'Well, my name is really Feran, but….'

Her eyes flashed. '*Feran*, is it?' she interrupted. She leaned back. 'That's an unusual name. But it's also an *interesting* name.'

She regarded him again with her penetrating gaze.

'The mystery of your presence here becomes clearer,' she said. 'You are Lord Feran, new Thane of Westerling.'

Fenn was too surprised to speak for a moment.

'I've been Thane of Westerling for three days,' he said incredulously. 'How could you possibly know that?'

'I do not always sit beside a fire here at Lumenthal,' she said. 'Galastan, tenant-in-chief of Westerling, came to Moloch Tor yesterday. I saw him. I heard him and his two ogres talking about Lord Feran of Westerling.'

'If you heard their plans to capture me, you could have warned me.'

'The Earth Mother does not need my interference.' She smiled her enigmatic smile. 'But I did help by setting my fire so that you might be guided to me.'

'How did you know I needed guidance?'

'Anyone who enters the forest of the Lesidhe and blunders about as you did when night arrives, needs guidance. It's an unusual forest, this one, and dangerous – until you know its ways. Not a place to be lost. I heard you and added some wood to my fire – maybe you would see it.'

'And that was not interfering with the… Earth Mother?'

'No. As I said, *maybe* you would see it – if you had not already given up hope as many do and if you happened to keep your eyes open and look in the right direction.'

Even with the hood back and her silver hair free of her face, it was difficult to determine her age – but her beauty was undeniable. Fenn caught himself staring at her rounded face with full lips, high cheeks, and soft but piercing blue eyes. It had a timeless quality, the sort of beauty that remains constant even into old age. She caught his appraising look and returned it in kind without embarrassment.

'*Fer-an*…' she said, elongating the name, savouring it. 'An old name. A relic from an old language. It tells me you will struggle to settle. You're a wanderer.'

She waggled a finger at him.

'Where have you wandered from, Feran the Wanderer?'

'I was raised on the Holy Island of Lindisfarne, in Northumbria.'

'The monastery at Lindisfarne was attacked by the Northmen two years ago. Were you there then?'

'Yes,' said Fenn. 'I was captured on that day by the Northmen, but I escaped.' He sighed. 'It's a long story….'

She sat back. 'I see that in your eyes. Your experience was… unpleasant and painful.'

He nodded, tired and unwilling to begin a tale that would take a long time to tell.

'Painful it may have been, but you overcame the trial and it made you stronger. However…' she waved a hand, '…we can leave it there.'

She stared at him for a moment, then tilted her head.

'You are young to be a thane,' she said, 'and you weren't born to it. But, although they couldn't say why, those around you *feel* your strength of spirit and will obey you without question. You're a leader.'

'A leader?' Fenn mused, half to himself. 'Maybe,' he conceded. On impulse, he asked: 'But I wonder… what makes a *good* leader?'

'I can answer that…' she regarded him with deep bottomless eyes, '…if you need me to.'

Fenn met her gaze. He had the feeling those eyes held the answers to all questions. He nodded.

'You can only be a good leader,' she said, 'when you desire for your people what you desire for yourself.'

Fenn didn't reply. After a moment, she added: 'But I think you already knew the answer to your question. You have a strong future in this land.'

'Can you tell the future? Are you a soothsayer?'

She blew a breath between her teeth. 'A soothsayer? If you're asking can I predict what will happen tomorrow using magic… that depends on what you think of as magic.' Her eyes crinkled with amusement. 'I use no magic, only knowledge available to anyone who cares to look and listen, who takes time to understand the *connections* around us….' She waved a hand in a circle to indicate the trees, the forest, the land – maybe beyond. 'I use *ancient* knowledge passed down. I *listen*, I *look*, and I remember, as my mother taught me.'

She turned her intense stare on him. 'But you are correct,' she said. 'For you, I *am* a soothsayer. I do say sooth; I say the truth.'

She clasped her hands together and sat for a long moment in contemplation, then she rose smoothly to her feet from her seated position. She gathered the long wooden staff and, turning her back to Fenn, held the staff at arm's length facing the three massive stones. He heard some muttered words but couldn't tell whether they were directed inward or to the stones. The fire crackled, talking to the forest, the burning branches popping and sighing. When she turned back she was frowning and seemed dissatisfied. She saw the question on his face.

'It's not clear to me yet how I should help you,' she said. 'But I'm sure it will become so before our paths part.'

'You've helped me already by providing a fire and warmth without which I'd almost certainly be dead, and… as you said… guiding me to it. I'm grateful to you for that, and in return, anything I can do for you – you need but ask….'

'That's the past. I'm talking about what I can do in the future.'

'Why do you think I need more help?'

'Our paths met at Lumenthal for a reason.'

'A reason other than to save my life?'

She nodded but didn't answer. Instead, she settled herself back into her seated position.

'You can call me Arielle.'

Fenn smiled at her abrupt return to his question.

'If it's not impertinent, which of your names is that?'

She shared his amusement. 'The name I think you should know me by. Others you may learn in time.'

Fenn hesitated. Many things about this woman and this place were strange and mysterious. She may consider some questions unwelcome. Given her sensitivity regarding her name, he felt he should tread carefully.

'Arielle, why are you at… *Lumenthal* – is that the name of this place? As you said, most people would never choose to enter this forest, let alone stay here. It is not an inviting place with its weird misshapen trees, its deathly cold air and snow-covered ground. It deserves its bad reputation.'

She was silent for so long that Fenn thought he *had* crossed a line and she was refusing to answer. He was about to apologise when she spoke.

'Lumenthal is a sacred place to me and my order, and it's located here beneath Moloch Tor for a reason. The cold you can ignore, if you know how.' She waved a hand. 'These sacred stones have stood on this spot since long before the first seeds of the forest were sown. To explain Lumenthal would take a long time – you need to *feel* it and you can't do that until you're ready. The stones are my history and my foundation. This is a place of solace for me and a place of healing and renewal should I need it.'

'Your order?' Edelred had mentioned that Moloch Tor was sacred to the Druids. 'Do you mean the Druids? I thought that order no longer existed.'

She grunted derisively. 'The Druids? No. They knew nothing of the Earth Mother. They concerned themselves too much with passing judgment on their fellow men. They coveted power and were inclined to use sacrifice and fear as their primary tools.' She looked at him. 'You've seen the altar at Moloch Tor. That was a site for Druid sacrifices.' She tilted her head and raised her eyebrows. 'Do you *know* the name Moloch?'

Fenn shook his head.

'Moloch is a cruel pagan god with the head of a bull – he deals in *child* sacrifice. The Druids made no secret of their love for that horrible practice.' She screwed up her nose. 'They're gone, no loss to anyone, and thankfully their altar will claim no more victims.'

'It almost claimed Olgood,' said Fenn under his breath.

'Olgood?'

Fenn looked up, surprised she'd heard him.

'A good friend. Galastan had him beaten and tied to the altar.'

'Ah… the big man. He was in a bad way when they brought him to the tor. I thought he was dead or soon dead. Did you free him?'

'He was freed, but not by me. If all's gone well, he's heading to Westerling.'

She looked at him, her eyes narrowed and serious. 'Good. I'm glad the Druid's stone didn't take him.'

'So if you're not a Druid…' said Fenn, '…then…?'

'Enough of names for now.' She stood up again. 'Are you warmed enough to believe you may live a while longer?'

'I think so.'

'Then the time has come to prepare some food. Let me unwrap you.'

THE MORNING SUN FILLED the day with promise, shining from a bright sky dotted with clusters of woolly clouds, a sight Fenn had recently wondered if he would ever see again.

He gazed in the direction of Westerling. Before him, the barren moor stretched to the horizon. Behind him loomed the tor, surrounded by the strange wreath of twisted trees that Arielle called the forest of the Lesidhe. A stiff cold wind filtered through the trees and was pushing insistently at his back, urging him to leave this place.

Even without his cloak, the chill of Moloch Tor was no longer threatening. He felt refreshed – whether from his unbroken sleep warmly re-wrapped in a blanket by the fire or, as Arielle suggested, from the healing power of the standing stones of Lumenthal, or both – he didn't know. In any case, the buffeting of the frigid air sweeping off the peak was only a minor distraction.

'How long will you stay at Westerling?' she asked.

Arielle stood at his side, leaning on her staff. Fenn knew a stout staff could be formidable in skilled hands. Was this her weapon of choice?

He considered her question. 'For a time,' he said. 'The land is good. It's a fine place with good people. There's a lot that can be done there.'

'Then the wanderer's story will continue to unfold in Wessex.' She nodded slowly and muttered something to herself. Fenn thought she said: '*It shall be so.*'

She turned to face him, her eyes sparkling. 'Now I know how I can help you.'

She regarded him – the eyes that contained such depth making their final appraisal.

'Another name I'm known by is *Anesidora*,' she said, '…*giver of gifts*. I have a gift for you.'

She lifted her hand and eased the red-stoned ring from her finger. She held it tightly enclosed in her palm and muttered some more words. Then, reaching down, she slipped it onto the little finger of Fenn's left hand. On her finger, it had looked too small for him, but it fitted perfectly.

'Now I will travel with you,' she said.

Fenn raised his hand to better see the ring. Within the blood-red stone, somehow carved into the interior, a design was visible – a triangle containing a spiral that wound into the shape of an eye.

'I can't accept….' He looked up and stopped, his protest silenced by her expression.

He returned his eyes to the ring. 'Are you sure? This is gold – it's a valuable ring.'

'Yes,' agreed Arielle. 'It is one of only two.' She raised a finger. 'One rule – never take it off or move it. It must stay where I have placed it.'

'Is the design significant to your order?'

'Yes.'

He looked up when she didn't elaborate.

'What does it mean?'

'Nothing you need to know just yet.'

Fenn shook his head. 'How can this ring help me?'

'It introduces you, announces your connection to me, and carries a message to those who recognise it.'

Members of her order? Her answers just raised more questions. When he frowned, she smiled and added: 'How dull this land would be without mysteries to be solved. Be patient.'

She turned away from him, staring out over the moor.

'You asked if I can tell the future….' She clasped the staff with both hands and held it before her. Her head lowered and her breathing became slower and deeper, seeming to tune to her surroundings.

Fenn waited. The wind chose that moment to swirl and moan around the towers of Moloch Tor. A strong gust rustled the forest trees and swept out across the moor. Arielle's hair was blown forward, concealing her face. She remained still, seemingly unconcerned, while her hair was buffeted back and forth. Fenn had the absurd thought that the wind, and perhaps the Earth Mother, was communicating with her.

She raised her head and a hand absentmindedly brushed the hair aside.

'I have three pieces of a picture, fragments, to share with you – and there is no order to them.'

She paused, seemingly awake and asleep at the same time, her body still but her eyes shining.

'First, there may come a time when your weary body is bloody. A friend is dying. Perhaps you could have saved this friend if you'd made different choices. It is your nature to worry about making the right decisions. But, heed this… the other way, the way of a different choice, was *never written*. You are only a part of the forces that choose the way. Remember me and remember Lumenthal at that time.'

'My body is *bloody* and a friend *dying*?' he exclaimed. 'Are you talking of injury? In a battle?'

'There is tension in this land…' she waved her hand across the moor, her gesture extending beyond the horizon, her movement slow as if in a trance, '…and tension will build until there is change. Nothing brings about change more than a battle.'

'So you see a battle coming?'

'In these times, a battle is always coming.'

Fenn drew a long breath through his nose and released it. 'You seem to want to tell me something, without actually telling me anything.'

She smiled, and seemed to emerge from her trance-like state.

'The mist will rise. Remember my words so you may recognise the moment their meaning becomes clear.'

Her golden cloak glowed in the early morning sunlight, and, augmented by her sparkling blue eyes and shining silver hair, her smile created such an image of beauty that Fenn could not help but admire the vision and return her smile.

After a moment, he said: 'You said there were three… ah… fragments?'

Her face became serious. She nodded and rested a hand on his arm.

'I believe you have a strong destiny – one that will play an important part in the future of Wessex. I expect your hand will influence the course of events at the highest level, maybe concerning the next king of Wessex.' Her hand tightened on his arm to emphasise her words, her eyes holding his for a moment before her hand released him.

'The *next* king? Beorhtric is not an old man. He should rule for many years.'

'Yes, of course,' she said. 'Unless he does not live to old age.'

What was she referring to? Murder? Accident? Conspiracy? Death in Battle? Was Arielle suggesting *Fenn* would be the next king?

He suddenly thought of Egbert's claim to the throne of Wessex.

'What do you know?'

'What do I *know*?' Arielle smiled. 'I'm not talking about what I know. I'm talking about what the Earth Mother reveals to me, what my ears hear and my eyes see, and what my reason and my knowledge of this land and its workings tell me. I'm talking about what I see in *you*, Fenn the Wanderer, who is also now called Blue-Eyes and Lord Feran, Thane of Westerling.'

She said she saw strength in him, but it seemed to Fenn that the actions he chose simply depended on what was in front of him and what he wanted to accomplish. How did that show strength? Was the measure of strength based on outcome? In his experience, outcomes often contained components that were outside his control. Even so, it was true that people expected him to lead. Or perhaps he just assumed leadership. Maybe that was his strength.

He caught his rambling thoughts and reined them in.

'Does the name Egbert have any meaning to you?' he asked impulsively.

'Egbert? Well, your question already tells me something about this man.'

'My *question*? How so?'

'You raise his name after I have talked about your role in the affairs of Wessex.' She raised a hand to again push strands of wind-blown hair from her eyes and her brow creased in thought.

'Egbert… Do I know an Egbert?' She reflected a moment longer. 'Could you be referring to Egbert, son of Ealhmund of Kent, exiled to Francia by Offa? Yes, I see by your reaction this is the man. So… has he returned to Wessex?' A grunt of satisfaction. 'Yes, again. Then he is probably at Westerling. Indeed… indeed. An interesting turn of events. I didn't expect such early fruit from our…' she paused to collect the right word, '…*connection*.'

A flash of suspicion passed through Fenn's mind. Was she expecting him to be just a source of information to her? He regretted mentioning Egbert. For now, he thought it best if the man's presence in Wessex was not generally known.

He was about to request her discretion when she held up a hand.

'Do not worry, Blue-Eyes. You need have no questions about my motives. I will never betray you or any confidences you share. We *are* connected, and we are one in more ways than you know.' Her eyes dropped briefly to the ring on his finger. 'I told you I speak only the truth to you. Look at me and you will see the truth in my eyes.'

Fenn did look into her eyes. They returned his gaze, frankly and honestly, but once again, he was disturbed by the power he felt lying within those deep caverns.

'I'm sorry for my reaction,' he said. 'I didn't expect your insight to be so quick and accurate and your talk of connection surprised me. It's an unusual way to refer to a relationship.'

'Unusual perhaps, but in our case appropriate.'

Fenn looked at her. Her tone and voice – her *presence* – displayed a calmness and serenity that seemed eternally imperturbable. Again he had the feeling she was perfectly attuned to her surroundings. Apart from admitting to possibly being overly defensive, Fenn could imagine no circumstance that would unsettle this woman or invoke an angry or even a hasty response. She portrayed an image of control and confidence.

He was staring longer than was polite and turned his eyes back to the moor. A sharp gust of wind, more insistent than the last, pressed on his shoulders and ruffled his hair. The tor wanted to be rid of him.

Arielle felt it too. Her expression became serious. 'And my last offering – the final piece I would present, is this….'

She turned her head to follow his eyes, gazing westward.

'You have matters that are unfinished….' She paused but continued her unblinking stare toward where the sun would set, as if the direction was important. Fenn waited, resisting the urge to hurry her. An instinct told him her words should be allowed to form at their own pace.

'The paths of important relationships are always circular,' she said. 'They have their start, then they curve away out of sight only to swing back from another direction, returning to where it ends. What is unfinished needs to be resolved….' she closed her eyes, '…in the place you call… or *will* call… home.'

Arielle remained with her eyes closed, facing west.

As usual, her words raised questions. Home? Where was Fenn's home? Lindisfarne? Witanceastre? Westerling? What matters did he consider unfinished? Or perhaps he should ask – what matters did the *Earth Mother* consider to be unfinished?

The forest of the Lesidhe moaned. A cloud drifted over the sun, briefly darkening the land with shadow. Time to take his leave. He could mull over the mystery of her messages later.

'You saved my life,' he said. 'But even apart from that, I have much to thank you for. Thank you for your words, even if I don't understand them. I hope *our* path is also circular and we meet again.'

Arielle opened her eyes and looked at him. 'Oh, we shall,' she said with certainty. 'My eyes and ears will be watching and listening.'

She'd talked about her eyes and ears before. This time she seemed to be referring to people. Members of her order?

Fenn looked back at her and smiled. 'Talking of confidences, I wouldn't want to betray any of yours. What can I tell people about you?'

Her eyes flashed. 'You can tell them the *truth*,' she said, stamping her staff on the ground to emphasise the word. She held his gaze. 'But I would ask one thing of you. *You* may be able to find Lumenthal again, but I would prefer that others did not come looking.'

'I think your stones are perfectly safe, protected by the strange forest of the Lesidhe,' he replied, 'but no one will learn their location from me.'

RATHER THAN WEAKENED by his ordeal of the night before, he felt refreshed and invigorated, easily able to maintain a long stride that ate up the ground at a speed rivalling that of his horses during yesterday's approach to Moloch Tor. Down from the peak, the chill was gone, and each breath tasted fresh and clean, filling him with energy. The wind too had lessened – it was now a caressing breeze, warm to the touch and boosted by the sun when it successfully dodged the patches of clouds.

He recognised Kaela as soon as the horse and rider came into view a half-mile away. A small figure bent over the horse's neck, moving at a fast gallop across the moor, trailing another horse in its wake. Galastan's black mares. It was her hair, flowing behind her, that marked her. He stopped walking and raised his arms, waving and calling to attract her attention. After a moment the figure sat upright, stared at him, and swung the horse in his direction.

She slowed the mare to a walk when she was fifty paces from him. At ten paces she pulled to a stop, slid from the saddle and held the horse's head, stroking its nose, calming the animal – still blowing from its race across the moor. She took time to softly thank the black mare for its effort while her eyes surveyed Fenn critically from top to toe.

He had never seen Kaela dressed as she was now and the sight took his breath away. Whether by design or not, she was a perfect match for the mares. She was clothed entirely in black, from her boots to her tight-fitting tailored trousers and flared jacket made from soft dyed leather. The ornate sword at her side stood out in contrast to the black, as did the wild red hair covering her shoulders.

She looked nothing short of magnificent.

'You have a bruised eye,' she said, 'and scrapes on your face and hands. Apart from that, you look surprisingly well for someone who should, by now, be a frozen block of ice. *Are* you well?'

'And *you* are a welcome sight to behold,' he said, spreading his arms appreciatively. 'Where did you get…?'

'Don't evade my question,' she interrupted. '*Are you well?*'

'Yes, I'm well. No lasting damage. Did you see Olgood and Gisele?'

'Yes. I met them last night and talked with them. All three are fine. They'll be at Westerling now. They told me of your foolish idea to search alone for Thorvald's axe, which, thankfully, I see you found. They told me of the conditions on the tor. How did you survive the night?'

Fenn's answer was to step forward and embrace her. Her response was immediate and just as fervent, strong fingers digging into his back. He held her tightly, resting his head on her hair, breathing her scent. His body relaxed for the first time in a while and melded with hers.

After a long moment, his voice muffled by her hair, he said: 'In short, I found a fire. The long story will take some time to tell.'

He felt her nod. She pulled back so she could see his face. There were tears in her eyes. She raised a hand to wipe at them.

'You had me worried. I was relieved when I encountered Olgood and Gisele, but when I saw you weren't with them, I thought you'd… I thought you might be….'

He held her head and kissed her. Her lips were soft and warm. He tasted her salty tears.

'I'm sorry to have caused you to worry…' he breathed against her cheek.

'Don't do that again.'

He didn't reply immediately. In other circumstances he may have been tempted to answer flippantly – '*Do you mean don't kiss you…?*' but he knew she meant don't be late in returning, and she was serious. Although she only sought reassurance, he couldn't promise never to be late again. His encounter with Arielle, for some reason, made him wary of even small lies.

'I'll try,' he said.

She seemed satisfied. She rubbed his arms. 'Are you still cold?'

'Not with you close.' He smiled. 'And the walking has warmed me.'

She smiled back at him, her eyes bright, looking him up and down again. Her eyes caught something and widened. She froze.

'Fenn…?' She was staring at him oddly. 'What is *that*?'

'What?' He glanced down at his clothing. Was something amiss?

'What are you wearing on your hand?'

'Ah… yes.'

He lifted his hand. Kaela took it in her own and studied the ring. She looked up at him expectantly, waiting for the explanation.

'It's a gift. I met a woman in the forest. An unusual and intriguing woman.'

At his pause, she prompted: 'And…?'

'As I said, the story will take time to tell. Why don't I do that on the way back to Westerling?' He gently removed his hand from hers.

She took some time to decide whether to accept his suggestion.

'Very well.' She untied the second mare and handed him the lead.

'By the way,' she said. 'The rider you sent to Lord Herewic of Somersaeteshire returned. Herewic's message said Westerling could wallow in its own pig muck for all he cared.' She looked at him. 'His own words were stronger.'

Fenn shook his head. 'I do wonder how the kingdom has lasted as long as it has with such rivalries festering within it.'

'It also has many good people,' she said.

He smiled. 'Of course.' He pointed at her. 'You haven't told me about your new clothing.'

'This…?' She fingered the hem of the jacket. 'A gift from Bronwyn and Erenweth.'

'Ah… Erenweth… Of course.' He remembered the beautiful gown Gerwent's daughter had worn when he'd first seen her in Westerling Hall. So, it seemed they had *both* received recent gifts.

'Yes. They thought my clothing was somehow inappropriate. Bronwyn prepared and dyed the leather and Erenweth did the sewing. She's quite a magician with a needle.' She turned to present him with a side view. 'What do you think?'

She had a gleam in her eye. A warning that he should put a little thought into his answer. That presented no problem to Fenn. He simply told the truth he'd seen at first sight of her.

'You look magnificent.'

Her smile told him she was happy with those words.

'Then let's be on our way,' she said. 'I can't wait to hear about your mysterious lady of the forest.'

CHAPTER EIGHTEEN

Balthazar stakes a claim, and unwelcome aid arrives

The sounds of the forest were typical for a lazy, sunny afternoon. Bird calls and soft tree rustlings. The swish of grass and the crackle of twigs and dry leaves underfoot. Sounds so common that Fenn, searching among the trees for mushrooms, ignored them, indulging instead in recalled memories of Lindisfarne and his childhood, when life was simple. Gathering mushrooms did not require much thought and his mind was free to wander.

He was grateful to have wrested some time away from the constant stream of incidents and concerns requiring his attention. While Olgood and Fenn had been talking, Gisele approached to inform Olgood that she was heading to the forest to collect mushrooms. Olgood laid down his tools and made to stand from the baby crib he was making, to accompany her, but Fenn seized the opportunity and laid a hand on his friend's shoulder.

'I know you'd like to finish the rockers today. Let *me* go with Gisele. I've just finished a session of sling training with Beric, and a quiet walk in the fresh air of the woods is just what I need. Balthazar also needs to stretch his legs. It gives me an excuse to ask Edelred to sort out the brewing dispute.'

He took Gisele by the arm before Olgood could raise an objection.

HE FELT SOOTHED BOTH by the quiet of the forest and by its noises. The sounds didn't intrude; even the sudden trill of birdsong fitted perfectly into the surroundings because it was expected. The calmness and the sense of everything being as it should be lifted a heaviness from his shoulders. The trees were ageless. They resisted the buffeting of the breeze with nonchalance, engaged as they must be in loftier pursuits, in concert with the sky above and the earth below. Every breath was refreshing and invigorating. He'd needed this break more than he realised.

He grunted with realisation – his thoughts of the forest were beginning to align with Arielle's description of the Earth Mother and the *connections* she'd talked about.

His roving eyes spied a group of shaggy inkcaps nestled among a patch of tall grass. They were mature – the rounded bell-like caps just beginning to open. A tasty mushroom, but they wouldn't keep – they'd need to be in the pot today. Inkcaps were delicate, so he took care when placing them in his shoulder bag. The black fringe at the bottom of the cap reminded Fenn that, at St. Cuthbert's Monastery, Master Nerian had experimented with making ink from these mushrooms, but the result didn't fix well on parchment, and it also had an unusual aroma. The Master disguised that with cloves but eventually decided the process was not worth the trouble.

The thought of inks led him to realise it had been some time since he'd been able to indulge in two related passions of his youth – calligraphy and drawing. Master Oswald, the monk in charge of the scriptorium at Lindisfarne, had been strict and demanded high standards. Nonetheless, Fenn found enjoyment and satisfaction in creating the beautifully-coloured intricate designs called illuminations in the manuscripts he'd been charged to copy. He found the steadiness and accuracy required to achieve the perfection his art demanded to be totally absorbing. He recalled the chapter page he'd been working on the day the Northmen had raided Lindisfarne, which led him to wonder if that work had ever been completed and if so, by whom.

His reverie was interrupted by sounds that were definitely not common or expected in the forest.

The first was a high-pitched angry squeal from an animal followed immediately by a cry from Gisele.

He jerked his head up, his hand reaching for his axe. Gisele shouted his name: '*Fenn!*' There was urgency in her voice.

'Balthazar!' – he yelled to alert the hound who was nearby but out of sight, and broke into a run, his heart pounding. Gisele was not far ahead; she should be just over the rise.

On the rise, he stopped to take account of the scene before him.

Gisele lay among the gnarled roots at the foot of a giant oak, its massive branches spread to either side like entreating arms. One of her legs was strangely twisted, caught in the roots. In front of Fenn, thirty paces away, a huge black-haired boar was headed directly *toward* him but trying to stop, sliding, scrambling, feet digging in – showering leaves and clods of earth into the air. The heavy grunts issuing from its throat were evidence of the beast's effort to arrest its momentum and turn about.

Edelred had said no wild pigs had been sighted in this part of the forest for weeks, but this animal was full-grown and in prime condition. It was bigger than any Fenn had seen in Northumbria – and it was angry; he could clearly see the bristles on the back of its neck standing erect. What had enraged the beast? Was it rutting season?

Gisele was frantically tugging at her foot. She looked to have escaped the boar's initial charge only to have become trapped in the tangled roots of the oak. Had she stumbled upon the boar unexpectedly? She must have been enjoying a sunny day's dream like Fenn because when Gisele entered a forest, she became part of it – it was unbelievable for her to have unknowingly surprised a forest animal.

Fenn leapt forward, raising his axe. He let out a guttural shout just as the boar came to a halt, hoping to distract the beast, but its intentions were set and although they were now only twenty paces apart, it paid him no mind. Its long thin snout twisted backwards and beady eyes fixed on a helpless Gisele sprawled at the base of the tree. With another piercing squeal of rage, the boar swung its hindquarters nimbly about and, its feet again raking up earth and leaves, pointed its tusks at Gisele and charged.

The boar moved incredibly fast for such a large animal. Desperately, Fenn pulled back his arm and let the axe fly. From the skill he'd developed with the sling, Fenn knew the coordination of his arm and his eye was excellent – most things he threw found their target – but as soon as the axe left his hand, two facts were evident – the tumbling weapon would miss the boar, and he could not reach Gisele in time to save her.

Gisele was defenceless and she knew it. She reached for her knife, then thought better of it. She drew her free leg up and twisted away, tucking her chin behind her shoulder and lowering her elbows to protect her body while still tugging at her trapped leg to free it.

The razor-sharp tusks were a heartbeat from striking her when a snarling grey whirlwind erupted from the undergrowth and crashed into the side of the boar. The impact collapsed the boar's front legs, forcing its snout to plough into the ground as Balthazar's snapping teeth sought its throat. The pair dissolved into a fury of twisting bodies, thrusting heads and thrashing legs – with high-pitched squeals and angry snarls issuing in equal measure from the throats of the combatants – the deadly embrace occurring a mere arm's length from Gisele, who recoiled as far back as her snared foot would allow.

The wolfhound's long canines sank in but the boar's neck was thickly protected with a mass of coarse hair and although the dog's jaw was closed and locked with as much pressure as the huge wolfhound could apply, whether the boar was wounded, let alone vitally, was unclear. As large as Balthazar was, this boar was massively thick in the shoulders and twice the dog's bulk.

The boar forced itself back to its feet, swinging its head to dislodge the dog and turning its snout to bring its lethal tusks into the fray, instinctively aiming for the hound's soft underbelly. Although violently jostled to and fro by the boar's efforts, Balthazar managed to elude the deadly thrusts, all the while maintaining his vice-like grip, his own head twisting and jerking, muzzle deep in the boar's neck, fangs tearing at the wound, fresh blood now spraying over the area of forest floor already flattened by the struggle.

With her need to escape no longer immediate, Gisele thrust her hands into the mass of roots to blindly examine her trapped foot, her eyes never leaving the fight that twisted and swayed back and forth, threatening to swing in her direction at any moment. Fenn arrived and waited for the right time to step in and free her foot from its entangled position. He saw how it was caught and eased it from the roots, then supported her as they stepped back, away from the conflict. She rubbed her ankle and smiled her thanks, raising a hand to show she wasn't hurt. His eyes flicked to her stomach where a bulge was just showing. Again she reassured him – she was unharmed.

Fenn retrieved his axe and circled the wildly struggling animals, unable to intervene for fear of injuring Balthazar. He stepped carefully around the perimeter, looking for an opening. It was difficult to tell which animal had the upper hand. Balthazar had wounded the boar; that much was now evident from the blood staining the forest floor, but at any moment, the boar's frantic contortions could tear the dog's hold free and the tables could turn. Even with Balthazar clamped onto its neck, the boar's tusks came dangerously close to their target time and again – each near-miss punctuated by a squeal of alarm from Gisele. Only Balthazar's surprising agility for such a large dog and his instinct to keep away from the boar's snout at all costs saved him.

Fenn raised his axe as he saw a chance, but it disappeared in an instant. He circled again, trying to get behind the boar.

The action slowed.

The boar still twisted and shook its head to dislodge the dog, and Balthazar still tore at the boar's throat, but the movements were at half-speed, with frequent pauses. Both combatants were exhausted but for the boar the blood loss was also starting to tell. Even so, Fenn was still unable to find an opening. Each time the action paused and a possibility arose, it was gone before he could intervene. He was continually raising and lowering his axe.

He leapt back as the boar pushed itself up and the struggle moved in his direction but instead of initiating another attack, the boar was now intent on escape. The change of intention surprised Balthazar. The boar's sudden lurch in an unexpected direction jerked the dog off his feet and he was dragged along the forest path on his side, his teeth still locked in the boar's neck. After a few paces, the extra weight caused the boar to stumble, and Balthazar was able to scramble upright. He used his legs and shoulder to push against the side of the staggering boar while pulling back with his teeth, dragging the boar's head in the opposite direction.

The boar collapsed with a grunt, straining for air, each breath now sounding as a hoarse gurgle in its throat. For the space of a half-dozen heartbeats, all motion ceased. Fenn took the opportunity to step in, bringing the axe up, but at that moment – his jaws still thrust deep in the boar's throat – Balthazar gave a low growl, and his eyes flicked up to meet Fenn's with an unblinking gaze. As surely as if the wolfhound had spoken, Fenn knew what the dog was telling him.

'No! Stay back. This is my *kill.'*

The boar convulsed, legs writhing and kicking towards Fenn. Fenn jumped aside, but it was the animal's dying act. Its desperate attempts to breathe stilled. The great body stiffened, held that pose for a heartbeat, then went limp. Balthazar growled deep in his throat. His head twisted once, then again, his growls inviting his opponent to continue if it could.

The boar gave no response. The dog slowly released his hold and lifted his head cautiously, panting heavily, steaming tongue lolling over blood-stained teeth – but his body remained rigid and tense, eyes fixed intently on the boar's head, every muscle taut, ready to resume the fight in an instant if the boar made the slightest movement. When there was still no response, Balthazar relaxed, accepting his victory.

He sniffed the animal at his feet from top to tail, then, still panting, turned his head to regard Fenn and Gisele. This time, Fenn read the message as: *'What do you think? Did I do well?'*

Fenn let out a long breath, replacing the axe on his belt. He walked toward Balthazar to give him the praise he deserved, but Gisele was there first. She knelt before the wolfhound and flung her arms around his neck, heedless that the blood covering his coat was now being liberally transferred to her face and hair.

'You save me, Balthazar,' she cried, her eyes misting. She drew her head back. 'You get only best cuts of meat from now.' Balthazar panted in her face, pleased.

Fenn checked the boar. It was young – the meat would be juicy and tender. He marvelled at the size of the animal stretched out on the forest floor. The carcass was too heavy for one man to carry; Fenn would need help. It would be a good feeling to arrive at Westerling bearing not only the mushrooms he'd gone to collect but an additional unexpected bounty for the pot. He had no doubt the meal Gisele would produce from the combination of wild pork and mushrooms would be magical.

Gisele drew her knife from her belt and knelt by the boar.

'I prepare 'im,' she said. 'You go bring strong men for take 'im 'ome.'

FENN HEARD EDELRED'S CALL from across the yard.

'Where's Lord Feran! Lord Feran!'

The tenant-in-chief burst into the hut where Fenn sat at the bedside of a woman. Beside him, Acwellan ignored the intrusion and lifted the woman's arm to show Fenn the swellings in her armpit.

'A cluster of boils only. It's not the plague,' he said.

Fenn sighed, leaned back, and turned his head to acknowledge Edelred.

'Wyllard has returned,' said Edelred excitedly.

'Already? That's welcome news.' Fenn rose and motioned Edlered back out of the hut. Acwellan bent to talk to the woman, patted her shoulder, and followed.

Outside the hut, Fenn looked about. 'Where is he? How many with him?'

'He's alone. He's ridden hard. I asked him to wait for you in the Hall.'

Fenn nodded and turned to Acwellan. 'Thank you. I'll talk to the people who were worried about the plague.'

He started to turn away but Acwellan put a hand on his arm.

'Lord Feran, I understand you've important things to do. I've been trying to talk to you about this situation for a while.' He inclined his hand toward the entrance of the hut. 'This poor woman has been shunned and humiliated….'

Fenn placed a reassuring hand on Acwellan's shoulder. 'I understand, and I apologise for not coming sooner. As I said, I'll explain to them.'

As he lifted his hand, the physician unexpectedly reached out and seized Fenn firmly by the wrist.

'*Where did you get that ring?*' he said sharply, his eyes locked on the red-stoned ring on Fenn's left hand, his grip painfully strong.

Fenn drew in a breath. Apart from Kaela, he'd told no one about Arielle.

'That would take some time to explain,' he said. 'It's a gift. We can talk about it later. I need to speak with Wyllard.' He attempted to withdraw his hand, but Acwellan held it tightly.

'A gift?' the physician said, his voice hard with suspicion. 'How could that be?' His breathing had deepened. His eyes were wide and his face strangely twisted as if attempting to solve an impossible puzzle.

Edelred had taken a step back, staring at Acwellan as though he had transformed into a devil. Fenn understood his concern.

Since Fenn had known Acwellan, a striking feature of the man had been his imperturbable nature. Nothing fazed him. Whatever situation confronted him, however unusual or bizarre, it was met with the same calm, methodical manner. It was probably related to his craft – the physician at Lindisfarne had been the same type of man.

The behaviour Fenn saw now was entirely out of character.

Fenn stopped trying to free his hand. 'Acwellan, what is it? What's wrong? Have you seen this ring before?'

Acwellan didn't answer immediately. Slowly, he calmed himself, his features relaxing.

He said softly: 'I know of it.'

Fenn waited for further explanation. Acwellan frowned, suddenly realising he still held Fenn by the wrist. He released his grip as if dropping a hot coal.

'My turn to apologise – for my reaction, Lord Feran. I hadn't noticed the ring before. It was a considerable surprise to see it on your hand.' He looked up into Fenn's eyes. 'A gift, you say?'

'Yes.'

Acwellan nodded.

'So you met Avarinthe the Fae on the moor,' he said matter-of-factly. 'You must indeed have emerged from the encounter high in her favour to be wearing one of her rings.' He shook his head slowly, his mind still arranging pieces of the puzzle.

Edelred stared back and forth between the two, his face a picture of bewilderment.

'I didn't know her by that name,' said Fenn.

'Of course not.'

Fenn hesitated, torn between wanting to continue the conversation and the need to hear the news from Wyllard.

He made a fist of his hand, the ring uppermost. 'We must talk about this,' he said. 'I'd like to know what you know. But, for the moment….'

'Yes, yes, go.' Acwellan waved Fenn away. 'It can wait.'

Fenn gestured for Edelred to follow and headed across the yard to the Hall. When he looked back, Acwellan was still staring after him with a puzzled expression.

'THEY ARE AN HOUR or so behind, Lord,' said Wyllard. 'I rode ahead to tell you so you wouldn't be surprised and could prepare for their arrival.'

Fenn sat on the Thane's chair. Beside him, Kaela leaned against the tall back of the chair.

'Well done, Wyllard,' said Fenn, 'You've brought the help we requested *days* quicker than anyone expected. You must have ridden like the wind.'

'I picked a good horse, Lord.' He raised a hand in acknowledgement. 'Not like the mares, of course, but not far behind.'

'Even so, a fine job. How many men did the King send?'

'The King is still at Tamworth, Lord. The *Queen* sent twenty.'

Fenn thought he heard a sigh followed by a chuckle from Kaela.

'*Twenty?* I presume you informed the Queen that at least eighty Cornish were preparing to attack Westerling?'

'Of course, Lord. She sent twenty. However, Lord Wulfstan, Ealdorman of Wiltonshire, supplied another thirty.'

Another low chuckle from Kaela. Fenn glanced at her with a frown.

Kaela bent forward so she could whisper in his ear privately.

'*Eadburg has to respond to a call for help if Wessex is attacked,*' she said, '*but nothing would please her more than for Westerling to be burned to the ground so soon after she had gifted it to me. She knows her relief force of twenty will not be enough, and I'm sure that even they will be the chaff of the men she has available. She'll argue that any competent leader should have been able to repel the Cornish with twenty brave men from Wessex.*'

She straightened. 'Wyllard,' she asked. 'Did the Queen request that you ask for more men from Ealdorman Wulfstan?'

'No, my Lady. We met Lord Wulfstan by chance on the road. When he heard of the Cornish raid and saw we had only twenty men, he offered to accompany us with the men he had with him. The Reeve initially declined, but he relented when the Ealdorman insisted.'

Fenn drew in a breath. 'The King's Reeve?' he asked.

'Yes, Lord.'

Fenn and Kaela shared a glance. So, *Grimbold,* the man whose purse Fenn had returned in the market at Witanceastre, was coming to Westerling.

Fenn pushed that thought aside as Kaela whispered again in his ear: '*I'll wager she'll be more than annoyed when she learns that Wulfstan added thirty men to the force she sent.*'

'How many archers are there?' Fenn asked Wyllard. 'How many footmen?'

'No archers, Lord. All footmen.'

'*No archers?!*'

'The Queen forbade the Reeve to take archers. She said her archers were needed elsewhere.'

'Did she say where?' asked Kaela sweetly. To Fenn, she whispered: '*The lack of archers will be deliberate.*'

'No, she didn't say,' replied Wyllard.

'And Wulfstan…' Fenn continued, '…did he supply any archers?'

'No, my Lord. He had none with him.'

Fenn sighed. 'So, fifty footmen only. Thank you, Wyllard.' He stood up. 'Edelred, please see he gets food and drink.' Edelred bowed and headed for the entrance. Wyllard touched his forehead and followed him.

Fenn turned to Kaela. 'I'd like Nyle and his men in the yard to receive Grimbold when he arrives, and Olgood, Edelred, and as many others as can be spared – and Wyllard, of course….'

Wyllard was fifteen paces away, but when Fenn mentioned his name, he uttered an audible groan and turned back to face the chair, his discomfort evident from the hat twisted back and forth in his hands.

Fenn looked up. 'What is it?' he asked.

'Please, Lord, if I may,' he said. 'I would rather *not* be in the welcoming group.'

Fenn raised his eyebrows.

'Ah… you see….' Wyllard said haltingly, '…when I said I would ride ahead… ah… the Reeve did not give his approval. He said he wanted to be the bearer of the good news himself. So, you see, I did not… exactly… obey him… I thought it was important to alert Westerling. I hope you don't think…?'

'Of course not. Thank you, Wyllard. You've done well.'

'Thank you, Lord. But…' Wyllard continued, '…I'd rather not be in his sight when he arrives. He'll be angry with me. I don't think he's a forgiving man.'

'I understand. Don't worry about the Reeve.'

Wyllard bowed, slipped his hat onto his head, and turned to follow Edelred.

'Oh, one moment, Edelred…' called Fenn.

Edelred turned back. 'Yes, Lord?'

'It may be best if Egbert is also not seen by the Reeve or the Queen's men.'

'Do you mean because of his claim…?'

'It just may be for the best.'

'Of course, Lord. I'll tell him.'

Wyllard and Edelred left. Kaela came to stand beside Fenn.

'I'm surprised Beorhtric is still with Offa at Tamworth,' she said. 'He's stayed longer than expected. But… on reflection… some good may yet come from the situation.'

'If we were under siege, it would definitely not be good. Even though they will add to our strength, fifty footmen would not have been effective against Hernam's archers in the field. And *Grimbold* is about to arrive at Westerling. What good can you see coming from that?'

Kaela smiled. 'Eadburg's feelings toward me have caused her to miscalculate this time. Her deliberately feeble response to a reported threat to Wessex will not have gone unnoticed at court.'

Fenn stared at her. The politics of the court of King Beorhtric were an unknown and unwelcome mire to him and far from his thoughts. He was happy to leave that area of conflict to her.

He smiled and reached out to take Kaela's arm, drawing her to him.

FENN STOOD IN THE yard facing the open palisade doors beside Kaela, her hair drawn back and dressed in her black leathers. Next to her was Nyle, his men lined up alongside him, fully armed with their spears and shields prominent. Fenn glanced at Olgood, Gisele, and Kuralin standing to one side. Olgood nodded back at him, his arm resting on Gisele's shoulder, holding her close. Kuralin smiled at Fenn. After a few days at Westerling, she'd regained her infectious good humour and with it, the spirit in her eyes. Fenn had talked with her. Her recent experience, losing her husband and being held captive at Moloch

Tor, had not been forgotten, but she had found the strength to put it aside.

Another incident had also shown Fenn that the events on Moloch Tor would not be soon forgotten. On the day Fenn returned to Westerling, he had an interesting exchange with Olgood.

'You look much better than when I last saw you,' Fenn had observed. Olgood's face was discoloured by bruising and the scars were still fresh, but apart from that, he moved freely and looked to have returned to full health.

'I feel better,' said Olgood. 'Up on the tor I thought I'd never be warm again. Arcwellan stitched the wounds in my scalp and applied a paste of myrrh, but it seems I was protected from more severe damage by a thick skull. I'm stiff and bruised but no bones broken. I'm under good care.'

'From Acwellan *and* Gisele, I've no doubt.'

Olgood smiled, nodding.

His tone became serious. 'Do you think we're likely to meet Galastan and the Ariochs again?'

'When he finds the box contains only river stones, he'll be angry and may seek revenge. We'll be ready if he comes.'

'Good. I hope he tries. I have my mark on all three of them.' He held up three fingers of one hand, circled the fingers with the other hand and made as if to crush them.

Fenn looked at Olgood, surprised by his actions and his flat menacing tone. Olgood was a good-natured, relaxed, and patient man. He knew his size could intimidate people so he made an effort to be friendly, smiling, and soft-voiced. But his size and strength did not disappear, and Olgood readily called upon both when necessary – Fenn had seen him bend thick bars of iron and lift weights that seemed impossible. But he had never known Olgood to previously consider anyone an enemy.

If Galastan or the Ariochs valued their health and their lives, they would stay well beyond the reach of Olgood.

FENN TURNED HIS HEAD to look over his shoulder across the yard. Most of the farming community of Westerling were in the fields, but about twenty from the craft rooms and trading houses had gathered in a curious group by the well.

His attention was brought back to the entrance by movement in the corner of his eye.

Through the arch, Fenn watched a double column of men led by two horsemen emerge from the eastern forest on the Roman Road. Each man in the column carried a spear and a round blue shield emblazoned with the golden Wyvern of Wessex – matching those held by Nyle's men.

When they reached the path, the horsemen turned from the road up the hill toward Westerling Hall. Fenn rapidly counted the men following, confirming the total of fifty.

Kaela groaned. 'I was hoping it wasn't true, but that *is* Grimbold on the lead horse.'

Fenn also recognised the man from the market. Grimbold had threatened to whip Fenn if they ever met again.

'If I were to report Galastan's abduction of Olgood and Kuralin and Olgoods' beating to the High Reeve, what would he do?'

'Ha!' said Kaela. 'He'd do nothing. He'd say those affairs are shire matters for the Shire Reeve and not worth his trouble.'

'I thought as much,' said Fenn. 'I presume the man on the other horse is Ealdorman Wulfstan?'

'Yes. That's Wulfstan. And now that I see him, I've realised his presence will complicate things.'

'How?' asked Fenn, not wanting to hear the answer. More complication was definitely unwelcome.

'Wulfstan is married to Alburga, who is Egbert's half-sister. He knows Egbert well.'

AS GRIMBOLD AND WULFSTAN passed under the arch together, Grimbold's eyes roamed over the people gathered before him. He sat high in the saddle, chin in the air, expecting a triumphant welcome. His disappointment with the silence that greeted him was noticeable.

When his eyes fell on Fenn, he frowned instantly and his eyes narrowed with recognition.

'*You, by God!*' He pointed an imperious finger at Fenn. 'That man is a thief!' he yelled.

He awkwardly rolled off his horse, landing heavily with a grunt. His dismount was made to look even more ungainly by the flapping of his ill-fitting clothing, which, while different from that worn in the market, still hung loosely on him. Fenn wondered if the man's image of himself was larger than the reality. Murmurs of amusement came from the group standing by the well.

Grimbold reached up, untied his whip from the horse, and shook it loose.

He looked up at Wulfstan and pointed at Fenn again. 'That man tried to steal my purse in Witanceastre. I warned him not to cross my path again. I mean what I say. I'll whip the cur until he's whimpering in the dust.'

Wulfstan frowned and an angry buzz arose from the people gathered at the well.

'I won't allow you to do that, Grimbold,' said Fenn calmly. He placed his hand on the axe in his belt.

'So *now* you know who I am,' Grimbold retorted. He laughed. With a wave, he indicated the men filing through the door behind him. 'How do you intend to stop me? I'll have you tied down if you're too cowardly to take a whipping like a man.'

Olgood removed his arm from Gisele's shoulders. He walked forward to stand in front of Fenn. 'You'll have to go past me first,' he said.

Grimbold's eyes widened as he took in the size of Olgood. He swallowed and glanced over his shoulder. The crowd of armed men still passing through the arch reassured him. His lip curled. He indicated his men should spread out, then he grunted and said: 'If you so wish.'

He raised the whip.

'And past us.' Edelred's voice came from behind Fenn, and the shuffle of feet as the group from the well moved forward.

'What is this? Don't be foolish,' Grimbold said disbelievingly. 'All together, you're less than half our number, and you're unarmed. Stay back, or some of you may get hurt.'

Wulfstan leaned down from his horse. 'Grimbold…' he said.

Grimbold glanced up and raised an open palm. 'Please, Lord Wulfstan, this is a *private* concern. It won't take long….' He directed his gaze at Nyle and motioned him to move away from Fenn. His eye moved to Kaela. 'You too, my Lady, if you would.'

Nyle didn't move. Neither did Kaela.

'Nyle!' the Reeve said sharply. 'You and your men move back.'

Nyle stayed where he was and did not speak. Slowly he reached behind his back for his bow. He placed one end on the ground and bent it to attach the string. That action caused an audible whispering among the men at the palisade door. Many of these men were probably members of the royal house-guards. Nyle and his bow would be well known to them.

'What are you doing, Nyle? Did you not hear? I said to move your men back!'

Nyle didn't answer.

Grimbold's face screwed itself into a mixture of disbelief and outrage. Fenn could see the man was struggling to determine which was more incredulous – a pack of unarmed farmers daring to oppose him or Nyle's disobedience.

'Sir…' Fenn began, but Kaela stopped him with a hand on his arm.

She stepped forward to stand in front of Grimbold.

'You do know who I am?' she asked.

Grimbold lowered his whip. His annoyance at being interrupted was obvious. 'Of course,' he admitted reluctantly.

'You were sent to *aid* Westerling, Grimbold,' she said, 'not to get into a fight with its inhabitants the moment you arrive.' She turned to Fenn. 'This man is the Thane of Westerling, Lord Feran, and he is no thief.'

'The Thane? Ha! What trickery is this? He's too young to be a Thane – and he's a *foreigner*. A rogue who lives in the streets or in the forest, more likely. What stories has he told you? What lies? He stole my purse in the market and I forced him to return it – with this!' He shook the whip in her face.

'I heard a different story,' said Kaela. 'I heard *he* is the one who apprehended the thief and ensured your purse was returned.'

'You were not there,' said Grimbold stubbornly. '*I was.*'

'Nonetheless, he *is* the Thane, as anyone here will tell you. You're holding the wrong end of the stick in this matter Grimbold, and you'd be wise to let it go.'

Wulfstan had dismounted while Kaela was speaking. As she finished, he walked towards Fenn, his hand outstretched. Olgood moved out of the way, his eyes never leaving Grimbold.

'Lord Feran,' Wulfstan said, 'I'm Lord Wulfstan of Wiltonshire. I'm happy to make your acquaintance.'

Grimbold opened his mouth and attempted to say several things at once. All that emerged was an unintelligible splutter.

Fenn took Wulfstan's hand.

'It seems Westerling is no longer under attack,' Wulfstan continued. 'I wonder if I can arrange refreshments for my men and care for my horse?'

Fenn released his hand. 'I'm also glad to meet you, Lord Wulfstan. Thank you for coming so swiftly to our aid. Yes, the matter with the Cornish has thankfully been resolved.' He indicated Edelred. 'This man will take care of your needs. I hope you will join me in the Hall when you're rested.'

Edelred stepped forward.

Wulfstan nodded to Fenn. 'I'm obliged,' he said.

Calling to one of his men, he returned to his horse. The man, in turn, talked to the men crowding the palisade entrance. Most then headed toward Edelred, but a smaller group remained, Grimbold's men, their eyes darting about, unsure whether they were included.

Grimbold stood with a frown etched on his brow, his mouth still open.

Fenn walked over to join Kaela, Olgood following.

'Reeve Grimbold,' Fenn said. 'Welcome to Westerling. I'm prepared to let this misunderstanding pass. I hope you will also.'

Grimbold closed his mouth and let a long breath out between his teeth. Fenn noticed the hand clutching the whip was taut with tension. The Reeve's eyes stared malevolently at Fenn. Olgood joined the group, his shadow falling on Grimbold, drawing the man's eyes away from Fenn to the mountain that had just blocked the sun. Olgood's presence up close could be daunting, and Fenn saw his effect on Grimbold. Olgood towered over the man and the Reeve was unable to prevent himself from swallowing and taking a step back. He controlled himself with an effort.

He wrestled with his options for a few moments.

'I'll let it go,' he said through tight lips. '*For now.*'

'Grimbold…' Fenn said firmly. 'I do not wish this scene to be repeated later.'

Grimbold looked at him. He saw the resolve in Fenn's eyes and something undefinable in his bearing.

The Reeve blew out another breath and jerked his head dismissively. 'It's of minor importance,' he said through gritted teeth.

Fenn was unsure what Grimbold felt was unimportant – the words he had just said or the matter in the market.

'I'd like to thank you for coming to our aid,' Fenn repeated his words to Wulfstan, 'and I'd also like you to join me in the Hall when you're ready. Your men should go with Edelred.'

'I'll take your horse,' said Kaela.

Grimbold's eyes moved back and forth between Fenn and Kaela. Fenn thought he might baulk at their suggestions just to oppose them, but Grimbold surprised him. His smile was cold, but he turned to wave at his men to follow Wulfstan's, then coiled his whip in a few quick motions and retied it to his horse. He handed the reins to Kaela.

'You had better have a good ale to compensate for my being sent to this desolate corner of the kingdom,' he said.

'We do,' said Kaela.

EALDORMAN WULFSTAN LOWERED HIS mug with an approving smack of his lips.

'You can't beat a strong country brew,' he said.

'Better by far than the weak cow's piss they serve in Witanceastre,' agreed a red-faced Grimbold. He was on his second mug and the effects were showing.

Wulfstan turned to look at Fenn. 'So, Hernam's son, Hopkin, is being held here? At Westerling?'

'Yes,' Fenn confirmed. He'd just completed relating the outcome of his meetings with Hernam.

'Bearing a wound on his cheek to remind him of his folly in crossing our border,' Wulfstan observed. 'I enjoyed that part.' He smiled at Kaela, who reluctantly acknowledged his appreciation.

'I trust your wife is well?' she enquired, to change the subject.

'Alburga? Very well, thank you. She is presently engaged in founding an abbey.'

'Indeed?' Kaela showed her admiration with a nod.

Grimbold looked up from his ale and struck the table with his fist. 'By God, Hernam must be punished for daring to attack Wessex.'

'He didn't attack us in the end,' argued Fenn. 'The situation was peacefully resolved.'

'Don't wave words at me, young man. He brought a group of armed men deep into Wessex with the intention of raiding and stealing grain and livestock. For that alone, he must be punished. A man of Wessex was killed. We'd be within our rights to kill his son Hopkin in retaliation.'

Fenn was about to respond that he had already exacted some compensation from Hernam but caught himself. That would bring Egbert into the conversation.

'As I explained,' said Fenn, 'Hopkin is *my* prisoner and I've given my word to return him.'

Grimbold's reply was a disdainful puff of air through his lips.

'A poor harvest forced Hernam's hand,' Fenn continued. 'The border has enjoyed many years of peace. It would be better to reconcile differences rather than inflame the situation.'

Grimbold allowed his hand to again fall on the table with a thump.

'If Wessex stood meekly aside every time it was attacked or its borders ignored,' he said vehemently, 'it would cease to be a kingdom in a very short while. Our enemies only respect us if we're strong and act forcefully.'

He sat back in his chair and lifted his ale to his lips. He took a strong pull, raising the mug and regarding it appreciatively before turning his gaze back to Fenn. He shrugged.

'When were you due to meet Hernam again, to….' Grimbold shook his head as if he found the idea unbelievable, '…to give him back his son?'

'Tomorrow.'

'How many men will Hernam have at the Tamar?'

'I don't know. He brought about eighty to Westerling, but he may not have the same number at the Tamar. He'll only be there to receive Hopkin.'

'Yes…' agreed Grimbold, with a strange tone to his voice, 'that's what he *thinks*, and that's what he'd like *us* to think.'

Fenn frowned. The man wasn't making sense.

'Forgive me,' said Fenn, 'but what are you planning…?'

'I forgive you nothing,' Grimbold retorted. Then he laughed and spread his hands. 'What is there to forgive? I'm planning to accompany you to the Tamar, that's all.' He turned to the ealdorman. 'Wulfstan, what about you? Do you fancy a ride in the country tomorrow?'

Wulfstan shrugged. 'Of course. I didn't come all this way just to turn straight about and return home again.'

'Good,' Grimbold rubbed his hands together with satisfaction. 'The matter is settled,' he said, lifting his mug.

Instead of drinking, he paused and lowered the mug as a thought came to him and he leered at Kaela. 'Where's your dancing fairy? You used to go everywhere with that annoying little *bug* of a man.'

'His name is Sergio. He's not here.'

'*Serg-i-o,*' Grimbold mocked in a sing-song voice. 'Ha. Stupid fancy *foreign* name for a foreign fancy-man.'

He completed the mug's journey to his lips and swallowed.

Kaela took advantage of the fact that while Grimbold was drinking, he couldn't speak. She addressed Wulfstan: 'My father has stayed longer than expected in Tamworth,' she said. 'Do you know when he's due to return to Witanceastre?'

'I heard Beorhtric has remained in Tamworth because Offa took ill before they concluded their business,' Wulfstan replied. 'I've not heard any more than that.'

Grimbold put his mug down heavily, ale spilling over the rim and onto the table. He raised his eyes to Fenn, a strange smile on his face.

'Talking of King Beorhtric and official business…' he said, '…I have one more important duty to perform.' He paused dramatically, wiping his mouth with the back of his hand. 'In my capacity as High Reeve, I'll take your oath of fealty to the King.'

Fenn stopped – about to sip from his mug. He looked up and frowned.

'An oath? Now?'

'Now,' confirmed Grimbold, smiling, pleased to have caught Fenn off-guard.

Fenn stared at him. He knew nothing about the protocol of oath-taking. He opened his mouth, but before he could speak, Kaela stood up.

'I'll leave you men to complete your *business,*' she said, 'but I need to discuss a minor problem with Lord Feran before I go. It will only take a moment.' She beckoned to Fenn and walked away from the table. Fenn rose and followed her.

'Can I refuse this?' he asked her when they were far enough away not to be heard.

'No,' said Kaela. 'He's within his rights as High Reeve and you cannot refuse. All thanes must take an annual oath of fealty. He's hoping you *do* refuse because then he'll have cause to arrest you. Watch him. He's ignorant and arrogant, but he's not as dumb as he looks.'

'What must I do?'

'He'll say the oath and you repeat the words.'

'What does the oath ask of me?'

'Nothing specific. You'll swear to recognise the King and to obey him and his laws.'

Fenn nodded. Kaela clasped his shoulders in a brief hug. 'I'll check on Egbert and give him news of his sister.'

Fenn paused for a moment in thought. He naturally baulked at swearing an oath to anyone, but he could do it if he was merely required to say he supported the King. He slowly walked back toward the table and caught the end of a conversation.

'…your men really are a poor undisciplined mob, Grimbold,' Wulfstan said.

Grimbold shrugged. 'You work with what you have.'

Wulfstan laughed. 'Sending a bunch like that – the Queen must have expected the matter at Westerling to be resolved one way or another before you arrived.'

Grimbold looked sharply at Wulfstan, but any retort was interrupted by Fenn's approach.

The Reeve's features relaxed. He smiled broadly.

'Aah, our thane returns. Has she prepared you for the ordeal? Are you refreshed and ready?'

'I'm ready.'

'Then sit down. No need to be too formal. Wulfstan, you will witness, of course?'

'I will,' said Wulfstan.

Grimbold lifted his mug and drained its contents. He belched and patted his stomach.

'Indeed a good drop. And *I* will swear to that.' He laughed.

He leaned forward, placing his hands firmly on the table.

'Now to *your* swearing.' He took in a breath. 'Lord Feran, Thane…' he cleared his throat, '…of Westerling, you will repeat the oath to King Beorhtric of Wessex after me.'

Hearing Grimbold acknowledge his title, albeit reluctantly, was both strange and satisfying.

Grimbold stared at Fenn, waiting for an acknowledgement. Fenn simply returned his stare.

'*Before the Lord,*' said Grimbold, '*I will to King Beorhtric of Wessex be true and faithful.*'

Fenn slowly repeated the words.

'*I will love all he loves and shun all he shuns according to the laws of God,*' the High Reeve intoned. Fenn again copied him.

'*Nor will I by word or deed do anything to harm the King or do damage to his property.*'

Grimbold sat back, signalling this was the final phrase. Fenn was relieved. As Kaela had advised – the oath did not commit him to anything specific.

When Fenn had repeated the final words, Grimbold scowled, giving Fenn reason to believe Kaela's assessment had been correct – Grimbold had been hoping up to that point that Fenn would refuse to take the oath or deliberately state it incorrectly.

The Reeve remained still for a few moments, seemingly in thought, then said abruptly:

'Can you muster twenty archers, Lord Feran?'

'We won't require archers tomorrow,' Fenn replied. 'This should be nothing more than a peaceful meeting to return Hopkin as agreed.'

'Is that what you think? You have experience in meetings with Kings, do you? Well, *I* don't trust Hernam. Who knows what that cunning

Briton may do when he has his son back? They're all the same in West Wealas – a barren and forsaken land of rocks, filthy tin miners, and ignorant dirt farmers. Remember your oath to King Beorhtric and through the King, to *me*.' He peered at Fenn through half-closed eyes.

'Twenty archers,' he said firmly.

Grimbold didn't wait for further discussion. He thumped his empty mug on the table and roared: 'More ale!'

Fenn groaned under his breath. Arriving at the Tamar with a large force of men and archers would indeed display a lack of trust. Fenn would rather have demonstrated the opposite – that he trusted and accepted Hernam's word.

He would have liked to rise and leave as Kaela had done, but hospitality required him to remain with the guests he had invited to his table.

He could only hope as Grimbold drank more, he wouldn't notice that Fenn drank less.

CHAPTER NINETEEN

Incident at the Tamar

The Roman Road met the Tamar where the riverbank flattened into a wide stony area. A similar stony protrusion on the other side formed a natural ford. Arrayed on the Wessex side of the river, thirty men stood casually in a loose group behind two horsemen. Hernam, in his helmet, his fine chain mail vest and regal cape, sat astride his grey horse with his familiar standard-bearer alongside. The King's tailored finery contrasted sharply with the ill-fitting clothing worn by the High Reeve of Wessex.

When the size of the force accompanying Fenn was realised, Hernam issued a bark of command and his men moved into a defensive formation creating a short line of spears and shields with a dozen archers arranged behind them. The archers could be seen rapidly stringing their bows.

Fenn rode one of Galastan's mares. He held a rope attached to another horse carrying Hopkin whose hands were bound in front. Beside Fenn, Kaela, in her black leathers, sat astride the other mare. A short distance away, Grimbold and Wulfstan were the only other riders. Behind the horses, all fifty of Grimbold's and Wulfstan's men followed, and, at the rear, Nyle and his men walked with nineteen of the twenty archers

Edelred had selected from the men of Westerling to satisfy Grimbold's request.

The twentieth archer walked at Fenn's side. This was Treddian, the man who had brought the warning of the Cornish raid to Westerling.

'By God,' Grimbold exclaimed indignantly, 'they're on the *Wessex* side of the river!'

'It's a concession,' Fenn said. 'So we wouldn't feel vulnerable crossing the river.'

'Bah. Concession? I think not. It's a deliberate provocation.'

Kaela caught Fenn's gaze and rolled her eyes.

Hernam moved his horse out from the line and the man carrying the standard of Cornwall followed him. The King stopped when he was close enough to be heard. Grimbold raised his hand and the men with him also halted, the two lines facing each other.

Directing his attention to Fenn, Hernam called in Latin: 'Why have you brought so many men?'

'What did he say?' asked Grimbold. Wulfstan leaned across to translate Hernam's words.

Fenn glanced at Kaela and she smiled back at him. For some reason, it pleased him that Grimbold was ignorant of Latin.

'Sire,' Fenn called to Hernam. 'I apologise for….'

'*I'll* do the talking!' Grimbold interrupted sharply.

He stepped his horse forward a few paces. 'My name is Grimbold,' he shouted. 'I'm the High Reeve of King Beorhtric of Wessex. You will speak with me.' He gestured to Wulfstan to translate his words for Hernam.

Hernam glanced at Grimbold but turned back to face Fenn. 'My agreement is with the Thane,' he said.

He called out something in his own language, to which Hopkin uttered a short reply.

'He asked Hopkin if he'd been treated well,' said Treddian quietly. Fenn nodded his thanks. He thought it would be helpful to have someone who knew the Cornish language at this meeting.

'*I* speak for King Beorhtric,' insisted Grimbold. 'Lord Feran, you will be quiet.'

He waved at Wulfstan to translate. Wulfstan repeated the sentence. When he uttered the words '*Lord Feran, you will…*', Grimbold turned on him: 'Not that part, you….' With an effort, he restrained himself from completing the sentence.

Fenn was quick enough to catch the twitch of amusement on Wulfstan's lips. Had his mistake been deliberate?

'Translate what I say *now*,' Grimbold said to Wulfstan. 'Word for word.'

He stared imperiously at Hernam. 'Hernam of Cornwall, you have raided into Wessex and killed a man.' Grimbold waved and waited impatiently for Wulfstan to translate.

'For that invasion into our territory,' he continued, 'I will take your son, Hopkin, to Witanceastre and hold him prisoner there for one year to ensure your respect of our border.'

Hernam stiffened immediately, before the translation, his face angry, probably objecting to Grimbold's tone.

Before Wulfstan could begin the translation, Fenn said quickly: 'Grimbold, that was not my agreement….'

'Silence, Feran,' commanded Grimbold. 'For the last time, *I* am in charge here. *I* represent the King. Wulfstan, go ahead, *word for word*.'

Wulfstan translated Grimbold's words. When he heard his intended fate, Hopkin's eyes became wild, casting about, looking desperately for a means of escape.

'Stay mounted, Hopkin,' Fenn said in Latin. He kicked his horse forward, pulling Hopkin's horse with him.

He called over his shoulder: 'I do this on my own. I ask no one to follow me.'

'What are you *doing*? Stop!' shouted Grimbold. 'Wulfstan, stop him! Come back, Feran.'

Treddian moved when Fenn's horse moved, remaining at its side.

Hernam sat as motionless as a statue, his eyes fixed on Fenn. He beckoned behind him and his men moved forward to join him.

Fenn heard Grimbold say: 'Bring up the archers,' then shout: 'This is treachery, Feran. Stop now, or face the consequences.'

Fenn called to Hernam in Latin: 'I intend to honour my word, sire, and return Hopkin as I promised.'

Fenn was still close enough to hear Grimbold.

'So *now* we see the true measure of this so-called *thane*,' the Reeve sneered, speaking loudly so all could hear. 'He flagrantly disobeys his King's Reeve. Beorhtric would be appalled.'

Kaela's voice answered. 'I agree. My father *would* be appalled.'

Fenn quickened the horse's pace.

Quietly, to ensure that only Treddian and not Grimbold could hear him, Fenn said: 'Tell Hernam – if Grimbold attacks, I'll stand at the King's side.' Treddian called out to relay Fenn's words.

Hernam replied.

'He says it would be an honour, Lord,' said Treddian, forced into a run to keep up.

Galloping hoofbeats sounded behind Fenn. Grimbold? He turned sharply to see Kaela approaching.

'I've said it before,' she said as she pulled alongside, '…where you go, I go.'

'Damn you both!' shouted Grimbold. 'The pair of you are traitors to Wessex. Wulfstan, *do* something! Where are my archers?'

'Can you free Hopkin's hands?' Fenn asked, glancing anxiously at Kaela. 'I don't want him to fall.' He knew it would be no easy task to cut the rope binding Hopkin's hands from a trotting horse, but a moment later, Kaela said: 'Done,' and Fenn heard a murmured appreciation from Hopkin. He tossed Hopkin the lead rope he held so they could both ride freely.

In the act of turning to toss the rope, Fenn noticed movement in Grimbold's ranks. Nyle strode out and broke into a run, followed by his five men and, behind them, the group of Westerling archers.

Grimbold let out a cheer. 'Well done, Nyle!' he yelled, raising a fist above his head. 'Bring them back and I'll see you rewarded. We'll follow you.'

He circled his arm to include the men around him. 'Move forward!' he cried. 'Follow those men. *For Wessex!*' He started his horse walking.

Fenn quickly covered the remaining distance to Hernam. He wheeled the horse to pull alongside the King and drew the axe from his belt. Hernam nodded an acknowledgement and reached down to free his own sword. He unclasped his cape with his other hand and passed it back to his standard-bearer. Hopkin and Kaela, the Lord of the Battle already in her hand, arrived at the same time as Treddian, breathing hard from his run. He wasted no time bending his bow to string it.

'Thank you, Treddian, but I release you from any obligation to fight,' said Fenn. 'This is my fight. You can withdraw.'

'If it's your fight, Lord, it's *my* fight,' Treddian said without looking up. He selected an arrow and notched it.

Hopkin rode up to his father and they clasped arms. Hopkin called out an order in his language to a nearby man, holding out a hand.

'He wants a weapon,' said Treddian at Fenn's side, looking up to see if Fenn still required translation.

Hernam barked a counter order, reaching behind him on his horse to retrieve a sword and scabbard. Hopkin waved the man away and gratefully accepted the sword, which Fenn saw was Hopkin's own, the one Fenn had returned. Hopkin leaned back on his horse to attach the scabbard to his belt.

Fenn returned his attention to the front. Nyle and the Westerling archers were closing, running towards Hernam's line.

'The men in the first group, the archers, are my men,' Fenn told Hernam in Latin. 'Don't loose any arrows on them.'

Hernam relayed his request and turned back to Fenn. 'Welcome, Saxon,' he said. 'This could be an interesting skirmish.'

'You have your son. You could withdraw,' said Fenn.

'I'll not run from this man,' Hernam said, but his wary eyes were on Nyle and the archers behind him.

Fenn called to Nyle: 'Nyle, where do you stand?'

'I stand with you!' called Nyle. 'For *Westerling.*' At his words, a ragged cheer sounded from the Westerling archers.

GRIMBOLD DREW BACK on his reins, slowing his horse to a walk, then to a stop. He held up a bent arm, halting the movement of his men-at-arms.

Instead of using the threat of his archers to stride boldly up and seize Hopkin's horse to return his prisoner to Grimbold, Nyle had turned about on reaching the Cornish ranks and, like Treddian, bent to string his bow. As the Westerling archers arrived, each performed the same action until all stood ready.

Including Hernam's men, Grimbold faced more than thirty archers with none of his own.

Hernam spoke a command in his language. His archers notched arrows and stood with their bows at the ready. Twenty pairs of Westerling eyes looked at Nyle who looked up at Fenn. He nodded and the Westerling men copied the action of the Cornish archers.

Hernam leaned toward Fenn. 'The Reeve's men do not look willing to fight,' he said.

Fenn agreed. Rather than focusing on their adversaries to the front, many were looking left and right, seeking avenues of escape.

Wulfstan drew up alongside Grimbold. The two were only fifty paces from Hernam's lines, well within range of the archers. Wulfstan's words were just audible. 'What's done is done,' he said. 'Our position is poor. We should walk away while we can.'

Grimbold turned on him. 'Walk away?' he said sarcastically. 'Is that your best advice?'

Wulfstan frowned at Grimbold, then shook his head in frustration. He turned his horse and signalled to his men. Wulfstan's leader gave the call, and his men turned about. This time Grimbold's men did not hesitate to follow their lead. As one, the men arrayed behind Grimbold headed away from the river at a fast walk, glad to be moving out of the range of the rows of archers confronting them.

Grimbold shouted hoarsely: 'Stop! You men, stop!' Some men did stop and look around, but when they saw most were continuing to walk away, they followed.

Grimbold watched the retreat in stony silence, his eyes narrowed, his face dark with anger. He turned abruptly, leaned forward in the saddle, and raised his fist.

'By opposing *me*, Feran, Thane of Westerling,' he roared, 'you oppose the King and show yourself to be a traitor to Wessex. You're in forfeit of the *oath* you swore just *yesterday*.' He shook his fist in the air. 'You've made your choice, so accept your fate. I declare you an *outlaw*, to be arrested on sight. You haven't heard the last of this — *or of me!*'

He looked over his shoulder and realised how isolated he was. He swung his horse and kicked it into a gallop to catch up with his men.

A cheer sounded from the Cornish and the men from Westerling joined in. Fenn looked at them, his mouth tight. Did these men realise by following him, they may now all be considered traitors to the King?

He leaned down to Treddian. 'Is there a way to bypass Grimbold and arrive at Westerling before him?'

'Aah…' said Treddian, thinking. 'Yes.' He pointed south. 'If you were to head into the southern hills…. you can cross the tributaries of the Taw, then up the valley behind the old Roman villa and across the moor to meet the road to Escanceastre, then north to Westerling. A fast horse could do it.'

Fenn clapped him on the shoulder.

'King Hernam,' he said in Latin. 'I apologise, but I can't stay. I must return to Westerling before Grimbold. I fear what the Reeve may do there if he holds onto his anger.' He reverted to his own language. 'Kaela, can you….'

'No!' Kaela interrupted him. '*You* can't return to Westerling just yet. If you're there when Grimbold arrives, he'll arrest you. If he recognises anyone from this group they'll be arrested — especially us three.' She indicated Fenn, Nyle, and herself. At Fenn's expression, she said: 'Yes, I think he would try to arrest even me.'

'I won't let him arrest anyone. Westerling will stand with me.'

Kaela shook her head. 'Then you'll be provoking the very confrontation you previously tried to avoid.' She looked at him earnestly. 'It would make things worse. Grimbold won't back down this time. You did disobey the High Reeve of Wessex…' her lips creased but the smile lacked mirth, '…we all did. Wulfstan was a witness, so the Ealdorman would be forced to back Grimbold no matter what he might privately think of the Reeve's actions.' She waited a moment for her words to be understood. 'It would be best if we wait here until Grimbold leaves Westerling.'

'She's right,' added Nyle.

Fenn groaned in frustration, but Kaela's words made sense. He noticed Hernam's eyes had moved back and forth with the conversation. It would have been more polite to King Hernam to have spoken with Kaela in Latin, but he didn't know if Nyle or Treddian understood Latin. In any case, it was too late now.

'Westerling must be warned,' he insisted. 'They need to know what's happened here before Grimbold arrives….'

'Treddian can go,' said Kaela. 'He knows the way and Grimbold won't recognise him. He wouldn't have taken any notice of a single archer.'

Fenn dropped his gaze to Treddian, who immediately bent his bow and unstrung it.

'You warned Westerling before,' said Fenn. 'Can you do it again?'

Treddian nodded. 'Yes, Lord,' he said. He swung the bow onto his back.

'Tell Edelred what happened here,' said Fenn. 'I don't expect Grimbold to remain long at Westerling. I can only hope he does not take his anger out on the people. Send someone back to tell us when he's left for Witanceastre.' Fenn dismounted. 'Take my horse.'

'No!' The objection came surprisingly from Hernam. 'You should not break up that pair. Take this one.' He spoke rapidly to his standard-bearer who dismounted and led the horse forward.

Fenn stared up at Hernam.

'Ha!' said Hernam, a broad smile on his face. 'Do you think I would live with Wessex at my border and not learn the tongue of the Saxons?'

'DID I BREAK MY OATH?' asked Fenn. 'I didn't oppose the King – just that idiot, Grimbold. I acknowledge I acted contrary to the commands of the King's representative, but I have a duty to myself and to Wessex first. Grimbold would have achieved nothing by imprisoning Hopkin – other than to inflame the tension at the border. I believe I still hold the King's interests and the interests of Wessex at heart.'

Kaela placed a hand on his arm.

'You do. Don't worry about the King,' she said. 'I can explain the events to my father. The *Queen*, on the other hand....' She shrugged. 'Who knows how she'll react? I fear she'll use this incident somehow – she'll twist it to suit *her* interests.... We can only hope the King returns to Witanceastre before Grimbold gets home. He, at least, will seek our side of the story.'

THE SHADOWS WERE LENGTHENING with the approach of dusk. Fenn squatted with a hand shading his eyes as he scanned the countryside for a sign of a rider from Westerling.

During the time he had been in this spot, the view had remained maddeningly unchanged. Only the shadows lengthened and the afternoon air on his bare arms became cooler. He shook his head in frustration and rose to stretch his legs, turning back to where Kaela and Nyle waited on the hill overlooking the Tamar.

'We should have had word before now,' he said. 'Grimbold will want to get back to Eadburg and tell his story. Why delay at Westerling?'

'Who knows how Grimbold thinks,' Kaela said. 'One time he took a whole day to....'

She broke off to stare over Fenn's shoulder.

Fenn turned. A rider had broken from the trees and was galloping toward the ford.

'THE HIGH REEVE ARRESTED Treddian,' said Wyllard, speaking quickly, 'accusing him of being a traitor....' He broke off to recover his breath.

'Slow down,' said Fenn. 'You did well to get here so soon.' He caught Kaela's wry smile. 'We can wait a few more moments.'

He frowned at Kaela. The side of Wyllard's face was cut and bruised. Had he fallen from his horse? That was unlikely – Edelred would have sent Wyllard because he rode well.

Wyllard leaned against the horse and took a series of deep breaths. 'Thank you, Lord.'

When his breathing had slowed, he straightened.

'Olgood resisted,' he said. 'He drew his axe and shouted for the doors to be closed but the Reeve's men prevented that. There was no one in the yard who could help Olgood. We were unarmed against swords and spears. He tried to stop them from taking Treddian, but the Reeve's men wouldn't fight him. They just backed away from his axe.' His words had gathered speed; Fenn waved at him to slow.

'Olgood got separated from Treddian, and they took Treddian and tied him onto a horse from the stables. The Reeve and his men then left quickly. I tried to pull Treddian from the horse but I had no weapon – no one had any weapons.'

He winced from Kaela's examination of his injured cheek.

'That's not a sword cut,' said Nyle.

'No,' Wyllard said. 'The blunt end of a spear did this.'

Kaela stepped back. 'Nothing serious. He'll live,' she said.

'What did Lord Wulfstan do?' asked Fenn.

'Lord Wulfstan stood by, Lord. He didn't help the Reeve, but he didn't interfere either. He followed when the Reeve left Westerling.' He paused, then said: 'Egbert, Gisele, and the new lady came running with bows, but Olgood told them not to shoot. He said it would do no good, and the men were not enemies.'

When Fenn was silent, Wyllard added: 'I'm sorry, Lord – they took Treddian and we couldn't stop them. It was all unexpected and happened so quickly.'

'I'm sorry, too,' said Kaela. 'I didn't think Grimbold would recognise Treddian.'

'Neither did I,' said Fenn.

'The Reeve didn't recognise Treddian, my Lady,' said Wyllard. 'It was one of his men who pointed him out.'

Kaela sighed in frustration. 'I'll bet Grimbold couldn't believe his luck,' she said.

Fenn nodded. He stared eastward. Not for the first time, he felt he was constantly reacting to events that pulled and pushed him in different directions. He was as far away from enjoying a quiet peaceful life as he'd ever been.

'Before the Reeve arrived, Treddian told us what happened at the river,' said Wyllard. 'He said you would be waiting for word that the Reeve had left. Edelred sent me. I came as quickly as I could.'

'What did Treddian say happened here?' Fenn had the sudden thought that Westerling may now consider their Thane a traitor.

'He said you acted with honour, Lord. You would not break your word. He told us you had given permission for him to leave the fight but he was proud to stand beside you.'

'Thank you, Wyllard,' said Fenn. 'Go with Nyle. He'll get you some food.' He looked at Nyle. 'Have the men ready to leave at dawn.'

Nyle nodded, beckoned to Wyllard and they walked down the hill towards where the men from Westerling were camped.

Fenn took Kaela gently by the arm, stopping her from following Nyle.

'You and I should talk with Hernam,' he said. He kissed her ear. 'But we have a moment or two and I'd like to enjoy the sunset.'

'KING OFFA OF MERCIA is dead…' said Hernam, '…after a short illness. His son Egfrith now rules.'

Fenn and Kaela looked at each other, absorbing the news.

'I hear the son is weak,' Hernam continued. 'Offa was ruthless in eliminating any opposition to his reign. I wouldn't be surprised if vengeance for the blood shed by the father comes to visit the son.'

'Egfrith is Eadburg's younger brother,' explained Kaela.

Fenn recalled Kaela saying Wessex would be a shackled kingdom while Offa and Eadburg held power.

'How will Offa's death change things in Wessex?' he asked.

Kaela smiled and looked away, and Fenn regretted his question. He should have known she would be unwilling to discuss her father and Wessex in front of Hernam.

Hernam was amused by the question and Kaela's reaction. He lifted an admonishing finger at her.

'I suspect you are *more* than a nobody,' he said, but his mood remained jovial. He waved his hand, telling her he didn't expect a reply.

'And you…' he addressed Fenn. 'I called you a Saxon, but you are not. You're a puzzle. You two fit together, but somehow… you don't fit.' He pointed at Kaela. 'You are Wessex born and high-born I'd say.' His eyes flicked down. 'Your sword and your manner betray you. But…' his finger moved to Fenn, '…how did *you* come to be in Wessex…?' He smiled. 'If you're willing to tell me?'

'That's a long story,' said Fenn.

Hernam sat back and raised his hands. 'I like a good story. We have all night.'

At Fenn's glance, Kaela shrugged.

'I was raised in the north – at St. Cuthbert's monastery on the Holy Island of Lindisfarne in Northumbria. But I don't know my place of birth.' He paused. How much did the King want to know? How much did he want to tell?

Hernam waved his fingers. 'How is it that you are so far from your home?'

Fenn sighed. 'Almost two years ago, two strange ships landed on a Lindisfarne beach. The fury of the Northmen had arrived to raid the monastery. Many were killed. I was captured and taken across the big sea to their home town as a thrall. I met Kaela there. She had also been taken a few years before from the south coast of Wessex.'

'These Northmen… do their ships have square sails and tall bows carved like serpents?'

'Yes.'

'I heard of the Wessex landing. The King's Reeve was killed.'

'Yes, he was,' said Fenn. 'Kaela was taken in the same incident.'

'So, you became thralls of the Northmen… How are you now sitting at my fire?'

'We escaped.'

Hernam laughed. 'As simple as that?'

'There was nothing simple about it….'

Fenn described their journey from Lognavik to Lindisfarne and then to Wessex.

Hernam was silent for a long while when Fenn had finished, then said: 'I agree. Not a simple tale.'

'But,' he added, 'one thing I don't understand. Why did the leader of the Northmen, Ragnall, kill the outlaw Lothar and toss you his head?'

'I don't fully know, but I think he didn't like how Lothar treated Kaela.'

Fenn glanced at Kaela and caught the slight nod of her head.

Hernam shook his head in wonder. 'This Northman, Ragnall, has an unusual relationship with his thralls. He hunts you through many lands, would probably kill you if he caught you, but then at the end, gives you the gift of your enemy's head.'

'They are a strange people with strange beliefs.'

'You know a lot about these Northmen.'

'Kaela knows more than me,' said Fenn.

Hernam nodded. 'That could be useful,' he said. He stared silently into the night, absorbed in his thoughts.

Fenn leaned back against the trunk of a tree and allowed his own thoughts to run.

A king had fallen – a kingdom could become unstable. Arielle had talked about tension in the land. Already, the landscape was changing. How far would this wave of change reach? He looked at the faces of the people nearby. Cornish and West Saxons sitting together – was it possible for change to happen faster than the land could cope?

Fenn examined the food spread before the King and reached for some bread. One of Hernam's men had caught a fox; Fenn selected a piece of back meat to chew.

'IT'S A TRAP,' said Fenn. 'Grimbold took Treddian so that we would follow him to Witanceastre. He'll be waiting for us to enter the town.'

'Of course,' agreed Kaela.

'They probably won't harm him. There's no gain in that.'

'I'm not so sure. If Grimbold is angry and frustrated, he may give Treddian a beating just because he can.'

Fenn nodded. 'Do we have any alternatives?'

'We have precious few. I need to speak to my father; therefore, *I* must go.'

Fenn shrugged. 'Then I'll go too.'

'It's *you* Grimbold wants; maybe it's best if you….'

'He wants you too. He labelled us both traitors. As you eloquently put it on the banks of the Tamar – where you go, I go.'

'But…'

Fenn raised a finger. 'I have a plan that will allow us to enter Witanceastre unnoticed.'

She smiled. '*Do* you…? The gates are guarded, and the guards are sure to have our description.'

'I know.' He gave her his 'do you trust me?' smile.

'And you don't want to tell me what this plan is.'

'Where's the fun in that?' His smile turned triumphant. 'Let me just ask… when did you last visit a tannery?'

She frowned and formed a fist, punching at him. At the last moment, the punch changed to a caress on his cheek. They laughed together.

'So the only question is…' she said, '…who else should we take to Witanceastre?'

CHAPTER TWENTY

Disguise and discovery

'Beorhtric's standard is flying at the gate, so he's in residence,' said Kaela, her voice muffled by the scarf wrapped around her head so only her eyes showed.

Fenn wrinkled his nose. How could she stand to breathe through that scarf? He walked with his head lowered, his hat pulled down so the floppy brim shaded his face, and the high collar of his coat turned up to cover his mouth and chin. The stink of the rags he wore grossly offended his own nostrils so he was confident it would be effective in keeping people at a distance. Already the group following had dropped back to find clean air.

Leading the same horse and cart Eadburg had provided for their journey to Westerling, Fenn followed another cart in a procession of people approaching one of the northern gates of Witanceastre. Their cart still looked ready to fall apart, but Olgood had replaced a spoke on each wheel and pronounced the vehicle fit for the journey back to Witanceastre.

Fenn glanced at the sky. The conditions were as perfect as they could have hoped. The sun was high in a cloudless sky and the gentlest of breezes thankfully lacked the strength to disturb the fetid air around the cart. Unfortunately, the foul smell did draw unwelcome attention in the form of a swarm of persistent flies.

Their forward progress was halted frequently as each group seeking entrance to the town was inspected and questioned at the gate. It was only a cursory inspection, but Fenn had no doubt the guards would have been instructed to watch for anyone matching his description and probably Kaela also. For this reason, they had chosen to enter the town from the north rather than the west.

To disguise his height, Olgood rode on the back of the cart. A shawl covered his distinctive shoulder-length blond hair, and his face was darkened with grime. Like Fenn, he wore a high-collared cloak which, together with the shawl, gave the big man a feminine appearance from a distance – much to Fenn's amusement, which for some reason Olgood did not share. A close look at the face beneath the shawl would have dispelled any such thought, but no one wanted to get that close. To complete the illusion, Olgood was curled up, his lower half covered by a blanket that emitted the same stench as their clothing.

The stench of a tannery.

All three were unarmed. Kaela's sword and the two axes lay concealed beneath a pile of blankets in the cart but within reach if needed. Also hidden beneath the blankets was a bag containing a change of clothing. Although some carts were being searched, Fenn was sure no one would willingly want to touch the stinking pile.

The cart ahead moved forward and Fenn pulled on the horse's rope. A man in front turned and waved for Fenn to move back, to leave more space between them. Fenn smiled. He hoped for the same reaction from the guards at the gate. They should want to clear the air as quickly as possible and hurriedly usher them through.

Kaela said she knew a place where they could safely change and discard the rags and blankets from the tannery. From there, a back entrance into the court kitchens and a corridor would take them to the door leading to the interior gardens. On sunny days Beorhtric liked to rest and take refreshments under the trees after his noon audience.

Grimbold should have arrived at Witanceastre the previous day. He would certainly have reported the incident at the Tamar to the Queen, but as Kaela was involved, Eadburg might prefer to deal with the situation herself and be in no hurry to inform the King. If that were so, Kaela may be able to put their case to the King without him being prejudiced by Grimbold's version of events. On the other hand, Eadburg may have jumped at the chance to present Kaela in a bad light.

Too many ifs and maybes to be sure of success, but getting quickly to Beorhtric seemed the best way, and the simplest, to clear Grimbold's charge of being traitors to Wessex and secure Treddian's freedom – if all went to plan.

The gap in the line ahead increased. Fenn waved his hand in front of his face for the hundredth time in a vain attempt to discourage the flies.

He pulled the horse forward.

'WHERE ARE YOU FROM? State your business.'

The words were spoken routinely as the cart approached the gate. When the tannery stench reached the guard he recoiled, stepping back, his hand automatically rising to protect his nose.

'From Andeferas,' answered Fenn, narrowing his eyes to conceal their colour, '…to buy hides.'

'Dear God, that stink is *awful*,' said the second guard, a younger man, turning away, also holding his hands over his nose.

'Go through and be quick about it.' The first guard waved them on.

Kaela walked ahead and Fenn drew the cart through the gate. The first guard peered into the cart as it passed and noticed Olgood.

'What's wrong with the woman?' he asked, his voice muffled by his hands. 'Is she ill?'

Fenn coughed to disguise his laugh.

'We've walked a long way. She's tired.'

'Tired? Huh, I'm not surprised,' the second guard said. 'Looks like she has a bit of extra weight to carry if truth be told,' He expelled a breath, waving his hands in front of his nose. 'Phew! She stinks worse than the rest of you.'

Fenn looked over his shoulder. Thankfully Olgood had the sense to ignore the remarks and remain still, although Fenn noticed his hand had crept under the blankets where the weapons were concealed.

'Does she?' said Fenn. 'I can't tell.'

The first guard waved his hands, urging them to pass through the gate quickly. He blew out a lungful of air to clear his throat and nose and turned away to beckon the next group forward.

Kaela directed the cart off the main way and down narrow streets but still headed toward the town centre. Fenn was soon lost but Kaela seemed sure of her direction. Anyone they approached made an effort to give them a wide berth.

At a corner, Kaela held up a hand to stop the cart.

'That's the third group of men to pass, walking quickly,' she said softly. 'They look like they're searching. Are they looking for us?'

'Seems unlikely,' said Fenn. 'Nobody knows we're here. They could just be in a hurry.'

Kaela grunted. 'Maybe…' she said and waved him forward.

After twisting seemingly at random from one street to another, she turned into a lane with dusty stones showing evidence of little use. Along one side of the lane stood abandoned animal pens choked with tall weeds. Kaela stopped beside a decaying barn with a roof that had partly collapsed. The door was leaning at an angle and showed a gap at the bottom.

She looked up and down the lane, then tapped Olgood on the shoulder. 'Olgood, can you pry this door open a little further so we can get inside? We can change our clothes here.'

Olgood sat up and tugged the shawl from his head, raking his hands through his hair. He threw off the blanket and levered himself from the cart.

'Thank God,' he said. 'I couldn't stay under those stinking rags any longer, and I need to escape from the incessant attention of these damned flies.'

Kaela laughed. 'We're only a few streets from the back of the royal kitchens,' she said. 'This place has been abandoned since the new pig market was built. I used to sneak away and play here as a child, but I was a little smaller then….'

Olgood grasped the edge of the door and pulled. The wooden door groaned as the gap widened.

Kaela bent down to peer into the interior. 'I'll check inside.'

She disappeared through the gap, and for a moment, there was silence. Fenn and Olgood looked at each other. Kaela's head reappeared.

'All good. Come on in. Bring our clothes.'

'We should take everything from the cart,' said Fenn.

'I don't want to touch those blankets any more than I have to,' said Olgood. 'And if we take them inside, the flies will come too. I'd rather leave them where they are.'

'I understand,' said Fenn, 'but although we may have entered Witanceastre unrecognised, I don't think the guards will forget us, so it's best if we don't leave suspiciously abandoned piles of stinking tannery blankets where they might be noticed.'

Olgood nodded reluctantly. 'What about the horse and cart?'

'I'll unhitch the horse once I've changed,' Kaela said. 'I know a stable nearby where we can leave him. The cart can stay here. It already looks derelict, just like the rest of this place.'

Fenn repeated Kaela's action, looking along the lane in both directions. No one was in sight. He took the dirty hat from his head and, like Olgood, felt the need to check his hair for unwelcome visitors. Then he pivoted and, in a smooth movement, threw the hat directly at Kaela, spinning the brim. Her speed of reflex allowed her to pull aside and easily evade the hat, which spun past her and into the gloom of the interior. She poked her head back through the gap to make a triumphant face at Fenn. He laughed.

Olgood rolled his eyes and pointed at the pile of blankets. 'You're closest.'

Fenn screwed up his nose and lifted the pile of filthy blankets to reveal their weapons and the leather bag tied at the top containing a change of clothes. He gathered the shawl and blanket that had covered Olgood and handed the pile to Olgood who held his breath and thrust it through the gap in the door where Kaela pulled it inside. Fenn then gave the axes to Olgood, taking the leather bag and Kaela's sword.

He took a last look along the lane before he crouched down to follow Olgood. He thrust the bag through the gap and entered the barn.

'YOU DID OPPOSE GRIMBOLD at Westerling, but you weren't at the Tamar so you're in less danger of arrest. We're the ones he's declared outlaws and traitors – it's *us* Grimbold wants; we need to use that fact to its best advantage. You should be able to wander freely in the town. Listen for any talk about Treddian or the Tamar....' Fenn paused at Olgood's questioning look.

'Don't you think it would be better to stay together?' Olgood smiled, but only half-jokingly. 'Bad things happen when we split up.'

'Kaela and I need to talk with the King,' said Fenn. 'If we encounter the wrong people in unfavourable circumstances before we get to the King, we could be imprisoned. Then we'll need someone we can depend on to help us or get help.'

'If I'm with you, no one would take us by force.'

'I know that, but....'

'And...' Olgood interrupted him, nodding at Kaela's sword. '...I don't see how anyone could take you if Kaela doesn't want them to.'

'That would depend on circumstances, as Fenn said,' said Kaela. 'I'll resist an improper arrest but I don't want to injure anyone just doing their duty.'

'You could always just disarm them. I've seen you do that.'

'Maybe, but those situations can quickly escalate.' She placed her hand on his arm and waved a finger at him. 'I know you understand. You made the same decision not to use the bows when Grimbold took Treddian. The house-guards are innocents.' She looked up at him. 'I agree with Fenn. If we're discovered, it would be better if you weren't there.'

Olgood stared silently back at her. He raised his eyebrows in acknowledgement.

Fenn stood up. 'I wish now we hadn't brought our axes,' he said. 'The idea is not to be noticed. They're unusual and too conspicuous.' His eyes flicked down to Kaela's sword. 'And that sword, worn by a woman, shouts to all who see it.'

Kaela looked at him. 'It's not like you to be negative. You always say we use what we have.'

'I'm trying to give our venture its best chance. Maybe we should leave our weapons here.'

'It's only a short distance to the kitchens,' said Kaela. 'If anyone sees me and recognises me, it won't be because of the sword. I'm not leaving it behind.'

'Better to have and not need than to need and not have,' agreed Olgood. 'Cover the head of your axe with your tunic like this. It's more difficult to get to but less noticeable.'

Fenn copied Olgood, folding his tunic over his axe. The iron-covered shaft was still visible lying against his leg, but with the wickedly curved blade covered, it wasn't obviously a battle-axe.

'Simple and effective,' he said. He grinned at Kaela, raising his hands in surrender. 'This might just work.'

He clapped Olgood on the shoulder, then reached out and grasped him by the forearm, using the grip of the Northmen.

'Good luck,' he said. 'If all goes well, we'll meet at the Prancing Pony at sunset.'

'You'll need the luck,' said Olgood, 'not me.'

Fenn nodded. He bent to lead the way through the door.

'Now…' he said, '…the first thing we must do is leave this stink behind and the flies with it.'

KAELA SLOWED HER PACE and peered around the corner.

'It's clear.' She moved around the corner with Fenn following.

Kaela headed toward a gate set into a high wall. Through the bars of the gate, Fenn could see into a large yard. A well stood beside a covered walkway which led to a door. The cackle of hens and the peep of chickens came from inside a wooden enclosure.

'The door leads to the kitchens,' said Kaela. She nudged his side. 'Walk normally.'

Fenn straightened from the slightly bent pose he had inadvertently adopted and smiled at her. He glanced about. Several people were in sight but none were paying them any attention.

At the wall, Kaela paused to peer left and right through the gate. She opened the gate and indicated with her fingers that Fenn should follow her through. The cackle of the hens increased at their appearance, but it was caused by curiosity rather than alarm. Maybe they were expecting to be fed.

Walking swiftly to the covered walkway, Kaela bent to lift a pot overflowing with parsley, retrieving a large key underneath. Other pots decorated both sides of the walkway, displaying a variety of recognisable herbs – basil… sage… a small rosemary bush…. Fenn had to duck his head to pass under bundles of dried herbs hanging from the roof of the walkway.

'If we meet cooks or servants, or even guards, act normally – as if you should be here,' she said. 'They won't be a problem…' she grimaced, '…as long as our status as outlaws hasn't been made official. We just don't want to meet any of the wrong people.'

Kaela listened at the door before inserting and quietly turning the key. She opened the door a crack and listened again. Satisfied, she handed the key to Fenn and he replaced it under the parsley pot.

The door opened into a storage area containing food sacks piled on the floor and shelves stacked with jars of preserved fruit. Fenn smelt cabbages and from a box came the sweet waft of tomatoes.

He also heard voices.

Kaela mouthed the word '*Cooks*' and waved him forward.

They entered a large kitchen area with a stone floor. Several long tables filled the middle, cupboards and shelves lined the sides, and a row of barrels stood against one wall. The voices were coming from an adjacent room, but the volume was too low for Fenn to distinguish the words being said. He passed in front of the first of two massive fireplaces with cauldrons hanging from chains. Kaela continued unhurriedly towards three doors set in the far wall. The cooks' conversation continued at a low level with no indication they had heard anything unusual. Still, Fenn found himself holding his breath as they crossed the last part of the kitchen, only releasing it as they exited through the rightmost door into a long corridor.

The corridor was lit only by small openings in the ceiling. Fenn slowed to allow his eyes to adjust to the dim light after the open space of the kitchen. When the corridor split in two directions, Kaela chose the right-hand path. She slowed at the next corner and carefully checked the way ahead.

'*We're almost there,*' she whispered.

Fenn followed as Kaela moved to the next bend in the corridor and repeated her actions.

She beckoned him forward. 'Good, the door's not guarded.' She pointed. 'That door leads to the King's gardens….'

She walked towards the door. Before reaching it, she turned to talk to him and stiffened, looking over Fenn's shoulder. Fenn followed her gaze.

A man was strolling nonchalantly towards them, a broad smile on his face.

'Aah… the wayward daughter,' the man said, his tone that of a teacher who'd righteously caught a child in a forbidden act.

'*One of the wrong people,*' Kaela whispered to Fenn. Aloud, she said: 'Ealdorman Ethelmund. What are you doing at Witanceastre?'

Fenn struggled to remember where he'd heard that name.

'I've come to see Eadburg, Queen of Wessex,' said Ethelmund.

'Eadburg? Why Eadburg?' asked Kaela sweetly.

'I bring a message from her brother, Egfrith, new King of Mercia.'

'And why would Egfrith send you and not someone from Mercia?'

'Egfrith and I are good friends as the sons of important people often are. We've known each other for a long time.'

Ethelmund didn't seem to mind Kaela's questions. His voice was light and conversational as if he didn't mind chatting all afternoon in the corridor. His broad smile did not diminish. He was enjoying himself.

Fenn realised who this man was. He was the son of Ingeld, former Ealdorman of Hwicce, the man Nyle was rumoured to have killed at the Taw before the battle with the Cornish. Cedric had warned Nyle that Ethelmund was as bad as his father.

Fenn frowned as he understood the reason for Kaela's questions. Offa's death would certainly affect the delicate arrangement between Mercia, Wessex, and Hwicce – what did Ethelmund's presence in Witanceastre mean?

'Very interesting,' said Kaela dryly, 'but, if you'll excuse us, I'm headed to the royal gardens to see the King.'

'Very furtively it seems,' observed Ethelmund. 'Which is understandable for a pair of *outlaws*.' His eyes switched to Fenn. 'And *this*, I can only suppose, is the *traitor* and oathbreaker, Lord Feran.'

CHAPTER TWENTY-ONE

A peaceful garden interrupted

Kaela's hand moved to the hilt of her sword.

Ethelmund brought both hands up, palms facing forward, fingers spread.

'Please…' he said. 'I will not be so foolish as to draw my sword. There are some in the land who have heard of your skill.'

'What do you intend to do?' asked Kaela.

Ethelmund lowered his hands. 'Eadburg said you would come to Witanceastre and try to reach the King.' He shook his head in admiration. 'She's usually right.'

Fenn caught Kaela's frown. Was it Ethelmund's reference to the Queen by her name or his regard for her? Either way, it seemed the ealdorman was close to the Queen.

'Despite Grimbold's assurances you wouldn't get through the gates,' Ethelmund continued, 'she has had men scouring the streets and the corridors of court. She invited me to join the hunt and I was only too pleased, and now…' he gave a slight bow of his head, '…I'm doubly pleased to have been the one to, fortuitously I might add, stumble upon you. Strange are the workings of fate…' he waved a hand casually over his shoulder, '…I was headed for the kitchens. I didn't want to come down this corridor – as you know, it's a dead-end, leading only to the gardens. But something whispered in my ear… intuition? …and I turned this way….'

Fenn and Kaela exchanged glances. He was too effusive – talking too much.

'That's all very interesting,' she interrupted him curtly, 'but….'

A noise came from around the corner of the corridor.

'What do I intend?' Ethelmund returned to her question smugly. 'There are men following me – they'll be here in a moment. I intend to escort you both to the Queen.'

Kaela flicked her eyes to the door. Beorhtric should be in the gardens on the other side.

Ethelmund followed her thinking. 'By the way…' he leaned toward her secretively, lowering his voice, '…sorry to disappoint you, but the King is not taking his meal in the gardens today.' His broad smile appeared again, and he spread his arms. 'That means you've nowhere to go – I believe your game is lost. You have no choice but to come with me peacefully. I trust you agree.'

The noises became louder. Footsteps.

Ethelmund straightened. 'Aah…' he turned to look over his shoulder, '…that will be my men….'

The sound of people approaching was accompanied by a soft whispering nearby.

Ethelmund turned back. 'Shall we…?'

He stopped. Kaela's sword was at his throat.

'Then we have no time to lose,' said Kaela. 'Walk ahead, Ethelmund.'

Ethelmund's smugness was replaced with surprise and then alarm. 'Are you mad? You can't threaten me like this. The Queen will not stand for it, and neither will Hwicce.'

'That's the second time someone's asked recently if I was mad. Maybe I am. I may not want to kill you, Ethelmund of Hwicce, but I can hurt you if you don't do as I say.' She indicated the door with her eyes. 'Fenn – the door, please.'

Fenn moved swiftly to the door and grasped the handle. He reached down with his other hand and freed the fold of tunic covering his axe.

Kaela used her sword to indicate the required direction for Ethelmund.

'*Move*,' she said, placing her blade against the side of his neck.

'*Move now!*'

THE DOOR OPENED TO brilliant sunshine.

The contrast between the dank, gloomy, stained-wood corridor and the vivid colours of deep blue sky, light green trees, and grassy areas threaded with white stone paths, was stark – Fenn's eyes reacted to the bright light by involuntarily shutting. For a moment, he was blind – and vulnerable if Ethelmund had been expecting the brightness. Fenn forced his eyes to open, squinting at the scene. Ethelmund had his hand up to his eyes, shading them, but he was looking away from Fenn.

Two men were seated at a shaded table under a tree – a tray of bread, cheese, grapes and apples set before them. Both men looked up as the door opened.

'I said I was not to be….' said one indignantly. He lifted his head higher. 'Kaela? What's the meaning of…? Ethelmund…? What are you…?' He took in Kaela's sword and came to his feet.

'Why do you carry a drawn sword in such a manner?'

'Give me a moment, father. I can explain.' She nodded to the other man. 'Ealdorman Worr, I'm pleased to see you again.'

Fenn had heard of Worr, the King's closest advisor, but hadn't met him. Kaela didn't seem surprised to see Worr in the gardens.

The Ealdorman returned her acknowledgement, his eyes still wide in reaction to the unexpected intrusion.

She motioned for Fenn to close the door and murmured to Ethelmund. '*So, the King is not in the gardens today.*'

Ethelmund stared back sullenly.

'Fenn, please take his sword. Then walk him over there by the wall and keep him under control. What I have to say to my father is not for his ears.'

Fenn reached around Ethelmund and withdrew the ealdorman's sword from its scabbard. He flicked a meaningful glance to the door.

'Don't worry, they won't enter without permission,' Kaela said.

Only when Fenn had stepped back did Kaela's blade leave the Ealdorman's throat.

'Sire, I must protest!' Ethelmund cried immediately. 'This is outrageous! To be forced here at the point of a sword. I'm an *Ealdorman* and I demand….'

'You will demand *nothing*,' said Beorhtric firmly. 'You'll remain silent until I ask you to speak.'

'But, sire…'

'*Silent!*

Ethelmund gritted his teeth but kept his mouth closed.

Beorhtric's gaze switched to Fenn, and the sword now in his hand. It dropped to his waist where the Northmen's axe hung exposed on his belt. He turned to Kaela with a wary expression.

'I trust there's a good explanation for all this.'

'Of course.' Kaela replied, sheathing her sword. She waited while Fenn marched Ethelmund down a path to one of the garden walls. When Ethelmund was seated with his back against the wall, she turned.

'Ealdorman Worr, do you mind if I speak to my father privately?'

'Worr can stay,' said Beorhtric. 'If there's something to be learned, then he should hear it. I have nothing to hide from him.'

Kaela nodded. 'Very well.'

She bowed. 'Hello, father,' she said formally. 'It's good to see you and to be able to talk with you. It's been some time. How long have you been back in Witanceastre?'

'Worr and I returned yesterday,' said the King.

Kaela paused, then said: 'I suspect you didn't know Ethelmund of Hwicce was here.'

Beorhtric glanced in Ethelmund's direction. 'I did not.' Worr also shook his head.

'Eadburg is up to something,' said Kaela. 'With the death of her father, she'll be wasting no time.'

'Kaela, I know your opinion of Eadburg….'

'Father, Offa's death will change everything….'

Beorhtric held up a hand. 'I'm aware of that. Worr and I were in Tamworth when he died. We've already talked with Egfrith.'

'What's Egfrith's relationship with Eadburg now?'

The King drew back, surprised at the question. 'They are brother and sister,' he said.

'*Younger* brother and *older* sister,' said Kaela. 'Knowing Eadburg, it may not be as you would expect….'

'It sounds to me like you're wishing that to be true, Kaela,' said the King.

Worr spoke: 'Actually, sire, I did hear….'

He was interrupted by three loud knocks on the door.

'Sire!' a voice shouted, 'Trevanian of the house-guards. Do you have need of us?'

'No, Captain,' Beorhtric called. 'All's well. But wait where you are.'

'Sire!'

Beorhtric regarded Kaela. His face softened. 'Please sit down. It's good to see you too.' He indicated a place beside him. 'We can talk of politics later. Time for an explanation of this,' he waved towards Fenn and Ethelmund. 'I hope it's worthy of disturbing my meal and my solace.'

Kaela sighed. Worr moved to give her room.

'What have you been told about recent Cornish activity?' she asked as she sat down.

Beorhtric frowned. 'I know about that. Hernam crossed into Wessex a week or so ago, but Eadburg sent some men and pushed him back to Cornwall. A minor skirmish.'

So Eadburg had taken the credit. Kaela coughed to cover the retort she was tempted to make.

'Have you heard of a subsequent incident with the Cornish at the River Tamar?'

Beorhtric shook his head. 'What incident? What has Hernam done now?'

'I suspect you've been deliberately kept in the dark about the most recent events,' said Kaela. She moved closer and placed a hand on his arm. 'Much has happened since I last saw you. I need to start with the murder of Lord Orvyn on the ides of last month….'

'Murder? What murder? He had a weak heart….'

'It was something he ate…' said Worr.

'Eadburg poisoned him.'

Beorhtric stiffened. 'That's enough! Even you cannot talk of the Queen of Wessex in this manner.'

Kaela sat back, surprised. She drew in a breath. It may be better to keep that discussion for another time.

'Very well….' She took a moment to compose herself.

'While you were away at Tamworth,' she said, 'Eadburg called for me and told me she was gifting me Lord Orvyn's Westerling estate.'

Worr said: 'Gifting you *what*…?'

Kaela continued: 'She ordered me to leave immediately for Westerling.'

Beorhtric looked disturbed at the revelation but said nothing. He glanced at Worr. Worr didn't hide his astonishment.

Kaela paused. Should she declare her belief that the so-called gift was part of the Queen's plan to rid herself of both Orvyn and Kaela?

'I was suspicious of her motives,' she said. 'I thought she wanted me out of the way for some reason. I sent a messenger to Tamworth, to let you know what she'd done – but Eadburg stopped my message from reaching you.'

'Eadburg *stopped* the message?' said Beorhtric. 'Why? How?'

'I don't know how. I was told….'

'Told? By whom?'

Kaela paused. 'It doesn't matter. What's important….'

'Told by *whom*?' Beorhtric insisted.

'By… by Cedric.'

'Cedric? Who is…?' Beorhtric straightened. 'Do you mean the *outlaw*, Cedric the Bald?' Kaela's expression answered his question. His face grew stern. 'Did you talk with this outlaw?'

'Yes. But… father… what's important is that Eadburg stopped my messenger. She didn't want you to know what she'd done.'

'You were told this by an outlaw – and you *accepted* it?'

'He had no reason to lie – quite the opposite, in fact.' She held up her hands, aware that her father's opinion of Eadburg would not be swayed by Kaela's suspicions alone.

'However… this is a diversion. I have more to tell you and little time. May I continue…?'

'Little time? What do you mean?'

'Let me explain.'

Beorhtric sighed and reluctantly relaxed. He fixed her with a look that said: *Go ahead but be careful with your accusations.*

Kaela described the days after her arrival at Westerling, keeping the narrative focused on the Cornish. She told about the initial meeting with Hernam when he threatened Westerling, and the subsequent capture of Hopkin, following up with Fenn's agreement with the Cornish King to return Hopkin if Hernam withdrew, then Grimbold's arrival with a mere twenty men….

At this statement, the King's eyes narrowed: 'Twenty?' he interrupted. 'Are you sure of that number?'

'I'm sure. And *none were archers.*'

'No archers?' said Beorhtric. 'That's absurd… Are you…?' He stopped himself before he repeated his question. He turned his head sharply. 'Worr, what have you heard of this?'

'Sire,' said Worr. 'I wanted to confirm it before I brought it to you, but, yes, I was told yesterday by a guardsman that only twenty were sent.'

'…and all of them worthless layabouts,' said Kaela.

'That may be your opinion,' said Beorhtric, but his unease was apparent.

'How many men were with Hernam?' the King asked.

'Eighty. About twenty archers.'

'And Eadburg knew this?'

'Yes.'

Beorhtric's emotions played on his face. He waved his hand. 'Please continue....'

'After a chance meeting on the road, Ealdorman Wulfstan supplied thirty more, but again, footmen only.'

'Wulfstan? Was Wulfstan at Westerling?' Kaela nodded. 'I'll talk with him,' said Beorhtric. He held up a finger. 'So, Grimbold and Wulfstan arrive, but the Cornish have already retreated – what more is there?'

Kaela told of the confrontation at the Tamar, Grimbold's threat to kidnap Hopkin and hold him for a year, and Fenn's refusal to abide by that course, resulting in Grimbold labelling Fenn and Kaela outlaws and traitors.

'It was not a traitorous action,' she concluded, 'quite the opposite. As Fenn said – holding Hopkin for a year would only have inflamed tensions between Cornwall and Wessex and resolved nothing. He'd given his word to Hernam; his honour dictated that he had no choice but to disobey Grimbold and return Hopkin as he'd promised. Doing that, and doing it in opposition to Grimbold, gained Hernam's respect. Fenn did what he thought was best for Wessex.'

'Does an agreement with an enemy override a lawful order of the High Reeve of Wessex?' asked Worr.

Kaela looked at him. 'It's not that simple,' she said. 'Not when you consider the consequences of Grimbold's proposed actions.'

'Nothing is simple,' the King said. 'But you're right – all actions have consequences.'

He was silent for a moment, then he said: 'You said Fenn...' he waved a hand in Fenn's direction, '...made an agreement with Hernam. Why did *he* make the agreement and not you?'

'Lord Feran is the Thane of Westerling,' said Kaela.

'Is that so? Who appointed him a Thane?'

'I asked him to act as Thane. In your name,' said Kaela. Beorhtric frowned.

'Father…' she said quickly, '…it was complicated. Eadburg bequeathed Westerling to me… but I thought it could be difficult for the people to accept a female thane.' She didn't think it wise to voice her suspicion that Eadburg knew that and expected her and Westerling to fail.

'Fenn has addressed the problems on the estate,' she said, 'and they were considerable – and everything is now working well. The people saw and approved of how he dealt with the Cornish and have welcomed him as their Lord.' She looked at him directly. 'I ask for your acceptance of his position and confirmation.'

The King sighed, blowing out his cheeks. He looked down the path at Fenn.

'Is this a good thing?' he asked.

Was Beorhtric talking about Fenn being a thane, about Kaela appointing him, about the situation with the Cornish, or about the current situation in the garden?

Kaela decided it didn't matter. 'A *very* good thing,' she said.

Beorhtric smiled and patted her hand. 'I expected you to say that.' He sat back in his chair and Kaela allowed him time to think. Worr also kept a respectful silence.

The King waved in Ethelmund's direction. 'You've given me valuable information. But you have yet to explain why you entered my gardens with Ealdorman Ethelmund of Hwicce at the point of a sword.'

'Grimbold couldn't arrest us at the Tamar, so he kidnapped a tenant from Westerling and brought him to Witanceastre to force us to follow him. Grimbold and Eadburg hoped to capture us and accuse us before we could reach you. Ethelmund came upon us just as we were about to enter the gardens. He'd come to visit the Queen, he told us, and, at the Queen's request, had gladly joined the hunt for us. He called us traitors.'

'I don't understand this. Ethelmund thinks you're traitors to Wessex. What has that to do with Hwicce? Nonetheless, he has only to bring the charge to me and I'd arrange a hearing to clear it up.'

'That was not his intention, Father. He said he was going to take us to the *Queen*.'

'The Queen? Why would he do that if he's here…' he pointed, '…on the other side of *that* door?'

'I can only repeat – he's acting on the Queen's orders and in the Queen's interests, not yours.'

Beorhtric frowned. After a moment, he shook his head and sighed.

'Grimbold kidnapped a tenant, you say?'

'Yes, a man named Treddian.'

'Where is this man now? Do you know?'

'No. Grimbold will be holding him somewhere.' She circled her hand. 'All this is happening within your court, father, but without your knowledge.'

Beorhtric took in a deep breath and expelled it slowly.

'Worr, what do you think?'

Ealdorman Worr wrung his hands together and took a moment to put his words in order.

'Firstly,' he said, 'as you're aware, Kaela has given voice to some of our own thoughts – with Offa gone, many things will change. Egfrith is not the man Offa was. The new King did not wish to discuss Hwicce while we were at Tamworth. I find it suspicious that Ethelmund of Hwicce comes so soon to Witanceastre and does not present himself immediately to you – the relationship between Mercia, Wessex, and Hwicce may be changing faster than we expected.'

'Ethelmund said he was delivering a message to the Queen from her brother,' said Kaela.

'Was he indeed?' said the King. 'Behind my back.'

Worr said: 'Also, sire, I was about to say earlier that at Tamworth I overheard some kitchen staff talking about the new King of Mercia….'

The King gave a short laugh. 'Doing your job, then.'

Worr nodded. 'They agreed that Eadburg had bullied Egfrith mercilessly when they were young, and Egfrith would give her no favour now. Just the opinion of a gaggle of cooks, but worth considering.'

When the King said nothing, Worr continued: 'So, we must ask what message would Ethelmund be delivering. Like Kaela, I find the Queen's involvement in this secret messaging… disturbing… it makes me wonder whether the communication came from Mercia as Ethelmund claims, or from Hwicce.'

The King again said nothing.

Worr continued: 'I also find the Queen's reaction to the Cornish incident… suspicious.'

The King's narrowed eyes fixed on Worr. 'How so?' he asked slowly.

Worr rubbed his chin, seeming not to notice the King's wariness of another suspicion cast against the Queen.

'The force she sent was inadequate in several respects,' he said. 'I question why she did that. Was it simply inexperience, or was it to ensure failure? Also, it seems Grimbold did not rout the Cornish as he reported….'

'To be fair, he said they withdrew,' said Beorhtric.

'He implied that was due to his presence, and that's worrying enough. And the Queen did not tell you about the subsequent meeting on the Tamar.' He paused and laid his hands on the table. 'Do you wish me to speak frankly…?'

The King nodded.

'It makes me wonder where her loyalties lie – with her King and Wessex, or with herself.'

This time there was no contradiction from the King. He closed his eyes briefly, then opened them looking first at Kaela, then at Worr.

Worr took that as an invitation to continue: 'Regarding the Tamar…' he said. 'On reflection, I think Grimbold has once again acted impetuously. I find Fenn's actions to be sensible and eminently in your interest. Indeed, he may have quieted the western border just when we need to be able to concentrate our attention elsewhere – to the north, for example.'

Beorhtric reached for a knife on the table. He picked up an apple and made two delicate cuts to slice a piece which he carried to his mouth using the knife.

'Regarding the suspicions aired here today about the Queen,' he said. 'They will not leave this garden.' He looked at each to elicit their acknowledgement.

He ate silently, then cut another slice and chewed thoughtfully, staring out over the gardens. A pair of sparrows flitted noisily above Beorhtric's head. He looked up as they flew from the tree, one chasing the other low across the grass to alight in another tree.

Beorhtric swallowed. He leaned forward, addressing Kaela. 'Orvyn's estate at Westerling… do I understand this correctly…? On his death, Westerling was forfeited to the crown, and in my absence, Eadburg gifted the estate to you….' he paused, his lingering worries regarding that transaction showing in his tight lips. He took a breath. '…and you subsequently gave it to Fenn.'

She hadn't thought of it like that, but….

'Yes,' she said.

Beorhtric nodded. 'It seems to me it was indeed fortuitous that you and Lord Feran were there to negotiate with Hernam when he came calling….'

Kaela breathed a sigh of relief at her father's reference to Fenn as *Lord Feran*.

Beorhtric continued: '…I'm pleased with how that was handled, and I agree Fenn acted throughout in the best interests of Wessex. Despite Hernam's incursion and Grimbold's interference, the outcome is acceptable and there's no doubt Fenn has performed an important service on our western border.'

A breeze ruffled the leaves of the tree overhead. Beorhtric looked up at the gentle rustling. This time there were no birds. He let his eyes roam the gardens, then leaned his head back and breathed deeply, savouring the fresh air.

'Today we have peace in the gardens,' he said. 'But change is upon us.' He breathed deeply again. 'Tomorrow… may well bring a different outlook.'

He nodded to himself; his decision made. 'Worr, draw up a charter for Lord Feran. I'll make him a King's Thane, so there's no misunderstanding.'

'Yes, sire.'

Beorhtric stood up and beckoned to Fenn. 'Come over here, young man,' he called. 'Bring Ealdorman Ethelmund with you.'

While Fenn got Ethelmund to his feet, Beorhtric took Kaela's hand.

'Thank you, Kaela. You always had a sharp mind. I should have taken you to Tamworth.' He reached down and picked some grapes with one hand. 'But, if I'd done that…' he mused, '…the fate of the kingdom would have unfolded differently, and we may now have serious trouble with Hernam.' The grapes went into his mouth and he chewed thoughtfully. 'You've opened my eyes to several issues. Maybe I should listen to you more often. I need a word now with Eadburg and Grimbold – and Wulfstan also. Some questions need to be….'

The door flew open and Eadburg swept into the garden, followed by a group of men with swords drawn.

'*Here's your chance,*' said Kaela to herself.

'*Her!*' the Queen pointed at Kaela, 'and…' she moved her finger in an arc to rest on Fenn. '…*him!* They're both traitors to Wessex. Seize them.' The men split to move toward their targets.

'*Stop!*' Beorhtric roared the word, rising to his feet. The men froze where they were, looking alternately at the King and the Queen for instructions. Fenn stopped also and reached out to halt Ethelmund.

The Queen looked at Beorhtric sharply, then composed herself and walked towards the table.

'Ealdorman *Worr,*' she purred in a voice Kaela knew well. It dripped with thinly disguised loathing. 'Why am I not surprised to find *you* here…?'

Worr's eyes narrowed, but without allowing him to speak, the Queen turned to Beorhtric.

'My dear,' Eadburg said, speaking quickly. 'I can prove these two, *including your daughter,* have acted against Wessex. They disobeyed the direct orders of the High Reeve in a time of conflict. There are impeccable witnesses to their actions. She's been misled by that boy. Together, they're a dangerous pair. Lock them away before they can do any further harm, and I'll bring you the proof.'

The King regarded his wife without speaking. As the unexpected silence grew, the Queen's demeanour changed from righteous anger to unease. Her eyes flicked to Kaela and back to Beorhtric.

'What has she told you? Has she begged for your mercy? What twists of the truth has she spun?'

Kaela laughed. 'Truth is truth; it cannot be twisted and remain the truth, Eadburg.' She echoed the Queen's phrase: 'Why am I not surprised *you* don't understand that?'

The King held up his hand to stop the conversation.

'Ethelmund,' he said, 'I want to talk with you later – wait for me in the Great Hall. For now, leave us.'

Ethelmund turned his gaze to Eadburg. He didn't move.

Beorhtric raised his voice. 'Ethelmund, go *now* if you would.'

Ethelmund looked again at Eadburg, but she stared back at him without expression.

Fenn raised the sword. The Ealdorman glanced at Fenn and snorted with annoyance. He held out his hand for his sword, his face dark. Fenn bowed and presented the sword hilt first. Ethelmund snatched at the weapon and Fenn had to draw his hand away quickly to avoid injury. The Ealdorman sheathed the sword, twisted on his heel and marched for the door. The look he gave the Queen in passing was smouldering – the man was not happy with the turn of events. He seemed to be expecting something from the Queen, but the Queen's gaze was stone.

'Leave us too, Trevanian,' said Beorhtric. 'Take your men.'

Beorhtric looked at Eadburg. 'Worr stays – and so do Kaela and Lord Feran.'

'*Lord…?!*' the growl of indignation that issued from Eadburg's throat was feral. Beorhtric waved her to silence.

'Eadburg,' the King said sternly, pointing to a chair, '…sit down.'

Eadburg glared first at Kaela then briefly at Fenn before resting her gaze on Worr who had a smug look on his face, seeming to enjoy her discomfort.

'Wipe that smile off your face, you bloodsucking leech!' she said with venom.

'Eadburg!' the King said firmly. He again indicated the chair.

Eadburg sat. She raised her chin to cast a defiant look at Beorhtric. Her curled hands and narrowed eyes gave her a distinctly feline appearance.

And there were few creatures more dangerous than a cornered wildcat.

CHAPTER TWENTY-TWO

Drama at the banquet

'She won't take Beorhtric's rebuke quietly,' said Kaela. 'Especially as it was delivered in front of witnesses.'

'Then I suggest we keep out of her way,' said Fenn.

'It's not me I'm worried about,' said Kaela. 'She knows the King gets his advice and information from Worr and because of that she hates the man.'

'Which one is Worr?' asked Olgood.

Kaela pointed at the top table. 'There, sitting on Beorhtric's right.'

As she spoke, Worr leaned in to whisper in Beorhtric's ear. The King at first smiled and then laughed loudly, clapping Worr on the back.

The King's table was set across the Great Hall at one end. All other tables were set lengthways. The Queen was seated to the King's left and beside her was Ealdorman Ethelmund of Hwicce, in whose honour the King had strangely decided to hold this banquet. Kaela had attempted to explain the diplomatic threads that Beorhtric was trying to weave by honouring Ethelmund, intended to strengthen the ties between Wessex and Hwicce, but to Fenn the idea of praising the Ealdorman, who was almost certainly plotting to undermine the kingdom, made no sense.

Kaela and Fenn had been offered seats at the King's table but had decided to join Olgood and Treddian at the table closest to the western wall of the Great Hall. The seating at the top table was completed by Ealdorman Wulfstan of Wiltonshire and his wife Alburga, next to Worr, and High Reeve Grimbold and the lady Fenn had seen on the wagon at Witanceastre market, presumably his wife, sitting on the other side of the King, beside Ethelmund.

The tables were covered in food – more food than Fenn had ever seen in one place. Roasted cuts of pork, beef, venison, chicken, and pheasant, dishes of salmon and eel, pies of many sizes, cheese, bowls of peas, beans, and onions. Bread was everywhere, and one had only to hold up a cup to have it refilled with wine.

As Fenn watched, Grimbold reached out an arm to claim a chicken leg, oblivious that his loose sleeve had brushed through a saucer of gravy. His face was already red from the wine which he consumed at twice the rate of his neighbours. He tore a bite from the leg and lifted his cup while still chewing, only to find it empty. His roar of '*Wine!*' was muffled by unswallowed pieces of chicken ejected from his mouth by the cry, but it was still loud enough to be heard throughout the Hall. Holding the cup high, he searched for someone to fill it. His roving eyes discovered Fenn watching him and locked there, his bloated face darkening with an immediate scowl. He slammed his cup on the table and held out the chicken leg in Fenn's direction. He raised his other hand and snapped the bone in two, exaggeratedly mouthing the words: '*That's you, thief*' at Fenn.

A girl carrying a pitcher came to attend to Grimbold's empty cup. Grimbold continued to stare at Fenn while she filled it.

Fenn dropped his gaze to find Kaela looking at him.

'Pay him no mind,' said Kaela, 'he's more bluster than substance.'

'I hope so. The man seems incapable of realising I did him a favour.'

'He likes to have someone to attack. It makes him seem to have an opinion. He throws his considerable weight around but it's mostly talk. Besides…' she gave a mock bow, '…you're a King's Thane now, and you answer only to the King.'

They both looked up at another loud laugh from the top table. Beorhtric leaned back in his chair, chuckling happily. Eadburg took him by the arm to get his attention but Beorhtric waved her away and bent back to say something to Worr. They both laughed again, the King banging his hand on the table. Ealdorman Wulfstan must have overheard what was said and he joined in the laughter.

The glare delivered by the Queen in response to the King's snub was hot enough to melt iron.

'Grimbold may be bluster, but that one is not,' said Kaela.

'I see what you mean,' said Fenn. 'She's not good at hiding her thoughts.'

'She'll bide her time, but if history is anything to go by, she'll have her vengeance,' said Kaela. 'In a few days or weeks, she'll move against Worr somehow. I've tried to warn him but neither he nor my father will listen.'

'Would she move against the King?' asked Olgood. 'She doesn't seem to mind scheming behind his back.'

'No… never,' said Kaela. 'Without Beorhtric, now that Offa, her father, has gone, she'd be nothing more than a dead king's daughter.'

'She eagerly acted as ruler of Wessex when Beorhtric was in Tamworth,' argued Olgood. 'Maybe she likes the role.'

'But *he* gives her that authority. Without him, she's nothing – and the Ealdormen of Wessex would be rid of her before the sun rose.'

'Does she have any forces loyal to *her*?' Olgood asked. 'Any good men under her control? We've only seen the worst of her house-guards – apart from Nyle and his men.'

Kaela paused to hold out her cup for a refill. She reached across the table with her other hand and worked a sliver of eel from the bone.

'The house-guards are the King's, of course, but I believe she's cultivated a group she considers loyal to her by rewarding that loyalty. Grimbold is always taking bands of men off for so-called training.'

Kaela replaced her refilled cup on the table and paused while she chewed on the eel. 'I've talked to my father about it – he thinks I'm overly suspicious.' She shrugged.

'How many?' Olgood persisted.

'If I added them together… I've noticed maybe forty or fifty.'

'That's… a small army. For what purpose?'

Kaela swallowed. 'I've no idea. Since we've been away from court, I haven't been able to keep my eye on her. But one thing I can always be sure of – she'll be up to something. And, also for sure, it'll involve that fool Grimbold. Look at them now.'

Eadburg was leaning across Ethelmund, talking intently with Grimbold, who was struggling to concentrate. Eadburg scowled at him, pointing at his wine cup. Fenn couldn't hear her, but from her lips he thought she said the words '*Be ready.*'

'Did she just say 'Be ready' to Grimbold? Ready for what, I wonder.'

'Be ready for whatever she next desires of him,' said Kaela. 'She's probably told him he's drinking too much. *That* at least is one man she has completely under her control.' She took a sip of wine.

Eadburg leaned back, and Grimbold appeared to forget her admonitions immediately. He clapped Ethelmund on the shoulder, saying something to him and raising his mug. The Ealdorman responded and raised his own. They touched their mugs together exuberantly, causing wine to spill from both. Each man reacted to avoid the splash of wine and laughed at the attempt of the other.

'Grimbold and Ethelmund seem friendly,' said Fenn. 'Do they know each other?'

'I wouldn't say so. They may have met but not often.'

'They're sharing something. I wonder what they have to talk about?' mused Fenn.

'I suspect the wine is doing most of the talking,' said Kaela. 'But… they are similar in one respect.' At Fenn's inquiring glance, she said: 'They think only of themselves and not of the people – which makes Ethelmund spectacularly unsuitable as a ruler.'

Fenn recalled Arielle saying the same thing about leaders – her words were coming to mind often – and Cedric the Bald had also given a poor opinion of Ethelmund. He looked to the top table. Both men wore a smug, self-satisfied expression, perhaps as Kaela suggested, due to the wine. Thinking of their similar natures led to another recollection – the incident at the Weyhill Inn on the way to Westerling. Those mercenaries had been heading for a meeting with Grimbold.

'Do you remember the men at the Weyhill Inn?' he asked Kaela. 'I don't think I told you, but before you made your dramatic entrance, Olgood and I overheard them talking about being paid by Grimbold. That was weeks ago.'

Kaela nodded at him, her face thoughtful. 'Grimbold hiring mercenaries. That *is* interesting.'

Olgood also nodded, remembering. 'Why would Grimbold be gathering men?'

Kaela shook her head, having no answer. If *she* had no answer, Fenn certainly didn't. He shrugged, reaching out to claim a piece of pork.

Not for the first time, he was glad to leave considerations of Wessex court politics to Kaela.

WHEN HE NEXT LOOKED at her, she was searching the room.

'What are you looking for?'

'I'm looking for Sergio. He doesn't like to attend these gatherings if he can avoid it, but I haven't had a chance to catch up with him. I hoped he might be here.'

'I'd like to talk with him too,' said Fenn, smiling at her. 'I'd like to ask him what kind of pupil you were.'

'The rebellious kind,' suggested Olgood.

'Not at all,' said Kaela. 'The energetic kind would be a better description. If Sergio said to do an exercise ten times, I did it twenty.' She shrugged. 'A stupid and futile attempt to send a message to Eadburg that she would not beat me down. I needn't have bothered as she didn't notice, but I'm glad I made the effort.'

'That attitude made you what you are,' said Olgood. 'A master of the sword.'

Kaela smiled. 'Now I think of it, those sessions could have been gruelling and exhausting, and the endless repetition could have been boring, but I didn't experience those feelings. I was always asking Sergio for more – better techniques, how to be quicker, how to fix a balance problem. I practised each move until I didn't need to think.' She reached for the hilt of her sword. 'And the Lord of the Battle is a perfect fit….' She finished with a grunt of embarrassment.

Fenn chuckled. Her searching hand had found nothing to grasp. No weapons were permitted at the banquet.

She laughed with him, then leaned forward to speak to Treddian, gesturing at the food on the table.

'Don't be shy, Treddian. Eat all you want. Drink. There's plenty of wine.'

'Thank you, my Lady. There's just so much….'

Fenn and Kaela shared a glance. A few short weeks ago, Treddian had left Westerling because he feared starvation. In front of him was more food than he could possibly eat in a week.

'I know. It's hard to understand….' She struggled to find the words to explain how one part of the kingdom could have so little and another so much.

Treddian didn't notice her difficulty. 'Three days ago,' he said, 'I was in a dungeon….'

'A misunderstanding that's thankfully been cleared up.'

'And I thank you and Lord Feran for that,' Treddian said. 'It's just that… *now* I'm in the Great Hall of Witanceastre and I'm dining with the King!' He waved his hand at the top table in the Great Hall.

Kaela smiled. 'You are indeed,' she said. 'You'll have a good story to tell that little baby of yours.'

FENN SAT BACK IN his chair. His stomach was full but he picked at a bunch of grapes. His other hand was engaged in idly swirling wine around in his cup. He would have preferred to be drinking mead or ale but he was becoming used to the wine.

'It's like watching a play being enacted on a stage for our benefit,' said Olgood, his eyes on the King's table. 'The Queen has barely taken her eyes off Beorhtric and Worr, but both are completely unaware of the intensity of her scrutiny.'

Fenn glanced up and nodded.

Ealdorman Worr drained the last of the wine from his cup. He placed it on the table and took a handful of nuts. While he was chewing, Beorhtric said something and Worr almost choked with laughter.

Eadburg tore her gaze from Beorhtric and swung around to Ethelmund. She spoke to him sharply, tapping her finger hard on the table to emphasise some point, then pointing at the kitchens. Her hand closed into a fist as she thrust some more words at him.

She abruptly stood, pushing her chair aside. Ethelmund looked up in surprise, frowning, and asked her a question. She picked up a knife and brandished it at him before giving him a terse answer. She flung the knife back onto the table, followed by her napkin, whirled, and strode towards the hallway and the kitchen entrance. The disturbance caused Beorhtric to raise his head to watch her go but he turned back at a remark from Wulfstan. Worr replied, and the three bent their heads together.

'What now? Has she left in a sulk?' asked Olgood. 'Is the entertainment over?'

'I don't know,' said Kaela. 'It's not like her to retreat.'

Treddian gave a loud belch, generating a gust of laughter at the table. He reddened and apologised profusely. Olgood laid a hand on his shoulder.

'No need to apologise,' he said. 'It shows you're appreciating the food.'

Fenn clapped Olgood lightly on the shoulder. 'And few people appreciate food as much as Olgood,' he said. 'That's because he eats enough for two.'

Kaela laughed. 'It's Gisele who should be eating for two.'

Olgood nodded, laughing with her. 'Well, this is good food,' he said. 'We should enjoy it while we can. You never know what lies around the corner….'

'Olgood…?' said Fenn in mock astonishment, '…taking a dim view of the future? I never thought I'd hear that.'

'It *is* good food,' agreed Treddian. He stood to reach across the table for a piece of venison and lifted his wine cup. 'It was worth spending two days in a dark, smelly room to be able to eat like this.'

'That's better,' said Fenn. 'You see, Olgood, Treddian's expecting the future to be an *improvement* on the past.'

Two girls entered the Hall from the kitchens carrying more pitchers of wine. The first girl walked behind the chairs of the top table, leaning across and filling the empty cups. Grimbold quickly drained his and held it out. The girl poured his wine and also topped up Ethelmund's cup. The second girl waited by the wall until the first had emptied her pitcher, then stepped forward and filled Worr's cup. She turned away without checking Wulfstan and Alburga. Beorhtric finished his wine and turned, cup in hand, for a refill. The girl didn't notice and Beorhtric opened his mouth to call her but was distracted by Eadburg re-entering the Hall. She caught Beorhtric's eye and smiled sweetly at him.

'Good,' she called loudly, waving her hand over the top table. 'Your cups have been filled.'

She turned to encompass the Hall.

'I propose a toast,' she announced forcefully enough to quieten the conversation.

She waited until the last murmur died, then lifted her chin and announced: 'A *toast* to our guest of honour, Ealdorman Ethelmund of Hwicce!'

She lifted the cup of wine she'd been carrying high then brought it to her lips and drank deeply.

Fenn glanced at Kaela, his eyebrows raised. She shrugged. He considered protesting by refusing to toast the Ealdorman but decided it would be a petty gesture. He raised his cup and sipped at his wine, his action copied by the other diners in the Hall.

Beorhtric lifted his cup and cursed, thumping the empty cup back on the table. He waited until Worr had finished the toast then took Worr's cup from him, stood, and drank to the toast from it.

'To Ealdorman Ethelmund of Hwicce,' he said, wiping his lips with the back of his hand. 'We welcome him as our guest today and tomorrow may Wessex and Hwicce long continue to share our Saxon values and our friendship.'

There was a crash as Eadburg's cup slipped from her hand.

'Beorhtric!' she cried. Her face seemed to drain of blood and she fell to her knees. 'My God….'

'What is it?' called Beorhtric. 'Grimbold. Help her up.'

Eadburg moaned. Grimbold pushed himself out of his chair and bent to help her to her feet. She tried to stand but couldn't. Grimbold lifted her.

'Beorhtric,' she cried again. 'No! Oh my God…' She gagged as her words caught in her throat.

'What's happening to her? Take her to her rooms and call the physician,' Beorhtric commanded.

Grimbold was unsteady on his own feet; he staggered but managed to lift and carry the Queen from the Hall accompanied by his wife fussing behind him, looking to right and left for help.

Fenn scanned the room. People had risen to their feet in alarm. Beorhtric tilted his head to watch Grimbold disappear, then looked out over the Hall. He seemed confused.

Kaela stood up. 'What *is* happening?' she asked. She frowned. 'Something's wrong.'

She pushed her chair back and ran along the wall toward the top table where the King was again staring after Eadburg, his expression pained. Fenn also stood and followed her. He heard the scrape of Olgood's chair.

Beside Beorhtric, Worr sat down heavily and coughed. His hand went to his throat.

'I can't…' he said, struggling for breath, coughing again.

Kaela reached the top table. She spared a glance at Worr, then turned to her father.

'Father… what is it…?'

Beorhtric looked at Kaela. 'That's not like her,' he said. 'She's usually hardy.' He raised the wine cup in his hand. 'This wine is….'

Worr collapsed onto the table, coughing hard. Wulfstan rose and reached out to help him. Worr's hands came up to his mouth. He pulled one away, grimacing, to clutch at his chest. The hand was stained red. It looked like blood, but Kaela saw it was wine. Worr's body heaved and more wine spilled from his mouth, spreading over the table. Wulfstan grasped Worr by the shoulders, helping him into a seated position.

'Worr, what's the matter?' he asked urgently.

Alburga brought a napkin to wipe the man's mouth. Ealdorman Worr groaned in pain and his head flopped to the side. Wulfstan tried to hold him but Worr slid from his hands. Alburga gave a short cry as the ealdorman toppled slowly to the floor, his body spasming, his hands clenching at his side, his face suddenly white and sweaty.

'*Poison!*' breathed Kaela. She turned to her father, her face stricken. 'My God… you drank from the same….'

Beorhtric swayed on his feet. He reached for the back of a chair, missed, and stumbled with a groan into her arms. He coughed.

Kaela cried out: '*Fenn! He's been poisoned!*'

Wulfstan bellowed: 'Close the doors! Nobody leaves!' He motioned to a guard standing by the doorway.

'The King is ill. Fetch the physician.'

'But…' the guard protested. '…the Queen…'

Wulfstan yelled in the man's face: '*For the King! Now!*'

CHAPTER TWENTY-THREE

Changes in the House of Wessex

'Treddian, get some milk from the kitchen,' said Fenn. 'Olgood, find the girls who served the wine.' He turned to Wulfstan: 'We need to get Worr and the King out of here. They shouldn't be seen like this.'

Olgood turned without a word and headed for the kitchens, Treddian on his heels.

'Worr's already dead,' said Wulfstan. 'Why have you sent for milk?'

'The physician at Lindisfarne told me it weakens many poisons.' He looked at Ealdorman Worr, curled into a ball on the floor, his eyes open, staring at nothing. 'We should still take them both out of the Hall,' he said. Then to Kaela: 'Where can we go?'

'The kitchen.' Her voice was almost inaudible. Beorhtric's head was cradled in her arms. The King groaned and his body contracted, his knees drawing up to his chest.

'Beorhtric may not have drunk as much as Worr.' Fenn waved to two men by the door. 'You two, carry the King to the kitchen. Be quick.'

'I'll help carry him,' Kaela said.

'Kaela, let them….'

'*I'll* carry him,' she said forcefully.

She reluctantly let one of the men take the shoulders of the King and lift him. The movement forced another groan from Beorhtric's throat – his eyes were closed tight and his lips drawn back in a grimace of pain. His arms were clutched across his chest as if to hold himself together. Kaela stood and took hold of his legs. The other man helped Wulfstan carry Worr and they followed behind Kaela.

'What about the Queen?' asked Wulfstan. 'Has she been poisoned too?'

Fenn looked for the Queen, but the corridor was empty. He looked back at the table for Ethelmund. Why hadn't he offered to help? But Ethelmund was gone.

A GROUP OF FOUR anxious kitchen staff were huddled in the corner of the kitchen, one still carrying a pot she'd been cleaning. Fenn went to them and ushered them from the kitchen into a side room.

'The King is ill,' he said. 'Please wait in here.'

'Something he's eaten…?' one asked, horrified.

'No,' Fenn said. He closed the door.

Kaela held Beorhtric's head up and tipped milk into his mouth. The King spluttered and choked. He groaned, his body twisting in pain, wanting to roll onto his side.

Worr's body was laid on a table. Wulfstan joined the gathering around the King.

'Please, father. Drink it.'

The King choked again and coughed, a mixture of wine and milk spurting from his mouth. His eyes opened and he looked at Kaela, his face creased with pain and shock. He tried to speak.

She wiped his face with her sleeve. 'Father…' she said.

The King's eyes closed tightly. He spasmed once, then fell limp. A cry of despair from Kaela. She lifted his head.

A man in a white gown appeared, walking purposefully past Fenn. He moved to Beorhtric's side, one hand pushing up an eyelid and the other feeling at the King's neck. He bent his head to place his cheek beside Beorhtric's mouth, remaining still for a moment. Then he straightened.

'The King is dead,' he said matter-of-factly.

Nobody spoke. Kaela looked at the man, her face white. Her mouth opened but no sound emerged. Fenn took her shoulders and drew her to him. He felt her sag and held her tightly.

The man, who Fenn assumed was Beorhtric's physician, returned Kaela's gaze. 'Where's the Queen?' he asked. 'Why isn't she here?'

'She was also ill,' said Fenn. 'Did you see her?'

'I heard shouting. I've come from the infirmary,' the man said, 'I haven't seen the Queen.'

'If she's also been poisoned, it may be too late,' said Wulfstan.

'Eadburg has not been poisoned,' said Kaela.

'What?' said Wulfstan. 'How do you know? She collapsed too.'

'Yes,' agreed Kaela, 'she did. But that was because she realised what had happened. *She* was not poisoned.'

Wulfstan looked at her. 'I don't understand.'

'Fenn,' Kaela said quietly. 'I need my sword.'

Fenn turned to Treddian. 'Do you know where our weapons were left? In the room beside the entrance to the Great Hall?'

Treddian nodded.

'You know Kaela's sword?'

'Of course.'

'Why do you need a sword?' asked Wulfstan. 'Do you think we'll be attacked?'

Fenn didn't reply. He said to Treddian: 'Fetch them quickly. Kaela's sword and our two axes.'

'Yes, Lord.' Treddian left at a run.

Wulfstan opened his mouth to speak again, but the physician spoke first.

'Why are you talking of the Queen being poisoned?' he asked. 'What happened here? The King doesn't appear to be wounded.'

Kaela straightened. 'The Queen poisoned Ealdorman Worr's wine,' she said tightly, 'and Beorhtric drank from the same cup.'

Alburga exclaimed: 'Oh my God….'

Wulfstan jerked his head back in alarm. 'What!?' You think… dear God. How could you know that…?

'The *King*? Poisoned?' The physician interrupted him. He bent down and opened Beorhtric's mouth, peering inside and sniffing. 'Yes… you may be right… foaming… vomiting, sweating… discolouration… probably Wolfsbane – the root must have been used and a large dose for it to act this quickly. You tried to give him milk…?'

'Yes,' said Fenn, 'I was told….'

'You did the right thing. It may have helped. It was just too late.'

'The King was poisoned?' Wulfstan shook his head. 'And Worr. And you say the *Queen*…? But….'

He was interrupted again by a door opening. Olgood appeared.

'Fenn, you need to see this.' He beckoned with his hand.

Fenn looked at Kaela.

'Yes, go,' she said. 'I want to stay here.'

Fenn followed Olgood through the door into the same herb walkway he and Kaela had used to enter the kitchens when they came to Witanceastre a few days ago. Olgood led him toward the hen house. There he stopped. The hens were strangely quiet.

Fenn saw a form lying on the ground, then another. He squatted down beside the first. In the moonlight, it was clear who was sprawled and abandoned here. The two serving girls, dark lines drawn across their throats, lying in pools of their own blood that shone as black as pitch in the silvery light.

Fenn stood up quickly, his hand reaching automatically for his axe. He grunted when he found it wasn't at his side.

'There's no one here,' said Olgood. 'I've had a look around.'

'These poor innocents….' Fenn said, feeling his voice choke.

Olgood nodded. After a moment, he asked: 'Why would anyone…?'

'To silence them – they knew or saw too much. Kaela thinks the Queen poisoned the wine one of these girls poured into Worr's cup, and the King drank from the same cup.'

'Is the King…?'

Fenn met Olgood's eyes. 'Yes.'

Olgood looked down at the bodies. 'Did you suspect this when you asked me to look for the girls?'

'No.' Fenn shook his head. 'I also thought it must have been the wine that was poisoned. Worr was affected first. I merely wanted to ask who told one of them to pour Worr's wine. But it seems we know the answer to that question.' He indicated the bodies by waving his hand. 'The taking of these souls…wasn't… it was just *unnecessary*.'

Olgood put his hand on Fenn's shoulder. 'No one can help them now. Whoever did this is gone. We should get back. Kaela needs us.'

'We can't leave them here like this.'

'We can for now,' said Olgood.

KAELA WAS STRAPPING ON her sword.

'Take good care of him,' she said to the physician.

'Beorhtric was my King, and Worr an ealdorman of Wessex,' the man said. 'They will both receive the best care I can give.'

'Of course.' Kaela drew in a breath and nodded to him. 'Thank you.'

She spoke calmly but her eyes were smouldering. She took Lord of the Battle from the scabbard and inspected the sword.

Treddian handed Fenn and Olgood their axes.

'Should I get a sword?' he asked.

'Do you know how to use one?' asked Fenn.

'I'm more comfortable with a bow, but I can swing a scythe and thrust with a hayfork. I do the same with a sword, don't I?'

'It's not quite the same,' said Fenn. He dropped his iron-handled axe into the loop at his belt.

He beckoned to get the attention of Kaela and Wulfstan and related Olgood's discovery of the bodies of the two serving girls.

Wulfstan cursed. 'What damned plot is unfolding here?' He gestured and one of his guards handed him a sword.

Alburga had her hands to her mouth, digesting the news about the girls. The physician acted as though he hadn't heard. Kaela also looked pained, but she recovered quickly and scanned the kitchen.

'Where are the pitchers they used?' she asked.

Olgood pointed. 'There on the bench, by the wine cask.'

Kaela walked to the pitchers and bent over them to examine their contents.

'As I suspected,' she said. 'There's wine in both.'

'Wine in both?' asked Wulfstan. 'Does that mean something?'

'It means,' said Kaela, her mouth firm, 'that the first girl didn't stop filling cups because her pitcher was empty – she stopped because she was told not to fill Worr's cup. Just as the second girl was told to *only* fill Worr's cup – with the poisoned wine. You're right; this is a plot – a plot to kill Worr that has also taken my father's life.'

'Are you suggesting the Queen did this?' asked Wulfstan.

'Yes,' Kaela said. 'Her hand is all over it. She was in the kitchen when the pitchers of wine came out.'

Wulfstan stared at her. 'Yes… but….'

Kaela held up a hand. She thought a moment, then added: 'Eadburg brought her own cup from the kitchens to be sure she didn't drink the wrong wine.'

Wulfstan's eyes widened. 'Yes, I saw that. I thought it was strange she had a new cup. She dropped it when she saw Beorhtric drink from Worr's cup. I see it now. She was in shock, not pain.'

'Her reaction proves her guilt,' said Kaela. 'Before either man had shown any effect, she *knew* the wine in that cup was poisoned and knew what would happen after Beorhtric drank from it.'

Wulfstan frowned. 'My God! She *must* have known. She called out to Beorhtric. Despair took the strength from her legs.'

'Yes, but her despair was not for her husband or her King – it was for herself. At that moment, she realised what she'd done. In a heartbeat, her position and her life were ruined.' Kaela grunted. 'And by her own hand.'

Wulfstan sighed, then nodded in agreement. He motioned to one of his men. 'Let the people in the Hall go. No need to keep them. We know how the King died.'

Kaela said: 'She killed Orvyn the same way.'

Wulfstan drew in a breath. 'Also poisoned? My God, where is this going…?'

Kaela placed her hand on the hilt of her sword. 'I swear she'll not get away with it this time.'

'What do you want to do?' asked Fenn.

'Find her.' She looked at Fenn. 'Will you come with me? Olgood? You'd better come too, Wulfstan – your authority may be needed.'

Fenn's mind raced. Wulfstan's *authority*, what did that mean? The authority to face the Queen? With the King dead, *who ruled Wessex?* The Queen? Kaela said that was so only while Beorhtric was alive. If not Eadburg, then Kaela – the King's daughter? Beorhtric had educated Kaela to rule, but she had told Fenn that the ealdormen of Wessex would not accept her. Who did that leave? Wulfstan – a senior ealdorman? He wasn't acting as though *he* now ruled. Maybe no one had had time to think about it.

'Wait here, Treddian,' said Fenn. 'Help Alburga and the physician. Get those poor girls in from the yard when you can.'

He strode after Kaela, Wulfstan and Olgood behind him.

OUTSIDE THE QUEEN'S ROOMS, Kaela knocked loudly on the door.

'If she's inside, why are there no guards?' she asked.

She knocked again and called: 'Eadburg!'

She tried the door. It was unlocked.

'No guards *and* the door unlocked….' Kaela said slowly. She pushed the door open.

The room was empty.

Kaela turned, her eyes searching the corridor.

'Where would she go?'

Fenn said: 'The stables?'

Kaela looked at him and nodded. She took two steps along the corridor then stopped. Turning abruptly back to the Queen's rooms, she strode to the door and thrust it wide.

'The jewellery's gone!'

The centrepiece of the room, Eadburg's tiered table, customarily strewn with evidence of her wealth, stood bare.

'She's leaving,' Kaela said. She set off along the corridor at a run.

'Where did Ethelmund go?' asked Fenn at her shoulder. 'Did anyone see him?'

No one replied.

Wulfstan: 'And Grimbold? Are they all in this together?'

'It's possible,' said Kaela. 'But Eadburg's attack on Worr was personal.'

She descended a flight of stairs and headed along a cloistered path. She glanced at Fenn.

'Whatever she intended, she killed the King and now she's running for her life. She'll keep Grimbold with her. I don't know about Ethelmund.'

'From the look of those three tonight,' Olgood said, 'they were hatching some plan together, but it's probably been thwarted by the death of Beorhtric…. ah…' he said quickly, 'I'm sorry, Kaela… I didn't mean to say….'

Kaela looked back at him and smiled grimly. 'I understand,' she said. 'Let's just find Eadburg and Grimbold.'

'What about Grimbold's wife?' asked Fenn. 'She left with him.'

Kaela shook her head without replying. She passed through the gates at the end of the pathway, turning right to cross a courtyard. Two horses standing freely at the far side of the yard backed nervously away from the sound of running feet. They spun away together and broke into a gallop, heading into the open fields beside the stables.

Kaela slowed to a stop.

'She was here,' she said. 'She's released the horses to slow any pursuit.' She looked at Wulfstan. 'Her intent is clear. She's leaving Witanceastre and making it hard for anyone to follow. We need to stop her. We need to close the town gates.'

'You won't get that order to the gates before the Queen,' said Wulfstan.

'She's not the Queen anymore!' retorted Kaela. Wulfstan acknowledged her statement with a nod.

'Where will she head?' asked Olgood. 'To Mercia? Or will she go into hiding?'

'She won't go to her brother,' said Kaela. 'She'll get no welcome there, especially not as a fugitive. She could go with Ethelmund to Hwicce, but I don't think she'd trust him. More likely to the south coast and across the sea to Francia. Offa had a good relationship with King Charles of the Franks.'

'It wouldn't be wise for the four of us to give chase on our own,' said Fenn. 'We don't know how many men Eadburg has with her. I agree with Olgood, and you've been saying it too – she's been planning for something like this.'

Kaela shook her head. 'Not exactly this, but yes, she's been planning something. She may have had her men ready to move.'

Kaela's remark reminded Fenn that Eadburg had said *Be ready* to Grimbold. Was there more to this affair than just a jealous Queen wanting to rid herself of a rival for the King's attention?

'Yes,' he agreed. 'So we need to organise our pursuit.'

Kaela looked to Wulfstan.

'Ealdorman Wulfstan. I think you're best placed to take charge of that.'

Wulfstan returned her gaze. He slowly nodded. 'Very well,' he said. 'It won't take long to gather my men.'

'And horses?' asked Olgood.

'Ours are tethered on the green,' said Wulfstan.

'*I'm* going with you,' said Kaela.

'No,' said Fenn. Kaela looked at him sharply.

'I understand you want to find Eadburg, but you must stay. The kingdom needs you here.'

Kaela drew a breath to reply, but Wulfstan held up a hand to stop her, nodding to Fenn.

'Thank you for that reminder,' he said. He turned to face Kaela squarely. 'Kaela, I'm addressing you as Beorhtric's daughter. Before we go any further, some things need to be said.'

He held up a hand while he gathered his thoughts.

'Beorhtric named no successor,' he continued, 'so I'm as unsure as anyone how the kingdom stands at this moment. But I agree that *you*, Princess Kaela, must be the one to hold it together for now. I'll support you… and you have good men at your side,' he waved at Fenn and Olgood, 'but the ealdormen will not accept that as a permanent solution.' He shook his head. 'If only….' He stopped, his head down, apparently lost in thought.

If only… what? Fenn asked himself. What was Wulfstan going to say? If only Beorhtric hadn't drunk from Worr's cup? If only Beorhtric had wed Kaela's mother, Aedra? If only Kaela had been born a male?

Wulfstan's head came up. 'There is one… possible… way,' he said, '…to save the kingdom from chaos….'

'*Wulfstan!*'

The call came from the other side of the yard. A figure was running toward them.

'Alburga, what are you…?' cried Wulfstan, walking to meet her.

'Wulfstan, I've been looking for you. You must come quickly,' Alburga gasped. 'People are demanding to know what's happened.' She paused to catch her breath. 'Your guards are keeping them out of the kitchen, but they're growing angry.'

Wulfstan looked at Kaela. 'You need to talk to them….'

Kaela drew in a breath, then nodded: 'The people in the Hall will be anxious. Yes, I'll talk to them. Fenn, you're right; I need to stay. Wulfstan, you must find Eadburg and bring her back.'

'One matter before I go….' Wulfstan placed his hand on Alburga's shoulder. 'Do you have any contact with your brother? We need him now.'

'Egbert?'

Wulfstan nodded. He glanced at Kaela to get her reaction to his words and caught Fenn and Kaela exchanging glances.

'What is it?' he asked, frowning.

Fenn looked at Kaela. She nodded.

'Egbert is at Westerling,' he said.

Wulfstan stared at him. '*What*…? *How*…?' His eyes widened. 'Was he there when I was…?'

'Yes, he was. It's a long story. No time to explain now.'

Alburga looked up at Wulfstan and shook her head to show she hadn't known. Fenn kept his eyes on Kaela. Did she agree with Wulfstan?

'Will the Ealdormen of Wessex accept Egbert?' asked Kaela.

'I think so,' said Wulfstan, but Kaela could see he had some doubt. 'Some may require persuasion,' Wulfstan continued, 'but some supported Egbert at the time of King Cynwulf's death when Beorhtric took the throne.' He spread his hands. 'There's none other with a better claim to the throne now.'

Kaela could see he was trying to convince himself as much as each of them. She took Wulfstan by the arm and looked around at the group.

'Wulfstan, Alburga – listen carefully. Beorhtric did not name a successor….' She paused, drawing a breath between her teeth, '…but, if you agree, it may be better for Wessex in these times if he *had*.'

'Egbert…' whispered Alburga.

'Yes,' said Kaela. She looked at Fenn, then Olgood. Was this the right thing to do?

Wulfstan looked at Alburga then back at Kaela. 'I agree,' he said.

He covered her hand with his own. 'If I ever had any doubt you are the daughter of a King, I have none now.'

'If it's to be so,' Fenn said, 'we need to get Egbert to Witanceastre without delay.' Olgood grunted approval and Kaela nodded her agreement. After a moment, Wulfstan nodded also.

For a moment, no one moved. The courtyard was silent.

'Ealdorman…' Kaela prompted.

'Of course,' said Wulfstan. 'We'll ride hard. If she stops for the night, we'll catch her.'

He squeezed Alburga's shoulder, gave a short bow to Kaela and ran for a door.

'Before I talk to our guests,' said Kaela, 'I need to see who remains in the guardhouse, and I'd like to find Sergio.' Her eyes followed Wulfstan thoughtfully. 'Can you…?'

'Olgood and I will do what we can to calm the people until you arrive,' said Fenn. He reached out his arm to include Alburga.

Kaela nodded her appreciation. 'I'll meet you in the Great Hall. I'll be as quick as I can.'

IF OLGOOD HADN'T BEEN there, Fenn wasn't sure he could have stopped the crowd outside the kitchens from forcing their way inside. The sight of the giant of a man blocking the door to the kitchens, blood-red axe in hand, served to dampen the bubbling frustration of the crowd. They were short of rebellious but they wanted answers to their questions.

Fenn and Olgood had inserted themselves in the doorway. Behind them, out of sight of the crowd, the physician was attending to the four dead bodies arrayed on the kitchen tables. Alburga had gone to join Treddian, assisting the physician. Both were casting anxious glances toward the noisy disturbance at the door.

Wulfstan's two men said they had been told to leave as soon as Fenn and Olgood arrived – Wulfstan wanted all the men he'd brought to

Witanceastre to join the hunt. Since then, the crowd's mutterings had grown in volume.

'Tell us what's happening,' called a man.

'Those men wouldn't talk to us,' said another, standing close to Fenn. 'No one's told us anything. What's happened to the King?'

Fenn cast his eyes over the people crowded in the hallway. Fenn and Olgood's arrival had signalled a change in the situation. That change and Olgood's stature had quieted them temporarily, but their frustration was increasing and could quickly turn to anger. He decided the truth was the best response. He raised his hands for silence.

'The King is dead,' he said. 'His daughter, Princess Kaela, will be here soon.'

The news of the King's death had probably been expected, but the announcement was still met with murmurs of astonishment and dismay.

A shout: 'Where's the Queen?'

'Eadburg is no longer Queen of Wessex,' said Fenn. 'She's accused of poisoning Ealdorman Worr and accidentally killing the King. She has admitted her guilt by fleeing Witanceastre.'

His announcement generated more murmurs – this time expressing disbelief and shock. The words *Poison* and *Mercia* were repeated. Someone cried: 'She killed the King!'

A woman at the front of the crowd yelled in Fenn's face: 'Who are you? Are you an ambassador? You look like a foreigner.'

'I'm Lord Feran…' Fenn was about to say 'Thane of Westerling', but the people of Witanceastre may not have heard of Westerling. Instead, he said: 'King's Thane.'

'King's Thane? Are you indeed?' the woman asked sceptically.

'Yes, *he is*,' confirmed Kaela's voice from the corridor. Heads swivelled towards her.

She came up to the crowd. Behind her was a short man who's smooth, perfectly-balanced gait Fenn immediately likened to that of a cat. That would be the Lombard swordmaster, Sergio. A group of about twenty men followed Sergio, all like him wearing a sword.

'You all know me,' said Kaela calmly. 'Please return to your homes now. Take food and wine from the tables for your families. There are changes tonight in the House of Wessex, but your lives will not change.'

Sergio stepped up to stand beside Kaela. Those nearest to him shrank back.

'Who is King now?' asked a voice from the back. 'Are *you* claiming the crown?'

'King Beorhtric named Egbert of Kent as his successor,' said Kaela. 'He's been sent for.'

The crowd's reaction was muted and questioning at first. Someone whispered: *'Egbert? Who's that?'* Another person replied. Several heads nodded. The volume rose, but the tone indicated the news was being accepted.

Some people turned and headed back to the Great Hall, satisfied. Others, hearing movement behind them, also turned. The remainder noticed their numbers were dwindling and one by one they followed.

Sergio watched the last of the crowd leave, then glanced into the kitchen.

'The King is dead,' he said softly. 'A pity. I liked him.' He turned to Kaela. 'And therein, I presume, ends my tenure at this court. No more trying to impart sufficient skills to the King's house-guards to preserve their fragile souls a few moments longer on the battlefield.'

Kaela lifted a finger to him. 'You stay right where you are,' she said.

Sergio grunted. 'Did I hear correctly that High Reeve Grimbold is involved with the affairs of the night?'

'It seems so,' said Kaela.

'Then I would welcome the chance to settle with that man for the indignities he enjoyed persecuting against me. Beorhtric, God rest his soul…' Sergio made the sign of the cross on his chest, '…called it playful banter, but it was far beyond that. He forbade me from responding with my sword – a fact Grimbold well knew.'

Sergio's implication was clear. The restriction no longer applied.

There was a commotion among the guards in the corridor. A rotund man with a chubby face pushed his way past the men. His small eyes and prominent cheeks reminded Fenn of an Arioch, but there the resemblance ended. Where the Ariochs' skin was pure white, this man's face was flushed red, and his appearance was as far from menacing as it was possible to be.

'Ah, my dear Kaela, is that you?' he said, squinting at her. 'Yes, good. I'm glad to have found you. I have something urgent to report. I heard the King is ill. If this is true, who shall I report to?'

'This is Bartholomew, the King's treasurer,' Kaela introduced him. 'You can report to me, Barty,' she said. 'Somehow, I doubt this is going to be good news.'

'Good news?' The man's hands came up to flutter in front of his face. 'No, definitely not,' he said. 'The treasury has been plundered. There's *coin* missing. I found the door unguarded and standing open. Four bags of the King's coin are missing. No, no, *definitely* not good news at all.' He pulled on a chain and dragged a key from his pocket. 'The room should have been guarded. I have the only key, so how could this happen?'

Kaela groaned. 'Eadburg.'

'They took all they could carry,' said Fenn. 'It seems that was *not* the only key. More evidence of planning and readiness.'

'Planning for a getaway at least,' said Kaela. 'Thank you, Barty. The door is relocked?'

'Of *course*.' The man looked shocked that she should think otherwise.

'What about the gold and the jewels in the Treasury?' asked Kaela.

Bartholomew folded his hands over his stomach and looked down at his feet.

'The Orb of Wessex is missing,' he said quietly.

Kaela grimaced.

'What is it?' asked Fenn.

'The ceremonial orb. A ball made of gold topped by a jewelled cross. It represents the office and authority of the King. It's handed to the King during the coronation ceremony to seal his right to rule.'

'Can Egbert be crowned without it?'

'I… think so. But if he doesn't have the orb… it could diminish his authority in the eyes of the people. I'm not sure how the people will view it.'

'Why would she take this orb?'

Kaela was silent for a moment. 'She knows its importance. I can only presume she has someone else in mind for the position.'

Kaela looked at Bartholomew. 'Anything else?'

'The rest is untouched as far as I could see.' He shrugged. 'Without a full check….'

'Please make that check now,' said Kaela.

'Yes, ah…' Bartholomew seemed unsure how to address Kaela. 'Yes, yes, of course.'

Kaela turned to the man behind her. 'Trevanian, post two guards at the Treasury.'

The man bowed and indicated the two men standing at the rear. The men made way for a muttering Bartholomew to return down the corridor. Fenn caught the words: '…*absolute outrage…*'.

'If she had access to the Treasury, I wouldn't have expected her to take coin,' Fenn said. 'If Eadburg is trying to get to Francia, the gold and jewels would serve her better there than Beorhtric's coin.'

'I can only suppose she's being practical with speed in mind. She's taken her own jewellery and the orb. The gold is heavy. The coin was already bagged and could procure a boat and men to sail it if she intends to cross the sea to Francia.'

Kaela turned from watching Bartholomew to face Fenn.

'*You* need to go for Egbert. It's a good moon. Good for hunting and good for travelling. You need to go tonight.'

'I'm not sure you'll be safe here. Treddian can go.'

'Fenn…'

'There's a lot to do here – questions that need answers….'

'I know…'

'*I'll* stay,' said Olgood. 'She'll be safe.'

Fenn looked at Kaela. He opened his mouth to speak, but Kaela stopped him with a finger on his lips.

'Please…' she said gently, '…I can take care of myself. I'll have Olgood and Sergio at my side. Leave the affairs of the court to us. You're the Thane. You must go to Westerling without delay and bring Egbert here.'

FENN OPENED THE TOP of the bag, pushed the loaf of bread inside and checked that the bag was securely re-tied. He pulled the axe from his belt and leaned across the horse to drop it into the leather sleeve attached to the saddle.

The light of a pale three-quarter moon bathed the courtyard with a steady glow. A cool wind pushed rustling leaves across the stones. As Kaela had observed, it was a good night for travelling.

A grunt came from a few paces away, accompanied by a creaking of leather – Fenn didn't need to look up to know that Treddian had mounted.

He performed a quick check – did he have everything he needed for the journey? His sling and stones were in place. He mentally listed food, water, clothing, weapons – including, at Kaela's insistence, a bag of coin inside his tunic and a sheathed seax that had belonged to Beorhtric attached to his belt so his left hand could reach it. The seax was shorter than a sword but longer than a dagger, sharpened on one side and tapering to a wicked point. It felt bulky on his belt – he wasn't used to it, and he wasn't sure how useful the extra weapon would be, but he didn't want to offend Kaela.

He heard her voice in his mind: 'This seax was made for my father shortly after he became King. Carry it in his memory. I want *you* to be safe as well.'

He chuckled and raised his foot to the stirrup.

The man's voice came from behind.

'Don't turn around, Blue-Eyes. I mean you no harm, but I wish to remain anonymous.'

Fenn froze. His axe was out of reach and his awkward stance made it difficult to draw the seax. An uncomfortable feeling between his shoulder blades emphasised his vulnerability.

Fenn forced himself to relax. Only one person called him Blue-Eyes. He let his foot fall from the stirrup to the ground but remained facing the horse.

'Avarinthe would like me to tell you three things,' the man said. 'The Queen left Witanceastre by the south road; the High Reeve's wife is sitting at home alone by the fire; and the two white ogres from Moloch Tor have caused quite a stir in the camp of Cedric the Bald.'

Fenn listened but heard nothing more. He turned.

The courtyard was empty.

CHAPTER TWENTY-FOUR

The High Reeve's wife

'I can only presume Eadburg's haste made her noticeable,' said Fenn, still breathing quickly from his rush to find Kaela.

'But how did this person know you were interested in Eadburg *and* Margareth tonight?' asked Kaela.

'The message came from Arielle,' he whispered, drawing her attention to his ring by tapping it with a finger. 'As to how she knew…?' He shrugged.

Thinking of Arielle triggered the memory of her standing with her shining silver hair and golden cloak at the edge of the forest of the Lesidhe, telling him he would play a part in the succession of the next king of Wessex.

'And the man said the Ariochs are with Cedric?'

Behind Fenn, Olgood growled the word '*Ariochs*' through clenched teeth.

'Yes, but neither Cedric nor the Ariochs would know of the other's connection to us,' said Fenn. 'Galastan wasn't mentioned.'

'Where they are, he will be,' said Kaela.

'Hopefully,' said Olgood quietly.

Fenn threw a glance over his shoulder at Olgood. 'The Ariochs are the least of our worries. We've more important matters to attend to tonight.'

Kaela breathed in and nodded. She pursed her lips. 'However it was obtained, we're grateful for the information. It confirms our suspicion of Eadburg's intention.'

Fenn wasn't sure whether Kaela was referring to herself in the royal way, or to the small group walking briskly down a narrow alley only wide enough for two people side-by-side. Behind Fenn, Olgood walked alongside Sergio – a marked contrast in stature with Sergio's head at the level of Olgood's chest. Behind Olgood, four guards were awkwardly holding their shields to the front to avoid the stone walls.

'Let's see what Margareth can tell us,' Kaela said.

The alley widened at an intersection with another street. Kaela turned to the right. A house stood apart at the end of the street, a wall enclosing a compound at the front. A man lounged against the wall at the gate. He came alert at the appearance of Kaela striding toward him.

'The High Reeve is not here,' the man announced.

'We've come to see his wife,' said Kaela. 'Open the gate.' Sergio glided up to stand beside Fenn.

'I cannot let....'

Sergio's sword was at the man's neck. Fenn was used to Kaela's skill with a sword, but he was surprised to see another person unsheathe his sword with the same blurring speed.

'We hope the Princess will not need to ask you twice,' Sergio said. The softness of his voice together with his accent made the words even more menacing.

The man fumbled to open the gate.

Kaela entered as soon as the gap was wide enough. She marched across the compound, Sergio at her side.

Fenn paused at the gate.

'Wait here,' he said to the four guards. 'Make sure this man stays and no one else enters.'

'Yes, Lord,' said one of the men.

The men stationed themselves two on either side of the gate with Grimbold's guard standing uncomfortably between them. Fenn followed Olgood across the compound. They reached the door just as it opened to Kaela's sharp knock.

Grimbold's wife, Margareth, presented a confused face to the visitors.

'What is the meaning of this? What do you want? It's late. My husband is not here.'

'It's you we've come to see,' said Kaela.

Margareth cast an uneasy glance at Sergio, then opened the door slightly wider, lifting her head to check Fenn and Olgood standing behind Kaela. When she saw Fenn, she looked momentarily puzzled, as if she recognised him but couldn't remember from where. Her eyes widened when she looked beyond Fenn to the men stationed at the gate.

'I'd like to speak with you inside,' said Kaela.

'If you want to talk with me,' said Margareth, 'I'd like the High Reeve to be here. Can you come back tomorrow?'

'Margareth, the King is dead and our business is urgent.'

Margareth's hand went to her mouth. 'The King dead…? No… it was the *Queen* who was ill, and she…. Is the King really dead…?' Her eyes frantically searched Kaela's. 'Oh, my God. How did he die?'

Kaela didn't answer. She indicated she would like to enter the room. Margareth brushed a nervous hand through her hair, hesitated, then reluctantly stepped back.

'We were hoping you could tell *us* where your husband is,' Kaela said, walking through the door, her gaze surveying the room and returning to rest on Margareth.

'I don't know where he is. With the Queen, I suppose.'

Margareth's eyes followed Sergio as he crossed the room to look through a doorway. He turned and shook his head.

'Margareth,' Kaela said, 'this is important. Please tell me what happened when you left the Great Hall earlier with Grimbold carrying Eadburg.'

'What is this about? Has someone accused me of something? I haven't done anything wrong, I swear. Oh my God...' her hand went to her mouth again. 'What has Grimbold done?'

Kaela held up a hand. 'Please... I just want to know what happened.'

Margareth looked at Kaela anxiously, wringing her hands. Any resistance she thought she should be offering to this intrusion into the home of the High Reeve disappeared. She took a step back, feeling behind her for a chair and sat heavily.

'Well... *nothing* happened,' she said. 'The Queen recovered immediately as if nothing was wrong. She and Grimbold spoke a few words. I didn't understand what she was talking about. They went off and I came home.'

Kaela sighed. 'I want to know what happened *in detail* and what was said – *word for word.*'

Margareth swallowed. Her hands clutched at her gown.

'Oh... well....' She frowned. 'Well... Grimbold carried the Queen from the Hall. I was following him. He'd drunk too much wine, as usual, and could hardly walk himself. As soon as we were in the corridor, the Queen demanded to be put down. She was angry with him. She had *miraculously* recovered from whatever had caused her to collapse....'

Margareth wrinkled her nose and shook her head to show her disbelief.

She looked apologetically at Kaela. 'Sorry,' she said. She took in a breath to calm herself.

'I asked Grimbold if he wanted me to get the physician as the King had requested. He asked the Queen and she snapped: *Of course not.*'

She looked up at Kaela. Was that what she wanted to know?

Kaela had winced at each reference to Eadburg as the Queen but hadn't interrupted.

'Was anything else said?' she asked.

'Nothing that made any sense to me.'

When Margareth stopped, Kaela said calmly: 'Perhaps it will make sense to me. Tell me *exactly* what she said.'

'Yes, of course. Well, she *admonished* him... ah... yes... she said she had wanted him ready, but for what I don't know.... She said he was in a poor state – which he was, of course. Grimbold said…. Do you want to know what Grimbold said?'

Kaela took in a deep breath. Her voice rose and took on a steely tone.

'My patience has its limits, Margareth. I'll tell you this for the last time. I want to know everything that happened in that corridor. *Everything*. And I want to know it without further delay.'

Margareth's face creased. Tears formed in her eyes and she dabbed at them with the edge of her sleeve.

She said hurriedly: 'It was a strange conversation. Grimbold said: *But you told me two weeks*, and she said: *Not two weeks, you…* – she called him a… a *fool*…. *Not two weeks, you fool, now!* She screamed that last word at him, but hoarsely, almost silently – it sounded horrible. I didn't know what they were talking about. I think they'd forgotten I was there. But then…' Margareth used her other sleeve to dry her eyes. Her hands were shaking.

'But then….' prompted Kaela.

'The Queen noticed me standing behind Grimbold. She gave Grimbold *that look* and nodded toward me. He told me to go home. He said not to go back into the Hall but to go through the kitchens.' She looked up at Kaela. 'The Queen was in a dangerous mood – I was glad to leave.'

'Did he say where he was going?'

'No.'

'Or what he and Eadburg were planning to do?'

'No. That's all I heard.'

'What did Grimbold and Eadburg do next?'

'My God, what has he done?'

'Where did they go?' insisted Kaela.

'They continued down the corridor towards the Queen's rooms. She was hurrying, dragging him behind her.' Her head dropped. 'That's all that happened. That's all I know, I swear.' She sobbed, her hands at her eyes.

'Was anyone else in the kitchens?' asked Fenn.

She lifted her head to him. Tears had streaked her cheeks.

'What? No, just the cooks.'

'What about the girls who served the wine?'

'Those girls? What about them?' When Fenn didn't answer, she shook her head: 'I didn't see them.'

'Did you go through the herb path to the back gate?'

'Yes.'

'Did you see anyone there?'

'Well, yes. In the herb garden, I'd just shut the kitchen door when the clang of the gate startled me. That Ealdorman from Hwicce had just closed it.'

'Did he see you?'

'He didn't look back. He was also in a hurry.'

AT THE GATE, KAELA reached out to take Fenn by the arm.

'You must join Treddian and leave for Westerling. We need Egbert here as soon as possible.'

Fenn nodded. He waved for the four guards to accompany them and followed Kaela through the gate and into the street. Grimbold's man hesitated, not sure if he'd been dismissed, then he stepped into the courtyard closing the gate behind him and hastily headed for the house.

The news of the King's death had spread and the town was deserted – their footsteps echoed off the empty cobbled streets and bare stone walls that were starkly outlined in the moonlight.

Kaela stopped on a corner. Time to part ways.

'We could have saved time by simply asking the cooks if anyone came into the kitchens,' said Fenn. 'I should have.'

'It's obvious now, but it wasn't then,' she replied. 'We had no reason to think Margareth or Ethelmund had been in the kitchen before us. At the moment my father died, finding Eadburg became our most urgent task. Don't worry, I'll talk to the cooks.'

'It's now even more obvious that Eadburg, Grimbold, and Ethelmund are working together,' said Olgood. 'But I don't think Ethelmund went through the kitchen. We would have seen him.'

When Kaela looked at him, he added: 'It doesn't make sense for Ethelmund to walk through the kitchen where he would be seen and then murder the girls outside.'

Fenn said: 'Are you suggesting he left the Hall and ran through the streets to the kitchen courtyard in the hope of meeting the girls?'

Kaela answered for Olgood. 'It would be Eadburg who arranged their death. We saw her give Ethelmund his orders at the banquet immediately before she left the Hall to poison the wine. She told the girls to wait in the courtyard and told Ethelmund where they'd be.'

When Olgood nodded, she looked up into Fenn's eyes, reluctant to say goodbye.

'What was going to happen, do you think, in two weeks' time?' Fenn asked her.

'I don't know. But I do know that whatever she had planned, that plan has now changed.'

'Perhaps brought forward.'

Kaela's reply was a grunt of agreement. 'Perhaps. But we're wasting time. We can think about that later.'

Fenn took her by the waist and rested his head on hers, then straightened and turned to Olgood.

'Take care of her, both of you.' He waggled his finger between Olgood and Sergio. 'These are uncertain times.'

He turned back to Kaela. 'Eadburg does not wish you well. With Beorhtric gone, there's nothing to stay her hand. Even in her desperation, she may still have enough reach to do you harm.'

'Look for an assassin around every corner?' Kaela smiled at him.

'To anyone who doesn't know of the events here tonight, she's still the Queen of Wessex. So don't make light of this.'

'She won't,' said Olgood. 'And neither will I.'

'No one will harm the Princess,' said Sergio.

'I'm sure Eadburg will have only one thing on her mind,' said Kaela. 'And that's getting to the coast and across the sea to the safety of Francia.'

'Let's hope so,' replied Fenn, 'but nonetheless, keep your guard up and keep your eyes open. There's Ethelmund to consider as well.'

'Fenn…' she said gently. 'Go to Westerling. We need Egbert here. The sooner he can be crowned, the better.'

Fenn took her by the shoulders and kissed her. He held her tight, feeling the warmth of her cheek and the pressure of her arms on his back.

Stepping back, he clasped Olgood's arm and nodded to Sergio.

'I'll try to be back within a week,' he said.

He turned and disappeared around the corner and into the night.

CHAPTER TWENTY-FIVE

To Westerling to fetch a King

Fenn pulled his horse to a halt.

He'd been in the saddle a long time. His body ached and his dismount was slow.

Treddian pulled up alongside. 'Wait here,' said Fenn, handing up his reins for Treddian to hold.

'Lord, may I remind you of the many times you hurried me along and told me we must reach Westerling without delay.'

'This is important,' said Fenn. 'I may not get another opportunity.'

'Yes, Lord.'

As Fenn walked away, he heard Treddian continuing his protest to the horse: '…wouldn't even stop at the Weyhill Inn – and I was thirsty for an ale….'

THE OLD MAN HAD not looked up at the sound of approaching horses. He was bent over, his attention directed at a shaded area beneath the curled roots of an ancient elm.

Fenn walked towards the man, his footfall silent on the carpet of soft leaves. When he was five paces away, the man straightened, turning and speaking at the same time.

'Welcome back, Lord Feran. I had heard you were on your way.'

Fenn smiled. 'It's good to see you again, Acwellan. Gathering medicinal stock, I presume?'

Acwellan held out a hand. 'Henbane and hemlock. Not normally found together but this particular place has areas moist enough for one and dry enough for the other.' He opened a bag tied around his neck and placed the plants inside.

Fenn looked about. It was a beautiful spot. The cluster of elms enclosed a small meadow covered in a carpet of white daisies. Fenn remembered noting the beauty of this meadow on his first journey to Westerling along the Roman Road. He was surprised to find Acwellan this far from Westerling – it would take half a day to walk from Westerling Hall to the elm meadow.

'You're a long way from Westerling,' he observed, 'but I'm glad to have found you. I wanted to talk with you.'

'This place is worth the walk,' said Acwellan. 'There are many treasures in these fields.'

'Are you not worried about being alone this far from home?'

'Worried? About what? I'm too old to be of any concern to anyone. I accept whatever the Earth….' He stopped.

'Whatever the Earth Mother brings?'

Acwellan shrugged.

'You said you heard I was on my way here. How did you hear that?' asked Fenn.

Acwellan shrugged again. 'Somebody…' He lifted a hand in the air.

'Avarinthe the Fae?'

Acwellan closed his eyes and breathed deeply. When he opened them, he looked directly at Fenn.

'Perhaps it was her,' he said. 'Not herself, of course, but….'

Fenn nodded. He held up his hand with the red-stoned ring prominent on his little finger.

'You know something about this ring, don't you?'

Acwellan didn't reply. Fenn waited. After a long silence, Acwellan said: 'As I said to you before, you must be high in her favour to be wearing that ring.'

'Yes, she gifted me the ring,' Fenn said. 'But I know nothing of its significance or why she wanted me to wear it.'

'I'm not sure it is I who should be telling you of these things.'

'Acwellan…' Fenn gently took the physician by the arm. 'I have an important task to complete and precious little time. I was surprised to see you so far from Westerling, and Avarinthe talked to me about the importance of paths that intersect. I'm sure she would say there is a reason you and I have met at this place at a time when we could be alone.'

'If she wanted you to know, why did she not tell you herself?'

'She said I would understand when I was ready. Maybe I needed to experience the spread of her influence. Also…' he paused, '…I think certain events needed to unfold.' He spread his hands. 'Acwellan, the King is dead. I've come to fetch Egbert, the future King of Wessex. I may need to be away from Westerling for a while. Now is the time to tell me what you know.'

'The King is dead…' repeated Acwellan. 'But how? How did he die?'

'He was poisoned…' Acwellan took a deep breath, and Fenn added: '…accidentally.'

Acwellan screwed up his face. '*Accidentally*…' he said, recognising that the word and how Fenn said it hid more than it revealed.

Fenn nodded.

'*Egbert*… you're calling him the next king – so you have reason to believe his story.' Acwellan sighed and shook his head. 'Offa gone, now Beorhtric. There are indeed grave changes in the wind.'

He lowered his head and brought a hand up to his chin in contemplation. He remained in that position, motionless, while a gust of wind rustled the tall elm under which he was standing as if in response to his words, dislodging a flurry of loose leaves which tumbled around the physician. His long hair and beard swirled in the sudden breeze. Fenn watched the gust move among the other elms and sweep across the meadow, the daisies briefly bending in obedient unison then springing upright again. A fascinating dance of nature orchestrated by….

'May I see the ring?' Fenn was startled by Acwellan's voice.

He held up his hand. Acwellan lifted the ring closer, his finger touching the blood-red stone.

'A spiral inside a triangle,' he said. 'The spiral is the eye that sees all, and the triangle represents the ear that's always listening. The design is drawn in one continuous line – the unbroken line of time. Her eyes and ears are everywhere, along the narrowest paths in the farthest corners of the land. The symbol is a request to all who know of it to provide whatever help they can.'

'Members of her order?'

'The web extends wider than that. For some people, the only thing they know is that they must provide help when they see the eye and ear of Avarinthe the Fae.' Acwellan paused. 'That you are wearing the symbol on her ring announces you as one of high regard. So, if you want anything, make sure that ring is visible and you will likely get it.'

Fenn thought a moment. 'Is there a difference between the red and the blue stone?'

'It is said the blue looks inwards and the red outwards, but what that really means – I don't know.'

'You know a great deal. Are you a member of her order, Acwellan?'

'If I were, or if I weren't, the answer would be the same.'

Fenn smiled.

He turned to look at Treddian, who pointedly glanced toward the sun.

Fenn hesitated, conscious of the need to make the most of this opportune meeting. 'Why is she called *the Fae*?' he asked.

Acwellan shrugged. 'She is a mistress of the forests where the fae dwell. But some folk call her that name because they believe she is just a legend.'

'Avarinthe the Fae… the name has a nice sound to it. She told me two of her other names….'

'*Stop!*' Acwellan's hands flew to cover his ears. 'I don't wish to know her names.' He lowered one hand in a gesture of apology. 'Excuse me, Lord, I don't want to be in a situation where I might reveal one of her names at the wrong time or place.'

Fenn shook his head. Arielle was not the only one who took her names seriously.

A feeling he had while he was with her resurfaced. Each time he gained more knowledge, he also learned there was still more he didn't know. A question answered – birthed yet more questions to answer.

'Can I offer you a ride back to Westerling,' he asked, gesturing toward the horses.

'Thank you, no. I have other places to visit before I return.'

'Very well,' said Fenn. 'I'll leave you to your discoveries.'

Acwellan nodded.

Fenn hesitated. 'One more thing… I'd like your opinion of Egbert. Have you talked with him?'

'I have spoken with him often. I found him a good companion, knowledgeable and thoughtful – he has depth. I believe he's an honest man – I see no guile or deceit in his nature. He has the foundation to make a good leader.'

'Thank you,' said Fenn. He inclined his head in farewell.

THE GATES OF THE palisade parted and a grey streak flew through the opening. The baying howl that had started the moment Fenn and Treddian exited the forest continued as the hound rapidly closed on the horses at full speed. Fenn tensed, expecting the horse to recoil from the charging dog but some communication between the animals let the horse know it was not under attack.

A few moments later, Fenn was glad he had tightened his grip on the saddle as Balthazar, seemingly without thought of the consequences, left the ground in a giant unrestrained leap and planted his paws squarely on Fenn's chest with an impact that bent Fenn backwards and would have toppled him from the saddle had the broad back of the horse not fortuitously intervened. The momentum of his leap carried Balthazar over the horse and he tumbled to the ground in a blurred mixture of hairy coat, thrashing legs, and a still yelping mouthful of teeth. The dog arrested its roll, planted its feet and was about to attempt another leap when Fenn decided it would be better to meet Balthazar on the ground. He freed his feet and rolled from the saddle.

Immediately Balthazar was on him, his tongue washing Fenn's face and his hot, panting breath filling the air. Fenn laughed, staggering under the onslaught, and wrapped his arms around the dog trying to quieten the wild enthusiasm.

'Good to see you too, Balthazar.'

Balthazar wriggled free and bounded away, still barking his joy, his excitement too much to contain. He turned his run into a wide circle and headed back towards Fenn. Again, Fenn tensed to receive the assault but Balthazar dashed by him, his barks now directed at the countryside, telling the story of his happiness to all who could hear.

Fenn watched the wolfhound running freely in the field, startling the birdlife and attracting the attention of the pair of nearby cows. Acwellan's words came to mind: *Without guile or deceit.* Those words could undoubtedly also apply to Balthazar.

His eye was caught by movement in the wheat fields. Alerted by the dog, people working there had stopped and were hurrying toward the palisade. Two men ploughing behind a team of six oxen set the plough and dropped the reins to also head for the road. Fenn noted some of the strips that had been poorly ploughed before had been reploughed, and the furrows were now straight and even. Would the lateness of sowing affect the crop? He smiled. The answer to his question was that these people had decided it was worthwhile.

Balthazar's circle brought him again to Fenn. Fenn held out his hand and the panting dog licked at the offering then raised his head and delivered three loud barks that rang in Fenn's ears. He held up his hand to quiet the wolfhound just as Edelred's voice said: 'We couldn't hold him back, Lord. He would have torn down the gates.'

Fenn turned to see Edelred, Bronwyn, and a group of Westerling people approaching.

Treddian ran forward to greet Edelred. After also embracing Bronwyn, Treddian moved on to talk excitedly with the people, many of whom reached out to touch him as if to be sure he had actually returned. Edelred walked up to Fenn.

'I had no doubt you'd bring Treddian safely back,' he said. He glanced to where the Roman Road met the eastern forest. 'But where are Lady Kaela and Olgood?'

Gisele came up to Fenn as Edelred asked his question. Her face eagerly awaited Fenn's reply.

'Olgood and Kaela are well, but they have stayed in Witanceastre.'

Their frowns looked for more explanation.

'Much has happened and much has changed in the last few days,' said Fenn. 'Let's go inside and I can tell you about it.' Addressing Edelred, he said: 'I need to talk with Egbert immediately.'

'Egbert?' said Edelred, puzzled.

'Yes,' he clapped Edelred on the shoulder. 'Can you bring him to the Hall? I'll explain everything.'

FENN LOOKED ACROSS THE table at Egbert who returned his gaze with a wary expression. Nyle and Gisele sat on either side of Fenn with Edelred opposite.

'You need not be worried, Egbert,' said Fenn. 'There have been changes at Witanceastre….' He waited while a woman placed four mugs of ale on the table. 'I've come to invite you to be the next King of Wessex.'

'Invite?' queried Egbert. 'Who is making such an invitation? Are you proposing a rebellion?'

Egbert's unease was reflected on the faces of Nyle and Edelred.

'No, nothing like that.' Fenn reached for his mug and took a sip, glancing around the table.

'I'm sorry to be the bearer of bad news. King Beorhtric is dead….' He held up his hand against the barrage of reaction, waiting for them to reluctantly quieten.

'I've quite a story to tell,' he said. 'I'll need to start at the beginning.'

He replaced his mug on the table and took a breath.

'Just over a week ago, Kaela and I managed to enter Witanceastre without being recognised and met with King Beorhtric in the court gardens….'

He told of the banquet and the deaths of Worr and Beorhtric, of Eadburg's flight, and of the decision that Egbert should assume the throne of Wessex.

'…so with the agreement of Ealdorman Wulfstan of Wiltonshire and Princess Kaela, I've come to fetch you to Witanceastre where, assuming you're willing, you will be crowned King of Wessex,' finished Fenn.

Egbert leaned back in his chair and brought his mug to his lips. He swallowed slowly. 'Beorhtric poisoned by Eadburg….' He shook his head. 'I didn't know the man well and held no love for him, but that is not a fitting end for a king.'

He narrowed his eyes in thought. Fenn allowed him time.

'Princess Kaela supports me?'

'She suggested you as Beorhtric's successor.'

'And Wulfstan also…' his head came up, '…did you see Alburga? Is she well?'

'She's well.'

Egbert nodded.

'But Eadburg…? What news of her?' asked Nyle.

'We had word she was headed for the southern coast. Ealdorman Wulfstan is pursuing her. He may have already brought her back to Witanceastre.'

He looked at Egbert. 'What becomes of her may be your first decision as King.'

'I SEEM TO HAVE hardly been at Westerling for any time,' Fenn said to Nyle, who stood with his arm around Erenweth's shoulders. 'Short stays and lengthy absences. I'm glad *you've* decided to stay.'

'With Eadburg no longer Queen, there's even less reason for me to return to Witanceastre. I've found my place here.' He lifted his hand. 'This land is good. I'll return to farming. But I still wish you'd let me accompany you.'

Fenn smiled. 'Gisele made the same request,' he said. 'You're needed here. Two travellers on the road will attract less attention than a larger group.'

He looked up. 'I don't see Edelred.'

'He was here. He dashed off a moment ago. I'm not sure what his hurry was.'

'Well, we shouldn't delay,' said Fenn. He caught Egbert's attention and called: 'Open the doors!'

Raising his hand, he acknowledged the crowd gathered in the yard to witness his farewell and nudged his horse forward, turning to confirm that Egbert was also moving. Peada waited by the entrance arch, a hand resting on Balthazar's neck. The hound looked up at Fenn, his eyes waiting for the command, but as Fenn passed his head lowered, accepting that he wasn't invited to join this hunt.

Outside the palisade doors, a group of boys stood in a line in the field, attacking a tree stump with slings. It was Beric and his friends putting Fenn's tuition into practice. In quick succession, the slings whirled and released, the stones striking accurately. Fenn watched for a moment and nodded approvingly. They were all progressing well.

He turned again to wave to the crowd. A running figure came into view, hand raised and calling: 'Wait! Wait, Lord.'

A red-faced Edlelred slowed to a halt beside Egbert's horse. He looked at Fenn.

'If Lord Feran agrees,' he said. 'A new king should have a king's sword.'

Fenn saw what Edelred was carrying. 'Indeed, I do,' he said.

Edelred handed Cormwurst's sword to Egbert. 'From King Cynewulf to Lord Cormwurst to you, sire,' he said.

Egbert leaned down to accept, twisting his body to fit the scabbard onto his belt.

'Thank you, Edelred, and thank you, Westerling,' Egbert said. 'I've admired this sword from the time I first saw it. I won't forget its history and where I received it.'

Edelred stepped back. 'You have a hard journey ahead, sire,' he said, '…and not just on the road to Witanceastre. Westerling sends you on your way. Go with our best wishes and with God.'

Egbert stared back at Edelred for a moment, then drew the sword and held it before him, the blade reflecting the sunlight.

'Thank you,' he said. 'I'm not the king yet, but this sword will always remind me of Westerling – and the people of Westerling will remind me of our great land of Wessex, which I swear, now and forever, to champion.'

'I AWAYS APPROACH WEYHILL in the evening or in the rain,' said Fenn. 'I've never seen the sun in the sky here.'

He completed his dismount and led his horse toward the stable, Egbert following his example. Fenn pointed to the adjacent building.

'…but I know the barn is dry,' he continued. 'I can only hope it's not as crowded as the last time I stayed.'

It had been raining since early afternoon, not heavily but persistent enough to make the ride uncomfortable. This was the fourth time Fenn had journeyed between Westerling and Witanceastre in two months and the road and this inn had become familiar.

The door to the inn opened to a warm blast of heat from the fire and a hum of conversation from well-populated tables, but a few empty seats remained.

Fenn waved at the room. 'Choose a table and I'll arrange our accommodation and some ales,' he said. Several people had looked up at their entrance, but they returned quickly to their own affairs. Fenn glanced around but saw no one he recognised.

He waited while the woman filled two mugs with ale and pushed them across the tabletop to a customer. She dropped his coin into a pocket, wiped her hands on her apron and looked up at Fenn.

It was the same woman who had served ales at Fenn's previous visit to the inn. There was no recognition in her eyes, and Fenn didn't expect it.

'Two beds for the night,' he said, 'and food and ales for that table.' He pointed to where Egbert was pulling up a chair.

'Huh?' she said, '*Beds*, eh? I can do the food and drink, darlin', but you'll need to see my man for the *be-eds*.' She inclined her head toward a room behind her. Her mocking tone confirmed that a patch of straw was all that could be expected.

He took a coin from his bag and placed it on the table.

'Ooh…' she said, raising her eyebrows. 'We don't see many of those round here.'

He smiled. 'Food and as many ales as that will bring,' he said. He nodded to her and walked around the table.

The door to the back room stood open. He knocked on the doorframe and ducked under the lintel. A portly man, his bald head encircled by a ring of white hair, sat at a table in front of a fire, sorting coins scattered on the table into piles. When he didn't look up, Fenn cleared his throat.

'Yes?' the man acknowledged curtly, still absorbed in his piles of coin. 'What do you want?'

'A place to sleep for two,' said Fenn, careful not to ask for beds.

'There's room in the barn; just pick a spot,' the man said. He finished his sorting and raised his head. 'Two pieces…'

He stopped talking and stared at Fenn, his eyes widening.

'Please excuse me,' he said quickly. 'I didn't realise who you were. I have two beds upstairs that should be suitable.' He gave a slight bow. 'No charge, of course.'

Fenn looked down at himself. He saw nothing that would indicate he was a King's Thane. How could the man possibly know?

The man continued: '…and can I offer you food and drink?'

'Thank you,' Fenn said. He half-turned back to the main room. 'But I've already arranged for food and ale for our table….'

'Payment will not be required,' said the man. 'I'll let Bethy know.'

'Thank you again, but I've already paid the woman.'

'Your coin will be returned, sir.'

Fenn frowned. He took a step back. 'May I ask why you're being so generous?'

'I think we both know the answer to that question.' The man tapped the side of his nose. 'We'll say no more.'

He rose and extended an arm, inviting Fenn to return to his table.

AS FENN RE-ENTERED THE room, his eye caught a man seated in a corner looking back at him. The man held Fenn's gaze without embarrassment before breaking eye contact and returning his attention to his bowl. Even in the shadow of the corner, the light colour of the man's eyes contrasted with his darker skin – but apart from that, there seemed to be nothing unusual about him. Fenn was about to dismiss it when he noticed the long staff leaning against the wall beside the man's chair. The last person he'd seen with a staff like that was Arielle. The man was now absorbed in his bowl.

It was an intriguing coincidence but not worth interrupting the man's dining to enquire.

He sat at the table opposite Egbert. Two ales had already been delivered. Egbert was leaning back in his chair, mug in hand, surveying his fellow drinkers. Fenn picked up his ale to sample the brew. He smacked his lips in appreciation.

'Not as tasty as Westerling ale, is it?' he observed. 'And not as strong. But a satisfying brew all the same.'

Egbert nodded in agreement.

'Good news,' Fenn said. 'It seems we may have real beds for the night.'

'If it's good news, why do you look worried?'

Fenn shook his head. 'A strange thing happened. The innkeeper offered me beds and also food and drink without charge. I've no idea why.'

Egbert smiled. 'Did you ask him?'

'Yes, but he wouldn't tell me. He seemed to think I should know.'

Egbert shrugged and spread his hands. 'When good fortune comes knocking, don't close the door in its face.'

Fenn screwed up his nose. He didn't like a mystery.

They reached for their mugs together, following their own thoughts. Fenn felt an uncomfortableness in his shoulders and lifted his eyes to the room. The man in the corner was looking away, but Fenn couldn't shake the feeling someone had been watching him. Maybe his suspicions were heightened from his encounter with the innkeeper.

'Will there be opposition to my accepting the throne?' asked Egbert.

'Perhaps, but Wulfstan believes it will not be sufficient. Beorhtric named you, and this time there are no other contenders.'

'…that you know about.'

Fenn conceded the point. 'That we know about.'

He looked up as the woman appeared carrying two steaming bowls on a tray. She placed the bowls and two wooden spoons on the table then reached into her pocket. She extended her hand and unfolded her closed fingers.

'The Master says to return this.' Her face clearly showed her disapproval of the decision.

Fenn's coin dropped onto the table with a rattle.

'I'll bring two more ales when you've finished those – but that's it!' she said curtly. She turned away, muttering to herself.

'Bah. I've never seen the like…. Why don't we just give it *all* away…?'

⸺◦⸺

'THAT WAS THE BEST sleep I've had in many years,' said Egbert.

Fenn laughed. 'Considering your situation these last few years, I'm not surprised.' He checked his axe and seax were secure on his belt. 'But I agree, it was a pleasant night. It was certainly better than my last experience at Weyhill.' He swung his leg over the horse and settled in the saddle, nodding toward the barn. 'In that place, I'll tell you, I couldn't even straighten my legs.'

He had said he would try to be back at Witanceastre within a week. It would require two days of hard riding to keep to that schedule. He adjusted his sitting position and turned his horse toward the road, relishing the warmth of the morning sun and the wind of movement on his face.

'At last,' he said, 'the sun shines over Weyhill. Maybe this is a sign your coronation is favoured.'

Egbert looked sceptical. His expression said: *Maybe… we'll see.*

Fenn kept the horse between a fast walk and a trot. There were few other travellers on the road. During the morning, they overtook only one group of people walking in the same direction, and three men had passed, heading west, carrying scythes. Fenn occasionally caught sight of another horseman following behind. He was riding at the same pace because the distance between them remained constant, the horseman neither gaining nor falling from view.

The sun rose higher as the miles passed, heating the air and, when the wind turned to the northeast, drying the throat. Fenn slowed his horse and waved Egbert to draw alongside. He handed the water bag to Egbert who drank from it and passed it back.

'Are there any towns or inns nearby?' Egbert asked.

'No,' said Fenn. 'It's forest for ten or more miles now. We can rest the horses when we reach the river.'

'I haven't ridden for some time,' Egbert said. 'I'm feeling the lack of it. A rest would be welcome.'

Fenn smiled. 'I understand, but we need to be in Witanceastre as soon as possible. I'm keen to know the turn of events since I've been gone.'

Egbert grunted his acceptance.

Fenn set his mount back to its previous gait. The dusty road passed steadily under the horse's hooves as the miles to Witanceastre were consumed. The heat of the midday sun bore down. Fenn thought about another pause for water and looked for a shady place to stop and wait for Egbert.

In the distance, where the road narrowed to pass between a pair of low hills, a group of men were gathered around a cart. One of the cart's wheels was in the middle of the road. Fenn was reminded of the problem with their cart's axle when they first came to Westerling. It looked like something similar had happened here. The group were in discussion with their backs to Fenn and didn't seem to hear the horses.

Egbert pulled to a halt.

'I think they could use some help,' he said, dismounting. He stretched his back and groaned, glad for an excuse to be off his horse.

Fenn wondered where the horse was that had been pulling the cart. The problem must have just occurred because no attempt had been made to clear the road. Were these people in disagreement about what to do?

He prepared to dismount but his instincts were alerted when two of the men simultaneously turned, reaching beneath their cloaks.

'Egbert!' He shouted a warning, pulling at his axe.

'That one!' one of the men called, pointing at Egbert.

The two men rushed at Egbert while the others also drew swords and headed for Fenn. Egbert recovered from his surprise and scrambled backward, away from the advance, reaching for Cormwurst's sword. His heel caught in a rut in the road and he stumbled, tried to regain his footing with two ungainly steps, then sprawled on his back in the dirt, his partially-drawn sword falling from his hand. Fenn urged his horse forward as Egbert twisted onto his side and scrambled for his weapon. One of the men raised his sword to strike at Egbert just as the horse's shoulder hit him, knocking him aside. Fenn swung his axe but the man ducked beneath the blow. The horse's movement had impeded the two headed for Fenn and they had to work their way around the rear of the horse. Egbert's grasping hand found his sword and he rose to his feet in time to block a thrust from the second man. Fenn pulled the horse's head around, whirling the animal in a circle, its swinging haunches again knocking Egbert's first attacker to the ground. With a roar, Fenn charged at his two opponents, who jumped to the side. Fenn swung the axe and felt it bite into the shoulder of one man, who spun away with a cry of pain. He couldn't tell if the blow was crippling.

Fenn thought of charging into the attackers again, but separating them from Egbert would be difficult. He freed the reins and slid from the horse. The second man brought up his sword, but Fenn could see he was unsure how to meet the axe. The man stepped back and tried to counter Fenn's blow but the iron-covered axe was a heavier weapon. Fenn used the hook of the axe blade to drag the sword aside. The man was momentarily wide open and defenceless. If Fenn had had a weapon in his other hand, he could have struck freely, but the seax was still sheathed on his belt. Fenn balled his fingers into a fist and hit the man in the face with as much force as he could muster, the blow twisting his head sharply. He dropped to the ground, stunned. Fenn dismissed him and leapt to aid Egbert who was managing to keep his two opponents at bay but needing to move continuously to the side to counter one trying to get behind him.

One of the men pressing Egbert turned to face Fenn's approach. With a start, Fenn recognised the man. It was the guard who had been outside Grimbold's house.

From behind, the sound of shuffling feet. Fenn whirled and ducked to the side in time to avoid the sword of the man he had left sprawled on the ground and seemingly out of the fight. Fenn backed away, circling around Grimbold's guard to join Egbert, who, now that he had steady footing and was only fighting one opponent, was demonstrating the skill Fenn had expected of him and getting the better of the contest, driving the man back.

The guard and the third man advanced together. Behind them, the fourth man was also approaching, his shoulder bloody but still willing to continue. Fenn swung his axe at Grimbold's guard who parried the strike and returned a thrust that Fenn swept aside. He ducked away from Fenn's return blow but halted his advance, waiting for the fourth man to join the circle.

Egbert paused his attack and he and Fenn exchanged a glance. Two against four were not good odds. They moved to stand so their shoulders touched, providing mutual protection. The fourth man joined the others.

'*There can be only one ruler of Wessex*,' snarled Grimbold's guard, raising his sword. On that signal, the attackers moved forward as one.

Above the resulting clash of steel and iron, thrust and parry, the sound of a galloping horse invaded the scene, pausing the action and drawing all eyes.

A horseman wearing a broad-brimmed red hat was approaching fast, a cape of the same colour billowing in the wind behind him. The man smoothly lifted his leg over the horse and slid from his mount, meeting the ground at a run. The horse continued unchecked toward Fenn's assailants, forcing them to scatter.

The man's clothing was unusual enough, his face shaded by the hat and his bright cape now settling around his body, but it was what he carried that drew Fenn's attention. In his hand he held the long staff that Fenn had last seen resting against the wall of the Weyhill Inn.

The man's momentum from leaving his horse carried him swiftly up to the fourth attacker, the man with the bloodied arm. While still beyond sword range, the staff whirled and struck the side of the man's knee with a crack. The leg crumpled and the man fell, but before his body had hit the ground, the staff moved again in a blur, striking first a glancing blow on the forehead of a second man and then a third man solidly on his wrist, the impact flinging his sword from his grasp. The first man staggered back, dazed, his hand rising to stem the blood flowing from the gash on his head. The second cried out in pain and leaned away, clutching at the hand now hanging limply at the end of his arm.

Seeing the fate of his companions, Grimbold's guard turned to escape but stumbled over the discarded wheel from the cart. Egbert reached out to stop him, dropping his sword to free both hands, catching the man by the shoulder and the wrist and shaking the arm to dislodge the sword. Fenn stepped up to help, but the man held on to his sword and pulled away from Egbert, driving his elbow into Egbert's face, knocking him back and breaking his hold. The man saw Egbert held no weapon and growled in triumph – he twisted from his hips and, in a smooth motion, swung his sword at Egbert's neck. The sword had three feet to travel – it had only to complete its arc and Egbert was dead.

Fenn reached around Egbert, taking the blade on the iron handle of his axe, a hand's width from Egbert's throat. He pushed Egbert aside to confront the guard. The sound of further blows and cries of pain came from behind Fenn, but he dared not divert his attention from the guard to his front. Fenn reached to draw Beorhtric's seax from his belt just as Egbert recovered his balance and stooped to retrieve his sword. The guard recognised his position was poor and he bent low, ducking out of reach of Fenn's axe, disengaging from the fray and turning away at a run.

Fenn raised both axe and seax and twisted his head to assess the threat from the remaining men.

He relaxed and let the weapons fall to his side.

The caped man was standing over the three attackers who were gathered together, seated on the ground. The man regarded Fenn impassively. His eyes flicked over Fenn's shoulder.

By the time Fenn looked back, the guard was fifty paces away.

'He's gone,' said Egbert, breathing deeply.

The guard twisted his head to look back. When he saw he was not being pursued, he stopped and waved his sword belligerently.

Egbert grunted in frustration. 'He must think he can get to his horse before we get to ours.'

The guard stood defiantly in the centre of the road. He spread his arms, mocking, inviting pursuit, shouting a string of taunts.

'I'll get the horses…' Egbert slid his sword into its scabbard.

Fenn let his axe and seax fall to the ground. He reached beneath his tunic for his sling.

'No…' he said, '…he hasn't gone far enough.'

Fenn's fingers extracted a stone from his bag and placed it in the pouch. When Grimbold's guard received no response to his insults, he shook his fist, then sheathed his sword, turned again and headed down the road at a fast walk.

Fenn steadied his stance.

The sling whirled. Even though the stone whistled as it left the pouch, the walking man did not hear it coming.

EGBERT AND FENN DROPPED the limp body beside the three others seated on the ground. When the man didn't move, Egbert checked that he was still breathing. With a nod, he acknowledged the caped man who was standing patiently beside the group, leaning on his staff, and turned to Fenn, placing a hand on his shoulder.

'You twice saved my life,' he said. 'I'm in your debt.'

'I undertook to fetch you from Westerling,' said Fenn. 'I would not be well received if I returned with a dead body.'

Egbert grunted.

Fenn looked at the four men. The fight had gone from them – they were all nursing wounds. The three who were conscious sat quietly, having learned that any untoward move would be rewarded by a sharp rap with the staff.

He walked over to pick up his weapons.

'They were waiting for *you*, Egbert,' he said. 'Somebody, probably the one with a lump on his head, knew of our plan and knew we would pass by here today, so we've probably been watched.' He pointed at Grimbold's guard. 'I know that man. He was a guard at Grimbold's house. He must have overheard that I was coming to fetch you. Grimbold is involved in this, and if *he* is, so is Eadburg.'

'Who's Grimbold?' asked Egbert, frowning.

'The King's High Reeve, but loyal to Eadburg.'

'But you said Eadburg fled.'

'Yes, but…' Fenn took Egbert by the arm, turning him. 'I can explain later. We're forgetting our manners.'

He stepped up to the man in red.

'Sir,' he said, 'we thank you for your intervention.'

Even under the shadow of his hat, the man's face was dark, enhancing the contrast with his light blue eyes – a complexion, Fenn suddenly realised, not unlike his own. The man had a gentle smile on his lips as if pleased with the outcome.

When the man did not speak, Fenn continued: 'I saw you at the Weyhill Inn. It's fortunate we're travelling in the same direction. You were under no obligation to place your life at risk to help us, but without your help the situation may have ended badly.'

He drew the bag of coin from his tunic. 'I'd like to reward you for your assistance, if you're willing.'

The man waved his hand in a firm rejection of Fenn's offer. He motioned to Egbert, requesting him to take his place guarding the men. Egbert nodded and drew his sword. The man took Fenn aside, out of hearing.

'You noticed me and I noticed you at the inn,' he said. The man spoke with a soft voice carrying a heavy accent. He pointed his staff at the man cradling a broken wrist. '*That* man was also in the room. He was watching *you*.' The caped man's eyes paused for a moment, regarding Fenn, then his eyes dropped to Fenn's hand.

'I also noticed the ring you wear.'

'*I also noticed the ring….*' The man's words hit Fenn like a hammer. He drew in a breath of realisation as he remembered Acwellan's explanation. *People who know of Avarinthe the Fae will help you if they see her ring.* The innkeeper's generosity was no longer a mystery.

The man continued: 'I don't need reward, and I *was* under an obligation. I'm bound by oath to help *you* when and where I can.'

'But you don't know me.'

'I know the ring, so I know you.'

Arielle's reach, or the reach of her order, must indeed be broad if it included this man who, by dress, voice, and appearance, was not of this land… Fenn drew his thoughts up sharply. He had previously been deceived by Arielle into thinking she was foreign and also a man. Was deception a mark of her order? Was this person what he seemed?

He pushed his suspicions aside. The man had almost certainly saved their lives.

'I am Lord Feran, King's Thane, and this is Egbert…' he paused. Was it wise to reveal Egbert's identity? He sighed, reminding himself again of the vital and timely assistance the man had provided. He continued: '…the future king of Wessex. The man whose imminent coronation these men were trying to prevent.'

The man bowed. 'So this was more than a simple robbery on the King's highway. Indeed. Then I'm happy to have been of assistance to such important people.'

'In no way more important than you, sir….' Fenn left the invitation for an introduction hanging.

The man gave a slight bow of his head. 'I am Tariq ibn Sulayman ibn Omar al-Arabi,' he obliged. 'I'm a trader from Faro Bregancio in Hispania – seeking wool and dyes on this occasion – my ship is moored at Hamwic.' He smiled. 'I don't expect you to remember my full name. Call me Tariq.'

'Then I thank you again, Tariq. Can I invite you to accompany us to Witanceastre as an honoured guest at the coronation of the next king of Wessex?'

Tariq paused to give Fenn's offer consideration. He nodded. 'You may need help to get these men to Witanceastre – if that is your intention?'

'It is.'

'Then I accept.'

'Good,' said Fenn. He held out his hand. Tariq grasped it and held it.

'A question, if I may…?' Tariq asked.

Fenn raised his eyebrows. 'Of course.'

Tariq released Fenn's hand and pointed along the road. 'Your target was moving away. If your stone carried too much force, you might have killed the man – too little, and you wouldn't stop him. How confident were you in your stone?'

Fenn thought about it. He couldn't explain his calculation. He knew he hadn't used the full power of the sling. His only explanation was he'd released his stone when it felt right.

'I was confident,' he said.

Tariq regarded him carefully. 'Then it was an exceptional slingshot,' he said.

Fenn smiled. He nodded his acknowledgement, then turned to the road, looking for the horses. Egbert's horse stood together with Fenn's on the side of the road and Tariq's was waiting patiently a little further away.

Fenn beckoned to Tariq and walked back to join Egbert as Grimbold's guard pushed himself up from his lying position with a groan and sat with his head in his hands. Egbert's sword hovered menacingly beside the man, but he appeared concerned only with his misery.

'These men will have their horses close,' Fenn said. He pointed. 'In the direction Grimbold's guard was headed. And I'd wager the cart is not as disabled as it looks. We can use it to carry this lot.'

He turned his attention to the four seated men.

'I know a yellow vine in the forest that's strong and flexible enough to be used as a binding.'

CHAPTER TWENTY-SIX

Threat from the North

'Don't worry,' said Wulfstan. 'These fools will be persuaded to tell us everything they know.'

'After having their injuries attended to first, I trust,' said Kaela.

Wulfstan hesitated. Fenn could see the Ealdorman considered that the injuries could be used to his advantage, but he bowed and said: 'Of course.'

'Thank you,' said Kaela. 'Any information they provide will be confirmation only. We're already as certain as we can be that Grimbold and Eadburg were behind the attempt.'

Wulfstan nodded and left the room.

'Is Eadburg here?' asked Fenn.

'Unfortunately not. Eadburg managed to keep ahead of Wulfstan on the road. Some fishermen at Hamwic confirmed she arrived in the night and secured a boat. She's no doubt headed for the court of Charles in Aachen. Wulfstan sent men to follow her, but she has a good lead.'

'And Grimbold? Any news of him?'

'According to the fishermen, he wasn't with Eadburg.'

'Where was he then?' thought Fenn. *With Ethelmund?*

'What of Ethelmund?' he said. 'He murdered those two young girls.'

'Yes. We need to talk with Egbert about Ethelmund. Egbert's been away from Wessex for many years; there's much he needs to learn.'

'And there's no better teacher…' said Fenn.

She smiled. 'The coronation is set for Saturn's day. The Archbishop will arrive tomorrow.'

He raised his eyebrows. 'You've been busy. What if I'd been delayed?'

'You said you'd be back in a week. I believed you.'

She slowly melted against him, wrapping him in her arms.

She breathed deeply. 'It's good to have you back. I've only been a half person this past week.'

'Then I'm glad to be able to make you whole again.' He bent to kiss her. 'I've missed you too.'

He raised his head. 'I didn't like to leave you,' he said, 'so soon after your father's death.'

She was silent for a while, then said: 'I've had time to myself. He was a good man, Fenn, and a good father. I loved him. He loved me and I know he loved Wessex.' She looked up at him. He saw tears in her eyes and was sorry he'd raised the subject.

'Now we're both orphans,' she said with a smile.

He kissed her wet cheeks. She kissed him back, then wiped her eyes.

'You'd better go find Olgood. He'll soon learn you're back.'

'Yes, I'd like to see him. I have some messages from Gisele.'

'The blacksmith's appreciated his help, and Olgood has enjoyed working at the forge, but he yearns to be back in Westerling with Gisele. He won't be satisfied with anything less than a long and detailed account of her, so you'd better be prepared.'

FENN MADE HIS WAY between two rows of market stalls. He walked quickly, swerving around groups of buyers crowded at the tables. He'd left Olgood at the blacksmith after being drained of news of Westerling and especially of Gisele.

There'd been little opportunity on the road to talk privately with Tariq and he wanted to question the Moor about his relationship with Arielle. They'd arranged to meet at the Prancing Pony.

He stopped and turned when he felt a tug on his arm.

He swept the crowd but couldn't see who had touched him. The market was thriving and this corner was a central intersection. He was surrounded by movement, his head jutting above the flow of people like a rock parting a river, people passing within inches, moving in all directions.

A gap opened for an instant and he spied an impish face framed with coal-black hair, beaming a radiant smile at him from an arm's length away.

Rowena.

She leapt at him and flung her arms around his neck.

He held her and laughed. 'Do I need to check for my purse?'

Her face took on a pained expression.

'Of course not! I only take what deserves to be taken.' She released his neck but held his arms. 'I hoped you'd come to the market. I've been here since this morning. I have a message from Cedric for the Princess – and you and Nyle.'

'Nyle's at Westerling,' Fenn said. 'I can take the message to Kaela.' He looked about and took her arm. 'We can sit over here.'

He forced his way to an empty bench shaded by the leafy umbrella of a tree.

'A message from Cedric?' he prompted when they were seated. 'What has he to say?'

The crowd still flowed by, but they were now an isolated island rather than an intruding rock.

'Cedric sent me to tell you he keeps an eye on Ethelmund of Hwicce, and to warn you that Ethelmund is right now gathering a fyrd. He thinks Ethelmund intends to take advantage of Beorhtric's death and is preparing with all speed to attack Wessex.'

Fenn sat back. 'And assume the throne?'

Rowena frowned. 'Of *course* take the throne,' she said indignantly. 'He won't be just calling in for ale and cakes.'

Fenn laughed at her sarcasm. 'Well said.'

'Cedric says he'd relish the chance to strike a blow at Ethelmund. He'll join you against Hwicce if you'll have him. He has fifty fighting men. I'm to take him your reply – to let him know what you want him to do.'

'Thank you, Rowena.' He stood up. 'I'll need to get this information to Kaela… and Egbert… and Wulfstan.' He shook his head in frustration. 'The sooner Egbert is crowned and we have a king, the better.' He looked at her. 'Did Cedric say how much time we have?'

'He said it will take Ethelmund a few days to gather his men.'

'I understand.' He beckoned with his hand. 'Come with me. We'll get you an answer to take to Cedric.' He grimaced, remembering Tariq was waiting at the Prancing Pony.

Rowena hesitated. 'Can you meet me back here? It's safe here. I've had run-ins with house-guards before. They know me, and I don't want to meet the Reeve. I'd rather not go anywhere I might be noticed and get arrested.'

'No one will arrest you… but… if it would make you feel safer….' He thought quickly. 'Can you take a message to a man waiting for me at the Prancing Pony alehouse? I'll meet you there as soon as I can.'

'The Pony? Of course. I can slip in there easy.' She flashed her sweetest smile. 'I've had their pheasant and herb pie before. It's tasty and filling. Stuffed with onions. Can I ask him to get me some?'

Fenn smiled back and nodded.

'One quick question,' he said. 'Have two large white twins come to Cedric's camp?'

'You mean the two freaks?' She hunched her shoulders, spread her arms, and puffed her cheeks in a recognisable imitation of an Arioch. 'How did you know that?'

'I was told. Why are they in the camp?'

'Cedric took them from the road – they were headed north. They had a sealed iron box strapped to a horse and those two big… men… interested him. He wanted to take them back to the camp and show them off. They looked soft but they were strong. He said they put up quite a fight. Even against swords, they didn't want to give up the box. It took several of his men a while to get them under control.'

'So Cedric has them held prisoner?'

'They can walk about, but they can't leave the camp.' At Fenn's frown, she added: 'Every eye is on them, and they stand out like an angry pimple on your nose.' She looked up at Fenn. 'Why do you ask? Do you know them?'

Fenn smiled then nodded thoughtfully. 'Let's walk while we talk,' he said. He invited her to precede him and she danced ahead.

'I know them,' he confirmed. 'And I know another man who may be with them.'

'*Him*! I call him the ferret,' said Rowena. 'I don't like that one. He has big shifty eyes and he makes me feel… dirty. Why do you ask about these strange people?'

'I heard they were at Cedric's camp. They were at Westerling when we arrived.'

'Westerling? Where's that?'

'A long way to the west. It's the place we were headed when Cedric captured us, and the place we went afterwards. I'm the Thane of Westerling.'

'The *Thane*…. Do you mean I know a *thane*?'

Fenn laughed. 'Yes, you do.' He raised a hand. 'But, listen… those three are dangerous and not to be trusted; you must warn Cedric about them.'

He reached to pull Rowena out of the path of a long-striding man carrying live chickens packed tightly into a wooden cage.

Her eyes thanked him. 'I'll tell Cedric what you said, but I think he already knows their type.'

'Good.' Fenn nodded thoughtfully. 'You said the box was sealed. Did Cedric open it?'

Rowena laughed. 'Yes, of course. There was nothing of value inside. The box they protected so fiercely was filled with *river stones*. You should have seen the ferret when he saw the stones.'

'Surprised, was he?' Fenn joined her laughter. They halted while the way ahead was blocked by a passing tinker's wagon.

'Surprised? Hah. He seemed to forget to breathe. I thought he'd die on the spot.' She stopped and looked at him. 'But you knew about the box, and you knew it contained stones.'

'I did. Galastan forced me to give him the iron box – he thought it contained something else. So hearing how he reacted is very pleasing…' he placed his hand on her shoulder. '… despite the message you've just delivered.'

'Galastan? Is that the ferret's name?' She made a noise as if spitting out something distasteful.

Fenn smiled at her. 'I must hurry.' He handed her a coin. 'Enjoy your pie. Tell the man I'll be there as soon as I can.'

She took the coin, her eyes widening. 'With this I could get a whole pheasant.' She danced a jig, circling, hands on hips, singing the words 'Lucky day, lucky day.'

He caught her by the shoulder, pointing. 'The Prancing Pony is this way.'

'I know that, but I need to let Silward know I've met you and where I'm going.'

'Silward is here too?'

She gave him an exasperated look. 'Didn't I just say that?'

Fenn laughed. 'You did.'

She glanced at the sky. 'We separated to find one of you. We're expecting another man from Cedric to come to Witanceastre later today. He may have more information about Ethelmund. If Silward has heard from him, I'll let you know.'

She twirled a few steps, then stopped and tilted her head.

'What's your man look like then?'

'IT TAKES TIME TO gather a fyrd,' said Wulfstan. 'We need to set a watch on the border and warn the other ealdormen, and we should send people to Hwicce to mix with the locals and find out what's happening in the villages.'

Egbert stood like a statue in the centre of the room, wearing a coronation robe dyed a deep red-purple with a thick white speckled fur trim that looked like foxtail. The fur trim circled the neck and continued down the front and around an ample hem spread on the floor behind him. On command from his attendant, Egbert raised his arms and held them out from his sides while the man checked the fit at the join under the armpit.

'Hold still,' the man said. He took a handful of pins from a container on the table and corrected the alignment.

'Cedric already has contacts in Hwicce,' said Fenn. 'His people will gather better information than strangers asking questions. He'll keep us informed.'

Wulfstan grunted. 'You're talking of the outlaw, Cedric the Bald, I presume. How can we trust *him*?'

'I trust him,' said Kaela. 'He is no friend of Ethelmund.'

Wulfstan looked at her warily but made no further comment.

'That's good enough for me,' Egbert said, lowering his arms and waving the attendant away. He turned to Wulfstan. 'Set your watchers on the border. We'll leave the infiltration to the so-called outlaw, Cedric the Bald.' He clasped his hands behind his back and wriggled his shoulders, checking the movement in the garment, then marched a few paces to the window, the rear of the robe dragging on the floor behind him. He stood staring for a long moment at the view, then drew in a deep breath. 'Will the ealdormen answer if I call on them?'

'All of them will be attending your coronation tomorrow,' said Wulfstan. 'You can ask them.'

'I'd like your opinion before then. Yours too, Kaela. Who can I depend on; who may prove to be a problem?'

'You may have difficulty persuading the ealdormen of the east,' said Wulfstan, '…those close to Sussex and Kent, that this need be their fight, and their loyalty….'

'If they are ealdormen of Wessex, by God, *this is their fight!*' Egbert growled. He shrugged out of the gown, handing it to the attendant who gathered the garment in his arms, his face forming a pained expression as he inspected the fur-trimmed edge that had trailed across the floor.

Wulfstan straightened, surprised by Egbert's passion. 'Of course,' he said. 'I agree. I meant they might consider they won't be needed and that now they've been forewarned, the ealdormen of the northern shires should be sufficient to repel Ethelmund.'

'Hmm. What were you going to say?'

'Sire?'

'I'm not king yet,' said Egbert. He waved a hand. 'I interrupted you. You were talking of the loyalty of the ealdormen.'

'Ah. I was going to say that the strength of their loyalty may depend on who leads them, and it cannot be an ealdorman.'

'Why not?'

'Relationships and rivalries run as long and deep in Wessex as anywhere. There is no one ealdorman, including myself, that all would follow.' He held up his hands. 'May I speak frankly?'

'Of course.'

'With due respect,' said Wulfstan, 'I do not think it would be wise for *you* to lead.'

Egbert turned his head slowly. 'Why?'

'It would be taking an unnecessary risk. You need time to prove yourself, and it would be best if you did not gamble everything on the outcome of a battle within a few days of your coronation. The eyes of Wessex would be upon you. Should all not go well on the battlefield – and these affairs can fail in a hundred ways – your reign as King of Wessex may be very short.'

Egbert stared at Wulfstan. A faint smile touched his lips, and he tilted his head. 'You didn't argue that I'm untried…' Wulfstan looked pained. Egbert held up a hand. '…but it happens I agree with you. It's not about the risk. I can accept risk when the prize is worthwhile or the threat warrants it. There's always risk.'

Wulfstan frowned, inviting Egbert to continue.

'I don't consider my leading our forces would be the best option for Wessex,' Egbert said. 'I know nothing of command on the field or battle strategy. I intend to learn and learn quickly, but at this moment, my heading an army would be more of a hindrance than a help. I'm sure there is more to it than just throwing men against each other and meeting force head-on with force. That said… do you know of a suitable leader, Lord Wulfstan?'

Wulfstan took a moment to reply. He shook his head. 'I'm sorry. No. Normally, in place of the King, the High Reeve….'

Egbert waved away the suggestion. 'What do you think, Lord Feran?'

Fenn frowned. Hernam came to mind, then Cedric – both absurd choices.

'No,' he said. 'I don't….' He looked at Kaela for support. She may be better placed to suggest someone. To his surprise, she made no comment, merely returning his look with an expression he had difficulty interpreting.

Egbert grunted. He stepped up to Fenn. 'It happens that I do know of one person I would trust with this task.' He paused.

'Lord Feran, *you* will lead my army.'

'What? *Me?* But, I…' Egbert stopped Fenn's protest. He leaned closer, half-turning and inclining a hand toward Kaela.

'I've already talked with Kaela,' he said, 'and with Olgood. They have faith in you, born from recent shared experiences, I understand. They tell me you have commanded in battle and that men will follow you. I also talked with Acwellan at Westerling. He has a faith in you as well, but a different, deep faith. His talk was somewhat cryptic – he said you'd been *chosen* by some mystical person. Despite that, I consider him both astute and wise, and his sincerity was undeniable.'

Egbert regarded Fenn solemnly. 'You showed me on the road that you're calm and decisive in times of conflict. I'm trusting my instincts because nothing I've seen of you deviates from what I've heard.'

Egbert grasped Fenn on both shoulders. 'I'm heeding Wulfstan's advice,' he said. 'The leader must be outside the established nobility. You will have my complete trust and support.'

He turned away from Fenn. 'The matter is settled. I have work to do before tomorrow. I'll leave you three to discuss the details.'

He beckoned to the attendant. 'The gown is still too tight across the shoulders. Apart from that, I'm happy with the fit.' Without looking back, he strode to the door. The attendant adjusted the gown in his arms to minimise the risk of crushing the fabric and followed. They disappeared from view, leaving three pairs of eyes staring at the door.

Although he had denied being a king yet, Egbert seemed to act exactly like one.

Fenn turned to Wulfstan. They stared at each other until Fenn said: 'I doubt this will sit well with the ealdormen either.' From the corner of his eye he saw Kaela smile.

Wulfstan nodded. 'Probably not,' he agreed, 'especially when they learn your age and your….' Wufstan stopped. Fenn suspected he was about to remark on Fenn not being from Wessex. The Ealdorman changed direction: 'However, youth is not necessarily a problem – if the appointment comes from the King…. *when* he's king….' He left the sentence unfinished and lifted his head. 'There are advantages in the leader being someone the ealdormen know little about.'

He assessed Fenn with thoughtful eyes. 'I'll say this for you,' he concluded, 'you seem to generate fierce loyalty very quickly.'

'Fenn is the right choice,' said Kaela.

Wulfstan regarded Fenn a moment longer, then waved a hand.

'By the way, the men who waylaid you on the road from Weyhill confirmed they were acting under Grimbold's instructions. I've issued an order he is to be arrested on sight.'

'And the men?' asked Kaela.

'They're locked safely away and will face a trial.'

'Very well,' Fenn said. 'Let's talk about Ethelmund.'

Wulfstan grimaced, stepping back and drawing an audible breath through his teeth.

'Damn him! To dare to attack Wessex! I never liked that man. He's as slimy as an eel. I've suspected him of many underhand things in the past. He taints the nobility of Wessex. It would give me great pleasure....' He caught Fenn's look, straightened his tunic and composed himself.

'My apologies,' he said.

Kaela touched Wulfstan's shoulder, showing her sympathy.

Fenn nodded to Wulfstan then leaned on the table.

'The River Thames is the border between Wessex and both Hwicce and Mercia, is it not?'

'Yes,' said Kaela and Wulfstan together.

'So, where will Ealdorman Ethelmund cross the river?' asked Fenn.

Wulfstan thought a moment. 'There are two or three possibilities,' said Wulfstan. 'I'll put watchers on them.'

To Fenn, Kaela said: 'I know that look. You have a plan in mind, don't you?'

Fenn smiled. 'It depends. We'll see what Cedric can tell us. In the meantime, as Egbert said, Wulfstan, set your watchers and gather your fyrd. I need to know what numbers we have. We'll talk with the other ealdormen tomorrow.'

DESPITE ROWENA SAYING SILWARD was in Witanceastre, Fenn was surprised to see him sitting at the table with Rowena and Tariq, and just as surprised to see that there were no drinks on the table – only the picked-clean carcass of a pheasant on a wooden plate.

He approached and nodded to Silward and Tariq. Silward regarded him warily.

'Can I get some ales?' Fenn asked.

They both shook their heads. To Fenn's raised eyebrows, Silward shrugged and said: 'Ale and I do not mix. People get hurt. I've sworn an oath to Cedric I'll only take ale to relax after a battle. I'm looking forward to doing so soon.'

Fenn nodded. The man may have a short fuse but his promise to Cedric would be solid. He turned to Tariq.

Tariq said: 'No, thank you. I don't drink such…' he paused, looking for the right word, '…such *potions*.'

Rowena looked up hopefully, but Fenn smiled and ignored her.

'Very well,' he said, pulling a chair to the table.

He moved his left hand forward on the table, showing the ring.

'We'll talk another time, Tariq.' Tariq's smile was enigmatic.

Fenn turned his attention to Silward who was watching him with an expression that suggested he was eating something distasteful.

Fenn frowned. 'What is it?'

'I've heard a rumour that *you* are to lead the Wessex fyrds. Is that true?' Silward's face displayed his disbelief. Rowena gasped. Tariq looked bemused.

Fenn shook his head in amazement. That announcement was to be made tomorrow. The decision had only been made a short time ago, and as far as Fenn was aware, only four people knew of it. He frowned. One other person could have overheard the discussion – Egbert's attendant tailor. It seemed one was enough, but even so, the news had spread faster than he would have believed possible.

He nodded. 'Egbert will announce it after the coronation.'

Silward shook his head in amazement. 'Someone must see more in you than I do,' he said with a scowl. He expelled a puff of air. 'But these things are not up to me.' He sat back, resting his large hands on the table. 'At least Cedric's message might get to the right person.'

'Do you have more information?'

'Cedric received news from Hwicce yesterday. Ethelmund has assembled more than three hundred men on the north bank of the Thames at Cymeresford. They're waiting for more men and archers to arrive from Mercia.'

'Three hundred,' Fenn observed grimly, '…and more from *Mercia*.'

Silward held up a hand. 'And there's more….'

Fenn raised his eyebrows.

'Some of the men on the northern bank are *Wessex* men. Cedric said High Reeve Grimbold is with Ethelmund.'

Fenn closed his eyes and sighed. His suspicions of Grimbold's involvement were being confirmed.

He assessed Silward. He knew the man had seen many battles – that experience could be helpful.

'I'd like your opinion,' he said. 'How long will Ethelmund wait there?'

Silward sat back. His scowl softened. 'I do the doing, not the thinking. Nobody wants my opinion.'

'I do.'

'Well…' Silward shuffled in his chair for a moment, then raised his head to look Fenn in the eye. 'He'd be foolish to cross the border before his full force is gathered. Three or four days – a week at most.'

'Do you know the area around Cymeresford?'

'I know it well. It's not a good place for a fight.'

'Why is that?'

'The land is marsh and swamp on the Wessex side – on both sides of the road. There's no firm footing.'

'That's better than I'd hoped for,' said Fenn. He leaned forward. 'Tell Cedric I want to know Ethelmund's strength in horsemen, footmen, and archers. Tell him to bring his fifty to Cymeresford. We'll meet Ethelmund there.'

Silward sat back and raised his chin. 'But I just told you….' He stared at Fenn. 'You're either crazy,' he said, '…or… you're clever. I'm not sure which.'

OLGOOD HELD UP HIS hand while he finished chewing the bite he'd taken from the apple. He swallowed.

'I think her plan was to destabilise the kingdom by killing Worr,' he said. 'Then induce Ethelmund to attack Wessex with her brother's help and somehow end up on top of the heap. She took the Orb of Wessex for a reason.' He looked at Fenn then Kaela. 'How else do you explain Grimbold's alliance with Ethelmund? Beorhtric's death changed the plan but also created an opportunity to be exploited.'

'You think she's poised to return to Wessex if her plans are realised?' asked Fenn.

'…and the fates fall in her favour.' Olgood shrugged. His expression said: *Why not?*

'It's possible,' said Kaela. 'It's all possible. Even Egfrith might be attracted to the idea of ruling Wessex directly. But knowing who's behind these moves doesn't change what we need to do to counter them.'

She turned to Fenn, taking his arm. 'Wulfstan and I have managed to persuade the ealdormen of Wessex to accept Egbert. *You*, however, are a different matter. We anticipated that not all ealdormen would accept your leadership immediately and without question. Ironically, those who agreed most readily may not be able to gather their fyrds and arrive in time, and two whose shires are close to the border have yet to agree. But Wulfstan is still working to get agreement from them, and I'm sure that as soon as Egbert is crowned, he'll also have a few words to say.'

Fenn smiled grimly. Egbert had made his expectations clear regarding the commitment of the ealdormen of Wessex.

A man entered the room and looked at each person in turn. His gaze rested on Fenn. 'Lord Feran?'

'Yes?' said Fenn.

'Lord Wulfstan sent me. He requests that you come to meet with Lord Herewic.'

Fenn closed his eyes. He remembered the name Herewic.

He grunted in resignation. At Olgood's inquiring frown, he said: 'Wulfstan thought my youth and appearance would work against me and didn't think it was a good idea for me to meet *any* of the ealdormen. We both agreed I should *especially* not meet with Lord Herewic.'

He could see from the expression on the messenger's face that the man agreed with his Lord.

Olgood's frown deepened.

Fenn explained. 'Herewic refused to aid Westerling when Hernam was outside the palisade demanding our grain. For Wulfstan to request a meeting now means things are not going well and he's desperate.'

'*Refused?*' Olgood said. 'Why? What possible…?'

'Historical disputes and grievances,' said Fenn. He nodded at Olgood's still bewildered expression. 'I agree. It's a problem for Wessex.'

He turned to Wulfstan's messenger. 'Very well,' he said. 'Lead the way.'

'The coronation will begin soon,' Kaela reminded him.

'I'll meet you in the Great Hall.'

THE MAN STOOD ASIDE and indicated the open door at the end of the corridor.

As Fenn approached, a voice came to him clearly.

'A new king I can abide,' the voice stated. 'That is the way of things and the proper order. But that is change enough. To be asked to stand aside and have a boy and a *foreigner* lead me and the men of Somersaeteshire in battle… a boy you tell me is the new Thane of Westerling! Despite our friendship, Wulfstan…' the speaker gave a sardonic grunt, '…or should I say our amiable association – *that* I cannot abide. And, by God, I *will* not.' He expelled a frustrated breath of air. 'I'll see him – that far our friendship will extend. But I tell you now, it will do no good. No *boy* from *Westerling*, King's favourite or not, will lead me and mine.'

Fenn hesitated at the doorway. It did not sound like a good time to enter. He decided there would be no good time.

The two men turned as he walked into the room.

Wulfstan held out an arm. He looked tired. The other man, Lord Herewic, did not seem concerned his recent words may have been overheard.

'Herewic, may I present Lord Feran.'

The man confronting Wulfstan was solid and broad at the shoulder but not as tall as Fenn. He was dressed for the coronation in a fine deep blue cloak that drooped almost to the floor, giving the man a barrel-like appearance accentuated by long hair and a full beard reaching down to touch his broad chest. The man's age was indicated by flecks of grey scattered in his hair and beard. His eyes were intelligent, stern, and calculating, immediately taking Fenn's measure, scanning him from head to toe.

An instinct told Fenn to use his height. He walked up to the man.

'Lord Herewic.' Fenn held out his hand.

To his surprise, Herewic backed away from him, a look of astonishment on his face.

'*Who are you?*' he breathed.

'What do you mean?' asked Fenn.

Wulfstan stepped forward, concerned: 'Herewic? What is it?'

Herewic looked accusingly at Wulfstan. 'Why did you not say anything? This is not a game.'

'About what…? I don't understand.' Wulfstan cast a confused look at Fenn.

'Oh, I *see*,' said Herewic, dismissing Wulfstan. 'You didn't know.'

He turned back to Fenn and stared. After a long moment, he raised a closed fist in a salute.

'My men and I are yours to command,' he said solemnly.

Wulfstan lifted his shoulders, staring at Fenn, then Herewic, his mouth open, eyes wide – at a complete loss to understand the man's sudden change of behaviour.

Fenn drew in a breath as the mists of confusion cleared.

The *ring*. It was the only explanation that made sense.

A sound of horns came from the Great Hall. The three men looked at each other.

'It's time for the coronation,' said Herewic. His eyes rested on Fenn's ring, then moved to his eyes.

'So *you* are Westerling now.' He stared silently for a moment, then said: 'I've never had reason to doubt. For all our sakes, I trust that will continue – and you prove to be worthy.' He held up a finger. 'But… I'll be watching.'

Herewic marched for the door. Wulfstan came up to Fenn, regarding him intently.

'Loyalty is one thing,' he said. '*This* is something beyond loyalty.' He waved at the room. 'That reaction from Herewic was incomprehensible. I find myself repeating his question… *who are you?*'

'I ACCEPT THIS CROWN as a symbol of my duty to lead the people of Wessex.'

Egbert's eyes moved across the crowded Hall, his hand resting on the hilt of Cormwurst's sword.

'I am Wessex, and I make this promise to you now. I intend to prosper, and as I prosper so shall Wessex, and so shall you all.'

He straightened his back and the Archbishop placed the crown on his head.

Wulfstan stood and raised his fist. 'To the King!' he called. 'Long may he reign!'

A shout of '*The King!*' rang throughout the Hall.

Fenn noted that the one remaining ealdorman who had yet to pledge him allegiance, Leofrith of Hanteshire, voiced the salute enthusiastically. Wulfstan had no doubt that with Herewic's help, he could persuade this man to join Egbert's alliance.

Fenn looked at Tariq seated beside him, seemingly absorbed in the ceremony.

Tariq noticed his glance. 'Thank you for inviting me,' he said. 'As well as getting to know the King, I've met many important people, which can only benefit my trade.'

'I'd still like to talk to you about this ring,' said Fenn.

'Time enough for that,' said Tariq. 'Time enough.'

Fenn smiled and settled back in his chair, reflecting.

Wessex had a new King. And, Fenn mused, as Arielle had foreseen, Fenn *had* played a part in placing Egbert on the throne.

But even before the crown could settle comfortably on his head, the new King of Wessex faced the challenge of an imminent invasion from the north.

CHAPTER TWENTY-SEVEN

Conflict at Cymeresford

Fenn crouched on the crest of a low hill overlooking the valley of the River Thames south of Cymeresford. The sun was well risen, but grey mist lay heavy and unmoving in the valley, shrouding all the low-lying features of the countryside. For the moment, not even the tops of trees showed above the thick blanket of morning fog. He could not see the river, let alone any evidence that hundreds of men were gathering on the far side.

Behind Fenn, across a narrow valley, rose another taller hill. A stream ran between the two hills, eventually feeding the marshes lining the south bank of the Thames.

'The mist will take a while longer to clear from the marshes,' said Cedric. 'The Hwicce will wait for that, but I was assured they intend to cross today.'

Cedric's head was uncovered. An angry scar in the shape of a cross — the result of his clash with the horse — was clearly visible, etched into his scalp. Cedric seemed to wear the wound with pride.

'We must keep most of them in the marshes,' said Fenn. 'But when we show our hand, they may think to outflank us by skirting around the marsh. I'm told there's another ford five or six miles west. Your task is to stop any who come that way.'

Silward grumbled. 'And if they don't, we'll be sitting here watching the birds while you have all the fun.'

Fenn was about to question whether 'fun' was appropriate, but Cedric held up his hand.

'I'll do as you ask. If any come that way, they won't get past us.'

That would depend on how many were sent, thought Fenn. What if taking the road through the marsh, the direct path to Witanceastre, was a feint, and Ethelmund's main force came from the west? He curbed his thoughts. He could ask such questions all day. His forces were concealed behind the cover of the hills. He had no reason to believe Ethelmund knew they were there.

'Keep an eye on the battle,' he said to Cedric. 'If I think you're needed, I'll circle my axe above my head.'

'If we're needed, we'll come. I do want a chance to even the score with Ethelmund.'

Fenn nodded.

'I also don't want to be too far from you,' Cedric added. He smiled. 'I've a debt to repay, and the way things are shaping, an opportunity may soon arise.'

Fenn turned to leave, but a thought stopped him.

'If you and your fighting men are here, who's guarding the Ariochs?'

'The *what?*'

'The Ariochs. The large pale twins with the iron box.'

'Is that what they're called? Rowena sent a message you knew those three. You needn't worry about those white monsters and that greasy man; they're safe. I have some reliable men watching them, and they're locked away at night.'

'Galastan, the 'greasy man', is unscrupulous and dangerous.'

'I understand. I know his type.'

Fenn nodded his farewell and dropped below the crest, walking quickly along the valley floor between the two hills to join a group standing by the stream.

Kaela looked up at his approach. Sergio was standing beside her. 'Is Cedric happy?' she asked.

'Happy? I'm not sure. But he'll protect the flank.'

Wulfstan and the other ealdormen glanced at each other, unable to hide their unease with an arrangement that required them to trust the notorious outlaw, Cedric the Bald.

Olgood stood beside Egbert with his axe drawn. He looked both relaxed and ready. Fenn had given him the charge of protecting the King, a task Olgood had immediately protested.

'I hope you're not asking this of me to keep me out of the conflict because I have a baby due?'

Fenn had denied it but could not truthfully say that the idea hadn't entered his mind.

Tariq stood nearby. When Fenn had reminded the moor this need not be his fight, he'd replied: 'I already have an investment in this King, which I would like to protect, and an interest in this battle. I'll stand with Olgood beside the King.'

So what's your plan?' asked Herewic. 'How do we deploy?'

Fenn brought his mind back to the task.

'There's only a single road across the marsh,' he said. 'So if we strike too early, they'll just retreat. It makes sense for Ethelmund to gather his forces before proceeding. We'll wait and let a good number, a hundred or so, get free of the marsh and onto the field on the other side of this hill, then attack them from the front and both flanks. The remainder will then try to come to their assistance, but they'll be constricted on the road and vulnerable if they enter the marsh.'

Leofrith frowned. 'And if they don't stop in the field to gather their forces?' he asked.

'From his position on the hill behind us, with a view of the field and the road, the King will make the decision to attack. Watch for the flags.'

Leofrith made no reply.

Fenn continued: 'You, Wulfstan, with your fyrd and I with Egbert's house-guards, will take the centre. Herewic will take the left flank and Leofrith the right. As well as attacking the flanks, your task will be to keep the rest of the Hwicce in the marsh.'

He looked at the ealdormen to ensure they understood. 'Be ready as soon as the mist clears.'

Kaela wore a slight frown. Recalling the battle at Hammaburg, she had suggested Fenn might be more effective using his sling from a distance, but Fenn had countered that if his leadership was to be respected, he must be seen to be with the men.

Fenn looked at her. Both wished the other could stay safe. She'd tied up her hair so it lay flat but there was no hiding her gender.

'You know I'd rather you didn't fight today,' he said. 'This will be no place for a woman.'

'And *you* know my sword will be useful,' she replied.

'There's no doubt of that.'

'I'll stand by her,' Sergio said.

'I thank you,' Fenn said. He shook his head in admiration. 'You two will make a formidable pair. I pity anyone who blunders within reach. Still….' He made a final silent plea.

She returned his gaze, unmoved.

Fenn sighed. He turned to Wulfstan. 'I trust your men watching the ford are alert.'

'They'll send word if there's any crossing.'

'Good.' Fenn nodded. 'Remember… On the King's signal, the archers loose two volleys of arrows. We attack with the third volley. Keep your men quiet and hidden until the last volley, but on the charge tell everyone to yell like the devil himself is inside them. If all goes well, Ethelmund won't have time to deploy his archers.'

He checked with Egbert. Did the King have anything he wanted to say?

Egbert took a step forward. 'I thank you for your service,' he said solemnly. 'You fight today for your King and for Wessex. It is unfortunate that I've called upon you so soon, but we do what we must.

I wish you all well. May God be with you and bring us victory on this day.'

Fenn nodded and the ealdormen moved to join their men.

The estimate from Cedric's spies was that Wessex would be facing four hundred men, including fifty to eighty archers and a few on horseback. Under Fenn's command, the three ealdormen had stationed three hundred men behind the hill. Egbert's house-guards numbered eighty, and with Cedric's fifty they should have a slight advantage in numbers – not enough to be decisive but hopefully Fenn's use of the terrain and the surprise of their attack would tip the odds in their favour.

Fenn nodded to Egbert, and the group retreated up the hill behind the stream to a shady grove of trees sitting on a flat area high enough to overlook the three fyrds hidden from view of the Cymeresford road. When they reached the plateau, Fenn turned to survey the river valley.

Over the top of the hill hiding his army, he could see the valley floor was still covered by mist – but there was a change. Instead of the heavy still air previously oppressing the valley, a wind rising from the southwest was already disturbing the edges and curling up the misty carpet. Fenn fixed his eyes on the point directly in front of the location where Wulfstan's fyrd and the house-guards waited behind the hill – the point where the Cymeresford road emerged from the marshes and from the mist and crossed a large green meadow before continuing into the hills.

In a short while, this quiet and peaceful scene would be disrupted and transformed.

He bent and picked up two large coloured flags, handing them to Egbert.

He pointed. 'The Hwicce should stop and regroup in that field. We've talked about it. When a hundred have emerged from the marsh, signal *get ready* with the yellow flag. Allow a moment for the archers to draw, then raise the red flag so they all loose the first volley together.'

He stared at the mist, trying to imagine the hundreds of men it concealed.

'If they don't stop to gather in the field, wait until as many as possible are in the field before you signal.'

'Yes, as you say – we've talked about it,' said Olgood. 'Several times. And it's remarkable that every time we talk, the instructions don't change.'

Fenn laughed. He clapped his friend on the shoulder, nodded to Egbert and Tariq and turned to descend the hill. Kaela clasped Olgood by the arm. They nodded to each other then, with Sergio on her heels, she followed Fenn to join the house-guards.

THE LEADING HORSEMAN DREW his horse to a halt allowing a second horseman to pull up alongside. The leader turned in his saddle and waved to the men following on the road, instructing them to disperse to the left and right. The field where he had stopped bordered the edge of the marsh – wide and inviting, covered in a swathe of daisies, a natural place to wait for the remainder of his force to gather.

Gradually the field filled with men. The road crossing the marsh was only wide enough for a single cart and men filed along it in mixed groups. A man astride a horse was followed by a band of archers interspersed with strings of footmen.

Fenn lay concealed behind a tree on the crest of the hill, this time with Wulfstan alongside him. The lack of formation while crossing the marsh and also in the field, confirmed that Ethelmund was unaware an army of Wessex was watching and waiting for him. He didn't expect to meet opposition this far north. Fenn breathed a sigh of relief. It seemed Ethelmund was feeling safe and, as Fenn had hoped, taking the time to collect his forces before proceeding.

The sun glinted on metal, indicating Ethelmund was wearing armour. Within the Wessex forces, only the ealdormen wore full armour, although some of Cedric's men displayed some pieces, notably Giffre in chain mail, and within the men gathered behind the hill, several heads were covered with a variety of helmets, some metal, some leather. Egbert had offered a suit of armour to Fenn, but he'd never fought in armour and he was sure he'd find it restrictive. For the same reason he had refused a shield. He hoped he didn't regret those choices.

At Egbert's insistence, however, Fenn did wear a leather chest covering decoratively studded with chains and circular patterned plates of iron, and, as a mark of his rank, a wolf's pelt covered his left shoulder. He reflected that, fittingly, his horse's only protection was also a layer of hardened leather across its chest.

He took his eyes from the field and regarded the men at his back, concealed behind the hill, each one carrying on one arm the blue shield of Wessex emblazoned with a golden Wyvern and a long spear in the other hand. Properly disciplined, an advance behind a shield wall with the long spears thrust forward was difficult to oppose. Once the spear was thrown or when the combat closed up, the men would resort to their swords.

He looked along the ridge of the hill to his left. He could just make out Cedric's men also waiting behind the hill to the west.

Ethelmund's men were arriving in a steady stream and the field was filling fast. The newcomers wandered from the road and sat or stood about in groups, relaxed. Now that the damp mist had all but dispersed, they would be glad to feel the warmth of the sun. Ethelmund also looked relaxed and unhurried. He leaned to the side to converse with the horseman next to him. Fenn's eyes narrowed.

Grimbold!

Ironically, the man who had accused Fenn of being a traitor to Wessex was now preparing to attack the kingdom.

Beside him, Wulfstan whispered fiercely: '*Ethelmund is mine.*'

'There are many who want his head,' replied Fenn. 'Including me.' He remembered the two young bodies lying in the moonlight by the henhouse.

Wulfstan caught and held Fenn's eyes. 'No, Lord Feran. I mean it. He's *mine.*'

Fenn nodded an acknowledgement and glanced again at the field.

It was time.

He tapped Wulfstan on the shoulder and slid down the hill, his eyes searching the trees on the hill behind for Egbert and Olgood's position.

He reached his horse and mounted, drawing his axe. He heard a man say: 'Feswick, look! The princess and the master fight beside *us*.'

He glanced down at Kaela, who already had Lord of the Battle raised and ready in her hand. She'd decided not to ride a horse, preferring to fight on foot. Their eyes met.

Sergio, standing beside her, looked up at Fenn. 'Is Grimbold on the field?' he asked.

'I saw him,' confirmed Fenn.

'Then he who was untouchable can now be touched,' said Sergio. 'My sword has a hunger for that man.'

Fenn shook his head in wonder at the stupidity and arrogance of Grimbold. What possible momentary gain was worth antagonising a dangerous man such as Sergio.

A voice from behind announced: 'Yellow!' The word was followed by a creaking of wood as the archer's bows were bent by taut strings.

'Red!'

A volley of arrows crested the hill with a sound like leaves rustling in a stiff breeze and descended on the men assembled in the field, accompanied by matching volleys from the left and right. In very short order, a second volley followed the first. The field deteriorated into chaos and commotion, men shouting and men screaming. Shields would be raised, but already casualties were evident by the screams.

The third volley of arrows flew overhead. Fenn dug his heels into his horse's flank, urging it forward and with a roar, a wave of screaming men in three solid lines of shields and spears erupted over the hill and descended on the field of battle.

UNMOVING BODIES ALREADY LAY scattered among the daisies. Men were cautiously emerging from behind shields, searching the sky for more arrows as the fyrds from Wessex bore down on them. They scrambled to gather their weapons and defend themselves.

With his horse moving at a gallop, swinging his axe from high on the horse's back gave Fenn an enormous advantage and attempts to block the axe with a sword were futile. Some managed to raise their shield and were simply knocked down, but the blade bit deeply into those less fortunate.

Wulfstan was ahead of Fenn, pushing towards the centre, already trying to reach Ethelmund. A man thrust a spear at Fenn's horse, but the axe blade was quicker, brushing the spear aside then reversing to bite into the man's neck. A spray of blood spattered horse and rider, some entering Fenn's eye. He shook his head and blinked to clear his vision. A man ahead shaped to throw his spear. Fenn turned the horse into him and the man was knocked sprawling. He screamed as a heavy hoof descended on his knee. Fenn glanced anxiously to his front. Wulfstan was getting further ahead, determined to get to Ethelmund and possibly end the conflict early, but he was outrunning his own men as well as Fenn.

A man appeared carrying a bow, looking frantically about – an archer trying to escape the carnage. He swerved away in the direction of the marshes. Fenn pulled on his horse's head to direct the animal to follow Wulfstan, but the creature was unwilling, its movements suddenly sluggish. He shouted and urged it forward. Wulfstan's idea was a good one. Ethelmund was unprotected. From the horse's back, above the heads of the men on foot, Fenn could see Ethelmund and Grimbold, a hundred paces away. Both mounts were twisting back and forth and the men were fighting to control them, seemingly unsure whether to flee or to fight. The day may well be quickly won if they could be taken off the field. But Wulfstan, in his eagerness and single-minded focus, was becoming isolated.

Fenn's horse took a faltering step, unwilling to carry its weight on the right foreleg. Fenn tore his gaze from Ethelmund. Blood was flowing freely from a wound on the animal's leg, possibly caused by the spear. He slid off the horse and slapped it on the rump – maybe without Fenn's weight, it could get clear of the fighting. As if it understood, the horse hobbled away to the side. Remembering his previous encounter on the Weyhill road, Fenn drew Beorhtric's seax. With a weapon in each hand, he headed for Wulfstan.

A man ran at him from the side. He carried no shield and both he and Fenn hesitated, unsure whether the other was friend or foe. Many men on the field were dressed alike. The shields of the Hwicce and the Mercians were also blue but instead of the Wessex wyvern, these shields showed a yellow saltire, the diagonal cross of St. Andrew. The blue was darker than the Wessex blue and the cross yellow, not gold, but in the movement and confusion of the battle, they weren't easy to distinguish.

Fenn saw the man glance at the wolf's pelt on his shoulder. Whether he recognised its significance or not, the man made his decision and turned away.

Fenn heard running feet approaching from behind. He whirled, but it was Kaela – Sergio on her heels. A man thrust ineffectively at Sergio with his sword, receiving Sergio's blade in his throat in instant reply. The action drew Kaela's brief attention; her step became a half-step, then the incident was dismissed and she arrived at his side.

Fenn realised with dismay that Kaela's black outfit and Sergio's neatly trimmed attire distinguished them. There'd be no one dressed as they were in the Hwiccan army and no hesitation around them.

'You left us behind,' she said, not accusingly, just stating why she'd been unable to stay with him on horseback.

'We need to help Wulfstan,' said Fenn.

He turned back. Wulfstan was still on his horse but he was hard pressed, slashing to left and right with his sword. His blows were effective, men falling away from the horse.

Fenn ran in his direction.

His way was immediately blocked by three men who moved to join their shields together to form a small protective wall. No doubt as to who was an opponent this time. Mercian shields. The men raised their swords above the shields, ready to strike over them, and moved forward together. Fenn knew Kaela was on his left. He would be exposed to the man on his right, so he glanced to confirm Sergio had taken that side. He ran at the centre man. Just out of sword range, acting instinctively, he reached out with his axe, hooked the edge of the blade over the top of the shield and dragged it to the side, exposing the man enough for a quick step and a thrust with the seax. The man dropped and his companions to left and right fell in unison, the swords of Kaela and Sergio having also found their mark.

Fenn nodded his thanks to Sergio and raised his head to see that Wulfstan had reached Ethelmund. All about, men were shouting and screaming, but above the noise Fenn was close enough to hear the clash of steel as the blades of the two ealdormen met. Wulfstan drove his horse into Ethelmund's mount, unbalancing the Hwiccan, whose free hand reached for his saddle to avoid falling, his sword arm flying high. Fenn leapt forward. Hwiccans were gathering around Wulfstan, drawn to the attack on their leader. One swung his sword ineffectively against Wulfstan's armoured back.

Fenn saw the moment when Ethelmund's eyes met Wulfstan's, saw the realisation in those eyes as Wulfstan's sword went under Ethelmund's flailing arm between the plates of fine armour and into his armpit. Wulfstan leaned his weight behind the thrust, screaming at his enemy, standing in his stirrups and following as Ethelmund, with eyes widening in shock, tried to pull away.

Fenn reached the fight. Two men were attacking Wulfstan, but the ealdorman's attention was solely on Ethelmund. The man with the sword swung again, the blade deflecting this time off the gauntlet covering Wulfstan's forearm. The second man was probing with a spear, searching for a weak spot in Wulfstan's armour. The spear was more likely to do damage. Fenn swerved toward the spearman. The man saw him coming and dropped his shield to block the swing of Fenn's axe. The blade was deflected by the edge of the shield away from its intended target of the ribs but still retained enough force to bite deep into the man's leg below the knee. He screamed, and Fenn used his momentum to kick him away from the horse. The man dropped his spear and fell, his attempts to clutch his leg awkwardly hampered by his shield.

As Wulfstan leaned forward to seal Ethelmund's fate, the first man's sword found a gap under his armour, high in his side. Fenn lunged at him with the seax over the rump of Wulfstan's horse, but the thrust was met and deflected by a shield. Fenn moved around the horse and swung the axe at another man about to throw a spear in Wulfstan's direction. The man ducked away from the axe but was met by Kaela's sword. Fenn turned, but the swordsman who'd struck at Wulfstan was gone.

Ethelmund toppled silently from his horse and Wulfstan fell back in his saddle with a moan.

A spear stabbed into the shoulder of Wulfstan's mount. The horse screamed and reared, kicking at the man and striking him solidly in the head, hurling him backwards. He crumpled and lay still. Wulfstan had slipped in the saddle when the horse reared. He pulled himself back with a groan of pain. Somebody fell against Fenn – Sergio, who regained his balance immediately; the corner of Fenn's eye caught the Lombard's sword flashing twice. Sergio examined a tear in his leggings and a shallow cut beneath. Fenn heard him mutter: 'I must be getting old.'

Fenn stopped a blade on the handle of his axe – he pulled the axe away, twisting the head so the sword was dragged with it and thrust at the man with the seax. The man blocked the seax with his shield, detached his sword from the axe and swung again. Kaela appeared in front of Fenn, parried the man's sword to the side and in the same movement, leapt high and drove her sword down behind his shield into the gap between shoulder and neck. A gush of blood flew into the air. Fenn stepped away, twisting his head, searching for an enemy, bringing his arm up to wipe blood from his eyes. He heard a grunt from Wulfstan and raised his eyes. The ealdorman's face was twisted in pain.

Sergio's voice said: 'Grimbold's running.'

The action stilled as those Hwiccans who had seen their leader fall withdrew and were replaced by more Wessex men – guardsmen and men from Wulfstan's fyrd. They surrounded Wulfstan, helping him from his horse.

Fenn looked about but couldn't see Grimbold.

Wessex shields were gathering around him.

'The day isn't over,' he called, pointing to the north. 'We need to push them back into the marsh.'

'Our Lord is injured,' one said.

Wulfstan was lowered to the ground. The action had been short but violent enough to churn the daisies to mud. A man turned Wulfstan on his side to examine his wound. Blood was smeared about Wulfstan's mouth and leaking from his lips. He grasped the elbow of a man beside him to help him raise his head. With his other hand, he urgently beckoned Fenn closer.

Fenn knelt beside him.

'I've done what I wanted to do.' Wulfstan's voice was weak. 'I'm content. The kingdom is in good hands.' His hand sought Fenn's. 'Take care of Alburga. Tell her I'll wait for her.'

Fenn frowned. He glanced beneath Wulfstan's horse at Ethelmund's spreadeagled body, the shiny armour now thickly spattered with mud and blood. Already a man had knelt by Ethelmund and was stripping the armour, untying the straps.

'That was brave work,' he said. 'It's probably won the day. But you can take care of Alburga yourself.'

He looked up at the man beside Wulfstan.

'Get his armour off. Stop the bleeding.'

The man held Fenn's gaze. He reached his hand behind his shoulder, indicating where Wulfstan had been struck. He slowly shook his head.

Wulfstan tightened his grip. 'Swear to me you'll deal to that cur Grimbold… deal him the fate that traitor deserves…' Wulfstan coughed, blood dribbling from his mouth. 'In the name of Wessex.'

'That I *do* swear,' said Fenn. He repeated Wufstan's words. '*In the name of Wessex.*'

Wulfstan's hand fell away.

The man beside Wulfstan leant forward, his head close to Wulfstan's mouth.

'He's gone,' the man said.

Fenn motioned to the men gathered around Wulfstan. They approached and Wulfstan was lifted, leaving behind a dark pool of blood blending into the muddy soil.

'Take him from the field,' said Fenn.

He shook his head as he watched the men move away. Had he condemned Wulfstan at that critical moment by choosing to attack the man with the spear over the one wielding the sword? An instant decision in the heat of the battle….

The memory struck him instantly. *Arielle's prophecy.* What had she said? A dying friend that Fenn may have been able to save. But the twists of fate were not his to understand. Her words: *The other way was never written.* He shook his head. He had to find the strength to accept what could not be changed.

Fenn blew a breath of frustration between his teeth and pushed himself to his feet.

'The rest of you follow me,' he said.

He caught Kaela's eye. She was looking at him with a slightly puzzled expression, wondering what he'd been thinking. He cast his eye over her. She looked unharmed.

He looked for Sergio. He'd heard him speak a few moments ago but now he was nowhere to be seen.

The struggle was continuing to the left and right and many of the men from both Wulfstan's fyrd and the house-guards had been dragged into the side conflicts. From his position, Fenn could clearly see the road and the steady stream of men still pouring onto the field. Herewic's and Leofrith's fyrds had failed to close that gap. Twenty or more men were visible on the road, with more coming. He used his sleeve to again wipe the sweat and blood from his eyes.

'We need to block the road,' he yelled.

He waved to the men around him and headed in that direction.

WITH THEIR BACKS TO the marsh, the men from Hwicce and Mercia fought fiercely. What forward progress the Wessex fyrds made was thwarted and rebuffed by the continual surge of reinforcements along the road. Fenn had expected the invaders to run when they heard that Ethelmund had fallen, but that news did not spread readily among men when their total attention was focused on staying alive. The Wessex men remaining in the centre didn't quite have the numbers to counter the Hwiccan and Mercian reinforcements and drive them back into the marshes. Rather than being forced to fight from the marsh, the

Hwiccans had gained a foothold on the field. The fyrds of Wessex were fighting separate battles and hadn't been able to combine as Fenn had hoped. Despite the reassuring words of pending victory Fenn had just given to Wulfstan, the conflict was in balance, surging one way then the other.

He was young and fit, but he'd been exerting himself strenuously. Every movement, whether in defence or attack, was necessarily delivered with maximum force. To try to conserve strength was to die, but that unrelenting effort was taking its toll. He was gulping in air, and his forearm and the hand gripping his axe were aching. For the first time, the seax felt heavy in his left hand.

Wessex needed its own reinforcements. It was time to signal Cedric. Fenn had said he would circle his axe when the time came, but that simple action required a free moment. Right now, he had none.

He blocked the high overhead sword with his axe, then swung it laterally. The man lifted an arm to protect his head and the axe blade sliced his forearm to the bone. The injury was ignored and the sword was twisted and thrust at Fenn's head. Fenn leaned back and away from the blow, stepping to the side to bring his seax into the fray, aiming under the man's extended sword arm.

This was the precise moment that Fenn's survival on the field at Cymeresford became precarious.

The foot he planted to provide a pivot for his attack with the seax slipped in the mud and slid from under him. He dropped to one knee — the thrust of the seax intended for the body instead striking the man's thigh. The sharp point sliced the muscle and again hit bone. The man grunted in pain but reversed his sword and swung it once more at Fenn's head.

Fenn leaned further, his back bent double, awkwardly and painfully wrenching the knee of the foot that had slipped. To keep his balance, he was forced to rest the head of his axe on the ground. The sword blade sliced the air a hand's width from his chin, but Fenn was left in a dangerously vulnerable position. The man was wounded in two places, but Fenn was almost defenceless if his opponent was able to continue his attack. Fenn struggled to regain his feet, pushing himself back and away from his foe, blindly bringing up a crossed axe and seax in an attempt to block the next blow, an act of desperation that would only be successful if that blow came from the expected direction – his foot slipping again, still not finding solid ground – bizarrely thinking it would be an ideal time for Kaela or Sergio to appear, but he hadn't seen either for a while.

A deep-throated roar sounded beside Fenn. He twisted his head to identify the source but caught only the arc of another blade swinging in his direction. He rolled away onto his elbow, unsure whether the move would be enough to evade the sword. His shoulders hunched involuntarily, expecting the searing bite of steel. A guttural yell and a clash of swords sounded above him. Fenn tensed, waiting for the pain, but it didn't arrive. A foot splashed into the mud in front of his face. There was something strange and also familiar about the foot. Fenn curled his legs beneath him and pushed himself to a crouch just as a swinging arm hit his face, knocking him back. He staggered, tasting blood. His heel caught on a discarded shield and he fell backwards, twisting and dropping again to one knee. Futilely, he raised his axe, knowing it would be unlikely to protect him, turning his body to face the new foe, his eyes searching. The same roar sounded in the man's throat and his sword cut through the air – but not in Fenn's direction. Instantly, Fenn recognised the man and his footwear.

Silward!

The foot was lifted and a violent kick drove Fenn's attacker back. Two more heavy blows with the sword and the man was down. Silward moved forward, stepping over the body, and Giffre in his chain armour appeared briefly in front of Fenn, before he too moved away.

Cedric's voice came from behind.

'This is no time to wallow down there in the mud and the blood. There's still work to be done.'

CHAPTER TWENTY-EIGHT

Aftermath, revenge, and resolution

'Have you seen Cedric?' asked Fenn.

'He's near,' said Kaela. 'I saw him a short time ago.'

'I need to thank him for his timely arrival on the field.'

She detected something in his voice and looked up at him. He nodded. 'It was not going well for me.'

Her face tightened, torn between asking for more and not wanting to know.

'And Sergio?' Fenn asked.

Kaela frowned. 'I haven't seen him. We were separated. I can only hope….'

Fenn and Kaela stood at the edge of the grove of trees on the plateau of the high hill. They gazed over the battlefield. Men were moving among the fallen, checking the bodies. The wounded were being carried to the side where tents had been erected. The field was also being scoured for discarded weapons – swords, spears, arrows.

Egbert, Herewic, and Leofrith were conferring a short distance away beside the body of Wulfstan which had been covered by a Wessex flag. Tariq crouched nearby, seemingly in contemplation.

Herewic turned away from Egbert and walked toward Fenn, pausing by Tariq. After a few words, the two bowed to each other and Herewic continued, nodding to Kaela before addressing Fenn.

'Lord Feran,' he said. 'In Witanceastre I told you I hoped you would be worthy. Firstly I apologise for my doubts, and secondly… although I didn't approve of the outlaw protecting our flank, I acknowledge that his men turned the tide of the battle – and furthermore they were properly held and brought onto the field at the correct time.' He looked directly at Fenn. 'You could have stood aside but you put yourself in the thick of the battle. You've proven yourself as a leader today, Lord Feran, in more ways than one. From this moment, if you ever have need of me I'll be there, and quickly.'

Herewic brought up a fist and clasped it with his other hand. It seemed like an unusual salute, but Fenn understood it was a reference to his ring. Was this the way members of Arielle's order greeted each other?

He was about to protest that Cedric's entry into the battle was not at his direction – he had wanted to signal Cedric but hadn't been able to – but it was too complicated to explain and he'd just seem foolish if he tried.

'Thank you, Lord Herewic. For myself and on behalf of the King, I thank you for your service today.'

Herewic brought his feet together, bowed formally, then turned on his heel walking quickly away.

'That was… interesting,' said Kaela, puzzled. 'You made an impression on him. You now have a strong ally there.'

Fenn nodded. He followed Herewic's retreat for a moment, then let his gaze return to the battlefield.

'What a waste of lives,' he said, sighing. 'All for ambition.'

'Ethelmund's assessment may have been different, had he prevailed. Then it may all have been worthwhile.'

He shrugged. 'Maybe. But he didn't.'

They stood in silence, watching the men at work in the field.

'How will King Egfrith of Mercia respond to this outcome?' asked Fenn.

'I've met Egfrith a few times. He's a weak boy who was totally dominated by his overbearing father. When he learns Wessex was not caught by surprise, he'll probably deny any involvement and hope it all blows away in the next strong wind.'

Fenn could still taste blood in his mouth. He took a moment to assess his injuries, feeling with his tongue for loose teeth and bending to check his aching knee.

Kaela saw what he was doing and smiled at him.

'Glad to be off that field with only a few knocks?' she asked.

'Of course.' He regarded her. She looked as though she hadn't been touched.

'I saw you hook the man's shield aside with your axe. That was neatly done.'

Fenn tilted his head in acknowledgement. 'You can't do that with a sword.'

Kaela snorted. 'That's true.'

They looked up as Olgood approached.

'Talking of seeing things…' Olgood said, 'I watched Grimbold and some of his followers leave the field, heading east, skirting behind Leofrith. They were in a hurry and looked as though they weren't going to stop until they ran out of land.'

'Grimbold. So, he's south of the Thames and still in Wessex?'

Olgood nodded.

'I want that man,' said Fenn. 'I gave my word to Wulfstan.' He turned to Kaela. 'Who can we send…?' Now the battle was over, he wasn't sure whether he still had the authority for such action, but that could be debated later.

'I'll tell Trevanian to go after him,' said Kaela. 'He didn't look kindly on Grimbold, so he'll be willing. East, you say? How many men?'

Olgood pointed. 'Between those hills. He was on a horse, so his tracks should be easy to follow. He had about twenty men with him. And…' Olgood paused. He had a puzzled look on his face.

'And what?' asked Fenn.

'I'm not sure, but I think the little Lombard followed Grimbold.'

'Sergio?'

Olgood shrugged. 'From where I stood, it looked like him.'

Fenn looked at Kaela. 'Would Sergio want his revenge on Grimbold so badly he would leave your side and follow him from the field?'

Kaela shrugged. 'Sergio's a fiercely proud man. Grimbold's insults annoyed him, and his inability to respond annoyed him more.'

Fenn frowned, perplexed. He still found Sergio's action strange – if the man Olgood saw *was* Sergio.

'It seems he was more than annoyed.'

Kaela offered no further comment.

'Grimbold must know he's taking a risk remaining in Wessex,' said Fenn. 'I wonder what he's up to? Wulfstan's order stands.... tell Trevanian to arrest the man on sight.'

Kaela nodded and moved away.

Footsteps from behind. 'Arrest who?' Cedric's voice. Fenn turned. 'Not me, I hope,' Cedric added.

'No. High Reeve Grimbold.'

'That arrogant oaf. He deserves it, whatever he's done.'

Cedric looked at Olgood. 'So, I meet the big ox again... I suppose I should apologise for trussing you up in the forest. My God, I thought Silward was big, but....'

Silward walked up to stand beside Cedric. Fenn nodded to him to acknowledge his help on the field. Silward did not react, appearing disinterested. He and Olgood appraised each other like two wild stags meeting in the forest.

Fenn turned back to Cedric. 'I just said to Kaela that I wanted to thank you and your men. I think, after the service you provided Wessex today, we could rescind your outlaw status if you wanted and you could leave the forest.'

Cedric stepped closer and lowered his voice. 'You know I didn't come here today for Wessex,' he said. 'It was personal. A chance to do damage to the House of Hwicce and Ethelmund in particular.'

'Nonetheless…' Fenn said, '…no one would deny you tipped the scales in our favour. I'm sure I could persuade Egbert to declare you no longer an outlaw.'

Silward snorted his disdain. Cedric smiled. 'I'll think on it.'

'And furthermore…' Fenn said slowly, '…your arrival not only proved to be at just the right time to seal the victory… but as you commented on the field, I wasn't in the best of positions myself. You probably saved me….'

Cedric raised a hand. 'I think you would have regained your feet, but any salvation was by Silward's hand, not mine….'

Fenn made to interrupt.

'…and no,' Cedric continued, 'it's *not* the same thing, so I do not consider the obligation I owe you for my life to be settled.'

Fenn glanced at Silward. Again he was met with indifference. Fenn realised Sliward's intervention had been totally fortuitous. He played by his own rules. The big man simply didn't care for the welfare of anyone else on the battlefield, save, perhaps, Cedric. If you weren't an enemy, you were insignificant.

Fenn had mixed feelings toward Silward. He would have killed Kaela had she not been so skilled, and yet he had probably saved Fenn's life. Fenn sensed that if he thanked him, the man would genuinely not understand why.

Fenn shook his head. 'Cedric,' he said, 'I helped you in the river and, in return, you promised to help me when you could. You have done that today. Your entry into the battle probably saved me and may have saved Wessex. I know you lost men today. You've done more than enough.'

Cedric regarded him silently. After a few moments, he nodded and said: 'I hear your words. I'll think on that too.'

Fenn clapped him on the shoulder. 'Please do.'

FENN WALKED AT A leisurely pace. Beside him, Kaela hadn't spoken for a while. He presumed she was contemplating the battle, maybe worrying about Sergio, who hadn't been seen but also hadn't been found on the field. Hopefully, he *was* the man Olgood had observed following Grimbold. Olgood and Tariq followed at a short distance. In contrast, that pair were in deep conversation. Tariq was twirling his staff and explaining its capabilities. Olgood had his long axe in his hand and looked to be drawing a comparison.

It was early afternoon. The air was cool and pleasant. There was thick forest to either side but the road was wide and flat and made for easy walking. Apart from Fenn's split lip, twisted knee, and a few bruises, he and Kaela had emerged from the day unscathed and he had to be grateful for that. As Wulfstan had observed, in the chaos of a battle things can go wrong in a hundred different ways.

Fenn thought of Wulfstan. He'd grown to like and respect the man – a worthy and capable leader and a great loss to Wessex.

No matter how quickly they walked, they would not reach Witanceastre today. Fenn had said he'd like to visit Andeferas, the town he'd given as his home town when they'd entered the gate at Witanceastre disguised as tanners. It was only a short detour.

Egbert had stayed to organise the wounded and the burials. He'd offered Fenn horses for the journey back to Witanceastre but Fenn had declined – they would be better used to transport the injured.

He rounded a bend and stopped.

Ahead, a lone horseman was waiting in the middle of the road. A horseman Fenn recognised.

It was Grimbold.

Fenn heard the whisper of Lord of the Battle before his hand reached his axe.

Grimbold raised his arm and a score of men emerged from the forest, at least ten on each side of the road. The four travellers were heavily outnumbered.

Grimbold nudged his horse forward. He held up a hand, motioning for everyone to relax.

'You need not die here,' he called. 'I have no quarrel with most of you… only one person – *him*.'

He pointed a finger directly at Fenn.

Grimbold narrowed his eyes, staring malevolently at Fenn. He slowly lowered his arm and dismounted in his usual ungainly manner, landing heavily. He straightened and reached for his whip.

'Lord Feran, Thane of Westerling – we meet again. I couldn't believe my luck when I saw you on the road.' He shook his head in mock amazement, unfurling the whip and letting it fall. 'I thought God had forsaken me, but now I understand. God *was* listening to my prayers and arranging this final meeting.'

Fenn glanced at Kaela. She was tense, watching Grimbold, eyes darting to the side, assessing the men, waiting to see what developed before deciding on a response.

Grimbold was enjoying himself and in no hurry. He slipped the loop of leather attached to the handle over his wrist to fasten it to his hand and took a fierce grip on the handle, raising it to brandish at Fenn, his face twisting into a scowl.

'My Jenny can now deliver the whipping she's long been denied – the whipping you deserve, you *foreign* upstart. I should have done it in the market when we first met.' He grinned cruelly. 'I do like it when I can settle an old score.'

Kaela stepped forward, but Fenn held her arm.

'No,' he said. 'It's me he wants.'

'Fenn…' she whispered urgently. 'I've seen him use that whip. He's an expert.'

'Fenn…?' Olgood rumbled.

'What will be, will be,' said Fenn firmly. 'This is *my* fight.'

He lifted his axe from his belt and drew Beorhtric's seax.

Grimbold laughed. 'Do you think you can reach me with your clumsy chopper? I can snatch a gnat from the air.' He flicked his wrist to extend the whip, then flipped it over his shoulder.

'I usually leave my victims whimpering in the dirt but alive to rue the encounter. But for you, I'll make an exception. You've disrupted my plans for the last time.'

Enough talk. Fenn raised his arms and moved forward.

The whip curled out like a snake. It was fast, blindingly fast. The end wrapped around the handle of the axe, just under the blade. In the blink of an eye Grimbold's wrist snapped back, and before Fenn had time to react, the axe was snatched from his hand, the jerk pulling him off balance. Grimbold shouted his triumph. Fenn corrected his stumble, transferred his seax to his right hand, and leapt forward to close with Grimbold. It would take the Reeve a moment to unwind the whip from the axe handle, and that may be all the time….

The whip snaked out again. It had seemingly uncoiled itself from the handle without effort. Fenn instinctively raised his left arm to protect his head. The whip was deflected enough so that it furled across Fenn's shoulders rather than around his neck. Still, at the speed it was travelling, the rough leather tore through the cloth on his back, breaking the skin beneath. The fastest moving part of the whip, the flailed ends, struck under his right arm with unbelievable force. Fenn felt the skin tear, and the blow staggered him to the side. The pain was instant and intense. He automatically brought his right arm in to cover the wound and staunch the blood. Again, the whip uncoiled freely and Grimbold flicked it back, ready for the next strike.

He was gleeful, confidant, used to seeing people cowering defenceless before the bullwhip.

'How do you like my Jenny's gentle caress?' he sneered.

The two strikes of Grimbold's whip had given Fenn's eye a measure of its speed. As the three-tailed end of the whip flicked out again, Fenn didn't crouch or hunch his body to protect himself. Instead, he stepped toward Grimbold to disrupt the range, leaning to the right and raising his left arm high and away from his body, intercepting the whip's path, deliberately allowing it to twist around his forearm. It ripped through the sleeve and bit into his flesh. Again the pain of torn skin was severe, but even before the deadly tails had completed their whirling flight, Fenn swiftly fastened his hand around the thick leather thong. In the same movement he leaned back, pulling on the whip with all his strength.

The handle was dragged from Grimbold's grasp, but the holding loop tightened around his wrist and he was jerked from his feet. He stumbled forward and was met by Fenn's advance and two quick thrusts of the deadly seax.

'*For Wulfstan…*' Fenn hissed under his breath.

The High Reeve's disbelief was still painted on his face as he slid to the ground.

There was a moment when nobody moved, each person absorbing the sudden conclusion.

Then a man stepped forward, raising his sword. Fenn recognised the man with his scarred forehead and broken nose. It was the mercenary he'd fought at the Weyhill Inn. The man opened his mouth to shout – but there was a blur of movement behind him and instead of words, a spray of blood erupted from his throat, bizarrely followed by the emerging tip of a sword blade. The mercenary toppled forward onto his face, revealing the form of Sergio, who wiped his weapon on the man's tunic before stepping onto the road and walking toward the next man.

'Are you next, Godwin?' he asked as if offering cake. The man's eyes widened and he uttered a cry of terror, recoiling from Sergio and backing quickly into the trees.

Sergio's appearance was astonishing enough and his calling the man by name more so. The man's extreme reaction was also weird until Fenn realised that Sergio would know many of Grimbold's men, and they would know the skills of the swordmaster.

The two closest to Sergio also lurched away from him as if he was diseased. Their panicked retreat, following the swift demise of both Grimbold and the mercenary leader – coupled with Sergio's steely glare and raised sword, Kaela's leap forward, a bellow from Olgood, and the sight of Tariq's staff whirling in the air above his head – were enough to scatter the rest. They jostled each other in their haste to escape – crashing into the forest, the sounds of their forced passage lingering, then fading, leaving Fenn's party alone on the road – in the company of a pair of dead bodies.

Sergio moved quickly to catch Grimbold's horse before it could bolt. Kaela turned in a slow circle, listening – to ensure none of the attackers had second thoughts. Satisfied, she replaced her sword in its scabbard.

Fenn felt under his arm. His hand came away bloody. Kaela helped him sheath the seax and lifted his elbow.

'Let me look at the damage,' she said. Tariq appeared beside her, offering a white cloth. Kaela eased the torn tunic away from the sliced flesh under Fenn's arm, turning him toward the sun for better light and bending to check the wound.

She grunted with relief. 'It's taken a strip of skin and bitten into the muscle but not deeply. You'll probably have a nice set of scars but in a place where no one will see them.' She smiled, but he could see the concern in her eyes. 'Another lash or two would have peeled the skin from your back… I wasn't going to let him strike again.'

She pushed the cloth under his armpit. 'Hold it there,' she said. Fenn obeyed, and she moved to check the bloody sleeve of his left arm.

'We'll need honey to help these wounds heal and keep them clean,' she said, fixing him with a look. 'If we don't see any hives before we get to Andeferas, at least we now have a reason to go there.'

Olgood bent to retrieve Fenn's axe and offered it to him.

'That's the second time this has been taken from you,' he said with a playful hint of reproach. 'I'd hold on to it if I were you.' He placed his hand on Fenn's shoulder. 'You've taken some damage, but that move to catch the whip was boldly done.' Olgood paused and regarded Fenn. 'It's been a long and difficult one, but… not today, my friend.'

Fenn nodded. 'Not today.'

He reached to take the axe and winced with the pain of the movement.

Sergio returned, leading Grimbold's horse. The Lombard paused by Grimbold's body face-down on the road, looking down at the High Reeve impassively.

'It's unfortunate I couldn't be here sooner,' he said. 'I'm glad this deed was done. I'm only sorry I wasn't the one to do it.'

Kaela straightened. 'I would say you arrived at a very opportune time.'

Sergio grunted his acknowledgement and gave Fenn an appraising look. Kaela nodded to him and waved her hand – telling him Fenn's injuries were not serious.

Sergio held up a finger. 'If all's well here, I've something to show you.'

Reaching behind the horse's saddle he retrieved a bag, untied it and held it out to Kaela.

'When Ethelmund fell, I was watching Grimbold,' Sergio said. 'He spared no thought for the ealdorman. Instead, he focused on retrieving this bag from Ethelmund's horse. It was obviously important. He put himself at considerable risk to get it – Wessex men were arriving. As soon as he had the bag, his only thought was to escape the field.'

Sergio had a strange expression on his face.

'I've already seen what's inside,' he said. 'I was watching from a distance when Grimbold took it out of the bag to check it. It's what I suspected.'

Kaela nodded to Tariq who took her place beside Fenn. He pulled Fenn's torn sleeve aside to bare the forearm and wrapped a cloth over the broken skin. As Kaela opened the bag, Tariq split the end of the fabric into two strips and bound the wound.

Kaela reached inside and pulled an object from the bag.

Even though he had never seen it before, Fenn recognised the object.

The golden Orb of Wessex.

'I FOLLOWED THEM AT a distance,' Sergio said. 'I planned to take the orb tonight when they slept.' He pointed to a hill. 'Then Grimbold spotted you from over there, and everyone's plans changed.'

Kaela said: 'Ethelmund had the orb? Why? How did he…?'

'It's the logical answer to the orb's disappearance,' Olgood offered. 'Eadburg planned for Ethelmund to take the throne of Wessex. The orb would aid his claim.' He raised a finger. 'Grimbold took it to him. On the night Beorhtric died, I'll wager Eadburg went straight to the Treasury, sent Grimbold on his way with the orb to join Ethelmund, and took the coin for herself. She then collected her jewellery and escaped to Francia. It's what I've been saying – they planned it together.'

'Yes,' acknowledged Kaela. 'But how would Eadburg benefit from Ethelmund being on the throne of Wessex?'

'Maybe marriage – maybe gold?' suggested Olgood. 'They must have made some arrangement.'

Kaela nodded thoughtfully.

'A more relevant question is – after Grimbold took the orb back from Ethelmund, where was he going?' asked Fenn.

'By the direction he was headed, not to Mercia and Egfrith,' said Kaela.

'Then…?'

'To the coast? To Eadburg?' offered Olgood.

No one could propose a better answer.

Kaela turned to Sergio. 'Have you seen Trevanian? I sent him and some men to follow and arrest Grimbold.'

'No, I haven't seen the Captain. But Grimbold changed direction abruptly when he saw you. That may have misled Trevanian.'

Kaela nodded. 'You're right. It doesn't matter now.'

She looked down at Grimbold sprawled on the road, the whip still attached to his wrist – as lifeless as the hand that held it.

'What shall we do with these bodies?'

'Throw them in the forest. Leave them for the crows,' said Sergio, 'they deserve nothing more.'

When no one disagreed, Kaela turned to Fenn.

'We have a horse,' she said. 'You should ride.'

Fenn looked at her. 'I can walk,' he said.

'Fenn… we have a horse,' she repeated. 'You should keep that arm still.'

Fenn sighed. His wounds were already settling into a dull ache.

'Very well,' he said. 'To Andeferas and then we'll take the orb to Egbert at Witanceastre, but after that, as soon as we can… back to Westerling.'

CHAPTER TWENTY-NINE

Race to Westerling

The girl perched on a fallen tree trunk, her legs dangling a foot from the ground. Her hands were resting in her lap and her eyes were closed, her head back, enjoying the warmth of the sun on her face.

At the sound of horses, she opened her eyes and smiled. She leaned forward and waved.

Fenn rode up to the girl and looked down at her.

'It's hard to get away from you,' he said. 'You turn up in the most unexpected places.'

'I saw you from the top of the hill,' she said. 'I heard you'd left Witanceastre by the west road. I've been waiting here a while.' She looked past Fenn to the person drawing his horse alongside Fenn's and her eyes widened with astonishment.

Fenn dismounted.

'Rowena, I don't think you've met Olgood. Olgood, this is Rowena, the girl from the market.'

'I've heard of you,' said Olgood. 'Good to finally meet you.'

Rowena's eyes were still wide. She gulped. 'I… uh… I've never seen….'

'…a man so handsome,' finished Fenn smiling, 'I know. He does have that effect sometimes. It's his fair hair, I think.'

'…a man so….'

'Olgood is bigger than most,' said Kaela. 'Fenn, stop teasing her.'

Fenn laughed. He stepped up to the tree and lifted Rowena from it. 'Good to see you again.' He looked about. 'Are you alone?'

'Of course,' she said.

'Isn't that dangerous?' asked Kaela as she dismounted. 'Surely, Silward or…'

'Bah. In the forest, no one can catch *me*.'

Olgood also dismounted. He stretched his legs and lifted his arms above his head. Rowena stared at him.

'Well, Cedric must believe that if he sent you to meet us,' said Fenn. 'Does he have a message?'

'Cedric didn't send me. I heard him telling Silward you'd left Witanceastre. I came on my own.'

'Why?'

Rowena's face turned serious. 'I have news I think you'll want to hear.'

'Cedric has decided to accept Egbert's pardon,' suggested Fenn.

'No. It's not good news.'

Fenn drew a breath through his teeth. 'Galastan and the *Ariochs*.'

'Yes. Those beasts escaped the camp. They broke out of the storehouse, took their horses and crept away in the night.' Rowena reached out for Fenn's arm. 'Fenn, I heard that greasy ferret talking yesterday. He knows about the battle at Cymeresford. He mentioned you and…' her eyes flicked to Olgood, '…Olgood by name. He was surprised you weren't dead…? Why would he think…?'

'It's a long story,' said Fenn.

'Anyway…' Rowena continued, '…they know you two and the Princess aren't at Westerling….'

'…and they'll think the gold is there,' finished Fenn.

Rowena's eyes widened. 'Gold?'

'The gold Galastan thought was in the box.' He frowned. 'When did this happen?'

'Sometime last night. They have almost a day's start on you.'

'What's Cedric doing about their escape?' asked Kaela.

'He says good riddance. He's tired of them. The white monsters ate as much as four men.'

'I'm surprised he'd just let them go,' said Fenn. 'He told me they were guarded by reliable men. Was anyone hurt?'

'No. They were locked in a storehouse for the night as usual. They broke through the wall.'

Fenn looked at Olgood. 'It looks like Galastan was able to control his dogs this time.'

'Gisele is at Westerling,' said Olgood. 'If they're headed there, we should be too. And without delay.'

'It's not likely Edelred will open the doors for Galastan,' Fenn said.

'He's a cunning man,' said Olgood. He regarded Fenn, his face set tight.

Fenn mounted his horse. 'On to Westerling,' he said.

'Wait,' said Rowena. 'I have a gift for you.'

She disappeared behind a tree and reappeared leading a small horse with greyed features. Tied to the horse's back was the iron box. She walked to Fenn and handed the rope up to him.

'You told me this box was yours. Cedric had tossed it aside, but I retrieved it for you.'

Fenn was about to refuse – he didn't need the box back, but the eagerness on her face changed his mind.

'That's kind of you,' he said. 'Thank you again. I'll send the horse back.'

'No.' Rowena stroked the horse's neck. 'She's been a good friend but she's old. I'd like her to have one last adventure, but she won't like to travel far. One journey is enough. Just give her a pasture where she can smell the wind and has someone to care for her.'

'I can do that,' Kaela said.

Fenn looked down at Rowena. 'You're a rare one,' he said. 'With understanding beyond your years.'

'We can't just leave Rowena alone here,' said Kaela, also mounting. She adjusted her sword, automatically checking that Lord of the Battle moved freely in the scabbard.

Rowena returned Fenn's gaze, chin up, head tilted to the side, daring him to try to tell her what to do. Her eyes were drawn to Olgood remounting, the crease of her brow indicating her sympathy for the horse.

Rowena's independence reminded Fenn of someone. For a moment, he couldn't recall who – then it came to him. Beric, the boy at Westerling. And there was someone else….

'You could come with us to Westerling, if you wanted,' he said.

She looked back at him, smiled, and shook her head.

'This life is my life,' she said. 'I like the freedom of the forest and the wide open sky.'

'I think she'll be fine,' Fenn said to Kaela. 'She reminds me of you.'

TWO DAYS LATER, as dawn settled on the forest, Fenn emerged from the trees on the Roman Road, and Westerling came into view. They had ridden through the night and Fenn could feel the lack of sleep as an ache behind his eyes. His wounds also ached and he knew the injury under his arm was bleeding again. When he'd been marked by the whip, Kaela had thought it best if he rode, but on horseback during the long ride west, he'd discovered it was difficult to avoid his arm rubbing against the wound.

Despite his aches, the sight of Westerling was welcome.

They'd kept the horses at a good pace, stopping only briefly on the first two nights and not at all last night. Fenn had some initial concern for Rowena's horse, considering her age, but it proved unfounded – the little mare kept up well, and true to Rowena's expectation, she seemed to take interest in her new surroundings.

By pushing the pace, Fenn had hoped to catch Galastan, but neither he nor the Ariochs had been sighted. He hoped that meant Galastan was not headed for Westerling.

Olgood urged his horse to a trot, passing Fenn, bouncing in the saddle as he hurried towards the palisade doors. Fenn looked over the fields and saw people waving. He waved in return and quickened his horse to follow Olgood.

The doors opened before Olgood reached them. Fenn expected Balthazar to bound through the doors, howling, but instead Edelred stepped out, Bronwyn at his side, followed by Nyle and Erenweth. Soon a small crowd had gathered around the horses as the people of Westerling came out to greet their Thane.

Olgood raised himself in the saddle and searched the gathering. He dismounted and strode up to Edelred.

'Where's Gisele?' he asked. 'Do you know?'

'Gisele? I haven't seen her this morning.' Edelred looked at Bronwyn. 'Have you…?'

'No, I haven't seen her since last night. I left her in the Hall with Kuralin. They were sewing.' Bronwyn smiled up at Olgood. She patted him on the arm. 'She's getting bigger. You'll have a strong boy there for sure.'

Nyle called. 'She's well and thriving, Olgood. Have no worries.'

Olgood grunted and headed purposefully through the doors, the crowd parting before him. Those he brushed past looked up at him, surprised by his uncharacteristic forcefulness.

Fenn called to Edelred. 'Edelred, has Galastan been here?'

'Galastan!?' Edelred said incredulously. 'No, I don't expect him to ever return to Westerling.'

'Thank the gods,' said Kaela, surprising Fenn with her use of the plural. Was she referring to the gods of the Northmen?

He'd expected Balthazar to be first through the doors, but the wolfhound wasn't among the welcoming crowd. He spotted the tall figures of Peada and his father, Merewyn, standing together and waved the boy over.

'Yes, Lord?'

'Where's Balthazar?' Fenn asked. 'I expected him to be first to greet us.'

'Gisele had some venison for him last night,' Peada said. 'He may have stayed with her. Looks like he doesn't know you've returned.' He looked around. 'That's strange – he usually knows what's going on. I'll look for him if you wish, Lord…?'

Fenn nodded. Peada ran off and Fenn dismounted as Nyle came up to him.

'Welcome back,' Nyle said, grasping Fenn by the arm. He reached out to greet Kaela as well. Kaela also dismounted and Erenweth enveloped her in a hug. Bronwyn stood by, waiting for her turn.

'Good to see you're all well,' said Nyle. 'We heard about the Hwicce and the fighting at Cymeresford. I'd like to hear more about that.' He paused, frowning, his eyes drawn to the blood on Fenn's tunic under his arm.

'It's nothing,' said Fenn. 'Just a minor wound aggravated by the long ride.'

'If you say so,' said Nyle. 'But…' he paused, frowning, '…why do you mention Galastan? Have you reason to think he may return here?'

'Yes,' said Fenn. 'Let's talk as we walk.'

Progress was slow as Fenn acknowledged the good wishes of the people of Westerling. He quickly related Cedric's capture of Galastan and the Ariochs to Nyle and Edelred, and their subsequent escape after discovering that the iron box Fenn had delivered to Moloch Tor contained only river stones.

'They also know we escaped from Moloch Tor and that we were at Cymeresford and therefore not at Westerling,' Fenn finished. 'So it was possible they could have taken the opportunity to come here for revenge or to find the gold.' He waved after Olgood. 'Olgood was worried about Gisele.'

'But they wouldn't know where the gold…' said Edelred.

'No,' Fenn agreed. 'But…'

'They may have tried to force me to tell them?'

'If they thought you knew.'

Edelred reflected, then said: 'Anyway, we wouldn't have let them in.' Nyle nodded his agreement. He reached up to tap the bow strapped to his back.

'Of course not,' said Fenn, sighing. 'It seems we've been worrying over nothing. They were headed north toward Mercia when Cedric came across them. They've likely gone that way again.'

He turned to wait for Kaela who was surrounded by women and being barraged with questions.

Peada appeared around the corner of the Hall and ran up to Fenn. He spread his hands.

'I'm sorry, Lord, I can't find Balthazar anywhere. He's not in his usual places. But don't worry…' he continued, '…I'll ask Beric and his boys to look for him. They'll find him.'

He turned away, leaving Fenn staring at his departing back.

Fenn held out his hand to Kaela as she freed herself from the circle. She accepted it and said: 'It's good to be back, Fenn… among friends.'

He smiled and took her by the shoulders, drawing her to him. She sighed. 'I only wish Sergio had agreed to come with us to Westerling.'

'Why didn't he?' asked Fenn.

'He said he wasn't ready to retire his sword, and Egbert asked him to stay in Witanceastre.'

'Egbert wanted us to stay as well. Luckily, he understood our need to return to Westerling, but he's still expecting us to consider his proposal. He wants a new High Reeve.'

'I know,' Kaela said reluctantly.

'Let Merewyn take your horses…' Edelred offered, '…and I'll arrange for refreshments to be brought to the Hall.'

'Ah, Merewyn…' Kaela said. 'Let me tell you about this little horse carrying the box.'

THE THREE COUPLES – Fenn and Kaela, Edelred and Bronwyn, and Nyle and Erenweth – headed for the Great Hall. They stopped at the entrance when Olgood's call came from across the yard, waiting while he hurried to join the group.

Olgood walked up to Fenn. 'I can't find Gisele,' he said anxiously. 'She's missing – Kuralin too. No one has seen them this morning.'

'They could be gathering herbs in the forest,' suggested Edelred.

'Not this early. Not without letting anyone know,' replied Bronwyn.

For a moment, no one could offer another explanation. Then Olgood growled.

'*Galastan was here,*' he said with conviction. 'Somehow, he was here. He's taken her. If he's hurt her I'll tear him apart.'

'That's not possible,' said Edelred. 'He couldn't enter Westerling without anyone noticing him – and he couldn't take Gisele and Kuralin by himself – they're fighters, those two. He'd need the Ariochs and they couldn't get within a mile of here without being noticed.'

Fenn was silent for a moment, then he looked at Kaela.

'When the Ariochs were last here,' he said slowly, 'they disappeared from the Hall unnoticed. Is it possible…?'

'A secret passage?' suggested Kaela.

Fenn glanced at Olgood. 'You may be right, Olgood,' he said. 'Galastan may have taken them. He's going to repeat Moloch Tor and try to exchange Gisele and Kuralin for the gold. Edelred, who would know about a secret passage from the Hall? Gerwent?'

'Perhaps. But he…' Edelred turned to Erenweth. 'What do you think?'

'I can ask him. He can sometimes talk now.'

'Please do so,' said Fenn.

'I'll come with you,' said Nyle.

Fenn continued: 'And Edelred….'

'Yes, Lord.'

'Please ask Merewyn and Peada to join us.'

'Merewyn? Oh… do you think his skill may be useful?' He nodded quickly. 'Of course.'

'But first,' said Kaela, 'you need to see Acwellan.'

FENN DRANK SLOWLY FROM a water bag. Bronwyn took a few apples from a sack and placed them on a plate. There was bread and cold hare already on the table, but no one was hungry. Olgood paced along the side of the Hall, inspecting the fitted tree trunks that made up the wall as a distraction. Kaela sat beside Fenn, leaning her elbows on the table.

'What did Acwellan say?' she asked.

'He said I will heal. I have new bandages.' Fenn managed a wry grimace. 'He suggested I not fight in any battles for a while.'

'That's good advice….'

She looked up as Nyle and Erenweth appeared at the entrance, followed by Edelred with Merewyn and Peada. Fenn queried Peada with a look, but Peada shook his head. No news of Balthazar.

Fenn shook his head. He had a bad feeling in his stomach.

Nyle pulled a chair out for Erenweth. She smiled at him and sat down.

'I'm sorry,' she said. 'I asked my father if he knew of a secret passage from the Hall. He seemed to understand me, but he didn't say anything useful.'

'What *did* he say?' asked Kaela.

Erenweth shrugged and looked embarrassed. 'He just kept saying the words 'the old broken chair'. It made no sense. He became quite agitated, so we stopped asking him to explain.'

'Broken chair…' repeated Fenn. There were many chairs in the Hall, some pulled up to tables, some sitting against the wall, but…

'I don't see any broken chairs.'

'A broken chair would be repaired,' said Edelred.

'I'm sorry,' Erenweth said. 'He must have been rambling.'

'But he *was* insistent,' said Nyle. 'It seemed to mean something to him.' Erenweth took his arm, thanking Nyle for his support.

Fenn stood up. Erenweth was right – a broken chair made no sense. If it was broken, it would either be discarded or repaired.

'Merewyn,' he said. 'Can you…' He stopped. Can you what? What he was about to ask was ridiculous. Scour the whole area around Westerling for Galastan's footprints? He looked at Kaela. Did she have any suggestions? He caught Olgood's eye, urging him to do *something*.

'Fenn, we need to search the forest,' Olgood said, 'and visit the villages. Find out if anyone has seen them. We shouldn't wait any longer.'

Ask at the villages? That would take a long time. He cast his eyes around the room, looking for inspiration, the words *broken chair* echoing in his mind.

It hit him like a bolt of lightning. There *was* an old chair that was broken and had not been repaired. A chair that had been *replaced*.

'In the storage room…' he said to Edelred, pointing. 'You said the old Thane's chair is kept there. *An old broken chair.*'

LORD CORMWURST'S OLD THANE'S chair stood against the wall towards the back of the small room, but when Fenn attempted to move it aside, it was found to be firmly attached to the floor. A swift search behind the seat cushion found the same indentation that when pushed allowed the whole chair and the square of the wooden floor to which it was attached to slide back, revealing a hole with stone steps and a passage leading underground.

Fenn stared at the tunnel. It was as he had suspected on the first day he'd arrived at Westerling. The Great Hall built by Hardwain had a secret passage to allow people to escape from the Hall if besieged or threatened.

He peered into the darkness. 'There's a ring at the bottom of the steps to hold a torch, but it's gone. We'll need a flame.'

Olgood growled with frustration at the delay.

They waited impatiently until Edelred returned with a flaming pig-fat torch.

Fenn asked Merewyn to descend into the hole first.

'They came this way,' said Merewyn immediately. 'The last footprints are three sets coming, three sets going.'

Olgood said: '*Three* going? But…'

Merewyn interrupted him. 'The Ariochs have big feet. They were each carrying something heavy on the way out.'

Peada was halfway down the steps. He joined his father at the bottom and pointed at two places on the ground. Merewyn bent to examine where Peada was indicating. He straightened and they conversed quietly.

'What is it?' asked Fenn, peering into the tunnel. The dancing flame made it difficult to see the floor of the tunnel in any detail from where he stood.

'Peada has pointed out that Galastan is also carrying something on his return journey. He's staggering – having difficulty with the weight.'

Fenn frowned. What would Galastan have taken from the Hall? Not the gold – that was safely buried in a location known only to four people – Kaela, Olgood, Edelred, and himself.

'They've taken a third person,' he said. 'But who?' Had someone else been in the Hall when the Ariochs entered through the tunnel?

Both Kaela and Olgood answered his questioning glance with a blank look and a shake of the head.

Edelred said: 'We don't all need to go into the tunnel. We'll find out who else is missing.' He motioned to Bronwyn and Erenweth.

Olgood descended the steps. Kaela bent and picked up an object from the storeroom floor. Fenn was about to follow Olgood when Kaela caught him by the arm. She held the object out for Fenn to see. It was a table leg that had only been partly shaped. One end of the leg was thickly covered in blood. Nyle touched the blood with his finger.

'It's dry but still sticky. Less than a day,' he said quietly.

'I also noticed blood outside the storeroom door,' said Kaela. 'There's been an attempt to wipe it, but....'

'Until we know whose blood this is, we say nothing to Olgood,' said Fenn.

THE UNDERGROUND BURROW WAS long enough to pass beneath the palisade and extend a significant distance beyond, and wide enough for two people to walk side-by-side. Immediately after leaving the stone steps, the floor sloped noticeably downwards. A framework of wooden planks shored up the tunnel roof every few paces. The earth walls between the shoring looked damp and smelt musty, but the air was breathable. In the flickering light of the torch, Fenn glanced warily at the parts of the tunnel roof that were not directly supported. They thankfully looked solid enough. He tried to curb his anxiety – if a craftsman such as Hardwain had built the tunnel, it should be stable and trustworthy.

Merewyn and Peada led, followed by Fenn and Olgood, with Nyle and Kaela at the rear. After a hundred paces, which by Fenn's estimate would take them to the edge of the forest, the floor levelled again, and light began filtering into the passage, increasing in brightness until Merewyn could see without the torch. He stopped and pushed the flame into the earth to extinguish it, dropping the torch. Fenn searched but couldn't see the torch Galastan had used. He'd expected it to be similarly discarded.

The passage emerged from a hillock in the middle of a group of trees in the forest, the entrance concealed behind dense bushes. Fenn had earlier thought the forest had been close on this side of the palisade, and now he realised it was to cover the exit of the tunnel.

Merewyn and Peada circled in different directions, examining the area. They came back together and conferred, pointing and nodding to each other.

'Five horses were here,' said Merewyn. 'They headed north. They'll be easy to follow.'

'Are you sure?' said Nyle. 'There are six people to carry.'

'Only five horses,' confirmed Merewyn.

'We'll need our own horses,' said Fenn.

'Shall I ready my men?' asked Nyle.

Fenn was surprised that Nyle should consider his men to still be under his command. He had expected they would be fully integrated into the Westerling farming community.

'No,' said Fenn. 'When the people learn what's happened, I'm sure we could raise an army – but we don't have time for that. The six of us should be enough.'

'Do we want to take the gold with us?' asked Kaela.

Fenn grimaced. If Gisele and Kuralin could be rescued safely only by exchanging the gold, it would be best to have the gold with them. But almost any other option would be better than that. Almost....

'No,' he said. 'I...' he looked at Olgood.

'You don't want to exchange the gold, do you?' said Olgood.

'No...' repeated Fenn. 'I don't....'

'You won't need to,' Olgood said, 'when we catch them, they'll have no need of gold.'

Kaela looked at one and then the other. She turned to re-enter the passage. Nyle followed, but Olgood headed in a direction that would take him out of the forest and around the northeast corner of the palisade to the palisade doors. Fenn stopped him.

'I think it would be best if this passage remains secret,' he said. 'People will wonder if you suddenly appear outside the palisade.'

'Why keep the passage secret? It'll be quicker if we go this way,' said Olgood.

'I...' Fenn began. He was having difficulty explaining himself. How could he explain it was just a feeling?

'You know Fenn makes good choices, Olgood,' said Kaela from the passage entrance. 'It'll take longer if we stand here and argue.'

Olgood stared hard at Fenn. 'Very well,' he said. 'But know this. When we meet again with Galastan and the Ariochs, I ask you not to stand in my way.'

He walked past Fenn and followed Nyle and Kaela. Fenn waved to Merewyn and Peada to precede him. They entered the bushes concealing the tunnel entrance leaving Fenn momentarily alone, the forest falling quiet as the noise of their passage receded. For some reason, he hesitated and took a last look around the area where the horses had waited – imagining the Ariochs placing Gisele and Kuralin on horses and Galastan struggling to lift the third person.

He heard a sound.

It was faint but unusual enough that curiosity took him a few steps in that direction. He opened his mouth to hear better. The sound came again. Now that Fenn was concentrating, he knew what it was.

A dog's whine.

Fenn knew who Galastan had been carrying.

'*Balthazar!*' he called, breaking into a run.

FENN'S FIRST THOUGHT WAS that the dog was dead – the last whine he heard had been its dying breath. Balthazar's great body lay stretched out with the stillness of death, his head and shoulders a matted mass of blood.

Fenn dropped to a knee, placing a hand on the dog's chest. Was he breathing? At his touch, a foreleg twitched, the paw raising an inch, then falling.

'*Balthazar* – my God, you're *alive*,' Fenn whispered. A noise in the dog's throat, a whine like the first but softer. A whine of recognition.

Fenn turned to call just as Kaela knelt beside him.

'Acwellan, quickly!' said Fenn. 'He's alive, but only just.'

CHAPTER THIRTY

A clifftop confrontation

'Why are they taking so long?' asked Olgood impatiently.

'They'll find where Galastan left the stream,' said Fenn. 'Give them time.'

Galastan was avoiding roads and paths, probably to avoid questions about his captives, and riding instead through forest and country, heading northeast.

Fenn turned his head at the sound of Merewyn splashing toward them, pointing upstream.

'Three hundred paces, Lord. Five horses on the northern bank.'

Merewyn put his fingers in his mouth and issued two piercing whistles, sounding just like the rising and falling screech of a hawk, calling to his son who'd headed in the opposite direction, downstream.

'How far behind are we?' asked Olgood.

'At the speed they're travelling, they're no more than five miles ahead. They're in no hurry. We're catching them.'

'Galastan must think his abduction won't be detected for a while,' said Fenn. 'He's only taking minimal precautions to cover his tracks, so I'd say he also thinks no one knows about the secret passage from the Hall and he doesn't expect to be followed.'

'Where are they going?' asked Kaela. 'They're not going back to Moloch Tor.'

'As Galastan himself said, the tor served its purpose, but maybe he feels like the rest of us that it's a cold, desolate, thoroughly uninviting place.' Fenn swept his gaze around the countryside. 'At the moment, they seem to be headed north and east. I presume he'll send a message demanding the gold when he feels he's safe.'

Galastan had been travelling north when Cedric met him, and that meeting had occurred further east. Was he headed to the same place now as then? Mercia? Or maybe Hwicce?

'Moloch Tor was an ideal location,' said Kaela. 'He'll need somewhere similar with good visibility to make the exchange.' Her eyes added: *And this time you're not going alone.*

Fenn turned in his saddle to look at Nyle. 'You've been in this area before. Do you know of any such place ahead? Where is he going?'

Nyle thought a moment. 'There are only a few small villages. If he continues in the same direction, there's nothing of note between here and the Severn Sea.'

'Merewyn?' asked Fenn.

'I agree – only villages.' He shrugged. 'The coastline is mostly high rugged cliffs. There's moorland to the north, but it's flat, rolling forested land; no tall peaks. There's no place like Moloch Tor that I'm aware of.'

Fenn shook his head. 'Where *is* he going?' he thought aloud. 'What's he intending to do?'

'They may split up,' Nyle suggested. 'Or he could hide Gisele and Kuralin somewhere.'

'I'd like to catch up with him before that happens.'

Fenn and Kaela rode the black mares who, like Olgood, were impatient with the slow pace. They were twitchy and wanted to run. Fenn patted his horse's neck, holding her, waiting until a splashing announced Peada's arrival.

He turned his mare upstream. The sky was being covered by clouds that were gathering a tinge of grey. The afternoon sun would be obscured well before it could set.

Why did Galastan carry Balthazar from the Hall, take him through the tunnel and abandon him in the forest? He could have dropped the dog in the tunnel if his idea was to leave no evidence of the kidnapping. And – another thought – how could they have surprised Balthazar? The hound had already shown his dislike and distrust of Galastan and the Ariochs. He would have detected their presence and warned Gisele.

Fenn shook his head. He'd find the answers when they caught up with Galastan. He leaned forward on his horse to speak to Merewyn.

'Can you still follow if it rains?'

Merewyn shrugged. 'The rain needs to be considered, Lord – like everything else.' He checked the sky. 'I also have a candle to see in the dark. But…' he smiled, '…even I find it difficult to track in the dark *and* the rain.'

Merewyn and Peada ranged ahead on foot, with the four horses following at a steady walk. Fitting Merewyn's description, the area was hilly and forested but not thickly, so a good pace could be maintained.

Fenn eased himself in the saddle to adjust to the mare's gait. Something else niggled in his mind – something Nyle had said.

MID-AFTERNOON. THE RAIN was still threatening but had not yet arrived.

Surprisingly, Galastan and the Ariochs had recently joined a narrow road. Merewyn said he thought the road led to a fishing village on an inlet at the bottom of a cliff. He didn't know its name. Galastan must think the area was not well travelled – remote enough to risk using the road.

Merewyn and Peada were waiting in a grove of trees.

Merewyn came up to Fenn's mare. 'We're less than a mile behind them,' he said. 'I wanted to show you this.' He pointed to an area of flattened grass beside the road. 'The horses stopped here. See *there*. One of the women has fallen from a horse. An Arioch has dismounted and retrieved her, and….'

'One tried to escape,' said Kaela.

'Escape? No,' said Merewyn. 'No… they were still tied – they weren't able to get up; they couldn't escape. But it's not the first time. The same thing has happened twice before.'

'Gisele and Kuralin are slowing Galastan. They know we'll be following.'

'They don't even know we arrived at Westerling,' said Fenn.

'They know *someone* will be following,' insisted Kaela. 'They're doing what they can to help. Gisele would do that.'

'But at what risk?' observed Olgood. 'To deliberately fall from a horse when she's….'

'It may be Kuralin,' Kaela said.

'It may be,' Olgood said softly. He straightened. 'We must catch up before they try again. Such a fall could injure….' He stopped.

'We'll catch them,' said Fenn. 'But if we're within a mile we don't want to come upon them unexpectedly and allow the women to be threatened or used as shields.'

'Merewyn,' he said. 'I want you to go ahead. Find Galastan and the Ariochs and follow until they stop or split up. Peada will lead us. Are you able to leave messages for Peada to let us know what to expect?'

'Of course,' said Merewyn. Peada nodded.

Merewyn clasped his son by the shoulders, then turned away, walking slowly at first, scanning the ground, then moving into a loping run.

AS THE ROAD CONTINUED northeast, Fenn asked himself again what the man's intentions could be. Nyle said the sea was close. There seemed to be no place suitable for effecting an exchange. If Galastan had such a place in mind, and it was close, he could have recruited a messenger at any of the villages they passed nearby. Fenn grimaced as he recalled the fate of Galastan's last messenger.

Galastan was running out of options. Until now, he'd deliberately avoided villages. Galastan joining the road and heading toward a small fishing village made no sense. Why *that* village? What was there?

Peada was waiting just below the crest of a hill.

The boy stood and waited for Fenn to pull up.

'You can see the sea from over that hill,' said Peada. 'But the forest stops here. It's clear land over there with no cover. Galastan has stopped on the top of the cliff and is resting or waiting for something. My father asks us to wait here for him.'

Fenn looked at the arrangement of sticks, stones, and lines drawn in the earth on the side of the road.

'You can read all that in those stones?'

'Yes,' said Peada.

Fenn continued to stare at the marks and items scattered on the road, trying to make sense of them.

Peada pointed. 'These three stones say beware of danger ahead, and this flat stick is the top of this hill. These two pieces set square with a cross say Galastan has stopped at the cliff. The wavy line is the sea. This circle and the line coming this way means we might be seen. This small upright stick asks us to wait.' He raised his head. 'I've looked over the hill, Lord. If we follow the road, there's no cover between there and the clifftop.'

Fenn shook his head, impressed. His eye followed Merewyn's message. When he reached the wavy line of the sea, something clicked in his mind.

'Thank you, Peada,' he said quickly.

He urgently waved for the others to gather.

'I *know* where Galastan's going,' he said, looking at Nyle. 'I should have remembered when you mentioned the Severn Sea.'

He drew in a breath.

'Galastan isn't seeking an exchange for the gold. He told us at Moloch Tor he was from Wealas. He's taking Gisele and Kuralin across the

Severn Sea back to Wealas to be his thralls, and thereby I presume exact his revenge.'

A growl from Olgood drew a look from Kaela, but he gave her a calming wave.

'Have no fear,' he said. 'I won't jeopardise things at this stage. I feel my time is coming. I can wait a short while.'

As he spoke those words, a gust of wind brushed the trees and the first heavy raindrops spattered onto the dusty road, disturbing the message Merewyn had so carefully constructed.

THEY WITHDREW TO THE shelter of the trees and dismounted to wait for Merewyn.

Olgood's impatience showed. For the moment he was standing quietly, but the thoughts he wrestled with were evident from the frequent shuffling of his feet and sighs of frustration.

The rain was persistent enough to be uncomfortable. Fenn had just changed his position again to seek better shelter when there was a rustle nearby and Merewyn stepped into view. Waving an acknowledgement, he walked to where Fenn held his horse, greeting his son with a hand on the shoulder as he passed.

'They've taken shelter in some caves just below the top of the cliff, Lord. Galastan left the Ariochs with the women. He roped the horses, took them with him and followed the road down to the village.'

'He's going to take the women across the sea to Wealas,' said Fenn. 'He intends to trade the horses to purchase his passage.'

'Then they'll probably wait for night to take Gisele and Kuralin into the village,' said Kaela.

Fenn nodded.

'How is Gisele?' asked Olgood, his voice betraying his anxiety.

'I saw them,' said Merewyn. 'Both women are covered head to foot in blankets and tied. The Ariochs are waiting in the first cave and the women in the next. They were lying quietly.'

'*Lying quietly!*' Olgood hissed the words. He looked at Fenn. 'You say he's taking them as thralls, but the man is mad… If he's given up on the gold, all that's left is revenge. I heard him at Moloch Tor – he thinks he's been thwarted at every step by filthy Saxons – that's what he called us. Yes, he talked about taking thralls, but….' He turned his head to Merewyn. 'Are they *alive*, Merewyn? Did they move?'

Merewyn hesitated. 'I… didn't see them move… but they were securely tied so movement would be difficult….'

Fenn could read Olgood's thoughts. They may know where Galastan intended to take his captives – but was he taking them alive or dead?

'Olgood,' he said. 'It makes no sense for him to kill them and still take them to Wealas.'

'Nothing that twisted little man does makes sense,' Olgood said.

Fenn turned to Merewyn.

'Can we get close to them without being seen?'

'We'll need to leave the horses here and go back the way I came,' said Merewyn. 'After a small detour, we can approach along the cliff top.' When Fenn nodded, Merewyn looked at his son. 'Peada, you wait with the horses. Take them further into the forest, away from the road.'

Peada was about to protest but was silenced by a look and a gesture from his father.

Nyle reached up and retrieved the quiver of arrows from his horse.

AS SOON AS FENN crested the hill under cover of the forest, the wind strengthened and the unruly sea boldly announced its presence. Over the steady patter of the rain, its rhythmic roar dominated as it pounded ceaselessly against the foot of the cliff.

Merewyn led the way through the trees until he came to an open field. He crouched beside an earthen bank topped by a weathered stone wall, an ancient structure built by a farmer long ago to protect his animals from the same relentless south-westerly that gusted along the cliff face today.

'This wall goes all the way to the cliff,' he said. He waited until everyone had arrived and then, keeping his head low, he led the way along the wall.

He dropped to the ground when the wall ended at the cliff and scampered along the cliff top on his hands and knees. His movements were smooth and effortless, born from long experience tracking game. After a hundred paces, he halted behind a group of boulders situated on a slight promontory of the cliff and waved for Fenn to join him.

During the crawl along the clifftop, the rain eased. It was still steady but light. An annoyance rather than a problem. Fenn's concern was that it not only affected visibility but also made the rocks slippery.

Uncomfortably close to Fenn's left, the land fell away in a vertical drop onto jagged rocks – an invitation to certain death. He focused a short distance ahead to keep his mind off that deadly prospect. From the top of the cliff, a path led a third of the way down to a wide ledge where the mouths of several caves could be seen.

Merewyn whispered in Fenn's ear. 'The Ariochs were sheltering in the first cave, Lord, and the women were inside the second cave. But now....'

Fenn completed his sentence. But now, the rocky ledge and the caves looked empty.

'Maybe they've moved further inside because of the rain,' said Merewyn. 'Or...'

Fenn nodded. In the time Merewyn had taken to report back to Fenn, the Ariochs and the women may have left the caves.

He scanned the countryside. The road they'd been following crested the hill and crossed the field between two stone walls, meeting the cliff a half-mile from where Fenn lay. At that point, Fenn presumed the road continued down to the village which was out of sight. The coastline formed an inlet there, and the fishing village would probably be nestled at its head.

He turned back to where Kaela, Olgood, and Nyle crouched behind him.

'We can't see the Ariochs or the women – they may have….'

A low bird whistle from Merewyn drew his eyes back to the clifftop.

A horse and cart had appeared on the road coming up from the village. A man led the horse, and another rode on the cart at the rear. The horse reached the top of the cliff and followed the road across the field, plodding slowly. As Fenn watched, the man riding in the cart gave a wave and jumped from the cart. He passed through a gap in the stone wall to follow a path along the top of the cliff, heading directly towards them. The other man returned the wave and he and the horse continued on their journey without changing pace.

'A man is coming this way,' Fenn breathed. He peered into the haze of the rain. 'It could be… It's… *Galastan.*'

Merewyn murmured confirmation.

'Is he alone?' asked Olgood.

'Yes. There's a horse and cart, but they've stayed on the road.'

'This is our chance,' said Olgood. 'We should take him.'

'We don't know where the women are,' said Kaela. 'Or the Ariochs.'

'If he's coming this way,' Olgood said, 'it means the Ariochs are still in the caves and if they are, so are the women. It won't take me a moment to wring their location from him.'

'We can't just walk down to the caves and confront them,' said Fenn. 'That would give the Ariochs time to harm the women or use them somehow. First, we need to confirm where Gisele and Kuralin are, and… *how* they are.' He glanced at each person. 'For the moment, we'll wait and watch. We'll see where Galastan goes.'

Through a gap between the boulders, Fenn watched the man walking towards them. He walked purposefully but not hurriedly. The fact that he no longer had the horses indicated his trade had been successful.

He tapped Merewyn on the shoulder and pointed to the caves. 'Can you climb down the cliff to the caves? Could you find the women if they're inside?'

Fenn knew he was asking Merewyn to descend a cliff slippery from the rain with the gusting wind threatening to pluck him from the face, then enter the dark caves to find the women, all without being detected.

Merewyn searched the cliff face, his eyes marking possible paths. Could it be done?

'I think so, Lord. I think I see a way.'

Olgood pushed himself alongside Fenn.

'It's too dangerous,' he said, peering through the boulders at the cliff face above the caves. 'There's no path down there.'

He shuffled back. 'As I said, I can take Galastan and find out what he knows. Then we can trade him for the women.'

'One shout from Galastan could alert the Ariochs,' said Fenn. 'Olgood… there're too many ifs… if the Ariochs don't come out… if only one Arioch shows… if they're not in the caves….' He raised his hands. 'What if they bring the women out with them – and threaten to hurt them?'

Olgood stopped him with a raised hand. He blew out a breath of frustration. 'I'll give you an if of my own… Gisele is with child… If he's hurt her in any way….'

Fenn could see the pain in his friend's eyes. He looked at Kaela.

'If Merewyn can climb down the cliff face…' she said. 'If he can find the women… If no one sees him… Also a lot of ifs.'

Fenn looked at the faces around him.

Olgood pointed towards the boulders: 'Galastan's right here, walking towards us. We can't let this opportunity go by.'

'He'll know where the Ariochs and the women are,' said Kaela. 'The Ariochs wouldn't do anything without him. I think the idea of trading Galastan is a good one. But, you'd better decide on a plan quickly.'

Beside her, Nyle nodded. 'I say take him,' he said.

Fenn said: 'Do we have something to tie him with?'

'I do, Lord,' answered Merewyn.

GALASTAN HAD HIS HEAD lowered to shelter his eyes from the rain, seemingly deep in thought as he turned from the cliff top to descend the path down to the ledge and the caves. The rain had plastered his straggly hair to his head, accentuating his gaunt face. He had taken only two steps down the path when he heard a noise behind him. His head came up and he started to turn, but a thick arm curled around his neck, a hand covered his mouth and nose, and he was jerked from his feet and hauled scrambling along the clifftop to the boulders. There, he was thrown to the ground, a knee planted in his back, and his hands drawn behind him while Olgood kept his hand firmly on Galastan's mouth. Galastan squealed but only a low whine escaped.

Merewyn stood up from tying Galastan's hands behind his back. Fenn took his place and stood over the former tenant-in-chief of Westerling.

'You're too far from the caves for your shouts to be heard in the wind, but try and you'll regret it.' He nodded to Olgood who removed his hand.

Galastan turned his head to stare angrily at Fenn but kept his mouth shut.

'We are going to take you down to the caves, Galastan, and you'll tell the Ariochs to release the women. Refuse, and Olgood will enjoy hurting you.'

Galastan twisted himself onto his shoulder and looked wildly about. His gaze rested on Olgood and he sighed theatrically.

'So… you survived Moloch Tor. I didn't believe the rumours until I saw the Kuralin woman in Westerling Hall. I'd like to know how….'

'What *you'd* like to know is of no importance,' said Olgood. 'I have a question, however….' His voice hardened. 'How is Gisele? If you've mistreated her, I'll snap your neck.'

'Gisele… who's that?' The corners of Galastan's mouth twitched into the beginning of his smirk when Olgood's hand took him by the throat, hauling him off the ground.

'If you think this is a game, you're more stupid than I thought,' Olgood snarled.

Galastan nodded frantically and Olgood dropped him to his knees. He coughed and swallowed, breathing hoarsely. He glared at Olgood, then dropped his gaze. 'They were both alive when I left them.'

Olgood growled in frustration, realising that's what he expected Galastan to say.

Fenn drew in a breath. Galastan had used the same phrase at Moloch Tor, and he'd looked away from Olgood as he said the words. *He's lying somehow.*

'The Ariochs, Galastan…' he repeated. 'You'll tell them to release the women.'

Galastan's big eyes turned to Fenn. He scowled and sighed dramatically. 'Very well,' he said. 'I'm not a fool.' His gaze flicked back to Olgood. 'I see my game is lost. If you promise to let me go on my way, I'll do as you ask.' This time he completed his customary irritating leer.

Fenn regarded him suspiciously. It was not like Galastan to surrender meekly.

'Cover his eyes,' he said. 'I suspect he can convey messages to the Ariochs by blinking.'

Galastan's reaction was immediate. 'What? That's simply ridiculous. Whoever heard of such a thing?'

Merewyn drew a kerchief from under his tunic. 'I'm sorry – it's not clean,' he said with a smile.

'Wait! You don't *believe* him, do you?' Galastan pleaded. 'The idea's absurd. The cliffs are dangerous – I can't go down there blind. You have to let me see. It's unnecessary and… and… *cruel.*'

Now he's protesting too much, thought Fenn. He nodded to Merewyn.

Galastan growled and puffed his protest through his cheeks. He twisted his head away, but Merewyn quickly tied the blindfold.

When Merewyn stood back, Galastan snarled: 'Damn you, Feran. How did you find me?'

When Fenn didn't answer, Galastan raised his head. 'Did you use magic? I heard another rumour that you'd joined the Fae.' He laughed. 'Although only ignorant pagans would believe that.'

When Fenn still did not reply, Galastan continued: '…or stupid *Saxons!*' He spat defiantly in Fenn's direction. Olgood moved swiftly and slapped Galastan on the ear with an open hand. The sharp blow knocked the man down and he fell heavily onto his side, sliding dangerously close to the cliff's edge. Fenn reached out to hold him.

Galastan groaned and struggled to a sitting position. 'Do you think you can defeat *me?* I've been chosen by almighty God. I've always done his bidding and he'll protect me now. You don't frighten me.' He sneered down his long nose. 'Damn you. You've taken everything from me. I should have just taken the gold the moment I found it – more riches than I'd ever seen.'

'Why didn't you?' asked Fenn.

'I wasn't finished with those stupid Saxon farmers.'

Fenn shared a puzzled glance with Kaela and Olgood. Galastan took his silence as an opportunity to continue.

'But I've evened the scale.' His voice took on a sarcastic tone. 'I've taken from you too, Lord Feran of Westerling. I wanted to send your damned dog's head to you as a farewell gift. It attacked one of the Ariochs like a werewolf from hell, but the other one managed to club it to death. I couldn't get it on the horse, the cur was too slippery with blood and the Ariochs wouldn't touch it. Good riddance to the animal. I left its body to rot where you'll never find it.'

'We already have,' said Fenn. 'You did your worst, but he's still alive.'

'The damned beast was *dead,*' Galastan retorted. 'I don't believe you.'

'What you believe is of no interest to me,' said Fenn.

Galastan blew out his breath defiantly. 'Well then, believe *this,*' he snarled. 'You'll never see your precious women again. They were too much trouble. They were willing to risk injury more than once by throwing themselves blindly off the horse. People with such little regard for their health make poor thralls.'

He gave a mocking laugh. 'I know this coast. The caves down there lead to a labyrinth of passages. I told the Ariochs to lose those women where no one could find them. They may have killed them already. I didn't say not to.'

A low growl sounded deep in Olgood's chest. He started forward but Fenn held up a hand.

'Get him on his feet,' he said, 'before he *accidentally* tumbles off the cliff.'

Galastan shuffled nervously towards Fenn's voice. 'The cliff? How close is the edge…?

His question was cut off as Olgood again took him by the throat with one hand, hauling him onto his toes.

'Do I think I can defeat you?' he asked sarcastically. 'Yes, I do. I'll kill you in the blink of an eye and take my chances in your labyrinth. All you need to do is say one wrong word or make one wrong step.'

Galastan gagged and coughed, twisting and squirming in Olgoods grip. Olgood deliberately squeezed tighter and the cough turned to a hoarse whimper as Galastan found he couldn't breathe and realised he was heartbeats from death. He grunted frantically, pleadingly, his shoulders shaking. Olgood opened his hand, and Galastan cried out with fear, his hands outstretched, as he stumbled a step before regaining his balance. He gasped, drawing air noisily into his constricted passages and coughed deeply.

'Damn you, you brute,' he said hoarsely. 'You could have broken my neck.'

'Yes,' agreed Olgood. 'Consider how easily I could have done just that.' He stabbed Galastan's forehead with the tip of his finger in time with his words: 'One… wrong… step.'

Galastan's head recoiled from each thrust of Olgood's finger. After the third word, the fight seemed to drain from him. Galastan's head fell to his chest, his shoulders sagging, the rainwater dripping freely from his hair. He breathed heavily.

'I hear you,' he said.

Fenn considered Galastan's words. If he'd told the Ariochs to dispose of the hostages, why didn't they all go into the village, trade the horses, and cross the sea? But then he realised that even Galastan might think it unwise for the Ariochs to show themselves in daylight. Kaela was right. With or without his captives, Galastan planned to wait until nightfall to set out across the Severn Sea to Wealas.

'Merewyn,' he said. 'I've heard you sound just like a hawk. Can you also make the cry of a kestrel?'

'Yes, my Lord, I can even fool another kestrel. Why?'

'We're going to use both plans. Come away from Galastan's ears, and I'll explain. You'll need your candle.'

OLGOOD LED GALASTAN DOWN the path leading to the caves. At first each of Galastan's steps was hesitant and fearful – feeling with his toes for solid ground before committing his weight. Olgood quickly tired of the slow progress. He lifted Galastan and carried him, releasing him when the path widened onto the ledge.

There was no response to Galastan's first call. At his second call, an Arioch appeared at the mouth of the nearest cave. He stared blankly at the small group standing before him on the ledge, either uncomprehending or unconcerned with what he saw.

'Only one Arioch has appeared,' said Fenn. 'We want them *both* out here.'

Galastan sighed dramatically. Fenn nudged him sharply with an elbow.

'Very well,' Galastan said grudgingly. He called: 'Where is Arioch?'

In response, the Arioch shook his head and uttered sounds like the squealings and grunts of a pig mixed with bird-like chirps.

'What did he say?' asked Fenn.

Galastan shrugged. 'I don't know....'

Olgood reached behind Galastan, took him by his bound wrists and pulled them high, twisting Galastan's arms behind his back. Galastan squealed with pain and rose onto his toes to ease the pressure.

'I'm in no mood to play your games. Tell us, or I'll break a finger.'

'Don't be stupid,' said Galastan. 'How can I…?' He screamed as Olgood snapped the bone in his little finger.

Fenn watched the Arioch to see how he would respond to Galastan's scream of pain. The Arioch didn't move or change his expression.

'I'm not in the mood,' Olgood repeated. 'Tell us *now*, Galastan. What did he say?'

Galastan whimpered in pain. He tried to pull his hand from Olgood's grasp. 'Please…' he said, 'I don't know…' Olgood took hold of Galastan's next finger.

'The Arioch spoke words to me in the Hall,' Olgood said. 'So they can speak our language if they want to. He expects you to understand his sounds.' He pulled Galastan's wrist higher. 'You only have nine more fingers and a few heartbeats to tell me what he said.'

'Stop, stop!' Galastan shrieked. 'I can't take pain. I *can't*. Please stop.' He turned his head blindly toward Fenn, pleading. 'Make him stop.'

'That's up to you,' said Fenn. 'We want both Ariochs.'

A figure appeared on the cliff face above the caves. Merewyn. Fenn was careful not to move his eyes so the Arioch wouldn't notice where he was looking.

Galastan made a whimpering sound in his throat. 'But how do you expect me to understand those animal grunts…?' He screamed again as Olgood snapped the second finger.

Galastan's knees sagged and he groaned in pain, his breath coming in quick bursts, each accompanied by a moan – but Olgood didn't let him fall, holding him upright by his wrists. His hand moved to the next finger.

'No, *nooo*…' Galastan squealed. 'I only know a few sounds. I think he said the other one is eating. I wasn't sure. It's hard to hear in the wind.'

'Tell him to call the other Arioch,' Olgood said. His hand tightened on Galastan's finger.

Galastan cried: 'No, no, *don't*. Please don't. I'll tell him.' He called out: 'Arioch! Bring Arioch!'

The Arioch turned to re-enter the cave.

'He's going back into the cave,' said Olgood quickly. 'Tell him to stop and just call. If he goes back inside, I'll break your arm.'

'Arioch, *stop!*' shrieked Galastan. 'Wait there. Call Arioch. Bring Arioch.'

Kaela gave a short cry. The Arioch had his back turned, so Fenn took the opportunity to look up. Merewyn had lost his footing and was sliding slowly but inexorably towards a steep part of the cliff. Fenn watched in horror as Merewyn's hands and feet scrambled frantically and silently to arrest his slide, the noise of his struggle masked by the swirling wind. Fenn tore his gaze back to the Arioch. If he disappeared into the cave, their advantage would be lost. If he happened to look up and to his left, he'd notice Mereywn. The Arioch stopped. Fenn flicked his gaze back to Merewyn – whose fingers had found a crag or a crevice just as his legs dangled over the precipice.

The Arioch called into the cave – uttering a string of animal noises, including a sound like a barking dog.

Slowly Merewyn drew his legs up and inched away from the danger.

'What did he say?' Olgood asked. '*Exactly.*'

'He called to him to come out. The other Arioch is coming,' said Galastan. He groaned again. 'It's over – he's coming. You can let me go now… *please*. My arm….'

'When I see the second monster,' said Olgood.

Fenn's thoughts raced. Did the other Arioch really not come to Galastan's call because he was *eating?* It was a weird reason. Had Galastan misunderstood the Arioch's noises? Or was the other Arioch with the women right now? Would he appear with one and threaten to harm her – or was it true that the Ariochs had left Gisele and Kuralin deep in the caves? What was truth – what was a lie? If Galastan was lying, he'd be more arrogant – wouldn't he?

He waited. The Arioch stared into the cave, unmoving.

Merewyn inched away from the precipice and resumed his descent, slowly creeping down the cliff face until he was above the mouth of the farthest cave.

'Why didn't the Arioch react when you screamed, Galastan?' asked Kaela. 'Do they not care about you? They don't seem very loyal.'

'I didn't expect them to react,' Galastan sneered. 'They don't. But – why should I explain it to you?'

'No,' she agreed, 'you don't have to answer, but I'd like to know. Shall I ask Olgood to squeeze your fingers?'

Galastan drew a quick breath and let it out between his teeth.

'No, that's not necessary. Mammon damn the fates – what does it matter? The Ariochs don't understand pain. They don't feel it like we do. They don't understand why anyone would cry out. It's almost like they enjoy it.' He shrugged. 'They had a cruel and isolated upbringing – they were put in a cage.'

Fenn watched the cave. For a long moment, the scene seemed frozen – the only change being Merewyn's exaggeratedly slow and jerky movements, one limb at a time, crawling across the cliff-face, searching for hand and foot-holds among the smooth surface of the rain-slicked rock. The wind often forced him to cling desperately to the cliff, unmoving, until the gust had passed.

The second Arioch walked out of the cave.

He stopped beside his brother, who turned. The second Arioch also stared at the group of people in front of him without expression. Once again, just as when Fenn first saw them, the twins resembled a pair of still and lifeless matching stone statues.

In time with the Arioch's appearance, the steady rain eased to isolated drops, which the wind swirled around the group of people occupying the ledge.

Merewyn completed his traverse around the mouth of the far cave and jumped lightly down to the ledge. He moved under the cover of the cave entrance, shook his head and stamped his feet, running his hands through his hair and shaking them to remove the rainwater. Fenn was momentarily puzzled, then realised it would be so drips of water did not disturb the tracks on the dry cave floor. Merewyn took a moment to peer out from the cave and survey the scene on the ledge before he disappeared.

Fenn silently wished him luck.

THE ARIOCHS WERE TOO close to the cave entrance; Fenn waved for them to come forward.

The second Arioch broke the image of lifelessness by casually lifting a hand to his mouth and taking a bite of something. It looked like an apple.

Neither Arioch took a step.

Fenn turned his head to Galastan.

'The twin is here,' Fenn said. 'Tell them both to come closer.'

Olgood tightened his grip.

Galastan groaned. He called: 'Ariochs *come*.'

The twins looked at each other, then moving in perfect unison, they lumbered out of the mouth of the cave. Nyle moved to the side to cover them, an arrow notched in his bow.

Olgood released Galastan's wrist and Galastan sank to his knees with a sob, landing with a splash in a puddle of muddy water.

Olgood stepped forward. 'My time has come,' he said to Fenn. 'I have a score to settle here. They won't surprise me again. I'll find out what they did and what they know.'

'*We'll* find out,' said Fenn. 'No axes. Until we find the women, we want them alive.'

Galastan broke off his groaning. He grunted, lifting his head.

'Hah… it won't do you any good. Even the Ariochs may not be able to find the women again. I said to lose them. The caves are vast and they're gagged. The wind whistles in there like a banshee, so you won't hear what little noise they can make. It's a maze. You won't….'

Kaela silenced him with a hard slap. Galastan cried out with surprise and pain and jerked away from her.

'Enough from you, Galastan,' she said. She looked from him to Fenn. 'Fenn, you're injured. Remember Acwellan's caution.'

'I remember,' said Fenn.

Kaela looked at him. 'Then be careful. Treat the Ariochs as a single creature with two bodies.'

Fenn nodded. 'Good advice,' he said. He indicated Galastan. 'Watch him.'

Galastan raised his head. 'You can take the blindfold off now, can't you? I need to see. Tell me how close I am to the edge.' His voice fell into a whine. 'Untie me, *please*. My hand is shattered… I've done as you asked.'

A whisper as Kaela drew Lord of the Battle. 'You stay where you are,' she said. 'As far as the cliff is concerned, you're close. I advise you not to move or talk.'

AS FENN AND OLGOOD approached, the Ariochs separated, each taking a step to the side as they had done in Westerling Hall. Fenn stopped in front of them. He noticed with satisfaction that one of the Ariochs bore the unmistakable marks of Balthazar's teeth on his forearm. On the Arioch's pale skin, the double line of deep wounds was starkly red and swollen. It looked painful enough even for an Arioch to feel.

'Do you understand me?' asked Fenn.

There was no response.

'Where are the women you took from Westerling?'

The Arioch in front of Fenn leaned to the side so he could see Galastan.

'Why Gal'stan tied?' he asked in his high-pitched voice.

'Where are the women?' insisted Fenn.

'Arioch talk to Gal'stan.'

'Talk to us first.'

The Ariochs exchanged a glance. The second Arioch threw the apple core onto the ground. He took a long look at Olgood and seemed to make a decision. He waved toward the cave entrance.

'Wo-men in cave,' he said. He pronounced 'women' as if it were two words. 'Long way in cave,' he added.

'Are they alive?' Olgood asked, his tone hard.

The Arioch shrugged.

Simultaneously, without warning, the Ariochs stepped to the side and headed toward Galastan. Olgood moved quickly, taking the nearest Arioch by the wrist and shoulder, halting him. Fenn moved to block the way of the other Arioch, putting a restraining hand on his shoulder.

'Stop!' he ordered.

The Arioch contemptuously knocked Fenn's arm aside and struck him hard in the chest with the other hand, pushing him back, continuing his plod toward Galastan. Fenn felt a stab of pain from the wound under his arm. He reached for the Arioch again, but the Arioch stopped walking before Fenn touched him. He stopped because the Lord of the Battle's blade was resting on the top of his chest, just under his chin.

Olgood spoke again, his words menacingly slow and even.

'I'll only ask one more time, Arioch. Are the women alive?'

Fenn turned to see Olgood had immobilised the Arioch as he had in Westerling Hall, an arm around his head and the Arioch's arm twisted behind his back. Whether he held the same brother as before was uncertain, but the Arioch had stopped struggling, aware of the futility and the consequences.

He made no reply to Olgood's question.

Fenn took a quick glance at Nyle. When Kaela had left Galastan, Nyle had moved closer to him. He still stood ready, an arrow notched. Nyle raised his eyebrows and asked a question with his eyes. Did Fenn need his help, or should he stay where he was? Fenn held up a hand. Stay there.

The Arioch in front of Fenn followed Fenn's glance at Olgood. A growl sounded in his throat as he noted the plight of his brother. Ignoring Kaela's sword, he turned toward Olgood and swung his thick arm, the one showing a jagged set of bite marks, to push past Fenn — but Kaela was quicker. Before he could complete another step, she had circled him and replaced her sword against his chest. This time the Arioch did not stop fast enough and drops of blood appeared at the sword point, the beads appearing overly bright against the white skin. The Arioch looked down. He brought a finger up to touch the blood, then lifted the finger to his mouth.

Bizarrely, the Arioch smacked his lips and grinned. 'Mine,' he said.

The Arioch looked at Fenn and then at Kaela. He brought his hand up and grasped the blade of the sword, lifting it from his chest. The sharp Damascus steel sliced into his flesh and blood immediately dripped from his closed fist. The Arioch didn't seem to mind.

'*Arioch?*' he said, addressing his brother. It sounded like a question.

Kaela tilted her head. She seemed more intrigued than worried that the Arioch had her blade in his fist.

'Don't tell them anything!' yelled Galastan. 'They won't kill you if they don't have the women.'

Nyle kicked Galastan in the head and he sprawled face-down in the puddle. 'Don't speak again,' Nyle said. Galastan lifted his head and spat water and mud from his mouth.

In response to his brother's question, animal sounds issued from the Arioch held by Olgood. They were cut short as Olgood tightened his grip.

'Do you have that one under control?' he asked Kaela.

Kaela twisted her sword quickly one way then the other, making the blade slick with blood. It slid from the Arioch's grip. He stared at the blood dripping from his hand, seemingly more interested in the flow than the injury.

She kept her sword raised. 'I have him,' she said.

Olgood lifted the Arioch and dragged him towards the cliff edge, heels scrabbling.

'Tell him to answer my question, or I'll drop this one over the edge. We only need one alive.'

'You heard him,' Fenn said to the Arioch. 'Are the women alive? *Where* are they? Can you find them?'

The Arioch stared at his brother; at Galastan tied and blindfolded, sprawled in a puddle; at Kaela and her sword. His eyes focused for a moment on the blood-stained steel.

He slowly turned his head to look directly at Fenn.

'Gal'stan say lose; Arioch lose. Long way in cave. Torch finish. Dark. Not find again.'

'Are they alive or dead?'

The Arioch shrugged.

Fenn rephrased his question. '*Were* they alive when you left them?'

The Arioch stared at him. Fenn worried he may not have understood the question, but the Arioch said: 'Arioch not kill. Arioch lose in cave like Gal'stan say.' He shrugged again. 'Dead now? Yes… no…? Arioch not know.'

Fenn stared into the mouth of the nearest cave. Somewhere in the depths of the labyrinth, Merewyn was trying to decipher marks on the floor of the cave by a flame of a candle that was threatened with imminent extinction by the wind that continually whistled and moaned through the caverns. It was an impossible task.

Olgood reached the cliff edge. The wind there was stronger, rising off the sea and rushing up the cliff, buffeting his hair and clothing.

To the Arioch, Fenn said: 'We're going to find them and you're going to help us.'

He called to Olgood: 'He says he doesn't know if he can find Gisele and Kuralin, Olgood, but he's our best hope. Kaela and I will go with him.'

He glanced at Kaela, noting her frown. Without a torch to light the path, their task was also impossible.

'You'll have to wait here to hold that one,' Fenn continued. 'Nyle can watch Galastan.'

Olgood didn't reply for a long moment, considering Fenn's words. Fenn feared Olgood might insist he change places with Kaela, but Kaela's sword may not be as much of a threat to the Arioch as Olgood's strength.

Olgood turned his head to Fenn. Fenn saw the resignation in his friend's eyes. And the frustration. And the despair. Olgood knew that searching blindly in the blackness of the caves for someone who cannot call out was hopeless.

'You know they won't give up. They'll help us in any way they can,' said Fenn. 'We won't give up either. We'll find them.'

'I hear you,' Olgood said. 'And I understand. Much as I hate to, I'll wait here.' He took a half-step closer to the edge, balancing the Arioch on the lip. 'Tell your Arioch to hurry. I don't know how long I can hold his brother.'

Olgood's Arioch twisted his head as far as it would go and looked down at the waves crashing onto the rocks below. His feet couldn't find firm ground and he squealed with fear, reaching up and behind with his free hand to claw at Olgood's arm, his body squirming, his heels trying to push backwards, his frantic fingers now scratching at Olgood's neck and face.

Olgood twisted his head away but not quick enough. He jerked back as a finger found his eye. He released the Arioch's wrist, his hand flying instinctively to his eye, and took a step back, away from the edge, dragging the Arioch with him. The Arioch felt the pressure under his chin lessen as his hand was released. He thrust at Olgood's arm, ducked his head free, twisted his shoulder into Olgood's chest and pushed Olgood away. He took a step back, forming a fist to strike at Olgood – and found only air under his foot.

He toppled over the edge of the cliff.

His shrill scream lasted a long time, the sound echoing off the cliff face until swallowed by the wind – ending in a stunned silence.

'What was that? What happened?' cried Galastan, squirming to regain his knees, his head twisting back and forth. 'Tell me what's happened.'

Olgood's hand massaged his eye. 'I didn't… I couldn't….'

The other Arioch uttered a series of distressed grunts, and before Fenn or Kaela could stop him, he moved faster than Fenn considered possible, lumbering toward the edge. Fenn feared he would push Olgood over the cliff – he started to cry a warning… 'Ol…!' – but the Arioch ignored Olgood, heading to the place where his brother had disappeared and peering over the edge. He placed both hands on his head, oblivious of the blood steadily leaking from his injured hand, streaming down his cheek and dripping off his chin. His despairing call, like the blood, was sucked away by the wind.

'Arioch!?' he cried – and again, softer; an enquiry: '*Arioch?*'

He let his hands fall. His head rocked from side to side.

'No Arioch.'

'Olgood…,' Fenn said, keeping his voice calm, '…get him back from the edge.'

He walked forward quickly, Kaela at his side, both not wanting to alarm the Arioch by running.

'What?' Olgood looked up, turning to face Fenn, one hand still covering his eye.

'Pull the Arioch back,' Fenn repeated.

Olgood realised Fenn's concern and reached for the Arioch.

Before Olgood's hand could touch him, the Arioch deliberately stepped over the edge of the cliff.

Unlike his brother, he fell silently.

NYLE WAS THE FIRST to move. He calmly replaced the arrow in his quiver and unstrung his bow.

Fenn released the breath he'd been holding. He waved at Galastan. 'Untie him,' he said. 'He can't do any damage now.'

Galastan said: 'What happened? Please… will someone tell me…?'

'Both Ariochs fell from the cliff,' said Fenn. 'One by accident, the other by his own choice.'

'*Fell…? Both* of them?'

Nyle removed Galsatan's blindfold and bent to untie his hands.

'Be *careful,*' Galastan snapped. 'The cursed giant broke my *fingers.*' He remained kneeling, bringing his hands to the front when they were freed, moaning and cradling one in the other.

He looked up at Fenn, blinking his eyes. 'One fell by *accident,* you say. What sort of *accident?*' He shook his head and his face twisted into the insolent smirk.

Despite Galastan's behaviour – and the pain and trouble he'd caused – Fenn felt sorry for him. He could give him the courtesy of an explanation. He walked over to stand beside the kneeling man, spreading his hands.

'An Arioch was with Olgood. He was too close to the edge. He stepped back… and… fell. The other one… jumped after him.'

'Olgood took him to the edge….' said Galastan sarcastically, '…and he *fell*. Is that so? The other one *jumped?*'

He glared at Olgood. 'They weren't wise in the ways of men and could be easily fooled.' He spat out the words. 'They were *children*. I took them into God's care and now you've taken them from me. I heard you drag one to the edge. You used him to lure the other, no doubt, and pushed them over. You coldly *murdered* them both.'

He muttered a curse, then, dramatically bowing his head, he lifted his uninjured hand high and pointed an accusing finger at Olgood.

'God's righteous wrath be upon you,' he snarled.

Olgood raised his fist in response. 'I didn't touch them and I couldn't save either one,' he growled. He started forward, shaking his head in frustration. 'We're wasting time, Fenn. Galastan, I swear, if you….'

Kaela said sharply: *'Fenn…'* Fenn's eyes were drawn to the flash of steel as her blade rose. He heard a cry of alarm from Nyle and felt a tug at his belt.

Galastan snatched Beorhtric's seax from its sheath and, with a scream of *'I am his instrument!'*, rose to his feet to lunge at Olgood, thrusting the sharp-pointed blade directly at his chest.

GALASTAN WAS QUICK. Olgood was quick, Fenn was quick. Kaela was quicker.

Olgood leaned away from the thrust and brought his hands up, one as a block, prepared to take the blade in his hand if need be, the other grasping for Galastan's arm. Fenn launched himself at Galastan, too late, as the seax slid past Olgood's blocking arm, and the pointed steel tip cut into his tunic.

But that touch was as far as the seax progressed. Galastan suddenly collapsed, folding away from Fenn's diving shoulder. Fenn rolled over Galastan's falling body, landed on his back and twisted to end on his knees.

Kaela withdrew the bloodied blade of Lord of the Battle from under Galastan's ribs and rose from her crouch. She looked alarmingly at Fenn.

'My blade could have struck *you* when you leapt for him!'

She let the sword slowly fall to her side.

'I'm sorry,' Nyle said. 'I couldn't stop him….'

Kaela raised a hand. 'I know,' she said. 'Too many people, too close. I had only a momentary chance and one choice.'

Olgood released a slow breath of relief. He rubbed at the tear left by the seax and curled an arm around her shoulder. 'Thank you,' he said.

Kaela rested her hand on his and looked up at him. Her eyes told him: 'No need.'

Fenn looked down at Galastan, crumpled lifeless in the mud, his head lying in the puddle of water where he'd previously knelt. The sight was both sad and pathetic.

'I saw him notice the seax,' Kaela said. 'I saw the idea come into his eyes even as he thought of it.'

Galastan would have killed Olgood if he could, but Fenn couldn't shake the feeling that the three deaths on the ledge were an unnecessary waste. Without an Arioch to guide them, finding the women would now be even more difficult. It was as if a heavy cloud had descended around him with no light for guidance – as if the hopelessness of the situation and his dread of a bad outcome suddenly had a physical presence. His mind felt numb – unable to think.

He picked up the seax that had tumbled from Galastan's hand, wiped the wet blade on his trousers and replaced it in its sheath, then straightened, gazing out over the sea. The sun was low and would soon be setting. He wished he had the wisdom of Arielle at this moment.

Behind him, Kaela said: 'Fenn, as Olgood said, we've no time to waste. We need to start the search....'

Fenn raised his head. 'Of course,' he said. Although it would provide minimal help inside the caves, it would be better to start with some of the sun's light rather than none. 'At least now we can *all* search.'

He glanced at Galastan, then headed for the cave entrance.

'We'll need to separate,' he said. 'But we'll keep in touch by calling.'

'Merewyn last saw them in the middle cave,' said Olgood. 'I'll take that one.'

'You go with him, Nyle. Kaela and I can start with this cave.'

His eyes were dragged once more back to Galastan. He couldn't shake the heavy feeling of foreboding. He forced his gaze to the front, away from the crumpled body, and stared into the black and impenetrable interior of the cave.

The screech of a hawk, rising and falling, came from deep inside the cliff.

Fenn's dark thoughts and the weight on his shoulders evaporated. He uttered a cry of joy and turned to clasp a startled Olgood by the arms.

'*That's Merewyn!*' he shouted in Olgood's face. 'He's found Gisele and Kuralin. And they're *alive*, Olgood. The call of the hawk means they're *alive!*'

Olgood stared at Fenn, eyes wide, not wanting to dare to believe what he was hearing. He put his hands to his head and exhaled a long audible sigh that turned into a groan of relief.

'Merewyn...?' he said incredulously. Nyle patted him on the back.

Kaela stood with her mouth open, her face creased with relief and tears forming in her eyes.

'The call of the hawk,' she repeated.

'Thank God,' said Olgood, his eyes looking upwards. 'Thank God.'

Fenn drew Olgood and Kaela together, reaching out to include Nyle.

'And thank Merewyn,' he said.

KAELA DREW FENN TO one side.

'You asked Merewyn if he could also make the sound of a kestrel. I presume that was for a different outcome?'

Fenn looked to where Olgood held both Gisele and Kuralin in a deep embrace. After Gisele had assured him several times she was well and the baby was fine, Olgood had not let her out of his arms. Merewyn and Nyle stood beside the group, Merewyn nodding and smiling, patiently answering Olgood's stream of questions and accepting his repeated gratitude.

Before Fenn could answer Kaela, Gisele pushed herself free of Olgood and ran to him. She halted before Fenn, her hands moving as if she wanted to say something but didn't know how. As Kaela reached out to her, large tears formed in Gisele's eyes and rolled down her cheeks.

'Oh, Fenn, I am so sorry…' she sobbed. She took his hands. 'He was *magnifique, vraiment magnifique*. He charge the monsters…. He fight for us…. He give 'is *life*. They kill 'im.'

'Balthazar is alive,' Fenn said.

'No.' Gisele shook her head. 'They kill 'im. I saw it. Kuralin and I, we try to stop the monster from 'itting Balthazar. We should 'ave run, per'aps, when Balthazar attack, he give us time, but we must try 'elp 'im. We get in the way, make 'im 'it me – just not 'it Balthazar more.'

Kaela put her arm around Gisele. 'Balthazar's strong,' she said. 'You *did* save him. You stopped them in time. They could not kill him. Balthazar is alive and with Acwellan.'

Gisele's tear-filled eyes widened and turned to Fenn, silently asking for confirmation. Can it possibly be true?

'We found him,' said Fenn. 'He was near dead, but the spark was still there. Acwellan is caring for him.'

Gisele gulped lungfuls of air, tears streaming down her cheeks, unable to speak. '*Merci, merci mon Dieu*,' she breathed.

She waved her hands, indicating she had more to say. Gisele wiped at her eyes and reached out to take both of them by the hand. They waited while she took a moment to compose herself.

'I already say to Olgood,' she said, 'but I want to say to you. Kuralin and me… and *I*… we always 'ave 'ope. I not know where you are, Fenn, Kaela…' she glanced over her shoulder, '…Olgood… not see you for long time… but no matter what 'appen, I know you come. I know you find us. You never give up. I *know* it. So *we* not give up.' She took a deep breath. 'Galastan say 'e take us to Wealas. I not care. I know you still follow there.'

All Fenn could do was nod. 'Yes,' Kaela said. 'We would have.'

Gisele beamed her wonderful smile. She squeezed their hands. 'And now I am two times 'appy.' She released them and clapped her hands together. 'Because Balthazar is *alive!* – I see 'im again.'

She spun around, thrust her hands in the air, and called: 'Kuralin! Balthazar – they not kill 'im, 'e is *alive!*

Fenn watched her reach Olgood and duck back under his arm.

'She could have escaped,' Fenn said, 'but she risked her life to save Balthazar. They both did.'

Kaela nodded. 'Are you surprised?'

Fenn shook his head. 'No.'

Gisele's happiness was infectious. He put his arm on Kaela's shoulders.

'To answer your question. Yes. A kestrel would have signalled that Gisele was dead. I wasn't sure how I'd tell Olgood if I'd heard a kestrel.'

'Fortunately, it doesn't matter,' Kaela said.

She was silent for a while, then added: 'If they had killed Gisele, Olgood would have killed them all.'

She looked into his eyes.

'And I would have helped him.'

CHAPTER THIRTY-ONE

Another alehouse, another ale, another surprise

'Someone will wonder why a man would exchange horses for a passage across the sea and not turn up to complete the agreement,' said Nyle. He spoke loudly to be heard, leaning close to Olgood and Fenn.

Fenn lifted a spoon of leek and bean stew to his lips, blowing on the spoon to cool its contents. The soup was thick and he chewed as Nyle continued: '…but then he'll thank God for his good fortune and not waste a second thought.'

'And neither will I, now that I have these two beauties beside me again,' said Olgood.

Gisele laughed as Olgood tried to reach his mug without removing his arm from around her neck. She found herself squashed against him. The endeavour was successful, and Olgood took a hearty swig of ale. He chuckled at Gisele's discomfort, holding her close even after returning the mug to the table.

Kaela leaned into Fenn. 'Nyle told me that Gisele and Kuralin have become inseparable. Olgood certainly seems to enjoy the company of both.'

Fenn looked at her and tilted his head. 'What are you suggesting?' he asked playfully.

She widened her eyes. 'Nothing. I'm just making an observation.'

Fenn put his arm around her shoulders. 'If it's affection you're seeking....'

'I'll know where to go,' she replied, enjoying his frown as he wondered if she meant Olgood. She reached up and kissed him. Fenn cradled her head.

He was silent long enough for her to look at him.

'What are you thinking?'

'He smiled. 'I was thinking we should replace the gold in the iron box and put it back under the chair.'

'Why?'

'It'll be safer and dryer there.' He smiled. 'And it'll be closer to hand.' He nodded thoughtfully. 'It's time we put it to better use than leaving it to lie in the ground.'

Kaela laughed and nestled into him, putting her lips close to his ear. 'When we have a quiet moment, there's something I want to talk about,' she said.

Fenn's reply was interrupted by a shout of alarm from the next table. A man stood quickly to avoid the wash of spilt ale. He wasn't quick enough, and his companions laughed at his discomfort.

It was raucous in the small room, with raised voices shouting just to be heard. Above the noise, the woman serving ale roared instructions to a younger woman clearing tables and delivering ales with a voice that would not have been out of place ordering men on a battlefield.

As usual, their weapons had caused some concern when they first entered the small inn, and for a while they were the main topic of conversation, with many eyes drawn to the axes and Fenn's seax, Nyles bow, and especially Kaela's sword. But once they had settled into a corner and kept to themselves, the concern had mellowed to mild interest.

'Drink up, Merewyn,' said Fenn. 'You're falling behind.'

'The ale is too weak, Lord. It's hardly worth the payment. I'll need to relieve myself many times before I can enjoy its effect.'

'I agree,' said Peada beside him. 'It doesn't have the taste of Westerling ale.'

'And when have *you* drunk Westerling ale?' Merewyn said sharply. Peada stiffened and looked guilty until Merewyn smiled and clapped him on the shoulder. 'Relax. You've proven yourself. You're a man now in my eyes, son. As our Lord says, drink up and enjoy.'

Fenn and Nyle exchanged glances. They both shook their heads and smiled in agreement. Not an ale worthy of settling a wager.

Fenn lifted the bowl to get the last of the stew and dropped the wooden spoon into the bowl with a clatter. He raised his mug and sat back contented.

Galastan's body had joined those of the Ariochs at the bottom of the cliff to be claimed by the sea. Merewyn told of tracking the Ariochs deep into the caves, deep enough for him to worry whether his candle would last. He said the women were well bound, so they could only move their limbs tiny amounts, but when he found them they had inched their way in total blackness more than twenty paces in the right direction toward the entrance. They were gagged but had somehow communicated and kept close together. Gisele had retained her sense of direction and heard the Ariochs laying stones as a guide for the return journey. She was confident she could follow their path, and they would eventually escape from the labyrinth.

Gisele said they had tried unsuccessfully to free each other's bonds using hands and teeth, but the blankets they were wrapped in made it impossible. They realised they'd been left to die and knew their chances of being discovered were better if they could make it to the ledge and then to the clifftop, rather than lying deep inside the caves.

Thankfully, neither showed any sign now of the discomfort and suffering they had endured.

'I'm ready for more ale,' Fenn said. 'Finish up and give me your mugs.' Kaela smiled at him. She lifted her bowl to her lips to drain the last of her stew. 'You can't carry them all. I'll help you.'

'The woman will come to the table,' said Nyle. 'Be patient.'

'She's busy. And I need to stretch my legs,' replied Fenn. Nyle grunted and raised his mug to down the last drops.

Beside him, Peada said to his father: 'Was the floor inside the caves earth or rock? Was the rock dusty?'

'Earth mostly. But there was one part….'

Fenn pushed back his chair, Kaela scooping up some mugs and rising beside him. Together they made their way between the chairs to the serving table at the head of the room.

Another customer was being served. Fenn and Kaela waited.

'Lord Feran?' The voice came from behind.

Fenn turned. 'Yes?'

The man bowed. 'Someone is asking for you outside. He said to mention the name Tareek.'

'Tariq? What is he doing here?' Fenn turned to Kaela. 'He should be in Hamwic by now, shouldn't he?'

Kaela said: 'Yes. He said he'd bought all the wool his vessel could carry – and the dyes…. Why would he travel this far west? How could he have found us?'

'No matter,' said Fenn. He made a beckoning gesture at the door. 'Tell him to come in and join us.'

'He'd prefer to meet outside, Lord. He said to bring… ah… he said… to bring the warrior princess with you.'

'The… who?' He looked at Kaela: 'Has he ever called you by that name?'

'No, he hasn't,' said Kaela, frowning.

'What can I get ye, me darlin'? Ales? How many?'

Fenn and Kaela dropped their mugs onto the table. The woman glanced at Fenn's ring but made no comment.

'Eight,' said Fenn.

'Right, darlin', I can count.'

The woman took four mugs in her fist and turned to the keg behind her.

Fenn swung back to the man. 'Where's Tariq waiting?'

'In the shelter beside the barn.'

'Fenn…' said Kaela warily.

'I know,' said Fenn, 'I'm getting the same feeling. Something's amiss.'

'I'll warn the others….'

The woman slapped four mugs onto the table, ale slopping freely from the brims and dripping between the planks of the table to join the puddle beneath. She took up the second four.

Fenn looked across the room at Olgood, laughing and nodding at something Nyle had said, his arms protectively encircling Gisele and Kuralin. Merewyn was huddled with his son, his hands painting a picture in the air, describing his journey through the caves.

'No, let them be. They deserve a moment's peace. If Tariq is acting strange and mysterious, you and I can find out why.'

The woman placed four more mugs alongside the others.

'Can we leave these here for a short while?' asked Fenn. 'We'll be back soon.'

'I'll have them delivered for ye, me darlin',' she said. 'Ye go and attend to yer business.' She bellowed to the room: '*Here, Brunny! Do these next, will ye? T'the top table.*'

Was she making the offer because of the ring, or… Fenn couldn't tell.

He dropped a coin on the table. It was swept up quickly, but not before it had been noticed. The messenger narrowed his eyes.

'He said you'd give me something for my trouble,' he said quickly.

'Of course he did,' said Fenn. He looked at Kaela. She shrugged and stepped back. Her hand went to her sword.

'Wait. I didn't mean nothin' by it,' the man said nervously. 'I just thought… well….'

Fenn smiled. 'That coin should be good for an extra ale,' he said.

The man looked at the woman expectantly. She blew out a breath of exasperation.

'One day, Pog, ye'll buy yer own!'

FENN SCANNED THE AREA.

A figure was standing in the shelter beside the barn, as the man had said. He was neither hiding nor standing in full view. There was no one else to be seen. For the moment, the man was half in shadow and half in the light of the moon – but tonight the moon was delivering its glow only in brief spells.

In the light there was, Fenn could identify Tariq by the staff he held at his side, although he wore a cloak with a hood instead of his customary wide-brimmed hat.

'Why the mystery, Tariq?' he called as he approached. 'It's good to see you, but you're far from….'

The figure stepped forward, and with that movement, Fenn knew this was not Tariq.

He also knew who it was.

He reached out to stop Kaela from drawing her sword.

'Kaela…' he said. '…I would very much like you to meet my lady of the forest. Arielle.'

ARIELLE LIFTED HER HANDS to ease back the hood of her golden cloak and reveal her face. Her silver hair glowed and the ring on her finger sparkled bright blue in the moonlight.

She bowed to Fenn. 'I'm glad to see you, Blue-Eyes… and to meet you, Kaela, Princess of Wessex, who should be Queen.' She inclined her head to Kaela.

'It's good to see *you* again,' said Fenn. 'Much has happened since we last met.'

Several questions formed in his mind. Kaela, a queen? Was that another prophecy? He decided to ask another question first.

'But… if you wanted to meet, why did you use Tariq's name?'

'I would not like my name shouted in a crowded inn. It could be heard by the wrong people.'

'I'm sure you could have entered the inn in any disguise you chose and approached us without risk.'

'It's noisy in there – an unpleasant place to hold a conversation. This is more suitable. I can hear myself speak.'

'I see,' said Fenn. He looked at her, but she made no move to initiate her conversation.

'Do you know,' he said, 'that all your prophecies have come to pass?'

Kaela frowned: 'What prophecies? You haven't spoken of any prophecy.'

'They seemed unbelievable. You would have thought I was mad. It's only now that I've been able to properly assess all three of Arielle's prophesies. You have a gift, Arielle.'

'A gift? No. The pieces I gave you were not prophecies, merely offerings – possibilities derived from knowledge, observation, and deduction. I called them fragments of a picture.'

'Yes,' Fenn said, 'I remember your words.' He turned to Kaela. 'Arielle gave me three *offerings* – whatever they're called – and they have all come to pass. She told me I would play a part in the crowning of the next King of Wessex before we went to Witanceastre and before Beorhtric died.'

Arielle waved her hand. 'I was aware of moves being made from Mercia to upset the throne of Wessex. There was a good possibility they would be successful. You were with the King's daughter – it was likely you would be involved.'

'Very well,' Fenn conceded. 'That's plausible.' He noted she had said the moves were initiated from *Mercia,* not Hwicce. 'But you also told me a friend would die on the battlefield. You described the scene and correctly foretold I could have saved him if I'd made a different choice.'

'I told you there would be a battle, but I also said a battle is always coming, so that was hardly a prophecy. Someone close to you may die – that's always likely in a battle. I heard that Wulfstan of Wiltonshire was killed at Cymeresford. I said you may make a decision that could have saved your friend, but I also said your nature is to question your decisions.'

'You could have saved Wulfstan?' queried Kaela. 'How? I didn't see that.'

'Wulfstan was being beset by two men. I chose to attack one, and the other killed him. That was my decision, and it was the wrong one.'

Arielle raised a finger. 'Your focus is too narrow, Blue-Eyes. Decisions on a battlefield are driven by circumstance. You react to what is happening around you. So you have searched and found a moment when a different decision may have had a different outcome. There were probably several such occasions. Your decisions are only partly your own, remember, so don't try to take full responsibility for them. There are many possible paths, only one of which is written. Who knows if your decision was the right one or not? Perhaps whichever attacker you chose to confront, the other would have killed Ealdorman Wulfstan.'

'Maybe… maybe… but however you explain the… *offering*, it happened just as you said it would.'

Arielle regarded him for a moment, then inclined her head in acceptance.

'The third piece she told me was that I had unfinished business – that a previous unresolved relationship would return to be resolved. That also has happened – Galastan disrupted our lives on Moloch Tor. He disappeared but came back to disrupt again. As you said it would be, Arielle – that page is now finished and complete.' He frowned. 'You said the resolution would happen at a place I called home, but I presume you meant Wessex.'

Arielle shook her head. 'I did speak of the circle of relationships, but Galastan…? No, you made only a brief acquaintance of Galastan, however unpleasant that may have been. I was referring to the nature of more important relationships, circles with broader scopes, ones with their beginnings farther in the past. My third offering had nothing to do with Galastan.'

When Fenn didn't reply, Arielle continued: 'You have interpreted my words as prophecy; I understand why, but prophecy is only one explanation. As to their accuracy – that is also an interpretation. Are you sure you're not making the events fit the words?' The corners of her mouth crinkled to a half-smile. 'At least you did not call it magic.'

She pointed a finger at him. 'You only need to open your eyes and ears and understand the language of the Earth Mother and her children, and you too can see as I see.'

Fenn shook his head in wonder. Arielle denied her words were prophecies, but that description perfectly fitted the place and manner of their delivery and the events that followed. Did she speak those words in that way to enhance her aura of mystery? He looked at Kaela. What did she think? She returned his gaze with puzzled eyes.

He turned back to Arielle. 'Very well,' he said. 'If you wish it thus, then so be it.'

He spread his hands. 'Now… why have you enticed us away from our ales?'

'Ah, yes. I was close and I heard you were here. I have some dark news that will interest you. I thought this inn would be worth a visit so our paths could cross again.'

Fenn looked at her with a smile. 'You were close…?'

She shrugged. 'Close enough.' She returned his smile, then her face became serious.

'The Northmen have raided the abbey at Iona in the land of the Scots, killing monks just as they did at Lindisfarne. And there are further changes in the wind. My ears and eyes are not only on this island. There are stirrings across the water to the east. The Northmen have also raided south, in Francia. They are stretching out their arms and feeling their reach and their power. Their greed for gold and their lust for new land are both growing.'

'I know of the island of Iona,' said Fenn. 'St. Aidan, the founder of the monastery at Lindisfarne, came from Iona. And I know the Northmen. I know they slaughter defenceless monks to show that the christian god cannot even defend his priests, so their gods must be greater. It makes them powerful.'

'You may need to draw upon your knowledge of the Northmen soon. They are spreading in this direction.'

Fenn looked at her. What did she know? Was this another prophecy?

'Do you know the names of the Northmen who raided the abbey?' he asked.

'I take careful note of names, but those I was not told.'

'Ragnall?' asked Kaela.

'The second night I was in Lognavik, after you had left with Askari to return to her hut, Ragnall asked me about our land, its climate, its kings, and its people. I don't think I told him anything useful, and it was information he could have learned from the other captives, but I hope it wasn't I who enticed him back here to raid again.'

'Did you tell him about the abbey at Iona?' asked Kaela.

'No.'

'Then, if it's him, he learned that from someone else.'

'So it seems.'

He looked at Arielle. 'Thank you for your warning…' he smiled, '…if that's what it was.' He paused and continued: 'You said Kaela should be a queen. What did you mean?'

Arielle held Fenn's gaze a moment, then switched her eyes to Kaela.

'You should be Queen of Wessex,' she said. 'You have the blood, you have the skill, you have the fibre, and you have this man at your side – but you and I both know that will never be.'

Kaela acknowledged the comment but made no reply.

'And what of Egbert?' asked Fenn.

'He'll do well. He'll become the greatest of the high kings – the legendary *Bretwalda,* the 'wide-ruler', and rule the seven kingdoms.'

She saw his expression and smiled.

'Offa's death has left a void,' she said. 'Beohtric's death has created uncertainty. Strong alliances have been shattered. Hwicce is broken. Northumbria is weak. The kingdoms are open for Egbert if he has the desire and the strength. He *could* become the greatest.'

She tapped her staff on the ground. 'I've said what I came to say. Keep a watch on the sea and the rivers.'

Fenn laughed. 'We have no view of the sea from Westerling.'

'You know what I mean.'

Fenn nodded. 'I do.'

'Then I'll let you return to your ales and celebrate the baby.'

Kaela turned quickly, but not before Fenn caught her expression of surprise. He stared after her as she walked steadily towards the inn without looking back. Fenn heard a tap of the staff behind him.

'We've already celebrated Gisele's baby....' he began, turning back to Arielle.

There was no one there.

CHAPTER THIRTY-TWO

Home is where the heart lies

'Your hand and your eye must learn to work together. They will – if you give them time.'

'My stones don't strike with the force yours do.'

'The force comes from the speed of the sling, and the speed comes from the strength of your wrist – but it's more than the wrist; it's the whole body working as one. You must teach your body what you want it to do. You'll find it's a willing pupil, and it will grow strong the parts that need to be strong and make flexible the parts that need to be flexible. Your body will learn through repetition and practice.'

Fenn stood in the field outside the Westerling palisade facing the edge of the forest where a row of trees formed natural targets. He motioned for Beric to try again and watched as he selected a stone, placed it in the pouch and set the sling whirling above his head. The stone was released but it flew just wide of the target, a broken branch jutting from a trunk.

'What were you thinking when you released the stone?' asked Fenn.

'If the sling was spinning fast enough.'

'Focus only on the target; think only of the target,' said Fenn. 'Trust your hand, your arm, your body to do the rest. That trust, that *connection*, is what you're trying to achieve.'

'Thank you, Lord.'

Fenn patted him on the shoulder, and moved on to the next boy.

A WHINE AND THE noise of a thumping tail greeted Fenn as he entered the hut.

Acwellan looked up. He moved aside so Fenn could view the patient.

Balthazar raised his head and started to rise but seemed to realise he shouldn't move and lowered himself again to lie on the blanket. His tail, however, continued its rhythmic drumming. He opened his mouth to pant happily, seeming to grin at Fenn.

'His eye looks good,' said Fenn.

'Yes,' said Acwellan. 'They cracked his skull for sure and broke some ribs. I say again he should be dead. The last time you visited, I told you he might have trouble with his eye but as you see, it's staying in place. It's only been two weeks, but look at him – he thinks he's almost ready to leave.'

Fenn reached out to ruffle Balthazar's neck.

'Take your time,' he said to the dog. 'No need to hurry. There's nothing for you to worry about. All our problems are behind us.'

Acwellan laughed. 'It would not be wise to believe *that*,' he said.

Balthazar panted his agreement and laid his head to rest on his paws.

THE SCENE AT LAKE Wealdemere was vastly different from Fenn's last visit. Beric had called the lake 'beautiful' and a favourite place of relaxation for Lord Cormwurst. Now that there were no Cornish in sight checking weapons on the grassy verges of the lake and building ladders to scale the palisade, the scene presented was indeed beautiful and peaceful.

Fenn and Kaela stood at the edge of the forest, where the trees stopped and the thickly grassed lake shore began. The area was hushed. The lake waters sparkled in the sunlight, ripples were visible on the surface, brushing the rocks gently and silently – a trio of ducks floated in one corner beside a group of reeds. There was only a hint of a breeze, and even the bird sounds were muted, respecting the sanctity of this idyllic enclave of the forest.

Fenn felt reluctant to step out from beneath the trees in case he disturbed the balance.

Kaela took his arm and pointed. 'Fenn, look, there are ducklings in the reeds.'

Bright yellow balls of movement with tiny orange beaks came into view, bobbing among the green stalks. A string of ducklings emerged but as soon as they were in open water, the leader swung back into the safety of the reeds, followed in a perfect line by the others as if they were tied together.

Kaela laughed. 'It's wonderful,' she said. 'If your aim was to cheer me up and remind me of the beauty of this place, you've succeeded.'

'Good,' he said. 'I thought this would do well for both of us.'

Fenn drew her to a rock with a flat side facing the sun. He sat on the grass and leaned against the smooth rock, pulling her down beside him. The stone was pleasantly warm on his back; he closed his eyes and let his head rest against the rock. He breathed deeply.

'You know Egbert wants me to return to Witanceastre and be his High Reeve,' he said.

'I do know that. And I know he left the decision to you.'

'What do you think? It's an important position.'

'You'd be a good Reeve. You'd be the Reeve Wessex needs.'

'But, what do you think? Would you be happy in Witanceastre? Should I accept?'

'I think it's your decision.'

'Does that mean you don't have an opinion?'

'I most certainly do. But what *you* think is more important.'

He opened his eyes to look at her. As usual, she gave no hint of her thoughts in her expression. He wished she would speak out, but he respected her resolve that she didn't want to influence his decision. He also knew that she would accept and support without question whatever he decided.

He turned his gaze to the lake's sparkling water, the trees, the ducks, and the little yellow balls still flitting among the reeds. He felt the warmth of the sun on his body. He felt the warmth of her body where it touched his.

'I came to Wessex to be with you,' he said. 'Since we arrived, we haven't been able to settle – we haven't found the easy road yet. We didn't come to Westerling by choice – that was forced upon us – and we've been wrested away from it more than once.'

He laid a hand on her arm.

'But now that I've been able to stay at Westerling for these last weeks with you, and Olgood and Gisele are here, and Nyle, and Kuralin, and Edelred….'

He waved a hand to encompass the lake, the forest – the estate.

'Everything I love is here. For the first time since the day I was taken from Lindisfarne by Ragnall, I feel I belong somewhere. Arielle speaks of the Earth Mother. I see the beauty of this lake, I feel the calm, and I'm close to knowing what she means – here in this place, in this land. And I know you and I are a part of it – a tiny part.'

He looked at her. There were tears in her eyes. He reached out to wipe them away.

'What I'm trying to say is… this is my….'

'*Our*…' she corrected him. 'Our *home*.'

'Yes,' he said. 'And I don't want to leave.'

Her eyes closed, her lids forcing the tears to spill down her cheeks.

'It's what I hoped you would say,' she said.

Fenn smiled and drew her to him, her head nestling into his shoulder. He closed his eyes again, savouring the beauty of the moment, not wanting it to end.

After a few moments, Kaela spoke.

'Fenn…' she said, her voice soft. 'Do you remember when we were at the inn a few weeks ago where we met Arielle?'

'Mmm,' Fenn murmured.

'I said I wanted to talk to you when we had a quiet moment.'

'Yes?' Fenn could feel the sun's heat on his eyelids.

'This is very quiet.'

Something in her voice alerted him. He opened his eyes to look at her.

She raised her eyes to meet his.

'Our child will also be born at Westerling.'

'SOMEONE IS ASKING TO see you, Lord Feran,' said Edelred. 'I told him to wait outside.'

Fenn looked up from the Thane's chair. 'Who is it?'

'I don't know him. He says he carries a message from King Hernam. He speaks strangely so he could be Cornish.'

'From Hernam? What could Hernam want? Very well, bring him in. Ask Kaela to join us; Olgood and Nyle too if you can find them.'

'Yes, Lord.' Edelred bowed and headed for the entrance.

'And, Edelred…' said Fenn.

Edelred turned.

'If he's an emissary from the King, we should show our hospitality. Ales, and some food to offer.'

'Of course,' Edelred replied.

Balthazar stirred at Fenn's feet and uttered a low rumbling growl as the man entered the Hall.

'Easy,' said Fenn, resting a hand behind the wolfhound's ears. He stroked the limp ear that was the only remaining evidence of Balthazar's beating by the Ariochs. 'We can at least hear what he has to say.'

Fenn waited while the man walked the length of the Hall to the Thane's chair. He walked slowly and purposefully. He was a big man, tall, thick in the chest, and wore a cloak made from patched animal fur tied under his throat with a cord. A large sword was visible at his side with an ornate hilt long enough to be gripped by two hands.

As he approached, he kept a wary eye on the dog. Fenn rose and waved the man to a table surrounded by six chairs. Balthazar came to his feet, tense, matching the man's stare.

'Welcome to Westerling,' Fenn said. 'Please sit. If you're thirsty, I'll have ales in a moment.'

The man grunted. He loosened the cord of the cloak with one hand, the other hovering beside his sword. When the cloak was free, he swung it away from his shoulders, again only using one hand, and draped it over an adjacent chair. He moved the sword so he could sit and lowered himself into a chair. He flicked a glance at Balthazar, who slowly relaxed his haunches to sit by Fenn's side, but the tension did not leave the hound's head and shoulders. He had yet to accept this man.

'You have a message from Hernam?'

The man turned his eyes to Fenn, studying him a moment before asking: 'You are Lord Feran?'

'I am.'

'My name is....'

The sound of footsteps interrupted him. He swung around, rising from his chair, one hand grasping his sword. Two women entered, one carrying a tray with mugs and two jugs of ale and the other with a platter of food.

The emissary released his sword and sat back down, but this time he chose a different chair so he could watch the entrance. His eyes, returning to Fenn, held no apology. It was just a cautious reaction from one who has experienced violence from unexpected quarters.

The woman leaned across a chair and placed the mugs one by one onto the table followed by the jugs. The man's eyes moved from Fenn to follow the ale, and he licked his lips. The other woman laid her platter of bread, cheese, and apples before Fenn. She bowed, and the two women left, leaning their heads together to whisper some remark no doubt regarding the visitor.

Fenn lifted a jug to pour ale into the mugs. He raised his own mug in salute.

'I trust the King is well,' he said.

The man's mug was already on its way to his lips. He paused long enough to say quickly: 'He is,' before taking a long draft. He sighed heavily and replaced his mug on the table.

His eyebrows raised. 'A welcome ale and strong,' he said appreciatively. 'I thank you. I've ridden hard. It's been a long dry morning.' The man spoke clearly with a heavy accent. His words came slowly and carefully as if unused to the language.

Another disturbance at the entrance marked the appearance of Edelred and Kaela, followed by Olgood and Nyle.

'I asked some more people to join us,' said Fenn. Balthazar lowered himself to the floor, relaxing, the threat of danger gone, resting his head on his legs.

The Cornishman watched the four people approach warily, his eyes spending a little longer appraising Olgood. Fenn waved to the chairs and poured more ales.

'These are friends,' said Fenn. 'I want them to hear what you have to say. Please, take some food.'

The man turned back to the table. He chose a piece of cheese and chewed on it. Fenn waited, encouraging the man to take more food as Edelred, Kaela, Olgood, and Nyle each took a chair.

'This man has a message from Hernam,' he said; then, to the man: 'You were about to tell me your name.'

The man swallowed the cheese and raised his mug again.

'My name is Brecan. Some know me as Longsword,' he said.

He took a breath. 'King Hernam asked me to find you and tell you that three ships with square sails were seen at dawn entering the sound at the mouth of the Tamar. He said you'd talked of these ships. The Northmen have arrived. He asks for your assistance.'

FENN GROANED.

The passing months had clouded Arielle's warning in his memory. Spring had brought excitement to Westerling with new growth in the fields and in the forests and among the people.

Fenn's contentment from watching the estate bloom, new life appearing, the people happy in their work, invited him to take the time to consider his future and the future of Westerling. At the start of summer, the winter wheat had yielded a bountiful harvest, the best for several years. Edelred said it was a sign that Westerling was again enjoying God's favour. As Fenn had promised, he asked for no tithe, allowing the grain stores to be filled and the excess used to trade for pigs and hens. He'd used Cormwurst's gold to strengthen the cattle herds and sheep flocks.

Fenn raised his head.

'Have you seen these Northmen?'

'Only as ships at sea. I watched them approaching the sound.'

'How many men were in each ship?'

'It was difficult to tell at the distance. Maybe forty or fifty.'

The ship Olgood had been helping to build at Lognavik was larger than the ships that had attacked Lindisfarne and was designed to hold up to seventy men. That ship would have been finished by now, and more could have been completed. If this was Ragnall, he could have more than two hundred men in his three ships.

Fenn turned to Edelred. 'Does anybody at Westerling know the valley of the Tamar?'

'Merewyn would know it best. He often visits his brother.'

'Good. Ask him to come to the Hall.' Edelred nodded.

'And…' Fenn continued, '…my apologies to Wyllard for interrupting him again in the fields. Send him and another rider immediately to inform Ealdorman Herewic and King Egbert.'

'Lord Herewic…? But…'

'The situation with Herewic has changed. He will answer.'

Edelred bowed quickly. 'Of course. What message?'

'Northmen have invaded Wessex up the Tamar. Tell Herewic Lord Feran needs his fyrd. Ask him to come to Westerling. Tell the King – Wessex needs to repel another aggressor. Give Wyllard the black mares – they need to move fast.'

Edelred nodded. 'Yes, Lord,' he said and hurried from the Hall.

'We need to keep a watch on the Northmen,' Fenn continued, 'and I need to know if it's Ragnall.' He glanced at Kaela. 'Could he know that we're in Wessex?'

'You're assuming too much,' said Kaela. 'You don't know it's him. Even if it is, he couldn't know where we are. We're not significant enough for him to come to Wessex because of us.'

'Who is this Ragnall? And how do you know him?' asked Brecan.

'He and his brother Olaf are leaders among the Northmen,' replied Fenn. 'We've met them. A long story. We have some knowledge of the Northmen.'

Brecan's eyes narrowed suspiciously.

'Treddian can go,' said Kaela. 'He speaks the language if he needs to communicate with the Cornish.'

'Treddian doesn't know Ragnall. I need to go. I need to know if it's him.'

Kaela frowned. 'I repeat… it's unlikely to be Ragnall, and even if it is, you have no reason to think that somehow *we* may be the reason Ragnall has returned to this land.'

Fenn didn't reply. Kaela was probably right. He knew it didn't make sense. But he remembered Arielle looking west across the moor when she talked about the circle of relationships. He could not shake the feeling she was talking about Ragnall, who was now coming from the west to complete the circle.

He saw Kaela share a worried glance with Olgood. Was he obsessed with Ragnall? Was he thinking too much of Arielle's prophesy?

At Fenn's silence, Kaela sighed. 'Then I need to come with you,' she said. 'You don't speak the language of the Northmen.'

'I'm not intending to speak with them.'

Kaela narrowed her eyes and placed her hands on her hips.

'But…' he said, 'you're….' he waved vaguely.

She didn't move.

'You'll come anyway, won't you?'

'If you go….'

He nodded slowly. 'Very well.'

'I'm coming too,' said Olgood. 'To keep you two out of trouble. We three know the Northmen and three sets of eyes are better than two.'

Fenn's first thought was that Olgood was too big to be creeping about in a forest, staying out of sight, but he remembered his effective disguise when they met leaving Cedric's camp.

He sighed and smiled. 'Does anyone want to stay behind?' He looked at Nyle.

'I will obey my Lord's command,' said Nyle.

'Good,' said Fenn. 'I'd like you to be in charge of raising a fyrd to help Hernam and also to prepare Westerling.'

'Prepare Westerling for what?' asked Olgood.

'In case the Northmen come this way.'

'Why should they come this way? I agree with Kaela. They can't know we're here, so there's nothing to bring them to Westerling. Undefended monasteries are the targets the Northmen seek — they'll use the Tamar to get inland, then search for monasteries and abbeys with easy takings in gold and thralls.'

'We can still be prepared,' said Fenn. Olgood hesitated, then shrugged and nodded.

Brecan had followed the conversation with a puzzled expression. When Olgood did not continue, he bowed his head to Fenn.

'On behalf of our King,' he said, 'I thank you for your offer of help. Hernam will already have eyes on these ships. I'll stay with you until we find the Northmen. I can help if you meet with Hernam's eyes. Then I'll report back to the King. Depending on what the Northmen do, we can plan where to meet again.' He paused. 'I rode hard to get here. I'll need a new horse.'

'So be it,' said Fenn. 'Fetch the horses. With each moment we delay the Northmen row further inland.' He turned to Nyle. 'But I first need to talk with you, Nyle, about preparations.'

CHAPTER THIRTY-THREE

Destination of the longships

'This man saw the ships. He says they turned from the Tamar and entered the Tavy,' said Merewyn. 'They're heading away from Cornwall, northeast, into Wessex.'

Fenn had ridden southwest from Westerling, skirting the moor, to the mouth of the Tamar where the ships of the Northmen had last been seen and then followed the bank of the estuary north. On the mud flats where the River Tavy entered the Tamar estuary, Merewyn had approached a lone fisherman casting a net into the tide.

The man gazed up at Fenn, holding his dripping net in his hands.

'Were the ships you saw under sail or rowing?' asked Fenn.

'Rowing, Lord,' said the man, 'with many oars. Who are these men? The ships were strange. I've never seen their like before.'

'They're Northmen. Raiders. How fast were they travelling?' Were they rowing hard to a known destination or at a more leisurely pace, looking for opportunities?'

'At a good walking pace.'

Fenn thought a moment. 'When were they here?'

The man pointed to the sky. 'When the sun was there, Lord.'

'Thank you, you've been helpful,' said Fenn. He handed a coin to the man who stared at the offering with wide eyes then bowed smartly.

Brecan muttered under his breath. He frowned. 'That's not good. The men Hernam sent to watch will need to go miles upriver before they can cross the Tamar with horses in order to reach the Tavy. They'll lose contact.'

Fenn acknowledged Brecan and turned to Merewyn. 'Do you also know this river? The Tavy?'

'Yes, Lord. What's harder for Hernam is easier for us. If they'd stayed on the Tamar, it would be difficult to catch them. But the Tavy is a lazy river – it switches back and forth, wandering across the countryside. If they stay on the river, we can travel a much shorter distance on land and gain on them quickly.'

'They'll keep to the river,' said Fenn. 'These ships only need chest-height water. How far up the Tavy can they take their ships?'

'To Tavistock, at least,' said Merewyn, 'where my brother farms. Maybe even to Lydford.'

'Is there an abbey in that area?' asked Olgood.

'The largest is Ordwulf's Monastery at Tavistock.'

'I'd wager they know about that monastery,' said Fenn. 'We'll go there. In what direction is Tavistock from here?'

Merewyn pointed a finger. Fenn frowned. Merewyn had indicated a direction close to the way they had just come.

'We'll be heading back towards Westerling?'

'Almost,' agreed Merewyn. 'But…' He hesitated, thinking.

'What is it?'

'Lord, there's a place south of Tavistock where a long arm of the river runs east before turning north. From what this man has said, if we ride fast, we should arrive at that bend before the Northmen, but then….'

He waved a finger in the air.

'But then….' Fenn repeated.

'The Tavy enters a gorge there. We cannot follow along the bank. Overland, there's a range of hills to cross, a difficult path. If we wait for the Northmen at the bend – from that point, the river will be a much faster route. They'll reach Tavistock well before us.'

'*We'll* wait at the bend,' Fenn said. 'You'll go on to Tavistock to warn your brother, the monks at the monastery, and the town reeve if Tavistock has one.'

He nodded again to the fisherman, turned his horse and urged it forward, waving to Merewyn to take the lead.

THE SQUARE SAIL BROUGHT back memories the instant it came into view.

As a captive roped in a line, being dragged across the sand dunes at Lindisfarne, Fenn recalled his first sight of the strange longships of the Northmen standing on the beach, tall carved dragon heads staring down menacingly – the turmoil and discomfort of the wild sea journey, the amazing seamanship and harsh cruelty of the Northmen, and the eerily majestic sail up the long *fjord* to reach Lognavik, a village so different from anything he'd known – so pagan, so primitive, and so completely *foreign*. Experiences from his time as a thrall in the land of the Northmen tumbled through his mind as the ships drew closer and were arrested only when Kaela laid her hand on his shoulder.

'Look in the bow,' she said.

Fenn focused on the two men standing beneath the sweeping carved prow of the ship, their attention directed upriver. Behind them, two rows of oars rhythmically dipped into the water and were dragged backwards in unison, propelling the vessel powerfully and smoothly forward. A second ship and then a third came into view around the bend, pulling just as strongly.

The two huge men were unmistakable.

'Olaf and Ragnall,' breathed Fenn. 'It *is* them. They'll be going to the monastery for sure.'

'It's incredible. How did you know?' asked Kaela.

'I didn't,' he said. 'But… I did.'

He shrugged. He felt no satisfaction that his suspicions had been confirmed. It made no sense that of all the Northmen who could have sailed into the mouth of the Tamar, it would be Ragnall. But, from the moment Brecan had spoken the words that square sails had been sighted, he *knew*. And he'd been unable to shake that feeling, no matter what others had tried to argue.

Being right brought no comfort. He knew the capabilities of these men.

Fenn took a quick count. His earlier estimate of two hundred Northmen was close.

'And Birgitta,' said Olgood. 'Look. She's rowing toward the front, on the left side.'

Fenn shared a glance with Kaela and Olgood. Their relationship with these Northmen was complex. All three had been thralls and subject to their harshness and cruelty – but they had also seen kindness and compassion. As Fenn had observed before, they were a people of stark contrasts – on one side, the Northmen were bloodthirsty, cruel, arrogant, and vengeful, but on the other, they were also gallant, generous, loyal, and honourable.

They knew some of the people who would be on these ships. Kaela had said that Askari – Ragnall and Olaf's mother – treated Kaela like a daughter. What would be her relationship with Ragnall and Olaf now? After all, along with Fenn, she had escaped from Ragnall, an action punishable by death.

Kaela had thought of Agatha – Birgitta's daughter but raised by Askari – as a sister. Fenn had saved Agatha from a bear, and Fenn and Olgood had helped Birgitta during a skirmish outside Ragnall's house. Birgitta acknowledged those debts by allowing them to escape Lognavik. Would she consider the debt paid in full? Or not?

The trio lay well-concealed in the treeline of a bluff high above the river where it entered the gorge. They had a good view of a half-mile stretch of the Tavy. Behind and below them, Brecan held the horses.

While Fenn watched, Ragnall turned his head to gaze along the top of the bluff. Fenn resisted the urge to duck his head as the man's eyes stared directly at him before passing by. He knew he could not be seen, and Ragnall gave no indication of noticing anything amiss.

Fenn had seen what he needed to see. He shuffled back and slid down the bank to join Brecan.

'We've confirmed where the Northmen are,' he said, 'and *who* they are. They'll be heading to the abbey at Tavistock. Do you want to return to Hernam now?'

'I haven't seen any of Hernam's eyes. They may have lost the Northmen. I'd like to know where the Northmen head next – *after* Tavistock.'

Fenn's attention was drawn to a muffled exclamation from Olgood, who tugged on Kaela's shoulder and slid down the bank.

'Fenn, *Nameth* is on Ragnall's ship.'

Nameth was a cook at St. Cuthbert's Monastery on Lindisfarne Island. He'd been captured along with Fenn and Olgood on that fateful summer's day when the Northmen had attacked. Fenn had not seen him after their arrival at Lognavik. He thought Nameth had been taken with other Lindisfarne captives to the Hedeby market and sold as a thrall.

'Are you sure? Why would Nameth be aboard?'

'I had to check, but it *is* him.'

Fenn stared at Olgood. Had Nameth joined the Northmen? And, if so, willingly or by force?

'Was he wearing a collar?' asked Fenn.

'I couldn't see.'

'Was this man Nameth another thrall taken from the monastery at Lindisfarne?' asked Kaela.

Fenn turned to her. 'Sorry, yes. I forgot you didn't meet him.'

'Ragnall would need someone who speaks the language.'

Of course. It was the role Hakon had played on the Lindisfarne raid.

Fenn took his horse from Brecan.

'Are you intending to go to Tavistock?' asked Kaela.

'Yes. But I'm not asking any of you to come with me.'

'To do what?'

'To provide what help I can. The monks will be unarmed.'

'Four against three ships of Northmen? We came to watch, not to fight.'

Fenn looked at her. 'I will not stand by and do nothing while more monks are needlessly slaughtered. I saw it at Lindisfarne, and I wasn't able to help. I don't know yet what I can do, and I'll probably be too late, but I intend to do what I can. Hopefully, Merewyn was able to warn the town.'

She matched his look. 'Then we'd better start without further delay,' she said.

She and Olgood mounted together. Fenn reached out for her hand, a gesture of thanks. Brecan waited beside his horse, frowning up at Fenn.

'You need not come with us,' said Fenn. 'Tell Hernam we will aid him if the Northmen head west, but I ask for *his* aid if they go further east.'

Brecan stepped into his saddle. 'I see what Hernam means,' he said. 'You're unusual Saxons. As I said, I'd like to keep the Northmen in sight. I think I'll stay with you a little longer.'

FENN CURSED THE SLOW progress. As Merewyn had indicated, the path crossing the range was narrow and rough. It looked to be rarely used – in some places barely formed. The descent from the ridge was as steep as the climb from the river.

Fenn divided his attention between the path being carefully picked by his horse and the valley stretching before him. Their immediate destination was visible on the valley floor – a clear road running the length of the valley alongside a meandering stream. The road to Tavistock.

For a long while, nothing changed. The snorting of the horses and the clip of their hooves on the rock. The buzz of insects. A hawk circled lazily. The road seemed to be getting no closer. The air in the valley shimmered in the dry heat of late afternoon.

The horse stepped carefully, Fenn letting him choose his own way down the hillside. He wanted to hurry. He needed to get to Tavistock as soon as possible before sunset, but there was nothing to gain from urging more speed from the horse.

The hawk suddenly ceased its circling, rapidly gaining height before disappearing over the ridge. Fenn searched for a reason for the hawk to break off its hunt. He pulled to a stop when a cloud of dust appeared at the far end of the valley, announcing movement. He glanced behind and Olgood nodded – also looking down the valley. After a few moments, the indistinct cloud resolved into a lone horseman riding fast.

As Fenn watched, the horseman turned from the road and headed directly towards Fenn.

'It's Merewyn,' said Olgood. 'He's in a hurry.'

'I WAS ABLE TO warn the monks. I'm not sure if they believed me, they wouldn't leave the monastery but at least they were cautious and decided to hide the holy relics and the sacred vessels. The town reeve was a different matter. He wouldn't listen. I begged him to have the people flee the town and take their livestock with them but he laughed at me and told me to leave or be arrested. I tried to tell some other people and they acted like I was mad.'

'What about your brother?' asked Kaela.

'I didn't see him. I was headed for his house when the Northmen arrived. The monastery is by the river; they went straight to it. There was a lot of shouting and I heard screams inside. The Northmen were everywhere....'

Merewyn stopped, trying to organise his words. He was breathing hard, appearing to want to say more but needing a moment to recover.

Fenn reached out to place a hand on his shoulder. 'Don't worry,' he said. 'Take your time. You couldn't have done anything. It's good you were able to give some warning, and I'm glad you withdrew and came back immediately to warn us.'

'No,' said Merewyn, 'I didn't leave. I hid. The Northmen gathered up some of the town people and held them in a group outside the monastery. It took me some time to move into a position where I could overhear them. I thought I might learn their plans – where they were going next.' His hands curled in frustration. 'But when I was close enough to hear them talking, I couldn't understand them.'

Fenn flicked a glance at Kaela. Maybe she should have gone with Merewyn. She knew the language. But he immediately dismissed the thought. Kaela would have been instantly recognised by many of the Northmen, even with her hair now long.

Merewyn spoke again. 'They brought the monks out of the abbey and forced them to kneel in a line before two big men who were the leaders. One of the men drew a sword and shouted at the monks, but they didn't understand him. They brought up another man who spoke to the monks in our language….'

'Nameth,' said Olgood.

Merewyn looked at him, surprised. 'You know this man's name?'

Olgood nodded. 'Yes, we know him and many of these Northmen.'

Merewyn frowned, then continued: 'I could hear him. He asked the first monk at the end of the line where the abbey's riches were hidden. The monk took the cross he wore around his neck and thrust it boldly forward. He said they were poor; they had nothing. He was a young man with fair hair. The big man, he… he… with his sword….'

Fenn waited, but Merewyn just shook his head.

'The big man threatened him… he wounded the monk?' suggested Fenn. He remembered Olaf threatening Master Nerian in the courtyard at Lindisfarne with the same question.

Merewyn stared at Fenn. 'No… No… He *slew* him, Lord, with one stroke. His blood….' He spread his hands wide and let a breath out through his teeth.

'I couldn't do anything. It was all I could do not to cry out.' Merewyn's expression was pained. Fenn nodded.

Merewyn clenched his hands into fists.

'They ignored the man's body sprawled on the stones, spilling his life's blood, and moved to the next monk,' he said. 'The man who had spoken to the monk… Nameth… refused to ask the question again. The big man knocked him to the ground but he still refused to speak.'

Merewyn looked away. Fenn glanced again at Kaela and Olgood, forcing himself to wait patiently to learn of Nameth's fate.

Merewyn continued: 'The big Northman dragged a woman from the group they held. She had a small child, a girl, clinging to her gown. He put his sword to the woman's throat, threatening her.'

'What did Nameth do?' asked Fenn.

Merewyn spread his hands in a sign of helplessness. 'He asked the question. He asked the monk where the abbey's gold was.'

'And the monk's reply…?'

'The monk lifted his head. He moved his eyes from Nameth to look defiantly up at the Northman and said…. he said, Lord….'

Merewyn drew in a breath.

'He told the Northman that the only gold he knew of was Lord Cormwurst's gold at Westerling.'

CHAPTER THIRTY-FOUR

Prepare to fight

The sun set quickly and nightfall caught the four riders ten miles from Westerling under a dark, cloudy sky that allowed no light from stars or moon to guide their way. Their pace slowed frustratingly as they picked their way through the forest in the gloom. The only comfort was the belief that the Northmen would wait until morning to take the road from Tavistock.

At midnight, a call from the palisade challenged the riders. Fenn noted with satisfaction that several men were on the palisade step. He identified himself, and the doors swung open.

Just before the horses entered the archway, their hooves clattered on wooden planks.

'This is new,' exclaimed Olgood. 'What is it? A bridge?'

'It's something I asked Nyle to do,' said Fenn. 'I'll show you in the morning.'

FENN CHECKED THE PALISADE in the cool morning air, then cast his eye over the barricade being resurrected in the courtyard in front of the palisade doors. Olgood was supervising the careful placement of items to maximize the difficulty of surmounting this final barrier should the doors be breached.

The dawn was painting the hills and treetops. Archers were already stationed where they should be, with a basket of arrows standing at the feet of each archer. Edelred had not yet returned from leading a party of the old and infirm and the young children once again to the sanctuary of the cave in the forest. Fenn had considered holding these people in the Hall to escape through the tunnel if necessary, but many were unable to move fast.

At first light, Fenn had taken Olgood and Kaela through the palisade doors to view a wooden bridge set across a wide trench dug parallel to the palisade walls in front of the archway and extending for twenty paces on each side of the bridge.

'The trench should foil any attempt to batter down the doors with a ram,' said Fenn. 'There are sharpened stakes underneath. When the time comes, four men can remove the bridge and add it to the barricade.'

Olgood frowned and shook his head. 'A worthwhile addition to our defences.' He turned to Fenn with a puzzled look. 'You asked Nyle to do this yesterday? How did you know the Northmen would come here? How did you know it was Ragnall?'

'I didn't *know* for certain,' said Fenn. 'I thought it was possible. I just considered what I did know....'

He stopped. He realised he was about to answer Olgood in the same way Arielle had answered him. He didn't know for sure, but he'd recalled his earlier thoughts of a trench when the Cornish had been here; he'd added his experience at Hammaburg, his assessment of the Northmen, and – maybe there was something else, a feeling that he couldn't put into words.

'It was possible the Northmen would come this way,' he repeated, 'and we had the time to prepare.'

Kaela took him by the arm. 'You still surprise me,' she said softly. 'That's a good thing.'

Fenn smiled. He took her hand and with his other he pointed toward the Roman Road. 'I also asked Nyle to place those.'

Set at regular intervals in the field, forming an arc, was a curved line of white stones.

'Our flour sacks,' said Olgood, remembering the white flour sacks Fenn had placed in the field outside Hammaburg Castle to give his archers their range.

'Yes,' said Fenn, 'Anyone inside that ring is a target for our arrows.'

Olgood remained staring over the fields, letting his gaze move along the road, assessing the terrain. His hand absentmindedly felt for the head of his axe, his fingers lightly touching the razor-sharp edge. He straightened, flexing his huge shoulders, and drew in a breath.

'Let them come,' he said.

NYLE HAD SENT TREDDIAN and two other men to hide in the western forest near the River Taw and bring warning of the Northmen's approach.

'I've sent the message to the villages,' said Nyle. 'All the men who can be spared will come on your call. I've also brought in our own livestock.' He indicated a group of women working around a table beside the well. 'We're increasing our stocks of arrows.'

Fenn twisted to face the table just as one of the women looked up. He recognised Brianne, the archer who had expressed a forceful desire to fight when Hernam had threatened Westerling. Fenn nodded to her and she responded by raising her closed fist.

Beside the table lay an ordered pile of thin branches and saplings, a variety of woods – Fenn could see yew, birch, and ash – all cut to the same length. Beside the pile were two baskets of goose feathers. On the table sat bowls of iron arrowheads, showing that the blacksmith had been hard at work. Beside the table, a covered cauldron of water was boiling over a fire where the wooden shafts were being straightened by steaming and then scraped smooth.

Fenn turned back to Nyle. 'Call the villagers in,' he said. 'The harvest can be left – hopefully for only a day or two – we need every person willing and able to fight, not just the men.'

'Of course,' acknowledged Nyle, nodding.

'And tell them to scatter or hide the animals and gathered crops,' said Fenn. 'We don't want to feed the hungry Northmen.'

Nyle nodded again. When Fenn didn't continue, he held up a finger. 'One more thing. Over the past few weeks, I've been training my men to be your personal guard. They're ready.'

'I don't need....'

'Please... Lord Feran. They consider it an honour. When I told them what their role would be, to a man they willingly put their total effort into the training, and I didn't spare them an inch. As I said, they're ready. They're as disciplined and well-trained with sword and spear now as any man in the land. I would ask you not to disappoint them.'

Fenn remembered the young farm boys he met on the first journey to Westerling. Bashful, raw, innocent – lacking experience in both life and battle. He had no doubt that Nyle would have turned those boys into worthy fighting men.

'I would be honoured,' he said. 'In return, I would ask something of you.'

'Name it.'

'You knew me before I was a Thane. You need not call me Lord Feran. Fenn is sufficient.'

'With respect, I will address you as Lord in public; the title is important – but in private... if you wish....'

Fenn clapped him on the shoulder. 'Good.' He glanced at the position of the sun. 'Send your riders. Bring the villagers in. Have you seen Kaela?'

'She's in the Hall with some women.'

Fenn nodded and headed for the Hall.

Kaela was standing before a line of six women. All were dressed in leggings and a loose-fitting tunic and had their hair drawn back and tied.

The other thing the women had in common was a sword buckled to a belt and their full attention on Kaela.

'We'll fight as a team, each looking after the other,' said Kaela. 'Alone, you cannot stand against a Northman, but *together* we can.'

She turned to face Fenn. 'Nyle said he wanted his men for other duties. So I've been training my own group.' She swept her hand along the line of women. 'I have my roving band, and we're prepared.'

HE WAITED WHILE KAELA laced the back of the iron-studded leather covering his chest. He hunched his shoulders to test its tightness.

'I don't think I'll need the wolf pelt. It has no meaning here.'

'You *should* wear it,' insisted Kaela. 'It's a mark of your rank in Wessex. Ragnall won't know what it means, but he'll know it's significant.'

Fenn smiled and nodded, pleased that Kaela was there to advise him. She fitted the wolfskin to his shoulder, then stood back and gave him an admiring look.

'Now you are every inch the Thane of Westerling and Protector of Wessex,' she said.

'At this moment, I'm solely concerned with Westerling.'

Kaela smiled indulgently. 'Really? You are what you are.'

She turned him around, giving a critical appraisal, then adjusted the leather at his shoulders to make it sit better. Fenn reached up and took her by her wrists.

'It's fine,' he said. 'You needn't fuss any more.'

She chuckled in her throat. 'I'd like you to look perfect.'

In reply, he rested his head against hers. 'Thank you, and I assure you I aspire to nothing grander than protecting Westerling.'

She pulled back and looked him in the eye. 'If that's so, have you considered giving Ragnall the gold so he will just go away? You may save Westerling without a fight.'

Fenn waved his hand in a negative gesture. 'Would he go? I can't be sure of that. But even if he did, then what? Where would he go next? He could ravage the countryside – attack the villages. You know the Northmen are looking for a fight.' He raised his hand to make his point. 'Brecan will bring Hernam and Wyllard will bring Herewic – if we can hold until they arrive, we can end Ragnall's raid here.'

'Ah ha! So you admit you *are* trying to protect Wessex.'

He widened his eyes and regarded her for a moment, then shook his head. 'Very well,' he conceded. 'Of course, you're right. I should know better than try to argue.'

She smiled. 'There's only a slim chance that Herewic will arrive today. We don't know about Hernam. Egbert…?' She shrugged. 'Can we hold?'

'We must,' said Fenn.

He looked toward a noise at the Hall entrance, turning when he saw it was Treddian. Fenn waved at him to enter. Treddian stepped forward and walked swiftly up to Fenn. He stared at the leather covering on Fenn's chest and at the wolfskin on his shoulder.

When he didn't immediately speak, Fenn raised his eyebrows.

Treddian bowed. 'Sorry, Lord. I've not seen you dressed like this before.'

Fenn nodded at him. 'You've seen the Northmen?'

'Yes, Lord. The Northmen have crossed the Taw on the Roman Road. They're headed directly for Westerling. They'll be here around midday.' He smiled. 'They're walking in good order but, as I've been told you predicted, they look tired. It's been a hot morning and a long dusty walk.'

'How many?'

'I counted one hundred and seventy or eighty.'

Some would have been left with the ships. When the villagers arrived, Westerling could have one hundred and fifty defenders. They'd be outnumbered, but Fenn remembered at the siege of Hammaburg Castle, Duke Widukind of Saxony told him that behind appropriate fortifications, the right force could hold off twice their number. Westerling was not a castle, but its walls were well-constructed and strong. It was as if Hardwain had foreseen this day and built his palisade to keep out not just wild animals, but also an attack of wild men from the north.

THE SUN WAS HIGH in the sky when the last villagers arrived and no more were in sight. Some, as before, had driven stock to Westerling, including the man with his flock of noisy geese. Olgood, Nyle, and Kaela had been busy organising and checking weapons and forming the people into groups and into positions.

Olgood came to him and said the people were ready. He was carrying an oversize round wooden shield, like the shields of the Northmen but with a pointed iron spike protruding from the centre dome and a sharpened iron rim.

At Fenn's enquiring glance, he said: 'I made it myself. It's bigger and has a few extras.'

'I can see that,' said Fenn. 'It's certainly large. I don't think anyone else could lift it.'

He jumped down from the step and placed a hand on Olgood's shoulder. 'How is Gisele?'

Olgood took a deep breath. 'Acwellan says the birth will be soon.' He grimaced. 'Maybe today.'

'It's not too late. If you need to be with her….'

'No,' said Olgood firmly. 'It's one more reason to fight. I won't stand to the side this time.'

He reached out a hand. Fenn grasped his forearm firmly and they silently regarded each other.

'Have you picked good men?' Fenn asked.

'I have. They know what's required of them. It's a good plan. We'll give the Northmen a surprise.'

With a nod, Fenn turned back to the palisade, climbing onto the step.

He stared out over the gathering. He noticed Beric and his boys at the back, standing together, buckets of stones at their feet. After several whisperings as the people saw how he was dressed, they quieted and silently returned his gaze.

This was a different crowd from the one he'd addressed when the Cornish were outside Westerling. These people were more confident. They'd been in this situation before, and it had been resolved successfully. Also, previously their leader had been unknown and untested. Now they knew him; he was their accepted and respected Thane.

'When the Northmen arrive, they'll be tired,' Fenn said. 'They are not demons or gods, despite rumours you may have heard; they are people just like us. They will have marched at dawn from Tavistock. I know the leaders of these Northmen, they are fiercely competitive, and they need to show their strength and endurance. They will not have walked their men slowly and easily so they arrive fresh. They will have forced the pace. They'll arrive tired and hot and the last thing the men will want is a hard fight.'

'I've asked this of you before. We must show these Northmen we are ready for a fight – ready and willing to protect our home and fight for Westerling.'

'The last time I spoke, when Hernam was here, I said you should fight for this land because it was *yours*. You've worked with this land, nurtured your crops and brought forth harvests. It's soaked with your sweat and the sweat of your fathers. Your children have been born and thrived on this land. I said *you belong here*.'

'Now, there's a difference. Now I say this is *our* land. I, too, am a part of Westerling.' He waved his arms to encompass Kaela, Olgood, Gisele and Kuralin, standing to one side and Nyle and his men on the other. '*We* are part of Westerling because, like all of you, this is our home.'

'*And we will fight for our home.*'

An instant cheer rose from the gathering; arms were raised, most brandishing weapons. At Fenn's feet, Balthazar happily joined in the noise with a series of deep-throated barks. Fenn looked down at the dog.

'Yes, you too, Balthazar. You can....'

A shout interrupted him.

A man on the step beside the palisade doors pointed and called: 'Two riders coming fast.'

Nyle's watchers.

The Northmen were close.

CHAPTER THIRTY-FIVE

Old friends and old foes

The noise from the crowded palisade and the courtyard when the first Northmen came into sight on the Roman Road was satisfying but also deafening. Fenn struggled to concentrate on the gathering numbers of Northmen emerging from the western forest. In weapons and appearance, they were a mixed lot. Most carried an axe and a round shield, but some had swords and others carried spears. Some also wore a helmet of metal or leather, but many were bare-headed. Several women scattered along the line were armed and dressed the same as the men.

Ragnall and Olaf strode at the head of the column. Beside Ragnall, the golden hair of Birgitta shone in the midday sun. Two men walked behind Olaf. Fenn recognised one of them as Nameth. He didn't know the other but presumed he would be someone to guide the Northmen to Westerling.

When he was opposite the palisade doors, Ragnall stopped. Those with him stopped also, but the men following kept walking, spreading out along the Roman Road. When the last of the Northmen had exited the forest, the men at the ends of the column moved forward until the Northmen had formed a semi-circle confronting the hilltop palisade of Westerling.

Fenn waited on the palisade step beside the curved arch of the doors. On the other side of the doors, Nyle stood with his bow strung and an arrow held loosely against the string. His other hand was free, ready to signal his archers. Nyle had given the same instructions to his archers as Fenn had on the walls of Hammaburg Castle: 'The Northmen archers and the leaders are your primary targets. Shoot only when you have a target.'

Fenn returned his attention to Ragnall. The big man seemed to be in no hurry. What was he waiting for?

Would the Northmen attack or negotiate? If it was the former, Westerling was as ready as it could be. Fenn checked his pouch and felt with his foot for the bucket of stones gathered for him by Beric and his boys.

If it was the latter, three horses stood ready beside the barricade.

Ragnall and Olaf stepped out of the line, accompanied by Birgitta and Nameth. Birgitta and the brothers were dressed alike, with a vest of chain mail over tunic and trousers – all three carrying round wooden shields. One difference was that Ragnall and Olaf held axes, whereas Birgitta wore a sword. They walked forward twenty paces and stopped.

Ragnall was standing close to a white stone.

Fenn and Nyle exchanged glances and Nyle nodded. His bow could make the shot.

Ragnall rested his axe on the ground and waited.

Fenn released a long breath and shrugged his shoulders to release the tension. He was sorry he wasn't able to ride one of the black mares to meet Ragnall. They would have impressed the Northman, but they would also have been a tempting prize.

MEREWYN MOVED ASIDE PART of the barricade to allow the horses through, and Fenn led Kaela and Olgood under the arch. In contrast to the last time he had left the palisade to negotiate with a threat to Westerling, this time Fenn was dressed for battle and wore both axe and seax.

At his back, the voices of Westerling roared their full-throated anger at the Northmen.

He kept his horse at a slow walk. He knew the Northmen in their thick sea-faring clothing and helmets, carrying heavy weapons and shields, would not be comfortable under the heat of the sun.

As he neared the group, Birgitta's hand came to her mouth and she let out an exclamation. She spoke urgently to Ragnall who lifted his hand to shade his eyes, an action mirrored by Olaf. Nameth also heard her and took a step back, his eyes widening.

Fenn pulled his horse to a stop in front of Birgitta so he didn't obscure Ragnall from Nyle's bow. As before, the roar from the people of Westerling subsided as they concentrated on the exchange.

Ragnall frowned. He spoke, and Kaela translated.

'I *know* you,' said Ragnall. 'By Odin's tail, you're the young pup with a bite, the escaped thrall – you've grown and acquired some status, I see, and…' his eyes took in Olgood, '…gods beware, so has the shipbuilder grown.' He frowned briefly at Olgood, his eyes lingering on Olgood's shield, before moving to look Kaela up and down.

'You too, Kael,' he said, 'who, by your appearance, can now be called Kaela. And you still have Alfarin's sword.'

He spoke again, but Kaela didn't immediately translate. Fenn looked at her. Her eyes were misted. She breathed deeply.

'He said his mother will be pleased to learn I am alive.' She swallowed, finding it hard to speak. She moved her eyes to Birgitta.

'Agatha…?' she asked.

Agatha was Birgitta's deaf daughter. According to custom, the Northmen left disabled or deformed newborn children in the forest for the gods to decide their fate. Ragnall's mother, Askari, had secretly rescued Agatha – and another foundling named Addo – and raised both babies as her own. When Birgitta discovered Agatha was alive, her feelings were a mixture of guilt, relief, and profound happiness. Kaela had lived with Agatha for four years as Askari's thrall. She had known Agatha since she was a baby and thought of her as a sister.

Birgitta stared back at her and replied. After a moment, Kaela said: 'She said Agatha is well and thriving. And she has grown into a young girl who has now seen eight summers. She said she… she misses her big sister….'

Birgitta looked up at Ragnall and said something firmly to him.

With tears in her eyes, Kaela said: 'Birgitta said she cannot fight on this day.'

Fenn frowned. Was Kaela also about to say she couldn't fight? Kaela wiped her eyes with the back of her hand but didn't respond. She sat back on her horse, raising her chin and looking calmly down at Ragnall.

Ragnall was about to speak, but Fenn spoke first in his language: 'It's good to see you again, Nameth. Are you well?'

Nameth didn't reply. He shook his head, but it wasn't a negative answer – rather, he was still absorbing the shock of seeing Fenn and Olgood.

'We'll talk later,' said Fenn. 'When this is over.'

He turned his gaze on Ragnall. 'Tell Ragnall that I know him too.' Kaela translated.

Ragnall stared at Fenn. His eyes flicked to the palisade then back to Fenn.

'So be it,' he said, Kaela repeating his words as he spoke. 'I've come for the gold. The people at the place called Tavistock told me of Lord Cormwurst's gold. We've come for it. Give me the gold, and we'll leave.'

'Tell him we have no gold. That's only a story.'

'Many people told the same story,' said Ragnall. 'And they insisted it was true under threat of death.' He paused, his eyes moving from Fenn to Kaela and back. 'They were weak. It only took a death or two to find their gold, but a few cups and bowls are not enough.' His eyes flicked again to Kaela and back. 'It's a pity we meet again in these circumstances, but you had gone from our lives and you can go again.' He raised his chin. 'I'll say this one more time – give us the gold. If you resist us, even if you are who you are, we will kill and continue to kill. I'll kill everything that lives, your women, your children, and your animals, and then I'll burn your little town to the ground.'

Ragnall stared at Fenn. 'But, you three…' he said, waving a finger between Fenn, Kaela, and Olgood, '…you're still my thralls, and I'll take you back to Lognavik.'

Fenn leaned forward on his horse and fixed his eyes on Ragnall.

'We're ready for you, Ragnall,' he said. 'This is our home, and we're not going anywhere. We knew you were on your way. You ask us to give you gold and you will go. I don't *want* you to go. I don't want you raiding in Wessex. I want you broken and defeated here for daring to invade our land.'

He paused to allow Kaela's translation to catch up.

'Westerling is not a defenceless monastery…' he continued, '…like Lindisfarne or Tavistock, and…' his voice rose, '…*we are not unarmed monks!*' He stopped and stared to remind Ragnall that in Lognavik he had called Ragnall a coward for killing the monks at Lindisfarne. 'We will fight and you'll lose many men here today – men and women who will not be returning to their families.'

Olaf laughed and shouted at Fenn.

'He said he sees only farmers with farm tools,' said Kaela.

Fenn ignored Olaf. He twisted in the saddle and pointed back to the palisade. 'We have surprises for you behind those stakes. Things you will not expect. You would do well to leave now – go back to your ships and back to your own land.'

When Kaela finished translating, Olaf growled, turning an angry face to Ragnall and brandishing his axe at Fenn.

Ragnall scowled. 'I see you have not lost your bite.' He lifted his own axe. 'We may lose men. That happens in a fight. But *you* will lose everything.'

Olgood sat forward on his horse, raising his axe to match the stance of the Northmen. Olaf stared at the weapon, recognising it as one of the pair with blood-red handles that he and Ragnall had owned.

'*Blod-ox,*' he shouted at Ragnall, pointing, the word needing no translation. Ragnall nodded.

'You have my axe, shipbuilder – I want it back.'

'I'll give this axe back to you…' said Olgood, '…I'll bury it in your skull.' Kaela hesitated, then translated his words.

Ragnall grunted, but a quick frown appeared as he assessed the massive form of Olgood astride his horse. His eyes moved to the axe in Fenn's belt.

'And you still have Thorvald's axe. He told me the story, but I'll take it back to him if you fall today.'

Olaf shuffled his feet impatiently. He shouted something that caused a stir among the Northmen close enough to hear.

'He said: *Enough talk, kill them now*,' said Kaela, her hand resting on her sword.

'*Nay*,' Ragnall said firmly, raising his axe higher.

He pointed the axe at Fenn, his eyes angry.

'You once called me a coward. I should have killed you then. We are no cowards. We will fight you where you think you are strong. Go back inside your wooden walls – *our* walls move with us.' He thumped his shield with his axe. 'Go back to your farmers. We've met them before. They're too scared to raise a fist against us – they expect their god to protect them, but we know he will not.' He gave a snort of disgust. 'A last chance – bring me the gold and we may let you live. You think on it. Tell your people what I've said. I'll wait a short while.'

He withdrew the axe, but his eyes remained angry.

In reply, Fenn turned his horse, Kaela and Olgood following.

Ragnall said something behind him. He raised his eyebrows at Kaela.

'He ordered someone to find water,' she said.

FENN DISMOUNTED.

'Bring in the bridge. Double bar the doors.'

He felt a tug on his sleeve and turned to see Brianne, the archer, her bow in one hand and a full quiver on her waist. Two children stood beside her, a boy and a girl, looking up at Fenn with wide eyes that shone with wonder but also determination.

His first thought was to ask why they had not gone to the cave with the other children.

Before he could speak, Brianne said: 'Excuse me, Lord. My twins want to help. With your permission, I've told them they can collect the arrows the Northmen send us and deliver them to our archers.'

'That's dangerous work,' said Fenn.

'I know that and so do they. But it will help Westerling. I've told them every arrow will help.'

Fenn looked into the large eyes of the children. These innocents should be covered and protected, not exposed to the deadly arrows of the Northmen. If he allowed this, how could he face it if one were to be killed?

He shook his head.

Brianne spoke first again. 'I know what you're thinking… How can I think of putting my children in such danger? I know the danger – I see the men outside our walls. All of Westerling is in danger – the men, the women, *and* the children. My son spoke to me as a man, and I could not disagree with his words. He said: My arrows will allow our archers to keep shooting. One of my arrows could kill a Northman chief; another of my arrows could stop someone from killing my mother. An arrow that I collect could win the battle.'

The boy took a step forward. 'Please, Lord Fenn, we want to help. We can do it.'

Fenn smiled. Lord Fenn was what the Westerling children called him.

He remembered the two girls at the siege of Hammaburg Castle carrying buckets of arrows across the courtyard. He knew the sight of those brave children had inspired him and the other defenders.

He knelt beside the boy.

———⟶ ❦ ——

532

The head of Ragnall's axe was resting on the ground with the handle leaning against his thigh. Ragnall stood, hands on hips, head tilted, surveying the palisade of Westerling. For a long while, he was still. Nothing moved. Even the birds were silent, anticipating the upcoming disturbance.

Time for Fenn to give Ragnall his reply. He caught Nyle's attention.

'Can you put an arrow at Ragnall's feet?' he asked. 'The tall one at the front next to the blonde woman.'

'He's standing by a marker stone,' Nyle replied. 'I know the distance. I can put it between his legs if you want.'

Fenn smiled. 'In front will be fine. I just want to get his attention.'

Nyle selected an arrow and bent his bow. As soon as the arrow was loosed, there were shouts from the Northmen. All eyes followed its flight. Ragnall raised his shield, Olaf and Birgitta following suit. The arrow thudded into the ground in front of Ragnall, close enough to cause him to step back.

Immediately, he pointed to the arched doors of Westerling and leaned across to speak with Olaf. Olaf nodded and Ragnall glanced up to the heavens, no doubt invoking the favour of his gods, before leaning down to grasp his axe and raising a fist in the air.

At each end of the line of Northmen stretching along the Roman Road, a man stepped forward, signalled to the men behind him and walked towards the forest. About fifty Northmen followed each man leaving the remainder of Ragnall's force to assault the north wall of the palisade.

Fenn saw Birgitta take Ragnall's arm and say something to him, then turn from his side. She pushed through the ranks of men behind her, beckoning to Nameth, who joined her as she ascended the hill, stopping beside the trunk of a tall tree and turning to face Westerling, her arms folded – a spectator only.

'Just as you said, Nyle,' said Fenn. 'They'll rush from three sides.'

The River Yule created a difficulty for the Northmen on the south side of Westerling. It was a wide shallow river, but opposite Westerling, the centre channel was chest-deep, forcing anyone crossing the river to be slow and vulnerable. Nyle had stationed men on the south wall but not as many as on the other three.

Fenn felt in his bag, selecting a stone by its feel. He slowly rubbed it in the palm of his hand, warming it. He turned in a circle, checking again the parts of the palisade he could see.

His eye caught Acwellan standing in a doorway, flanked by Kuralin and Bronwyn on one side and Erenweth on the other. The physician looked calm, leaning against the frame of the door, his instruments, supplies, and medicines ready, with nothing more to do than await the first wounded. Fenn wondered if Gisele was inside the hut. He returned his eyes to the defenders lining the palisade.

The palisade, while solid and thick, was not ideally designed to defend against the force now confronting Westerling. The walls formed a square with slightly bowed sides, but, as Fenn had noted previously, there were no towers or protrusions to allow defenders to easily shoot at attackers attempting to scale the palisade. To do so, a man needed to lean over the stakes, thereby exposing himself to the enemy.

Fenn completed his circle. Ragnall hadn't moved – waiting for his men to get into position so they could assault the three walls simultaneously.

A growl, curious and enquiring, came from Balthazar who'd stationed himself below Fenn, by the barricade, beside the five men of Fenn's guard. The hound could feel the tension in the air.

Not long now, Balthazar, thought Fenn. He acknowledged Nyle's men standing in full Wessex colours, each carrying spear, sword, and the Wyvern shield. One raised his spear in salute and the others immediately followed his lead.

Fenn looked for Kaela. She stood with her group of swordswomen just behind two rows of people manning the barricade. The defenders carried a variety of weapons. At the front stood those with spears or makeshift spears, knives lashed to poles. Some in the second rank held swords, but there were also pitchforks and scythes. These were not usually seen on a battlefield, but in the hands of a skilled worker could cause serious injury.

Kaela was talking to Beric. She pointed to the nearest building. Beric nodded and gathered his slingers, each picking up their buckets of stones. *Enough stones for an army,* thought Fenn. From the roof, Beric's slingers would overlook the barricade and the courtyard and could shower stones on anyone who came through the doors or over the palisade.

From the safety of the doorway of the same building, Brianne's twins searched the sky with their big eyes, waiting for the first of the Northmen's arrows to arrive.

His eyes flicked to the northwestern corner of the palisade where he knew Brianne would be standing. She was there. Interspersed between her and the other archers, men with long spears stood ready to repel anyone climbing the palisade. The Northmen had no ladders – they would attempt to climb on top of each other. He saw Brianne cast an anxious glance at her children, then she looked towards Fenn. When she saw he was watching, she straightened and gave her clenched fist salute. Then she faced the Northmen and added her voice to the cries of defiance.

Olgood stood to one side near the Hall. His axe was drawn, his massive shield on his arm. He was flanked by ten men, well-armed, also with round shields like the Northmen – big men, men Olgood had chosen himself. Each man wore a band of red cloth tied to their arm below the shoulder.

The man beside Fenn yelled: '*Here they come!*'

Automatically, Fenn dropped the stone he'd warmed into the pouch of his sling and let the pouch fall to his side, bringing his attention to the front, raising his arm to start the sling whirling.

The Northmen were charging across the field, screaming – and their screams were reflected in matching volume and intensity by the throats inside the Westerling palisade.

CHAPTER THIRTY-SIX

Fury of the Northmen

As soon as the charging Northmen passed the ring of white stones, Nyle's arm dropped and Westerling bows hummed. Several Northmen archers fell before they could loose their first arrow. This was noted by a ragged cheer among the Westerling archers.

Ragnall and Olaf had the experience to conserve their energy now the battle had begun; they were overtaken in the race across the field by more exuberant younger men, eager for glory. Fenn had hoped to send his first stone at one of the pair but instead chose an archer who had stopped sixty paces out to draw his bow. Fenn's stone took the man in the head, a killing blow. The man dropped just as an arrow also struck him in the chest.

Another stone, another archer down. As a missile, a stone had a significant advantage over an arrow – the stone was invisible, the arrow was not. Westerling did not have enough archers to employ the tactic Fenn used at Cymeresford against Ethelmund of sending flights of hundreds of arrows at the enemy, making it difficult to counter them all. Many arrows already sprouting from the shields of the Northman testified to the unfortunate fact that the flight of a single arrow could be seen and blocked by a shield.

He couldn't waste time searching for Ragnall or Olaf – Northmen were already close to the palisade. The corner of his eye caught movement and he instinctively ducked as an arrow flew past his shoulder. Another struck the palisade. The angle of the arrow told him where to search. He rose and found the archer but hesitated. It was a woman. His stone flew but the woman was turning away – it struck a glancing blow. She fell but was still moving on the grass. He heard another arrow pass close, followed by a cry of pain nearby.

A man heading for the doors was only twenty paces away. He ran in a crouch, weaving across the field with his shield raised high to protect him from the arrows. Another stone selected. The sling whirled, but the man's shield dipped and the missile aimed at his legs hit the lower rim. The man slowed enough to hurl his axe at the doors, then noticed the trench. He tried to stop his momentum but stumbled onto the stakes and screamed in agony. A second man also tossed an axe at the doors, falling immediately with an arrow in his stomach. Another stone took out a third before he could throw his axe, but more were filling his place, passing him. A man picked up the fallen axe and threw it and then his own before two arrows took him down. Another stone. A hit. Another stone. Two more axes thumped into the door.

Fenn understood the tactic. They would try to climb up the axes, over the arch and open the doors.

He reached into his bag – and was surprised that it was empty. He bent to retrieve a handful of stones from the wooden bucket at his feet. Bronwyn was helping a man down from the step, an arrow in his neck, his shoulder bloody. She was pulling at the bow he still held but he refused to let go. Fenn looked for Olgood, but he was gone, already heading through the tunnel from the Great Hall to emerge in the forest and engage the Northmen from behind. A blonde-headed girl, Brianne's daughter, appeared with three arrows clutched in her hand. She dropped them into the bucket of the archer beside Fenn, her eyes meeting his briefly; she nodded an acknowledgement before scurrying away across the courtyard.

He dropped the stones into his bag, selected one, and the sling was whirling as he rose above the stakes. An arrow grazed his cheek, a sharp pain. Another deflected off the top of a palisade stake and struck the hardened leather on his chest but without the force to pierce it. He took a half-step to the side, picked out the archer and his stone hit the man in the face. A man was climbing the axes. The air was suddenly full of arrows as the Northmen archers tried to protect the climbing man. Cries and the sounds of a struggle came from further along the palisade. The Northmen had reached the top.

Fenn rose again. More men were on the doors, climbing the axes. He had no shot at these men, unable to bring his sling to bear on them. He saw Olaf, heading for the doors, his shield high. Fenn's carefully aimed stone caught him on the leg bringing the big man crashing to the ground – not a fatal blow. He couldn't see Ragnall. Fenn ducked below the palisade as more arrows sought him. It had been a mistake to still wear the wolfskin. It marked him.

He took a moment to survey the courtyard. The defenders on the east and west walls were fully occupied, the archers still loosing arrows, the spearmen thrusting over the palisade. They looked secure, holding the Northmen. Fenn could not see any breaches. A cheer from the northeast corner drew his attention. The men on the step were cheering action outside the walls. He took a quick look over the palisade – one look was all he needed. The massive form of Olgood, followed by his men, strode among the Northmen, creating destruction with both axe and shield. The red band on their arms identified them to the Westerling defenders. Fenn had witnessed Olgood wielding his axe at Hammaburg. His blows were so powerful no man could parry them or stand against him and, very quickly, none were willing.

But even the strongest could fall to an arrow.

An arm reached over the top of the arch, pulling a body behind it. Instantly, a rain of stones pelted the body and clattered against the doors. Beric's boys. Fenn hoped they could conserve their enthusiasm, or the vast supply they had hauled onto the roof would be quickly exhausted. But the barrage was effective and the man dropped lifeless at the foot of the doors. Two more arms appeared over the arch.

Fenn tucked the sling in his belt and jumped down from the step, drawing his axe and seax. The blonde hair of Brianne's daughter ran past him toward the corner of the palisade, this time with arrows clutched in both hands. She thrust the arrows into the empty bucket at her mother's feet, her hand reaching out to gently touch her mother's ankle before turning away. Fenn hadn't seen her brother. He hoped the boy wasn't injured. Brianne looked down at the touch, her eyes briefly following her daughter before she bent to take an arrow, straightening, drawing her bow.

The sight of Brianne, her long auburn hair swirling, her bow at full stretch, her eyes wet with pride and worry for her children, but her face set with determination, filled Fenn with resolve. When Fenn had saved Agatha from the bear, Thorvald, the man who had given him the axe he now carried, had paid him the compliment of saying he would stand with Fenn in battle. Fenn looked at the faces of the men and women manning the barricade. Ordinary men, ordinary women, farmers, craftswomen, brewers, an innkeeper, a tanner, a cooper, sturdy and reliable, people to fight with and fight for – *his* people, the people of Westerling.

He would willingly stand beside them all in battle.

'They will not take Westerling,' he roared. *'Hold them at the barricade. Kill all who dare enter.'*

A man dropped to the ground before the doors, and another. They reached to unbar the doors but were met with another hail of stones and both fell before they could move the bars. But like water escaping a breach in the riverbank, another man dropped from the arch, and another, another. A Westerling man made to climb the barricade to attack them but Kaela pulled him back.

The boys on the roof were slinging a steady stream of stones but even through the torrent, men were reaching the barricade. They were met by the spears of the first rank and those that fell added to the obstacle, making access more difficult for their followers. The attackers rushed the barricade in a group but the unwavering spears and long pitchforks drove them back. The shouts of defiance, mixed with screams of pain and death and clashes of weapons, created a maelstrom of noise.

Men scrambled up the barricade in front of Fenn. He stepped forward, but two boys of his guard were faster, their spears slipping skillfully under the shields, knocking the Northmen back. A following Northman stumbled over a body and was struck solidly with a thrown spear, collapsing on top of the first victim.

But the Northmen were over the archway in sufficient numbers. The bars were flung aside and the doors swung open. With a roar, more Northmen rushed through – but not as many as Fenn had expected. They straggled into the courtyard rather than charge in a concentrated group. The trench had slowed them. Nyle jumped from the step and took a handful of arrows from Brianne's boy. Within moments he had loosed the arrows into the surge of Northmen from a few steps away, each shaft dropping a man. His supply exhausted, he let his bow fall and drew a sword.

The defenders were taking a deadly toll on the Northmen. Fenn calculated he had seen twenty Northmen fall, more than a tenth of their number. Surely they couldn't sustain such losses. Perhaps Westerling could win this battle without help.

An axe came hurtling through the air toward Fenn. The man beside him stepped in front. His raised shield deflected the axe, but it rebounded to strike the guard in the head, knocking him to the side. Fenn's glance caught Kuralin running towards the fallen man.

A loud cry spun Fenn's head.

A group of screaming Northmen rushed the centre of the barricade and were repulsed by spears and stones. They rushed again. Fenn saw Merewyn and Peada fighting side by side to repel the rush. A Northman tumbled over the barricade and landed on his knees. Before he could rise or bring up his shield, he was met without hesitation by the blade of a sword wielded by one of Kaela's women. In her eyes, Fenn saw what he hoped he would see, anger and determination, not fear.

There was a skirmish at the back of the group manning the barricade. Northmen had breached the palisade and were coming to aid those at the doors. Fenn saw Kaela and her women move to intercept, he saw Kaela's blade flash, but then two men were on top of the barricade in front of Fenn. One escaped the spears and leapt into the courtyard, his axe raised. Fenn met the axe with his own and swept the seax under the man's arm. The blade bit deeply.

The Northmen were over the barricade.

A man came from the side but was knocked back by Balthazar, growling fiercely, his teeth seeking the man's throat. The man screamed and died, blood gushing from his ripped throat. Others backed away from the snarling hound.

All at once Fenn and his guards were beset on three sides, and his guards turned away from the barricade to protect their Thane. Balthazar's deep snarls told Fenn the hound had found another victim.

One guard cast his spear at an advancing Northman who took it on his shield, the point piercing the wood and lodging there. The weight of the spear impeded the man's movement and he attempted to cut the shaft away with his sword but could get no purchase on it. He rested the end on the ground and raised his sword, but at that moment, Fenn jumped forward, stamping on the shaft and forcing the Northman's shield further down, exposing his head and chest. Fenn's axe rose over the lowered and pinned shield, striking the man and driving him to the ground.

He looked about. The flow over the barricade had slowed. For a moment he was in the clear with no assailants nearby.

His searching eyes found Ragnall advancing to join a group of Northmen engaging Kaela and her women. Kaela was holding her own, her blade flashing with incredible speed, several bodies of unfortunates scattered around her, but the addition of Ragnall could tip the scales. He saw one of the women fall. He knew at once there were too many — Kaela was being surrounded.

'*With me!*' he shouted to his guards, his heart pounding, leading the way around the barricade.

A man stepped in his way. Fenn's axe and seax struck together almost without thought, his focus on Kaela. Fenn kicked the man aside, pulling his weapons free. His guards flowed past him to engage the Northmen. Balthazar was there, his teeth finding a leg. A cry of pain and a curse.

He saw an axe swing.

In front of Fenn's anguished eyes, Kaela fell to one knee, her face bloody. He couldn't get to her; she was being overwhelmed and Ragnall would reach her first. She was at the Northman's mercy.

'*Ragnall!*' Fenn shouted the name at the top of his voice.

Ragnall heard him and turned in midstep. His face creased with immediate recognition and anger and he started towards Fenn, Kaela forgotten, his shield and axe raised, growling curses in his language.

Over the noise, Fenn heard a strange sound from outside the palisade.

Ragnall was a huge man, taller and broader than Fenn. Fenn had no shield and knew he would not fare well in straight combat. He was alone, his guards engaged in defending Kaela and her women, Balthazar was elsewhere – he couldn't hear the hound. Fenn backed away, moving to the side, drawing Ragnall away from Kaela.

Ragnall roared at him. Fenn did not need to understand the language to know he was being mocked – probably called a coward.

The strange sound came again. A horn.

Fenn continued to circle around Ragnall, looking for an opening. His circling brought the archway entrance into view, and he was astonished to see Olgood enter. That momentary distraction was almost his undoing as Ragnall swung his axe. If Fenn's reaction had been a fraction slower, the blade would have taken his head. The Northman was trying for the kill. Fenn leaned away from the blow just as the horn sounded a third time, louder, closer.

This time Ragnall heard it. He stepped back and turned to the entrance, noting with widening eyes, as Fenn had, Olgood standing under the arch – also noting the numbers of bodies of Northmen sprawled on the ground and stacked two and three high on the barricade.

He crouched, his axe and shield still raised should Fenn attack.

A group of Westerling defenders on the northern palisade step broke into cheers.

Fenn and Ragnall make the connection together. The horn and the cheers signified the arrival of help for Westerling. Herewic or Hernam – it didn't matter – and if Olgood was at the arch, the reinforcements were free to enter. The Northmen were split, some inside, some outside the palisade, fighting in small groups. Ragnall would not be able to rally them to meet the newcomers.

Balthazar appeared beside Fenn, crouching, snarling up at Ragnall, his lips pared back to show his teeth, his body tense, ready to leap if Ragnall dared to move.

Ragnall looked down at the dog then back at Fenn. Anger and frustration showed on his face.

He lowered his axe.

Olgood walked into the courtyard. He was an imposing sight, a giant, taller even than Ragnall or Olaf – axe, shield, body, face, and hair bizarrely covered in blood as if he'd been painted. The Northmen near him backed away from the apparition in awe as if he were a god. Fenn couldn't be sure how much of the blood was Olgood's, but he walked steadily and looked unharmed. Three of his men, then two more, appeared behind him in the archway, similarly spattered from head to toe, their appearance a testimony of the havoc they had wrought.

Fenn met Ragnall's eyes. Ragnall stared at him, his lip curling with the sour taste of defeat. He shouted a command and let his axe fall to the ground. His command was taken up by others.

The noise of the battle died.

The silence was filled by the unmistakable cry of a newborn baby.

CHAPTER THIRTY-SEVEN

A wager settled, a future sealed

It was Herewic who rode under the arch at the head of several mounted men – one was Wyllard, and another carried a standard bearing the golden Wyvern of Wessex. They were followed by Herewic's fyrd in a long column. Two more mounted men brought up the rear of the column. Behind one of these men sat Birgitta, her hands tied. Nameth was carried on the other horse, his hands also tied.

As soon as he cleared the arch, Herewic stood in the saddle, his eyes darting around the courtyard, assessing the state of the conflict. Slowly he relaxed and waited while bodies were moved and part of the barricade was hauled aside to allow the horses through.

Fenn searched for Kaela and found her with Erenweth, who was gently dabbing with a cloth at Kaela's head. Kaela's face was streaked with blood but it didn't look to be a severe injury. Nyle was close by, talking with Brianne, her two children at her side.

Ragnall stood at the front of a gathering of a hundred or so Northmen, many with visible wounds. All had laid their weapons on the ground. Some Northmen and women were tending to their wounded in the courtyard. Olaf sat behind Ragnall on a folded blanket, in obvious pain, his leg bruised and possibly broken.

Fenn was joined by Olgood, his eyes also on Kaela.

Fenn looked him over. An attempt had been made to wash the blood from his face and hair, but his body was still streaked and spattered with red. His axe was in his belt but he no longer carried the shield.

'Are you hurt?' asked Fenn.

'A few knocks. Nothing serious,' said Olgood. 'But two of my men gave their lives.'

Fenn didn't reply. In the time it had taken Herewic to reach the palisade entrance, Fenn had been told that, so far, fifteen other men and one of Kaela's women were known to have been killed. Many others were injured. A small number compared with the losses of the Northmen but a tragedy for Westerling.

Were the losses worth the gain?

'Is the baby well? Have you seen…?'

'I held him for a moment,' said Olgood, his eyes shining. 'A boy.'

Fenn breathed deeply. 'A boy,' he repeated. New life had arrived. Westerling and Wessex were safe. That answered his question about loss and gain.

Olgood returned Fenn's gaze. 'You have a scrape.'

Fenn remembered the arrow that had cut his cheek. He felt for the wound – it was the length of his finger but thin enough to be already sealed with blood.

'Not today,' he said.

Olgood looked at him somberly. 'Not today,' he said. 'But this time it was close.'

Fenn silently agreed. One slip, one misstep, an unseen arrow, even a hesitation – could have been fatal. He'd wondered before how much luck he had left in his bag. One day it would run out. But not today.

When a wide enough path through the barricade had been cleared, Herewic rode through and spent several more moments surveying the scene before he walked his horse up to Fenn and dismounted.

'Lord Feran.'

'Lord Herewic. I thank you for getting here so quickly.'

'I'm not sure we were needed,' said Herewic. 'It seems you had the better of them. My God…' he looked at Olgood's bloodied body, '…I saw you outside the palisade… the carnage you wrought was hard to believe….'

'This is Olgood,' said Fenn. 'And the outcome was by no means certain. Your arrival stopped further blood being shed.'

'I'm glad to be of service.'

Herewic turned to gaze at the Northmen. 'What do you want done with the invaders?'

Fenn caught the puzzled frown of the closest man still on his horse. Herewic was an ealdorman and outranked Fenn as a thane, even a King's Thane. The man didn't understand why his ealdorman was not taking charge and making the decisions.

Before Fenn could answer, Herewic said: 'If we let them go, they'll just return another day; if not here then somewhere else.' He held Fenn's gaze steadily. 'There's only one way to make sure they don't.'

'I know the leaders of these Northmen…' said Fenn, holding up his hand against Herwic's reaction, '…it's a long story which I'll tell you another time. We'll talk to them. I think we'll reach an understanding.'

Herewic stared at Fenn. He shook his head. 'An *understanding*? With these….'

'Yes.'

Herewic took in a breath. 'As you wish,' he said. He bowed. 'What do you want of me?'

'Untie these two,' said Fenn indicating Birgitta and Nameth. 'The man is a friend, captured by the Northmen. The woman is… not a threat.'

'The woman fought us like a she-wolf, and it was only because she was alone that we were able to capture her. Why were these two on the hill, taking no part…? Was she guarding that man?'

Herewic saw Fenn was reluctant to answer. He waved his hand.

'Never mind. Another time.'

His puzzled expression deepened. 'There's more to you than even I suspected,' he said. 'Someday, I hope to understand.'

Herewic pointed at Birgitta and called: 'Free them both.'

Birgitta and Nameth slid from their horses. Birgitta looked up at the man on the horse and held out her hand. The man looked astonished and leaned back, shaking his head in denial.

'Give her her sword,' said Fenn.

Herewic grunted. 'Lord Feran, with all respect, you do not give a rabid wolf the gift of teeth. These people are pagan barbarians. They have no honour. I've heard about their women warriors. She's an animal. She'll try to kill someone.'

'She has more honour than most. It's important for her to have her sword.'

Herewic grimaced. 'You must know something I don't.'

'I know *her*. That's enough.'

Herewic signalled. With an expression of disbelief, the man untied a sword attached to the horse and handed it to Birgitta. She immediately headed for Fenn. Herewic moved to block her but Fenn laid a hand on his arm.

'Let her pass.'

Birgitta stopped in front of Fenn. She held out her hand. Fenn clasped her forearm in the style of the Northmen. Birgitta bowed her head, she stepped back and thumped her chest with her right fist as a salute. She next turned to Olgood, again offering her hand. As Olgood took it, Birgitta reached out her sheathed sword and touched the hilt to his forearm as a mark of respect. She withdrew and gave him the same salute – then she pointed at Kaela, silently asking Fenn's permission. Fenn nodded and Birgitta buckled her sword to her waist.

With Herewic's bewildered eyes following her, she walked swiftly to Kaela, checked her wound, then embraced her. They fell into a rapid conversation.

Nameth had remained where he was, looking about, confused. Olgood called his name. Nameth took a few stumbling steps, peering up at Olgood warily. Olgood met him and enveloped him.

'Welcome home,' he said.

Tears rolled down Nameth's cheeks. He found his voice.

'Olgood. It *is* you. I thought I was dreaming. It's good… it's good to be… at last….' He gave up trying to express his feelings.

Herewic looked bewildered. 'You *do* know these people. What was this conflict really about?'

'This was simply about gold, and about old friends, and old enemies.' In his mind, he thought: *And about relationships and circles.*

When Herewic just shook his head, Fenn said: 'We'll tend to the wounded. Then I would ask you to escort the Northmen back to their ships and ensure they leave this land.'

'Escort invaders from the land?' Herewic said incredulously. 'Say goodbye and fare thee well? This is a day I never thought I'd see.' Herewic's eyes bored into Fenn's. He lowered his voice. 'I'll say this straight, Lord Feran. It's a mistake. I wouldn't do this for any other man, not even the King.'

His eyes left Fenn, flicked to the group of Northmen, then to Birgitta still in conversation with Kaela, finally returning to Fenn.

He kept his voice low so only Fenn could hear. 'There's much I don't understand. But here again, as at Cymeresford, you've proven yourself worthy, so I'll do as you ask. I'll do it because that ring, *who* it stands for and *what* it stands for, is important to me and, I believe, also important for Wessex. I'll do it, but I don't have to like it.'

As Herewic moved away to confer with his men, Fenn noticed another man patiently waiting beside the arched entrance. A tall man wearing a sword with a long handle. Fenn beckoned to him.

Brecon Longsword walked the few paces to Fenn. Fenn held out his hand and Brecon took it. The Cornishman turned slightly to nod through the open doors to the forest beyond.

'Hernam is in the forest,' he said. 'We arrived to see your ealdorman approaching the palisade with his colours flying and horn blaring. We thought it best not to proceed. We couldn't be sure of his reaction to Cornish on this side of the Tamar.'

'A wise decision.'

'King Hernam asked me to check all was well and he was not needed.'

'Thank the King on my behalf. Tell him I appreciate his rush to our aid. I'll not forget it. I'm in his debt – but the situation is contained.'

'When we didn't know where the Northmen were headed, you were willing to aid our King. I don't consider there's any debt owed, and I'm sure the King will agree.'

Brecon Longsword stepped back. 'We'll meet again, no doubt.' He bowed. 'With your permission….'

Fenn nodded. When Brecon turned away, Fenn searched again for Kaela. She was still talking with Birgitta, but noticed him.

KAELA TRANSLATED RAGNALL'S WORDS.

'You were right,' Ragnall said. 'You did hide surprises behind your walls. More archers than I expected and they were *better* archers than I expected. Your farmers fought well and to your credit, they didn't run. You also had slingers and a hell-hound.'

Ragnall's eyes flicked to Olgood. 'But… your greatest surprise was *him*…' Ragnall allowed his eyes to move up and down Olgood's massive frame. 'In Lognavik, I saw a gentle giant lacking a warrior's heart. He seemed to enjoy building ships.' He shook his head. 'He's already a legend. He killed many – fifteen or twenty died today by his hand. Many good men… Tostig… Lothgrin….'

'You were a threat to his unborn child.'

Ragnall raised his eyebrows. 'The baby's cry?'

'Yes.'

'Then that is how it was written. It was time for these men to die with honour, and they'll be happy it was against a mighty hero. They can walk proudly in Asgard, in the Hall of the Fallen, Valhalla, with respect, their heads high and their axes in their hands.'

Ragnall stopped. He asked Fenn a question. Kaela hesitated with the translation.

Fenn looked at her. 'He asked if you did have any gold,' she said. 'He would like to see it.'

Fenn didn't answer. He stepped back. 'It's time for you to go. Don't come back.'

Ragnall grunted. He picked up his axe.

'I know *that* man would have killed us all,' he said, pointing the axe at Herewic.

'What would you have done in his place?' asked Fenn.

Ragnall stared at Fenn without answering and that was an answer.

After a moment he nodded to Fenn. Fenn knew Ragnall was not thanking him for saving the lives of the Northmen – that had been determined by fate. He was merely acknowledging Fenn had played a part.

'You have earned the mark of the wolf,' Ragnall said. 'It is fitting.' He drew in a breath. 'You were well organised. Aid should not have reached you so quickly. Was that due to fortune or planning?'

'It doesn't matter,' said Fenn.

Ragnall puffed his cheeks. 'No,' he agreed. 'It doesn't.'

He nodded to Kaela and then back to Fenn.

'I free the three of you,' he said, including Olgood. 'You're no longer my thralls.'

He flicked his head dismissively.

'I won't return here. This place holds nothing worth remembering.'

'YOU AND YOUR BOYS did very well,' said Fenn. 'I'm proud of you, and Westerling thanks you.'

Beric beamed. 'Thank you, Lord. I thought at first our buckets might fall through the thatch of the roof – they were so heavy.'

Fenn smiled. 'You did your best to lighten them.' He rested a hand on Beric's shoulder. 'You did what was expected of you, and I ask nothing more. Without you, things would have been worse. You saved lives today. Tell your boys.'

'YOU'RE RIGHT TO BE proud. They're both *heroes*, Brianne – there's no better word. As your son said, the arrows they collected almost certainly won the battle, but… it's more than that. The sight of those young children delivering vital extra arrows and the sight of *you*, fearless at the palisade – I saw you – gave *me* the strength to believe in Westerling, to believe we could win the battle.'

'Thank you, Lord. But I was so scared for them.'

'So was I,' said Fenn. He leaned over to embrace her.

THE NIGHT WAS CLEAR, the stars bright in the company of a full moon.

Fenn had drawn a table and chairs to the entrance of the Great Hall so he could look over the courtyard and also see the stars. Beside him, Kaela leaned back in her chair, her eyes closed. Covering a linen bandage which circled her head, her long flame-coloured hair was spread behind her, shining in the moonlight. He reached out to stroke it.

'You saved my life,' said Kaela softly, in response to his touch. 'Ragnall had only to take another step… I couldn't have stopped him.'

'I'm not sure he would have killed you. How could he explain that to his mother?'

'Maybe… we'll never know.'

To change the subject, Fenn said: 'Aerlene is my mother's name. She's a strong woman. It would be a worthy name.'

Kaela laughed, opening her eyes. 'And if it's a boy?'

'If it's a boy, then….'

'Stop,' said Olgood. 'The child does not need a name yet. You can choose one when it's born.'

'I think Aerlene is a nice name,' said Gisele mischievously.

Olgood grunted at her.

Olgood and Gisele had welcomed a healthy son, whom they named Marcelet, after Gisele's father. Both glowed with happiness – a particular type of happiness that Fenn hoped he would experience himself soon.

He moved his hand from Kaela's hair and used it to gently draw her head closer to kiss her. She returned the kiss, lifting her hand to touch his face.

'It is a nice name,' she agreed. 'But let's leave that for today. I'd like to enjoy the peace of the night.'

Fenn tilted his head, conceding.

The moonlight shining on Kaela's hair reminded him of Arielle. Was the confrontation with Ragnall the completion of the circle, the resolution of a relationship that Arielle had foreseen – the third of her fragments? Or was that still to come? How could he be sure?

Perhaps that was the nature of prophecies – never to be sure.

His thoughts were interrupted by Nyle clearing his throat and rising to his feet.

'I have an announcement to make,' Nyle said.

He paused dramatically, waiting for their attention.

'Westerling is prosperous again, and tonight is peaceful with no threats at our doors. It's time for something to be done that has been too long undone.'

He raised his mug. 'We know our Westerling ale is the best in all of Wessex, and the best ale is the ideal ale for an outstanding wager that's still to be settled.'

Nyle extended his mug toward Fenn.

'This is *my* mug of ale. No one would dispute it belongs to me. It's untouched. I find it worthy. I'd like to give it to *you* as settlement of our wager – if you're willing to accept it.'

Fenn laughed. He stood up. 'I *do* accept,' he said and formally took Nyle's mug from him.

Fenn solemnly presented the mug to each person at the table – Olgood, Gisele, and baby Marcelet nestling in his mother's arms; Nyle and Erenweth; Edelred and Bronwyn; Kuralin and Nameth; and, lastly, he extended the mug of ale to Kaela.

He looked deep into her eyes, eyes that still held the same promise, the same mystery, and the same attraction he'd seen outside the gates of St Cuthbert's Monastery on the day of new beginnings, the day they'd started their journey from Lindisfarne to Wessex.

Behind and above Kaela, Fenn's eye caught a flash in the sky.

A bright serpent appeared, streaking through the night across the dark fabric of the heavens. Fenn followed the fiery trail as it carved its path among the stars. He smiled.

Sky serpents were a sure sign of good luck.

He raised his mug – saluting the heavens, saluting the future, saluting Westerling.

'*Wassail.*'

HISTORICAL NOTES

The following information was researched and compiled using literary and internet sources during the creation of the novel to provide the author with historical accuracy and the reader with interesting background information.

A major source of information from this period is a collection of manuscripts written in Old English in the form of annals (i.e. entries year by year) known as the Anglo-Saxon Chronicle. The original is thought to have been compiled during the reign of Alfred the Great.

Where possible, the data has been corroborated from more than one source, and where two or more sources conflict, the version used was based unashamedly on personal preference. Many names of the people and places in the late 8th century are recorded with various spellings — again, personal preference ruled the choice.

The information is as accurate as the author can determine but is intended only as helpful or interesting notes regarding the prominent figures, events, and practices in these times.

All dates are CE/AD unless stated.

The notes have been ordered according to the timeline of the novel.

*Some notes relevant to both novels have been extracted in full or abridged form from the Historical Notes of the prequel novel — **Lindisfarne: Fury of the Northmen.***

Queen Eadburg of Wessex (c770-c830)

Eadburg was the eldest daughter of Offa, King of Mercia, and his wife Cynethryth. She married King Beorhtric of Wessex in 789 to seal an alliance between Wessex and Mercia. Under this alliance, the two kings cooperated in the exile of Egbert (a contender for the throne of Wessex) to the court of Charlemagne, the King of the Franks, in Francia (France).

Queen Eadburg's nefarious career was presented almost a hundred years later by Asser, Bishop of Sherborne, in his *Life of King Alfred*. It's possible Asser fabricated his account regarding the Queen to discredit both Mercia and a rival family, but the story is too good not to be retold.

According to Asser, Eadburg was jealous of friends that the King favoured. She falsely accused them so that Beorhtric might have them exiled or put to death. If this didn't work, Eadburg removed them with poison. Furious at Beorhtric's attachment to a young ealdorman named Worr, the queen poisoned his cup at a banquet but accidentally poisoned her husband when he drank from the same cup.

With Beorhtric's death, the ealdormen of Wessex rose against Eadburg, who gathered her treasure and fled to Aachen and the court of Charlemagne, who'd had a good relationship with her father, King Offa. Charlemagne's fifth wife had just died and he offered her the choice of marriage to himself or his son. When Eadburg tactlessly chose the younger man, Charlemagne reportedly replied: "Had you chosen me, you would have had both of us. But, since you chose him, you shall have neither."

We can only assume Eadburg was attractive because with her father King Offa's death six years earlier, in 796, and the death of his successor, Eadburg's brother Egfrith, less than a year later, she would be without the family connections necessary to be a desirable bride.

For her indiscretion regarding his marriage offer, the King sent Eadburg to the convent of Ober Altaich in Bavaria, where she became a nun taking the name of Salome. However, her behaviour proved so disgraceful – she seduced an Englishman in exile – that Eadburg was ejected from the convent. She travelled with only one maid-servant to Pavia in Italy, where she was seen begging for food in the streets.

Such was the resentment of the nobles toward Eadburg, the status of subsequent queens of Wessex was diminished. They were not titled 'Queen' but 'King's Wife' and were prohibited from sitting beside the King on the throne.

Ealdorman

An Anglo-Saxon noble of high status, second only to the King. In Wessex, these were the leaders of the individual shires.

Ealdormen were expected to attend court, manage and defend their shires, lead in battle, and raise an army (fyrd) if requested by the King.

By the eleventh century, the term ealdorman had been replaced by *earl*, a change influenced by the Danish equivalent *Jarl*.

Earl remained the highest rank below the King until 1337 when Edward III created the title of Duke and made his eldest son Edward the Black Prince, Duke of Cornwall – an appointment traditionally held by the eldest son of the monarch since.

Damascus steel

Kaela's sword, Lord of the Battle, was made of the famed 'Damascus steel', a type of steel used in the manufacture of sword blades in the Syrian capital of Damascus, where a weapons industry thrived for centuries.

The 'Damascus' process was based on Wootz steel – a high carbon alloy steel imported from Southern India, but the actual method used to create the renowned steel has been lost.

Damascus steel swords are characterised by distinctive swirling patterns on the blade reminiscent of flowing water. Such blades were reputed to be very strong and capable of being honed to legendary sharpness.

The Sling as a weapon

The sling was used by many cultures throughout the world for both hunting and warfare from as far back as 2500 BCE. A pair of slings were found in the tomb of the Egyptian pharaoh Tutankhamun (died ~1325 BCE), probably to be used for hunting game in the afterlife.

A sling shot could equal and even exceed the range of an arrow. Chris Hamson in *The Sling in Medieval Europe* says '*a sling bullet lobbed in a high trajectory can achieve ranges in excess of 400 metres (1,300 ft).*'

Many armies contained specialist slingers. The people of the Balearic Islands off the coast of Spain were considered particularly skilful. Strabo, a Greek historian (~63 BCE-24 CE), records that the islanders carried three slings of varying length (for different distances) wound around their head and bodies and that they were trained from infancy for a life as a mercenary warrior – their mothers allowing them bread only when they had struck it off a post with a sling.

The Persians, Greeks, and Romans all used slings as range weapons in ancient times, as did the Franks more recently. The Greeks used 'bullets' moulded from lead and inscribed with symbols such as lightning bolts, snakes, and scorpions, and words such as 'for Pompey's backside' and other insults like 'Ouch' or 'Catch'.

Hammaburg

The early name for Hamburg (Germany). The name derives from *Ham* (meadow) and *burg*, which in medieval times could mean a walled town, a fortress, or a castle – hence 'Castle in the Meadow'.

In *Lindisfarne: Fury of the Northmen,* a significant battle was fought at Hammaburg Castle.

Reeve

A Reeve was an administrative official appointed to implement the decisions of a high noble or a court. Each level of court from town to shire appointed a reeve. At the shire level, this official was called the shire-reeve, the predecessor of the word *sheriff.*

The King's Reeve, or High Reeve, was an enforcer of the King's laws, whose duties included the collection of taxes and the taking of oaths of fealty to the King.

Thane (also spelt Thegn)

Thanes were Anglo-Saxon nobility of the second rank, below the Ealdormen. It is equivalent to the position that later became a Knight.

A King's Thane was considered similar to a Prince. He served the King directly and was higher in rank than a 'median' thane.

The title could be inherited, awarded by the King for military service, or could be earned if a man strove to own five hides or more of land. A *hide* was the amount of land believed sufficient to support a family (~120 acres). Such a man would be considered thane-worthy.

In the same way, a successful Thane might strive to become an Ealdorman.

Thrall

A Thrall was the term used for a slave or serf in Viking society and by the Anglo-Saxons after the Viking invasions and the Danelaw division (see **The Great Heathen Army** below). The equivalent early Anglo-Saxon word was *Theow,* but *thrall* was retained in this novel to be consistent with the first novel.

Both Viking and Anglo-Saxon societies followed the three-tiered hierarchy of social order of their shared Germanic origins:

Nobleman – Freeman – Thrall or Slave

The word 'slave' derives from the diverse and populous *Slavs* of Eastern Europe who were enslaved in such numbers that their name became synonymous with the condition.

One could become a thrall:

- by capture during a raid or after losing a battle,
- to pay off a debt – either voluntarily or by court order,
- as punishment for a crime, or
- by being a child of a thrall.

The universal sign of a thrall was the slave collar around the neck, made of leather or iron.

Thralls were considered property and could be bought and sold. They had no rights and their living conditions depended entirely on their owner or master. Wergild was not payable if a thrall was killed, but compensation for loss of property would be expected as if, for example, the damage had been done to another person's pig.

A thrall could gain a measure of freedom in times of conflict by fighting and killing enemies, by being freed by their master (e.g. in a will), or by buying their own freedom (some were paid small amounts for their services). They then became a 'freedman', a status between thrall and freeman, but still owed allegiance to their former master. They would be expected to ask permission to marry or change residence and to vote, if necessary, according to their master's wishes. If a freedman had no descendants, his former master would inherit his land and property.

It took at least two *generations* for freedmen to lose this allegiance and become full freemen (minus the 'd') with the same rights as free-born men.

The term is still in common usage (with a slightly changed meaning) in the verb 'to enthrall', but only the imagination is captured in this sense.

Forest of the Lesidhe (pronounced *Lay-shee*)

Arielle called the forest surrounding Moloch Tor the *Forest of the Lesidhe*. In Celtic folklore, the Lesidhe were self-appointed mischievous forest guardians who made life difficult for mankind by mimicking the call of a mockingbird to entice travellers into the forest and then causing them to lose their way by deforming the trees.

Black Dye

Kaela's clothes were dyed black. No black pigment was available, so the common blue pigment *woad* (from the dried and fermented leaves of the woad plant) was used to dye leather a dark blue. A reddish pigment called *madder* (from the root of the madder plant) was added to remove the blue tinge leaving a deep black colour.

Andeferas (Andover)

Andeferas is the Old English name for Andover in Hampshire.

Located approximately twenty-five kilometres northwest of Winchester, the word is probably of Celtic origin from *onn dwfr* or *onn dubr*, meaning 'ash tree stream'.

The author worked in Andover and lived in nearby Weyhill for two years, 1986-88.

Medicinal Herbs

Herbs formed a large part of the treatment of many ailments in early medieval times.

Vapour and herb baths were common, and the sick would often be 'smoked' with fragrant woods and plants. Scented garlands of flowers and herbs decorated most homes to combat 'bad air'.

Headaches were treated with sweet-smelling herbs such as rose, lavender, and sage.

Henbane and hemlock were applied to aching joints. Coriander was used to reduce fever.

Stomach pains were treated with wormwood, mint, and balm.

Lung problems were treated with liquorice and comfrey.

Wounds were cleaned with vinegar, and myrrh and honey were applied as antiseptics.

Faro Bregancio (Hispania)

The ancient name for La Coruña in the province of Galacia, Spain; today a city but then a town at the northwestern tip of the Iberian peninsula. The Moors invaded and occupied Iberia from the early 8th century, but this region was remote, and their rule there consisted at most of an overlordship.

In the novel, Faro was the home town of Tariq ibn Sulayman ibn Omar al-Arabi, the wool trader.

Seax

Pronounced *se-ax* or sometimes *sax,* the Old English word for 'knife', the seax was typically a single-edged short sword with a blade up to 55cm long.

The name **Saxon** derives from this weapon.

There were many variants in shape and length – earlier seaxes (~450) were short, light, and narrow, becoming longer, broader, and heavier around 800.

In the novel, Fenn's seax is a long, broken-back style seax. The cutting edge is straight and parallel to the back, and at about two-thirds of its length, the back tapers sharply to a point which is below the centerline of the blade (hence the name 'broken-back'). This was the typical style of seax seen in the United Kingdom and Ireland.

The seax was often wielded in one hand in conjunction with a shield, spear, or in Fenn's case, an axe, in the other.

King Egbert of Wessex

Egbert became King of Wessex a few years later than portrayed in the novel. King Beorhtric died in 802, supposedly accidentally poisoned by his wife, Eadburg. Egbert claimed the throne and reigned until his death in 839. He was the grandfather of King Alfred the Great.

When King Cynwulf of Wessex was murdered in 786, Egbert contested the succession against Beorhtric, but Beorhtric and Offa of Mercia conspired to exile Egbert to Francia. Egbert returned to take the throne after Beorhtric's death.

The death of King Offa of Mercia six years earlier, and a succession of weak Mercian rulers, freed Wessex from the yoke of Mercia and allowed Egbert to significantly increase the influence of Wessex in the southern part of the island.

In 815, he conquered Dumnonia (Cornwall), also known as West Wealas (West Wales). In 825, he repelled an invasion by King Beornwulf of Mercia at the battle of Ellendun (now Wroughton, Wiltshire). The victory destroyed Mercian supremacy and made Wessex the strongest of the Anglo-Saxon kingdoms.

Four years later, in 829, he invaded Mercia itself and drove the King of Mercia, Wiglaf, into exile. At this time, he was described by the Anglo-Saxon Chronicle as *bretwalda*, meaning wide-ruler, indicating that he ruled all of the country now called England south of the Humber River. Later in 829, he invaded Northumbria and received the submission of King Eanred.

This was the height of his dominion and he could justifiably be called the first King of all England.

Egbert's control of Mercia was brief, however. In 830, probably due to a rebellion in Mercia against Wessex rule, Wiglaf returned to the throne of Mercia, but Mercia never regained the supremacy it once had. Wessex was clearly now the dominant Anglo-Saxon kingdom.

Even after conquest, territories were hard to control, and the Vikings were always a threat. After suffering a defeat by the Vikings at Carhampton in Somerset in 835, Egbert subsequently defeated a force of Danes allied with the Cornish at the Battle of Hingston Down in 838 (see **Vikings on the Tamar** below).

Egbert's military successes fundamentally changed the political landscape of Anglo-Saxon England. The southeastern kingdoms of Kent and Sussex were absorbed into Wessex and were never again independent.

Egbert was succeeded by his son, Ethelwulf – a measure of the stability of the kingdom as this was the first time in two hundred years that a son followed his father as King of Wessex.

Egbert's descendants ruled Wessex and, subsequently, all of England continuously for more than two hundred years, until 1013, when Ethelred the Unready was unable to organise resistance against an invasion by the King of the Danes, Sweyn Forkbeard, who forced Ethelred and his sons to flee to Normandy. Sweyn Forkbeard's reign was brief, however – he was pronounced King on Christmas Day, 1013, but died only five weeks later. Ethelred returned to rule England after Sweyn's death.

Ethelred's unfortunate nickname, 'the Unready', is a misnomer; it derives from the Old English *unraed* meaning 'poorly advised'.

Hamwic

The Anglo-Saxon name for the settlement that became Southampton, deriving from *Ham* meaning meadow or field (or village, or home) and *wic* – a trading settlement.

The name 'Hamtun' is also used by chroniclers to describe the same area. Some references say Hamwic and Hamtun existed as separate settlements, with Hamwic located 'South of Hamtun', which became known as South Hamtun and eventually Southampton (spelt with only one 'h', but pronounced as if there were two).

Hwicce (pronounced like *Witcha*)

Hwicce was a small sub-kingdom of Mercia lying between Mercia and Wessex.

On the day Egbert succeeded to the throne of Wessex (after the death of Beorhtric in 802), the Hwicce under Ealdorman Ethelmund crossed the Thames at Cymeresford (Kempsford), which translates as *Ford of the Great Marsh* and were met by Wulfstan of Wiltonshire (Wiltshire).

The invasion was defeated, but both Ethelmund and Wulfstan were killed in the conflict.

The Saltire – the cross of St. Andrew

In 60CE, Saint Andrew (later known as the Patron Saint of Scotland) was crucified. Legend has it that he felt unworthy of being crucified on the same shaped cross as Jesus Christ, so he asked to be crucified on a diagonal cross (shaped like an X), known in heraldry as a *saltire*.

A yellow saltire on a blue background as portrayed on the Mercian shields was used as a symbol of Mercia around the time of King Offa.

The Severn Sea

The Severn Sea was the former name for the Bristol Channel – the stretch of water separating Wales from Cornwall and West Wessex, culminating at the mouth of the River Severn– the longest river in Great Britain.

The name was changed to the Bristol Channel by Henry Tudor in 1485.

The Severn Sea is the name still used for this stretch of water in Welsh (*Môr Hafren*) and Cornish (*Mor Havren*).

Iona Abbey

The abbey on the island of Iona, located in the Inner Hebrides on the west coast of Scotland, was established in 563 by St. Columba and was a centre of Celtic Christianity for three centuries. It was raided by the Vikings four times over a period of thirty years.

The first attack was in 795, two years after the Lindisfarne raid. Further raids occurred in 802, 806, and 825. In 806, 68 monks were massacred at Columba's Bay which was renamed Martyr's Bay. After the massacre, many Columban monks relocated to build the new Columban Abbey of Kells in Ireland.

In 825, St. Blathmac and those monks who had remained with him in Iona were killed in the last Viking raid, and the abbey was burned. Even then, Iona was not abandoned, as it was only in 878, more than fifty years later, that the notable Ionan relics were finally moved to Kells.

Vikings on the Tamar

The Vikings did use the Tamar River to launch a raid on the southwestern peninsular during the reign of Egbert, but that raid happened in 838. Discounting the previous minor incursion at Portland in 789 (probably not a planned raid but more likely an opportunistic landing), this was the first Viking attack on Wessex.

The accord reached between Wessex and Cornwall (between Fenn and Hernam), as portrayed in the novel, did not occur. On the contrary, the Anglo-Saxon Chronicle records that in the 838 raid, the local Britons (Cornish) joined forces with a Viking 'ship army' against King Egbert of Wessex, and a battle was fought at Hingston Down in east Cornwall. However, the Viking/Cornish army was soundly defeated by the West Saxons.

Despite this defeat, the Vikings remained a threat to Wessex for hundreds of years.

The Great Heathen Army and the Viking Invasion of Wessex

The Vikings, also known as the Northmen or Norsemen, originated in the modern-day Scandinavian countries of Norway, Sweden, and Denmark.

For more than 250 years from the end of the 8th century, the Vikings fought with the Anglo-Saxons. Some conflicts involved small raiding forces and were resolved in one battle, such as at Hingston Down (see **Vikings on the Tamar** above). Others became extended campaigns that lasted for years.

In 865, twenty-seven years after the Tamar raid, a much larger force, later termed the Great Heathen Army, arrived on the shores of East Anglia to begin a campaign that would last fourteen years. At first, they struck north to capture the Northumbrian capital of York (which was renamed *Jorvik*) and subsequently raided deep into Mercia. The size of this force is disputed, with estimates from one thousand to ten thousand, but it would be reasonable to say it numbered in the thousands.

The Great Heathen Army was led by Ivar the Boneless, Halfdan Ragnarsson, and Ubba, three of the sons of the legendary Danish King Ragnar Lothbrok (*'Ragnar Shaggy-trousers'*). The invasion was supposedly to avenge the killing of their father, Ragnar Lothbrok, whom King Aella of Northumbria had captured and thrown into a pit of vipers.

After five years of raiding in Northumbria, Mercia, and East Anglia, the Great Heathen Army turned south and invaded Wessex using the Thames, reaching Reading in 870. At Reading (then called Readingum), they were met by King Ethelred of Wessex and his brother Alfred (later King Alfred the Great) – the grandsons of King Egbert.

Over the course of a year, the Anglo-Saxon Chronicle reports that *nine* battles were fought in the area and Alfred and his ealdormen also made several *incursions* against the Danes, but these, according to the Chronicle, 'were not counted'. In eight of these battles, the Chronicle reports a Danish victory – *'the Danes had possession of the place of carnage'* – but on 8 January 871 they were defeated by Alfred at the Battle of Ashdown.

Three months later, King Ethelred died and was succeeded by Alfred, who paid off the Danes to buy time as his army had been weakened by the continuous battles.

Alfred was forced into hiding until he again gathered an army and won a decisive victory at the battle of Edington in 878, after which a treaty was signed to set territorial boundaries and trade terms between the West Saxons and the Danes, effectively dividing the island south of the Humber into Wessex and the area known as the *Danelaw*.

Raid on the Monastery at Tavistock

In 997, more than a hundred and fifty years after the first raid up the Tamar, another Viking force, after raiding around southern Wales, sailed around Land's End and up the Tamar and Tavy rivers as far as Lydford, attacking and plundering Ordwulf's monastery at Tavistock which was burned to the ground – and later rebuilt in stone.

The Anglo-Saxon Chronicle for the year 997 reads (in part):

The Danes … went into the mouth of the Tamar, continuing up until they came to Lydford, burning and slaying each thing they met - they burnt down Ordulf's (sic) monastery at Tavistock and brought with them to their ships indescribable plunder.

The Viking attack on Westerling is based on this raid.

Monastery vs Abbey

The terms Monastery and Abbey describe similar institutions.

A monastery is a place where people can live a communal monastic life. The Rules of St. Benedict, promoted by Charlemagne throughout Europe, provided a set of governing principles for this life.

St. Cuthbert's Monastery at Lindisfarne was a monastery led by a Bishop.

An abbey (the name comes from the Aramaic *abba* or 'father') is a title granted by the Holy Church in Rome to a monastery with sufficient religious worshippers. If inhabited by monks, it is led by an Abbot (the Father) and, if by nuns, by an Abbess (the Mother Superior).

Wassail

The toast *Wassail* derives from the Old English phrase *Wes Hal. Wes* is from *wesan,* one of the verbs meaning 'to be', and *Hal* is related to the English 'Hale' meaning whole or healthy, so *wassail* means 'Be well'.

LIST OF CHARACTERS

***Indicates a historical person**

Main characters from the prequel

Lindisfarne: Fury of the Northmen

Fenn (Feran) — Orphan, apprentice scribe at St. Cuthbert's Monastery, Lindisfarne. Captured in a raid by Northmen (793). Kept as a thrall (slave) in Lognavik (Norway) for over a year, escaped, journeyed back to Lindisfarne and then to Wessex.

Kaela — Illegitimate daughter of King Beorhtric of Wessex and Aedra of Mannin. Captured by Northmen on a Portland (Wessex) beach (789). Thrall of Askari for four years. Escaped Lognavik with Fenn.

Olgood — Carpenter and Blacksmith at St. Cuthbert's Monastery. A boyhood friend of Fenn. Captured with Fenn by Northmen (793). Escaped with Fenn and Kaela.

Gisele — Frank (French). Captured as a young girl by Northmen during a raid in Francia. Thrall of Ragnall for many years. Escaped with Fenn, Kaela, and Olgood.

Yseld — Milkmaid, Kitchen servant, St. Cuthbert's Monastery.

| **Nameth** | Cook, St. Cuthbert's Monastery, taken captive in Lindisfarne raid, translator for Ragnall. |

Nameth — Cook, St. Cuthbert's Monastery, taken captive in Lindisfarne raid, translator for Ragnall.

Ragnall — Northman (Viking). Leader of the raid on St. Cuthbert's monastery, Lindisfarne. Headman of Lognavik village.

Olaf — Northman (Viking). Ragnall's brother.

Hakon — Thrall of Ragnall, interpreter on Lindisfarne raid.

Birgitta — Viking shield-maiden from Lognavik.

Askari — Mother of Ragnall and Olaf.

Thorvald — Askari's husband.

Agatha — Daughter of Birgitta, foundling, deaf, raised by Askari.

Lothar the Hun — Outlaw leader, Skyrvid forest, Land of the Danes.

Gunther — One of Lothar's outlaws, joins Fenn.

Widukind* — Duke of Saxony during the Saxon wars (772-804) against the Frankish King Charlemagne (Charles the Great).

Charles the Great* — King of the Franks (768-814). Appointed Holy Roman Emperor in 800 by Pope Leo III. In Latin he was known as *Carolus Magnus* and later as Charlemagne.

Westerling: Prince of Wessex

***Indicates a historical person**

In order of appearance

Eadburg*	Queen of Wessex, wife of King Beorhtric, King Offa's daughter.
Orvyn	Thane of Westerling (murdered).
Beorhtric*	King of Wessex (786-802), Kaela's father (*in novel only*).
Aedra	Kaela's mother, from Mannin (Isle of Man) (deceased).
Purdy	Household servant, court of King Beorhtric, De Facto mother to Kaela.
Offa*	King of Mercia (757-796), father of Eadburg and Egfrith.
Worr*	Ealdorman at King Beorhtric's court, Witanceastre, advisor to Beorhtric.
Sergio	Swordmaster at King Beorhtric's court, from Lombardy (northern Italy).
Rowena	Thief, a girl in outlaw band of Cedric the Bald.
Grimbold	King's Reeve (High Reeve of Wessex).
Margareth	Grimbold's wife.
Nyle	Leader of King's House-guards, Bowman, brother of Cedric the Bald.
Ine*	King of Wessex (688-726) (deceased).
Ingeld*	Ealdorman of Hwicce, killed before battle with Cornish (*in novel only*).
Hernam*	King of Cornwall (780-810), Oswallt's son.
Cedric the Bald	Outlaw leader, Nyle's brother.

Ethelmund*   Ealdorman of Hwicce (796-802), Ingeld's son.

Silward   Cedric's Reeve.

Galvaron   Outlaw in Cedric's band.

Giffre   Outlaw in Cedric's band, Frank.

Balthazar   Irish Wolfhound.

Edelred   Tenant Farmer, Westerling.

Bronwyn   Edelred's wife.

Cormwurst   Previous Thane of Westerling (deceased), Orvyn's uncle.

Galastan   Tenant-in-Chief, Westerling.

Ariochs   Albino Twins, Galastan's guards.

Gerwent   Tenant, Westerling, former Tenant-in-Chief.

Erenweth   Gerwent's daughter.

Hardwain   Builder, craftsman, Westerling (deceased).

Treddian   Tenant Farmer, Westerling.

Myfanwy   Treddian's wife.

Oswallt*   King of Cornwall (775-780) (deceased).

Wyllard   Tenant Farmer, Westerling.

Merewyn   Tenant Farmer, Westerling.

Peada   Merewyn's son.

Acwellan   Physician, Westerling.

Hopkin*   Hernam's son, King of Cornwall (810-830).

Herewic   Ealdorman of Somersaeteshire (Somerset).

Brianne   Woman archer, Westerling.

Beric   Youth, Westerling.

Alfric   Messenger sent by Galastan.

Kuralin   Alfric's wife, hostage of Galastan.

Egbert*   King of Wessex (802-839).

Son of Eahlmund, half-brother of Alburga.

Thrall of Hernam (*in novel only*).

Eahlmund*   King of Kent (784), (deceased), father of Egbert and Alburga.

Cynewulf*   King of Wessex (757-786) (murdered), succeeded by Beorhtric.

Arielle, Anesidora, Avarinthe the Fae

    Mystic woman, Forest of the Lesidhe.

Wulfstan*   Ealdorman of Wiltonshire (Wiltshire) (?-802).

Alburga*   Wulfstan's wife, Egbert's half-sister.

Egfrith*   Offa's son, King of Mercia (796).

Trevanian   Captain of the King's House-guards.

Bartholomew   Beorhtric's treasurer.

Tariq ibn Sulayman ibn Omar al-Arabi

    Moor, Wool-trader, member of Arielle's order.

Leofrith   Ealdorman of Hanteshire (Hampshire).

Brecan Longsword   Cornish emissary of King Hernam.

Marcelet   Olgood and Gisele's baby son.

ABOUT THE AUTHOR

OWEN TREVOR SMITH

I live on the Kapiti Coast of the North Island of beautiful New Zealand, but I have lived and worked for several years in Australia, England, Germany and Switzerland.

I share my home with two dogs (Harry and Jacko) and three guitars (not named). I've travelled throughout the world for extensive periods and sailed the Atlantic from England to Brazil in my (part-owned) 41-foot ketch 'Adastra'.

I have written novels, poems (that rhyme!), short fiction in diverse genres, children's stories, and a two-act play.

Westerling: Prince of Wessex is my third novel and is the sequel to

Lindisfarne: Fury of the Northmen.

Visit: www.owentrevorsmith.com

Email: owentrevorsmith@gmail.com